The skeleton ra............
hand was the B.............. Dave had seen in the
painting outside the Ghost Train. Its eight-inch blade
glittered in the white flashes of the strobe as he raised
it. Each time the light flashed the skeleton raised the
blade a little higher over Phil and Judy's heads.

'Look out!' Dave screamed at Phil.

In quickfire instalments of bursting white light, the
skeleton raised its other arm and buried its bony fingers in Phil's ginger hair. In the next three frames of
light, it pulled Phil's head backwards so that he was
staring up into its eyeless sockets. In the three that
followed Judy's head swivelled round towards Phil.

The knife began to descend towards Phil's neck in
the next two frames.

And the strobes went out.

As their cars passed, Judy let out a single lung-
bursting shriek.

He grabbed his right arm. Clutched in his hand was the bowie knife that Dave had seen in the

AdventureLand

Steve Harris

First published in 1990
by HEADLINE BOOK PUBLISHING PLC

First published in paperback in 1991
by HEADLINE BOOK PUBLISHING PLC

A HEADLINE FEATURE paperback

10 9 8 7 6 5 4 3 2 1

ISBN 0 7472 3394 2

Typeset in 10/11½ pt Plantin
by Colset Private Limited, Singapore

Printed and bound in Great Britain by
Collins, Glasgow

HEADLINE BOOK PUBLISHING PLC
Headline House
79 Great Titchfield Street
London W1P 7FN

AdventureLand

Dedicated, with love, to:

Caroline 'Razor Girl' Vaughan
The best . . .

and

Reg Harris
Who begat me (or so he says!)
And who has had to put up with me ever since.
You won't lose by it!

Who says there's no such thing as magic?

Also dedicated to:
Richard 'actually I was just leaving' Evans
For his good taste, enthusiasm and patience.

Special thanks are due to: P.J. Lockley, B. Johnsister, Geoff, Sarah, and Paul & Sheila (for years of entertainment and friendship), Mike Bailey (for his pain-free surgery), David Grogan & Co, (who went out of their way to please me), Sian Thomas and her team and all the very nice people at Headline, Sooty Asquith (for encouragement, long ago), Paul '20 minute' Pyrah and Robert 'EFI' Gould (for making life fun) and Bob & Jon (for putting up with me), Elizabeth 'really, really good' Curthoys, Colin 'Hedge' Rowe and 'Bramble' (for spotting errors), Hil (for being Hil), Florence (without whom . . .) and Cindy (who looks after me).

'Die a thousand deaths and live to tell the tale!'
– AdventureLand funfair hoarding

'Faith is not closing one's eyes to the facts of life, but opening one's eyes to the wonders of them.' – Calendar motto.

'I'M A TROLL FOL DE ROL!' – Jon Kott

Chapter One
The Claw

It was midnight on the day of his nineteenth birthday and exactly a week before the funfair arrived that David Carter saw The Claw.

July the sixteenth was a *weird* day.

And one that got steadily weirder as it unfolded.

Southern England was three weeks into what would eventually turn out to be a five week heatwave with the temperature rarely dipping below eighty, even at night. The roads were slick and sticky with melted tar which hadn't been made to withstand such unlikely Mediterranean temperatures. They hadn't set solid for almost fourteen days, and deep runnels had formed on some of the most heavily used junctions. The Council regularly sent out lorries to throw yellow sand on the melted tarmac – presumably to aid traction – but this made no difference at all, and traffic accidents had soared.

During the day, the concrete-shelled buildings and stone paving slabs that composed Basingstoke town centre became hot enough to cook on (and to prove it, the TVS television network had prepared a somewhat elementary and unappetising meal on the flagstones outside the Sports Centre) and remained warm enough to feel through the soles of your shoes all night.

Contrary to his usual practice, during the heatwave Dave had been sleeping on the outside of the bedclothes with the windows wide open. Even so, he still woke up in the morning sheened with sweat and the bed sheets damp beneath him.

Dave didn't really like sleeping that way because of the things that were out there in the night that could come in and flutter around his defenceless head.

Moths, for instance.

Dave, who liked to read for a while before he went to sleep, had recently been plagued with them. They came spiralling in on the stray beams of light that slipped through the chinks in the curtains as if they were drawn down by sci-fi tractor beams. To make things worse, the illumination in the room came from a small spotlight directly above the head of the bed, and they would flutter around it scorching their wings until, tired and singed, they fell on the pillows beside his head. The mere sight of one of the small brown moths trespassing on his property was enough to bring Dave out in cold shivers, and he couldn't relax until it had been dispatched.

At first, he had kept an empty jam-jar and a square cardboard Heineken beermat on the table beside the bed so that when he heard the chilling flutter of wings he could leap from the bed, neck hackles bristling, and capture the moth in the jar. He would slam the open end of the jar over its revolting body, slide the beermat between the wall and the jar, hold it at arm's length and take it to the window to release it.

He had given up this practice though, a fortnight ago, when he had shaken the jar out of the window, brought it back in and seen the moth still inside and no longer trapped. After a second of horror, during which Dave realised that the beermat was not in his hand and was nowhere to be seen, the moth had fluttered out of the jar and alighted just above the rim of his glasses on his sweat-dampened forehead. The single yelp he let out before batting it away and trampling it into the carpet with his bare feet, had brought his parents running, convinced (so they said, ha ha) that a child molester had shinned the drainpipe to interfere with their little boy.

The urine was still being extracted at every available opportunity.

Dave had dispensed with the jam jar and Heineken mat that same evening and now kept a rolled-up copy of the *Sun* beside his bed instead. This was much more violent, but quicker and more efficient.

He had been told off several times for the growing pattern of squashed insects that now adorned his wallpaper (*and that wallpaper was new only the year before last!*) but he was unrepentant.

But the moths weren't the only reason Dave didn't like sleeping with the window open. There were other night creatures at large in the sultry summer air. Spiders for example. Beetles, small enough to get in your ears or crawl up your nose. Then there were the things that didn't exist at all that might find an open window inviting. Nameless things that you laughed at when you saw them in movies or read of them in books, but which would make your flesh creep when you had to pad down the landing to the toilet in the dark.

This night was different though. For one thing, there was none of the regular Friday night racket going on outside as drunks staggered home from pubs and discos. He and Sally had spent the evening in the pub with their buddies Phil and Judy and then it hadn't seemed any different to any other Friday night. It was noisy and crowded and very hot. At half past eleven Sally had brought him home in her pride and joy – a badly rusting 1972 Mini – stayed for fifteen minutes for a coffee and a cuddle then gone home. She had to be up early in the morning because the cosmetics company she worked for were doing a promotion in the Owen Owen store in the town centre. Sally was a make-up artist and would have to spend all the following day painting pretty faces for free on anyone who showed an interest in buying make-up. She had done these promotions several times before and discovered that it was generally women over fifty that wanted to sit in the middle of a crowded department store and have themselves painted up by an expert.

Reg and Doreen Carter – known either as (fondly) the Old Farts or (not so fondly) the Nag Twins – had gone to bed before Dave and Sally had arrived home. Dave flicked through the t.v. channels, didn't see anything that looked worth staying

3

up for and decided to go to bed. As he climbed the stairs, or The Wooden Hill as Doreen would have put it (as in The Wooden Hill to Bedfordshire) he could hear his old man snoring. *Sawing logs again, Reggie*, Dave thought and wondered how on earth his mother could sleep with that droning in her ear. Reg slept on the left side of the bed, so perhaps she had gone deaf in her left ear or something.

He threw himself onto his single bed and the headboard rattled against the wall – another bollocking offence if anyone heard it. On the other side of the landing, the snoring stopped, but he didn't think the old man had woken up.

Christ knows what we're going to do with all those logs tomorrow, Dave thought, throwing his clothes in a heap on the floor. He nodded hello at his Amstrad CPC computer which rested on a desk in the corner of the room amongst an array of screwed-up print-out paper and manuals, and picked up his book. The time was five past twelve.

Happy birthday, Davey, he congratulated himself. *Nineteen years old today, and not a grey hair on the old guy's head*. He wondered what Sally would get him. She was going to take him out for dinner tomorrow evening – or since it was past midnight, *this* evening.

A few seconds later he noticed the silence.

There was no traffic noise outside. This was unusual because their house was situated in Worting Road, one of the main routes in and out of the town centre. Also, there was Sunny's Chinese takeaway two hundred yards down the street which generally attracted a lot of late night custom from drunks in cars. The roaring engines, squealing tyres and sounds of good ole boys having a good ole time usually went on until Sunny's closed at half past one.

Tonight there was none of this; not even the distant sound of a motorbike with a baffle-less silencer and a high lift cam red-lining it up through the gears as it rushed around the ring road miles away. No high heels on their way home from Martine's – Basingstoke's one and only night club – clattered and scraped their weary danced-out way home.

Dave cocked his head to one side and listened, his Kurt Vonnegut novel lying open against his bare chest. Basingstoke was soundless. He frowned and wondered why.

By twelve seventeen he had read five pages and no moths had entered his bedroom. This was a record; the most he'd managed up until now was a page and a half. He nodded knowingly to himself and decided that the word must have gone around in the moth world that this particular house in Worting Road was no place to go and boogie around the lightbulb.

Two pages later he put the book down, turned off the light and went to the window. The street outside was empty and desolate; as if a killer virus had struck the population down. The air was still and heavy, laden with darkness. Dave looked down the street towards Sunny's. If he leaned out of the window, he could see a section of the tarmac parking area in front of the shops and half of Sunny's plate glass shop front. The lights were burning in there, but the car park was empty. He shrugged mentally and looked at the nearest streetlight which was about forty feet from his bedroom window. Usually there was a swarm of flying insects darting back and forth around it. Tonight there was nothing.

'Everyone's dead by the look of it,' Dave muttered and went back to his bed.

Thirty miles away, in a house on Lewden Road – the new part of the South Hill Park housing estate in Bracknell – a six-year-old boy called Tommy Cousins was also sleeping badly. Tommy – Tiger to his friends and parents – was sweating heavily and tossing and turning beneath a single sheet. His shock of golden hair was plastered to his suntanned forehead and occasionally a small hand would worm its way out of the tangled sheets and try to push it away. Tommy would sigh and moan softly in his sleep as he did this, but the quiet noises of desperation were not enough to rouse his parents.

Tommy's dad had promised to take him to the big funfair tomorrow. The one that had been in Easthampstead Park all week. The one that had all the big rides like the Octopus and the Waltzer and the Big Wheel with the egg-shaped cage compartments that had a brake you could put on so that it went upside down at the top. They even had a thing called a Rotor, which was like a big tub that spun around. You went inside (Tommy's dad had said) and the tub would start to spin and the floor would rise until you were halfway up the inside of the tub. Then it would turn even faster and the floor would go down again, leaving you stuck in mid-air on the wall. Tommy's dad had promised to take him on everything – twice if he wanted to go. Even – and this was against his mother's wishes who seemed to think it would make him sick – on the Rotor itself.

But Tommy wasn't entirely happy about tomorrow's trip to the funfair. He didn't really know why, and he hadn't been able to articulate the thoughts. It was just that something felt *wrong*. Something about the funfair – which he hadn't even seen yet – frightened him. Not the good kind of fright you felt going on the rides, which was a nice and exciting fear – but a kind of musty, empty terror that felt as heavy as lead and which lingered in your mouth like bad medicine.

As Tommy had fallen asleep that night, the exhilaration he had felt about the visit to the funfair vanished, leaving him feeling very small and alone and wanting the comfort of his mummy and daddy. But he had been too tired to get up and go to their room where he could snuggle up between them in their big, warm bed and feel safe. And although his parents wouldn't have been angry if he had done so, the unspoken feeling these days seemed to be that he was now big enough not to get spooked by every little thing he imagined and that he should stay in his own bed unless it was an emergency. Tommy himself sometimes wondered if his folks really thought he was a big baby. He didn't want them to think that: No, *sir*!

So he stayed in his own bed. Even though he had nightmares that the Big Giant had come up the Beanstalk and was looking for him. Even in his dream he knew that the Giant should have come *down* the Beanstalk, but this giant didn't seem to be the same one as in the storybooks. This one came *up* from a great dark yawning hole which had opened up in the middle of the fairground in Easthampstead Park and he was twice as mean. It said the same old thing though.

> 'FE, FI, FO FUM. I SMELL THE BLOOD OF AN ENGLISHMAN!'

The Big Giant's words rolled out from its bearded mouth like thunderclaps. The sheer volume hurt Tommy's ears. He ran and shrieked in terror, but it was pointless. In one earth-crunching stride, the Giant was in front of him again. It turned quickly, swivelling on one massive brown leather boot while the other flew through the air with a terrifying *swish*. The air-borne foot came down on top of the big wheel, smashing it flat as if it were made of matchsticks. Tommy froze.

> 'FE, FI, FO FUM. I SMELL THE *BLOOD* OF LITTLE TOMMY COUSINS!'

The Giant roared. Its fetid breath howled down on Tommy like a gale. His trousers whipped his legs and his hair flew back. The helter skelter collapsed. People screamed. The Giant's terrible face glared down at Tommy. Beneath its prominent brow, its eyes were black as coals. And they sparkled. Its lips were drawn back, showing yellow tombstone teeth, each as big as the front door of Tommy's house. It leaned forward and a hand came wooshing down and plucked up Tommy between thumb and forefinger. The Giant's hands were covered with black hairs as thick as steel cables. It hoisted Tommy into the air and held his quivering body before its face, examining him with those huge watery eyes.

'I EAT LITTLE BOYS LIKE YOU FOR MY SUPPER!' the giant declared in an ear-shattering whisper.

Then The Big Giant popped Tommy into its mouth. He missed its front teeth and fell on to its slimy tongue. Then he was sliding into the darkness and there were doors in front of him. Big wooden doors with a terrible monster painted on

7

them. There were large coiled springs on the outsides of them between the hinges.

They made a wooden *crash* as Tommy's feet hit them and swung open. He slid inside into total darkness.

In his sleep, Tommy Cousins moaned.

The following day, while Dave Carter was playing the new computer game Reg and Doreen had given him for his birthday, and while Sally Harrison was painting the fifteenth ugly face of the afternoon, little Tommy Cousins became separated from his parents at the funfair in Easthampstead Park and vanished.

Dave Carter learned of his disappearance on Sunday.

But the weird Saturday hadn't passed yet.

The postman's heavy footfalls on the path to the house woke Dave at eight thirty that Saturday morning. Dave had slept fitfully – which was highly unusual for him. Staying asleep until midday was one of his greatest talents and he had honed it to perfection since finishing his A level exams in June and leaving school.

He realised he'd had some vivid and terrifying dreams in the night, but he couldn't remember what had happened in them, except that it was bad.

The postman stayed on the step for a long time while Dave waited for the thump of birthday cards falling on the mat. Lucy the dog didn't bark at the potential intruder because Lucy had died three months ago; run over by a lorry while she was crossing the Worting road in a hurry, having spotted a cat on the other side. She had died instantly and the vet had taken her crushed body away. Dave morbidly wondered what vets did with animal corpses.

The brushed steel letter box flap rattled, snapping Dave out of his depressing reverie. But no thud followed.

Where are they then? Dave wondered. There should have been at least ten; you should have been able to hear them hit the mat. He rolled off the bed, poked his metal-framed NHS spectacles onto his nose and put his head out of the window.

It was hot out there already; the sky was travel brochure blue and a heat haze shimmered over the paving slabs on the far side of the road. Birds were circling high over the old people's flats. A car sped by on an early-morning-beat-the-rush shopping mission. On the sticky tarmac the wheels made a noise like masking tape being ripped from a window pane after the paint job.

Dave padded onto the landing and down the stairs. He could see the doormat from the fifth stair from the bottom. There was one buff envelope lying there and his heart sank. No birthday cards then. Was this a terrible injustice or what? He couldn't believe that *no one* had remembered his birthday. There were four uncles and aunts, three grandparents, and an elder sister, married and living on the Isle of Skye with hubby and three children. Then there was Phil and Judy and Sally, Billy Martin his old school chum (who could be forgiven as he'd recently moved in with a gorgeous Danish language teacher who was ten years his senior and apparently banged like the proverbial shit house door in a gale) and Karen, who he had gone out with for three months in the second year and who had never missed Christmas or a birthday yet. Apparently the candle she had been holding for him for these past four years had burnt itself out. He was dumbfounded. Surely *all* of those bastards couldn't have forgotten?

The letter that had arrived was a phone bill from Telecom addressed to Reggie. Dave quickly searched his memory for any long distance, long-winded phone calls he might have made in the last quarter which could put the day on a bad footing if itemised on the bill. There was nothing though. The phone call he'd made to Denmark had been done at a crazy all night party of a friend of a friend and was unlikely to be traced back to him.

Dave sighed and placed the bill on the radiator shelf at the bottom of the stairs, then went to get dressed.

The day got better when the Old Farts got up, because they'd got him a card each. Doreen's had a picture of a smiling old man sitting in a deck chair next to a shady wady pool in which he was fishing. Inside it read 'Have a Happy Retirement – You

9

deserve it!' This was obviously a dig at Dave's postponed promise to find a job – he hadn't yet made up his mind whether or not he wanted to go to university (he wasn't sure his exam results would allow him to anyway) and he had decided to take a year off from education first. He was supposed to be looking for work, but he'd decided a rest would be in order first. After those exams his little brain was frazzled. The outside of his father's card read: ON YOUR NINETEENTH BIRTHDAY, HAVE A PARTY! GET PISSED! THROW UP! and on the inside it said: BUT NOT IN *MY* HOUSE. He had signed it, With love from one Old Fart to another.

They gave him a new pair of Levi's slimfits – the ones with the drainpipe legs that Sally liked – and a computer game: Space Pirates, for the Amstrad. Dave beamed, forgot about being let down by his friends and asked them how he could ever repay them. They told him to get a job then give them money.

But this wasn't all. As he was about to go and try on his jeans, Reggie informed him that they'd booked him a course of driving lessons and the first one was at ten thirty.

Counting the absent moths the previous night, and the cards that didn't come, the third odd thing of that day happened at eleven thirty. The driving school car hadn't turned up and Dave's father had been trying to contact them for the last half hour. He gave up trying to get a reply at eleven twenty-nine and the moment he put the phone down the woman from the driving school rang. She was apologetic and concerned, and her voice had a tearful edge. Later they found out that she was the instructor's wife. She spoke to Reggie and told him that their instructor would not be able to keep the ten thirty appointment because he'd had an accident. It seemed that he had been on his way to their house when he'd heard a strange noise from the engine. According to his wife, and Reggie didn't know why she told him all this, it had sounded like the cries of an animal. She supposed he'd thought something had crawled up into the engine compartment during the night and was now trapped there being roasted to death. Apparently it was quite common for cats to do this, but neither Reggie nor Dave had ever heard of it.

He had stopped the car, pulled the bonnet release catch and got out to look at the engine, which was still running. He'd lifted the bonnet and peered in.

There was some question about what he'd seen at this point, but the ambulancemen had insisted there was no sign of any kind of animal having been near the engine. What they thought had happened was that the instructor – who was an ex-Automobile Association mechanic and should have known what he was doing – had somehow knocked the bonnet prop away as he leaned forward. The bonnet had fallen on him and driven him down far enough for the fanbelt pulleys to grab his tie and drag him right down onto the engine. His right hand had found its way into the spinning fan blades and the left side of his face had hit the rocker box cover, then slid down onto the hot exhaust manifold. He had lost two fingers and suffered severe burns to the face. To compound the matter, the accident had also brought on a minor heart attack. A passing motorist saw him and stopped to help.

Reggie asked the woman why there was some doubt about what the instructor had seen when he opened the bonnet. He hadn't expected the reply he got, but the woman was obviously in deep shock and unable to stop herself telling him things that under normal circumstances she would have laughed off.

She told him that on the way to the hospital her semi-conscious and extremely distraught husband kept moaning about the 'ebony nails' which were going to get him. He made the para-medic promise not to let them near him again. The ambulanceman promised, but even this didn't shut the instructor up. He insisted there had been a huge black arm in there which rose from the depths of the engine, the fingers outstretched. It was this that had been making the noises. The shoulder seemed to merge with the side of the engine, but the bicep and forearm bulged as the arm moved. As he tried to pull away, the hand suddenly shot forward, grabbed his tie and yanked him down.

Reggie sympathised with her and mumbled about shock and hallucinations and delirium. Eventually she rang off.

Dave wasn't as amused as his father was by the tale of the ebony nails, and halfway through the story he slipped into a kind of *déjà vu* where he knew everything his father would say next. The unlikely events that were just the product of a mind unhinged by pain as far as Reggie was concerned, seemed too *right* somehow to him, and it gave him a few spooky moments.

When his father started discussing alternative arrangements for driving lessons, the power of the story and the odd feeling of having already known it faded and let normality back in. In five minutes the ebony nails and the black arm seemed ridiculous to him, too.

Sally phoned during her lunch hour and sang 'Happy Birthday To You' in a falsetto. He told her about the missing birthday cards and the driving instructor's accident, and she sympathised and promised to make it up to him.

She said she hadn't posted *her* card because she was going to give it to him tonight when she took him out for the meal. She had a present for him too, and wanted him to guess what it was. He ran through a list of the most expensive things he could think of, including a Ferrari car, a trip to Disney World and a huge country estate. Apparently, his present was none of these – Sally assured him that it was far superior to any of them. Perhaps it was her body then? She tittered, told him he knew all the right things to say, but no, it wasn't that. He'd just have to wait and see. Sally told him she would pick him up at eight that evening, but still wouldn't tell him where she was taking him for dinner. If it wasn't a surprise, it wasn't worth going, she said.

Doreen shouted that lunch was ready, and Sally heard it, too. She decided she was hungry as well and had to put something in her stomach so she could face up to this afternoon's lot of uglies coming to have their faces done. Sally was one of those people who came over faint and shaky if they didn't eat regularly. But first she got ill-tempered. She wished him a happy birthday again, blew noisy kisses that sounded like watery farts down the line and rang off.

After lunch, Dave retired to his bedroom, changed into the slimfit Levi's and cranked up the Amstrad with the game his folks had given him.

It was a corker – sharp graphics, good sound effects and plenty of excitement. By three thirty he had killed ninety aliens, plundered their ships and become a dollar billionaire in the process. The spacecraft took a lot of skill to handle, and Dave was sweating profusely and chewing his bottom lip as he concentrated on working the joystick. He played away, totally unaware that his feet drummed on the floor and his head darted from side to side like a prize fighter dodging blows as he weaved in and out of a meteor field.

While this was going on, little Tommy Cousins and his parents were parking the car in Easthampstead Park in Bracknell.

'What can we go on Dad? What ones can we go on?' Tommy yelled, clambering out of the Volvo across his mother who was still sitting in the front seat, his eyes already glued on the big wheel which was turning quickly less than three hundred yards away. One of the big wheel's chairs was being rocked back and forth so violently by its occupants it looked as if it might tip them out any second. The air thrummed with the sound of diesel engine generators and working machinery mixed with dozens of different pop records all being played at once: sirens, yells and girlish screams.

'Everything Tiger!' his father replied taking the keys from the ignition and smiling at his son who stood with his back to him, his little hand holding onto the wing mirror. 'Whatever you want to go on!'

'Wow! Can I?' Tommy said without turning round. He started to weave his way forward through the ranks of parked cars, drawn by the hum and throb of the funfair like a pin to a magnet.

'Wait on Tiger!' Anne Cousins yelled. 'We'll lose you!' She looked at her husband Derek and found it hard to believe that this thirty-four year old, thinning on top, sedate and calm

13

chartered accountant was the same man. His face had taken on a madly enthusiastic, somehow innocent look, that mirrored Tommy's. He looked twenty years younger. All it took was the sight of a funfair. *Me and my two kids!* she thought, smiling to herself.

'Nothing too dangerous mind!' she warned Derek, memories of Sunday paper disaster stories flitting through her mind. 'He *is* only six.'

'There isn't anything dangerous here,' Derek replied. 'They've got an engineer's certificate. The town council made them get one before they would let them come.'

'Even so . . .'

'Yeah, I know.'

'And not the Rotor. Definitely not the Rotor.'

'Your wish is my command, oh massah.'

'Mistress,' she said, getting out of the car and slamming the door.

'My mistress is here too? I didn't know she was coming. What'll I tell the wife?' he quipped as he locked up.

'I wanna go on the Big Wheel!' Tommy said, taking Derek's hand with one of his and gesturing with the other.

'That one, or the one that you can go upside down on?' Derek asked, ignoring the look Anne shot at him.

'Both!' Tommy said, beaming up at his dad.

There was a huge wooden helter skelter in the centre of the fairground – you got a doormat to slide down on. Tommy and Derek both went on. Tommy's mat came down ahead of him though as he'd fallen off halfway down. Derek managed to stay on his mat, but being far heavier than a child he gathered so much momentum he shot off the end of the slide, his mat beneath him like a magic carpet and mowed down three teenage boys who had been watching attentively and tut-tutting at the spectacle of a grown-up on a kid's ride. They were impressed afterwards, and completely forgave him. Anne pretended she was alone until the crowd of onlookers had dispersed.

Tommy loved the big wheel, but the one with the egg-shaped cages you could make go upside down was a different story.

Anne had watched worriedly from the ground as the two of them whizzed around, first facing the ground, then upside down, then up the other way, then into a spin which seemed to go on forever, and she could hear Derek yelling with glee.

Tommy was sheet white when they got off, and his hands were trembling, but he swore he liked it. Derek was flushed and happy. 'What about the Rotor?' he asked.

'No!' Anne said. 'I told you . . .'

'I meant what about going up to the viewing gallery and watching them all sticking to the sides. How about that Tiger? Wanna?'

Anne bent down and looked in Tommy's eyes. 'You're not going to be sick are you?' she asked.

'I'm okay,' Tommy said. 'The egg ride made me dizzy, but I'm alright now.'

The Chairoplanes followed the Rotor. Anne went on that one too. She rode on the Noah's Ark after that; declined an offer of the Waltzer and stood on the sidelines praying for Tommy's lunch to stay down. She drove her own bumper-car and attacked the one Derek and Tommy were driving with relish. After that they walked around the perimeter and watched people shooting air rifles and trying to knock coconuts off impossible stands with wooden balls.

They walked past the Ghost Train and watched the people climbing in to the little engines. Two roustabouts then shoved the engines to get them going and they clicked along the rails and banged the wooden doors open then disappeared as the doors swung shut again. There was a huge man in the box taking the fares and he spotted the three of them watching.

'Hey kid!' he yelled in a growling voice. 'You coming on? Best ride in the fair! C'mon and scare yer mum and dad! They'll have grey hair when they come out!'

'Want to go?' Derek asked.

'Not me,' Anne said, shuddering. 'I hate the Ghost Train.'

'Tiger?'

Tommy didn't answer. Something about those doors banging open scared him badly.

15

'C'mon folks, give your kid a ride!' the man in the booth yelled petulantly. He smiled a ghastly smile.

'Tommy?' Anne said.

Tommy took a step back, hid behind his dad.

Derek shrugged at the proprietor, held his hands out in a sorry gesture. 'Not today, thanks,' he called.

As they walked away, Derek said, 'Hows about some candy floss?'

'Yeah! I want some, I want some!' Anne said, jumping up and down.

'Yuk!' Tommy said.

'Toffee apple?'

Tommy nodded.

'Okay, apples and floss coming up!' Derek scurried away through the throngs of people towards the nearest stall selling goodies to eat. Anne and Tommy gravitated towards the Frogger game, just in from the perimeter of side stalls.

The Frogger game worked on a similar principle to hoop-la. The stall contained a pond on which plastic lily-pads floated. You paid your fifty pence and were handed three large and slimy rubber frogs and a rubber-headed mallet. You put your frog on the far side of a balancing device then smashed the near side of it with the mallet. The frog would fly through the air for several feet and – if you were lucky – land on a lily-pad which won you a prize. The playing area was very damp, the noise was deafening and no one seemed to care whether or not they won.

And in the five minutes that Tommy and Anne stood there watching, no one *did* win.

'Want a go, Tiger?' Anne asked, itching to have a go herself.

'Okay,' Tommy said, looking as though he thought she'd never ask. The colour that had left his face during his big wheel trip had now returned and Anne didn't think he was going to throw up after all. She breathed a sigh of relief and waved a pound coin at the old woman stallholder who was handing out frogs from a wicker basket like there was no tomorrow.

'Three for fifty, seven for a pound. Any lily-pad wins a prize,' the woman yelled as she approached. 'Have a go, dear?'

16

'I'll have a pound's worth,' Anne said.

The woman took the coin, dropped it into a leather change bag at her waist and unloaded the seven frogs from her basket. Their wet and shining bodies were about the size of a man's hand, coloured a dull green and made a sickly *thwack*! as she slapped them down on the shelf next to the launching device.

'C'mon, Mum!' yelled Tommy, waving the mallet above his head.

Anne picked up the first frog and was disgusted by its slimy, squishy texture. It was damp and cold and weighed about a pound. 'Yukky, mukky!' she said with feeling and quickly put it down on the far side of the launcher. Tommy moved the device so that it faced the nearest lily-pad, raised the mallet above his head and hammered it home. The frog leapt into the air, its trajectory almost vertical, hit the blue canvas roof of the stall leaving a wet, frog-like mark, and fell limply to the walkway.

Anne laughed, 'Have another go!'

The next frog made it to the water and entered in a perfect dive, hardly making a ripple. Cackling in a clear high voice, Tommy loaded another.

'Turn it to the left a bit,' Anne suggested, but the frog was already airborne. This one hit a pad on the third row from the centre, balanced on the edge for a second, then plopped into the water.

'Oh Tommy, bad luck!' Anne said, but Tommy didn't seem to mind. The mere sight of the frog flying was enough for him.

A small group awaiting their turn had gathered around them, and one of them, a bald man in his fifties said, 'Never mind, tacker. Just turn the launcher to the left about half an inch and you'll get it to stay on next time.'

Tommy took the man's advice, but the flying frog missed the pad by five inches this time. 'You and your big mouth!' the man's wife admonished him.

'Sorry tacker,' the man said, looking sheepishly at him.

The sixth frog fell short again and lay on the walkway

quivering. By this time Tommy had lost interest and laid the mallet down.

'What about the last one?' Anne asked.

'You do it.'

'It's yours. You might win a prize with this one.'

'You have a go. Go on Mum, you do it.'

So Anne gingerly picked up the last slimy frog and placed it on the launcher, wiping her wet fingers on her dress afterwards to take the slick feel away. Face grim, she took the hammer in both hands, raised it, and brought it down hard. The frog crashed into the air, described a perfect arc and landed square and firm on the lily-pad Tommy had been aiming for. 'Yeahh!' she squealed, shaking the hammer above her head in both hands in a victory gesture.

'Raaay!' Tommy yelled, grasping her dress at the hip and waggling it like a flag.

The old woman walked round to see what the commotion was, her face a picture of suspicion. Anne half expected to be accused of cheating.

'Goldfish,' the woman grated, as if the cost of the prize was going to give her a few sleepless nights. 'You win a goldfish.' She unhooked a tiny plastic bag filled with water and containing a minute goldfish from a hook below the counter and held it out for Anne to take.

Anne turned round to present the fish to Tommy. 'There you go, Tiger. A new friend for you. I suppose we'll have to buy a bowl and some fish food now, because . . .'

Tommy, who had been right by her side, had gone.

'Where'd he go?' she asked, puzzled.

The bald strategist and his wife and grandchildren were still there. 'Did you see where my little boy went?' she asked, searching the sea of people for him.

The bald man shook his head. 'He was here one minute and gone the next,' he said. 'I never saw him go. Did you?' he asked his wife.

'I was looking at the fish,' she replied.

'He went that way,' one of the children – a boy about

Tommy's age – said, and pointed into the depths of the fairground. It was in the opposite direction to where Derek had gone.

'Did he? Are you sure?' Anne asked, bending to address the child directly. Why had he gone *that* way, for God's sake?

The boy nodded.

Anne remained bent double, the fish hanging from her left hand, as she peered through the sea of legs, hoping to see a smaller pair trotting back towards her.

'Oh, you won a goldfish. Good work.'

Anne straightened up. Derek stood before her holding two toffee apples and a huge multi-coloured candy floss. 'Where's the midget?' he asked.

'Gone,' she replied, pointing in the direction the boy had indicated. She had intended the remark to sound light and unworried, but her voice already bore an edge of hysteria and she knew the blood had drained from her face. Derek was now looking at an extremely worried wife.

'Why?' Derek asked. 'Was he upset or something? Sick?'

She shook her head. 'He vanished while the woman was handing me this fish. We won it on the Frogger. Oh Christ, let him come back.'

'Don't worry,' Derek said, putting his free arm around her waist and hugging her to him, 'we'll find him. He can't have got far.' He handed her the candy floss, but her appetite had dried up along with the spit in her mouth. 'I don't want this now,' she said, handing it back to him. He dumped the apples and the floss in a nearby bin.

'Right,' he said when he came back. 'We'll check the perimeter first. You go round one way, I'll go the other. We'll meet midway round. Keep your eye on the big rides. The chances are he'll be watching one of them.'

'Shouldn't one of us stay here in case he comes back?' she asked.

'Okay, you stay, I'll go around.'

'I can't stand to wait. *You* stay.'

Derek nodded, then kissed her. He looked determined

and confident. 'We'll find him,' he said. 'Don't worry.'

Fifteen minutes and three circuits of the fair later, Derek's self-assurance had evaporated. His eyes were wide and dark and his face was pallid. Anne knew exactly what he was thinking. He was thinking what she had started to think five minutes ago – ten if she was honest with herself. He was thinking of little boys that sometimes went missing at funfairs and were invariably found weeks later, miles away in fields or ditches, tortured and starved and very dead.

They started to ask the fairground people if Tommy had passed by. He had no money of his own, so he couldn't have decided to go on any rides alone. He had not been seen. Derek checked the car park and the Volvo. There was no sign of him here either.

Anne was crying when he returned. 'We're not going to find him, are we?' she sobbed, clutching at his shirt front. 'We've been everywhere. I've looked and looked and looked. I've seen everybody in the whole place three times and Tommy isn't here. He's gone, isn't he? He's not coming back.'

'Shut up! Stop being stupid!' Derek said grasping her shoulders and shaking her gently back and forth. 'Of course we'll find him!'

She looked in his eyes then and saw her own desperation reflected, saw his bottom lip trembling like his son's did just before tears fell. That was when she knew for certain Derek felt exactly the same way as she did.

That was when she knew Tommy *wasn't* coming back.

The police started to search for Tommy Cousins at the same time as Dave Carter clocked up his third computer game million that afternoon.

By the time Dave and Sally Harrison arrived at the new Ziegfeld restaurant in Basingstoke at eight that evening to celebrate his nineteenth birthday, Anne Cousins was under sedation in Bracknell hospital and her husband was tramping the fields near Easthampstead Park with twenty-seven policemen.

But Tommy was nowhere to be found.

'What about a birthday kiss then?' Dave said as Sally shut off the Mini's engine in Ziegfeld's car park. The Mini's engine refused to stop. It whirred and chuntered and shook the car. Sally swore at it, then promised it a de-coke. Dave made a magic sign with his hands. The Mini finally backfired and stopped.

'Magic,' Dave said, examining his mystical waggling fingers.

'Bullshit, you mean!' Sally replied, taking the keys from the ignition and thrusting them into the depths of her handbag. 'You're full of it.'

'I put the 'fluence on it,' Dave insisted. 'These hands have the power.'

'Those hands will have eight broken fingers and two broken thumbs if you don't get out of this car!' Sally said, prodding him in the ribs.

'Ow!' he said recoiling. 'You're cruel to me.'

'You always hurt the one you love, the one you shouldn't hurt at all . . .' Sally sang. 'Come here dickhead, and let me give you this birthday kiss. If you still want it, that is . . .'

They noticed the quiet when they got out of the car.

The Ziegfeld restaurant occupied a position on what used to be the A30 road toward Winchester and Salisbury. Originally a pub, five years ago it had been remodelled and the restaurant added. Now it had been taken over by a London consortium, rebuilt once more and decorated in the swank thirties style.

Although the M3 motorway took the bulk of the through traffic by about half a mile behind the Ziegfeld this road was well used by cars travelling in and out of town from the Kempshott and Brighton Hill estates.

Tonight, though, the road was empty.

'It's gone quiet now,' Dave said. He stood in the middle of the car park staring at the empty road. The traffic had been heavy on the journey here.

'Saturdays ain't what they used to be,' Sally replied, putting on a heavy Hampshire accent. Sally was an out of towner, having moved here from London ten years ago, and constantly took the mickey out of Dave's occasional lapses into country-speak.

He whirled, hands poised over imaginary six-gun holsters. 'Say that again kid and you'll die!' he hissed. His voice sounded very small and flat in the huge silence that had settled.

'There are only four cars in this car park besides mine,' Sally said. 'And this is the place you have to book a week in advance because it's so busy. What's happened?' She looked bemused.

Dave looked up and down the car park, the scarlet sunset reflecting in his glasses so Sally couldn't see his eyes.

'What can't you hear?' he said, his voice now serious.

'What d'you mean?' Sally asked.

'Okay, tell me what you *can* hear.'

Sally thought for a moment, then shrugged. 'Nothing,' she said.

'No cars?'

'Nope.'

'No wind in the leaves.'

Sally looked around the car park which was bordered on two sides with sycamore trees. They were dead still. 'No wind,' she said lightly, 'what's so unusual about that?'

'No dogs barking, no music playing, no jets flying over. No birds in the sky. Look!' He pointed up. 'There are always birds wheeling about at this time of night. They catch the insects that rise on the thermal currents. Where are they tonight?'

In spite of the warmth of the evening, Sally shuddered. 'Gone to bed early?' she suggested.

Dave ignored her. 'No people,' Dave said. He shook his head slowly.

'What do you want people for when you've got me?' she said, smiling. 'C'mon turkey, let's go inside. You're giving me the creeps.'

He came back to her and kissed her gently on the lips. 'I love you,' he said.

Sally hugged him, felt his bony hips and ribcage press

22

against her. She put her face against his warm neck. 'First time,' she murmured.

'What?'

'That's the first time you've told me you love me.'

He drew away from her, looked at his feet. 'Slip of the tongue, as the actress said to the Bishop's anus. I didn't mean it.'

'Then why are you blushing?'

'I'm embarrassed.'

'Don't be,' she said, taking his arm and leading him towards the restaurant. 'I love you, too.'

The inside of the Ziegfeld was as expensive looking as Dave had been led to believe. They walked down the thick-carpeted corridor taking in the ornately framed photographic prints of Fred Astaire and Ginger Rodgers, Clark Gable, Vivien Leigh and Greta Garbo to the walnut-veneered reception desk. There was no one there. The two oak doors to the dining room stood open and, while Sally pinged the brass bell on the counter, Dave peered through them. It was carpeted in the same red plush as the corridor. There were perhaps twenty tables in there. They were made of dark wood and laid with silverware and white linen. The electric lighting was dim, and on each table, in a low silver holder, a candle flickered.

But the restaurant was empty.

Dave groaned inwardly. 'Come and look,' he said to Sally.

She wandered over, obviously awed by the place. Dave wondered how she was going to afford the meal. It looked as though it was going to be expensive.

Sally peered around the empty dining area, her mouth open in astonishment. 'I don't believe it,' she said.

'Did you get the time wrong?' he asked. 'It doesn't look as if they are open yet.'

'No, of course I didn't. I booked the table for eight thirty. Where is everyone? They told me when I booked that Saturday was their busiest night. There's no one here, for God's sake!'

She strode back to the counter and rang the bell again, sharply this time.

A neat woman in her fifties appeared through a sliding door in the panelling behind the counter. Neither of them had noticed it until it opened. The woman was dressed in black and sported a string of pearls that looked real. Her hair was blue rinsed. 'Can I help you?' she asked politely.

'I booked a table for eight thirty,' Sally said. 'The name's Harrison.'

The receptionist raised her eyebrows and regarded them suspiciously. Dave waited for her to say, '*I'm sorry, there must be some mistake . . .*' but she didn't. She said 'Hmm,' and opened a leather-bound appointments book.

'You *are* open, aren't you?' Dave asked.

The woman looked at him for a moment. 'Yes, of course we are. Why do you ask?' she said as if an empty restaurant at eight thirty on a Saturday night was nothing unusual.

'It's just that there's no one in there,' Sally said, nodding towards the dining area.

'Oh,' said the woman, and went back to leafing through her book.

'Where is everyone, then?' Dave asked. 'Why is no one here? Is it too early or something?'

'We don't appear to have any bookings this evening,' she said, adding, 'except yours of course. Ah, here it is. Table for two in the name of Harrison, eight thirty. Would you like to sit down now, or would you like to go to the bar for an aperitif first?'

Dave and Sally looked at one another. 'Drink?' Dave asked.

'I think we'll sit down now,' Sally said, addressing the receptionist. 'And we'll order some drinks from the bar to be brought to our table.'

'Fine,' the woman said, smiling. 'Follow me.'

'She's wearing cheap make-up,' Sally whispered as they followed her through the room. She was holding on tight to his hand, making it sweaty. 'Her foundation is coming off and her lipstick is bleeding.'

'Her lipstick is *what*?' Dave hissed.

24

'Here we are,' the woman said, stopping at a table in the centre of the large room. She pulled back the chair for Sally, then did the same for Dave who muttered a thank you. 'The maitre d' will be along in a moment,' she said and waltzed off, leaving them alone in a sea of empty tables and chairs.

'This is weird,' Sally said, staring around the room goggle-eyed.

'What did you say about her lipstick?' Dave said, more to hear some comforting sound in the silence than because he was interested.

'It's bleeding. It runs into the tiny lines around your lips if you're not careful. Makes them look feathery around the edges. My God, this is odd. I've never been the only person in a restaurant before.'

The maitre d' appeared beside them with two huge leather-bound menus and handed them out like a school master. He had a sallow complexion, a pencil moustache and slicked-back black hair. He was probably in his early thirties but looked older. 'I'm Sergei, the maitre d' . . .' he said.

I'll bet you are, Dave thought.

'. . . and I'll be looking after you tonight.' He leaned forward slightly as he spoke and unconsciously did an elaborate hand-washing gesture. 'I understand you wish to have some drinks while you are deciding,' he said.

'Scotch and Coke,' Dave said.

'And your wife?'

'Just a lemonade for me,' Sally said. 'I'll be driving my husband home tonight.'

'Thank you,' Sergei said, and walked quickly away.

'I don't like it in here,' Sally complained when the maitre d' was out of earshot.

Dave sighed. 'I know exactly what you mean,' he said and shuddered.

'It's *spooky*.'

'Don't worry about it. At least we'll get the best service.'

'This could only happen to us, y'know,' Sally said. 'Weird things like this just don't happen to other people. Who do you know that's gone to a new and popular place to eat and found it empty?'

'No one,' he said, uncomfortable that Sally was voicing his own thoughts.

'It feels like it was *meant* to happen. Like we've been selected for something. How else can you explain it?'

'I can't. It's an unbelievable coincidence that no one turned up tonight except us. And there's an atmosphere . . .'

'Like something is going to happen,' she finished for him.

'Something nasty. I've felt it since last night. Something's coming.' Dave didn't feel at all hungry any more.

'I could believe anything at this moment,' Sally said, her eyes huge and dark. The candle light danced in them, made them look a little mad. Dave wished she'd leave it alone and change the subject, but she seemed to want to worry at it like a dog with a tough bone.

'If that waiter came running through here brandishing an axe, I wouldn't be at all surprised,' she said. 'Or if a bomb went off and we were the only two killed – that wouldn't surprise me either. I'm scared.'

'Happy birthday to me, happy birthday to me,' Dave sang softly.

Sally's face lit up. 'I'm sorry,' she said. 'Happy birthday and let's quit the fantasising. Sally loves you.'

The maitre d' came back without the axe but with the drinks. This took the edge off the heavy surreal atmosphere, and both of them cheered up.

Dave ordered Entrecote Diane (in the special Ziegfeld sauce). Sergei even cracked a smile when asked if it was made of dead film stars. Sally asked for Dover sole and ordered a bottle of champagne which, she insisted, should be chilled to exactly forty-nine degrees, no more, no less.

Sergei actually laughed at this. At least, it approximated a laugh; his shoulders went up and down and a wheezing noise came from his nose. 'Yes madam, forty-nine degrees. I'll do my best,' he said.

After a few minutes, Dave began to feel uncomfortable

again. Someone was watching him, he was sure of it. He could feel the gaze burning into the back of his neck and it felt hostile somehow. He wanted to turn around and see who was there, but couldn't force himself to do it. For one thing, he reasoned, there was no one else in the restaurant who *could* be looking at him. No one could have come in unnoticed because he was facing the entrance, so if it wasn't a customer, it must be a member of the staff. He could see the receptionist from where he was sitting, and Sergei was adjusting a table cloth at the other side of the room. He didn't know who else might be looking at him, and he was too frightened to look now in case it was some-*thing* rather than someone. He had no reason to suspect there was anything terrible surveying him from way back in the shadows other than the fact that the whole day had been weird in one way or another. He remembered the driving instructor then, and imagined him in the ambulance, burnt and disfigured and begging for protection from the *ebony nails*.

Doesn't seem so ridiculous now, Davey boy, does it? he asked himself.

'Okay buster, what's up now?' Sally said, stopping in mid sentence.

Dave shook his head. 'Nothing,' he said. 'I'm having a great time.'

'I keep feeling as if there's someone watching me,' Sally said. 'My back has gone all shivery and the little hairs on the back of my neck are standing up.'

Dave looked at her for a moment, then turned and looked into the gloom behind him. Someone opened a door at the end of the room, and light spilled out, illuminating the back of the dining area. Sally jumped.

The chef stood there in what until a second ago had been Stygian gloom. He wore a white coat, a tall chef's hat and a blue and white striped overall. He was short, fat and aged about forty. His lower jaw sported a neatly clipped, pointed beard and his chubby features were pig-like.

A meat cleaver dangled limply from his left hand.

Dave's heart filled his throat and his head began to pound. A small, but insistent inner voice repeated, '*there you are, told you so, there you are, told you so . . .*' over and over as he gasped for breath.

The chef nodded and smiled at them, turned and went through the door, back into what must have been the kitchen.

'Jesus come and save us,' Dave said, breathing a sigh of relief. His heart slid back down to its rightful place, but still hammered away, annoyed at being disturbed. 'Shit? I need a change of underwear!' he said, taking a large gulp of his Scotch and Coke.

'How did he get there? That's what I want to know,' Sally said. 'I didn't see him come out. I didn't even know there was a door there until it opened.'

'Perhaps he came in another way,' Dave suggested, eager to rationalise it.

Sally shook her head. 'Either you or I would have seen him. That door has definitely not opened since we've been here. What *is* going on?'

They had calmed down by the time the meal arrived, two more drinks and a glass of champagne each (which, Sergei assured them, was chilled to precisely forty-nine degrees) had done the trick.

The food was gorgeous when it came.

By the end of the meal, they had even grown used to the gloomy emptiness of the restaurant, and were relaxed and content – if a little tipsy.

'I'm full,' Dave said, sipping what was left of the champagne and belching. 'That was the best steak I've ever tasted.'

'Good,' Sally said, 'it's going to cost enough.'

'But I'm worth it, aren't I?' Dave said, smiling dopily at her.

She took his hand across the table, squeezed it. 'Since you've started to tell me you love me, you're worth more than that. Want a present?'

'Yes please!' he said, jiggling up and down in his chair. 'What is it? What is it?'

'Close your eyes and open your hands,' she commanded.

Dave shut his eyes and held his upturned hands out about three feet apart.

'Not that far apart dummy!' she said, taking his hands and placing them together. 'That far!'

'Oh, I wanted a *big* present,' Dave whined from behind his closed eyes.

'You want what I've got you,' she said confidently and placed a small package in his hands. 'Okay, you can open them now.'

Sally had wrapped the rectangular box in candy striped metallic paper. Sally's wrappings were usually works of art, and Dave inspected this one for creases in the paper or chewed up pieces of Sellotape sticking the ends down like they would be if he'd wrapped the carton. The paper was perfectly smooth and the ends were neatly and precisely folded, stuck down from the inside. 'Good work,' he said admiringly.

She breathed on her fingernails and polished them on her blouse, looking pleased. 'What d'you think it is?' she asked.

'It's small and heavy,' he said turning the package over in his hands and weighing it. He shook it from side to side. 'And it doesn't rattle,' he added. 'Dunno.'

'Open it then.'

'And ruin your paper?'

'Don't worry, it only took about an hour to get it right.'

He ripped the paper off, and instantly knew what it was. The box was white and printed with the name VICTORINOX. 'Oh Sally,' he said, delighted, 'it's a Swiss Army knife. Thanks.' He leaned over and kissed her.

'The one you wanted. The Explorer model.'

He slid the inner tray out, tipped the knife out and examined it. It was red and marked on one side with a silver cross inside a shield. There was a tiny key ring attachment at the back end where the toothpick and the little tweezers were inserted. Enthralled, he opened the blades and examined them one by one. The knife was four blades wide. There were bigger knives which included saws and files, but he'd wanted this one. Phil had the biggest model but it was too fat to carry comfortably in your trouser pocket and weighed a ton. The Explorer model was just right.

'Thanks,' Dave said again. 'I love you Sally. Specially when you give me presents.'

'Okay, have another one,' she said, scooping a package from the floor. This one – also perfectly wrapped – contained a pair of Hi-Tec *Slammer* basket ball boots. Dave was ecstatic. He took off the shoes he was wearing, placed them on the linen cloth of the next door table and put the Hi-Tecs on. 'Four wheel drive for your feet!' he said, quoting an advert that hadn't been run for years. He did a test sprint down the aisle between the tables while Sergei looked on interestedly from a distance. He came to a stop by Sally's chair and dropped to his knees. 'Thanks Sally!' he said, 'my feet just had an orgasm! What more could a guy want on his birthday?' She bent over and kissed him, skewing his glasses.

'A guy could want one more presnt,' she suggested, straightening them again.

'Not more, surely?' He hugged her.

'I don't know if you'll like this one. It's only little.'

'Of course I will, of course I will!' he said, bouncing up and down.

'Behave yourself or you won't get it! Now, come and sit next to me.'

When he was settled she handed him another box. This one was smaller and lighter but just as carefully wrapped.

He carefully peeled the paper off to reveal a white box with an overlapping lid. It was about three inches by two. 'It's a jewellery box,' he said distantly. His mind was working overtime, trying to guess what was in it. A ring?

He lifted the top and his mouth dropped open. 'Wow!' he breathed. The most stunning item of jewellery he'd ever seen lay inside the box.

It was a silver cross three inches high and two inches across the horizontal. The strips were about half an inch wide. The silver was old and dull and looked soft. It was quite thick and Dave knew it would feel heavy if he picked it up. Indented tramlines ran all the way around the outside edge and there were faint hieroglyphic markings engraved between them. The marks were almost too small to be seen with the naked eye. In the centre, where the vertical crossed the horizontal, a heavy lidded eye stood out. Its pupil was a smooth, black, perfectly circular stone; its iris, which was partially covered top and bottom by the eyelids, was a faultless ring of clear red which looked as if it glowed, even in this dim light. Just below the eye was an eye-shaped hole which went right through the vertical section.

'It's lovely,' Dave whispered, not taking his eyes from it. 'It must have cost a bomb.'

'It's not new,' Sally replied from what seemed like miles away. 'Pick it up. Feel it.'

Dave hesitated for a moment, vaguely aware that to pick up the cross was to complete some unseen jigsaw of events from which there would be no escape. To hold the cross would give the lock one final turn and the door would close forever behind him. There would be no turning back now if he accepted the gift, no coming back and starting all over again.

And yet he *wanted* to hold the cross, wanted to weigh it in his hand and feel the goodness that seemed to shine from its single eye.

The doubts passed and then there was no question of his refusing it. He reached into the box and took it out. It was as heavy as he had expected and it felt good in the palm of his hand.

It felt *right*.

'You can't afford it,' he muttered, staring into that welcoming eye. It gave him a feeling of safety; of serenity.

'I did, didn't I?' Sally said.

He looked up at her then. She was holding an identical package to the one she had given him and she was smiling. Her eyes shone in the candle light.

'I've got myself an unbirthday present,' she said, starting to unwrap it. 'Watch!'

Dave looked on transfixed as she took the small white box from the paper and opened it. Inside was an identical cross to the one he had, except Sally's was half the size and its eye was slightly higher up and green.

'Look at the back of yours,' she said, holding the cross up. Its eye shone.

Dave turned his cross over and was amazed to find an indentation in the back where the smaller cross obviously fitted. The hole in the vertical piece of his was for the eye in the smaller one to show through. At the top of the vertical piece there was a smooth, raised eyelet to attach a chain to.

'They're parts of the same thing,' she said, bubbling with delight. 'Isn't it romantic? I've got one half, and you've got the other. Together we make a whole! It was love at first sight when I saw them this morning. I just had to have them! I knew you'd like them.'

'Where on earth did you find them?' Dave said. 'And how did you pay for them? They must have cost the earth. This is some sort of antique silver.'

'Y'know what I was telling you about coincidences?' Sally said. 'Well, this is another one. If I tell you what happened, you've got to promise not to get mad at me when I get to the bit about how much they were. Promise?'

'I promise.'

'I got a bonus,' Sally said. 'It's almost like someone arranged for me to have it at the right time, isn't it? Last week, I got a bonus of a hundred pounds due to the amount of sales I've clocked up in the past three months. I didn't even know there was a bonus scheme operating until I got this month's wage slip. No one had mentioned it to me before. The bank cleared this month's money yesterday, so there I was, a hundred quid up and nothing to spend it on. I'd already got your other presents.

'I wandered around town in my lunch break, looking in the shops. Eventually found my way to Joice's yard, which is strange, because I hadn't intended to go there and when I arrived I couldn't remember walking all that way from Owen Owen.'

'There aren't any shops in Joice's yard,' Dave said. 'It's just a

32

big tarmac car park behind the shops in Church Street. There's only that Chinese restaurant there.'

'Remember Ned Scrumpo's Emporium?'

Ned Scrumpo's was a second hand shop, one of the only two shop units in Joice's yard if you didn't count the hairdresser at the top exit. Ned Scrumpo's Emporium had closed down several years ago and the shop had stood empty ever since.

'They haven't reopened it, have they?' Dave said. 'I thought old Ned had moved away.'

'It's a jeweller's shop now, run by a little old deaf man. I didn't know it was there until today. Anyway, I found myself outside this jeweller's which is called Anstey's. The windows are full of lovely hand-crafted items. Rings, bracelets, earrings, you name it. They were all priced, and all out of my range. I was standing there drooling at some of that stuff, when a little bony arm with a gnarled old hand on the end appeared from the back of the display. It was the owner, Mr Anstey. He was putting the crosses in the window. He laid them out separately, next to one another. I stood and stared at them for a while, knowing I had to have them, and realising I could never afford them. He hadn't made out a price ticket for them yet, so I didn't know how much they were, except that it was going to be expensive. I waited for a while for the tag to appear, but it didn't, so I decided to go in and ask.'

The door was hard to push open against the return spring, and Sally felt silly as she leaned her weight on it. She couldn't *possibly* afford the crosses and was going to have to walk away embarrassed when the old man told her the price.

The door opened with a click, and an old-fashioned bell on a curly spring tinkled as it moved. The inside of the shop smelt musty, and the blue carpet on the floor was old and worn almost threadbare. The shop was narrow and long, and a glass display cabinet-cum-counter ran the length of it, taking about a third of the floor space. On the wall behind the counter was a collection of intricately constructed pendulum clocks, the largest of which ticked slowly.

There were tiered, blue velvet shelves inside the glass cabinet, and these were strewn with all kinds of gold and platinum jewellery, each tray holding various examples made from the same materials and stones. One shelf was devoted entirely to gold rings encrusted with rubies; another contained white gold with emeralds. Pendants, bracelets, necklaces all had their own shelves. The prices were ridiculous. Surely no one around here could afford such extravagance? Sally followed the cabinet to its far end, mouth agape as hundreds of thousands of pounds worth of hand-fashioned finery sparkled and glittered at her under the cabinet's display lights. At the far end were the most dazzling matching sets of rings, earrings and bracelets she had ever seen. There wasn't a piece of silver in the shop.

'Can I help you?' a voice boomed.

Sally jumped and, tearing her eyes away from the emerald and diamond combinations, looked up into the grey eyes of Mr Anstey. He was old, tiny and wearing a dirty apron. A pair of clear plastic protective goggles were pushed up high on his lined forehead. There were two red circles around his eyes where they had been.

'I don't know,' she said, feeling the blood rise to her cheeks. 'It's all a bit beyond my price range.' The man cocked his ear toward her as she spoke and she saw the button hearing aid inserted in it. It trailed a wire to a microphone attached to the top of his apron. Apparently, Mr Anstey had developed his ear-cocking habit long before he got his hearing aid. Old habits were hard to shake. He made no reply and Sally wondered if he knew what she'd said.

'Do you make all this yourself?' she asked, her voice louder this time.

'Every item,' he said. 'Been doing it for forty years. Not rich yet.' He shook his head. 'Wife nags. Says I don't charge enough. Materials expensive, see? Prices just cover materials. Don't charge enough for labour, she says. I charge fair prices, says I. Make enough money to get by. What's wrong with that? I love my work.' He shrugged. 'Maybe I'm wrong. Like people to have quality see? No substitute for quality. Can I help you?' he said suddenly, as if remembering what he was here for.

Sally draw a breath to ask about the crosses, but Mr Anstey's mind had gone off at a tangent. 'Was in the back polishing a new piece when you came in,' he said. 'Didn't hear you. Gold solitaire. Want to see it?'

'Not just now Mr . . .'

'Anstey, like it says on the door,' he boomed, putting out a grubby hand for Sally to shake. She shook and was surprised at his firm grip.

'Been here two months now,' he said. 'Sold fourteen pieces. New carpet soon. What piece did you want to see, young lady?'

'It's a pair of crosses. You put them in the window just now. There's no price on them.'

Anstey folded his arms and smiled at her for a time. 'The talisman,' he said. 'Only item in the shop not made by me. Got it this morning, not five and twenty minutes ago. Selling for an old friend as a favour. Don't normally sell other people's work.'

'There are two of them,' Sally said, confused by his reference to *it*.

'Parts of the same thing. They fit together. Eye in the small one shines through the hole in the big one.'

'How much is it?' Sally asked.

'It's an antiquity, that's what it is. Never seen one before in all my puff. Greek or Egyptian or something. Supposed to guard the wearer against the evil eye. That's what she told me. She's ninety-one now, wanted to sell it, see. Fixed the price for some reason. Odd old girl. Told her it was worth a hundred times what she asked. Value not monetary, that's what she said. George, she said, it's value is not monetary, just find it a good home. Will you give it a good home?'

Sally nodded. 'If I can afford it.' Her heart was sinking steadily as the old man spoke. If the cross *was* antique – and it looked as though it was – the price was going to be way out of the window. She had already made up her mind that she would keep the little one and give the big one to Dave, now she was telling herself to forget it.

'Ninety-nine pounds to you,' George Anstey smiled.

'Sorry?'

'I've got the hearing problem, not you!' he chuckled. 'You heard right. Ninety-nine pounds. Ask no questions. I knew it'd go today. It's a lovely piece. Make a good present. It's yours, isn't it?'

'Yes,' Sally said, excitedly.

Dave looked at Sally across the restaurant table. The cross was still clutched in his hand, the silver now warm. 'He knew you were going to buy it?'

'He seemed to be expecting me. It was weird. It was like I was *meant* to buy it.'

'It's not stolen or anything, is it?' he asked.

Sally shook her head. 'I have a receipt. It's all official.'

'Then why was it so cheap?' he said, but he had a feeling that he was going to find out soon.

Sally shrugged and smiled happily. 'Just accept it as a bit of good fortune. Christ knows we deserve a bit of good fortune.'

'I love you.' Dave blew a kiss at her. 'I've always wanted a talisman against the evil eye. What *is* the evil eye?'

'What the chef's got. He's looking at us again.'

Dave turned and peered into the shadows. 'Hi there!' he yelled at the lurking chef. 'Nice meal!' The man nodded curtly and slunk away.

'Something else weird,' Sally said.

'What now? I can't take much more. I'll wear out my brain before I'm twenty if I'm not careful.'

She handed him the small cross. 'Fit them together,' she said.

He took the little cross and inspected it closely. It was identical to the larger one in every respect except for the position of the eye which was slightly higher and more prominent, and the fact that there was no indentation in its back to accept a smaller one. The back of Sally's was smooth and had no markings. Dave could feel the warmth it had picked up from Sally's hands and this made him smile and decide that he really did love her after all. There was no doubt about it.

36

The little cross was only half the weight of his, but it seemed to give off the same feeling of serenity and gazing into its green eye made him feel great. The tense atmosphere that had plagued him all evening had dissolved and taken the feeling that something bad was about to happen with it.

'S'nice,' he said, wondering if it really was the crosses making him feel good, or just the effects of the alcohol he had consumed during the evening. He did feel a little drunk if he was honest with himself.

He turned his cross over and placed Sally's face down in the indentation. It fitted into the groove easily and slid home with a little metallic *snick!*

'Fits well,' he said, examining it. It was precision engineered to a minute tolerance and he wondered how they had made it so well all those years ago. The back of Sally's cross laid exactly flush with the back of his own and the line where they fitted together was barely visible. He ran his finger across it and couldn't feel the join.

'Turn it over,' Sally said, enthusiastically, 'it won't fall out again!'

And it didn't. Dave gazed at the front of the combined cross in amazement. The smaller eye looked as if it had been built into the surface as the larger one had. Now the two eyes were together, the cross seemed to have taken on a hypnotic quality. The red and the green irises complemented one another in a way that went far deeper than mere colour co-ordination. The talisman felt powerful now and Dave experienced an excitement that sharpened the edges of his serenity.

'What holds it together?' he asked.

'Love,' Sally said, laughing. 'It's great isn't it? It's a puzzle cross. Try and take it to pieces again.'

He took hold of the eyelet in the smaller cross, and tugged. Nothing happened. 'It's stuck,' he said, trying again.

'You don't do it like that.'

'How then?' He turned it over and pushed against the smaller eye. Still nothing happened. He rattled it, but the little cross stayed resolutely inside the big one.

'There *is* a way,' Sally assured him. 'I went through all this in the shop.'

'I'll bet you had to be told how to do it,' Dave said. 'You didn't work it out on your own. Did you?' he added.

'No, I didn't. You have to hold it upright and tap the bottom on the table three times.'

'You're joking, surely!'

Sally shrugged. 'Same reaction as mine,' she said in mock boredom. 'Try it and see.'

'It's not possible,' he protested. 'There's no mechanism in there that's holding it together, it's just a push fit.'

'Well you've tried to push it out again. What happened?'

'Nothing,' he admitted.

'Well, tap it three times on the table then and see what happens.'

'I don't have to say a magic word or anything as well, do I?' he asked, now resigned to playing her game.

'No magic involved,' she replied. 'Just cunning engineering. They weren't stupid, y'know, those ancient Greeks.'

'Or Egyptians.'

'Or whatever they were. No one knows for sure. Apparently it was in the old lady's family for hundreds of years – a sort of heirloom – and no one knows its history.'

He held the cross upright by the horizontal and tapped the bottom of it gently on the table three times as she had instructed. The smaller cross fell out after the third tap and lay on the table, its green eye glinting at Dave.

'What?' he said, astonished.

Sally laughed. 'I told you so,' she said merrily. 'Works every time.'

'There's some kind of a trick involved, isn't there?' he said.

Sally shook her head. 'Nope.'

'It's not possible.' He picked up the little cross and inserted it again. It went in as easily as before, and still wouldn't come out, no matter how hard he pushed on the eye or pulled on the tiny ring at the back. 'If it comes apart when you tap it, you must only have to tap it until it gets loose, right?'

'Three times, that's what Mr Anstey said. No more, no less. Try it. I did.'

He tapped the cross once on the table and waited. Nothing happened. He examined the back expecting the smaller insert to be protruding slightly, but it wasn't. It was still perfectly aligned and flush. He tapped a second time.

'You have to do the taps together,' Sally explained. 'If you tap once, wait and tap again, that's one tap each time. It doesn't count as two.'

'Oh,' Dave said, frowning. He tapped twice in quick succession. Nothing happened. Then he tapped four times. Nothing happened. 'This is impossible,' he said.

'No it isn't,' Sally replied. 'It works.'

He tapped it three times. The small cross fell out again. 'But how does it distinguish between three taps and four taps? How does it know you're going to tap again?'

'Something to do with the movement, I expect,' she said. 'You do it three times and stop.'

'But how does it *work*?'

'It just does, that's all,' Sally said, shaking her head and looking at him as if he was the slowest person in class.

He pulled out the magnifying glass of his Swiss Army knife and scrutinised the indentation in the big cross. There was nothing to see. The shoulders were perfectly smooth and had no hidden catches – neither did the rim of the smaller cross. 'Magic,' he said finally, resigned to his bafflement.

'But do you like it?'

'I love it. Thanks. I'm having the best birthday ever!'

'I was going to buy two silver chains to hang them on, but Mr Anstey said not to. He said the quality of this silver is different to the stuff his chains are made of and they wouldn't go together. He doesn't normally sell silver chains, but he showed me some he had in a drawer and he was right. The crosses look awful on silver chains. The old woman told him they had to be hung on leather, but she'd lost the ones she had. He didn't have any leather straps in the shop so I decided to go and buy some. I had to walk the length and breadth of the town before I could find these.' She pulled two thin leather laces from her handbag and gave one to Dave. 'You've got to hang it on this or it won't work against the evil eye,' she assured him. 'And you've got to keep your cross away from other metals or its power will be reduced. Got it?'

'Yeah, I've got it,' Dave said, threading the lace through the eyelet and tying the ends together. 'Now all I need is an evil eye to see if it works!'

Outside in the car park, Dave noticed something. 'Listen,' he said, standing in the same spot as he had three hours ago.

'What?' Sally stood still and listened.

'What can you hear?'

'Cars on the motorway,' she said, realising the silence they had experienced earlier was gone. They were surrounded by all the sounds of a normal Saturday night, the kind of cluttered distant background noise of cars and dogs and people that you didn't notice until it stopped. It was comforting to have them there again.

'Voices,' Dave said. 'I can hear someone yelling from miles away.'

A car sped past the car park. Dave smiled. 'It's finished, whatever it was,' he said.

'The talismans,' Sally replied. 'Or is it talismen? They work!'

The journey back to Dave's parents' house was uneventful, and it wasn't until he took the cross off later that evening that he saw The Claw.

His parents were in bed and asleep when they arrived nursing their distended bellies. It was ten past eleven. They went into the lounge and turned on the television. *The Creature from the Black Lagoon* was showing on BBC2 in black and white. Dave waved his talisman at the monster. It pawed the air and the scene ended. 'It works,' he told Sally.

'Come here, dickhead!' she said, catching his arm and pulling him to her. She kissed him passionately, then broke away

40

and stared into his eyes while her hips ground against him. 'Happy birthday, Mr Hard-On,' she said, then pushed him away. 'Go and make me a cup of tea.'

'What's it worth?' he asked.

'I'll think of something,' she smiled.

When he returned with two mugs of steaming tea Sally was sprawled across the settee. She was naked. 'Happy birthday,' she said again.

The tea got cold.

At three minutes to midnight while Dave and Sally were lying contented in one another's arms, Detective Inspector Grogan trudged to the middle of the cornfield and gently told Derek Cousins that they were calling the search off for the night.

'But you can't!' Derek protested. 'We haven't found him yet!' He shook Grogan's arm away from his own, and staggered two paces forward through the long corn. 'Tommy!' he shouted. 'Come on Tiger, time to go home!'

'Leave it,' Grogan said quietly. 'There's no more you can do tonight.'

Derek Cousins turned back to face him. His face shone a ghastly white in the moonlight and his eyes were brimming with tears. 'I can't leave it,' he sobbed. 'That's my *son* you're talking about. He's gone. Vanished. I've got to find him!'

'I'm sorry Derek, but you're not going to find him out here tonight,' Grogan said sympathetically. His heart went out to the man and he wished he could offer some comfort. Grogan had kids of his own and could easily imagine how Cousins must be feeling. Christ knew how *he'd* react in this situation. It didn't bear thinking about. He'd probably end up in hospital under sedation like this guy's wife had if it happened to him. 'He's not in any of the fields surrounding Easthampstead park, anyway, Derek,' he said. 'Go home and get some sleep and start again in the morning. I'll drive you.'

Derek Cousins stood before him, his hands clapped over his eyes and his shoulders heaving as he sobbed. 'I've g-got to find him,' he said in a high pitched child-like voice. 'I've *got* to.'

41

Grogan sighed, went to Derek and put his arm round the man's shoulders.

'Help me,' Derek sobbed. 'Please help me!'

Grogan didn't know what more they could do. Easthampstead Park had been thoroughly searched. The houses had been examined from attic to cellar and the fairground employees had all been questioned. No one had seen Tommy except a woman running a darts stall who thought (but couldn't swear to it) she had seen him watching the people going through the Glass Maze. It was his unruly shock of golden hair she remembered. The times added up – the one she gave Grogan was about five minutes after Tommy had vanished, but no one had spotted him since then.

Grogan had taken a serious view of the missing child; just recently kiddies always seemed to be going missing at funfairs. Four had disappeared this year so far. One body had been found. It wasn't really so surprising though, in this day and age – funfairs were purpose-built hunting grounds for the child molesting perverts that abounded just lately.

But Grogan was an optimist. Earlier in the day, he hadn't really believed that Tommy Cousins had been kidnapped at all. Not here in Bracknell. Lots of kids went missing every day and turned up safe and sound after a while. It was more likely that the child had wandered off and got lost. There was a possibility that he had found his way into one of the surrounding fields and injured himself somehow. Now darkness had fallen that hope was fading and the other alternative was seeming more and more likely.

'All the patrol cars in Bracknell and Wokingham have been told to keep an eye out for him,' he said, leading Derek back to the road. 'We'll probably have found him by the morning. Leave it to the experts, eh?'

'Gotta go to the toilet,' Dave muttered. He peeled himself away from Sally and their sweaty skin made a noise like a plaster being ripped off as it parted. She grabbed a skinny leg. 'Don't leave me,' she said in a pathetic voice and pulled him back, her right hand finding his lower abdomen and quickly applying pressure.

'You sod!' he said, trying to wriggle free as Sally pressed on his full bladder. 'I knew you were going to torture me!' He shook her off and left her giggling on the sofa as he staggered around the room pulling on his underpants and trousers.

'Guard my cross,' he told her as he left the room. 'With your life if necessary!' The crosses were on the low table next to the sofa. After five minutes of lovemaking Sally's had whacked him in the front teeth so they had taken them off. He wanted to go and put his back on, but he knew if he went near the table Sally would attempt to make him wet himself again, so he decided against it.

'Yessir!' Sally said and saluted making her right breast wiggle. Dave leered at her and left the room.

He trudged up the stairs in the dark, realising how weary he felt. His legs were like lead tubes. The cord for the bathroom light proved hard to find and he groaned, waving his arm about in front of him like a blind man feeling for obstacles. It wasn't until he'd managed to turn the light on and locked the door that he realised something was wrong. In his still slightly inebriated and tired state he couldn't quite put his finger on what it was though and decided it wasn't important. He was a little unsteady on his feet and reached the conclusion that pissing sitting down would be preferable to standing and having to support himself by holding onto the pipes that ran down the wall next to the toilet. He undid his trousers, pulled them and his underpants down together and sat on the toilet, peering around the room suspiciously. Nothing seemed to be out of place; the bath and shower were still placed along the right hand wall where they had always been; the sink unit was still mounted on top of the little cupboard to his right and at the back of the room, the pink-painted radiator was draped with towels as usual.

But the lid was askew on the linen basket.

Dave realised this halfway through relieving himself and his muscles instantly clamped off the flow. For a few seconds he was certain that the lid of the Ali Baba wicker basket where all his dirty jeans and tee shirts lived between washes had been on properly when he came in. He half expected the chef from the Ziegfeld restaurant to pop up from inside, his piggy eyes shining and his meat cleaver glittering dangerously while he drooled and sang 'Happy birthday to you,' one last time.

Then the moment passed, and Dave's muscles allowed him to finish urinating. Of course the lid of the basket had been half off when he came in. Things didn't move of their own accord, did they?

He was about to get up when the lid fell from the basket. 'Shit!' he breathed. *Just you coming into the bathroom, that's what disturbed it, wasn't it? Wasn't it?* he asked himself.

The basket itself wobbled. The movement was slight and he couldn't swear that it *had* moved at all. Although his mind was racing and he could feel the blood silently leaving his face, he sat still and stared, unbelieving. The basket couldn't possibly have moved.

The basket creaked and leaned toward the radiator.

This isn't happening! This is not possible! Dave shouted inwardly at himself. *It's your eyes, they're playing tricks.* He gulped in a lungful of warm air that seemed as thick as treacle. His heart started to batter his ribcage. A putrid stench rose and filled the room so quickly that Dave inhaled it on his next breath. The basket leaned even more. Its top end was now against the wall. Then the loose floorboard over by the radiator creaked and Dave looked down at the blue carpet. There wasn't someone in the basket at all, but what was causing it to move scared him even more.

A lump had formed in the carpet beneath the basket and was tipping it up. The bulge was semicircular, as if someone had placed a small upside down bowl between the floorboards and the carpet. And it was moving; pulsating in a slow, steady rhythm like a beating heart. Above it, the wicker basket rocked back and forth, creaking.

Dave stood and was frantically pulling his trousers up when the lump zoomed across the room towards him with a sound of rending floorboards and tearing carpet adhesive. It passed right beneath his feet, and it was solid. It lifted his right foot first, then his left, throwing him off balance and sending him crashing to the floor. He rolled and got up quickly, his ears singing. Whatever it was had been heading for the edge of the carpet where it was cut to accept the toilet pedestal. It was probably out by now – whatever it was – and stalking him.

He peered at the base of the toilet, but nothing was there and the carpet seemed to be undisturbed. 'Oh, God,' Dave said, wishing someone would come and rescue him. Surely the noise must have alerted his parents. Sally must have been able to hear it from downstairs, for Christ's sake! Why didn't someone come and hammer on the bathroom door and make reality come back?

On shaking legs he approached the toilet bowl and peered round the back. Nothing was there. He checked the ceiling and the sink, but couldn't make himself open the cupboard beneath it. The disgusting smell started to fade as he stood there and he began to suspect he'd had some kind of hallucination. His pulse steadied – although it was still far too fast – and his breathing relaxed.

That was when he heard the noise in the toilet. *GLUP*! it went, as though air had somehow blown back through the hidden bend where Domestos killed all known germs. He took a pace forward and looked down into the water which was yellow where he'd pissed. There was a long thin black object lying on the bottom of the porcelain. It was about three-quarters of an inch wide and perhaps six inches long. Dave couldn't tell for sure because it seemed to extend up around the U trap where he couldn't see. It didn't look like a turd that had escaped the flush, that was for sure. He peered down at it in the murky water and shuddered. It looked like a long black finger. He reached over to the cistern and pulled the flush. When the replica Niagara had abated, the black thing had gone.

'Christ,' Dave said. Sweat was pouring off him so he went to the sink, filled it, then wiped his face with his flannel, relishing the feel of the cool water on his skin. He bent over the sink and cupped his hands, bringing the water up to his face. His eyes were closed, so he didn't see the lump form again at the base of the toilet. He felt it pass beneath his feet though, and staggered back as the plug blew out of the basin and the sinkful of water gouted up. The force of the rising water knocked the tooth-brushes out of the rack and emptied the small shelf above the sink of its contents. It soaked the first aid cabinet and smeared the mirror with his mother's Signal toothpaste which she never bothered putting the top back on. A lot of the airborne water came down in Dave's eyes, blurring his vision. As he wiped them, the stuff from the shelves descended and clattered into the empty sink.

The lump shot across the carpet again, towards the bath this time. Dave followed it with unbelieving eyes. There was a pause, then a violent gurgling noise and the murky water from the bath U bend was blown forcefully into the air.

Then Dave noticed the bulge in the shower pipe which came out of the wall just above the taps. It was an electrical shower and the pipe was the inlet from the mains water supply. Whatever had caused the water to blow out of the plug hole in the bath couldn't have travelled up here through the pipes because they weren't connected. The pipe was copper – Dave knew that, because he'd helped Reggie plumb the shower in – and although copper was malleable, there was no way that it could possibly bulge like it appeared to be doing without breaking. The lump in the pipe was just above the tap which turned it on and was moving slowly upwards. As it travelled, the piece of pipe where it had been returned to its former shape. Dave watched in horror as the half inch bore tube flexed and expanded to allow the lump to move. Finally, it vanished into the workings of the shower unit itself. Dave knew where it had gone. The shower worked by piping in cold water and turning it in a tight spiral through a seven thousand watt heating element so that it was hot when it came out. This all took place behind a white plastic cover that had a knob on you could turn to make the water hotter or cooler. The bulge was now in the works of the shower, gradually squeezing its bulk through the spiral towards the shower head.

Dave listened carefully, and found he was able to hear the small noises as the pipes stretched and shrank again inside the shower unit. Although he was terrified, he found himself unable to look away from the shower. A small voice in the back of his mind had begun to assure him that all this was probably a temporary mental aberration, and even the water which still dripped from the ceiling would probably vanish when this all finished.

A few droplets of water dribbled from the shower head, then the stench came back, driving the small voice away almost instantly. This was *real*.

The shower head began to bubble and gelatinous black strands of the evil smelling substance poured out of the rings of tiny holes in the shower head. They glistened as they grew longer and became entwined, sticking together and forming a gooey lump which piled up in the bottom of the bath. Dave was transfixed. His mind had stopped trying to understand what was happening, and was reeling crazily. He gasped and groaned quietly as he watched the slime fall from the shower, unsure of what he should do next. There was a scream in his throat, but it was stuck there like a jagged piece of glass. He didn't feel real any more and only knew he was alive because he kept on breathing in that *stench*.

The stuff stopped coming out of the shower then, and the pile in the bath became liquid and flowed down towards the plughole, where it oozed through.

Then the lump was under the carpet again cruising across the floor towards the toilet. Dave knew in his heart that this was its final action. He knew that it was going to come out of the toilet and kill him if he didn't stop it.

There was a toilet brush in a plastic holder in the cupboard under the sink and without thinking, Dave opened the door and got it. His Swiss Army knife was in his trousers pocket. He took it out and opened the big blade, then advanced on the toilet.

The black thing was in there again, but he could see what it was now. It was a long black finger. It was bottom up and had two joints like a human finger, but this one was three times the

47

length. Its skin was smooth and shiny and had no fingerprints. As he stared at it, it curled in a beckoning motion and he could see its long, pointed ebony fingernail. It was just as he had imagined it when Reggie told him about what the driving instructor had said.

He moved quickly, reaching out for the toilet cover with the nylon bristle brush. His arm was only over the toilet for a split second, but it felt like an age and he mentally visualised the clawed finger breaking the surface of the water and shooting upwards so that it pierced his arm like a poison dart.

The toilet cover clattered down over the seat and Dave put his foot on top of it to prevent whatever it was down there from escaping. He pulled the flush, waited for the cistern to fill and flushed it again. Then he stood back and carefully lifted the cover and seat with the brush. He waited for a few seconds then went forward enough to see the water at the bottom of the pan.

'Guh!' he said and froze to the spot, his face a contorted mask of fear and every hair on his body standing erect.

There was a whole hand down there now. It was spread out, palm up and the spindly fingers were out of the water. There were no creases in the finger joints which were slightly bulbous and the narrow palm looked like it was made of slick black rubber. The ebony nails were hooked like talons. When it moved, Dave knew that it wouldn't be soft to the touch like a joke-shop monster hand. The thick tendons and muscles that bulged beneath the taut skin looked hard and powerful.

Jesus, it's The Claw! Jesus, it's The Claw! Jesus, it's The Claw! Dave's mind screamed.

The clawed hand slid out of the water like a snake, propelled by a sinewy wrist and forearm that seemed to slide around the hidden bend in spite of its muscular firmness. The fingers cleared the rim of the toilet bowl and kept rising. The arm swivelled then, so that the hand was raised and drawn back as if to strike at Dave, the clawed fingers spread and the dangerous ebony nails glimmering darkly.

Unthinking, Dave struck at the hand with his Swiss Army knife, leaning forward as he brought it around in an arc. The fingers snapped shut, but not quickly enough to catch the knife. When they opened again a gaping wound was revealed across the palm. Dave clearly saw purple tendons pulling deep inside, then dark green pus welled up and obscured them. The pus dribbled from the gash and fell on the rim of the toilet. The hand closed and opened once more, and the skin was faultless again. The wound had gone. The arm slid even further out of the toilet. Now the hand was almost at the same height as Dave's head and the elbow joint was visible just inside the pan. Dave took a step back as the hand reached out for him. He brought the knife down again, slashing wildly. The knife caught the wrist this time, but it might as well have hit a steel post. The force of the blow jarred the knife from Dave's hand and he stared incredulously at the undamaged wrist.

The Claw slashed at him, moving with incredible speed. He leaned back, sucking his stomach in reflexively and it missed by a fraction of an inch.

The next strike missed him completely, but he wasn't ready for the hand to change direction as quickly as it did. It seemed to have no momentum to overcome and just stopped going one way and came back the other with no pause in between. The ebony nail on the long middle finger hooked in the front belt loop of Dave's new drainpipe legged jeans and dragged him across the floor towards the toilet. He dug his heels in, but he was no match for the incredible strength it possessed.

The Claw was freezing cold. He could feel the cold coming off the arm in waves which increased as he drew closer to the porcelain bowl. The belt loop in his trousers grew a coat of frost. Still the arm pulled him closer.

He could see down into the bowl now, see the muscular black shoulder which filled the bottom of the pan. Suddenly, his mind cleared.

'Get away from me!' he hissed, striking pathetically at the arm with the nylon toilet brush. 'Getawayfrommeee! Let go or I'll kill you, you motherfucker!' He hit it again with the brush.

It stopped pulling. He hit it again, harder this time.

The Claw slipped from his belt loop and the arm retreated, stood ready to strike.

'Motherfuckingbastard!' Dave spat. He lunged at it with the brush. Its little finger snapped off with a sound like a carrot being broken in half. Dave heard it plop into the water. The green pus oozed from the wound. Dave poked at it again. 'Kill you, I'll kill you!' he promised it, now feeling rage replace his fear.

The hand shot forward and grabbed the bristle end of the brush, then slid back into the toilet, dragging Dave towards the bowl. He didn't let go of the handle, but tugged back although he was losing ground. The hand went back down the pan until all but two of its fingers were beneath the water. The broken one lay on the bottom, and its stump bled pus into the water, clouding it.

Dave stood with one foot on either side of the toilet, pulling for all he was worth. Then the brush snapped and he lurched backwards and fell heavily, striking his head hard on the floor. It bounced once, but he was already unconscious and didn't feel the second blow.

On his wrist, his watch bleeped midnight.

The weird Saturday had finished.

Chapter Two
Lucky

Sally was starting to get worried about Dave. He had been gone for ages. She had heard the flush go three times (the pipes were old and made enough noise to wake the dead as the cistern refilled) and she thought she had heard Dave cursing. Evidently, Ziegfeld's Entrecote Diane had not agreed with him.

The Creature from the Black Lagoon was almost finished but she'd lost interest in it now, and she turned down the sound in order to hear what was going on in the bathroom. Although the toilet was at the other end of the house from the lounge, the sound filtered through. There were a few seconds of silence, then several splashing noises which she interpreted as Dave throwing up. This was followed by two heavy footsteps and a noise like something breaking. The thud – which was obviously Dave collapsing – reverberated through the whole house.

'Oh God,' Sally said, 'he's passed out.' Reggie and Doreen were sure to wake up, so she quickly retrieved her clothes. Reg and Doreen didn't appear, however, and after a while of wondering just how heavily some people could sleep, she went upstairs to the bathroom.

The light was on in there; she could see it shining through a small gap at the bottom of the door. She stood outside the door and listened, but there was no sign of life inside. 'Dave,' she whispered, 'are you alright?'

Dave didn't reply. What if he'd fallen over and banged his head on the toilet? He might be lying on the floor bleeding to

51

death. Or perhaps he was suffocating, his own vomit blocking his throat and getting sucked into his lungs as he tried to breathe. She'd heard of that happening. *But he wasn't drunk enough for that to happen, was he?* she asked herself hopefully.

She tried the door handle and was amazed to find that the door opened. Dave was lying in the middle of the floor on his back, his face ghostly white. His hair and chest were soaked with water and there were splashes all down his new jeans. Even as she watched, the blue dye was probably coming out and staining his legs. His bare feet were pressed together and the black plastic handle of a toilet brush lay against his chest, gripped firmly in both hands. He looked like a skinny dead Crusader laid out to rest.

Sally breathed a sigh of relief when she saw that his heart was beating. It pulsed the skin up and down in the gap between his ribs and was quick but regular. She didn't notice the frayed belt loop at the front of his jeans. He took a deep, shuddering breath and sighed it out again. Behind their closed lids, his eyes flickered.

That'll teach you to drink too much champagne, she thought. The room didn't smell of sick though, which was strange. It smelt more like rotting vegetation. She knelt next to him, put her hand on his stomach which was cold and damp. 'Dave,' she said, pressing gently with her hand. 'Dave!'

He groaned and his eyes flickered. Then he came round and looked puzzled. 'What are you doing in here?' he asked, sitting up staring at the broken brush handle as if he'd never seen it before. He put it down and massaged his eyes with his hands.

'What happened?' Sally asked. 'You're all wet.'

'Shit,' Dave muttered, looking quickly around the room.

'Lost something?' she said, following his gaze.

'I dunno,' he replied, thinking: Wasn't I doing something terribly important just a minute ago? Wasn't something coming after me?

'You been sick?'

That sounded about right, Dave decided. 'Yeah . . . I s'pose I must have been.' He was almost certain he hadn't been.

52

There was no taste in his mouth, no sicky smell in his nose.

'And then you tried to have a shower with your trousers on and then you fell over,' she said, looking at the mess in the bath and the wet patch on the ceiling. 'You must have knocked all the stuff off the shelf when you fell, right?'

Dave nodded and struggled to his feet. He felt drained and had no idea what was going on.

'Only one question,' Sally continued. 'How did you manage to break the lavatory brush? And did you do that before, or after your shower?'

Dave went to the toilet and peered down into the water. The bristle end of the brush was wedged into the U-bend. There was a layer of stuff that looked like black mud coating the bottom third of the pan.

Sally had started to pick up the fallen razor blades and tubes of toothpaste so she didn't see the look of fear that passed across Dave's eyes as he stared into the toilet. He wanted to take the broken brush out of there, but for reasons he couldn't fathom, he was scared to put his hand in. He thought about it for a while, but no answers came. He pulled the flush, hoping that the muck down in the pan would go away.

'What *is* all this?' Sally asked in a tone of disgust. She was holding the Swiss Army knife up by its key ring attachment, keeping it well away from her. The sticky black substance coated the exposed blade. It dripped while Dave stared blankly at it, oozing like melting toffee. A black gob of the stuff descended to the bathroom floor on a shiny, ever-stretching strand.

'You didn't sick this up, did you?' Sally asked, horrified. She put the knife in the sink and turned on the hot tap.

'I don't know where that came from,' Dave said. *It's dead now, whatever it was,* he thought, not knowing why he was thinking it. He steeled himself to look in the toilet pan. The muck had been successfully flushed away. He reached in and grabbed the broken brush head, tugged it out of the U bend. Sally had the handle and he gave her the brush. 'Shove it back in the cupboard, Sal,' he said.

She looked at him, her concern apparent. 'You're ever so pale,' she said taking the wet brush head. 'Why don't you go downstairs and sit down. I'll finish clearing up in here.'

The sudden *crash* on the bathroom door startled both of them. Dave let out a little yelp of fear.

'Wassamatter?' a tired voice demanded. Reggie had finally woken.

'It's okay Dad,' Dave said, not opening the door. 'I just fell over. Knocked some stuff down. Bit drunk I suppose. Did I wake you up?'

'Noise,' Reggie declared sleepily. 'Heard a noise. Where's Sally? Gone home?'

'She's in here with me,' Dave admitted. 'Helping me clear up.'

'Oh yeah,' Reggie yawned in a heard-it-all-before voice. 'Kids – Christ help us,' he muttered to himself. 'Well hurry up will you, I want to get in there.'

'Won't be a minute Reggie,' Sally said cheerfully.

'In the toilet for God's sake,' they heard Reggie mutter as he stomped across the landing back to his bedroom. 'What will they think of next?'

Sally tittered, but her face was beet red.

'He thinks we came up here to have it away,' Dave said, amused. 'Shall we?'

'You're in no fit state,' she told him, turning him round by his shoulders and pointing him at the door. 'Go downstairs and sit. If you're still awake when I come down we'll see what we can do about your libido.'

Dave raised a smile in spite of the confusion he was feeling. 'That's a part of my intestines, isn't it?' he said.

She nodded. 'I'm going to have your guts for garters. Now go downstairs.' She opened the door, thrust him out and set about clearing the place up.

The smell had almost cleared now, but she opened the window anyway. A moth flew in instantly and fluttered around the light. Insect disposal was normally Dave's job, but she could handle it if she needed to. The insect was no longer whizzing around the light now, it was on the carpet, creeping along the strand of black stuff that had dropped from the knife blade. She bent over and peered at it. The insect had reached the dollop at the end now, and was feeding on it. It was disgusting. Sally's skin began to crawl up and down her spine. She caught a whiff of the black substance then, and could stand it no more. Reaching out, she caught hold of the toilet roll and yanked a few sheets off. She wadded it and brought it down hard on the moth, crunching it up in her hand afterwards. Strands of the black stuff followed the paper as she lifted it. She flushed the dead moth away, then tried to get what was left of the substance off the carpet. The toilet paper was no good; the stuff just came up in sticky strands, and the smell was awful.

Then she remembered the knife in the sink. The water was still running over it and it was clean. The substance was apparently water soluble.

What is this stuff? she wondered. She had never before seen anything like it. It was repulsive and it scared her somehow. It certainly hadn't come up from Dave's stomach, so where had it come from? *Stuff like that shouldn't be allowed to exist,* she thought, wetting some more toilet paper and dabbing it on the carpet.

But the stuff had got here, wherever it had come from, and she had a nasty feeling in her guts that before long she was going to find out everything she never wanted to know about it.

When she got downstairs again, Dave and his libido had fallen asleep. Sally covered him up with a blanket that Doreen had crocheted, retrieved her underwear and her cross, kissed him goodnight and went home.

'Here you are, you dirty little sod!'

Dave opened his eyes and was surprised to find himself in the lounge and peering through what seemed to be a veil. He was still wearing the jeans he'd got for his birthday and the blanket was over his head. He was drenched with sweat. Reggie stood in front of him holding a cup of tea and the Sunday paper.

'What time is it?' Dave asked, fighting to remember how he had come to be here.

'Eleven thirty, about time you woke up,' his father said, setting the tea and paper down on the coffee table. 'Sally's gone home,' he said. 'Your mum and I thought she might be in your bed, but she wasn't. She must have left you here when you fell asleep I suppose.'

'Oh,' Dave said, feeling the colour rise to his cheeks. He didn't remember her going. 'Have you seen my glasses?' he asked, trying to move the subject away from what he and Sally might or might not have been doing last night.

'On the table,' Reggie said, nodding at them.

Dave put them on and picked up the paper.

'So what was all the rumpus last night? What were you both doing in the bathroom?' Reggie said.

'Nothing.' Dave couldn't remember being in the bathroom at all. *Which might be just as well by the sound of it, Davey,* he thought. *Surely not screwing? Were we?*

'You were making a lot of noise about doing nothing,' Reggie persisted, apparently enjoying seeing his son squirm. 'Dirty little sod,' he said again.

'Did you see my cross?' Dave asked, knowing that his guilty face was shining like a stop light.

Reggie picked it up and admired it. 'That's funny,' he said, peering at it. 'I came in earlier, and I could have sworn that its eye was closed.'

'I expect it was asleep,' Dave quipped, sipping the tea.

Reggie dismissed the matter with a shrug. 'Right, your mum and I are sitting in the garden,' he said. 'If you want anything to eat, you can damn well get it yourself.'

'Shitter,' Dave murmured as he left.

'I heard that,' Reggie called back happily. 'Not so much of the shitter if you don't mind!'

Dave started to leaf through the paper which contained the usual Sunday morning fare. The front page headline story was about a Conservative member of parliament who had been exposed as a paedophile and was currently under arrest. Page two contained boring city news, and page three was mainly taken up by a picture of a girl with breasts so huge she could never fall flat on her face. It was a small item at the bottom of page four that captured Dave's attention: **Child Vanishes From Fairground**. And underneath the subheading read Fourth Reported Missing This Year.

This seemed to hold some special significance for Dave, although he didn't know why it should. The article read:

A trip to the fairground ended in tragedy yesterday when a couple's six year old son disappeared. Little Tommy Cousins – known as Tiger to his parents – vanished when his father went off to buy sweets. Mr Cousins, 34, a chartered accountant, said he left the child with his wife for a few moments while he went to a candy floss stall. According to Mr Cousins, his wife Anne, 30, became distracted while playing a game at a sideshow with her son and didn't notice him wander off.

After a thorough search of the fairground, Mr Cousins called in the police who quickly organised a massive search of the area surrounding the fairground in Easthampstead Park, Bracknell. The child was not found.

A police spokesman said 'We are taking a very serious view of this incident. This is the fourth disappearance of a child from a fairground this year. So far none has been located. These incidents have a very similar pattern and we are almost certain the kidnappings are the work of the same person.'

The police would not comment on the physical risk to Tommy Cousins or the other children, although a source inside the police force is quoted as saying that although no bodies have yet been found, the suspect is likely to be psychopathic and detectives are currently checking records of recently released serial killers.

A tearful Mr Cousins – whose wife is under sedation in hospital – appealed for the kidnapper to return his son unharmed. 'Life isn't worth living without my Tommy,' he told our reporter.

Dave read the report and was appalled. What motivated these people? What sort of a guy hung around fairgrounds and kidnapped little kids? he shuddered as he realised that a part of him had *expected* to read something like this in the paper. It seemed to fit into his consciousness too easily – in the same jigsaw-like way as the present of the cross. In the same way as what had happened in the bathroom last night.

Except that you don't know what happened in the bathroom last night, Davey, he told himself. Perhaps Sally would be able to help him out on that one when she came round today.

Sally couldn't. She turned up at three thirty that afternoon with Phil and Judy and took him to the river at Laverstoke where they swam in the freezing water.

He lay next to Sally on a towel on the riverbank. They were both dripping wet in the hot sunshine, shivering for the first time in weeks. Phil and Judy were still in the water, splashing and screaming as Phil tried to remove Judy's bikini top and she tried to pull down his trunks. Phil seemed to be doing marginally better than Judy at the moment. This was undoubtedly due to his size – although he was only five foot nine tall, Phil weighed almost fourteen stone and was using his extra weight and strength like a battle-tank. Like many fat people, Phil moved with a speed and grace that belied his size. Sally had recently found out that Phil was heavily into old James Brown records, and had nicknamed him the Fat Groover. Phil was, in turns, delighted with his new name and offended by it, depending on the mood he was in at the time.

Dave turned back to Sally. 'Okay, so what happened?' he asked, toying with the silver cross that hung from his neck on its leather cord. The sun glinted in its red iris, making it look fathoms deep. He got the feeling he could poke something small through that shining eye and it would go on forever, perhaps into another dimension.

'What happened when, my little dickhead?' Sally asked, turning on her side so she faced him.

She was taking a tan. She was being dedicated while the hot weather lasted, spending every free minute sitting in the sun.

Her flat belly was golden brown and her back was a mass of freckles which had now almost joined up. She called them sun-kisses.

'What happened in the bathroom?'

'You were sick.' She pushed her brown hair away from her face, struck a model girl pose.

'No I wasn't,' he said. 'What happened?'

'Don't you know?'

'No.'

'Well how do you expect me to know? You sounded as if you were being sick or fighting or something. There was a lot of crashing about. I heard you fall and I came up. You were out cold on the floor. Everything was on the floor – toothpaste, toothbrushes, razors, you name it. There was water everywhere. Half the loo brush was in your hand, the other half was wedged in the toilet bowl. Your Army knife was out.'

He shook his head. It all sounded familiar, but the reasons wouldn't come.

Judy squealed. They turned around. She was in the middle of the river trying to cover her naked breasts with her hands. Phil waved the bikini top triumphantly over his head. 'Get a load of those jugs!' he yelled, and started to try and pull Judy's tiny briefs down. An old man with a little white dog on a blue lead stood on the far bank smiling toothlessly and watching with interest. The threat of being stripped completely made Judy forget her modesty and she started to fight back.

'She's a big girl,' Dave said, smiling.

'Nipples like chapel hat pegs,' Sally laughed. This was one of the expressions Reggie sometimes used when he was in what Dave called *crude mode* and watching scantily clad girls on t.v. 'Phil's getting burnt,' she added. His back was facing them now and his pasty white shoulders looked red and angry.

'Ginger, see,' Dave said. 'People with ginger hair have that milk-coloured skin that never tans. It always burns. He'll be whingeing all the way home. I once spent the day on Bournemouth beach with him, and his skin actually *blistered* that evening. I had to take him to the hospital.'

Judy was fighting for all she was worth now, her hands clenched in the elasticated waistband of Phil's blue trunks while she danced and twisted, keeping his hands from her bikini briefs. Little by little – and accompanied by much high-pitched screaming from Phil – his trunks began to descend. His skin was even paler underneath them, and a distinct line showed where the waistband had been.

'He has got tanned!' Sally said. 'It's just that he hasn't changed colour much. Where the sun's been on his back, his white has gone whiter.'

The tops of Phil's buttocks were now on view, along with the deep crack in his ass. 'You've heard all about the boils on his bum,' Dave said. 'Now you're going to get to see them!'

'I sincerely hope not,' Sally replied. 'I've not digested my lunch yet.'

Phil lurched round to the left and made a desperate grab at Judy's briefs. His fingers caught, dragged the waistband down enough to reveal her pubic hair, then lost their grip and it snapped back up again.

'She's a natural blonde then,' Dave quipped. 'And I thought she dyed her hair.'

On the far river bank, the old man's dog began to bark. It stood right on the edge of the bank looking as if it was weighing up the pros and cons of joining Phil and Judy in the water. The old man seemed to have lost interest and was facing down-stream feeding a brown pipe with tobacco from a plastic pouch.

Judy gave a war cry and leapt at Phil, catching his trunks and dragging them down to his thighs as she sank in the water. Phil, hobbled by the trunks around his legs, began to stagger. The old man's dog finally worked up the courage to jump, and did so, flying in a yapping arc towards the centre of the river about three feet upstream of Judy.

Sally cheered. 'I saw 'em!' she yelled. 'I saw his bits! Good old Judy!'

The dog hit the water, bellyflopping and making a huge splash. It began to swim towards them, barking through jaws clenched against the water. Its top lip puffed out each time it yapped. Its tail worked crazily behind it, not aiding its propulsion at all.

Phil tottered round to face the far bank and save his vital organs from Sally's gaze. This gave them a full view of his huge, white ass. It shone white in the sun like an obscene full moon (which Dave supposed it *was* in a way) that someone had taken an axe to and split in half. Phil's famous boils weren't evident though – just a few red spots, peppered here and there.

That was when Phil went down.

He yelled first. The cry was short and sharp and Dave thought he'd stepped on a piece of broken glass, or a sharp stone. Phil's arms shot above his head as though he was about to dive forwards, and his pale buttocks tensed. Then he entered the water in the opposite direction to the way Dave expected him to go. It looked as though his legs had been dragged backwards from beneath him, and he slid beneath the surface slowly and gracefully. For a second, his mop of ginger hair floated in the current at the surface like a sea anemone in an ebb tide, then that too vanished from view.

The dog reached Judy. It was growling and yapping happily as it paddled along. Judy – who as yet did not realise anything was wrong – was shrieking with laughter and punching the air with her fists. The dog bumped into her back, and she turned and faced it in the other direction like a motorised toy boat, so she didn't see Phil's arms reaching out from beneath the river, grasping at thin air.

'He's gone under!' Dave said, standing up.

'He's playing,' Sally said. 'He can swim, can't he?'

Phil didn't surface.

'Judy!' Dave yelled. She was still watching the dog, who was making a looping turn and heading back toward her. The old man on the bank was busy lighting his pipe.

'What?' Judy said, turning to face them.

'He hasn't come up!' Dave craned his neck and could see Phil's body on the river bed, and although the flowing of the river distorted the light, something seemed to be dragging Phil upstream against the current.

Judy went to the middle of the river where it was deepest, the dog followed hot on her trail. 'Where is he?' she screamed. 'I can't see him!'

'There, there!' Dave shouted, pointing at the spot where his friend was lying full stretch on the riverbed. *Don't let him drown, for Christ's sake don't let him drown!* Dave thought. *It's only five feet deep in there right in the centre. He can't drown in five feet of water!*

Forty seconds had passed since Phil went down. Was that long enough for him to die? Surely not. *If he's been breathing river water all that time, I'd say yes, it was long enough for him to die*, Dave's mind coolly informed him.

'Get him out!' he screamed.

'I can't see him!' Judy wailed, trying to part the water in front of her with her hands to afford a better view.

'There! There!' Dave yelled.

He heard movement behind him, and then Sally had entered the water with a perfect dive that hardly disturbed the surface. Dave watched her pull and kick. She was a strong swimmer and reached Phil in five strokes. Judy waded towards her, the dog bumping her back with its nose. She looked terrified.

Sally struggled with Phil's bulk for a few seconds, then surfaced. 'Can't move him!' she said breathlessly. 'Stuck! Help!' She gulped in a breath and dived again.

Phil's body was definitely moving. It had travelled three yards upstream since he went down, and Dave was starting to remember what had happened in the bathroom last night. He stood on the bank, not wanting to dive into the river because he knew what was *really* happening down there. The Claw. It had got hold of Phil's leg and was dragging him away to God knew where. He had defeated it last night and now it wanted revenge.

But he had to help. His friend was drowning. No matter what it cost, he had to try and help.

He got the Swiss Army knife from his trouser pocket, opened the big blade, clamped his teeth on the knife like a pearl diver, and jumped into the water, Judy's screams ringing in his ears.

The shock of the freezing water – worsened by the warmth

of the sun that had been on his skin – almost dragged the breath from his lungs, but he held onto it and swam.

The water was flowing faster where Phil lay, and Dave fought against the current, not even thinking how Phil's body could be moving against the flow. When he reached it, Sally had Phil under the armpits, and was trying to pry him from the bottom. Phil's head was up, his mouth was open and his eyes were closed. He looked dead. A big bubble of air protruded from his mouth as Dave swam by, but it didn't leave, just hung there proving respiration had failed.

Dave swam down the length of Phil's body, to where he knew the trouble was. He *knew* what was holding Phil down, knew what he had to do.

A minute and a half, Davey boy. It must be all of that by now. He's either dead, or he's gonna die. Crazily, he found himself thinking, *But sponge divers in the Med can hold their breath for over three minutes!*

Phil's no sponge diver though, is he? he answered himself. *He's nineteen years old and overweight and not very fit in spite of playing squash once a week. If you get him up he'll die of a heart attack.*

He swam over Phil's bare buttocks – there was a pebble wedged tightly between them now, where had that come from? – and down his short, stocky legs.

And there was The Claw, just as he'd expected, growing out of the stony riverbed on its wiry wrist and clamped down tight around Phil's left ankle. The black slender fingers reached all the way around Phil's leg, and then had some to spare. The nails overhung and had apparently missed his flesh.

The river bed swirled and moved as the wrist slid through it, moving slowly upstream. Dave almost lost his breath again when he saw The Claw, and his lungs started to ache with a vengeance.

He took the Swiss Army knife from between his teeth and dived down at the claw, slashing at the fingers. Phil's body heaved up and down and Sally tried to drag him off the bottom. The gravel that was raised obscured Dave's vision for a second as the knife went in. He felt it connect though.

His lungs had reached bursting point, and he let out a little air which rose in silvery bubbles. The water cleared, showing The Claw again. Its first two fingers had been laid open and the green pus was bubbling out and rising through the water in a sticky streamer. Still it tugged at Phil's leg. Dave struck again. And again.

And Phil started to rise.

Sally had got him off the bottom. Dave allowed himself a mental cheer, which died in his mind when he saw that The Claw hadn't let go at all. It was still hanging on, but the arm had extended out of the riverbed. Dave's lungs screamed but he bobbed down again and slashed out at the fingers one more time. This time they let go. Phil rose. The Claw came after Dave.

His feet found the bottom of the river, and he thrust his legs down, driving himself up and away. His head burst through into daylight, and he gasped in the warm summer air, realising that The Claw might – even now – be searching for his feet beneath the surface.

'Get him to the side!' he shouted pointlessly at Sally who was doing just that. Against his better judgement, he dived again, knife ready.

The Claw was gone.

He swam to where Sally and Judy were moving Phil to the side, floating him like a barge. His face was still in the water. In their panic, neither of them had thought to turn him over.

'Get his face out, for fuck's sake!' Dave screamed, grabbing Phil's shoulders and pulling them over. 'He'll die!'

Phil wasn't easy to invert. It took the three of them to do it and when they did, Phil wasn't breathing and his eyes remained closed. They dragged him to the bank.

'How are we going to get him out?' Sally said. 'He's too heavy.'

Dave scrambled up the bank and started to pull on Phil's arms. The old man had seen what was happening, and was wading across the river, still wearing all his clothes and still smoking his pipe. He looked like a human river boat steamer. His dog was swimming along behind him, yapping and having a great old time.

With his help they got Phil on the bank. 'Put him on his front,' the old man commanded, 'and press on his back. Gets the water out of him.' They rolled him over and Dave pushed down between his shoulder blades. Dank river water spurted from Phil's mouth.

'Again!' the old man said. His dog sniffed interestedly at the water from Phil's lungs.

Dave pushed again. More water came out. Not so much this time, though, he noted.

'Again!' Hardly anything this time.

'Roll him on his back!'

Dave and the old man did this – the two girls were holding on to one another and having quiet hysterics. Judy seemed to be worse than Sally though, Dave thought proudly.

'Pulse!' The man crouched down next to Dave, shooed his dog away.

Dave put his hand on Phil's cold chest. '*I can't feel it!*' he said, a cool hand of panic flashing down his spinal cord. *He's dead*, he thought. *I knew he would be*!

Then, just when he had given up hope, Phil's heart beat. 'Yes! There it is!' he yelled. The pulse was faint and slow, but it was there.

'Pull his neck up and tilt his head back,' the old man said. 'And open his mouth. If there's anything in there, get it out, then blow!'

There was a strand of green weed in Phil's mouth that went right down his throat. Dave pulled it out, tossed it aside, clamped his mouth over Phil's nose and mouth like they had taught him to do at school with the rubber dummy's head and its single football bladder lung, and blew. Phil's chest rose, just like it was supposed to.

'That's enough! Let him breathe out now,' the old man commanded.

Dave stopped blowing and watched Phil's chest fall. He still looked dead and he didn't breathe in on his own. His chest just stayed where it had fallen.

'Again,' the man urged. 'Do it again!'

After twenty-four breaths, Phil started breathing on his own. Dave sat back, exhausted. Sally cheered. The dog barked. Judy bent and kissed Dave, embracing him and pressing her naked breasts against his chest. Dave blushed to the roots of his hair and pulled away, embarrassed.

Phil groaned. He opened his eyes and looked confused. Then he rolled over and threw up.

'You got me out,' he panted, when he had finished. 'The fucking weeds got tangled around my feet. Fuck! I haven't got any clothes on!' he said, sitting up and covering himself with his hands.

'Your trunks are lost, I'm afraid,' Sally said. 'They came off when we dragged you off the bottom. We couldn't get you up. You were stuck fast down there. Dave had to dive and cut the weeds from round your feet before I could move you.' She gave him her towel to cover himself with.

'Did you *see* the weeds?' Dave asked her.

'Yes, of course I did, they were tangled all around his ankles,' she said.

'Oh,' Dave said, and thought, *Is it my mind going bananas, or was it only meant for me to see?* Perhaps it had only been weeds then.

'Thanks guys,' Phil said, 'I couldn't shake the bastards off, no matter how I tried. I got well and truly fucked up there.'

'It doesn't matter,' Dave said, 'I just thank Christ you're still alive. We thought you were a goner.'

Phil coughed and spat out some more water. He was getting some colour back in his face now.

'Did we ought to take him to hospital?' Sally asked. Dave shrugged.

'Did we ought to take you to hospital?' he asked Phil.

'No, no I'm going to be okay now, I think,' he said. 'I just feel a bit sick and a lot knackered.'

'Okay, we'll get you home then,' Sally said.

Judy went and got his clothes and towel. She had calmed down now, but her face was still puffy and her eyes were red where she'd been crying. She was still unaware that she was topless. The old man stood on the path in his soaking clothes, puffing his pipe and eyeing her body. The dog was curled up at his feet in a little damp ball.

'Right, I'll be off then, if you don't need me any more,' he said finally.

'Who's he?' Phil muttered.

'He's your saviour,' Dave replied. 'We couldn't have pulled you out without his help. He waded across the river with all his clothes on to help.'

The old man smiled and nodded at Phil.

'And he gave me a quick refresher course on mouth to mouth. My mind was so blank I couldn't think what to do. He told me.'

'You gave me mouth to mouth?' Phil asked incredulously. 'Was I that far gone?'

'You'd been down there a couple of minutes at least,' the old man said. 'You weren't breathing at all when we dragged you out. You owe your friend here your life.'

'Thanks, man,' Phil said, grabbing Dave's calf and squeezing it with his cold damp hand. Dave had to fight with himself not to pull away. *That's how it would feel*, he told himself. *That's how it would feel if The Claw got you.*

'And thank *you*,' Phil said to the old man. 'Listen, can I give you some money or something? You deserve a reward.'

'Reward enough to know that you're still in the land of the living,' the man said. 'And besides, you've given me some rare excitement this afternoon.' He looked directly at Judy when he said this and she suddenly became aware of her nakedness, and quickly folded her arms over her ample bosom.

He nodded towards Dave and Sally. 'Those are some nice pieces you have around your necks,' he said. 'You don't want to lose those. I shouldn't wear them swimming if I were you, you may need them one day. Right then, I'm off home to get out of these wet things. Bye! C'mon Lucky!'

He turned and wandered off up the path, the little dog following at his heels.

'What did he mean we may need them one day?' Dave said suspiciously as they watched the man walk away.

Sally shrugged, pulled him to her. 'Give me a kiss, my hero,' she said.

'You didn't do so badly,' he said, kissing her. 'You were in the water before me.'

'But I never had the presence of mind to get the knife, did I?'

'True,' he said, not wanting her to ask him: *What kept you so long Buster? What were you afraid of?* He thought perhaps she was being kind here, not mentioning his delay on purpose. Maybe he was just fooling himself. Although it had felt like hours before he could make himself jump into that water, in reality it was probably only a few seconds; a few seconds in which he thought to get the knife because he could see those weeds down there, trapping Phil.

Yeah, he thought, *that's more like it*!

'But you've got to admit it was lucky,' Sally said, 'that I bought you that knife for your birthday. If this had happened yesterday, it would still have been wrapped up in my handbag and Phil would have drowned.'

'Yeah, lucky,' he said, 'like the man's dog. Lucky.'

There seemed to be too many lucky and coincidental things happening just lately. Lucky. There was a word to conjure with.

He looked it up that evening in his St Michael Oxford Dictionary:

> **Luck**. Chance; thought of as a force that brings either good or bad fortune.

Somehow, he didn't like the sound of that. Neither did he like the fact that the word fell between **Lucifer** and **luckless**; if anything was an omen, that was.

Chapter Three
Bad Eddie Gets Called

Derek Cousins appeared on *News at Ten* on Tuesday evening. Here was another coincidence that Dave would have to think about later. He walked into the living room and sat down at precisely the same time as the newscaster started to talk about the missing boy.

He and Sally had been upstairs in his bedroom all evening playing the Space Pirates computer game that his parents had given him for his birthday. Or rather, Sally had been playing it and he had been sitting behind her, resigned to offering advice and shouting encouragement. Six months ago when they had started going out together, Sally had told him that she hated computers and the people who played with them. Computers, according to Sally, were for kids and pimply Joe 90 boffin types; eggheads who didn't fit into the real world or care about it. Joe 90s she said (referring to the Gerry Anderson puppet programme of the early seventies whose star was a wooden-headed cleverdick in huge glasses and was controlled by strings that sometimes showed) never had girlfriends and thought girls were cissies because they didn't understand the secret world of peeks and pokes and Z80 processors – let alone the sixteen bit stuff. And all they did with their gadgets, when it came down do it, was play silly little games.

Dave had been wounded; his new girl was hacking him down already. That didn't usually happen for weeks. 'Get into one of those silly little games, and you'll get addicted,' he had told her, 'and it won't seem at all silly then.'

Of course she had pooh-poohed the idea – and managed to avoid his computer completely for the first month or two. Then she started waiting for him in his bedroom while he finished a game before going out in the evening. At first she brought a book with her, then she started watching the screen from the far end of the room where she sat on the bed. Then she moved down the bed until she was peering over his shoulder. Eventually she had wanted to sit in the hot seat and 'have a little go – just to see if I can do it.'

Addiction, as Dave had promised, followed.

Now – like tonight for example – she hogged the machine all evening and he was lucky if he got a game at all.

But she had run out of lives and patience at ten o'clock and they had gone downstairs to watch the t.v. Reggie and Doreen were in the lounge, sitting in their armchairs in opposite corners of the room. Doreen was asleep, curled up in a ball in a semi-foetal position. Her mouth hung open and she was almost – but not quite – snoring. Reggie was doing the crossword in the *Daily Mirror*. He looked up over his glasses as they came in and nodded at his wife, smiling. Dave and Sally sat down on the sofa. The newscaster was saying:

'. . . son Tommy Cousins who went missing at a funfair in Bracknell on Saturday. As yet no trace has been found of the boy and police are linking his disappearance with several others across the country. All the missing children were attending funfairs when they vanished and none has yet been found. Mr Derek Cousins, the boy's father, requested that we show this appeal.'

Dave remembered the newspaper report on Sunday, and leaned forward in his seat as the picture cut from the newscaster to what was apparently the Cousins' home. Derek Cousins was standing on the lawn at the back of his house. He was pale and drawn and looked as though he hadn't slept since Saturday. He was twitchy in his movements and his bottom lip was trembling even before he started to speak. When he did, his voice held a distinct tremor and Dave knew he was going to crack up and cry before he'd finished what he was going to say.

'I'd just like to say that someone out there knows exactly where Tommy is and what has happened to him,' the image of Derek Cousins said. 'All I ask is that y-you let him go. Let him come home to his mum and m-me. I don't want anything else from you, whoever you are. All I w-want is my little boy back. Please don't harm him – he's only six. He's t-too young for all this. Just send him back home safe and sound. *Please*. And if there's anyone out there who knows who's got my boy please tell the police, or even, or e-e-even . . .'

At that point, Derek's shoulders started to jiggle up and down with the sobs that escaped his chest. They kept the cameras rolling though, knowing that showing this despairing man was doing their ratings no harm at all and also knowing that the more he cried, the more people would remember the story of the missing Tommy Cousins; more people who just might spot him whizzing by in a car, or walking down a side street holding a tall man's hand and looking frightened.

The picture cut back to the newscaster who looked pained. 'Police are appealing for anyone who saw Tommy Cousins at the funfair in Easthampstead Park in Bracknell on Saturday or has seen him since the time of his disappearance to contact them,' he said. 'Now, we go to Westminster where members of parliament are demanding a full inquiry into the circumstances behind the Royston Groves paedophile case. We ask: has there been a cover up?'

Sally was next to Dave on the settee. She reached over, took his hand and squeezed it. He knew what she was thinking; the same as he'd thought when he read the newspaper report on Sunday, a few short hours before Phil nearly lost his life: *what sort of a guy hangs around fairgrounds and kidnaps little kids?* He glanced over at her, but she didn't look at him, just stared at the telly. Her eyes were brimming. He wondered if she had come up with the same answer as he had to that question. On Sunday, the answer had been vague and without substance, but even so, it had been there. Now he was able to articulate it to himself, and although it made no logical sense, it seemed to fit into the jigsaw of random events that perhaps weren't *quite* so random after all. The answer his mind so kindly provided him with was this: *maybe you don't know what sort of a guy hangs round fairgrounds and kidnaps little kids, nor why, but you're going to find out pretty soon, believe me.*

Looking at Sally, he didn't think she'd had that thought yet; she didn't look pale and worried enough. If she was lucky (and he was cracking up or something, which was quite possible after all those mind-bending exams crammed into such a short space of time) perhaps she would never have that thought.

She moved closer to him then, snuggled up. Her eyes were glassy, but the tears had gone, drained away before they overloaded the ducts. 'It's terrible, isn't it?' she said. 'That poor man.'

'That poor kid,' Dave replied. He pulled his cross out from under his shirt and stared into its deep, shining eye. It comforted him somehow.

'Bad . . .' Doreen murmured. They all looked over at her. She was still sound asleep. 'She doesn't usually talk in her sleep, does she?' Dave asked Reggie quietly.

'Only if she's really tired and worried about something,' Reggie said, laying the paper down on the arm of his chair and watching his wife in case she said anything else.

'What's she worried about now, then?' Dave whispered.

Reggie shrugged. 'Search me,' he said.

'. . . mmm, Eddie . . .' Doreen said.

'Milkman?' Dave suggested, his sombre mood lifting with the promise of some domestic entertainment.

'Milkman's called Bill,' Reggie said. 'And he's sixty-four and mad as a hatter. I doubt if she's having an affair with him. I've never heard of Eddie.'

'An old boyfriend, perhaps,' Dave goaded. Sally dug him in the ribs.

Reggie chuckled. 'She should be so lucky,' he said. 'I started going out with her when she was fourteen.'

Doreen stirred. 'Oh,' she said. She sat up, her eyes still closed, her face drawn into a deep frown. 'Bad Eddie's got it,' she said in a loud voice. Then her eyes popped open. She looked surprised.

'Bad Eddie's got what?' Dave asked her.

She looked from Dave to Sally to Reggie. 'Eh?' she said, yawning.

'What's Bad Eddie got?' Reggie repeated. 'You were talking in your sleep. Bad Eddie's got it, you said. We want to know, one, what has Bad Eddie got? And, two, who did he get it from?'

'I don't know, I was dreaming. It's all gone now,' Doreen laughed, easing herself out of her chair and standing up. 'Who wants tea?'

Bad Eddie had got The Knowledge. He had waited a long, long time for it to happen. Ten years – or it might have been more. Time was very slippery. You tried to grasp it, and it tromboned out or concertinaed in, leaving you nowhere, in the middle of where it had been and wasn't any more.

He remembered the book. That was a long spiral thread of time ago, when he had been old enough to write, young enough to know what was going on. That was even before the dolls. The book had started The Knowledge happening. He wrote the book, the book wrote him right back, burrowing into his head and depositing things that weren't there already, things of its own. The Knowledge. He wrote till his fingers bled, pages and pages magically filling themselves. It may have taken two years to finish. The book was Good. And the book paid him back handsomely. When it was done, it had put in more than it had taken out. But the book was gone, lost in some incinerator in a backwater in time.

Because they hated it. 112 was the magic number. 112 was the fire number. 112 times they hated it and it came back with notes appended, comments written in the margin; rejection photocopies hidden beneath the title page. The book had burned. He could smell the charred pages if he put his mind to it, the odour sifting up through dry, honeycombed years. The rejections had burned with it and the flames were ugly and yellow.

But the doors the book had opened inside his head did not close up. They stayed open, wedged in place by the beginnings of The Knowledge the book had put in there. Across the confused stream of time, they had stayed open. Waiting.

Waiting while his job went west. Waiting while his skin turned grey and started to break up. Waiting while his hair started to fall and his friends drifted away and his mother died and the Social Services had christened him Bad Eddie.

The path had stretched out before him, and Eddie had followed that path, even though it seemed to go on forever, even though it seemed there would never be any relief from the anguish and torment the book had started. The Knowledge would have come sooner had the editors understood. But they didn't. They knew no more than him – less in fact. Their minds were sandbagged when he wanted them to fly with him, negative when he needed positive, empty when he wanted substance. They had closed that avenue, but there would be others. The path would end and he would be completed. He had known that all along and he had kept walking.

Because there were pits inside his mind that needed to be filled. Gaps in The Knowledge that rendered it useless, made nonsense out of it. But he was hungry and it was too late to stop now. So he followed the path and waited, ravenously soaking up each new morsel of information as it came his way. Knowing that the big blast would come, by and by.

And he was right. It did come.

But not before the dolls. The dolls went right back down that cloudy stream of time to just after his mother and just before his face broke out. The first was a Sindy. He told the woman in the toy shop that it was for his daughter. Sindy had long blonde hair and blue eyes. She was beautiful. He took her home and stood her on the mantelpiece over the empty fire. He sat and watched her until he fell asleep, but The Knowledge didn't come shining out of her glassy eyes that day. The days started to grow shorter and the first itchy scab appeared on his face, but Sindy didn't speak to him and The Knowledge didn't shine forth from her sweet little face. He realised he was mistaken about her, but by then she'd found a place in his heart, and he kept her dusted and clean. She made him feel safe.

At Christmas he bought another Sindy to keep her company, and in the months that followed, he purchased a Tiny Tears, a Barbie and a New Born Baby doll. The Tiny Tears wet herself and cried which was fun, but the methylated spirit he filled her bottle with stained her nappy and made her insides go brittle. He didn't much like the New Born Baby because its realistic little face looked too much like one of the wise old men that appeared in science fiction films. He hid New Born in the cupboard under the sink.

His face worsened as time passed, blistering and developing sores and lesions that didn't heal. He gave up shaving and washing; partly because he suspected an allergy to soap might be causing this, and partly because it hurt so much.

People began to cross the street to avoid him when he went out – which wasn't often – but he was not offended because he knew they knew he had some of The Knowledge. They were frightened of him, and that was to be expected after all.

As he waited for enlightenment to come, the doll collection grew. None of them worked. Even the ones with the real glass eyes that closed when you laid them down didn't work, and he wondered about trying the real thing. It was too dangerous though. People would not understand. He knew that. They would come and get him and put him somewhere where The Knowledge would not be able to get to him. It was imperative that he remain free, so he kept collecting the dolls.

One Saturday earlier this year he had taken the bus to Aldershot and gone into Argos where he blew what he'd saved of his Social Security money on two Fisher-Price dolls and an Adam one. The Fisher-Price ones were called Cherry and Julie, and the Adam was called Heart to Heart. The Adam – which was a little girl, in spite of the manufacturer's name – was the most expensive. You put a battery in it, hugged it to you and you could feel its heart beating against your chest. You could adjust her pulse too. He fell in love with Heart to Heart and took her to bed with him each night, her beating heart soothing him to sleep.

He was sitting in front of the t.v. cuddling Heart to Heart

when what he had been waiting for all that time finally happened.

The Knowledge came to him while the Cousins guy was talking on the t.v. It beamed forth from the set on a wide pink ray which struck the centre of his forehead and stole through, finding those chasms, filling those gaps. The process was completed by the time Cousins started sobbing and the wave band ceased. Now he knew everything there was to know. All knowledge was his. He sat in front of the t.v., his head as chock-full as was physically and mentally possible. His head was a dictionary, an encyclopedia; an archive of all knowledge. His skull was tight with the volume, heavy with the mass, pounding with the power. He now possessed so much information that it was no longer possible to process thoughts. That way of existence had gone now, gone to join the concept of time in the scrap heap. It was no longer necessary to think because there was no longer anything to think about. He *knew*.

Bad Eddie picked up the bottle of methylated spirits that sat beside his armchair and took a swig. The fluid burned a path down his throat, and he gasped at the instant warmth. He laid Heart to Heart gently on the sofa, went to the coat cupboard, found an old greasy overcoat, put it on his bare back. He was already wearing trousers and his battered old desert boots and would need nothing else.

He went back into the lounge, got Tiny Tears' bottle, filled it with meths and gave her a drink. Then he sat her back on the mantelpiece and lit her crotch with the Zippo lighter that lived alongside her. He poured more meths from the bottle over the Sindys' long blonde tresses and lit them too. Avoiding the strands of burning plastic that were descending to the hearth from the mantel, he stacked most of the other dolls in the fire place, setting Cherry upright in the centre. He lit the Zippo again and placed it, still burning, in Cherry's hands.

He gently picked up Heart to Heart and took her to the window which he opened. He leaned through and dropped the doll on to the ground outside, then closed the window again.

He took another swig from the meths bottle and emptied the

rest over the ragged furniture in the room. There was a gallon can of the stuff in the kitchen, and he got this and unscrewed the lid. It smelled good as he tasted it from time to time as he sprayed it around the kitchen, then the hall, then the two bedrooms and the dining room that he never used. There was no upstairs to do, so he took the half empty can to the front door and doused that. He walked down the path and turned back to look at his place of residence for the past forty-one years. He realised with a start that he remembered time. His last lucid thought struck him then. *Forty-one years, was it* that *long?*

The thatch would go up like a tinderbox. He gazed up at it, and *knew*.

A box of Swan Vestas matches were rattling in his jacket pocket just as they were supposed to be. He took out the yellow and red box and pushed the inner tray open. There were six red-headed matches inside. He took one out and pressed it against the sandpaper side of the box, twisting it to and fro. The match spat and crackled. Bad Eddie smiled. He twisted the match again and it burst into life with a tiny *bang*! He waited until he could feel the heat on his fingers and then threw the match against the front door of the cottage. It hit the coating of meths he'd given it and went out. He repeated the process. The second match died. Bad Eddie didn't swear, he was patient. As patient as Job. He took the third match and showed the door to it, mentally explaining what was required of it. The match went out. Eddie waited. And waited. Then he saw the transparent flicker of heat which meant the flame had caught. A clear blue flame grew and expanded quietly across the splashes of methylated spirit on the door. The green paint began to blister. Eddie lit another match and threw it onto the hall carpet. The carpet caught instantly and the blue fire cruised down the hall, branching off into the bedrooms, the dining room and the bathroom on its way to the kitchen.

Eddie walked round to the back of the house and picked up Heart to Heart. He tucked her under his arm, realising that her mechanical heart was still beating in her rubber chest. He peered in through the lounge window. *News at Ten* was still flickering on the t.v. in the corner. Fire was licking up the legs of its stand. The easy chair he had been sitting in was ablaze and gouting thick black smoke; tongues of flame were scattering this way and that, following the meths pathways across the yellow nylon carpet and turning them black.

Eddie pulled his coat around his thin frame, turned on his heel and walked down the garden. There was a hedge at the bottom and trees behind. The trees were part of the forest that extended for miles – all the way to Bracknell, in fact. Eddie pushed through a thin part of the hedge and strode out into the darkness of the trees.

There were tracks in the woods, but Eddie didn't use them. They meandered, and added miles to what was already going to be a long walk; instead, he followed his instincts, followed his weighty knowledge to where he knew he had to go. He neither tripped on tree roots, nor fell in holes as he walked, just strode along effortlessly, his feet light and sure.

He arrived at Easthampstead Park at dawn, crawled into a thicket where he wouldn't be seen, cuddled up to Heart to Heart whose reassuring pulse still thudded away in her chest and slept the day away.

That evening, at the same time as Roddy Johnson and his friends entered the Dragon pub in Basingstoke, Bad Eddie woke up and walked to the nearby fairground which was in full swing and very busy. He strode across the fairground, oblivious to the flashing lights and loud music, walked up the steps to one of the rides and got on. No one seemed to notice him and no one asked him to pay.

Thirty seconds later, Bad Eddie vanished from the face of the earth.

Chapter Four
Roddy Comes Back

'How're your sinuses?' Dave asked Phil, sipping at his Bacardi and lemonade. 'Or is it sinei?'

They were sitting round one of the wooden tables in the saloon bar of the Dragon, Phil and Judy on one side perched on little stools, and Dave and Sally on the other in the good seat. The good seat was actually a velveteen-covered bench seat that ran the length of the back wall of the bar. Their table was one of two that the bench seat served, and the one nearest the end of the L-shaped bar which ran from end to end of the small pub. The bar carried on straight through the partitioning wall which separated the saloon and public bars and the staff spent most of the time darting from bar to bar.

The other table along the back wall was surrounded by half a dozen leather jacketed and denimed greasers. A row of battered skid-lids ringed their table like a low retaining wall. They were involved in a discussion concerning the drawbacks of fitting a high lift cam to a Kwak.

On the other side of the pub – the door side – there was a smaller bench seat and two more tables. A couple Phil knew vaguely sat at one of the tables and the other was empty.

The Dragon was Dave and his friends' local, and the place where they spent most of their evenings. They usually sat in the public bar, but there was a darts match on in there tonight and even though the pool table had been pushed right up against the wall, the members and supporters of the visiting team had crowded the place out. From time to time, a raucous cheer erupted from the public bar and drowned the conversation. 'WUUNN HUNDRIT AND FORTY-YYY!' someone had earlier yelled in a passable imitation of the t.v. darts commentator.

The Dragon was the kind of pub you could relax in. It had no pretensions to class or sophistication, the beer was okay and Jim the landlord and his wife Miriam were friendly and could remember your name and what you drank after two visits – even if you didn't spend hours talking to them.

The clientele seemed to be composed mainly of people who didn't fit in anywhere else. The disco kids had the Red Lion and the Bass House, the wealthy had any number of country pubs within three miles drive, Mr Average had most of the other town pubs and the oldsters had The Bounty and the Hare and Hounds. The Dragon got the in-betweenies and made them welcome. Irish navvies working on local building projects mixed with throwback punks; punks played pool with certified accountants; accountants chatted with the bikers who had recently moved here from the New Inn. No one gave you a second glance, no matter what you looked like or how old you were. Mostly, there was no trouble and if an alcohol-fuelled meathead happened by and started to throw pint beer glasses, he would be swiftly and neatly ejected.

'My sinei are fine, thanks,' Phil said, sniffing to prove it. He was back to his normal self now – in fact, he'd been back to his normal self by the time they had arrived home from the river on Sunday, although his sinuses hadn't forgotten the ordeal. A thin stream of river water had gushed down his nose in the car on the journey home. Judy had screamed. Phil had been non-chalant and explained that it was quite normal for his sinuses to retain water after he'd been swimming. This had provoked a lot of speculation about his physical make-up. Sally swore that this feat was impossible and that Phil must have been made wrongly. She suggested that God might have made him on a Friday afternoon, after an extended lunch hour spent downing pints of cider with large whisky chasers.

'Water-free now, are they?' Dave asked.

'It finally stopped coming out yesterday,' Phil said. 'But I can still smell the river sometimes though.' He sipped his pint of lager and let out an earth-shattering belch. Sally giggled. One of the bikers looked over admiringly.

The door between the two bars opened and Dave peered over to see who was coming in. His heart sank. The tall figure, whose shape had been distorted by the bubbled glass panel in the door, was Roddy Johnson. No one else had noticed him yet except Dave, and he froze, his drink midway between the table and his lips. He could feel the blood draining away from his face, leaving it cold and tight like a rubber mask. *Trouble*, Dave's mind needlessly informed him. *Here comes trouble, spelt V-I-O-L-E-N-C-E.*

The door swung open again and the squat, beefy figure of Jon Kott followed Roddy into the bar. Two of their cronies came in after them, then Randy Sandy – Roddy's sister who was currently being squired by Kott. All of them were carrying full pint glasses.

They can't have got served, Dave's terrified mind screamed. *Not after last time! The bar staff have specific instructions not to serve them! Miriam said that!* Miriam and Jim had not yet taken over running the Dragon when Roddy and his friends had caused the last lot of trouble in here, but they'd heard about it and knew of Roddy's reputation. They had promised not to serve Roddy or his friends.

But they had been served, and here they were all carrying drinks to prove it. They must have sneaked in on the tail of the visiting darts team, and got served by the new barmaid, Dotty, who didn't know her ass from a hole in the ground.

Roddy Johnson was one of those people who had a habit of turning up and terrifying you just when you didn't want to see him. He was one of those people with whom Dave's life seemed to be inextricably entwined. No matter who moved into town, or who left, there was always Roddy, lurking somewhere nearby and ready to pop up again. This was the third occasion in Dave's nineteen years that Roddy had appeared before him sending out waves of hatred that struck a chill of abject terror right through him.

The first time had been at a school-organised disco when Dave was fourteen. The disco was on the top floor of the school's new building and ran from seven until nine thirty. Dave made it to nine o'clock before he was visited. He was alone, sitting in an easy chair in a room adjoining the disco; just lounging, minding his own business and mooning at the occasional young lady who walked by, when Roddy appeared. Roddy was six feet tall even then. He was dressed in the only clothes Dave had ever seen him wear – faded denim jacket over a white tee shirt and drainpipe jeans, rolled up at the bottom to show off his black pointed-toed, Cuban-heeled boots. Roddy had strolled up to him, smiling an evil smile. He reached Dave's chair, got down on his knees and whispered in Dave's ear, 'I'm going to see you later on.' His voice was low and calm but those seven words promised more pain than Dave could imagine. *I'm going to see you later on*, when spoken by someone you didn't know personally meant they were going to kick seven shades of shit out of you.

And then some.

Roddy had walked away, back into the disco, leaving Dave bolted into his armchair with fear. There was a fire door in the corner of the room, and Dave slipped out of it a few minutes later and slunk home across the dark playing fields. He had not attended the disco again.

The second time their paths crossed, the outcome was much worse. Roddy and Jon Kott had visited the Dragon, six months ago, just before Dave started going out with Sally. He had been in the public bar that time, sitting with Billy Bowen and a group of his classmates. They were getting sozzled before going to the party at Billy Bowen's girlfriend's friend's house. There were six of them in his little group that night and none had made it to the party. Four of them had made it to the hospital though, and Billy Bowen still had the scars on his neck to prove it.

Dave had tried to make himself invisible when he spotted Roddy, reasoning that Roddy would remember that he had an old score to settle. Roddy apparently didn't recognise Dave, but he kept his head down anyway, hoping that the gang would pass him and his friends by.

They didn't.

Roddy and Jon Kott positioned themselves in the doorway and hung in there looking menacing, while their smaller friends moved in on Dave's group.

Comments muttered loud enough for Billy Bowen to hear about his girlfriend, Tish, had started the trouble. The atmosphere had cooled and the conversation all but dried up. Roddy and Kott were two years older than Dave and his friends, and an immeasurable amount meaner. The three that were with them – the ones making the snide remarks – were around Dave's age, but he didn't know them. These guys looked mean enough on their own, and Dave could tell by looking at the pale faces and nervous gestures of his friends that none of them fancied trying to mix it with them – even if they did outnumber the meatheads two to one. The meatheads knew the psychology alright, even if it was only instinctively. The aggressor has the upper hand. It was one of the basic psychological laws of the universe and it was called: *nobody here wants to get hurt*.

This gave the meatheads the edge. They were the ones that were going to *do* the hurting. It was the same principle that allowed a few men with guns to keep thousands of unarmed people in prison camps during wars or famines. They couldn't shoot everybody, but nobody wanted to be the ones they *could* shoot.

These guys who understood the principles of terrorism so well had learned something else from years of bullying, namely, that if you didn't care about pain, you didn't often get hurt. It was the ones who *did* care who suffered.

Dave knew that it would be quite possible for one of the meatheads to drag either him or one of his friends off their stool and bludgeon him to an untimely death while the rest of them sat there like statues thinking, *please don't let it be me next. Oh God please don't let it be me!*

'She's fucking gorgeous,' the smallest of the meatheads said, nodding at Tish. The three of them were standing right next to Dave's table. Everyone had found something interesting to look at now; fingernails that needed cleaning, shoes that were getting scuffed; patterns of butts in the ashtray. Everyone except Tish. She stared right back at the thug, fuming. She was on one of the bench seats which faced the bar and the guy pushed his way in there and sat down next to her in a space which miraculously formed as he approached. 'You have a lovely bone structure,' the meathead said. Dave stole a look at her and wished he had half her bottle. She was glaring at him with an obvious hatred.

'Why don't you fuck off and leave us alone?' she spat at him.

The thug was surprised at the venom with which she said this, and got up looking stupefied. He pushed his way back to his mates, glowering and colliding with as many people as possible on the way. Dave happened to look up as he passed, and although the guy didn't see him, one of his mates did. He shoved Dave in the back and said, 'What are you looking at, you four-eyed little twat?'

Dave neither turned around nor acknowledged the comment. His mouth was too dry to speak, and the blood was pounding through his empty head like a flood down a storm drain. Each beat of his heart made his body judder as he sat there, powerless to do anything. All the staff seemed to have vanished into the lounge side of the bar. That meant six against five and no referee if all Dave's friends decided to act together.

'What are we going to do?' someone hissed in Dave's ear. It was Mike Little, who was even skinnier than Dave and who probably didn't have one good punch in him. Dave shrugged, said nothing. His voice would waver if he spoke, he knew that. Mike's face was grey and his eyes were huge. 'Christ, someone should call the police!' he said. 'Where's the landlord? Why doesn't someone help us?'

Then meathead number two started swinging the pool cue about. The thick end of it whizzed past Stan Tichener's head. Stan flinched, but his face remained expressionless and he didn't turn around to look at the cue-wielding meathead, didn't seem to be at all interested in the fact that the next swing might quite easily stave in his skull.

Stan's friend George muttered, 'Fucking scumbags.' His voice was louder than he had anticipated. Dave heard it plainly from his end of the table and his heart sank. That was it! Now the shit would hit the fan!

But the meathead didn't bring the cue down on George's head, just wheeled back to face the pool table. *He didn't hear! Thank God he didn't hear!* Dave thought, a wave of relief surging through him.

'I'm leaving,' the sixth member of their group said. His name was Tony Turner and he had remained silent until now. Tony was the biggest of them and their only hope in a fight. Dave wanted to plead with him to stay, but his mouth had gone on the blink and no words came out.

Tony got up, skirted the meatheads and made for the door. The action was accomplished so quickly and easily that Dave wished he'd gone too. The yobs didn't even look around as Tony went. Their pool game had died out now, but they still had the cues and were making threatening movements with them, apparently enjoying themselves immensely.

Billy Bowen leaned forward toward Dave, Tish's face was nestled against his neck. 'I think we'd better go too,' he said.

'Good idea,' Dave agreed. Then he remembered who was keeping the door. Would Roddy remember him? Or would he stand aside and let him pass? It had to be worth a try. After all, what was the alternative? Staying here and getting a pool cue wrapped around his head, that was what.

Then Tony came back. He sat down on his stool and took a deep draught of his lager. His face was the colour of Wensleydale cheese.

'You were going,' Dave said.

'I came back,' Tony replied. He sounded like he wasn't too far from crying.

'Why?' Billy Bowen asked.

'Because that tall guy at the door promised to put my head through the glass panel in it if I wanted to leave,' he said.

'Fuck,' Billy said.

'Roddy,' Dave sighed.

That was when the fat end of the pool cue came down on George's head.

George's eyes closed. Blood bloomed from a point just above his hairline and trickled down his face. George swayed. George toppled backwards off his stool and hit the floor. People began to rush down the bar toward the door.

The meathead with the pool cue raised it above his head in both hands and brought it down hard on George's belly. George didn't move.

'Teach you to call me scumbag, you cunt!' the guy hissed.

George's friend Mike Little rose from his seat, his face aghast, his hands in the air. The pool cue came flying down and snapped in two when it hit his bony shoulder. Mike squealed, bent double, then punched the meathead in the nuts, his skinny fist flashing out and driving home. The troublemaker dropped the cue and staggered forward holding his lower abdomen. Mike got two more punches in before the second meathead's Doc Marten boot flew up and caught him under the chin. He fell heavily on top of George.

Billy Bowen and Tish were on their feet heading towards the door by the time Dave and Tony got up. One of the meatheads went after them, and the other – the largest one – punched Dave in the face. Dave saw blue spots form before his eyes, then white sparks as he took another blow.

Tony screamed and launched himself at the biggest meathead who now had hold of Dave's collar and was headbutting him in the face. They collapsed in a struggling heap.

Dave worked his way free of the tangle, his vision returning, but blurred now; somewhere in there his glasses had fallen off. Blood ran freely from his nose and mouth. It felt hot as it trickled down his chin.

The landlord had appeared now. His name was Ron and he was in his fifties. He held a baseball bat in his hands and was coming though the flap in the bar down by the door. He was shouting. Back at their table, the three meatheads had selected a victim each from the fallen Tony, Mike and George and were kicking frenziedly at them. The small one had retrieved the broken pool cue and was stabbing the blunt end into George's guts.

Ron sailed by Dave, missing what was happening at the door as he sped toward George's lifeless form.

Dave reached the door and wished he hadn't. Jon Kott had hold of Tish and was swinging her casually back and forth, crashing her against the wall, and Roddy had Billy by the shirt collar. Tish was screaming for help. Amazingly, there were people standing at the bar with their backs to her, totally ignoring what was happening. Roddy was peering into Billy's face and grinning. Dave skidded to a halt just as Roddy butted Billy. Roddy's action was smooth and practised. When his head came up again there was a smear of Billy's blood on his forehead and Billy's eyes were blank. Dave saw his body go limp. Roddy didn't let go of him though, just pulled him close and gazed interestedly into his eyes.

'Let him go, you fucker!' Dave yelled, clenching his fists. Anger was overcoming his terror. At the other end of the bar a beer glass smashed and Ron the landlord bellowed.

'I know you, don't I?' Roddy said quietly. His words were almost drowned as Tish's head hit the wall again and her screams increased.

Dave threw a right, which Roddy dodged easily, ducking just as smoothly as he had butted Billy. Dave swore and punched again. His fist had got halfway to Roddy's face, when Jon Kott's own fist smashed into his jaw.

Dave staggered sideways, but managed to keep his feet. Staying upright was a bad move, because Roddy's free hand shot out and grabbed his throat. His breath was cut off as Roddy dragged him closer.

Roddy stared at him for a moment as if seeking an explanation from his frightened face, then his head ducked forward in that fluid way again and Dave's mouth exploded with pain. He fell this time, Tish's screams ringing in his ears as he lost consciousness.

Roddy turned then, brought Billy Bowen's head around toward the door. 'Whoops!' he said, and let go of Billy. Later, in court, Roddy would swear that Billy Bowen had charged at him and he had stepped aside. Nobody witnessed him throwing Billy at the glass panel, so he got away with it.

Billy's head hit the pane. The pane broke and Billy's head went through. What nearly killed Billy was the fact that he was only semi-conscious. The glass broke where his head hit it, but there was a section between his head and the bottom of the pane that didn't break. This was the section that sliced into Billy's neck when his knees buckled.

Dave dimly heard the shouting, and felt more blows to his body, but afterwards he couldn't remember anything that happened until the ambulance arrived.

They told him later that Ron, the bat-wielding landlord, had knocked out all three of the meatheads despite being hit in the face with a glass. Ron needed thirty-two stiches in his wound. Roddy and Jon Kott had left when Billy Bowen fell back from the door with his neck gashed open and hot blood pumping from the wound. Tish had sealed the wound with fingers and thumbs until the ambulance arrived. By that time Billy had bled three pints over her. According to Ron, the bar had looked like a scene from a horror movie when everything had finished.

There were broken ribs, hairline cracks in skulls, gashes, abrasions and Mike Little's collar bone was snapped clean in two. Dave had got off lightly with three loosened front teeth, cut lips and a broken nose. But it was Billy who nearly died and was in intensive care for three weeks, teetering on the edge. The rest of them were lucky compared with Billy.

There was a court case. All of them (except Billy who stayed in hospital for eight weeks) were witnesses at the trial. Two of the meatheads got two years. One was given six months. Jon Kott who had done nothing (he swore) except try and restrain Tish, got a year's probation, and – mainly on Dave's evidence – Roddy got a two year sentence suspended for two years.

And now here they were again six months later, bright

as buttons and looking just as dangerous as always.

Roddy had come back.

Dave looked over at them, his teeth aching already. Surely Roddy wouldn't risk two years imprisonment just to beat him up again? Or would he?

'What's the matter?' Phil asked. 'You've gone all white.'

Dave nodded towards Roddy and Jon Kott. Phil and Judy turned around to look.

'Is that the guy who beat you up?' Sally asked. She had never seen Roddy before. Dave nodded.

Roddy Johnson was dressed in his usual denim jacket, jeans and pointed boots but he looked even taller now. He must have been six feet four or five and he looked as lean and lithe as a panther. His shoulders were wide and his waist was tiny, his legs long and slender. He had a reputation as a womaniser, and looking at him, Dave could understand why. He looked danger-ous – but it wasn't only that. His face was handsome in a gypsyish way. His hair was black and wavy and he wore it swept back from his face in a kind of grown out teddy boy style. His face was long and his features were even, his chin slightly pointed, his nose perfect for the face. His eyebrows were dark and looked as if they had been shaped; his eyelashes were thick and the same blue-black colour as his eyebrows, enhancing the blue-grey of his eyes. From his left ear hung a tiny gold cross.

Kott was the exact opposite. He was muscular and squat and bulged in his clothes like a body builder. His blond hair was cropped so short his head might as well have been shaved, and his face was moon round. In contrast to Roddy's swarthy skin tone, he was English Rose pink with a tendency to red around the back of the neck.

'Who is the girl?' Sally asked.

'Randy Sandy, Roddy's sister,' Dave told her. He wasn't aware of it, but as he spoke, his head was ducking lower and lower in a subconscious attempt at hiding.

Sandy Johnson was gorgeous. She was shorter than her brother, but still tall enough to be striking. She had the same overall shape as Roddy, but with rounded hips and a medium-sized bust to break up the angular lines. Her face was a copy of her brother's except that it seemed to have been more finely wrought. Her legs (which she always made a point of showing off in tiny skirts) were slender and went on forever. And she was as randy as her nickname suggested. Dave had once been at a party where he had come across a bunch of nervous looking guys hanging about by the telephone table at the bottom of the stairs. He had thought that they were about to do the old calling up your relatives in far away lands trick, and he hung about to see who they were going to phone. After a while, a red-faced guy emerged from the bedroom at the top of the stairs and came down. He looked sweaty and tired. 'You next,' he had said to one of the bunch, and wandered off. The chosen guy had gone upstairs and reappeared ten minutes later. He selected another, who trolled up the stairs. Dave had asked a friend what was going on. 'Sandy Johnson. She's up there pulling a train,' the friend had said. Dave had asked what pulling a train was. The friend told him that Sandy was fucking one guy after another to see how many she could cram into an evening. Dave kept score from time to time during the evening and counted fifteen. He might have missed some though, he realised. Around midnight, he had seen a flash of naked Sandy heading for the toilet, and he considered joining the dwindling queue himself (this was before the trouble in the Dragon). Then he started to wonder about what Sandy might be filled up with by now, and knocked the idea on the head.

Phil turned back, his face now as pale as Dave's. He hadn't had any trouble with Roddy personally, but was a good friend of Billy Bowen and knew all the grisly details off by heart. Boils up your ass paled into insignificance when contrasted with a gaping throat wound.

'Let's go,' Phil suggested bravely. He drained the remains of his drink.

'Can't,' Dave said. 'He'll see me. He hasn't noticed me yet. Maybe he won't if you move to your right a little and block me out of his field of view. If I get up to leave, he'll see me for sure and probably follow us out. There are four of them, Phil – five

90

if you count Sandy. I wouldn't fancy our chances against Roddy on his own, let alone him and Kott.'

'Surely he wouldn't do anything, not now,' Sally said.

'Yeah,' Judy agreed, 'he'll get two years inside if he does.'

'Some consolation to me if he sticks a switchblade through my throat, that'll be,' Dave said. Phil nodded.

'Maybe they'll leave in a minute,' Judy said hopefully. She turned around and scrutinised the group for a few seconds. 'They look bored, perhaps they'll go soon.'

'Or perhaps they'll try and liven the place up a little,' Dave said sipping his drink in spite of the fact that his stomach was sending up messages that it didn't want anything else thank you until the threat had passed.

'Well folks, I've got to go to the loo,' Sally announced, getting up. She looked at Judy, 'Coming?' she asked, hoping for company on her trip past the louts.

Judy shook her head, 'Just been,' she said.

'You've got to go,' Phil told her, 'Women *always* go to the toilet together – in pairs at the very least.'

'Ha ha, very funny,' Judy said and remained in her seat.

Dave knew full well why she didn't want to accompany Sally on this occasion. It was because of the simple fact that one of Roddy's friends (Jon Kott for example) might just grab hold of her as she went past and fling her up against the wall repeatedly until she lost consciousness and fell to the floor with concussion and a hairline crack in her skull.

Apparently Sally was made of sterner stuff. *Either that, or she just hasn't considered the possibility that something might happen to her*, Dave thought. *After all, why should it? She has done nothing to upset them, so why should they do anything to upset her?*

But it didn't work like that, as he knew to his cost. These people didn't care who you were or what you'd done. Stuff like that didn't enter into it at all.

Not in the first instance anyway, Davey boy, he told himself. *But when you've got them a two year suspended jail sentence, it might do.*

The toilets were at the far end of the other bar. The thugs

stood between where Dave's group were sitting and the partition door.

Sally walked up to where Roddy and his friends were blocking the aisle. 'Excuse me,' she said politely. The two unidentified meatheads stepped aside to let her pass. Sandy Johnson followed her progress until she went through the door then turned her attention back to the group of bikers sitting round the table next to Dave's. She had been staring at them since she came in. Roddy and Jon Kott were smiling as they talked to one another and their two friends had started shovelling twenty pence pieces into the one arm bandit in the corner by the door.

'We should go while they're not looking,' Phil said. 'We can go to the Red Lion.'

'Yeah, I know, but we'll have to wait for Sally to come back first,' Dave said miserably. His stomach was wrestling with the rum and lemonade he was forcing into it. His mouth had dried up and felt like an approximation of the Gobi desert.

He was still trying to hide behind Phil's bulk, peering round it occasionally, to see if they had noticed him yet. When he glanced around again, Sandy had gone. He didn't known where to.

He took a deep breath and assured his stomach that everything was going to be tickety-boo, then poured some more drink into it. He had broken into a cold sweat and his cross felt hot against his chest. The skin where it lay itched, and he pulled it out from under his tee shirt, wondering if it was really solid silver after all. Cheap alloys had a way of irritating your skin when you started to sweat.

The cross looked different somehow, but he couldn't put his finger on what it was. Its red iris still shone and looked much deeper than it really was, and the metal still looked the same; it hadn't worn off the back to reveal brass underneath or anything. He held it in his hands, examining it and enjoying its warm smoothness. Was the pupil larger now than it had been before? Had it encroached on the ruby red iris part?

'Let's go!'

Dave looked up at Sally. Her eyes were huge and her hands were trembling visibly. 'What happened?' he asked.

'That girl. Sandy or whatever her name is. She came into the toilet after me. There was no one else in there. I was doing my make-up in the mirror when she came in. She said, "Get your squeaky little cunt out of here before I put the toe of my boot up it." I got out.'

Dave slid his cross back into his shirt and looked around Phil. Sandy was back now. She was talking to Roddy and Jon Kott animatedly. The pair of meatheads had finished with the bandit and were listening to the conversation.

'Sit down,' Dave said to Sally. 'We can't go yet. They'll get us.'

'They'll get us if we stay in here,' Phil moaned.

'Too many witnesses,' Dave muttered. 'That's what I'm hoping. They won't pick on us in here.'

He was wrong.

Sandy sauntered over and sat down next to him, squeezing in between the bikers and him. Her bare thigh pressed against his leg. It was hot. She smelled of Poison, a perfume which didn't suit her at all. Dave went rigid and sat staring directly in front of him at the ginger chest hairs which poked up through Phil's open collar. Sandy leaned close to him. Her lips brushed his ear. Her breath was hotter than her leg. 'Roddy wants to fuck your little girlfriend,' she whispered. 'How about it?'

'Uh – I don't think so,' Dave said in Phil's general direction.

'I don't think Roddy cares what *you* think,' Sandy breathed. 'I think he's gonna fuck her whether you like it or not.' She kissed Dave's ear, got up and walked away.

Sally shook Dave's arm urgently, 'What did she say?'

Dave sighed. 'A wind-up. I hope. She said that Roddy wants to fuck you and he's going to whether I like it or not.'

Sally looked horrified.

'Oh God,' Judy said. 'What are we going to do?'

'Sit tight,' Dave said, sounding braver than he felt. If it wasn't just a wind-up, and Roddy *did* intend to rape Sally, the

93

worst thing they could do would be to go outside. Nobody was going to do any raping in here.

The cross started irritating Dave's skin again, and a burning sensation spread across his chest. He pawed at the front of his tee shirt. Sally looked at him, questioningly. 'Tell you later,' he said. He leaned over to the nearest biker and said, 'We may have a bit of a problem here, will you guys help us if we need it?'

'What's wrong?' the biker asked. His mates leaned across the table to hear what Dave was going to say.

'The people over there. Roddy Johnson and his friends. They may be intending to start something with Phil and me. Help us out?'

'Roddy Johnson,' the biker said doubtfully. He shook his head, 'He's hard.'

'That's why we need help.'

'I dunno. If anything starts, we'll see.'

Dave appealed to the other bikers, but they didn't look at all interested. The tale of Billy Bowen's throat had got around.

'Christ,' he said, turning back to Phil and shrugging.

'I'll go and tell Miriam and Jim there's going to be trouble,' Phil said. 'Jim will throw them out.'

Neither of them was in the room though – Jim was playing in the darts tournament next door, and Miriam was serving on the other side of the partition, presumably in order to shout support at her husband.

'You'll have to go next door,' Dave said. He unhooked his glasses and nervously polished them on his tee shirt.

'Hmm,' Phil said, looking at the knot of people in the middle of the bar who were obviously discussing him and Dave and Judy and Sally. He didn't get up.

Roddy Johnson went over to the table in the far corner of the room. There was a couple sitting there doing the crossword in the *Daily Mirror*. Phil knew them vaguely, but they were a few years older than him and didn't come in much. They were Danny Stafford and his wife Suzie. Danny – whom Phil had once played cricket with – had several long scars on his chest which were reputed to have been put there by a madman in Brighton.

'He's going to have a go at Danny and Suzie,' Phil said.

Danny Stafford was about six inches shorter than Roddy and a softly-spoken, bookish type. He looked up quizzically when Roddy spoke to him.

'What did he say?' Judy asked.

'Christ knows, I can't hear from here,' Phil told her.

Danny was shaking his head now and smiling.

Roddy stood there, his legs apart, his fists clenched above his hips like a gunfighter ready to draw. He said something else and Danny stood up.

Dave felt a flash of heat spread across his chest from the cross, but he didn't acknowledge it; he was transfixed by the expression on Danny Stafford's face.

'He's a dead man,' Phil said sadly.

Dave shook his head in disagreement, but said nothing. Roddy was twice the size of Danny, but the man didn't seem the least bit intimidated. He stood there smiling at Roddy, his arms hanging loose at his sides, as if daring him to strike out. He looked as though he was used to facing up to much worse things than Roddy before breakfast. Dave wondered if the madman tale might be true after all. The two of them faced one another like statues, Roddy glaring, Danny Stafford smiling. Seconds ticked by.

'He hasn't blinked yet,' Dave said in wonderment.

'He's had it,' Phil replied.

Finally, Roddy turned and walked back to his friends. He shrugged and shook his head. Danny Stafford sat down, kissed his wife and returned to his crossword, not even giving Roddy a second glance.

'He did it!' Dave said. 'He psyched him out!' It *was* possible after all. 'Let's get out of here before he recovers,' Dave said, suddenly getting up. The others followed his lead.

But Roddy's recovery time was quicker than they had bargained for. He got to the door ahead of them and barred their way. 'Hiya, Foureyes,' he said to Dave in that terrifying soft voice. 'We got some stuff to discuss.' Roddy glanced over at his friends and smiled. Dave followed his gaze and was outraged to see Phil slipping through the door into the next bar. Sally took hold of Dave's elbow and squeezed it. The hot blast from the cross rippled over his chest again and he found himself momentarily thinking *how can that be?*

'So what about it, squirt?' Roddy said.

'What about what?' Dave said trying to keep his voice level. It didn't work and although there were only three words to say, his voice had slipped up nearly an octave by the last.

'What about letting the young lady discuss your future with me. If she's good to me, I might not have to rip your neck up like I did your little friend's.'

The cross surged again. It burnt and Dave flinched. 'Go fuck your sister, she's willing!' Dave spat, instantly regretting the outburst and wondering at the same time where those words had sprung from. That had done it; Jim and Miriam were going to have to buy a new glass pane for *this* door tomorrow.

Roddy grabbed the front of Dave's shirt and dragged him close. His head went back. Dave waited for it to snap forward again.

'Two years inside, you bastard!' Sally shouted from behind him.

Randy Sandy leaped on Sally's back. Sally staggered backwards, clutching at Dave. Roddy had hold of the cross's leather strap somewhere beneath his tee shirt and Dave was almost strangled because Roddy didn't let go of him.

Behind Dave, the bikers got up and stood between him and Jon Kott and his cronies. None of them moved. One of the greasers separated Sandy from Sally and got three deep gouges down his cheek from her sharp nails for his pains.

Roddy brought his right fist back, slowly and deliberately, making sure that Dave had a good long time to see what was shortly going to remove most of his front teeth.

Then the door opened behind Roddy and an arm snaked in and wound around his throat.

At first, Dave saw The Claw coming in through the door,

straight out of his previous hallucinations. It was long and black and tipped with Ebony Nails.

But then it was only Jim's arm and it was attached to Jim's body. *That* was where Phil had snuck off to, to get Jim. He could see Phil, for Christ's sake – out in the alley at a safe distance.

Jim yanked on Roddy's neck and Roddy let go of Dave and flew out through the door backwards.

Three seconds later – just as the spring of the door had pulled it closed – it flew open again. Jim came in, followed closely by Phil. 'Right you lot!' he said, pointing at Roddy's cronies. 'Out!'

Kott and Sandy and the other two slunk out, glowering.

'Are you okay?' Jim asked Dave.

Dave nodded. 'Yeah, I'm fine. Nothing happened.'

'What about you?' Jim said to Sally, who was smiling triumphantly.

'No problem,' she said.

'Good,' Jim said, and went outside to make sure they'd gone.

'They're not in the alley,' he said when he came back in. 'I'm sorry about that – I thought everyone knew not to serve them. It won't happen again. Let me give you all a drink on the house.'

Phil looked worried.

'It's okay,' Jim told him, 'they won't come around here again. They're gone now.'

But Jim was wrong.

They left the Dragon just as Miriam called last orders, their free drinks drunk, and their spirits lifted. Dave was feeling quite pleased with himself. He had told Roddy to go fuck his sister and lived to tell the tale. The question of what might happen the next time Roddy saw him had not yet raised its ugly head.

An alley ran past the Dragon's doors – and was in fact the only access to the pub. If you went down the alley, you came out in Winchester Street. If you went up it, you came out into the tarmaced service access area for the Winchester Street shops. There was much more room there, and that was where Sally had parked her Mini.

'I want to go for an Indian,' Phil said as they made their way up the alley. 'Who wants to come?'

'No one,' Judy said. 'And anyway, you've eaten tonight, your fatship.'

'But I'm hungry,' Phil whined.

'Yeah, he's got to keep his stretch marks going,' Sally said. 'If he doesn't keep well fed, they'll disappear.'

'Go and buy a kebab,' Dave suggested. There was a mobile doner kebab van that haunted the service area during the evenings. No one ever saw it come, and it stayed so late that no one ever saw it go again, but it appeared every night after the shops had shut. There were two swarthy guys that ran it, who might have been Turkish or Greek, and they happily sawed bits of meat off the grey cone which spun slowly over an oven, shoved it in a pitta bread envelope and sold it until the last drunk had gone home.

Dave had tasted one once and vowed never again, but Phil loved it.

'I haven't got enough money,' Phil said. 'Lend me thirty pence someone.'

Judy sighed and fished about in her handbag for her purse. 'Forget I mentioned equal rights for women,' she moaned. 'Give me a man who will open doors for me and buy me nice things and not expect me to stand my round in the pub.'

'Hear, hear!' Sally agreed, linking arms with Dave.

'You lot wanted equality,' Dave said, 'now don't blame us if you have to look after us for a change.'

'For a *change!*' Sally said with mock indignation. 'I've been supporting you since we met!'

'I'll see you're alright when I'm rich and famous,' Dave said. 'You'll never have to go out on the streets again.'

They came to the end of the alley and veered to the right. Sally's car was parked over by the market traders' toilets. Phil was in the lead, his money clenched tightly in his hot chubby hand.

'Oh,' he said as he rounded the Harris Carpet Centre's loading bay wall. He stopped dead in his tracks. The others piled up behind him.

'What?' Dave said. But he didn't need an answer – he could see for himself.

Roddy Johnson was leaning up against Sally's Mini smoking a cigarette, his bottom perched on the bonnet, his long legs extended out before him so that the heels of his boots were on the ground and the pointed toes stuck up in the air.

'Hello, Foureyes,' he said. 'So we meet again.'

'Oh Christ,' Dave moaned, feeling the blood run from his face for the second time that evening. His stomach informed him that it really was going to puke this time and it was all his fault so there was no need for him to start carping about it. He felt a brief flash of heat across his chest again, and wondered if it was his heart trying to tell him something rather than the cross getting warm. *After all*, he thought, *it has been beating like billy-o all evening. There must be a limit to how long it can go that fast and carry on working.*

'About turn,' Sally said.

They wheeled around in unison. And stopped dead again.

Jon Kott and the other two meatheads were behind them in the alley. They had come up past the Dragon's door, so there was no chance of fleeing back in there.

'Hi, folks,' Kott called. He was grinning. They turned back to face Roddy, who had got up off the Mini and was taking his denim jacket off. His white tee shirt had capped sleeves that showed off his wide shoulders and well developed biceps to good advantage.

'Oh shit,' Phil said heavily.

Dave glanced over at the doner kebab truck. Amazingly, there were no customers waiting for their food to be carved. It would be pointless running over there for shelter.

Roddy started toward them. Behind them Jon Kott laughed. His voice was high and sounded slightly hysterical.

Sally squeezed Dave's arm. 'Where's your ugly sister gone then?' she yelled at Roddy. Dave looked at her, astounded. Here was good old Sally the wimp bad-mouthing someone who would put your head through a glass door for fun – and perhaps, in Sally's case, rape you afterwards.

Sally was pallid and her eyes were as huge as they had been earlier, but there was a kind of defiance in her expression. She looked as if she was quite prepared to fight Roddy tooth and nail, even though she wouldn't stand a chance.

Roddy came towards them, the steel inserts in the heels of his boots clacking on the tarmac. He looked faintly amused.

'Here I am, sweetie.' Sandy stepped out from behind Harris Carpets' big green metal gate which was never locked. She was less than six feet away from them. Dave caught a whiff of her sickly perfume. Behind him, he could hear Kott and the other two getting very close.

'Run!' Judy shouted, and made a break for it. She headed straight for Roddy who outstretched his arms to intercept her, but suddenly veered right, back towards Harris Carpets' gate and Sandy.

Phil went at the same time, running straight across the inner service area road to the pavement at the other side. From there it was only fifty feet to the main road. One of the meatheads darted past Dave and Sally and gave chase.

Judy dodged Sandy, crashed into the gate, bounced off and hammered away towards the doner kebab van.

'Which way you going?' Sandy asked Sally.

They were hemmed in now. Kott was right behind them and Roddy and Sandy in front, too close to dodge.

'Oh, go fuck yourself,' Sally said to Roddy's sister. She took two paces forward, balled her fist and punched Sandy in the stomach. The blow was short and sharp and Sandy said, 'ooof!' but she didn't fall down and she didn't double up. What she did do was catch hold of Sally's arm as Sally tried to pass her. She swung Sally round into the big metal gate and it clanged as she hit it.

Up on the pavement on the main road, Phil shot by, heading in the direction of the doner van, with the meathead hot on his heels. Dave had never seen him moving so quickly.

Kott's hand grabbed Dave's shoulder. He wriggled free

from it and ran, ducking low. Behind him Sally screamed.

Roddy's punch caught his cheek as he passed and lit up blue stars before his eyes. At the same time as this happened, his legs got cobbled up with the one Roddy had put out, and he lost his balance. He hit the ground and slid a couple of feet on his knees and elbows. What hurt him most though, was the burning sensation across his chest.

There was a metallic *snick!* behind him. He turned his head around and saw Roddy's famous flick-knife for the first time. It glinted orange in the light from the streetlamps.

'Now you're in trouble,' Roddy said.

But Dave's legs had taken on a life of their own. One sight of the knife and Dave was upright and charging. A part of his mind wondered coolly why he was heading towards Roddy instead of in the opposite direction, but it was too late to stop now. He ran full tilt into Roddy's left side, expecting to feel the cold steel of the knife blade between his shoulders at any moment. The knife didn't have time to come down on him before the collision and the force of the blow unbalanced Roddy. The hand with the knife flailed in the air as Roddy staggered backwards, trying to stay upright.

By the time he was ready to strike, Dave was bounding across the tarmac towards Sally.

Sally pushed herself away from Sandy before he got there and began to run. Sandy, Dave noticed as he turned sharply and followed Sally, had most of Sally's new yellow shirt in her hands.

Jon Kott and the second meathead chased Sally and Dave across the service area, but Kott wasn't built for running and they easily outpaced him. The meathead gave up the chase at the kebab van. Dave tried to keep up with Sally, but she left him behind as they passed the traffic lights, and by the time he got to Brinklett's car park on the Winchester road, she was a hundred yards in front of him, her ripped shirt flying out behind her like a pair of wings.

He stopped by the Chinese takeaway, gasping for breath.

Okay if I puke now? his stomach asked and didn't wait for an answer.

By the time Sally wandered back, Dave's stomach had finished rebelling and he was sitting on the low wall which fronted Brinklett's, feeling light-headed and giddy.

'I wondered where you'd got to,' Sally gasped, clutching at her side. 'I've got a stitch,' she said wincing.

'Are you okay?' he asked.

She nodded. 'I got slammed against that gate, but it didn't hurt. I hit Sandy a couple of times, and she let go.'

'Good for you,' Dave said. 'Roddy punched me in the face. Then he got his knife out. I thought I was a goner.'

Sally looked worried. 'He didn't get you, did he?'

'No. I charged him and bounced off.'

Sally took him in her arms and kissed him. 'We got away,' she said.

'But what about Phil and Judy?'

'I didn't see where they went. Should we go and look for them?'

'There were heading in this general direction, the last I saw of them,' Dave said. 'I expect they'll be okay.'

'Yeah,' she said. 'For some reason that sounds right. I've got a feeling they're okay.'

'Your shirt is ripped,' he said putting his hand between the torn flaps and on to her sticky back.

'Doesn't matter. Davey?'

'Yeah?'

'If I ask you something, you promise not to laugh?'

'What?' He looked down the road towards the traffic lights, half expecting Roddy and Kott to come charging around the corner.

'You've got to promise not to laugh.'

'I promise.' He looked at her. She was sweating, her hair was a tangled mess, her make-up had run and she looked embarrassed, but there was something else in her face, a kind of excited *glow*. There was a wild look about her, as if she had enjoyed the ordeal they'd just been through.

'It's something about my cross.'

'What about it?' Dave thought he knew what she was going to say.

She shrugged, unable to find the right words. 'It *does* something. In the pub earlier on, it seemed to burn my chest, like it had got hot, or become electrical or something. When it did that I wasn't scared anymore. Then it did it again outside, when Roddy was there. That was when I shouted at him. I didn't mean to, not really, but suddenly I felt like I could take him on. Then it happened again, just before I punched Sandy. I didn't know I could do it and normally I wouldn't even have considered it. It just happened. It was the cross, I'm sure of it. It seemed like it shot power through me, like it was magic or something. Does that sound stupid? It does doesn't it?' She buried her head in Dave's shoulder and started to cry.

'I dunno what to say,' Dave said as Sally heaved in a sobbing breath. 'Either we're both going mad, or someone spiked our drinks. It happened to me too.'

She looked up at him. 'Did it?' she asked.

'Yeah. Exactly the same feeling. Burning, then instant verbals. That's why I told Roddy to go and fuck his sister. I felt this hot flash, then I was mad at him. It didn't last long though.'

'Are we crazy?' she asked in a small voice.

Dave shrugged.

'What worries me is that it felt so . . . so *right*. Like it was meant to be.'

'Yeah,' he said darkly. 'That worries me too. Maybe we ought to take the crosses off and lose them somewhere.'

Sally shook her head. 'I think it's too late to stop now. I think we'd be in worse trouble if we took them off. We were *meant* to have those crosses, Dave, we were supposed to wear them.'

Dave shuddered. 'Too weird for me,' he said, but he knew exactly what she was saying. He remembered the feeling he'd had on his birthday in Ziegfeld's when she gave him the cross. That was the point when he'd made the decision to accept it and whatever it brought with it; that was the time where he'd had a chance to reject it and walk away. Deep down, he'd known that all along. And in spite of the fact that the whole sequence of events concerning the cross had been far too odd to put down to mere coincidence, he mentally said *Yes! Let's go!* Perhaps he should have thought about it more back in the Ziegfeld, because now he was in too deep to escape, just like Sally said. And he didn't much care for the turn events had started to take.

'What does it all mean?' Sally asked.

Dave drew her to him and sighed. 'That's a good question,' he said. 'A very good question indeed.'

Chapter Five
Arrival

The funfair began to arrive on Friday at midday.

Dave was standing beside the A30 London road beside the Black Dam roundabout which linked the bottom end of Basingstoke's ring road to the M3 motorway. He had been at a loose end all morning – the computer hadn't called to him today, it was too hot to lie in bed and the lunchtime t.v. was boring.

He had left home an hour ago, having decided to go for a walk through town and clock up the office girls who would be out on their lunch breaks. Sometimes he met Sally in the Dragon, but today she had gone to a Leichner training seminar in London. The hot concrete town centre held no appeal for him today and he had passed through it quickly and walked to the Memorial Park instead. For a while he watched kids on swings and sweaty mums with pushchairs and sunburned arms doing their things, then he had crossed what was left of the common, skirted the Ladbroke Lodge hotel and wandered down to the London road with the vague idea of hitching a lift to the Big City and meeting Sally.

He knew all along it was pointless though, and after twenty minutes of half-hearted thumbing, he gave up, sat down on the grass verge in the sun and watched the traffic roar by.

The episode with Roddy and his buddies seemed like ancient history now, even though it was only the day before yesterday. He wondered idly what Roddy was doing now.

He and Sally had gone back to the car that evening, ready to run should Roddy and Sandy and Kott still be waiting there. They weren't. Phil and Judy were though, sitting on the Mini's bonnet where Roddy had sat half an hour earlier. Phil was munching his way through the kebab he had wanted so badly. The experience hadn't affected his appetite at all.

It turned out that he had out-run the guy chasing him then fled into the other Chinese takeaway at the top of Sarum Hill. He had waited in there for a few minutes, then gone back along Winchester Street looking for Judy.

Judy had run down the alley at the other end of the service area, crossed Winchester Street, and fled along the pathway that led into Joice's yard where, four days earlier, Sally had gone into Anstey's jewellers shop and purchased the crosses. She hid behind some large plastic dustbins until she was sure her pursuers had been shaken off, and then headed back to Sally's car. She had met Phil in Winchester Street where he was hiding in a shop doorway because he thought he had heard Roddy shouting. None of them was the worse for wear afterwards except Dave, whose cheek was sore where Roddy had hit him. Sally had later told her parents that she'd ripped her shirt on the corner of her car door.

Dave's cheek was slightly bruised (although Reggie and Doreen hadn't noticed it) and, sitting here in the sun, it began to ache. Dave didn't really mind; Sally and the others had started treating him like he was some kind of a hero, and it was a lot less than the damage he'd copped the last time he and Roddy had met.

He lay back in the dying grass and looked at the cloudless sky, wondering about the part his and Sally's crosses had played in the other night's little episode. In spite of the flashes of heat he'd felt, his chest showed no signs of having been burnt. Neither did Sally's. He kept a close watch on the eye in the cross since he'd thought it had changed on Wednesday and, although he couldn't swear to it, it had not appeared to change since. In fact, the doubts he and Sally had had about the crosses seemed silly now. They hadn't taken them off, and the scary effects they'd felt seemed steadily less real as time had passed, until now it appeared more likely that their fear had made those things happen than the crosses. All that stuff they'd said to each other about things being 'meant to be' seemed silly in the daylight.

As silly, in fact, as the hallucination he'd had of the driving instructor's Ebony Nails, tipping the fingers of that creature of his own imagination, The Claw. It was obvious now he thought about it. Before he hallucinated The Claw, he'd been watching *The Creature from the Black Lagoon*. He'd swooned – probably due to the drink and the sexual exercise – and his mind had chucked up a combination of the horror film and the driving instructor's vision to keep him entertained while he was unconscious. The mess in the bathroom and the broken toilet brush could be explained away too. Who knew what a person could get up to while their brain was out of order? He'd probably staggered about in there, living out his nightmare. And the slime on the floor and in the toilet bowl was puke. What else could it have been?

The vision of The Claw he'd seen clamped around Phil's leg the following day must have just been a hangover from Saturday. Everyone else saw green weeds and he was prepared to accept their judgement on the matter.

See, he told himself, *everything has a way of working out alright in the end, doesn't it?*

The dull roar of the first Scammell truck heading down the hill to the Black Dam roundabout made him sit up. He could plainly feel its vibrations through the earth. The truck was massive and painted purple. Its vast chrome radiator grille looked like gnashing teeth. Dave had always thought of cars as having faces made up of headlight eyes and radiator grille mouths (or noses in some cases). This lorry had a happy look about it in spite of its bared teeth. It was old, but it had been kept in good repair. The Scammell had a flat-bed back with a huge diesel generator mounted on it. It was towing a forty foot trailer which was painted the same colour as the cab. There were three men in the Scammell's cab and they looked hot and tired.

The signwriting on the lorry's door said: *George Dale's famous Octopus*.

Written in three foot high, red letters down the side of the trailer was the legend: *AdventureLand – Europe's Premier Funfair*. Beneath it, in smaller, joined-up writing, was a copy of what was written on the cab door.

The lorry passed and ground down through the gears as the driver approached the Black Dam roundabout.

George Dale's Octopus wasn't *that* famous, Dave reasoned. It couldn't be – *he'd* never heard of it.

A brand new Range Rover towing a large ornate caravan followed the lorry down the hill. A young woman in a halter top was driving. The caravan was heavily chromed and had lace curtains in the windows. Dave felt a sudden urge to be in that Rover and travelling, going somewhere.

He took off his glasses and polished the sweat from the rims and lenses with the bottom of his tee shirt. Another lorry breasted the hill and accelerated towards him. This one was an ancient maroon Foden, it too bore the AdventureLand legend, but this one was enclosed and had no other signwriting. Dave supposed it must be one or more of the side stalls.

The cumbersome procession of heavy lorries continued sporadically for the next hour, and Dave watched with interest, reading the sign on the side of each, and wondering where they were going. It was the first time he had seen a funfair whose disparate elements were – it seemed – all a part of the same company. Each lorry bore the AdventureLand logo and on every single one it was written larger than the owner's own name. The fair that usually came to Basingstoke at carnival time (and had this year, several weeks ago) was known collectively as Wall's funfair, but the rides were owned by individuals who sometimes grouped together and sometimes worked with fairs from other areas.

At about four, Dave began to tire of sitting by the roadside. He was hot and sweaty, the back of his neck was starting to burn in the relentless sun, his mouth seemed to have run out of saliva, and since the stream of AdventureLand lorries had all but died out (there were mainly caravans going by now) he decided to wander home again.

He crossed the road and walked up the hill which bordered the football pitches and connected the common to the Memorial Park. When he crested the hill, he saw that the trucks had pulled into the park and formed a rough circle on the very area that the carnival funfair had recently used. Dave had read nothing in the local papers about a funfair coming to town, and AdventureLand wasn't the right one, even if one *was* coming. Forgetting his dry mouth, he walked closer to the circle of lorries and caravans and watched the ride owners starting to unpack.

There were perhaps twenty-five lorries, about fifteen caravans and lots more cars hauling trailers. Judging by some of the new cars there was plenty of money to be made in this line of work, Dave decided.

An old man with sun-tanned skin and wrinkles like a road map stepped out of a nearby caravan carrying a tray of large tea mugs. He wore grey trousers with a waistband that was halfway up his chest. These were held up with wide maroon braces, the dye from which had seeped into his grubby white shirt. On his head was an ancient felt hat that looked like it had been moulded in place since nineteen sixty.

He distributed the mugs to three men who were much younger and stronger-looking than he was and who, Dave decided, must be his sons. Then he spotted Dave and shuffled over.

'Busy son?' he asked. He sounded even older than he looked.

Dave shrugged.

'You out of work?'

'Yeah. I was just watching you set up.'

'You look like a strong young man,' the ride man said. Suddenly his right arm shot out and grabbed Dave's left bicep. Dave looked down at the old man's hand as he began to squeeze. His fingers were long and clawed with lengthy nails that each sported a crescent of dirt. His knuckles were misshapen – swollen and arthritic. But he was strong. His fingers sank into Dave's muscle and it hurt. Dave wanted to pull away, but he couldn't – the hand seemed to be hypnotising him and all he could do was stare down at it, wait for it to lengthen and turn into The Claw.

'Give you some work if you want it,' the man said, letting go of Dave and breaking the spell. Dave's right hand flew to his left bicep which felt as though it had been penetrated by sticks of ice. But he didn't rub it – couldn't while the man was watching – just covered it with his fingers and kept his face blank.

'It'd be strictly casual,' the ride man said. 'The dole don't have to know. We can always use a hand setting up and taking down. Got my three boys, but we got the Octopus and the Waltzer to cover.'

'You must be George Dale then,' Dave said. 'I saw your lorry coming down the A30.'

'That's me.' George Dale put out his arthritic hand to shake, but Dave couldn't make himself take hold of it again, and after a short time it was withdrawn. 'Like I said, there ain't enough of us to manage really, not with the putting up. Some of the others help out running the rides, but they're always too busy getting their own stuff together when we arrive somewhere. Want a job? If you turn out any good, maybe there's a place for you collecting the ride money during the week.'

'Uh, well I don't think so,' Dave said.

'Fifteen pound a day,' the old man offered.

Yeah, and what will you be making while I do all your hard graft for you? Dave thought. *That's just over a hundred pounds if they're staying all week, thirty if I just help put the stuff up and take it down again. What will they make? Ten – a hundred times that much?*

But he had to admit to himself that a hundred pounds would be useful, even if it did amount to slave labour. *Think what you could do with a ton, Davey boy,* the other half of his imagination told him.

He almost gave in. Would have, if the old man hadn't tipped his hat back and started to scratch his head with one gnarled hand. The real hand frightened Dave almost as much as the hallucinations of The Claw.

110

'You could use the money, I'll bet,' Dale tempted.

'Sorry, I'm going to be busy,' Dave replied.

George Dale shook his head and spread his hands, palms out. 'I offered,' he said simply, then turned and walked back toward the trailer where his three sons were busy unloading canvas and machinery.

Dave shuddered as he watched the old man's sweat-stained back. Dale turned around as if he'd forgotten something. He waved. 'We're open tomorrow and every night for the next week. Hope we'll be seeing you!' he called.

Dave nodded, waved back, then turned and headed across the grass toward the swings. He didn't relax completely until the park was far behind him.

'But it won't do any good!' Anne Cousins shouted. 'It won't do any good at all! Why don't you just leave it alone? He's not coming back. Don't you realise that? He's gone and he's not coming back. Ever!' She got up from the kitchen table, and bumped into it as she fled into the lounge. Her half-drunk coffee cup fell over and the dark liquid spilled out and ran across the scarred – but still neat – pine in an ever-widening stream. Derek stood there, back against the sink, arms folded, watching the coffee reach the edge of the table and start to drip onto the floor. His insides felt as if someone was running them through a mangle, and he wished he could stop thinking, stop hoping, the way his wife seemed to have done. But that wasn't the way to be. How *could* she be like that while there was still hope that Tommy might come back?

Tears filled his eyes for the third time that day and for the thousandth time that week. And that was how long it was. Or at least, that's how long it would be tomorrow. A week since Tommy vanished. Even though it felt like forever, it was only six and a half days. So there was still hope. A child could last six and a half days with no food or water. Longer probably. Of course Tommy was going to come back. Everything was going to be alright.

He pulled another Kleenex from the box, dabbed his eyes

111

and blew his nose, then mopped up the coffee with it. He put the cups in the sink where the dinner plates were. Dinner! That was a joke. Neither of them had eaten a proper meal since Tiger vanished. He hadn't felt like eating for the three days Anne was under sedation in hospital and, since she'd come home, it didn't seem right to eat while poor Tommy was gone. How could they stuff their stomachs while a madman held their son and was probably torturing him or subjecting him to some horrific sexual ordeal? It wouldn't be right, not with the house so *empty*.

Derek Cousins was convinced that Tiger had been kidnapped. The police had said as much, and the area had been thoroughly searched. All the small secret places a boy might become trapped in, or fall down, had been checked from here to Wokingham, and beyond. Ascot, Windlesham and all the woods in between had been searched and there wasn't a trace of his son.

So Tiger had been kidnapped. And it had happened at the fair.

That was why he was going to follow the fair to Basingstoke.

He squirted Fairy Liquid into the sink and began to wash the crockery slowly and methodically, his mind running through various scenarios that had one thing in common: they all ended with him rescuing his son from the kidnapper.

Anne's sobbing started again. The lounge door was shut, but he could hear her plainly, even with the taps running. Would it ever end?

He pulled the plug and went into the lounge where his wife was curled up on the sofa, crying into one of Tommy's tee shirts. The little tee shirt was blue. Derek had bought it for Tommy's last month when they were on holiday in Falmouth. Big black letters on the front said: PLEASE EXCUSE MY PARENTS, SOMEONE ELSE CHOSE THEM. Anne's face was buried in the shirt and her shoulders were heaving as she sobbed. Another bolt of pain shot through Derek's guts. 'Annie,' he said gently, sitting down next to her and smoothing her tangled hair. 'C'mon, calm down.'

Anne looked up at him, her pretty face drawn and gaunt. Her eyelids were swollen from the constant crying and her blue eyes were bloodshot and red-rimmed. 'All that's l-left,' she said, lifting the tee shirt for him to see. 'All that's left of my s-son. It n-needed washing. You c-can smell h-him on it. It's all there is now.'

She held out the damp shirt and Derek sniffed it, smelling the distinctive aroma of Tiger Cousins as clearly as if he had just peeled it off his wiry body. Tears sprang instantly to his eyes, and he dimly wondered where they kept on coming from and when they would stop.

'He's dead, isn't he?' she said.

'No!' Derek exclaimed, banging his fist down on the sofa's armrest. 'HE IS NOT DEAD!' He said this slowly so the words could sink into Anne's fuddled mind. The tranquillisers the hospital had supplied her with seemed to be doing more harm than good. They'd taken the edge off her hysteria sure enough, but they'd left her hopeless and defeated and he wasn't able to communicate with her properly any more. Her personality had undergone a huge change and he didn't know whether it was because of the drugs, because of the guilt she felt about losing Tommy (she blamed herself entirely) or a combination of the two. Nothing he said seemed to make sense to her while she was in that drugged state; all she seemed to want to do was forget about trying to find Tommy. Perhaps that was something to do with what she might discover if Tommy was found, he thought. If they found his corpse and he'd been sexually abused and murdered, what would that do to her? How could she carry on, knowing that?

'Tommy is alive,' he explained patiently. 'In spite of what the police say, I think that someone from the fairground – one of the employees – is the kidnapper. Someone has Tommy locked away in their caravan and that's why I must follow the fair to Basingstoke. We have to get him back. I'll die to get him back if that is necessary but, believe me, I will get him back.'

Anne shook her head. 'He's not there. He's gone. We can't get him back.'

'Okay,' Derek said, boiling with frustration and resisting the urge to slap Anne hard across the face in the hope of waking her up, 'where is he then?'

Anne looked up at him, her face empty and bleak. 'Dead,' she said.

'But what if he's not? What then? Do you agree that – in theory, at least – there's a chance he might still be alive?'

Anne nodded her head, the movement slow and ponderous. Her eyes were distant.

'Then I've got to look for him, haven't I? Even if you don't help me.'

She looked at him blankly.

'Well?'

'You don't love me any more, do you?'

'*What?*'

'You don't love me now. You blame me for losing Tiger and you don't love me any more.'

'Christ, of *course* I love you.'

'You haven't told me since . . .'

'Since what? Oh God, I know. The reason I haven't told you, is because other things have been on my mind. I'm sorry. I love you. Okay?'

'But it's my fault.'

'No it isn't. It's nobody's fault. Except Tommy's maybe. He was the one who wandered off.'

'Oh.'

'Will you come with me? To Basingstoke?'

She shook her head slowly. 'No,' she said, emphasising her point.

'Why not, for Christ's sake?'

'Because I'm scared.'

'Of *what?*' Derek's voice was rising as his temper flared. Now wasn't the time to be playing guessing games.

'I don't know. I'm just scared that it will happen to us too. If we go.'

'What?'

'What has happened to Tommy.'

'You're . . .' You're crazy, he was going to say, but he kept the words from spilling out. It seemed too close to the truth to be spoken aloud. He realised that this was what his subconscious had been muttering about all week. This was the reason he could no longer communicate with his wife. It wasn't the drugs that had changed her personality at all. Tommy's disappearance *had* pushed Anne over the edge. He wondered if anything other than Tommy's reappearance would make everything all right again. 'What do you think *did* happen to Tommy?' he asked, being careful to keep his voice level.

Anne looked up at him, her eyes distant and unseeing. Her eyebrows creased to a frown. She began to say something, but stopped before the first word came out.

'Well?' Derek asked.

Anne shook her head and put Tommy's unwashed tee shirt back over her nose and mouth. Two big tears formed in the corners of her eyes, grew large and trickled down her face into Tommy's shirt. Derek felt a sudden surge of love and pity for his wife and took her in his arms, rocking her back and forth as she sobbed.

Gradually, she quietened. Derek held her, looking around the room that was full of things it had once seemed important to have. The twenty-six inch screen television on which he had watched his tearful appeal a few days ago. It didn't seem at all right that he'd been electronically broadcast into his own house. The JVC video – bought mainly to show Tommy the Tom and Jerry cartoons he had loved so much. The leather three-piece suite they had paid a fortune for and scolded Tiger each time he bounced on the fat cushions. The radio-controlled car that sat in the corner, its flat-batteried controller lying next to it. All this stuff seemed so pointless now that Tommy wasn't here.

'I had this d-dream,' Anne said, her voice muffled by Derek's chest.

'Yeah,' Derek said softly. He knew what she meant. He had had dreams every night this week. Dreams of him and Tommy and Anne, together and happy and contented. That made it even worse waking up in the mornings. As soon as you became conscious again, the reality descended and hung on you like a lead blanket.

'It w-was a bad d-dream,' Anne said. 'We were just outside the fairground. I could see the rides in the background. Tommy was alive, but I couldn't get to him. I could see him as if I was next to him, but he w-was miles away. It was like there was a glass barrier between us. H-he was so frightened. He kept on calling "Mummy, Mummy, save me!" but there was nothing I could do to help him. Then . . . then the g-ground started to open up behind him. It cracked and split open like there was something huge underneath and Tommy started screaming that it was going to eat him all up again, then the ground burst open and a huge giant's head came up and . . . and. Oh God, its *teeth!*'

'Shh,' Derek said, holding on tight against her struggles as she relived her nightmare.

'And Tommy ran and ran and the head . . . the head. . . . And its hand came out of the ground and it came through the barrier and grabbed me and I could feel my ribs – oh my ribs. *Snapping!* And my b-breath I tried to scream oh I tried and blood was in my mouth and it was hot and thick and tasted nasty. And it picked me up and I was dying already and my back broke and I went into there into its mouth and *its teeth!*' She stopped then, gasping for breath.

'It's okay, I'm here,' Derek soothed, pushing the damp hair back off her face.

'And that's why we c-can't go to Basingstoke,' Anne said suddenly. 'It'll happen to us too.'

'I'm sorry Annie, but we've got to go. Someone has got him, and it's not someone from your nightmare. It's one of the fairground people and Tiger is in one of their caravans. Nothing will happen to us if we go, there's nothing to be frightened of.'

'We'll die,' she said. 'Like Tommy. Only we won't be dead. We'll be like he is. Trapped on the other side.'

'On the other side of what?' Derek asked. A tiny warning bell

had begun to sound in his mind. The image of the giant breaking up through the ground seemed to make some crazy kind of
sense to him. Her telling him about her nightmare seemed to
have awakened something in his own mind. A deep-seated race
memory, or more likely, a forgotten fairy tale from his youth.
Whatever it was, it sounded familiar.

Too familiar.

'What do you mean, on the other side?' he repeated. 'On the
other side of what?'

Anne looked at him for a second, then buried her head in his
chest again. 'On the other side of the fairground,' she murmured. 'In hell.'

Chapter Six
The Ghost Train

'So what if he *is* working on one of the rides? What do I care?'
Dave said as he and Sally walked across the War Memorial Park
towards the funfair. It was Saturday afternoon and they were
discussing Roddy again. That particular topic of conversation
never seemed to be far beneath the surface just lately. Any quiet
space in the flow of words between Dave and Sally, and them
and Phil and Judy, and *bang* – there was the ghost of Roddy
Johnson, filling the void and hanging there, waiting to be
discussed.

'So you're not worried?' Sally said lightly. She took Dave's
hand and smiled at him admiringly. Dave kicked an empty
Coke can which flew into the air and landed behind a dog that
was sleeping in the shade of one of the nearby trees.

Too hot for dogs, Dave thought.

'I asked you a question,' Sally said, tugging on his arm. He
realised that he'd inadvertantly changed direction so that he
was dragging Sally across to the dog. Dogs were one of his main
weaknesses. He found it almost impossible to pass one by without making friends with it.

'What were you saying? Oh yes, wasn't I worried about
Roddy being at the fair? Why should I be?'

'Because he just might take the opportunity to dot you one
on the nose, superman, that's why.'

'Don't worry my little wimpo, I have laid contingency
plans.'

'And what might they be?'

'If I see Roddy Johnson, Jon Kott or Roddy's ugly sister, I run. When the going gets tough the tough fuck off a bit quick!'

'You wouldn't leave me behind would you? You know I can't run as fast as you can.'

'Every man and every woman for themselves, I'm afraid. I believe in women's lib, as you know.'

'Thanks custard guts,' she said digging him in the belly with an extended knuckle.

Dave swore. 'C'mon, let's go and see that dog!' he said, tugging Sally's arm.

'No time!' she said and dragged him toward the hum and buzz of the fair.

Now the fair was set up, it looked quite impressive. The parked lorries and caravans had formed a circle which extended right out onto the cricket green. The circle enclosed the rides and side shows except for a point just past the park's swings where a big wooden arch, painted to look like a castle wall, straddled the entrance. The AdventureLand logo was written over the top of the arch in huge red letters and beneath that Dave could see something else written in black. As they got closer he read: *Die a Thousand Deaths and Live to Tell the Tale!*

Both Dave and Sally quickened their steps as they drew nearer to the entrance, the noise of screams and sirens calling to them to join the hundreds already milling about inside.

'Looks like a good one,' Sally said, 'I hope you brought your life savings. I want to go on everything and I want you to win me a coconut and I want . . .'

'Want want want!' Dave mimicked, dragging her past the hoop-la stall. 'Where are we supposed to be meeting the Fat Groover?'

'By the helter skelter,' she said. 'Oh look! There's that Frogger game, I've never seen one before! I want a go! I want a go!'

'In a minute. Be patient!' he scolded.

Phil and Judy were waiting in front of the Helter Skelter as promised. Judy was pale and Phil was munching a toffee apple.

'Hi guys,' Sally said. 'What have you been on?'

'We haven't been here long,' Phil said from behind the apple. 'We went on the Big Wheel.' His mouth was smeared red with the toffee. He looked like a drunk had been at him with a lipstick.

'And the Waltzer,' Judy added.

'Is that why you're so pale?' Sally asked her.

Phil shook his head. 'Nope,' he said through another mouthful of toffee apple. 'She's so pale because she went on the Ghost Train. It's her own fault, she was the one who wanted to go.'

'It's terrible,' Judy said. 'It's the most scary Ghost Train I've ever been on. The effects are really horrible and it's huge. I thought it was never going to stop.'

'What was so bad then?' Dave asked watching a little kid come hammering round the last bend of the Helter Skelter and whizzing off the end onto the pile of mats.

'There's a man in there dressed up in a skeleton suit,' Judy said, her eyes like saucers. 'I've never heard of that before. He wanders around and jumps up in front of you and screams and his eyes light up red.'

'She had to go and empty her drawers when we came out,' Phil chuckled.

'Scared me half to death,' Judy said, shuddering. 'Yuk!'

'I want to go on,' Dave said. Phil nodded his assent.

'Sally?'

Sally didn't look keen. She shrugged and said nothing.

'Well I'm not going again,' Judy said. 'I'll stand outside and wait. I don't like it!'

'Oh come on Jude!' Phil said.

'No. I don't like it.'

Phil looked at Dave. 'Fucking women, eh?' he said rolling his eyes heavenwards.

'Let's go on something else and think about the Ghost Train later, shall we?' Dave said, eager to make a compromise.

'Bumper cars,' Judy said.

'Rotor,' Phil said.

'Okay, but first we have to go on George Dale's famous

Octopus,' Dave said, pointing at the machine.

'Whose famous Octopus?' Judy said.

'George Dale. I was watching him set up yesterday and he offered me a job for the week. I told you in the pub last night.'

They pushed through the throng of people that were gathered around the Octopus and joined the queue. The ride was working as they took their places, and Dave looked up at the spinning cars on the eight long metal arms as they rose and fell. Apart from the fact that the cars were freshly painted in bright colours and had circular canopies mounted on a curved pole that came out of the back, George Dale's Octopus looked much like any other. George himself was in the control booth, his felt hat tipped back on his grey head and a dead roll-up planted firmly between his lips. One of his sons was the money collector and he was leaning up against the outside of the booth waiting for the ride to finish. There was a leather money bag hanging from the front of his trousers and he had one hand thrust deep into it as he idly watched the revolving cars. The front of the money bag bulged and twisted as his hand worked inside it. Dave decided that he was either picking up the coins and letting them run through his hands, or using the bag as a cover while he scratched his nuts.

The Supremes' 'Where did our love go?' blared out scratchily through two ancient speaker cabinets mounted on either side of the glass on the control booth. Dave wondered if George had bought the original back in the sixties and had been playing it ever since.

The old man leaned forward in his booth and banged his hand down on a red button. A siren screamed, drowning the Supremes. Far above Dave's head someone yelled that they were going to be sick.

'Twenty pence says we get the car with the sick in,' Sally said smiling.

'Yecch,' Dave said.

And then it was all over. The Supremes stopped in mid verse and the ride slowed quickly. Ten seconds later Dale junior was dropping the front of the first car and letting the riders out. The guy who had promised to be sick jumped out laughing and not looking ill at all.

Sally and Dave were the fourth couple on. Dave paid their fares, and Junior tipped the front up and shot the bolt that held it in place. George Dale stood up inside his booth and yelled at his son over Bachmann-Turner Overdrive's 'You ain't seen nothin yet'. Junior went over to him. Dave watched George speaking to his son and pointing at the car. When Junior turned to come back, George waved and smiled then indicated the sky.

'He says he's going to give you a special ride,' Junior said. 'Gonna put you in orbit. No extra charge.'

Sally grabbed Dave's arm and made a show of biting all her fingernails at once.

'Oh, thanks,' Dave said, nonplussed by the heavy undertone to Junior's message.

Junior grabbed hold of the side of their car and swung it around hard. The world spun in a garish blur before their eyes and George threw the lever so that the car began to rise. The Octopus stopped again when their car was about fifteen feet above the ground to allow Phil and Judy into the next car. The spinning took a while to die down though and both of them were dizzy when it finally came to a halt.

'You're breaking my wrist,' Dave said, looking down at Sally's tightly clamped fingers. Her nails were digging into his skin and when she let go there were four crescents indented in his skin.

She chuckled nervously. 'I couldn't focus on anything,' she said. 'Sorry.'

Below them, Junior was giving Phil and Judy the same treatment. Judy screamed.

The seventh and eighth cars were loaded, Stevie Wonder began singing 'Superstition' and the siren sounded. As the Octopus began to move, the initial drain on the generator's current slowed Stevie down and made him drop a couple of keys. When their car reached the bottom again Junior was waiting. He grabbed it as it passed and spun it hard. The other stalls and rides streaked by them in a crazy rush of colour as

George piled on the power and their car began to rise. The centre cam came into play then, revolving in the opposite direction to the turn of the arms and increasing the frequency and speed of the car's rise and fall. Now the cars spun of their own volition, fast enough to press Dave's insides against the back of his spine.

'Help!' Sally shouted.

Dave opened his eyes and looked over at her, trying to keep his head still enough to see if she was enjoying it. Her hair was whipped to and fro by the wind, and on the machine's downstroke it stood on end. Her hands were now clenched on the rail at the front of the car and Dave was grateful for that. Her eyes were wide and streaming and her mouth was open, screaming in fear and delight. And she had that look he'd last seen after the Roddy Johnson episode. That wild, *dangerous* expression.

For five minutes Dave's body resisted the conflicting fields of force and his vision remained blurred. Then the siren went and he breathed a sigh of relief. Soon he would be able to get off. But instead of the Octopus slowing like it had done last time, it speeded up.

'Oh God,' he groaned, pushing his feet to the end of the car and forcing himself against the back of the seat so that he locked into as solid a position as possible. He no longer knew whether he was going up or down or what direction he might be facing. The car began to wobble as it revolved, the forces at play on it too great for its bearings to withstand.

We're going to come off. I knew it. The silly old sod has pushed it too far and we're going to come off!

'Yesssss!' Sally shouted orgasmically.

The bearings began to squeal.

Dave's ears were filled with the screams of the other riders and the sound of grinding metal. His hair whipped his face and his glasses had came askew. He was sure he was going to die.

The car dived and rose, spun and dived again, its bearings pleading for mercy. Dave began to feel faint. The blood was slowly being drained from his brain by the centrifugal force and the jolting motion. Either the ride would break, or everyone on it would be dead when it stopped, he told himself. It was too much, it was just too much.

'More!' Sally yelled.

The siren sounded again.

Not faster, he thought. *It can't be going to get faster!*

The music stopped suddenly, and the Octopus slowed.

'Oh God!' Dave said as his car gradually ceased revolving. His brain was empty and a huge stupid grin filled his face.

'That was great!' Sally enthused, grabbing his cold hands with her even colder ones.

'Yeah, wasn't it?' he agreed.

'I want to go on again,' Sally said.

'Later,' Dave replied. 'I'd like my guts to fall back into place first.'

Junior was grinning when it was their turn to get off, but it looked like it was forced. 'Whadidya think?' he asked, sounding relieved. 'Like it?'

'Ace,' Dave said, turning to look towards Dale senior. The old man tipped his hat and nodded.

'Wasn't fast enough,' Sally said drily.

Junior chuckled. 'Last time he took her up to there, one of the cars flew off,' he said. 'Flew right over into the Noah's Ark. You should have seen the mess it made. Old fart's crazy as a coot. Swore he'd never do it again, he did. Never has until today.' He leaned over and looked closely at the car. Then nodded. 'Yep, this was the car that came off. Had to rebuild it meself.'

'You made a good job,' Dave said, levering himself out of the seat.

'Yeah, thanks,' Sally agreed.

They tottered down the steps unsteadily.

'Let's go and stand against the barrier,' Sally suggested. 'I can hardly keep my feet. The ground seems to have gone all spongy.'

They leaned against the Octopus's mesh safety barrier waiting for Phil and Judy to get off. 'I hope that guy was only winding you up,' Sally said. 'I got the feeling that he meant every word of what he said. Doesn't his dad like you or something? What did you say to upset him?'

'Nothing that I know of,' Dave replied. 'Only that I didn't want to work for him.'

'D'you think a car *really* came off?' she asked, putting her arm around his waist and drawing close.

'Nah,' Dave said. 'Course not.' But that was a lie.

Phil and Judy followed them out, hanging on to one another for support.

'That was worth fifty pee of anyone's money,' Phil said breathlessly. 'What next? How about the Rotor?'

'I've got to win madam here a coconut,' Dave said. 'I think we'll have a go at that first. Tour the side shows and let the stomachs settle.'

'Good idea,' Judy agreed.

No one won anything on the Frogger game, but Phil got soaked. Judy tried to get less than forty with five darts on a darts stall and got forty-nine and Dave just missed a goldfish, complete with bowl, on a hoop-la game.

They wandered around the perimeter, gazing at the stalls. Sally prevented Dave from entering the amusement arcades on the grounds that he'd be stuck there all afternoon if he went in, then they arrived at the coconut shy.

'Here we are,' Sally said. 'Win me a coconut!'

'Me too!' Judy yelled.

Phil looked doubtfully at the coconuts which were mounted on red and white striped stands with cups at the top. 'I dunno,' he said, 'they look an awfully long way away.'

'Yeah,' Dave added, 'and those cups are higher at the back than they are at the front. You haven't got a chance of knocking one off.'

'Have a go gentlemen?' the stall-holder asked, spotting them lingering. He came over with his wicker basket full of wooden balls. 'Four for fifty, nine a pound! Win the little lady a coconut.'

'How about we go down to Sainsbury's and I buy you one?' Dave said to Sally.

'C'mon spoilsport, have a go!' the man said. 'The lady wants you to win her one. These are fresher than Sainsbury's too. I only picked them this morning!'

'Okay, give us a quid's worth,' Dave said.

'Me too,' Phil said, groping in his pocket for a coin.

Despite much cheerleadering from Sally and Judy who worked out a quick routine, neither of them hit a coconut at all with the first four balls. Phil hit one with his fifth, but it was low and the nut stayed firmly in its holder.

'Up a bit, up a bit, rah rah rah,' the girls chanted, leaping up and down behind them. A small knot of onlookers had gathered (drawn mainly, Dave thought, by the fact that neither of the girls was wearing a bra). One wag advised Dave to put backspin on the next ball. He tried and it missed the coconuts completely and thudded into the canvas backcloth.

'Ooh, close!' the adviser said. 'Try again!'

But Phil was taking up all the play area and he decided to wait until he'd finished before throwing again. Phil's last ball tipped a coconut but the nut just swivelled and stayed put. 'Shit,' Phil said, grinning sheepishly and dusting off his hands.

'My go,' Dave said and took careful aim down his thumb. The ball struck the coconut dead centre with a sharp crack and bounced off. The nut split and thin milk trickled out, but it didn't fall. The crowd cheered.

The next three balls went wide.

'One left,' Sally shouted. 'Go on Davey, you can do it!'

Dave waited. He became aware of the cross which felt heavy and cool against his chest. A tiny tickle developed on the skin beneath it, and the noise and shouting faded into the background. Dave picked his target.

And closed his eyes.

And leaned back and threw the ball. He heard it strike, wooden and loud.

Sound came crashing back into his consciousness as the onlookers went wild. Sally grabbed him from behind and planted a sloppy kiss on his ear. 'You did it!' she yelled. Dave opened his eyes. The coconut was on the ground. The cross tickled him once more and then he stopped being aware of it.

'There you go kid,' the stall-holder said, picking up a big coconut from a pile at his feet and handing it to Sally. 'You look after him. He's the first one we've had that won with his eyes shut.' He shook his head. 'I'd never have believed it possible,' he said.

'Thanks Davey,' Sally said, hugging him again.

'I want to see the fish woman,' Phil said sullenly.

'Don't sulk,' Sally said, 'you can have my coconut if it makes you feel better.'

Phil shook his head, 'I don't even like coconuts,' he said.

'Nor do I,' Judy said, taking his arm. 'It's just as well you didn't win one really. Let's go and see the fish woman. I'll pay.'

'What's all this about a fish woman?' Dave asked, scanning the side shows to see if he'd missed anything.

'Half woman, half fish,' Phil said. 'I'll bet she's got enormous knockers,' he added enthusiastically.

Judy poked him. 'And what's wrong with mine?' she asked sticking her chest out. Phil eyed her lasciviously and made grasping motions with his fingers.

'Nothing apparently,' Sally said. 'He just wants to make a comparison.'

'In the interests of science,' Dave added.

The sign above the small tent proclaimed that THE AMAZING FISH WOMAN was THE SEVENTH WONDER OF THE WORLD and that YOU'LL BE AMAZED when you wonder HOW CAN SHE SURVIVE? Below it, chalked on a small blackboard were the words: 'Step inside and meat the fabulos Jean – half woman, half fish. 40p each adult, 20p children.'

They paid the forty pence admission charge and walked into a tent which couldn't have been much bigger than eight feet by eight. Inside it was hot and smelled of mildew and sea water. The grass on the floor had been worn bare by many feet. A glass cube ran from the ground to the top of the tent and was somehow fixed to narrow wooden partitions. It was filled with a translucent blue liquid, and in the centre, floating three feet above the bottom, was the fabulous Jean.

Jean was aged about forty and was naked. Long blond hair cascaded down her shoulders and covered her breasts. From just below the navel, Jean had a fish tail which was scaled and shone silver.

'Christ,' Phil said, pressing his nose up against the cold glass and peering in.

'How do they do it?' Sally asked, genuinely astonished.

'Dunno,' Dave said, looking for any wires that might be suspending the fish woman. He wandered why they hadn't advertised her as a mermaid. 'Mermaid' sounded much more up-market than 'fish woman' which had a kind of nasty ring to it. It sounded too much like fish-*wife* he supposed.

Jean the mermaid floated there, smiling. From this distance she looked slim and pretty in spite of her apparent age. Her fish's tail swished gently back and forth as she hovered in the water.

'Her hair's moving,' Phil observed hopefully as the mermaid adjusted her position. And her hair *did* move as though she were swimming, but it didn't move enough for them to see anything more than a gentle swell of pale flesh.

'She's got tits anyway,' Phil said. 'All we need to know now is how big they are.'

'Speak for yourself!' Sally said. 'I've got some of my own thanks very much.'

'How do they do it?' Sally whispered again. 'Her tail – it looks as though it's actually part of her body. You can't see where her skin stops and the false tails starts.'

Jean waggled her tail and slowly revolved. She came right up to the glass and hung there at head height. Dave could see the lines on her face now, although she was well made up. She smiled down at Phil and began to toy with her hair.

'I think she can hear what we're saying,' Judy said.

Dave inspected her waist line closely, trying to see where her body stopped and her tail began. The tail looked like a real one and seemed to behave like a real one too as it swished back and forth.

The mermaid took both hanks of her hair in her hands and lifted it.

Phil groaned with disappointment.

Two huge clam shells covered her breasts.

'She looks like a petrol advert,' Phil complained.

'Thanks very much,' the mermaid said. Her tinny voice came out of a loudspeaker high in the corner of the tent.

'So you *can* hear us,' Judy said.

'Yes dear,' the mermaid replied.

'You're not under water at all,' Dave said.

'Yes I am,' the mermaid insisted.

'How can you speak then?' Sally asked. 'There aren't any bubbles coming out of your mouth or anything.'

Jean the mermaid looked stumped. She thought for a while then said, 'Telepathy.'

'You're in there suspended on wires, aren't you?' Phil said. 'I can't see them, but that's how it's done.'

Jean shook her head. 'No wires dear. If it was wires, how could I do this?'

She swam from side to side of the tank, then somersaulted, swam upside down and finally stood on her head. All this was accomplished with a slow grace that could only be achieved under water.

'I don't like it,' Judy said. She was standing against the canvas side of the tent, as far away from the tank as she could get.

'It's magic, see dear?' Jean said, propelling herself back to their side with a flick of her tail.

'Trickery!' Phil yelled good-naturedly.

'If you're going to take that attitude, I'm going,' Jean said. She waggled her bottom half, dived toward the front of the tank where it was mounted in the partition and vanished.

'Show over,' Sally said, and they made their way out of the tent.

'Why didn't you like it?' Sally asked Judy when they were back in the sunshine.

Judy shrugged. 'I dunno. It was just weird. Like it was impossible.'

'It was only a trick,' Phil scoffed. 'You're a real scaredy cat.'

'Where did she go?' Sally said to Dave. 'She just vanished.'

'Optical trickery, I s'pose,' he replied. 'She probably wasn't in that cube at all.'

'Come on,' Judy said, aware that she'd attracted some curious looks from her friends and eager to change the subject, 'I want to go in the glass maze.'

'I'm not going in there, it's dangerous!' Dave said as they stood in front of the maze. The maze was a low wooden-sided building with a glass front. There was a pay booth in the middle and an entrance one side and an exit the other. The idea was to go in, then find your way out again. The only problem was that all the walls of the maze inside were made of glass and you couldn't tell what was wall and what wasn't. There were about fifteen people inside, all of them bumbling around like zombies and feeling in front of them for the space into the next corridor. Occasionally one would crash into a wall and cry out. The yells and comments were picked up by a microphone suspended from the ceiling and broadcast so that those watching could have a good laugh.

Sally wondered aloud if the panes ever broke. 'You could gash an artery in there,' she said, 'and by the time help got to you, you would have bled to death.'

'I expect the glass is toughened,' Dave said. 'They wouldn't use window pane stuff in a thing like that.'

'Are we going in?' Judy asked.

They all looked at one another. 'If we can go on the Ghost Train afterwards,' Sally said.

Judy nodded, realising that she'd never live it down if she refused.

Dave entered the maze with Sally hot on his heels and the other two following close behind. It was stiflingly hot inside and Dave found that an odd claustrophobic feeling had settled on him, in spite of the fact that he was still in the first corridor and could easily turn and go back out of the entrance. He felt his way around the first four turns and found himself face to face with a rather flushed Phil on the other side of a glass partition. Judy was nowhere to be seen.

'I'm lost,' Phil shouted through the glass panel. His voice was both muffled and tinny, and Dave realised he could hear it through the glass and across the speaker system from outside. The two sources were slightly out of phase with each other, and this increased the peculiar feeling of unreality.

Sally came up behind Dave and poked him in the ribs. He jumped.

'What's wrong?' she asked, kissing the back of his neck.

Dave pointed at Phil, who was feeling the glass panel for an opening which wasn't there.

'Why didn't you stay behind us?' Dave called.

Phil shrugged. 'Looked like a better way this way!' he shouted.

'Where's Judy?'

Phil pointed towards the front of the maze. Judy was in a corridor right at the front. Only one sheet of glass separated her from the onlookers outside. She had obviously made her way there thinking that it was a quick way out but the people who had designed the maze had thought of that one. It was a blocked-off corridor that ended right next to the exit. You could see the way out, but you couldn't get through. There was obviously only one way around the maze. To get to the front, you had to go right to the back first. That was elementary.

Phil turned around and went back the way he thought he'd come. He bounced off one of the glass walls and swore colourfully. Some of the people outside laughed and pointed at him.

'Which way?' Dave asked.

'Go left.'

Dave turned left, feeling in front of him like a blind man. 'Now what?'

'Straight ahead.'

Judy was in the next corridor along from them now, following a middle-aged man in a suit. The man hit the end wall of the corridor and fell over. Judy bent down to him, her hand over her mouth as she stifled a giggle.

131

Dave cackled and looked at Sally to see if she was watching. When he turned back, he walked into a wall too. His knees, forehead and nose took most of the impact, but his pride suffered the most damage. The glass wall wobbled rapidly. 'Shit!' he said, feeling his nostrils for blood. From outside he could hear muffled laughter.

'Are you alright?' Sally asked, wheeling him around and inspecting his face.

'Yeah, I'm fine,' Dave said, glaring at the people outside. 'Broken nose, fractured skull, but that's all.'

'Let me lead,' Sally said after she'd kissed his nose better.

'You think you can do better?'

'I'll have us out of here in thirty seconds.'

'How are you going to do that?'

'I know the way.' She juggled her coconut from one hand to the other and back again.

'Lead on,' he said, stepping aside to let her pass.

Sally set off at a fast pace, her coconut clutched to her bosom. She walked halfway up the corridor and turned left without even putting a hand out to feel if there was a gap there. 'C'mon!' she called as she accelerated away down the next lane. Dave found himself almost trotting to keep up with her. She veered right, took two steps and turned left. They were right in the centre of the maze now. Dave allowed himself a quick look around. Phil was near the entrance, one corridor in. He was on his knees feeling the bottom of the glass for a gap big enough to crawl under. Judy was right at the back of the maze, still following the man in the suit who was waving his arms about so much that Dave thought he ought to take up a second career as a mime artist.

'Phil's doing some lateral thinking,' Dave called to Sally who was increasing her pace and drawing ahead of him. 'He'll try climbing over next.' Sally didn't answer and her steps didn't falter. She kept on walking, her arms cradling the coconut, her head down as though she was studying the movement of her feet. Dave was forced to run a few steps to catch her up. The thought of losing her in here and having to find his own way out chilled him.

Sally turned left just before the end of the corridor and did a little zig-zag so that she was in the rear path of the maze where Dave had just seen Judy and the mime artist. He followed her, catching his shoulder on one of the panes and stumbling.

How is she doing this? he asked himself. *She's not hitting anything. It's as if she's memorised the route. This just isn't possible!*

But possible or not, he found he had complete trust in her ability to get him out of there and kept right up close behind her.

They took two more rapid turns and Dave realised Sally was saying something. Her voice was low, and he couldn't quite make out what it was, but she repeated it over and over as she walked. It sounded as if she was chanting, 'Icon dit, icon dit,' in time with her footsteps.

'Sally,' he called. 'Sally, what are you saying?'

But she didn't even acknowledge that she'd heard him, just increased her pace until they were flying along. Her voice increased in pitch and volume to match her pace and now Dave could hear her. She was chanting 'I can do it!' but it didn't sound like a cry of hope or self-assurance. Her voice was all wrong and it didn't sound like Sally at all. It was harsh and driven as if she was speaking in spite of being strangled.

Somewhere behind them, Phil hit another pane of glass and yelled. Muffled laughter filtered through from the outside once more. Dave began to sweat heavily as they twisted and turned their way through the maze. It seemed to go on forever, corridors and gaps, panes and spaces, the occasional person approaching from one side or the other as they sped by.

Sally took a left and overtook two kids almost knocking the larger of them over as she brushed by. Dave muttered an apology as he passed the little boy, and the boy glared at him as if he had no right to be there at all.

Then he could see natural light – *sunlight* – blazing in at the end of the passage. They charged out of the exit and into the real world again. Dave breathed a sigh of relief, the oppressive heat of the summer sun had never felt so good.

Sally took a good five paces before stopping when they were

outside, ploughing right through the wall of onlookers. Dave followed her, shouting, 'Sal! We're out!'

She stopped dead like a machine that had been turned off and spun around looking dazed. The coconut was still clasped to her chest, but her eyes were half closed and looked empty. Her mouth was still working as she silently repeated her chant to herself.

'Sal! It's okay! We're out!' he repeated, wondering what had happened to her. He walked up to her and took hold of her shoulders. 'Sal?' he said.

Her hooded eyes seemed to stare right through him.

He shook her gently. It worked. The lights came back on in her eyes. Sally was in the driving seat once more.

'Where were you?' he asked, feeling the worry drain from him.

Sally smiled and her face bore that dangerous look once more. Suddenly she looked very sexy indeed and Dave pulled her to him.

'Hiya Mr Hard-On,' Sally said, thrusting her hips gently at him.

Dave smiled. 'Where were you?' he asked again.

'Getting you out of the maze, wasn't I?' she said as if the altered state of consciousness she had experienced was an everyday occurrence.

'Yeah, but you went weird, didn't you? The lights were out when we got out. I looked in your baby blues and no one was home.'

Behind them, Phil's voice, made tinny by the public address system, yelled, 'BOLLOCKS!' The crowd chortled.

Sally ground her hips against his erection. 'I feel sexy,' she said.

'So do I. What happened?'

'I don't really know. It was when you bashed into the wall. I suddenly knew I could get us out. I thought: *I can do it*, and I just knew I could. The cross started to feel funny as well. I don't know, it all just seemed to flow into a path, like I'd found a groove in the floor which led out. All I did was follow the groove.'

'You were chanting "I can do it." Did you know that?'

Sally looked vague. 'I could hear it, I just didn't know where it was coming from. That was me, was it?'

'Yes, it was. What did you mean about the cross?' he asked.

She smiled again, and pulled him close. She kissed him and then said, 'The same as how you won this coconut, that's what I meant. My cross got us out, just like yours got the coconut. You had your eyes shut when you won it, I was watching you.'

Dave nodded.

'Well, the cross started to feel funny, and you hit the glass, and I knew the way out.'

'Did it burn you, like when Roddy was after us? Electric shocks or anything?'

'No, it just tingled and felt good. You know when it's telling you something, because it feels *right*. If you accept it and let it guide you, it does.'

She let go of him, and pulled her cross from under her shirt. 'Oh, Dave!' she said.

'What is it?' he asked. He was wondering what made the crosses work, and if it was a good or a bad thing. He hadn't liked that blank expression he'd just seen on Sally's face. He hadn't liked it one little bit.

'The eyelids! Look!'

She held the cross out for him to see. Dave gasped. The green eye of the cross was fully open. Usually, the silver eyelids masked the extreme bottom and top of the iris but, somehow, they had pulled back so the whole of the shining green circle was visible. He looked for creases in the metal where the silver had been forced back, but found nothing. It just wasn't possible.

'This can't happen,' he insisted.

'It can and it did!' she said. She looked delighted.

'But it isn't possible. Those eyelids are solid silver and they're not hinged or anything, so how can they have moved?'

'How about magic? How does that sound?' she said, seemingly ready to accept the idea.

'That sounds very scary,' Dave said. 'I'm not at all sure I like the idea of magical crosses.' He remembered the blank look on her face again and said, 'How about we take them off and forget about them?'

'Oh Dave,' she said, crestfallen.

'They scare me. I think it's a hallucination. There's something about them that makes you see and do funny things. They might be poisoning us. What if they're contaminated or something?'

'*Contaminated?*' Sally demanded. 'What do you mean. Contaminated with nuclear fallout or what?'

Dave looked sheepishly at her. 'Perhaps they have a large lead content or something. Perhaps it's soaking into our skin – that would explain why our chests feel funny from time to time; it probably happens when we sweat more than usual. Maybe the lead gets in your bloodstream and makes you think weird things.'

Sally shook her head. 'It's not that and you know it,' she said.

'Whatever it is, perhaps we ought to take them off.'

'We can't,' she said, still shaking her head – thoughtfully this time.

'Why not?' But he knew why not. Because he had been offered the chance to refuse in Ziegfeld's and that was the one and only chance there was going to be. He knew this intuitively.

'It's too late to stop now,' Sally said. She put her cross back in her shirt. 'What about yours? Has that changed?' she asked.

'I don't know.'

'Let's have a look then.'

'I don't think I want to know right now. Let's just forget about it for the moment, shall we?'

Sally nodded. 'Okay,' she said. She took his hand and led him back to the maze to watch Phil and Judy struggling to find their separate ways out.

'I'm bruised and confused and I want to sit down,' Phil said when he staggered out. Judy had followed her mime artist all the way through and managed to get out unscathed as she had adopted a policy of hanging back and offering advice whenever

136

there was a complicated bit to negotiate. She had finished five minutes ahead of Phil who had covered every square yard and each dead end of the maze – and hit his head on most of the panes.

'I thought they were going to slap a surcharge on you when you came out,' Dave said. 'You must have reduced the life expectancy of their show by at least fifty per cent. I didn't know glass could withstand such mistreatment. The owners were out here reading through the small print on their insurance policies, for God's sake!'

'Oh yeah, ha, ha, very funny,' Phil said, putting his arm around Judy. There were huge dark sweat-stained patches under his arms that reached almost to the waist of his lumber-jack shirt. Large droplets of moisture dribbled down his nose from his forehead. He flicked his hair out of his eyes and sprayed Dave and Sally who jumped away making noises of disgust.

'It was hot in there, wasn't it?' he said conversationally. 'Let's get a drink and go on the Ghost Train for a sit down.'

There was a queue for the Ghost Train, and they joined it, each of them sipping from chilled drinks. Sally and Dave had Cokes, Judy had a 7Up and Phil was slurping a Vimto that he'd made them walk the length and breadth of the funfair to find. There was nowhere you could buy beer in a funfair, and Phil wouldn't drink anything else except Vimto.

The Ghost Train's facade bore the AdventureLand logo and the words Dave had already seen over the funfair's entrance – *Die a Thousand Deaths and Live to Tell the Tale* – but on this ride 'AdventureLand' was written beneath the owner's name. *Fred Purdue's Terrifying Train of Death* was written in ornate golden letters high on the cross section above the rails, and Dave wondered if Fred Purdue was Mr AdventureLand himself. The rest of the facade bore gaudy illustrations of skeletons, hooded and sinister-looking monks carrying sickles, and corpses in various states of decay. Beneath one particularly gory scene of a young woman having her throat sliced open by

137

a skeleton with a bread knife, were the words: *Will You Survive the Ride of Death?*

The engines were pretty standard Ghost Train fare: a wooden respresentation of a railway engine with a padded bench seat inside that two adults could just about squeeze into. Their smoke-stacks were low and the roof was only waist high, so there was no sheltering inside. The ride looked old and well used but in good repair. Each of the engines had recently been painted in a different colour and sign-written across the back with Fred Purdue's name.

As far as Dave could make out there were four wooden engines; there might have been more but they were running non-stop and it was difficult to tell which was which. At most, only two of them were outside swapping passengers at the same time. Two roustabouts of about Dave's age held the engines while they were unloaded and loaded again and then shoved them back through the double wooden doors. They were sweaty and dishevelled in tattered, greasy Levis and grimy vests. Both of them looked like they wished they were somewhere else.

The queue gradually dwindled and they moved nearer the pay booth at the bottom of the steps to the railway platform. An engine bearing two pale-faced fourteen-year-olds banged out through the double exit doors. The girls' wore fixed expressions of terror and, although they blinked a lot at the sudden change from darkness to light, their faces didn't relax. One of the roustabouts grabbed hold of the back of their engine as it clicked slowly by, dug his heels in between the railway lines and brought it to a halt. If he hadn't gone around to the side and helped them out, Dave thought, they probably would have stayed woodenly in place for the rest of the afternoon.

'Us next!' Sally said, shuffling forward towards the pay booth as the two people in front went up the steps and got into the vacant engine.

And then they came face to face with Fred Purdue.

Purdue was huge. He filled the small pay booth as if he had been poured in. Dave judged him to be in his mid-fifties, and decided that the man had to be more frightening to look at than anything that might lurk inside his Terrifying Train of Death. The first thing you noticed about Purdue was his sheer bulk; the second his hare lip. His mouth was wide and slack, his lips pale. They rose in the centre and just below his large, purple capillaried nose, they joined in a mound of scar tissue so they looked as if they'd been split, then crossed over and stitched into place. Purdue's head seemed far too massive to be normal; it was as round as a football and its size was accentuated by the fact that he was almost bald. Only a few wisps of shortly trimmed, grey hair existed on the barren, liver-spotted waste that was his scalp. These ran from just above his ears to somewhere out of sight on the back of his head. His bottom half was invisible, lost from view beneath the counter, but his upper torso was crammed into a white shirt, the sleeves of which were rolled up to the elbow. His forearms were crossed in front of him and they were the size of hams. His fingers were stubby and strong and on the third finger of his left hand was a gold ring which bore a red stone. The stone seemed to be made of the same material as the iris in the eye of Dave's cross. It reflected the light in the same way so that it gave the impression of being endlessly deep.

But it was Purdue's eyes that scared Dave the most. They were blue; small piggy eyes with pupils the size of pinpricks that bored through you and sought the secret inner stuff that lurked deep inside.

Purdue looked at Dave long and hard, his breath whistling in and out through his nose, his penetrating eyes boring in. Dave began to think he *knew* the man. Purdue looked so familiar it wasn't true. He stared back at Purdue, realising that something – some hidden flow of information he wasn't able to pick up – was passing between them, linking them in some obscure way. Fear began to develop in the pit of his stomach, not the sharp panic he'd felt during the Roddy Johnson episode, but a more basic and pervading kind. The kind that wasn't easy to shake off. Dave knew that he would lie awake in bed tonight and remember this moment and that the dull feeling of fear would come back amplified.

Purdue blinked, but his gaze didn't falter and his eyes never lost their hypnotic grip on Dave. He tapped a sausage-like finger on the Formica counter top. *Thunk*, it went as though it weighed a ton. He did this twice more, and Dave began to think he was frozen to the spot. His flesh felt cold and stony and his muscles had turned to inoperative boulders as though he had suddenly been turned into a statue. He tried to swallow, but his throat was as seized up as the rest of him. Then he suddenly remembered that night in Ziegfeld's. The sound of Purdue's finger rising and falling echoed through his mind. Three taps. No more, no less. *Just like Sally taking the crosses apart*, he thought. *Three taps – the magic number.*

He heard the chink of money as, unaware of the one-sided silent exchange that was taking place, Sally rooted through her purse for their fares.

Then the familiar flare of heat surged across Dave's chest. It loosened his limbs and he took an involuntary step backwards.

'Look out!' Phil shouted, as Dave trampled on his feet.

'Hello,' Purdue said. His voice was a low growl that Dave felt reverberate through his own chest. The man had finished with him apparently – either that or the cross had freed him somehow. Dave's mind raced, wondering what had been going on. His brain felt disturbed, as though Purdue had been inside it, riffling through all his memories, searching for the information he wanted.

'Hi,' Dave said warily.

Purdue threw him a knowing look then growled at Sally. 'That'll be a pound for the pair of you.'

Sally gave him the money and they started up the steps. 'What was that about?' she asked.

'What?' Gates were already closing in his mind, shutting the unpleasant experience away in a place where it could do no harm. Rationality had begun to assert itself and fill in the gaps.

'You and that guy were staring at one another like you were weighing each other up for a fight.'

Dave shook his head. He felt much better now. 'I just felt a little bit dizzy,' he said, and it sounded right as he said it.

Sally looked at him closely for a second. 'Are you alright now?' she asked suspiciously.

Dave nodded. 'Yeah, fine,' he said. His thoughts were now running freely and as smooth as silk. It felt good to be alive.

'He's an ugly son of a bitch, isn't he?' Sally said as they stopped on the edge of the platform.

Dave found that he couldn't even remember what the ride owner looked like. 'Yeah,' he said vaguely. 'He is.'

'Nothing happened, did it?' Sally said insistently.

'Like what?'

'Well, I think my cross flared up while you and that guy were looking at one another. It wasn't very powerful though and it didn't last long, it was only a tingle. I just wondered if yours did it too.'

Dave thought about it. He shook his head. 'No, I don't think so, Sal. I expect you just imagined it.'

A siren sounded, the doors crashed open and an engine emerged, its ratchet mechanism click-clicking as it turned the last bend to the platform. While the people were getting out, the siren sounded again and another engine came out. This one was empty and Dave wondered what had happened to its occupants.

'That's ours,' Phil said. 'We've got the white one.'

'I like our blue one best, so there,' Sally said.

'Where did the white one come from?' Dave asked no one in particular.

'Dunno,' Phil said. 'I think they've probably got a little siding in there with some more cars on. They probably push another one out when it gets busy.'

'Who pushes it out then?'

'Little Johnny Stout,' Phil said. 'I dunno, probably the guy in the skeleton suit that runs around inside.'

'There *is* someone in there then,' Dave said. 'I thought you were joking.'

'Why would I lie to you?' Phil said, finishing the sentence with a belch. ' 'Scuse me,' he said to the woman behind him in the queue.

141

They squeezed into the car with some difficulty. It was a tight fit and there was no room at all to move their legs. Dave leaned forward and folded his arms on the low roof of the engine. The roustabout shook his head. 'You gotta keep your arms and legs inside the car at all times,' he explained patiently. 'You could get caught up on something and hurt yourself if you don't. There's a hand rail to hang on to just underneath here,' he said, slapping the roof where Dave's hand had just been. 'Keep 'em underneath.'

Dave nodded and dutifully obliged. Sally squeezed his thigh. 'I'm frightened,' she said, but she was smiling and didn't looked at all worried.

The second roustabout called Phil and Judy over and much good-natured banter followed as he shoe-horned Phil into the car which was about three inches too narrow to accommodate both him and Judy. His left hip bulged over the side of the engine's cutaway door. Dave craned his neck to see what was happening behind. 'He's much too big for that poor little car,' he told Sally. 'He looks like a wrestler on a kiddie's tricycle.'

Sally looked behind, 'Poor Judy,' she whispered. 'She'll be six feet taller and three inches wide when she gets out again.'

'If she *can* get out again,' Dave said.

'I heard that!' Phil called out. 'What did you say?'

'Just admiring your splendid physique,' Dave told him.

'He said you were fat,' Judy chimed in. 'Go and hit him!'

'I would but I can't get out again,' Phil complained. 'I'm stuck.'

'He'll hit you later!' Judy informed Dave.

'He'll have to catch me first!' Dave said.

The roustabouts went to the rear of Phil and Judy's engine and pushed. Their car hit the back of Dave and Sally's and stopped. 'Christ, they're heavy,' one of them exclaimed. Sally giggled. 'It's not me,' Phil told them. 'It's the two in the front car. All their money is weighing them down.'

The two workers altered their positions, putting their backs against Phil's engine and walking backwards. Dave's car was bumped again and started to roll forward down the platform, making that familiar click-clicking noise.

'Look!' Sally said suddenly, pointing out into the fair-ground.

'What?' Dave asked, following the line of her finger.

'That man! That's him!' The engine was picking up speed now and there was only another couple of yards before the right angle bend and the double wooden doors.

'Who?' Dave said. And then he saw. The old man was down there. The one that had helped pull Phil out of the river last Sunday. He was facing the other way, but Dave was sure it was him. Wafts of pipe smoke trailed over his shoulder and his little white dog was leading the way, its blue lead pulling tight as it dragged the old man along.

'Lucky!' Sally said. 'That was the dog's name. It's Lucky and his dad!'

Then the engine took the sharp turn and the doors were in front of them. The doors were orange and painted on them in life size was a man with a wolf's head. His outstretched arms ended in long hook-nailed fingers that looked like talons and his grinning mouth was wide and slavering. Dave wondered why he hadn't noticed this particular picture before and realised that if he had, he probably wouldn't have gone on the ride at all.

The little blue engine crashed into the doors with a wooden *THWACK!* and they flew inwards, splitting the wolf man in two. Inside were two more doors. These were black and a huge skeleton was painted on them. One arm was raised over its head in a threatening gesture. It was holding a lengthy Bowie knife in its skeletal fingers.

The engine clicked slowly forward and the first doors closed leaving them in darkness through which shone chinks of light. A strobe light flashed as they approached the second set of doors and the skeleton appeared to come alive and dance, the hand with the knife jiggling back and forth crazily. Sally screamed. Her yells were drowned as an ear-splitting siren sounded. The strobe went off and the engine crashed into the second set of doors and through into the stale total darkness of the Ghost Train's interior. The engine took a sharp right hand turn as the doors swung shut behind them and because of the lack of room in the engine Sally was pressed right up against Dave. The engine shimmied as it came out of the bend, then straightened, picking up speed. Behind them, Phil and Judy's car hit the first doors and the siren sounded. Dave heard Judy squeal and Phil give a low laugh.

Demonic laughter issued forth from a speaker concealed at head height and Dave and Sally both ducked. But they didn't duck low enough to escape the curtain of wet material that dragged over their heads. 'Oh, yuk!' Sally shouted. A peal of hysterical laughter escaped Dave's lips. The car pulled another tight turn – to the left this time and almost came to a standstill. A spot light flicked on. They appeared to be in a dead end and before them was a lifelike model of a man with his intestines hanging from a rent in his waist. The intestines were red and blue and looked damp and real. The light went out and Dave was left with the impression that the guts had been swinging gently as if blown by a slight breeze. *That wasn't for real*, his mind insisted. *This is only a fairground ride, no more, no less.*

The engine turned right again and began to accelerate. 'We're going downhill,' he yelled at Sally as the cool breeze began to ruffle his hair.

'We can't be,' she replied. 'We haven't gone up yet. Unless they've excavated the ground in here!'

He turned to look at her, but could see nothing. If he hadn't been able to feel her pressed up to him, he might just have begun to think he was in there on his own.

Beneath the engine's roof, her hand found his and squeezed. 'My cross,' she said. 'It's getting hot!'

'So's mine,' he replied, feeling the metal warm against his chest. Then there was a single flash of light and he was able to see the track. Phil and Judy's engine was coming down in the opposite direction. Their heads were pressed together like two lovebirds, but their faces were screwed up and their mouths wide open. Dave guessed that they'd just gone under the wet material.

'Phil!' he called, waving, but the light had already gone. Judy began to squeal. 'Help!' Phil shouted.

Dave and Sally's engine began to slow down again and something hit the front of it with a bump.

'What was that?' Sally said, her grip tightening on his hand.

'Dunno,' Dave said as the car began to turn again. The strobe lighting began to flicker and they were treated to the sight of a young woman's crushed body standing inside an Iron Maiden. She was wearing a white dress which was doused with blood. Spikes from the back of the torture instrument protruded from her breasts and navel. These too dripped blood as if the killing had recently taken place. As the car turned to pass the sight, the Iron Maiden's lid began to close, driving still more spikes into the woman. Recorded screams rang out from the coffin as they left it behind.

'This is incredibly realistic,' Dave shouted over the rising wail of another siren. The car began to speed up again.

Something gently touched Dave's head and he yelled. Beside him, Sally began to yell too. A distinctly human chuckle, low and menacing, came out of the darkness in front of the engine. 'Was that you?' Sally said. She sounded genuinely frightened now.

The deep laugh pealed again. 'What *is* it?' Sally shouted.

Then the lights came on for a second. They were travelling down a long dark empty corridor. Dave glanced over at Sally who seemed to have gone rigid. Her eyes were wide and fixed on a point just in front of the engine. Her mouth was a gaping O. Finally she let forth an ear-splitting scream. Dave turned to look in front of him and froze. There was a skeleton on the front of the engine. It must have jumped on earlier – when they heard the bump. It had crouched low on the front bumper of the engine and remained out of sight until they had passed the last set piece. Now it was swarming up the wooden tank of the engine and over the funnel and reaching out for them with bony fingers.

'Christ!' Dave said as he came face to face with the skeleton's grinning skull. A hand came up to touch his face and he knew then that he was going to die. The shock of feeling those cold bones against his skin would strike him dead instantly. But when the hand brushed over his face it was warm and soft and he suddenly knew what it was and wanted to laugh with relief. It was the man Phil and Judy had told him about. The fairground man in the skeleton suit that chased you about in the dark. The need to laugh increased, but Dave checked it, knowing that if he laughed it would sound hysterical and mad and make him even more terrified.

Beside him, Sally was wailing in a high, never-ending pattern, her voice rising and falling like one of the Ghost Train's sirens as the skeleton reached out for her head. Her wailing stopped the moment she felt the warm nylon of the skeleton suit and changed to the crazy laughter Dave hadn't wanted to hear.

The skeleton chuckled again and leapt off the engine, disappearing into the darkness as the lights went out once more.

'It was the man, it was the man!' Sally laughed crazily as the engine turned again and headed deeper into the heart of the Ghost Train.

'We're going up now,' Dave said, feeling the engine slow and tilt. The ratchet underneath the car caught a chain between the rails and the engine jolted as the chain began to pull them up. The climb into the blackness got steeper and steeper. Another strobe started to flash and Dave peered over the side of the engine trying to see the ground below. It felt as if they'd risen at least twenty feet, but that was impossible because the building housing the ride was only ten or twelve feet tall at the most. There didn't seem to be any ground at all beneath the car; just the rails glinting in the strobe lighting and total darkness. *Perhaps we haven't gone up at all*, Dave thought. *Perhaps it's just an illusion caused by tipping the engine backwards. Yes! That's all it is!*

'An octopus!' Sally shouted. 'Up there! Look!

In spite of the feeling that the engine was labouring up hill, the track in front of them looked flat. Ahead, a massive green octopus with eight waving tentacles was descending from the roof and they were heading straight towards it.

'It's going to fall on us!' Sally said. 'Duck!'

Both of them crouched as low as was possible in the tiny engine but the octopus's heavy tentacles trailed up over the engine's boiler and hit their heads. The tentacles were soft, slimy, cold and damp.

'Oh God let me out!' Sally said fending off a tentacle that was sliding up her face.

A nest of huge, animated Black Widow spiders lurked on the next corner and on the one after that was a scene of a man being stretched on a rack. One of his arms had been pulled clean out of its socket and bloody muscle and tendons hung out of the shoulder. Sally moaned and put her head on Dave's shoulder. He took his right arm out from beneath the engine's roof and managed to work it along between the seat back and Sally's shoulders. He pulled her tight against him.

'I don't like it,' she moaned.

'It's only a ride,' Dave said. 'We'll be out in a moment.'

Another ear-splitting siren sounded and the engine crashed into some more swinging doors. 'See, we're out!' Dave said.

But he was wrong.

The engine veered around to the left and went down a long straight, wheels clacking against the rails. 'Where are we now?' Sally said. 'I thought it was over.'

'I dunno,' Dave said, thinking, *it can't be going on this long, it's not possible. There just isn't enough room in here for it to go on for as long as this. We must have been in here for five minutes at the very least. Are we going round and around in circles?*

'Oh,' Sally said from the darkness.

'What is it?' Dave asked.

'Your cross. It's shining.'

'What?'

'Your cross is shining. Its eye is, rather. I can see it glowing red through your shirt.'

Dave looked down and could see the red ring of light radiating through the thin material of his tee shirt. It looked as if there was a torch beneath his shirt and he could distinctly see the weave of the shirt's material. He knew without checking that if he took the cross out the red rays would shoot off into the distance in a pencil-thin beam like a laser. He looked over at Sally. Her cross was doing the same thing, except the light was green. He put his hand over the site of the cross's eye, hoping to drive the hallucination – or whatever it was – away. Perhaps when he removed his hand, everything would be back to normal again.

But the light of the eye illuminated a small spot on his hand like a powerful torch, showing dark tendons beneath the bright red of his flesh.

'It feels hot,' he said miserably as the beam warmed his palm. Things weren't going back to normal after all.

Sally put her hand over her cross and agreed with him. 'But why is it happening?' she said, awed.

'I don't really want to know,' Dave replied.

The engine began to pick up speed again and it felt as though they were going downhill. Dave peered out into the darkness, straining to see where they were. Judging by the amount of time that had passed since they went through the last set of doors, they should be halfway round the fairground by now – if not right over into the nearby common.

'We must turn soon,' he said. 'We must.'

'It's wrong,' Sally shouted to him over the rising noise of the engine's wheels. 'We're going too far. Much too far! It feels all wrong!' Her grip on his hand tightened.

I know just what you mean Sal, he thought. He didn't speak the words, because he'd noticed something that terrified him when Sally spoke. Her voice had borne an echo. It had assumed the quality it would have had if she had shouted to him across a huge cavern.

'What's going on?' Sally yelled, a frightened note in her voice. 'Why doesn't it stop?'

You don't like this as much as George Dale's famous Octopus then Sal, he told her mentally as he stared into the darkness that lay ahead of them. *I thought you liked it when things got weird. Don't tell me this is too scary even for you! What's the matter, run out of guts, have we?*

He tried not to look down at the red glow shining through his shirt, and stared fixedly in front of him, willing the engine to crash through the wooden doors and let them out. The wind whipped his hair as the engine gathered speed.

'It's getting colder!' Sally shouted.

And if we're going down to hell it should be getting warmer, Dave replied mentally. *Ha, ha, good joke, Davey boy!*

The temperature had dropped dramatically and the cold breeze chilled Dave's cheeks. A fleeting memory crossed his mind, but he could make no sense of it. It was a brief picture of one of the front belt loops of his new jeans. The loop had a coating of frost that shouldn't have been there at all in his hot bathroom.

The air now felt as if it was laden with moisture, and it stank like a stagnant pond.

'Let's get out!' Sally suggested.

'Can't!' Dave managed to reply. 'Moving too fast!'

Then Sally got her cross out. He didn't see her do it in the pitch black, but he could see the results as plain as day. The brilliant green beam flicked up towards the roof like a searchlight scanning the skies for enemy aircraft. The slender belt of light seemed to go on forever. It shone upwards into the darkness until it became invisible. No roofing timbers showed up in the beam, no canvas ceiling reflected the light. There was just empty darkness up there that went on forever.

'Put it away!' Dave said urgently, his mind reeling. If she altered the direction of the cross's beam, they were going to find out there were no walls in any direction, and no floor for the rails to run along. They would be hammering along through an empty void to God knew where. He knew that would finish him, hallucination or not. If that happened, the chances of getting out of here with his sanity intact were very slim indeed.

'I've gotta see,' Sally said hysterically, her fingernails digging into his arm. 'I can't believe it! I've gotta see what's in front!'

The beam started to descend. It came far enough down before Dave reached out and covered it to allow him a glimpse of the emptiness that lay ahead.

'What is it?' she screamed. '*Where are we?*' She let go of him

149

then and started to struggle. Dave grabbed her and pressed her back into her seat. 'You can't get out!' he hissed as he fought to maintain his grasp on her wriggling body. 'Just sit tight!'

Then he remembered the sign written on the outside of the Ghost Train: *Will You Survive the Ride of Death?* 'Good one Fred Purdue,' he muttered. 'They won't be able to get you for contravening the Trades Descriptions Act.'

'What?' Sally said.

The engine's wheels locked then, and they were thrown forward with the G-force as it decelerated rapidly. The wheels squealed and a shower of orange sparks rose from beneath the engine, cascading down behind them in fiery waterfalls.

The engine stopped moving altogether and the strobe lighting started again. There before them on a platform – which was apparently attached to nothing – was a huge Cyclopean creature.

It's alive, Dave's mind screamed. *Whatever the other ones were, this is alive!*

The thing had no limbs and no feet and yet it stood erect on the platform like a huge pink worm. Where its base touched the stand, there was a pool of a shining slimy substance which bubbled and oozed in the flashing lights. Its trunk had the ridged texture of a worm and was about two feet in diameter. Short spiked black hairs protruded from the creases in its skin. It stood about six feet tall from its base to the top of its body, but what was above that struck a bolt of pure terror through Dave. It had a human neck and an outsized hairless human head. Its features were human except that above its bridge-less nose was a single eye twice the size of a normal eye. The eye was cobalt blue and bloodshot, and as they watched in horror, a translucent lid flicked down over it then flicked away again.

'What *is* it?' Sally moaned.

The worm's eye focused on them and its body bent forwards as it peered at them.

'It's going to get us!' Sally yelled. 'Do something!'

But Dave was paralysed.

The worm extended its body so that its head was just above

150

the short smoke-stack of the engine. It opened its mouth revealing rotted stumps of teeth, and a thick strand of drool descended onto the boiler.

'Help!' Sally shouted. 'FOR CHRIST'S SAKE HELP ME!' her voice went rocketing out into space and the last two words came back again a second later, distorted with the echo.

The worm's head tilted to one side as it cocked a malformed ear. 'Eeeep!' it said in a growling voice. 'Eeeep meeee! Fcreesh sheek eeep meee!'

The engine jolted forwards and hung a sharp left. The worm ducked back as it passed, but a strand of the gelatinous drool brushed Dave's face. It was cold and sticky. The cross flared on Dave's chest.

Dave screamed.

Then they were heading into the void again. Behind them the strobes went out. Sally was sobbing softly and Dave was fighting himself trying to stay calm and repeating over and over that this was *only a ride*.

The engine turned two more corners and went back into a long straight. Dave didn't know if they were going back the way they'd come or somewhere else, but it felt as if they were going uphill and the temperature seemed to be rising.

'We're going to be alright,' he assured Sally. 'It's all over, we're coming to the end now.' They had to be, he reasoned. Nothing could be worse than the worm thing.

The hidden strobe lights began to flash again, but slowly this time, pulsing about twice a second. They were in a corridor now that had walls and a low roof. The rails ran over wooden floorboards. There was another set of rails to their left and ahead of them, coming towards them, was the white car containing Phil and Judy. They were still leaning on one another and from this distance their faces looked pale and scared.

As they approached, Phil spotted them and called out.

Dave tried to shout a greeting back, but his throat was dry and all he made was a little rasping noise.

'Ohhh Godddd!' Sally moaned.

A shape was rising over the back of Phil and Judy's car.

It's the skeleton man, Dave thought, but as he watched he realised that there was something different about him this time. The skeleton man was not wearing a black suit with the bones painted on the front. This skeleton man was made of real bones. He knew because the light was shining right through the skeleton's ribs and shoulders. The skeleton raised his right arm. Clutched in his hand was the Bowie knife that Dave had seen in the painting outside. Its eight-inch blade glittered in the white flashes of the strobe as he raised it. Each time the light flashed the skeleton raised the blade a little higher over Phil and Judy's heads.

'Look out!' Dave screamed at Phil.

In quickfire instalments of bursting white light, the skeleton raised its other arm and buried its bony fingers in Phil's ginger hair. In the next three frames of light, it pulled Phil's head backwards so that he was staring up into its eyeless sockets. In the three that followed Judy's head swivelled round towards Phil.

The knife began to descend towards Phil's neck in the next two frames.

And the strobes went out.

As their cars passed, Judy let out a single lung-bursting shriek.

'Ohhh Godddd!' Sally wailed as the engine hung a right.

There was a crash, the two wooden doors opened and the little blue engine click-clicked out onto the platform.

Squinting in the sunlight and looking out over the fairground as the roustabouts slowed the engine, Dave saw the little old man and his dog Lucky. Wafts of pipe smoke trailed over his shoulder as Lucky dragged him along on the tight blue lead. The old man was in exactly the same place as he had been when they entered the Ghost Train. Dave followed his path between two darts stalls until the roustabout cut off his view as he arrived to help them from the engine.

Sally looked sick. Her bottom lip was trembling and her mascara had run. She didn't need any help getting out of the engine though. By the time the roustabout got around to her side she had clambered out and was making her way quickly down the steps.

Dave's helper pulled him out, and he stood there for a second, wondering what exactly had happened to him. By the time he thought of looking for the slime that must have been deposited on the front of the engine by the worm thing, the car was already heading back into The Ride of Death with two new passengers.

The exit doors banged open again and Phil and Judy's car clicked out into daylight.

Phil and Judy were not in it.

Chapter Seven
The Model

Dave stood on the platform watching the empty car roll up in front of him. His mind reeled and bucked as he tried to understand what he was seeing. Reality seemed to have fled. This was impossible, unimaginable; it couldn't be happening. The little white engine simply could not be coming out of the Ghost Train empty. But the more he blinked and squinted, the more apparent it became that Phil and Judy were not going to reappear. On his neck, the cross's eye pulsed steadily, seeming to have taken on the timing of the last strobe light he'd seen. Steady flashes of pain spread out across his chest, and later Sally would tell him that she could see the ruby light shining dimly through his shirt, but at the moment Dave wasn't aware either of the pain or the light. His whole being was focused on the empty engine.

He tottered back a step, feeling as though he was surveying the scene through thick glass which distorted his perception and made all the angles of the ride wrong. The daylight was too sharp and bright and threw the Ghost Train's facade and platform into an unnatural relief. Without realising he was doing it, Dave's right hand went up and touched the steel rim of his glasses, confirming that they were still on.

As the white engine click-clacked around into the waiting arms of the roustabouts, Dave spun around and looked down at the sea of faces in front of the ride. Sally was down there, looking up at him, her face a picture of terror. Of the hundreds of others milling about in the fairground, he recognised only two. There was the old man with his dog who was still walking between the stalls and a man he'd seen somewhere before – a man whose face he should have recognised but didn't. The man was standing two rows behind Sally and to the left of her. He was wearing a sports jacket and his hair was tousled. His face was gaunt and lined and his hands were thrust deep in his pockets. He bore the attitude of someone who was waiting and watching and who was prepared to wait and watch for as long as it took. He was the only person in the crowd other than Sally whose eyes were trained on Dave.

Dave turned back and walked the few paces over to the two workers who were bent over the white engine peering at its seat.

'Where are they?' Dave said to the younger of the roustabouts.

'What?' the youth said, looking up from what he was doing. In one of his hands was Phil's empty Vimto can, and in the other was a fifty pence piece that had probably fallen from Phil's pocket when—

When what, Davey? When what happened? he thought. When the skeleton with the big knife killed him and Judy and dragged them out? Be sensible, that can't have happened!

'Where are my friends?' he demanded.

The youth shrugged and looked at him as if he was a madman. 'I don't know. They could be anywhere. Where did you last see them?'

The other roustabout came round from the far side of the engine. He had a large wad of white cloth in his hand. He put his free hand on the younger man's shoulder and shot him a warning look.

'I last saw them in this car!' Dave yelled, pointing at the seat.

'When?' the young roustabout asked. Dave saw the older one's grip tighten on his arm.

'When we went in the fucking Ghost Train five minutes ago. We were in the car that just went in, and my friends were in this one!'

The older of the two shook his head slowly. 'You must have been mistaken pal, this one's only just come into service. They just pushed it out from inside. I'm wiping the dust off the seat.'He showed Dave his white cloth as if to prove his point. There was a little devil tattooed on his forearm. It was dressed in red and wore a slim moustache and a pointed beard. One hand was on its hip, and the other carried a black trident. Dave's eyes lit on the devil and followed its progress as the roustabout dropped his arm to his side.

'They pushed it out *before* we went in,' Dave insisted. 'They got in *this* one. He was drinking a can of Vimto. Your mate has got it in his hand.'

They all looked at the can of Vimto. The older man shook his head again. 'We get hundreds of empty cans left in these cars,' he said. 'How do you know this is the one your mate was drinking? This car has only just come into service, I tell you.'

The next two customers arrived and joined the group. They were a bare-chested, crop-haired youth dressed in jeans and braces and wearing Doc Marten's boots and his girlfriend who was a carbon copy of him except that she was wearing a purple vest beneath her braces.

'They were on it, I tell you!' Dave shouted. 'What has happened to them?'

''Scuse me guv, alright if we get on?' the skinhead asked. No one paid him any attention.

'If they were on this engine, where the fuck are they now then?' the younger roustabout challenged.

'Shut the fuck up!' the older one told him. He turned back to Dave. 'Look pal, if your friends were on this car – which they weren't – they'd have come out through those doors just like you did, okay?' He looked at the skinheads. 'Get in,' he told them.

'Oh no you don't!' Dave shouted. He darted in front of them, blocking the engine's doorway.

'Get out of it!' the skinhead said, annoyed. 'He said we could get on!'

'I'm not letting this ride go on until I find out what happened to Phil and Judy!' Dave yelled.

'I'll tell you what happened to them, they only ever existed in your imagination, that's what pal!' the larger roustabout shouted. 'Now get out of the fucking way before I have to throw you over the side!'

'Yeah, fuck off!' the skinhead snapped, pushing Dave in the stomach. Dave teetered backwards, but the wooden roof of the white engine stopped him from falling.

The exit doors swung open again, and the next car came out, rounded the bend and crashed into the back of the white engine. Its occupants – a middle-aged man and a girl who might have either been his daughter or his lover – climbed out and walked away paying no attention to the gathering in front of them.

Two more customers appeared on the platform. They studied the group with some concern.

'You'll have to wait while we get rid of sonny boy here,' Tattoo told them. He turned back to Dave who was squaring up to the skinhead, fists clenched. 'Okay, pack it in! If anyone's going to knock out anyone's teeth, its going to be me doing the punching. I'll give you five seconds to leave, Foureyes, and then it's hospital time for you.'

'I'm not going,' Dave insisted, glaring at the roustabout. 'My friends were on that engine and they didn't come out of the ride. I saw someone attack them with a knife in there as our engines passed. I want to know what's happened to them and I won't let anyone else go in there until I find out.'

The skinhead took advantage of Dave's distraction while he spoke to the roustabout, grabbed his shirt and flung him out of the way. Dave fell and rolled across the platform. When he came to a halt he was looking up at the rear of the white engine. The curved back was neatly bisected by a thick stream of bright red blood which started at the top of the glossy paintwork and zig-zagged its way down. It ran across the rear bumper and dripped onto the platform right next to Dave's head.

'BLOOD!' Dave screamed. 'YOU'VE KILLED THEM!' He struggled to his feet as the big worker started to mop the blood off the engine with the white cloth. The younger roustabout was helping the skinhead and his girl into the car.

157

'YOU'VE KILLED THEM, YOU FUCKERS!' Dave cried, launching himself at the one with the cloth.

'What the hell is going on here?' a deep voice rasped.

Dave let go of the struggling roustabout and came face to face with the immense bulk of Fred Purdue. 'What do you think you're doing son?' he growled at Dave. His heavy hand clamped down on Dave's wrist and squeezed hard.

'You know!' Dave spat trying to shake his arm free. He could vaguely feel the bones in there bending and protesting. The dull pain added to his rage. 'You fucking well know! My friends! Someone in there has killed them. LOOK AT THE BLOOD!'

Purdue held his arm firmly in his crushing grip. His piggy eyes regarded Dave knowingly, then flicked over to the back of the engine where the one with the cloth was getting busy. 'Can't see any blood,' he said, smiling. 'Where's the blood?'

For a second, the back of the engine looked clean, and the red stains on the white rag seemed to be black. Then there was a subtle shift of Dave's perception and the blood was back again, although most of it was gone from the engine and was now on the rag.

'There!' Dave said, pointing at the red rag.

Purdue took a deep whistling breath through his nostrils. 'Oil, that's all I can see. Charlie just wiped some oil from the back of the car. It's been inside on the siding up until now. We only just brought it into service. Getting busy, see? He's wiping the oil away so the punters don't get their clothes mussed. Simple.'

And for a second Dave could see just how simple it was. How could he have got so upset about a little oil stain?

'Some kind of trouble sir?' Two policemen had arrived. Or rather, one policeman and a special – one of those part-timers that helped at functions where the police didn't have enough men to go around. Both were jacketless and in summer uniform of short-sleeved blue shirt and dark blue trousers. Both wore flat-peaked caps but only the real cop had a radio. This was stuck into the breast pocket of his shirt and was hissing harshly.

The real cop, Dave noticed, had a sebaceous cyst the size of a large pea growing from the side of his nose.

Purdue let go of Dave and looked the policemen. He smiled and growled, 'This here kid thinks we killed his friends. He's a bit touched if you ask me. We were trying to get shot of him.'

The real policeman looked at Dave, his eyebrows raised. 'Is that an accurate summary of events?' he asked.

Another engine crashed out through the doors and ran into the queue. Its occupants left, smiling and animatedly discussing the horrors they'd seen inside.

'My friends went in behind me on this engine,' Dave said. 'I came out, their car came out but they weren't in it. I saw someone attack them inside. A guy dressed as a skeleton with a knife. I saw him stab my friends. Look at the blood all over that cloth. That guy was mopping it up!'

Everyone looked at Charlie who had the cloth between his hands. Charlie looked innocent and passed the cloth from hand to hand. The two cops studied the cloth and then exchanged looks.

'Oil,' Purdue explained, shrugging.

The real cop nodded.

'Looks like blood to me, Keith,' the special said. Horror shone in his eyes.

That's it! Dave thought. *I was right, it is blood*!

'Black blood, Sam?' the real cop said.

The special coughed and looked embarrassed. 'Just joking, Keith,' he spluttered. Dave knew what he'd seen and what he was seeing now. He didn't know how Purdue had accomplished the trick, but a trick it was. Some kind of hypnosis probably. It had just taken a little longer to work on good old Sam.

'You straight son?' Keith the real cop said. 'Haven't been at the little blue pills, have we?'

Tears of frustration sprang from Dave's eyes. 'For Christ's sake, I saw someone in there attack them!' he pleaded.

The policeman turned to Purdue. 'Is there someone inside?'

'Yeah, but he didn't kill no one,' Purdue rasped. He stood

there glowering, his breath whistling in and out through his nostrils.

'Then where are Phil and Judy?' Dave cried.

The policemen looked at Purdue, waiting for an answer.

'They didn't get on,' Purdue said.

'Just supposing they did get on,' the special said. 'Would it be possible for them to have got off again inside?'

Purdue looked at him long and hard. 'Yeah, I suppose so,' he finally agreed.

'Then maybe your friends got off inside and got out through the back or something,' the special said to Dave.

'Or maybe they're still in there, dead,' Dave sobbed.

The blue engine he'd ridden on came out then and knocked the queue along the platform some more. One of the roustabouts helped the riders out.

'Mind if we take a look in there, sir?' the special said. 'Just to settle this dispute. If they aren't in there, perhaps our friend here will be satisfied.'

'Go ahead, the cars are all out now,' Purdue said, waving toward the entrance. His face bore a sly expression. 'I'll turn the interior lights on so you can see there's no blood on the floor.'

'I'm going too,' Dave said firmly.

'Be my guest,' Purdue said, scowling at him. 'Then get lost.' There was a hint of dark humour in this last remark that the policemen seemed to miss. It wasn't lost on Dave.

He followed the policemen down the platform of the Ghost Train, searching the crowd for Sally's face as he walked along the platform. Sally didn't seem to be there any more, but the watcher was still appraising him, and the old man and Lucky the dog were still making their way between the two stalls where he'd last seen them.

The cop called Keith tugged his radio from his pocket and radioed in a brief report telling the control centre what was going on. He didn't seem at all concerned. He finished his call as they reached the double doors and turned back to face Dave, stuffing his radio back in his shirt as he did so.

'Ready?' he asked.

Dave nodded. The special pushed on the right hand door.

'Mind the skeleton with the knife, won't you?' the cop quipped as he went in.

The Ghost Train was different inside.

The small procession followed the rails through the second set of doors and turned right. The partitioned-off track ran along a corridor which was parallel with the outside wall. It was only twenty feet to the far end where the wet rags hung that had fluttered around Dave and Sally's heads not fifteen minutes ago. Beyond that was the first display. It was the disembowelled man. In the yellow glare of the sixty watt bulbs that now lit the corridor, the man looked crudely fashioned and his guts, that had looked so real, appeared to be made from inner tubes of various sizes.

Surely this isn't the same as we saw? Dave thought. He couldn't believe the difference the flashing lights had made.

'No bodies in here, are there?' the real cop called over his shoulder as he passed the display.

'No blood spattered about either,' the special added.

Dave followed the two men, round the corner and down the next straight, wondering how the Ghost Train could have got so much smaller now that the lights were turned on. There didn't seem to be any distance between the displays, and there were no sections of track that either rose or fell.

They passed the Iron Maiden and turned left into a straight that ran along the back of the ride. The outside wall was canvas.

'We never came this way,' Dave thought aloud.

'Do what?' the special said.

'If you never came this way, then where *did* you go?' the real cop called back. 'There *is* nowhere else to go. If you were in here, you came this way. Are you sure you haven't been taking any drugs?'

The special chuckled.

'Forget it,' Dave mumbled.

The policeman led them around the winding track which serpentined up and down the length of the building. On each turn was a new horror. None of them vaguely resembled an

161

octopus, there were no Black Widow spiders and no torture rack pulling a man's arms off. All the display pieces looked waxy and badly made. Dave had seen none of them before.

It took them as long to walk around the Ghost Train as it had for Dave and Sally's ride. Nothing was out of place. Finally they rounded the final bend and saw the man dressed in the skeleton suit. He was sitting on a small platform smoking a cigarette through the mouth hole in his mask.

'Boo,' he said in a bored tone.

'Hello,' the real cop said.

'Hi,' the skeleton man replied. 'Got trouble?'

'This young man reckons his friends got off the ride in here. Have you been here all the time?'

'Yeah,' the skeleton said, pulling on his cigarette.

'You didn't go out at all when the ride stopped and the lights came on?'

'Nah, Fred doesn't like it. He wants to keep it a secret that I run around in here. Scares the punters more if they don't expect it, see? I'm not allowed out unless the ride catches fire or something drastic like that.'

'You didn't think anything drastic – as you put it – was going on then?' the special asked officiously.

'Leave off. The lights go on five times a day at least. Usually girls losing their handbags inside and stuff. They get a scare and throw it over the side. One of the outside guys usually comes in and looks for it. First person we've had who's lost some people though,' he said.

'And you haven't seen them?'

'No. There's a chance they might have slipped out under the canvas at the back. I don't usually go down that stretch. I confine myself to the middle normally – there's more room to leap about. Last guy worked this job lost a couple of toes in that back stretch. Engine ran over his foot. Nowhere to leap away to, see?'

'Have you got a knife, sir?' the real cop asked.

'What would I want a knife for in here?' the skeleton man said.

The cop smiled broadly, 'Our young man here thinks he saw you killing his friends with a knife.'

The skeleton began to laugh, starting with low chuckles that sounded like a machine throbbing into life, and ending in a coughing fit which blew sparks from the hot end of his cigarette. Finally he took the cigarette from his lips and butted it on the platform.

'You're joking of course,' he said.

'I think our friend has been suffering from hallucinations,' the cop said. 'Thanks very much. We'll leave you in peace now.'

'Okay,' the skeleton said, holding up one hand in a kind of salute.

The real policeman went through the crash doors and held them open for the special and Dave to pass through. When they came out into the bright sunlight shielding their eyes, all the waiting engines were full of riders and the interested crowd had mostly gone: The line of people queuing had vanished too; obviously they had not wanted to be kept waiting. Only Sally and the watcher were still down there peering up at Dave and the cops from the milling crowd.

Purdue came across the platform. He was sweating heavily and one of the buttons of his white shirt had come undone across the bulk of his stomach revealing a profusion of grey hairs. 'Done?' he asked, glowering at Dave with those piggy eyes that had pin-holes for pupils. On his wedding finger, the ring with the red stone shone.

Dave said nothing. He was totally confused and beginning to wonder if he *had* hallucinated what had happened in there during his ride. The gory scenes he'd seen certainly weren't present, and there was no way the ride could have gone on as long as it seemed to have done.

'Yeah, he's done,' the cop said. 'Well done I should think. I expect he feels like a fucking idiot.'

'A cunt,' Purdue suggested.

The cop nodded. 'He's been taking something, that's for sure. Acid, I expect. For two pins I'd run him in and throw him

163

in the slammer over night. Let him cool his heels for a while. As it is, I'm sick of the sight of him and can't be bothered with the paperwork he'd generate. So I'm going to let him go.' He turned to Dave then and said, 'Listen, son, why don't you just piss off while I'm still in a good mood.'

'Yeah and don't come back or there'll be trouble!' Purdue warned in that grating voice.

Dave wandered towards the steps back down to the fairground. He looked back when he reached them. Purdue and the cops were conversing. As he watched them, Purdue muttered something and made a quick chopping motion with the ledge of his stubby hand. They all laughed and turned toward him. Purdue's expression changed from merriment to one of hatred in a split second. He nodded his head towards the steps and mouthed the words 'Fuck off', to Dave.

Dave went down the steps and made his way towards Sally whose face was pale and frightened.

And the watcher grabbed him.

The man caught hold of Dave's elbow from behind and swung him round through one hundred and eighty degrees. Dave found himself staring at a person he almost recognised. The man's lined face was grey and his hair was dishevelled. He was aged about forty and very thin. His sports jacket was greasy and had patches of what looked like mud plastered on it. He smelled of sweat.

'What happened?' he asked, digging his fingers into the flesh of Dave's arm. His voice was high and thin and his eyes wild. 'You must tell me what happened. It is imperative that I know.'

'Get off me!' Dave wailed trying to shake the man's arm off. This was the straw that was going to break the camel's back. He knew that for certain. Any attempt at conversation with this loony who had accosted him was going to end with him sitting in a nice room in Park Prewett mental hospital, weaving baskets. His mind just couldn't take any more. Finding it impossible to escape the loony's clutches, he began to cry. 'Salleee!' he called, peering over his shoulder for her. 'Help meee!'

'Listen!' the loony said in his high madhouse voice. Dave's

head was rolling on his shoulders now and he thought he was going to faint. His glasses were steaming up, blurring the world in front of his eyes even more. The loony grabbed both his shoulders and shook him hard. 'Listen to me!' he screamed.

'Let him go you bastard!' Sally shouted. She flew at the loony from behind Dave and ripped his hands from Dave's shoulders. Dave fell to the ground and his glasses fell off. Above him, blurred by the tears and the lack of his specs, he saw Sally's slender fist ram into the loony's face. The blow caught the man on the cheekbone and unbalanced him. He took a tottering step to the side and fell over, his head striking the wooden kick-panel of the darts game behind him.

Up on the platform of the Ghost Train, the two policemen started forward.

Dave felt his glasses being pushed back on his face. Then Sally was yelling, 'Get up for God's sake, the police are coming! Run!' She dragged him to his feet and began to run through the stalls. Dave followed her unsteadily, his mind still reeling.

They ran right round the circumference of the fair to the entrance arch and back out into the main area of the park where they fell to the ground gasping for breath. Sally turned away from Dave and began to heave. Nothing came up.

She turned back to Dave when the retching had subsided. 'Sorry,' she said.

'Don't be,' Dave said miserably.

'I don't think the police are following us,' she said, surveying the way back to the fair. 'What happened?'

'Starting from when?' Dave said heavily.

Sally took his head and cuddled it against her breast. 'Oh God,' she moaned. 'What's going on?'

'Dunno, Sal. Did you see what happened to Phil and Judy?'

'The skeleton. With the knife. I didn't see it stab them. It didn't, did it? Please tell me it didn't!'

'I saw the knife come down, but I didn't see it stick in either of them,' he said. 'But that was only because the lights went out. There was blood on the back of their car,' he said.

'It got them!'

165

'I think it did, Sal.'

'What *was* it though?'

'I dunno. It looked like a real skeleton. It couldn't have been one, but that's what it looked like.'

'But what happened when you went back in?'

He told her, taking deep shuddering breaths between each sentence. When he finished, she pulled his head back so she could look into his eyes.

'Why was it different when we went through then? What *was* it in there?'

'I've got no answers, Sal. Not yet. Maybe we'd better wait and see what happens before we try and think about it any more. Every time I try and think out what is going on, I start to feel like I'm going insane.' He started to giggle.

'What?' Sally asked, her eyes huge with worry. 'What is it?'

'You,' he spluttered.

'Me? Me what?'

'You hit that guy. Punched him right in the face. Who taught you how to punch like that?' He rolled away from her and curled up in a hysterical ball of laughter that felt as though it would never end.

Eventually, Sally began to laugh too.

The dog that Dave had kicked the Coke can at earlier noticed them and came trotting over to investigate. Neither of them noticed it approaching and Dave screamed when it thrust its cold, wet nose into his ear. He sat bolt upright, the laughter having been choked off in his throat. The dog leapt back and cowered, its ears flat and its tail between its legs.

'Oh shit,' Dave said after taking a shuddering breath. 'It's only a dog. Here boy!'

The dog looked at him through huge brown eyes, and its tail wagged uncertainly. 'Come here!' Dave called to it. The sight of the dog caught his ragged emotions and soothed them somehow. Dogs were real things that had nothing to do with Ghost Trains and skeletons. Dogs wanted to be liked, wanted to be your friend. Dogs were *good*.

The dog came up to Dave cautiously, its tongue lolling from

the side of its mouth, its ears pricked. It sniffed his outstretched hand and looked up at him with that friendly canine smile that Lucy used to have when Dave came home from school. Its teeth were yellowed and its breath smelt, but it was the most natural thing that had happened to him all afternoon and he welcomed it into his arms. The dog jumped on his lap and pressed its head up under his chin.

'He likes you,' Sally said.

'What are we going to do?' Dave asked, tickling the dog's ears.

'Wait, I s'pose,' Sally replied. 'What else can we do? Will the police be looking for us or anything?'

Dave shook his head. 'I doubt it. I don't think there is anything they can charge me with, except perhaps causing a disturbance. They won't do that. Fred Purdue was too glad to get shot of me to make an official complaint, and the cops were too knackered to want to take it further. I doubt if they could actually. They can't even do me for wasting police time – I never called them over.'

'Purdue. That was the fat man, wasn't it? The one in the pay box?'

Dave nodded. 'The guy who owns the ride.'

'He had a ring. Did you see it?'

'Yeah.'

'It had the same kind of stone in it as your cross. Do you think that's just a coincidence?'

'No, I don't. It's related. Purdue and the Ghost Train are what it's all about. This is what it has all been leading up to; it's all a part of the same thing, the same jigsaw. I just can't work it out at the moment. It hurts my brain when I try and think about it. Purdue knows something alright. He knows just what's going on. I'm *sure* of it.'

Sally nodded thoughtfully. 'Phil and Judy aren't dead,' she said. 'They'll be alright. We'll sort it out.'

'How?'

She shrugged. 'I think Judy got scared and they got off. She probably got sick. I was so scared when we came out that I

167

threw up. I had to dodge in between the stalls. I expect the same thing happened to Judy. They probably went out the back like the policeman said, so she could throw up. They'll turn up again. I don't know about the rest, the size of the inside of the Ghost Train and all that stuff. I expect it just seemed bigger in the dark.'

The dog gave a low woof.

'Yeah,' Dave agreed, but his mind told him: *it was bigger inside Davey boy. It was much bigger when the lights were out. It was far too big to have fitted inside that building and it wasn't just because the lights were out. What d'you think about that then?*

'Look after me, Dave, won't you?'

'What?'

'I'm frightened. Things are going to get worse, I know it. Promise to look after me.'

'I promise. But you have to promise to look after me too.'

'I'll do that,' she said, taking his arm. The dog looked around and licked Sally's hand. Its tongue was rough. 'Good dog,' she told it.

'Oh God,' Dave said, looking behind him in the direction they'd come from.

'What is it?' Sally said, peering over his shoulder. 'Oh,' she said when she saw what he was looking at. The watcher – the one she'd punched in the face – was ambling across the grass towards them.

'Who is he?' Sally asked, realising she didn't know what had passed between the man and Dave.

'I dunno,' Dave sighed. 'I thought I recognised him, but I didn't know where from.'

'What did he want?'

Dave shrugged and in spite of the heat, he shivered. 'He's just a loony. He wanted to know what had happened inside the Ghost Train.'

'He's not going to beat us up, is he? I mean, I did clout him one.'

'If he's as crazy as he looks, he probably won't even remember us by now,' Dave said hopefully.

'I think he does remember us, he's heading straight for us,' Sally said, getting to her feet. 'What shall we do?'

'I'm not running away any more,' Dave told her. He felt weary and leaden. 'If he's mad at us we'll just hit him again. That's a good right you've got there Sal.' He levered himself off the ground and got to his feet to watch the man approach.

'Hey!' the man called, waving his hands over his head.

Dave and Sally remained silent and stood their ground.

'He doesn't look very happy, Dave,' Sally said worriedly. She wasn't sure if she had another punch where the last one had come from, and Dave didn't look fit enough to handle the man.

'Don't run away,' the man called breathlessly, 'I won't hurt you!'

The dog looked at him and cocked his head to one side. He began to growl.

The loony stopped while he was still a few yards in front of them, and stood there mopping his brow with a grubby handkerchief. 'It's okay,' he said. 'I just want to talk to you. I'm sorry I scared you earlier.'

'He doesn't sound loony,' Sally said. 'And he does look familiar. Who is he?'

He came toward them, and the dog flew at him, a black and tan monster with hackles raised and teeth bared. When it was close enough, it launched itself at him and clamped its teeth firmly in the bottom of his sports jacket. The loony yelled and tried to shake the dog off. When this didn't work, he tried to run away and found himself dragging the dog behind him, its front paws waving in the air, and its back ones tearing up clumps of grass as it dug in its claws.

'Call him off! Call him off! I don't like dogs!' the man yelled. 'He's going to bite me! For heaven's sake call him off!' He sounded genuinely frightened.

'LEAVE!' Dave shouted, not knowing whether the dog would take any notice of him and not really caring. The dog immediately let go of the man's jacket and laid down on its belly, its head between its front legs. It looked up when the man called, 'Thank you!' and when he started towards them, it got up and followed him, but it didn't attack him again.

'Who are you?' Dave said when the loony stopped in front of them.

'I have to talk to you,' the man said. 'Please talk to me.'

'Tell us who you are then,' Sally said. She didn't think he was dangerous at all. He looked pathetic somehow, and absurd and she began to feel sorry she'd punched him.

'My name is Derek,' he said.

'I know!' Sally said grabbing Dave's arm. 'I know who it is. It's that guy off the *News at Ten*. The one whose son vanished at the fair in Bracknell.'

'Derek Cousins,' the man said, sounding very close to tears. 'My boy is called Tommy. We call him Tiger sometimes . . . when . . .'

'I'm sorry about your son,' Sally said, now realising why the man looked so dreadful. 'I take it you haven't found him yet.'

'He got lost . . . I must find him . . . or . . .'

'But why here? Why are you looking for him here in Basingstoke?' Sally said. She glanced over at Dave who was stony-faced and wanted to ask him what was wrong now. He looked like someone had just given him a death sentence.

'This is it,' Derek said quietly. 'This is the funfair. Tiger went missing in the middle of this funfair.'

'AdventureLand,' Dave said dully. 'It came straight here after Bracknell, didn't it?'

Derek Cousins' face clouded. His eyes took on a distance and he stared unseeing at them. 'Yes,' he said. 'It came straight here. I had to follow.'

'But *why*?' Sally asked.

'I forget now,' he replied.

Dave groaned. 'Your son can't still be here,' he said, but he didn't believe his own words. It was beginning to fall into place now; the crosses, the hallucinations of The Claw, all those impossible things. He thought the jigsaw was almost complete now. Soon it would be answer time. Soon he would find out. This untidy man that stood before him in a daze was one of the final pieces, one of the last things that had to happen. Pretty soon now the shit would hit the fan. AdventureLand was at the centre of it all. AdventureLand was what it had all been leading up to.

'Tiger,' Derek Cousins said distantly. 'I must find Tiger.'

'He can't still be here!' Dave said, trying to make the words sound more likely, trying to drive away the feeling of terror that was growing in him. He thought he knew what Derek Cousins was going to say next. Good old Derek, whose son's disappearance had pushed him over the edge, was going to tell them that little Tommy Tiger was lost in the Ghost Train. And if he did that, it would mean that what they had seen happen to Phil and Judy was correct and not a trick of their eyes or a shared hallucination.

He didn't want that to happen. He didn't think he could face going back into The Ghost Train again.

But Derek Cousins didn't say what Dave feared, he just stood there and stared through them.

'What do you mean?' Sally said to the man. 'Has one of the fairground people kidnapped him or something?'

'He won't answer, Sal,' Dave said, looking at Derek. The accountant seemed to have turned to stone. He was rigid and unblinking. 'He's gone. He's not with us any more.'

Finally, Derek Cousins shrugged, his shoulders moving jerkily as if they had a great inertia to overcome.

'He can hear me!' Sally said. 'Have you been looking for him? Is that how you got dirty?'

'Fell over,' Derek said distantly. 'Pushed me.'

'Who? Who pushed you?' Sally said as though her life depended on it. Dave looked at her and saw that the dangerous gleam of excitement was back in her eyes.

'I can't go back inside,' Dave said, but Sally didn't seem to be hearing him.

Derek said nothing.

'Was it Purdue? The Ghost Train man. Was it him who attacked you?'

Derek sighed and went rigid again.

'I'll bet it was!' Sally said, turning to Dave. 'I'll bet Purdue is mixed up in this. He knows something, that's for sure. I'll bet he attacked Mr Cousins. It's bound to be him!'

'My wife,' Derek said.

'What? What about your wife?' Sally asked.

'There's something wrong with my wife,' he said, frowning. 'She keeps dreaming. She's frightened. Wouldn't come to look for Tiger. Wouldn't let me use the car. Had to hitchhike. Sleep rough in the trees. She keeps dreaming.'

'What of? What does she dream of?'

'Don't ask him Sal!' Dave said, knowing it was too late. Things were moving too fast. They were getting right out of hand and there seemed to be nothing at all he could do to stop them. If only Cousins wouldn't answer it would be alright. If only he would stay frozen in position and keep his mouth shut. Fear gnawed away in the pit of his stomach like boiling lead. *Too late*, he thought. *Too late to stop now. Why didn't I think when she gave me the cross? Why didn't I refuse?*

'Coming up out of the ground,' Derek Cousins said. 'They keep coming out of the ground.' He shook his head on rusty pivots.

'Who do?'

'The giants keep coming up out of the ground. All I can think of is expansionist policies. Like the Russians. Taking over. They want to take over.'

'The Russians? Or the giants?' Sally asked.

'Leave it, Sal,' Dave warned. 'It's better not to know.'

'I've got to know,' Sally told him, her eyes blazing. 'I've *got* to!'

Derek Cousins shook his head again. 'No, it's not like that. The giants are Anne's, not mine. My wife dreams giants, I think of expansionist policies. Not Russians. Much, much worse than that. Russians are people.'

'And the giants aren't?'

'Not giants. Something else. Only one. But worse.'

'Where? Where is it?'

Here we go, Dave thought. *C'mon Derek, tell us it's in the Ghost Train. Make our day for us.*

'I don't know what I mean,' Derek said. 'I can't remember. I need help. The Giant has got Tommy, that's what she thinks. Tommy is in hell, she said. I can't understand it. I've got to find him. He's only a little boy.'

'You'll find him,' Sally said with conviction.

'I've got to go and look for him. I don't want to. I need help.'

'We can't help you, not now,' Dave said. 'We have our own troubles.'

'Take me with you,' Derek said.

'Where to?' Sally asked.

Derek shrugged that mechanical shrug again. 'When you go, take me with you. I can't go alone. I'll be here. Waiting.' He turned around and walked away, stiff-legged. The dog growled and when he was at a safe distance gave a single bark.

'What was all that about?' Sally said, watching him march back toward AdventureLand.

'Trouble, Sal, and I can't make myself think about it now. Let's go home.'

Dave was asleep when the phone rang. He was dreaming of giants and invading Russians and skeletons with Bowie knives clenched in their bony fingers. He woke instantly, the images fading as the shape of his lounge filled his eyes.

The clock on the mantel read a quarter to two. Big Audio Dynamite were playing away on the television, but the sound was low so as not to wake Reg and Doreen. Dave had been sitting here since Sally went home just after midnight and must have fallen asleep before one because he hadn't seen the start of the show. He had stayed up to await news of Phil and Judy.

They hadn't turned up that afternoon, nor had they appeared in the Dragon that evening. Dave and Sally had phoned Phil's and Judy's parents twice each between arriving home that afternoon and closing time at eleven. They had restrained themselves from phoning more in case their parents should be unduly worried. After all, they hadn't been missing for *that* long and, once they were away from the fairground, the fact that they might have been murdered seemed unlikely to say the least.

But the fear began to nag away again after Sally had gone home. Both of them had avoided discussing the afternoon's events when they left the park, having made an unspoken agreement to wait and see what happened. Both of them were prepared to deny the evidence of their eyes and their inner senses until the situation became clearer. But, as Dave sat alone in the lounge with the television on, doubts began to invade his mind once more. Reality seemed wrong suddenly, and the alternative began to seem more and more likely, impossible as it was. He had sat and tried to make sense of it all, and eventually his eyes had grown heavy.

He jumped to his feet and ran into the hall to answer the phone, hoping to get it off the hook before Reggie or Doreen came steaming downstairs, eyes full of sleep and disgruntled expressions on their faces. This would be Phil phoning with a long and complicated explanation of their disappearance. Perhaps, he imagined as he picked up the receiver, they had slipped out the back of the Ghost Train and come face to face with Roddy Johnson and Jon Kott and had to run for their lives.

'Hello?' he said, putting the receiver to his ear. He never gave the number. People who were phoning knew what it was, and it made life more interesting for those who had dialled wrongly.

'Hi, it's me.'

'Sal,' he said, unable to keep the disappointment from his voice.

'You haven't heard anything then?'

'Nah, I thought it was Phil ringing now. You heard anything?'

'Nope,' she said sadly. 'I don't think they are coming back. I want to come over. Can I?'

'It's almost two o'clock, Sal.'

'I know. I've been lying in bed trying to go to sleep, but I can't. My mind won't let go of it. I want to talk it out. Can I come over?'

'Yeah, okay. Don't make too much noise, you'll wake the

Old Farts. I'll leave the front door open so you can come straight in.'

'Dave,'

'Yeah?'

'I love you. Remember that won't you?'

'Yeah. Love you too, Sal.'

Sally snicked the front door of her parents' house closed behind her and went quietly up the path and out of the front gate. Her folks would hit the hat rack if they had known she was going out again, so she would have to roll the car down the hill before she turned on the engine. They were both light sleepers and would probably get up if they heard it.

Out in the yellow light of the streetlamps, she unlocked the Mini's door and got in. She put the key in the ignition and turned it to the first position so that the warning lights came on but the starter didn't turn. She released the handbrake, knowing the car would roll down the gentle hill. When she was two hundred yards away from the front of her house, she would start it up.

The car didn't move.

'*Sally*!'

The urgent whisper came from the back seat. The voice was not one she recognised. She froze, waiting for the touch that would follow. Waiting for the tug on her hair that would tip her head back far enough for the blade to caress her exposed throat.

Nothing happened.

Oh Christ, she thought. *I didn't hear anything. Please. I didn't hear anything and why won't this damn car roll?*

The springs in the rear bench seat creaked and popped beneath someone's shifting weight. Sally could not make herself turn around, could not force her eyes to look in the rear view mirror. The skeleton would be sitting there if she did, grinning at her with its rows of yellow teeth. Its arms would be folded and the Bowie knife would be jutting up under its chin.

'Salleee!' the voice called, hissing through her veins and turning her blood to ice-water. Sally tried to scream, but squeaked instead. The weight on the back seat shifted again and something very cold parted her hair and touched the back of her neck. The cold seemed to filter directly into her spine and she felt her whole body freezing, becoming numb and immovable. The burning sensation of extreme cold went on for what seemed like a very long time. As her blood cooled first her body and then her extremities, she had time to notice that there was a black cat in the road. It was standing still in the centre, right on a white line and it was looking towards the car. Its back was arched, its ears were pressed flat against its head and its tail was stiff and erect. Its mouth was open in what looked like a sneer. She could see its pink tongue and its sharp white teeth. She became aware of the little tell-tale lights in the speedometer. One amber, one red. Oil and generator. They were growing dimmer as the cold increased. The bunch of keys that hung from the ignition swung slightly from side to side, and the boot lid key made a tiny metallic clinking as it tapped her front door key at the end of each oscillation. The car smelled of the Mr Sheen she had used last weekend to clean the seats and take away the rank smell of the river water Phil had been soaked in. The figures on the odometer jumped out at her and she noted that the Mini had done sixty three thousand four hundred and five and seven tenths miles.

And the cold hand on the back of her neck took the leather strap on which the cross was hung and tugged.

The cross burst into life and its green beam shone through her shirt, its power pulsed across her chest, drawing star shaped patterns of heat in the intense cold.

'*Salleee*!' the hissing voice said.

Sally's tongue became loose and she swore. 'Leave me alone, you fucker!' she shouted, and for a second the cold was gone. It came back almost instantly and seemed to have twice the crushing, lung-freezing weight. The hot cross slid up her chest until its head was pressing against the hollow of her throat. The unseen hand behind her tugged on the leather strap and pulled the cross into her throat. Its emerald rays glinted and sparkled in the windscreen and bounced back diffused and diffracted, lighting the inside of the car in a crazy display of pyrotechnics.

The springs in the back seat squealed and complained as whatever was sitting there bounced up and down, pulling at the leather strap. The head of the cross bit through the soft skin of Sally's throat and she felt fluid begin to run. The tension was now so great that she had to fight for each breath, and the temperature had dropped to such a low degree that each breath was expelled in a gust of vapour. The inside of the windscreen grew a patina of frost which rapidly thickened and fell into spiky patterns.

'Huucker! Het ho!' Sally gasped. Her mouth tasted bitter and her fingers were numb and ached deep in the bones. 'Huuck off!' she grated.

The cross flared. And the grip loosened.

'I'll kill you!' Sally roared as her breath came back. Then she shouted something that surprised her. 'You don't belong here! This is my place! You can't exist here! You're not allowed!'

It was a few seconds before she realised she was alone again.

And a few more seconds before she started to scrape the ice from the windscreen.

Dave had two cups of tea ready when she arrived. She looked tired and drawn.

'What is it, Sal?' he said, sitting down next to her on the sofa and sipping his tea.

'Something was in my car.'

'What?'

'I don't know. I think it was the skeleton or . . .' she shook her head. 'I don't know what it was except that it was evil. It tried to get the cross off me.'

Dave's eyes were huge. 'What happened?' he asked.

'I fought it off. Mentally. It tried to freeze me and then strangle me by pulling on the thong that holds the cross. I'm surprised it didn't break.'

'You fought it off?'

'The cross came to life and shone all over the place. It gave me . . . I dunno. It gave me faith or something. I knew I could

177

beat it. All I had to do was believe it couldn't exist and it went away. But I did believe it existed, that's the weird thing. I shouted at it that it wasn't allowed to exist here and it went. I didn't mean to say those words that made it go away. I think the cross put them in my head.'

'Christ. Are you okay?'

'Yes, I think so. It pulled the cross up so that it dug into my neck. It pierced the skin. It bled, but it's healed up now. I think the cross did that too.'

Dave inspected her neck. There was a small red patch in the hollow, but no scar or break in the skin.

'It's happening, Dave,' she said, looking up at him.

'What is?'

'You know what is,' she said. 'It's been going on since I bought the crosses on your birthday, but it's started in earnest now. I can tell. My cross. It's changed.' She pulled the leather thong around her neck, drawing the cross up through her shirt. Dave watched its bulge rise between her breasts and then its silver top appear at the neck of her shirt. She took it in her hand and showed it to him. Its green eye no longer showed. The silver lids had closed over it.

'It isn't possible,' Dave said, probing the join where the eyelids met. He could just get his fingernail between them, but it was impossible to prise them open again.

'It is possible. It is all possible. All you have to do is believe in it. When you start to believe in it, it doesn't hurt so much. It doesn't make your brain want to explode any more.'

'I don't think I can do it Sal,' he said miserably.

'You must. We've been chosen.'

'What for?'

She shook her head. 'It isn't clear yet, but I think there's something we have to do. You know as much as I do really. I think it's to do with the Ghost Train. It's killed them, hasn't it?'

Dave set his cup down on the table. 'Yes, I think it has,' he said, listening interestedly to the steady tone of his voice.

178

It sounded right. The Ghost Train – or the person in it rather – had killed Phil and Judy, and very likely killed little Tommy Cousins too.

'So what do we do next?' he said.

'I don't know, but I think we're going to have to go it alone. I think my cross is worn out; it feels dead, like its power has been exhausted. What about yours?'

He took his cross from his shirt. Its eye was closed firmly too. 'Shit,' he said.

'What about if we put them together. Maybe that'll make them work again. Maybe the eyes will open.' She took off her cross and handed it to Dave.

He took his off and slotted her smaller one into the groove in the back of his. The eyes didn't open. 'Perhaps we should leave them together for a while,' he suggested. 'I expect they'll take some time to re-charge or whatever it is they do.'

Sally nodded. 'That man this afternoon. Derek Cousins. Remember what he said?'

'When you go, take me with you?'

'Yeah.'

'You want to know where he thinks we are going?'

She nodded.

'You know, don't you? He thinks we are going into the Ghost Train again. He thinks his son is inside, still alive.'

'What if he's right?'

'He's mad, Sal. He's gone overboard.'

'But what if he's right?' she persisted. 'What if Tommy Tiger is still alive in there somewhere?

'Then Phil and Judy are probably still alive in there too.'

She nodded and smiled.

'But I saw the guy with the knife. He was stabbing them.'

'You never saw the knife go in.'

'But I saw the blood on the back of the engine.'

'Perhaps that's what Purdue wanted you to see.'

'That's what he *didn't* want me to see Sal.'

'We've got to go back in.'

'Yeah, I think you're right. I don't know why I think you are right. All this is logically impossible. Look Sal, I don't know if I *can* go back in.'

'Then I'll go alone. The Ghost Train is the root of it all. You know that. Purdue has a ring like the eyes of our crosses, for God's sake.'

'What does that prove?'

'That proves that he knows what our crosses do. He *knew*, Dave. As soon as he saw us he knew who we were. I don't know what he wants from us, or what we are supposed to do, but I intend to find out.'

'Let's go upstairs,' Dave said.

'What for?'

'That's where the computer is.'

'Why do you want the computer?'

'I've got an idea. I want to make a model. Of the Ghost Train.'

'Why?'

'Just to prove something. Look Sal, the more I think about it, the more ridiculous it seems. How long did that ride last this afternoon?'

'Ten minutes. It seemed longer though.'

'Ten minutes is an incredibly long time for a Ghost Train ride. The building that houses it is far too small for the ride to have taken ten minutes, and when I went through with the cops, it didn't look at all familiar. I want to program a model of the Ghost Train in my computer and see how long the ride could last – maximum and minimum. If there's any discrepancy in the timings, that'll be hard proof that something is really awry with it.'

Sally nodded. 'Okay. I can't see the point in it, but okay anyway.'

They went up to his bedroom, making as little noise as possible. Sally laid herself down on the bed and Dave sat in front of the Amstrad on his swivelling, low-backed programmer's chair, known as the Hot Seat.

The rest of reality blanked out for Dave as he slid the CP/M system disc into the drive; when he was in front of the screen, everything else took a back seat. His parents would often come in and carry on a one-sided conversation with him while he was playing a game or putting a program together and most times he wasn't even aware of their presence. Once he had started, it took a very loud noise, or a thump between the shoulder blades to break his concentration.

So he wasn't aware, as he loaded the program that Sally's eyes had closed and her breathing had become deep and regular.

It took a long time to set up the program to calculate the maximum length the ride on the Ghost Train could possibly have taken, but Dave was not aware of the minutes and then hours as they passed. He wrote the program to display a representation of the walls of the ride as seen from above. This bit was simple, even though he had to include a facility to alter the size of the walls. After this was done, he set about writing the track part. He estimated the rails of the track to be about two feet six inches apart and started with this size (although here, too, he wrote it so the size was adjustable) and then he began work on the curves. These were more difficult; at the end of each run of track there had to be a U-bend to enable the track to come back in the opposite direction, and he also had to take into account the width of the engines – the tracks would have to be spaced so that two of them could pass on the straight sections. He estimated that the engines were three feet six wide.

By dawn, the program was complete and saved to disc. It was five fifteen. He shut the computer off, reloaded it and called up the program. It worked. The screen cleared and a message asked him to: ENTER LENGTH OF FRONT WALL IN FEET:

He tapped 40 and hit the enter key.

The screen cleared and the next message came up: ENTER LENGTH OF SIED WALL IN FEET:

'Shit,' Dave muttered, noticing the spelling error. He couldn't be bothered to change it now. He entered 30.

WIDTH OF TRACK:

2.5

AVERAGE ENGINE SPEED IN MPH:

3

At times the engine had gone faster than walking pace, but it had slowed almost to a standstill on the turns. It would have taken far too long to calculate the variations in speed, so he had settled on an average.

The screen cleared and Dave was left staring into nothingness. 'C'mon!' he urged, imagining all the thousands of tiny silicon chip gates inside the computer, all the minute pathways the current would be following.

The computer bleeped and the back wall of the ghost train formed, one row of t.v. screen dots at a time. The side walls formed, then the front wall. There was now a black rectangle shown on the screen against a white background.

'Yes!' Dave said punching his right fist into his left hand.

Everything stopped then, and Dave nervously fiddled with his spectacles as he waited for the rails to appear. There was no guarantee that the program would do it at all. It only took one tiny mistake, one command placed wrongly – or even something as small as a colon – in one of the hundred or so lines he'd typed in and the program wouldn't work. It might even crash and vanish from the computer's memory completely. Dave had played that game before, and now saved everything to disc prior to trying to run it. Programs seldom worked first time out anyhow; there was always some glitch that would at the very least give you a SYNTAX ERROR message.

Dave waited and polished a thumb mark from his glasses with his sweaty shirt. The mark smeared, but he could see better so he left it as it was.

Two tiny parallel lines formed at the bottom left hand corner of the rectangle and grew. There were no sleepers tying them together, that was an unneccessary refinement. The tracks ran the length of the front wall, turned in a U bend and ran back the other way.

Dave nodded and inwardly congratulated himself.

It took two minutes for the track to fill the rectangle representing the walls of the Ghost Train, then another thirty long seconds to calculate the time the engine would take to go around it.

'Crap programming see, Dave,' he muttered to himself. 'Your stuff never was very elegant.' But he was pleased. He had accomplished quite a sophisticated program in one night and it worked first time out.

The computer bleeped again and words formed at the top of the screen.

TIME TAKEN TO COMPLETE RIDE: 3.24 minutes.

That was confirmation. He was pretty sure that he'd guessed the right size of the ride and got the speed near enough correct, so that meant there was something wrong with the Ghost Train.

But suddenly he wasn't sure. The *what ifs* invaded his mind. What if he'd got the wall sizes wildly wrong? What if the speed was way out? What if he'd messed up the calculations?

Check 'em, he told himself, realising that it meant another two hours work on the program and a visit to AdventureLand to measure the actual size of the ride. He resolved to do this tonight and refused to think about the consequences of anyone finding him hanging around the Ghost Train.

'Sal,' he said. 'I've done it. It's finished. Sal!' He turned around and looked at her. She lay on her back, arms at her sides, eyes closed. Her mouth was slightly open and her breathing was deep and regular.

'Wake up, Sally, it's time you went home,' he said.

She didn't move.

Down on the street he heard the familiar whine of the milk float and the clinking of bottles. Dave checked his watch, which was an old fashioned digi-analogue job.

The hands had stopped at five fifteen, the time he'd saved the program. The really strange thing was that the little l.c.d. display at the bottom had stopped too. The black numbers still showed (so it wasn't a flat battery) but they were frozen at 05:15.

'Christ,' he said, staring at the watch and waiting for the digits to change.

The colon dots between the hour and the minute display flashed off and on once a second as they were supposed to, but the figures stayed the same.

183

He tapped on the glass face, knowing that it wouldn't work before he tried. He shrugged away the feeling of unreality that had crept up on him and tried to work out what time it really was.

He never had a very good grip on time when he was computing but he thought that about fifteen minutes had passed since he had saved the program, which meant that it was now about half past five. It was quite light outside and looked like being another fine day.

'Sally,' he said. 'Wake up woman!'

She didn't stir.

He got wearily out of the Hot Seat and went over to her motionless body. Her nipples were erect and showing through her white shirt and he had to resist the urge to tweak one of them. He looked at the base of her throat where the cross had broken the skin last night, and wasn't really surprised to find that it was completely healed. There was no trace of a mark, not even the tiniest blemish. The skin was lightly tanned and smooth. *Good old Sal*, he thought, and put his hand gently on her face.

Which was as cold as ice.

He snatched his hand away and took a pace back, gasping in air through clenched teeth and making a noise in the back of his throat which went 'Eeeeeeee!' The noise was quiet enough not to wake his parents, but he had to struggle to keep it that low. *It's alright*, his mind kept telling him, *she's breathing. She's not dead because she's breathing. She's not dead*!

He shook her shoulder gently, then harder, knowing that she wasn't going to wake up no matter how hard he shook her. It was more than just plain sleep, that much was obvious. He shook her again, then picked up one of her cool hands and let it fall. There was no reaction. The feeling of dread that seemed to be permanently lurking in the pit of his stomach just lately began to rise again. He clapped his hands next to Sally's ear, but there was no response. She seemed to have gone into a kind of suspended animation.

He put his warm hands on her marble-cold face again and remembered the coating of frost on the belt loop of his new jeans. What had done this? The same thing? Had The Claw crept out from under the bed and touched her pretty face while she was sleeping? Had her spirit been stolen from her while he was clattering away on the Amstrad's plastic keyboard? Her face looked shiny and the skin seemed to have taken on a blueish tinge as if she was being starved of oxygen. Dave knew he had to act.

He rushed into his parents' bedroom. 'Mum,' he said softly.

'Eh? What is it?' Doreen said, waking up and squinting at him.

'Who did? Who did?' Reggie said, throwing back the cover and sitting up before he was fully awake. He was wearing a vest and striped pyjama bottoms in spite of the heat and his hair stood on end.

'It's you,' he said, spotting Dave. 'What's up?'

'It's Sally,' Dave said. 'Something is wrong with her. She won't wake up.'

'She's here?' Doreen asked. 'Has she been here all night?'

'We were messing about with the computer. She fell asleep on the bed. I can't wake her up.'

'That's that damn screen,' Reggie said. 'I've told you about it before, but you won't listen, will you? I knew something like this would happen. I told you it flickered, but you wouldn't have it. It's given her a fit or something, I'll bet that's what it is.'

Dave was about to tell him that Sally hadn't been using the computer, but he didn't want to get into a discussion about it. Best to let Reggie think they had been playing Space Pirates all night.

Doreen and Reggie went into Dave's room and looked at Sally's sleeping form. She was still breathing deeply and slowly.

'Well she's not dead, at least,' Reggie said. Doreen dug an elbow into his ribs and called, 'Sally! Sally Harrison! Time to get up!'

Sally didn't stir.

'It's no good, she won't wake,' Dave said.

Reggie took Sally's arm and tugged it. 'She's stony cold,' he said in amazement. 'Still, it doesn't look like a fit. She's not moving or anything. Her eyes aren't rolling under her lids.'

She took the cross off! Dave thought. *She took the cross off and it got her*!

'I think we ought to call the doctor,' Doreen said. 'I don't like the look of her. She's too pale.' She touched Sally's forehead. 'And she shouldn't be as cold as this. It's all wrong. Call the doctor.'

Sally stopped breathing. There was no warning. She exhaled with a slight gasp, her chest fell and it didn't rise again.

They stood there silently, their eyes all focused on Sally's chest.

But it didn't move.

Chapter Eight
A Trip To The Funfair

The tap was dripping.

The rate was slow, but regular. It took a count of thirty for the flow of water to gather into a tear drop and fall, hitting the bottom of the stainless steel sink with a metallic *tock*! There were no ticks to balance the sound.

She sat at the kitchen table watching the drips form and fall, form and fall, knowing that each drop of water meant another tiny section of her life had passed. Two drips equalled a minute. One more minute nearer death. Strangely, this thought comforted rather than depressed her. With her head in this condition, it was difficult to find anything depressing any more.

Her mother sat at the kitchen table on her left, with her back to the door. She was sitting stiffly upright, her hands entwined on the table in front of her. She studied them through her thick-lensed horn-rimmed glasses, observing them as though seeing them for the first time in her life. From time to time she coughed – a wheezing rattle that spoke of years of dedicated cigarette smoking. She was seventy-nine now and had become a mother late in life. Never before in all her long years had anything like this happened to her.

Anne Cousins ignored her mother and stared at the tap. The more drips that fell, the sooner it would be dark and she would be allowed to go to her bed and leave this sad and crippled old world behind her. Sleep was what she wanted most out of life. Sleep was escape.

Even through the haze of tranquillizers, her mind still thought things. And even though the things she thought seemed distant and didn't make her mind rebel any more, they still hurt. Things would never be the same again. That was irrevocable. Even if Tommy did come back, and even if Derek came to his senses, things would be different. Because she had refused to help him in his search.

She remembered what she had said. Just five words: *I'm not coming with you.*

That one short sentence had changed things forever. She had sensed that in Derek's face as he had left the house on Friday evening. There would be no picking up the pieces now, even if he came back and was his old self. Some families would have weathered the storm, even if their son turned out to be dead, or was simply never seen or heard of again. In some families that would have drawn husband and wife even closer together.

But not in this one.

Because she had denied him the thing he needed most with those five words. He needed to search for Tiger and he needed her support while he did it. She had been aware of that, even as she spoke. But she had still spoken them, there was no changing that. Now, the reason she had refused to go seemed ridiculous, but even that didn't make any difference.

She hadn't gone because she had been frightened. Scared that Tommy wasn't dead at all. That would have been bad enough, but what she thought – was *sure* – had happened to him was far worse. She was certain that Tommy was alive and trapped in the land of the Giants, in a place that could only have been hell. He was in a place from which there was no escape, a place where he didn't belong, a place where only the dead should be. And Anne couldn't accompany Derek on his quest because she was sure they would both end up there too.

What hurt most of all was the fact that she was scared. Too scared about what might happen to her own sweet ass to help her husband and son. Weren't mothers supposed to be instinctively prepared to lay down their lives for the sake of their children?

She was a failure as a mother and a coward of the worst sort. She had seen this in Derek's face too. She would be judged a coward in the eyes of both man and God.

And God knew, there was no doubt about that. God had set the test and she had failed it. Eventually, she would have to answer for that, give account of herself. There was even the possibility of having to explain her actions to Tommy himself. And what would she tell him? *Sorry Tiger, your mum's got a yellow streak that's so wide she would let you suffer eternally rather than risk her own skin.* How could she?

'Darling, it's not your fault,' her mother said as if she'd been reading her daughter's mind. The old lady was avoiding looking at her and was pushing a few grains of spilled sugar around the pine table top with a long yellow fingernail.

Anne didn't take her eyes from the tap.

'He'll be back soon, and so will Tommy,' Mum said, not sounding quite so certain about the last part of her sentence as she did about the first. 'And if anything should go wrong, I'll look after you. Don't worry about a thing. Mum will take care of you, just like she used to.'

Anne turned to her slowly, her head full of shifting cotton wool. 'You'd like that, Mum, wouldn't you?' she said quietly. 'You'd like to get me back again, to have me all to yourself again, without Derek and Tommy cluttering the place up. You never liked Derek did you?' She said all these words slowly and as distinctly as she could manage. Her speech was a little slurred and her mental processes sluggish.

'Don't be like that, Anne,' her mother said. But she didn't deny it. She stared at the grains of sugar on the table.

'Super . . . supercilious, that's what you said he was, didn't you, Mum?'

Her mother looked at her, her eyes magnified by the thick lenses of her glasses. Her face was impassive. 'I don't feel well, Annie,' she said. 'Don't make it worse.'

'Don't start that again, Mum,' Anne said. 'Don't start that old game. It's exactly what you always do when I disagree with you. You get sick. I had it all the time before I got married and

189

I don't want any more of it now. Whatever happens, whether Derek and Tiger come back or not, I'm not living with you again. Oh, you'd like it if they didn't come back, wouldn't you? Men have never agreed with you, Mum, have they? You weren't happy with Dad until he died, were you?'

'Annie, don't! It's just that I don't like to see you like this. You're upset.'

'I'm upset because I've lost Tiger and now Derek has gone, too. I'm upset because you've been lurking like a vulture all week. Most of the time you don't even call us on the phone, but ever since this trouble started, you've been hanging around, putting your tuppence worth in and stirring it up with Derek. Don't think I haven't noticed how happy you've been all week, now you've had a chance to start organising my life again.'

'I only want what's best for you love. It's time to take your pill, Anne. Go on and take one, it'll calm you down and things will look better. Your Mum's here, she'll look after you.'

'I've got to go and look for Derek,' Anne said. She didn't know if she meant it or not, but she wanted to upset her mother if possible. Her mother who had disliked Derek from the very start and hadn't gone out of her way to disguise the fact. Her mother who never came to see her grandson except at Christmas and then ordered him about all day: *Don't do this, stop that at once young man, Thomas, will you please be quiet!* She always called him Thomas, never Tommy. She didn't like Tommy because he was his father's son, and she hated Derek because he'd stolen her little girl. She had fought to retain her daughter right up to the last moment and, when the wedding day was close, had used the ultimate in emotional blackmail by developing a phantom – and untraceable – liver complaint. She hadn't blamed either Anne or Derek of course, but the message was plain for all to see; *Look, my daughter is killing me! How could she leave me to fend for myself while I'm infirm?* Anne had almost forgotten but never forgiven her. Now the memories returned and she realised what the triumphant look her mother had been wearing all week meant. She thought she had won.

'You can't go,' her mother said sharply. 'It's madness to even think about it. You are in no fit state to drive and you don't even know where he's gone.'

'You never use his name, Mum, did you know that? You always say "he" or "him", never Derek.'

Her mother glared at her, pale faced. 'I'm feeling extremely unwell now Annie,' she said. 'I want you to stop all this nonsense and take your pill. You make so much more sense when you've taken your pill. It's doctor's orders you know, I'm only thinking of you.'

Anne stood up and went to the sink in what seemed like slow motion. The floor seemed soft under her feet and she felt terribly confused. A small slug of bright fear flared in the pit of her stomach and she didn't know why. A drip of water fell from the tap as she stood before the sink and hit the bottom with that terrible *tock*! Another thirty seconds were gone out of her meaningless life, her cowardly existence. She reached for the glass that was on the drainer.

'Good girl,' her mother said as she filled it from the cold tap.

The capsules were in a translucent brown bottle on the window sill behind the sink. She reached forward and took the bottle with numb fingers. It was light, too light for the contents to have such an effect on her. The capsules rattled comfortingly as she brought her hand back, promising the salvation of a wad of warm cotton wool where her brain should have been.

Then she remembered the AdventureLand funfair, remembered leaping up and down with excitement like a little girl at the prospect of getting some candyfloss to eat. She remembered the thrill of catapulting the green rubber frog into the pond. She could almost feel the splash of cold water on her face. These were good things. Clean things. Real things. Now she was stained and dirty and ashamed of herself.

She unscrewed the childproof cap (childproof, that was a giggle, she really needed a childproof cap on her pill bottle. A childproof cap was a must) and tapped the bottle until one of the green and red gelatine capsules rolled out into her palm. She looked at the capsule for a long time. It may have been three drips, or it may have been four, she wasn't really paying attention. Then she took each end between her thumbs and forefingers and pulled the two halves apart. The fine white powder poured from the separated halves of capsule into the sink where it promptly turned to sludge. She laid the empty halves on the sides of the sink, the red one on the left and the green one on the right.

'Annie! What on earth are you doing?' her mother bleated. 'Stop it, stop it at once! Have you taken leave of *all* your senses?'

The second capsule was in her hands now. A quick flick of the wrists and the powder poured into the damp sink. It was easy.

'What are you *doing*?' her mother said, getting up from the table and hopping from foot to foot in agitation.

'I don't know, Mum,' Anne said, opening the third capsule and watching the cotton-wool-head powder pour out. *My, my, the sink's going to be stoned,* she thought as she emptied the fourth and this made her chuckle.

Anne's chuckling turned to laughter and she tipped the bottle upside down and emptied the rest of the capsules straight into the sink.

'Stop it!' her mother cried and Anne turned to look at her. She looked terrified. 'You're not getting me back, Mum,' Anne said. 'I love Derek and I love Tommy and I can't let them get away from me.'

Her mother came over to her, and pushed her away from the sink. Anne let herself be propelled to the other side of the room and stood there waiting to see what was going to happen next. She had resolved to tear the phone out of the wall, cable and all if her mother should try and call the hospital or the doctor. She had made up her mind and she wasn't going to be stopped. She thought that if her mother had done that, she might even have taken the handset out of her hands and stuffed it down her throat. She began to giggle again, then she saw what the old woman was trying to do. She had rushed back over to the sink and was busy fishing out the soggy capsules.

'Leave them Mum, I won't be needing them anymore,' Anne

said. She felt good; a little light headed perhaps, but much better than she'd felt since losing Tommy last week. She had decided on action, and now things felt right. This was what she had been supposed to do all along. The fear was there, glowing cold in her stomach, but the fear had to be faced.

She ran across the kitchen and turned the hot tap on all the way, ignoring her mother's feeble efforts to stop her. The capsules her mum had gathered fell back into the sink and instantly went soggy. Anne didn't know whether her mother had dropped them or if she'd prised them from her hands, and she didn't care. Her head felt clear and hot.

Her mother screamed.

'Stop it!' Anne commanded. She went to the door and took the car keys down from their hook thinking, *I'm sorry Tiger, I'm sorry Derek. I'm coming now. Please wait for me!*

'Where do you think you're going?' her mother wailed.

'I'm going to help my husband get my son back, that's where I'm going. And I don't *think* it, I *know* it! Don't be here when I get back!'

She walked to the front door, opened it and stepped out onto the shingle drive where the Volvo was parked. She slammed the front door on her mother's agonised wailing – slammed it so hard that the panes rattled. It gave her a good feeling.

It was hot outside and the sun was high in the sky. Here and there birds wheeled in the sky, catching high-flying insects. Anne smiled at the Volvo and imagined it smiling back at her. It was going to be hot inside, she knew.

She would have all the windows open on the drive to Basingstoke.

Dave knew he'd forgotten, as soon as Sally's father's voice penetrated his subconscious and started dragging him back from the safe darkness of his dreams.

'I've brought you a drink,' Ed Harrison whispered loudly. 'Wake up.'

Dave's eyes opened and for a second he caught sight of the memory. It had escaped the confines of his brain and was winging its way off into the distance to a place where his conscious mind couldn't get access to it. He caught only its hugeness and importance as it fled; no details about it were forthcoming.

'What?' he said, finally realising he was not asleep on the sofa in Sally's house after all. He sat upright in the hard plastic seat realising he was in the reception area of Basingstoke Hospital's casualty department. He groaned as he realised what he was doing there.

'Tea,' Sally's father said, offering him a steaming plastic cup. He took the cup, sipped from it and burnt his tongue.

'Careful, it's hot,' Ed said.

Dave checked his watch. It was stopped at five fifteen. This seemed significant somehow, but he couldn't remember why. 'What time is it?' he asked Sally's father.

'Ten past four,' Ed replied. 'I'm not surprised you fell asleep if you really were awake all night. C'mon Dave, what were you and Sally really doing all night in your bedroom? You can tell me.'

Dave looked up at Ed who was a huge, bearded rugby player with an ex-boxer's crooked nose. In spite of his physical size and his intimidating looks, Edward Harrison – known as Teddy by his wife, Marie, and Daddy Teddy by Sally – wasn't a bad guy. Dave called him Ed, just to be different. Dave liked Ed a lot.

He ignored Ed's question about what they had *really* been doing in his bedroom and said, 'Any news?'

Ed shook his head. 'Marie's gone to look for someone to try and get an update. She'll be back soon.' He scowled. 'I don't know what's taking them so long, Dave, I didn't think she looked that bad.'

You didn't see her when she stopped breathing though, did you Ed? Dave thought. He remembered that then. They had stood transfixed, staring at Sally's still chest. Doreen had said, 'Oh my God!' That broke the spell and Dave went to her, intending to give Sally the kiss of life, just like he had done for Phil a week earlier. As he leaned over her bracing himself for the cold touch of her lips, she had taken a deep, ragged breath. Her breathing had continued from then on, but they were still unable to wake her. Eventually Reggie had called an ambulance and Dave had phoned Edward and Marie. All of them had gone to the hospital, but his own parents had left around lunchtime, having been assured that their presence was not necessary.

Dave had remained though, and he had stayed on tenterhooks all day, waiting for a doctor to emerge and tell him that Sally's breathing had stopped again and there was nothing they could now do for her.

That hadn't happened and somewhere in that timeless waiting area, Dave had fallen asleep in spite of his determination to stay awake.

'C'mon Dave, what were you doing all night?' Ed insisted. 'I won't be mad, I just want to know.'

If you think I'm about to tell you we were up all night screwing, Ed, you can forget it, Dave thought. *Even if we were, there are some things you don't tell your girlfriend's dad – especially when he's built like a brick shithouse and has cups for boxing standing on his mantel shelf.*

'You weren't doing any kind of drugs, were you?' Ed asked. 'I mean, if you were, it's important to let the doctors know. If she's taken anything they'll be able to fix it. They just have to know what it was.'

'No drugs, Ed,' Dave said. 'We don't do drugs. Never have done. Don't even smoke.'

Teddy nodded. 'Good for you, boy,' he said. 'You've got more sense than I had at your age. What were you doing then?'

Dave thought about it for a time and found he couldn't really remember. He could remember being in his room all night while Sally slept on the bed, but he couldn't quite get at the bit of his memory where what he was doing was stored. He imagined that he must have been playing Space Pirates on the Amstrad, but he couldn't think why he'd stayed up all night over it, nor why Sally had been there.

'We were playing a computer game,' he said. That was what he had told his parents. He could remember that bit. It didn't sound right somehow, though. It would have to do, he decided. It was as good an explanation as any.

'Why should that have sent Sally into a coma?' Ed asked, a pained expression on his face. 'I've heard those screens can flicker and give you fits, but a coma . . .'

Marie Harrison came around the corner then. Dave was pleased to see her, sad as she looked. Physically she was just like Sally. Her age suited her. At forty she still had a trim figure, and she had something Sally didn't. Although her years had given her a few lines on her forehead and slight crow's-feet at the corners of her eyes, they had filled her face with warmth and intelligence. If daughters grew up to look like their mums, as his own mother insisted, then Sally would improve with age.

'Hi,' she said, sitting down in the chair next to Dave.

'What did they say?' Ed asked.

'They didn't say anything,' she replied. 'They wouldn't let me into the room and there was no one willing to talk to me. A nurse said someone would let us know the score as soon as possible.' She turned to Dave. 'Are you okay?' she asked, taking his hand. Her hand was warm and soft, plumper than Sally's. As soon as she touched him, Dave could feel her sadness and anxiety and that gave his own concern a sharper edge.

The doctor came out at six thirty. He was youngish for a doctor – about thirty, Dave thought – and he had sandy hair and blue eyes. When he spoke, his voice was quiet and refined. 'Mr and Mrs Harrison?' he enquired politely.

Sally's parents stood up. Their faces said they were thinking the worst. Dave got up, too.

'I'm Doctor Sharp,' the doctor said. 'I've been involved in your daughter's case.'

'How is she?' Marie asked breathlessly.

'It's alright Mrs Harrison, she doesn't appear to be in any danger at present.'

'She hasn't stopped breathing again?' Ed asked.

The doctor shook his head. 'There has been no sign at all of any respiratory difficulty,' he said. He looked directly at

Dave then. 'Perhaps you were mistaken earlier,' he suggested.

Dave shook his head.

'Well, she's had no problems on that count since she's been here.'

'But what's wrong with her?' Marie said.

'Ahh, that's the sixty-four-thousand dollar question, I'm afraid.'

'You don't know,' Dave said.

'To be candid, no, we don't know exactly what it is. It's a very unusual case and we have called in two specialists. Mr Parker and Mr Smythe are very experienced researchers into problems of this kind.'

'Problems of what kind?' Ed said suspiciously. Things seemed to be taking a turn for the worse.

'Well, at first we thought Sally was suffering from some kind of a fit, as suggested by the fact that she's been up all night working at a computer screen. That didn't seem to be the case. All the outward signs seemed to show that she is in a coma, but that doesn't seem to be the case either, I'm afraid. Sally just appears to be asleep. We have run EEG tests on her brainwaves and the results indicate that she is sleeping. She has exactly the wave patterns one would expect to find in a perfectly healthy sleeping person.'

'So what's the problem?' Dave asked.

Doctor Sharp cleared his throat. He looked embarrassed. 'The problem is, we can't wake her up.'

'But there's nothing physically wrong with her?' Ed said.

'Not apparently, no. It's just that we can't seem to rouse her. Her vital signs are reduced somewhat, but steady and although her temperature is rather lower than we would like, it is stable and safe – it's just that we can't wake her up. It's rather a mystery, I'm afraid.'

'She won't die then?' Dave said.

Sharp shook his head and smiled.

'And these specialists, what do they know about it?' Marie asked.

'Well, they've done a lot of research into catalepsy and

related conditions, and they're looking at her now. I imagine they'll run some tests on her. I'm afraid we don't expect her to wake up today, and there's nothing else to tell you. We may know more tomorrow when Mr Parker and Mr Smythe have had time to assess the results of their tests. For the time being, I would suggest you go home and rest. There is nothing you can do here. We have your telephone number and will call you if there is any change, but we really aren't expecting anything tonight. Perhaps you would contact us in the morning, say about ten thirty?'

Ed nodded.

'And don't worry,' Sharp said. 'She's in no danger.'

Ed and Marie gave Dave a lift home in their new BMW. They drove to Dave's side of the town in silence, each of them lost in their own imaginings. Dave's, however, were darker and wilder than those of Sally's parents.

They arrived outside Dave's house and Ed pulled the BMW up to the kerb. 'Here we are, boy,' he said, not turning around to Dave who was in the back. Dave thought Ed might be crying. Marie didn't turn around either, but she had been sniffing into a handkerchief all the way home.

'Yeah,' Dave said. 'Thanks.' He wanted very badly to say something to Sally's folks that would make them feel better. He wanted to assure them that everything would turn out fine and that Sally would soon wake up so they shouldn't worry, but he didn't even believe that himself. He was getting an idea of what he and Sally were up against now, and he wasn't sure either of them would survive it. Especially now the crosses had died on them. Now he was alone. Whatever was going to have to be done, he was going to have to do it on his own.

He didn't think he could manage without Sally to spur him on. He wished he could discuss the weird goings-on with Ed and Marie. He felt sure that Ed would be receptive to the half-formed ideas that were whirling around inside his head, but he felt that to say it out loud would diminish whatever magic he had left on his side and probably endanger Ed and

Marie too. He wished he was eighteen again and still at sc

'Don't worry Ed,' he said. 'Sally will be fine. I'll make su
of that.' He felt guilty now, as if it was all his fault.

In a way, Davey boy, it is your fault, he told himself. *If you
had paid more attention last night, you might have been able to
stop it getting her, whatever it was.*

'W-we'll ring you,' Marie said. 'As soon as we hear something from the hospital, we'll l-let you know.'

'You'll want to come tomorrow when we go to visit, won't
you?' Ed said. His voice was low and husky.

'Yeah, can I come with you?' Dave said, blinking back his
own tears.

'Sure, boy,' Ed said. 'Now clear off and let a grown man have
some privacy while he weeps.'

Dave scrambled out of the car into the evening sunshine and
went down the path to his house without looking back. He
heard the BMW drive away five minutes later.

Reggie and Doreen were in the back garden. The sprinkler was
on, spraying the lawn with a fine mist, and Reggie was poking
about in the flower border. Doreen was sitting in a deckchair
just outside the range of the spray and supervising. When he'd
washed his face, Dave went outside and told them the details.
He realised he must have still looked stricken because they
were sympathetic and didn't try to apportion blame. Doreen
told him not to worry and that there was a tuna fish salad
waiting for him in the kitchen if he wanted it. He went back
inside and took the salad to the lounge.

The two silver crosses were still on the coffee table where he
had put them last night. They hadn't re-generated themselves.
The eyes were still closed and the dull gleam of the metal
seemed to have faded. The crosses look well and truly worn out.
He picked them up and passed them from hand to hand, hoping
to feel some of the emotions they normally produced in him,
hoping to feel the same thrill he had experienced the first time
he'd held them. There was nothing. They didn't feel special at
all. There was no life attached to them any more. They might as

well have been a cheap piece of sterling silver from the Cut Price Jewellery shop in town.

He put them back on the table, wondering if they really would have saved Sally last night in this condition. He doubted it. He also doubted that the crosses' eyes would suddenly open again. They wouldn't re-charge after all. Apparently they were a one-time-only, disposable variety. When the magic ran out you just put them in the bin. He considered this action for a moment and then decided against it. Not while there was a chance, however slim. *You never know, they might re-charge. Perhaps they just haven't had enough time yet*, he told himself. But deep down he didn't believe.

He turned on the television and picked at the salad while he tried to interest himself in a documentary about underwater volcanoes. But he couldn't concentrate on the programme and, although he hadn't eaten all day, his normally healthy appetite seemed to have vanished. Everything seemed wrong and uncomfortable and it was all because there was something he'd forgotten. Try as he might to force the information out of his brain, the memory wouldn't come back. It was an important piece of information and he could pinpoint the moment he'd forgotten it – when Ed woke him up in the hospital – but he didn't have a clue what it might have been.

He looked at his wristwatch then and realised the time it showed was important. This was the key to what he'd forgotten. The watch had stopped and read five fifteen, both by the hands and the digital display. But what was the significance of that? What had he been doing at five fifteen? *Waiting in the hospital, that's what*, he told himself. But that felt wrong, and he wondered if it meant five fifteen in the morning.

Wasn't that when I realised I couldn't wake Sally up? What was I doing at that moment? Playing Space Pirates, that's what, he told himself. He inspected the watch. The colon flashed on and off, but neither the seconds nor the minutes would advance. He pressed the mode button and looked at the date. It read "Sun 23rd July", which was right, but there was no way of telling if this too was stuck. He pressed the button again and brought up the stop watch facility. This read $00:00_{00}$. He pressed the start button and then grunted with satisfaction as the counter started to run. The satisfaction lasted for precisely five point one five seconds. That was when the display jammed.

'Shit!' Dave swore, stabbing at the cancel button. Nothing worked; the $00:05_{15}$ wouldn't clear. Eventually he gave up trying to cancel it and brought the time display back again. This too still read 05:15.

He took the watch off, shook it and banged it on the table. The second hand didn't start moving and the digital display didn't even waver. He got his Swiss Army knife out, opened the small blade, levered off the back of the watch and inspected the mechanism. Nothing appeared to be out of place – no dead ants or biscuit crumbs or droplets of water were inside – and nothing seemed to be broken. The battery was still firmly secured in place and there couldn't be anything wrong with it because the shop had only put it in a month ago.

The clasp securing the battery was tiny, but he managed to work it away without damaging it, and he tipped the battery out onto the table. The digital display cleared. He picked the battery up with the tweezers from the Swiss army knife and re-installed it. Then he clipped the back on again and turned it over.

Something had gone terribly wrong.

The second hand still wasn't working and the digital display read $05:15_{00}$. This wasn't possible. It should have been flashing and reading $00:00_{00}$. He checked the stopwatch again. This still read five point one five seconds, too. Apparently it was trying to tell him something.

He put the watch back on his wrist thinking, *if only I could remember*.

He picked up the joined crosses, put them around his neck and lay back on the sofa, closing his tired eyes to rest them.

By eight o'clock he had fallen into a deep dreamless sleep.

'Dave! Wake up Dave!' His mother's voice penetrated the wall of sleep and Dave's eyes opened. They felt as if someone had been rubbing grit into them all the time he'd been asleep.

'What time is it?' he asked blearily, peering at his watch which still said five fifteen.

'It's half past ten,' Doreen said. 'I think you ought to go to bed. You're tired.'

Dave sat up and looked around the room. Reggie was asleep in his armchair. Melvyn Bragg was on the television, talking about a ballerina.

'Are you hungry or anything? I can make you something to eat if you like,' Doreen volunteered. 'You've hardly touched your dinner.'

'I'm not hungry, Mum,' Dave said. His stomach felt shrivelled and tiny. The thought of food made him want to heave. 'I'm going upstairs,' he said. 'Wake me up in the morning before you go to work. I'm going back to the hospital with Sally's folks.'

Out in the hall, the telephone rang.

'I'll get it,' Dave said, getting up quickly. 'It might be Sally's dad.'

The caller was Mrs Lawrence, Phil's mother. She was worried. She wanted to know if Dave or Sally had heard from Phil or Judy yet. Dave was unable to remember what had happened to Phil and Judy. He knew he'd seen them yesterday, but no more.

'What exactly do you mean, Mrs Lawrence? Have I seen them? I saw them yesterday.'

'They haven't come home yet,' Phil's mother said. 'They've been missing for over twenty-four hours now. They met you at the fair, didn't they?'

Dave remembered meeting Phil and Judy, but not what had happened afterwards. It seemed that each time he went to sleep he forgot something else. He couldn't remember when he last knew he'd met Phil and Judy yesterday afternoon. The problem with Sally seemed to have expanded so much inside his mind that there was no room left for anything else. 'Yes, I did meet them,' he said, stalling for time.

'And you got separated, didn't you? You lost them. Judith's mother is frantic. We are about to report them missing to the police, but I thought I'd phone you and Sally first, just to make sure they hadn't turned up.'

Mrs Lawrence disliked Judy intensely. She thought that Judy was leading her son off the straight and narrow path. Judy, according to what Phil had privately told Dave, was thought by his mother to be 'loose'. They presumed this meant that she thought her son was having sex with her. Mrs Lawrence was as anti sex as she was anti everything else that teenagers did. Booze, drugs, music, you name it. And not only did she dislike Judy, she disliked Sally, who she had decided was a bad influence. Sally was too flippant for Mrs Lawrence's liking, but the rot had well and truly set in when she and Dave had visited Phil one Sunday afternoon shortly after the hot spell had started. Sally had been wearing a tiny pair of white shorts that revealed the bottom of her buttocks and a tee shirt with no bra underneath. Dave and Phil had been delighted; Mrs Lawrence had been thunderstruck.

'Sally's ill. She's in hospital,' Dave said.

'Is she? What happened?' Mrs Lawrence sounded both worried, and suspicious somehow. Dave suspected she was making the connection that had just occurred to him. He was now the only one of their group that was still around and Mrs Lawrence was undoubtedly wondering why.

'She went to sleep and no one can wake her up,' Dave said. Suddenly he felt too frightened to go upstairs to his room. It had happened to Sally in his bedroom, so what was to stop it happening to him? Perhaps by this time tomorrow he would be in hospital too, in the same room as Sally and in the same condition.

'Oh,' said Mrs Lawrence. 'I've not heard of that complaint before. I'm sorry to hear that. So you haven't heard from Philip or Judith?'

'No, I'm sorry,' Dave said.

'Are you sure? There isn't anything you are hiding from me David, is there? You see I keep getting the feeling that you know more about this than you're letting on, young man. Now is your last chance to tell me before the police get involved.'

'I don't know anything,' Dave insisted.

'Are you telling me the truth?'

'Yes, Mrs Lawrence, I am.'

'Well, if I find out you're hiding anything from me, there'll be trouble. Have I made that clear?'

'What do *you* think has happened to them?' Dave said tiredly. 'Do you think they've run away together or something?'

Phil's mother's voice rose to something approaching a scream, 'You'd better not be telling me they've eloped!' she yelled.

'I'm not, I'm not,' Dave said. 'I just wondered where you thought they'd gone. I don't know anything about it, I'm afraid.'

'Goodbye, David,' Mrs Lawrence snapped. 'I expect you'll be hearing from me again!' She put the phone down then.

'Who was that?' Doreen said, coming out of the lounge.

'Phil's mum. They haven't turned up yet and she thinks I'm to blame.'

Doreen looked at her son owlishly. 'And are you?' she said.

'Christ, Mum, of course I'm not! I don't know where they went. I'm as worried about them as anyone!'

Doreen nodded. 'She's highly strung, that's what she is,' she said gravely. 'Are you going to go to bed now?' she said, brightening.

Dave nodded. Then remembered what had happened to Sally in his room. 'I don't know,' he said. 'I'm going to go to my room. I might read for a while. I don't feel very tired any more.'

The room didn't feel as threatening as he had expected it would. He took off his shirt and trousers and laid down on the bed, wondering what was happening to his memory. He *knew* what had happened to Phil and Judy; he was sure of it. But something was keeping the memory out of his grasp, just as he couldn't remember why five fifteen on his watch was so important.

He closed his eyes, knowing that if he slept now, more of his memory would vanish into thin air; suspecting that as soon as sleep took him, a cold hand would sneak out from beneath the bed and steal his ability to wake up again.

What would it be like to sleep forever? he asked himself. Then he thought, *What would be so bad about that? Wouldn't it be nice to be warm and cosy and relaxed for ever and ever?* He had to fight that thought, drive it away, because he couldn't allow himself to think like that. That was giving up. That was the way something *wanted* him to think.

He turned his attention back to his watch, idly stroking the upright of the cross as he thought about five fifteen.

Wasn't five fifteen the time taken?

The time taken for what though? Sally to wake up? The car to arrive here from the hospital?

The time taken for something.

Or was it 3.5 minutes?

Dave sat up, staring in front of him at nothing. *Five fifteen was the time it was finished!*

The game! It had to be the game! He'd finished playing Space Pirates at five fifteen, the exact moment that his watch stopped. Although why that should be significant, he didn't know.

He got up and went over to the Amstrad, settled himself down in the Hot Seat and turned on the machine. He put the CP/M disc in and booted it up, then picked up the disc with Space Pirates on it. It felt wrong in his hand though, so he put it back in its box and started lifting each disc in turn, feeling it, judging it with his unconscious mind. The next four also felt wrong, and he was beginning to doubt himself when he picked up the Basic disc. That was the good one. He knew it. He slotted it into the computer's drive and loaded the Basic program, then checked the disc directory. In amongst all the garbage and half finished programs he'd been messing about with was something entitled: "GHOST.BAS"

He didn't recognise it, but it seemed familiar. He typed Run "Ghost.bad" and hit enter at the same time as he realised he'd made a mistake.

GHOST.BAD? the error message said.

He retyped it. Hit enter.

The screen cleared.

ENTER LENGTH OF FRONT WALL IN FEET: the computer said.

Dave remembered. It came crashing back like water from a dam bursting through the walls.

40 he typed.

ENTER LENGTH OF SIED WALL IN FEET: the machine requested.

A few minutes later Dave knew that he had to go and measure the Ghost Train.

Just to be sure.

It was dark in the Memorial Park. Dave approached AdventureLand from the safety of the trees which surrounded the perimeter of the main park area. He had contemplated entering AdventureLand from the rear side, where it backed onto the fence that separated the park from the common, but had decided against it since it was too far from there to the Ghost Train. He would be spotted for sure if he went that way.

He stood hidden in the trees and watched the entrance. The fair inside was dark and deserted. Dave didn't know whether he should go in through the entrance, or if he should walk down the Ringway, which ran along the back of the park. If he went in over the fence off the Ringway he would be right behind the Ghost Train. But he would have to work his way through the caravans and lorries parked behind the rides to get to it.

He waited for a few minutes. No one passed by and there was no movement around the outside of the caravans he could see from this side. Some of the lights were still on inside the caravans, but most of the fairground people seemed to have retired for the night. He checked his watch, which still showed five fifteen, and swore to himself. He estimated that it must be twenty past twelve by now.

He'd sneaked out of his house at midnight when he was sure his mother was asleep and he could hear Reggie snoring gently. Reggie kept a fairly large shed at the bottom of the garden, and Dave had taken the key off the hook in the kitchen, a three cell rubber torch from the cupboard under the stairs, gone down the garden and let himself in. Here, in the depths of Reggie's toolbox was a sixty foot metal tape measure that had never been used that he knew of. He had found a pair of dark blue overalls and put these on, thinking that it might make him harder to see. He put the sixty foot tape measure in the overalls pocket, then forced the torch into the other pocket. He locked the shed again, and took the key indoors in case he lost it while he was out, and set off for the park.

It had seemed like a good idea at the time; now, lurking here like a burglar, the thought of crossing AdventureLand – however he did it – didn't seem quite so appealing. He wondered if Derek Cousins was here somewhere, perhaps sleeping under the trees. The thought of actually seeing the man lying there terrified him and he didn't want to be there any more.

But he knew it had to be done.

Behind him, somewhere in the trees, a twig snapped. Dave started, and pressed himself up against the tree trunk he was peering round so he couldn't be seen. It sounded as if something heavy had broken the twig – something like a man's foot. He held his breath and listened for any other unusual noises, but none came. The night was perfectly still with not even the lightest breeze to disturb the leaves. A chill ran up Dave's back as he stood there, his face against the rough bark. He could feel unseen eyes boring into him. Someone was out there in the darkness, watching him.

Then something shot towards him from the base of a nearby tree. It was small and fast. Dave gave a single yelp as he saw the dark shape approaching and tried to dodge.

The animal spotted Dave and veered off to the left, scampering through the soft covering of dead leaves underfoot.

It was only a rabbit! Dave told himself, fighting to control the pounding of his heart and suck in a breath in spite of the fact that his chest seemed to have been paralysed.

That made up his mind for him. He decided to leave the park and walk around the outside to the Ringway. He would have to be careful getting past the caravans, but the Ghost Train was much nearer that way. He also told himself that the extra time taken to get around the other side would allow the fairground people more time to go to sleep.

A Volvo police cruiser passed him as he walked down Hackwood road toward the Ringway. It came from behind and when he turned to look, intending to dodge away if it was the police, the headlights blinded him and he couldn't see if it was trouble or not. He groaned when the white car passed him, and groaned again when he saw the cop in the passenger seat turn and look at him out of the car's back window. For the first time that evening, it occurred to him that he must look very suspicious wandering about in the middle of the night dressed in a pair of overalls.

The Volvo's stop lights lit up and Dave saw the back rise as the driver stood on the brakes. He wondered what he should do, and considered jumping over the park wall and hiding in the trees. If he did that, he realised, they would see him scaling the wall and their curiosity would be well and truly piqued.

He walked toward the cruiser, having decided it was silly to run away. His mind was working overtime as he tried to think of a plausible excuse for being out this late and dressed this way.

The Volvo's lights went out and the engine stopped as Dave approached. When he reached the back end of the car both the front doors opened and the cops got out. The passenger blocked his way and waited for the driver to join him. Both men were about the same age as Sally's dad, Dave thought. The driver (who was only now putting his hat on) was grey-haired and balding and a little overweight. Dave knew he could outrun the man if it became necessary, and this gave him a little more confidence. The passenger cop looked marginally fitter, but not much faster.

Dave grinned at them.

'Hello, son,' the driver said. 'Where are you going then?'

'I've just been in the park,' Dave said truthfully. He hoped his expression looked concerned and innocent. It felt like it should, but you could never be sure. Lying wasn't one of Dave's fortes, but he felt sure he could spin these two a line.

Usually when a policeman spoke to him, he all but collapsed with guilt, even though he was near enough law-abiding. This time he felt sly and clever, confident that he could handle the situation. Things were different now. Since he had become nineteen a lot of things had changed. Policemen were no more than a minor hindrance to him now that the stakes were getting so high. For a moment he wondered if this new found artifice was a good thing or not. All his innocence and guilessness seemed to be disappearing like snowballs in the summer sun.

'What were you doing in there then?' the passenger cop asked. He looked tense, as though he was ready to spring should Dave make a break for it.

'What's your name, son?' the driver asked before Dave had time to answer.

'Dave Carter,' he said.

The cop wrote it down in his notebook. 'Address?'

Dave thrust his hands in his overall pockets and told them. A sad expression had come over his face now. Inside he felt gleeful.

'And what are you doing? What's that you've got in your pocket? A torch?'

Dave pulled out the rubber three cell and turned it on, then off again. 'My dog,' he explained. 'She's gone. Her name was Lucy.' This was also the truth.

'And you were looking for her? In the park at this time of night?'

Dave nodded.

'When did she get lost?' the driver said tipping his hat back and looking concerned. He was obviously a dog man too.

'Earlier,' Dave said. How much earlier Lucy had gone, Dave didn't say. He hoped that if Lucy was watching him from her great kennel in the sky, she would understand and forgive him. Lucy had always liked a good game.

'So why are you all the way up here?' said the passenger. 'Why aren't you looking nearer your home?'

'I've already searched King George's Playing Fields near where I live,' Dave lied. 'But she wasn't there and the park was her second favourite place. I thought she might have found her way up here.'

'She wasn't in there then?' the driver said, thoughtfully.

Dave shook his head. 'I was just on my way round to the common. Maybe she's wandering about over there.'

'Why didn't you go on to the common from the park then?' the passenger said suspiciously.

'Funfair,' Dave said. 'Those people give me the creeps.' He shrugged and did his best to look sheepish. 'They frighten me to tell you the truth,' he said. 'I always give them a wide berth. Some of them look pretty mean.'

The passenger looked disappointed. The driver nodded. 'Well I hope you find your dog,' he said. 'What was her name again?'

'Lucy,' Dave said.

'Lucy,' the cop repeated. 'If I see her, I'll take her in and telephone you. I wrote down your name and address, didn't I?'

'Yeah,' said Dave adding mentally, *if you see her, you'll be lucky*.

The policemen got back in their car and left Dave standing on the side of the road holding the three cell. He watched the car as it sped away down the Ringway in the opposite direction to where he was going. He suddenly felt very lonely and sad. And unclean somehow.

A few minutes later he vaulted over the low metal fence that ran between the park annexe and the Ringway. The caravans and trailers came right up to the fence, and he chose a huge trailer with a diesel engine generator on its back as cover. There were caravans either side of the trailer, but both were unlit and he had decided to crawl underneath it and come out on the fairground side, keeping well away from them.

He hit the grass and dropped so that he was lying on his belly, the trailer in front of him. It wasn't quite dark – the lights on the Ringway took the edge off the blackness – and he was able to read the name on the side of the trailer. George Dale's Famous Octopus, it said. Thick power cables ran from

210

the generator and trailed along the ground towards the perimeter. Dave realised that the Ghost Train couldn't be far away from where he now was. It was quite near the Octopus.

He slid across the grass like a snake. Under the trailer it smelled of old grease and diesel oil. He worked his way to the far side. From there he could see the back walls of the side stalls that formed the perimeter of AdventureLand. They were about twenty feet away and he was easily able to work out which was the back of the Ghost Train. It was two stalls over to the left. The only problem was that there were three caravans, a couple of Range Rovers, and several small vans crammed into the area. There was almost no space between them; just enough to enable the ride owners access to their caravans and generators. The thick cables ran every which way in a complicated tangle. Some were suspended in the air, hanging from metal posts. Most ran across the ground.

Dave groaned. He would either have to pass directly by the caravan nearest to the Ghost Train or go a long way in the opposite direction to avoid it. If he went the other way, he knew he would run into other difficulties. They might even be worse ones. He decided to pass the caravan. If he was quiet there should be no problem.

He made it to the caravan without any difficulty. The van was a long, chromed thirty-footer, and he thought it might be the one he'd seen coming down the A30 on Friday. The lights were out inside, and he imagined the occupants lying there snoring in comfortable beds. He could see the back of the Ghost Train from under the caravan and he decided the safest bet would be to go underneath (there was just about enough room) and crawl up the length of it. It was only a matter of a few feet from the end of the caravan to the ride. And it provided cover. Should anyone wake up, he could hide here and not be seen.

He crawled under the caravan to the left of its steps. There were three steps. They had been crudely made of hardboard and there were two empty cans of Miller Lite on the middle one, and several crushed-out cigarette butts. The occupant had probably sat on that step not two hours ago, relaxing in the warm evening and passing the time talking to his friends.

Dave shimmied under the caravan, turning to the right to face the back of the Ghost Train. He crawled forward another yard.

And put his hand down on a broken beer bottle.

He didn't yell. It didn't hurt all that much, just stung a little. He withdrew his hand quickly, hissing quietly. It was too dark under there to see the extent of the damage, but he could feel the blood running down his wrist.

He felt in front of him for the broken glass and carefully moved it out of his path. His hand felt sore when he put it down on the grass again, but he hardly noticed the pain. He was too worried about being discovered for the cut to matter.

Things went okay until he reached the far end of the caravan. That was when he heard the noise. It was a familiar sound. He froze, waiting for it to happen again. It sounded like something metal jingling. He lay there stock still for five minutes and then moved forward again. The noise might have happened again. He wasn't sure whether he'd heard it, or if his hearing had played a trick on him. He was so tense he was beginning to doubt his senses.

He crawled out of the far end of the caravan and stood up. The back of the Ghost Train loomed in the dark before him. It seemed to be made out of hundreds of different bits and pieces of canvas and sheet steel and hardboard all strung together with ropes and strings. The mains cable disappeared under the centre of the canvas wall which was creased and didn't reach the ground. He wondered if this was where Phil and Judy had come out, and for a second toyed with the idea of going in that way and doing the measuring from the inside where no one would spot him. The memory of the stalk thing with one eye came back to him then and he immediately vetoed the idea. He didn't know whether or not that caterpillar thing was real, and even if it wasn't he didn't much like the idea of coming face to face with it again.

There was a cardboard box in front of him. Balanced on the top of it was the fuel injection meter from the Ghost Train's generator. The meter was in pieces and had been left there overnight, ready to reassemble the following morning. Dave didn't see the box or the bits of machinery that lay on top of it.

And he walked into it.

The box tipped up and the meter parts fell to the ground with a clatter.

That was when Dave realised what the jingling sound he'd heard was and why it had seemed so familiar. It was a dog chain. The metallic jingling started again, and Dave knew the dog was coming to investigate. He had disturbed its sleep earlier; now he had woken it up. He groaned inwardly and cursed himself for not remembering fairgrounds always had dogs. How could he have forgotten something like that?

Dave tottered backwards and forwards, frantically looking for a quick escape route. The chain jingled and he saw the shape of the dog emerge from the far end of the caravan. He must have passed within a few feet of it just now, he realised with a cold shock. It was a Dobermann. A very big dog.

The Dobermann spotted Dave and gave a long hoarse bark which seemed to go on for ever in a continuous "Woowoowooo". It ran toward him and leapt into the air.

Dave closed his eyes and waited for the weight to hit him.

The dog's chain was too short for him to get at Dave, and as it flew through the air, the slack ran out. It yelped as the chain went taught and its choke-chain collar tightened. Had Dave opened his eyes he would have seen the dog stop in midair and be swung into the side of the caravan by its momentum.

Dave looked when he heard the crash. The dog yelped again, then it was back on its feet and straining at its chain while it roared at him.

The lights inside the caravan came on.

Dave ran.

There was a small gap between the edge of the Ghost Train and the start of the next ride, and he headed for this, not caring about measuring the damn thing any more. If he could get away now, he could come back any time. He leapt over a guy rope and entered the alley, just as the caravan's door opened and a man emerged. He yelled at Dave and started down the steps.

Dave almost made it. If he hadn't misjudged the steel cleat holding the last guy rope, he would have been through into the fairground and away.

The cleat caught the toe of his Hi-Tec basketball boots as he leapt over it and brought him crashing to the ground. He tried to get up, but the breath had been knocked from his body and his arms seemed to have lost all their strength. In spite of this, he was on his hands and knees when the man's foot drove up under his ribs.

The kick was hard, and caught him in the guts just a little higher than his navel. The force lifted Dave momentarily from the ground. There seemed to be no air left in the world as his arms and legs buckled and he fell to the ground. A crushing weight seemed to have settled on his chest and his guts felt as though someone were injecting them with concrete under high pressure. The real pain, Dave knew, would come later.

'And what are you supposed to be doing sneaking round our van?' the man hissed. Dave looked up at him through eyes that were blurred with tears and recognised the features. This must be one of George Dale's sons. It wasn't the one that was working on the Octopus when old George had given them the ride of a lifetime. The guy was six foot tall and dressed only in a pair of blue Y-fronts. His feet were bare, but that hadn't stopped him kicking like a donkey.

'Ahh,' Dave groaned, clutching his stomach with his hands and fighting for breath.

'What were you doing, you little bastard?' He aimed a kick at Dave's crotch and Dave, seeing it coming brought his legs up to protect himself. The man's bare foot struck the area around Dave's hip pocket.

Where the three cell rubber torch was.

He yelled and hopped about clutching his foot, while Dave tried to get back on his feet. He made it up to all fours again, just in time to see the blond man hop into one of the steel tent pegs holding the guy ropes. He screamed this time and went down like a sack of coal.

'Sean? What is it? SEAN!' A young girl came out of the gap between the rides just as Dave got to his feet. She was quite pretty from what Dave could make out of her features and she appeared to be naked except for a bedsheet which was wrapped around her like a shroud. She saw Sean rolling about on the ground, and Dave standing there. She screamed at the top of her range. It was one of the loudest screams Dave had ever heard.

'*What have you done to him, you fucker?*' she shouted shrilly.

Dave gasped, but could say nothing. The weight seemed to be lifting from his stomach and chest a little now, but it was being replaced by a stabbing pain which screwed into his ribs like a white-hot blade each time he tried to draw breath. His legs badly wanted to take him out of there, but his chest wouldn't let him move just yet. He looked at the screaming girl, and then he looked at his left hand. The cut was short but deep. Blood was running freely from it and dripping from his wrist. The cut looked as if it might need a couple of stitches.

He turned away from the girl and the writhing Sean and took a few steps toward the exit from AdventureLand. He could just see the tip of the arch over the top of the Chairoplanes, but it seemed a long long way away.

'Hold it!'

Dave looked back over his shoulder and saw one of the Ghost Train roustabouts behind him. It was the older of the two ride men: Charlie, the one with the little red devil tattooed on his arm; the one who had promised to knock out some of his teeth. Dave groaned, and broke into a trot which hurt his ribs.

'Come back here!' the roustabout yelled. Dave ignored him and kept right on going, even picking up a little speed. The man started after him. He was bigger than Dave and much quicker. In a fit state, Dave could have outpaced him but, now, each breath tore at his body.

He glanced over his shoulder when he heard the thudding footsteps closing on him. Tattoo was fully dressed and wearing Doctor Marten's boots and he looked mad. Dave didn't much fancy the thought of having one of those heavy boots thudding into his sore ribs – the bare foot had hurt enough – so, ignoring the agony, he accelerated to his best pace.

The entrance arch was less than a hundred yards away but he knew he wouldn't make it. Tattoo was right behind him, and George Dale's son was coming up the rear, hobbling some but still moving very fast.

Tattoo leapt at him like a rugby player and he went down again, the man's arms encircling his legs. Dave fought. He ignored the pain in his chest and fought Tattoo tooth and nail. He bit, he scratched, he kicked. The two of them rolled back and forth across the grass, the roustabout trying to get a purchase on Dave, and Dave struggling to get free. Tattoo hissed and swore. His face was rough and unshaven against Dave's and his breath smelt of onions. Then Dave found his cut hand pressed against the roustabout's genitals through his jeans as the man straddled him. They felt lumpy and big. Dave grabbed hold and twisted hard clockwise. For one glorious moment the man let go of him and screamed.

Dave wriggled out from under him and tried to get on his feet.

White stars lit in front of his eyes and he felt himself falling. The passage down to the grass seemed to take a long time. When his vision came back, his right ear began to sing and he realised that George Dale's son had kicked him again.

The men were both on their feet now, towering over him.

'I'll teach you to come spying on my missus and me!' Dale's son yelled. His foot thudded into Dave's hip again, missing the three cell this time.

'Hold on,' Tattoo said, grabbing Sean's arm. 'I recognise this one from somewhere.' He bent down and grabbed hold of the front of Dave's overalls and yanked him to his feet. 'What are you doing here fuckhead?' he said right into Dave's face.

'Who is he?' Sean demanded.

'Dunno. He was causing trouble on the Ghost Train yesterday though. What are you doing back here, you little shit?' he demanded.

'Spying on me!' Sean answered for him. He stepped around

the side of Tattoo and punched Dave in the ribs again.

Dave blacked out.

He almost regained consciousness when someone kicked him in the crotch. The pain corkscrewed right up through his middle and tried to turn the lights back on in his brain. He dimly felt blows raining down on him and he tried reflexively to make himself into a small ball, curling his legs up and his arms in.

That was when his semi-conscious brain informed him that the crosses were gone. They had been around his neck when he came out, but they were gone now. The last thing he thought before the blackness came crashing back down was, *I'm fucked now. Yes I am, oh yes I am.*

Dawn was breaking when Dave came to his senses again. It was the rustling noise in the fallen leaves that woke him up. It sounded like moths. He sat upright, visions of creeping things filling his mind. He opened his eyes and thought, *what am I doing here?*

A rabbit scampered away through the woods, and the sight of it brought back last night. Perhaps it was the same rabbit.

Everything he had hurt like hell and he sat there rubbing his ribs, wondering how he had got to be back in the trees. He supposed the two fairground men had dragged him there and dumped him after they'd finished using him as a human punchbag.

The wound on his hand was throbbing, but the bleeding had stopped and a crust of scabbing blood had dried over it. His left arm was dark with dried blood and it felt stiff when he tried to move it. He got to his feet, ignoring the dull ache from his bruised ribs and stomach. His hand went to his face and he was mildly surprised to find his glasses still on.

Then he remembered the crosses were gone and that thought filled him with dread. Now he had absolutely nothing to help him. Even though the power of the crosses seemed to have expired, they had given him a sense of protection that he no longer felt. He was alone.

217

He checked his pockets. The metal tape measure and the three cell rubber torch were still there. They hadn't robbed him then, that was something. He stood there for a few minutes, checking himself. Everything hurt, but nothing seemed to be broken – why, he didn't know. Surely *something* ought to have been badly damaged. He wasted a few more minutes before he realised he wanted to go home but was too frightened to leave the cover of the trees.

Fuck off Dave, he scorned himself, *if they had wanted to kill you, they could have done that last night. All they wanted to do was beat you up because they thought you were spying on them or wanted to steal something from them. They aren't the types to call the police. They just do what they did to me and forget all about it. They aren't waiting out there for me so they can do it again.*

The other half of his mind hoped he was right, because he was in no condition either to run or to fight. He had been lucky last night. If they got him again, it would almost certainly mean hospitalisation.

He limped out of the trees onto the wide expanse of grass and made his way towards the park gates, being careful to keep a lookout for anyone approaching him.

He arrived home at five thirty and sneaked the overalls and the tape and torch back into their rightful places, and let himself into the house. Walking past the mirror at the bottom of the stairs in the hall gave him a shock. A wild-eyed maniac stared back at him from the glass – a bespectacled vision with sunken, bruised cheeks and a fat bottom lip. His hair was dirty and full of bits of dead leaf and one of his ears seemed to be twice the size of the other. The sight of his poor, tired and battered face brought tears of self-pity to his eyes. He was worn out. Completely and utterly ground down. He hadn't slept properly for over forty-eight hours, his crosses were gone, his girlfriend was in a type of coma that no one seemed to know anything about and he'd been badly beaten up. His tearful reflection reminded him of how Tommy's dad Derek Cousins had looked on Saturday when he followed them out of AdventureLand. Now he knew *exactly* how the man felt. Whipped.

And it hasn't started yet, Dave, his mind told him. *You know that, don't you?*

'Y-yes,' he sobbed at his reflection. The realisation that there was much more to come settled inside him like a lead weight. He wondered if he would die. If he was going to, he hoped it would be soon.

Wearily, he trudged up the stairs and went into the bathroom where he turned the bath taps on and took off his clothes. He wouldn't have to hide these – the overalls had stopped the blood and dirt getting on them. He threw the clothes into the washing bin and looked at his naked, skinny body in the mirror. His stomach and ribs were a mass of ugly purple bruises and abrasions. There were several friction burns on his skin between the proper bruises and scrapes. These, he realised, were where Tattoo's Doc Martens had missed their target and skidded across his clothes, rubbing them against him. He stood and looked at himself until the bath was full and the mirror steamed up.

He turned off the taps, suddenly knowing that the aching in his bladder was because he needed to urinate. He stood in front of the toilet and was unable to piss for a while. When the stream started, it was tinged brown and by the time it had stopped, he could no longer see the bottom of the U bend. He knew the colour was due to blood in his urine, but he didn't know how serious it was. If it continued, he would go and see someone about it, but that would cause a lot of questions that he didn't want to have to answer. He hoped it would get better on its own. The dull ache from his bladder subsided after he'd pissed, and he hoped this was a good sign.

The hot water stung his skin when he got in the bath, but after a time it eased the pain in his ribs and made his breathing easier. The scab on his hand wound dissolved, leaving the gash open and angry looking, but it didn't bleed again. He was thankful for this too.

After a while he fell asleep.

Chapter Nine
Going Back Again

Ed Harrison phoned at eleven wanting to know if Dave needed picking up. Dave was still in bed sleeping and Reggie had answered the phone.

Ed told Reggie that he had phoned the hospital on the dot of ten thirty, but there was nothing to report. Sally had not woken. Reggie sympathised with him and told him yes, Dave would want to go to the hospital with them when they went at lunchtime. He didn't tell Ed that he wasn't sure Dave would be in any condition to go.

He had got up to go to the bathroom at eight that morning, and was surprised to find his son asleep in the bath. He had looked at Dave carefully for a few seconds, instantly alert. Dave didn't seem to be breathing and at first he thought his son was dead, perhaps of a drug overdose. Then he saw the mass of bruises on Dave's chest and thought he might have died of the beating he had obviously taken. As he stood rooted to the spot, he saw Dave take a deep breath. He hadn't been happy until he'd woken him up though – thoughts (stupid though they were) of the same thing happening to Dave as had happened to Sally had immediately filled his mind. He had shaken Dave gently until he had woken.

Dave's eyes blinked open and he looked up at Reggie. 'Uhh?' he said. Reggie watched goosebumps break out on Dave's skin.

'What happened?' he asked.

'When?' Dave countered, sitting up in the grimy water and shivering.

He was like that, Reggie knew from long experience. Getting the details about anything out of him was worse than trying to extract whisky from a housebrick. God only knew why kids were so loath to tell you anything. Normally he would have become cross at this point, but the state his son was in and what had happened to Sally took the edge off his annoyance.

'Last night,' he said. 'I presume you didn't get in that state asleep in bed, so you must have gone out. I didn't hear you go. Did you go out late?'

'Yeah,' Dave replied. 'Couldn't sleep. Went for a walk. I was worrying about Sal.'

Another thing Reggie knew from long experience was when Dave was telling him fibs. You didn't make a child, help him with his homework, play with him and then put up with him all through his nasty rebellious teenage years without learning something about his personality and psychology. Dave didn't know that Reggie knew when he was lying, and Reggie kept that one under his hat. So far, Dave had done nothing which Reggie thought it was worth pulling him up on, and blowing his cover. So the secrets had stayed secret. Dave didn't get into any fights (bar the Roddy Johnson episode), he didn't steal (as far as Reggie knew) and though he was often sullen and withdrawn while he was home with his parents, his schoolwork had been good and there were no drink or drugs problems.

But something strange was going on here. Reggie was alert enough to know that. Things had been different since Dave's nineteenth birthday. At first, Reggie had put it down to the stress of waiting for A level results. Now he was beginning to wonder what else was going on.

'Where did you go?' he asked.

'Up towards the park,' Dave said. 'Just walking, that's all.'

'And you got into a fight? You've had a right royal working over by the look of you.'

Dave looked up at him, long and hard. 'I got mugged,' he said.

There you go, Reggie thought. *What really happened*? 'Who by?' he asked, playing the game.

221

'Didn't see 'em,' his son lied. 'They jumped me from behind. I was going along Southern Road past the carpet place. They must have come out of the car park there. They knocked me down and kicked me about a bit. I'm alright though, really I am. It doesn't matter.'

It wasn't alright, and it did matter, but if Dave didn't want to tell him, he wouldn't.

'It wasn't Roddy Johnson and his friends, was it?' he asked. That was more like it. They had probably been hanging about up there, seen Dave passing and decided to repay him for the trouble he had got them into.

'I don't know who it was,' Dave said. 'There were about four of them, but it was dark and I didn't get a good look at them.'

'Did they take anything from you?' Reggie said.

'I lost the crosses,' Dave said. 'The ones Sally got on my birthday. I had them on when I went out and they're gone now. I don't think they took them off me though,' he added quickly. 'I think the straps got broken and they fell off. I went back and looked for them afterwards, but I couldn't see them.'

'You'd better report it to the police,' Reggie said. 'That jewellery was expensive, wasn't it? Even if you don't say anything about the fight, you'd better report the crosses missing.'

Dave nodded. 'I'll go down later on and do it,' he said.

'Are you sure you're alright? That looks like a pretty nasty cut on your hand. How did that happen?'

Dave inspected the cut. 'Fell on some glass. Broken bottle or something. It's sore, but the bleeding has stopped okay. I expect it'll be alright with a plaster.'

Reggie nodded, feeling more worried than he looked. There was a whole lot more to this than he was hearing. He couldn't quite put his finger on what worried him so, but he knew it wasn't the fact that Dave had been done over or even the fact that he wasn't prepared to talk about it – those sort of things happened when you were that age – it was something else. Dave seemed to be in some kind of trouble which was bigger than he could handle and the crosses and Sally's coma and lots of other stuff were involved in it too. He decided the best policy was not to push for too much information. He would just have to wait until Dave was ready to talk about it. Eventually, he knew, Dave would ask for his help. He always had done before.

'You'd better get yourself to bed, Dave,' he said. 'I'll wake you up later, when you've had a good rest. If there's anything hurting badly later on we may have to get you looked at.'

'I'll be alright,' Dave said.

'Okay,' Reggie said. 'I'll tell your mum you've had some aggro. Try not to show her how badly you got damaged, or she'll have a fit.'

He had gone back to bed then, and waited until he heard Dave go into his room before he went back to the bathroom to empty his bladder. He still couldn't get back to sleep though, even with the pressure gone. He lay in bed and wondered what was going on.

Ed and Marie Harrison sat on one side of Sally's bed in the hospital room, and Dave sat on the other. Sally lay under a single sheet, sleeping peacefully. Her arms were outside the sheet and her hands were one on top of the other on her tummy, but they were not clasped. The hospital staff had done a job on her before they arrived, Dave knew. Sally's hair had been carefully brushed and looked glossy and neat; the tanned skin of her face and arms was washed and shone clean in the light from the window behind her bed. But her tan looked streaky and faded already and there were sticky electrode pads on either side of her forehead and on her chest with thin red wires that ran to the bleeping machines that surrounded her.

It was a nice room, small but somehow bright and cheerful in spite of the monitoring equipment that half filled it. There were two pictures on the walls, one of a misshapen dog and the other of a snowman, painted by kids from the children's ward.

The two specialists, Parker and Smythe, were standing at the foot of the bed, holding court. Both men were dressed in suits, rather than the white lab coats that everyone else wore, and both were middle-aged. Parker was tall and thin and had sharp features and a hooked nose. He was bald to the crown of his head, but the hair around the sides and back was dark and woolly. Smythe looked like a Californian executive type, right down to his gently toasted tan and his swept-back white hair. He wore a chunky gold signet ring on the middle finger of his left hand.

Dave didn't like them much. They seemed too pleased about having Sally here in this condition. They looked as if they would be happy to keep her here forever, just to study her.

'We have seen several cases identical to this one just recently,' Smythe was saying happily. 'We have christened it Sleeping Beauty Syndrome.'

Yay, let's have a round of applause for the clever doctor, Dave thought bitterly. *All we have to do now is hire a male member of the Royal Family to come and kiss her.*

'For some reason,' Smythe continued, 'the frequency of these cases seems to be increasing. This kind of complaint wasn't heard of until the mid-seventies, and there have been very few since. Suddenly it seems to be becoming popular.'

'How many have you seen?' Dave cut in.

Smythe looked at him and smiled. 'So far, ten. Four of them recently. Now, Sleeping Beauty Syndrome is a peculiar complaint because it doesn't seem to be a complaint at all. There are no unusual signs in the EEG charts and the only way in which her condition differs from that of ordinary sleep is her lowered temperature. This, in itself, is not dangerous at this point in time. We will, however, be keeping a close eye out for any further drop in temperature. We have taken the precaution of performing a lumbar puncture and we have processed the results. I can assure you, Mr and Mrs Harrison, that Sally has nothing wrong with her disease-wise. Her condition is not caused by infection of any kind. Neither is it caused by physical damage to your daughter.'

'So what *is* it caused by?' Ed said. Dave could tell from his tone that he didn't much like Smythe either.

'To be quite candid with you, Mr Harrison, we don't know precisely. Having ruled out infection and physical damage, there is only one possible explanation and that is a psychiatric one.'

'She's had a nervous breakdown, is that what you're saying?' Ed asked.

Parker took over the conversation. 'Not as such, no. This, you see, is the problem. This malady appears to have no set cause, either medical or psychiatric. It may be a combination of things, possibly it is an offshoot of a psychiatric disorder known as catalepsy, but it bears no real relationship to it. In the cases we have seen so far, there seems to be nothing which links up, no common factor. The other patients we have attended have come from all walks of life and all social backgrounds. Some of them had been previously treated for depression but, on the whole, their medical records differed considerably.'

'What you're saying is, you haven't a clue what's wrong with her, right?' Ed said.

'Not exactly,' Smythe said. 'We just don't know what caused it.'

'But you know what it is?'

'It is sleep, Mr Harrison, nothing more, nothing less, other than the lower than normal temperature, that is.'

'And the slightly reduced vital signs,' Parker added.

'But she won't wake up, so it must be something more,' Ed insisted.

'If there is more to it, it is something we are as yet unable to detect.'

'What happened to the others?' Dave asked. His ribs hurt each time he spoke.

'Six of them woke up.'

'And the others?'

'Two died. One of heart failure, the other of hypothermia. The rest are still sleeping.'

'Oh, God,' Marie moaned.

'But there is no reason why that should happen to Sally,' Parker said quickly. 'We are keeping a close eye on Sally's heat loss and, anyway, the more recent cases are the ones that woke up.'

'How long were they out for?' Ed asked.

'Between five months and two years,' Smythe said.

225

Marie took a shuddering breath and began to sob softly.

Dave remembered Fred Purdue's piggy eyes with the gimlet pupils and wondered if he had had anything to do with it. 'Could this condition be caused by hypnotism?' he asked suddenly.

Parker shook his head. 'It is impossible for a hypnotist to make one do something that is basically against one's wishes.'

Dave wasn't sure about that, but he didn't challenge it.

'So what do we do?' Ed asked. He sounded terribly depressed.

'Well, Mr Harrison, we have lots more tests to run on Sally. At the moment we are sure she is quite safe, but we don't know when she will wake up. There are several things we intend to do to try and stimulate her into wakefulness.' He looked at Marie who was hiding in her handkerchief again. 'Don't worry Mrs Harrison, I'm sure we'll be able to wake her in the very near future,' he said.

When Ed and Marie finally left Dave stayed behind to be alone with Sally.

He spoke to her for a time, hoping that the sound of his voice might rouse her. He told her about the disastrous measuring trip to AdventureLand, and he moaned about his bruises and his painful ribs. He waved his cut hand in front of her closed eyes and asked her to please kiss it better.

Sally did nothing. She just lay there, still and quiet. There were no movements at all, just the slight rise and fall of her chest as her slow, shallow breathing continued.

'Wake up Sal, I don't think I can do it alone. I've got to measure the Ghost Train and I can't go back again. Not alone. I *need* you, Sal. C'mon, wake up now,' he said.

The cardiac monitor bleeped slowly, evenly. Somewhere at the back of the room a pen slid back and forth across a continuous flow of paper, recording Sally's beta waves.

Dave reached out and took one of Sally's hands, peeling it away from the other. It felt as cold as ice. Her arm was limp but her fingers were straight and stiff. Dave massaged her hand, trying fruitlessly to bring some warmth back into it. After a while, he pinched the skin on the back of her hand, hoping to get some kind of a reaction, but knowing there would be none. Finally he worked up enough courage to lean over and plant a kiss on those chill lips. It was like kissing a corpse. Sally didn't wake. Perhaps she would never wake again.

Dave cried. Then he prayed – something he hadn't done since he was a little boy. He didn't really think there was anyone up there listening to him, and he knew that at times like this everyone did the same thing, but he still did it.

Afterwards, he sat and looked at Sally and wondered about Fred Purdue and the Ghost Train and the skeleton that had made Phil and Judy disappear. If all this really had happened, and this wasn't just a protracted nightmare, that stuff was evil. And it followed that if there was an evil force making all this happen, there might also be a force on the side of right and good. If there was, he needed its help, and he needed it right now. He prayed some more.

But there was no answer.

The police were waiting for him when he got home. Two CID men in plain clothes who wanted to ask him about Phil and Judy. They grilled him for over an hour before they left him alone. They seemed to be of the opinion that Judy had talked Phil into eloping with her and that he and Sally knew exactly where they'd gone and why. Dave pointed out to them that both his friends were over the age of consent, but they didn't seem to be very interested in that. He repeated the story of the Ghost Train over and over again, but the men didn't want to hear it. What they wanted to hear were stories of pregnancy and abortion, or of debt troubles or of anything related to crime. They left, promising they would be back and assuring Dave darkly that they would get to the bottom of the matter.

Dave spent the remainder of the afternoon checking the program that calculated the size of the Ghost Train. There were no mistakes in it. All he had to do was furnish himself with the final proof that Fred Purdue's ride was the centre of all this, and then he would act.

He was already quite sure that there was something dreadfully wrong inside the Ghost Train – he didn't need the figures to tell him that – but he was back-pedalling. He was aware that he was just putting the moment off when he would have to go back inside, but he insisted to himself that he had to *know* for sure first. He wouldn't admit to himself that he was hoping to be able to prove himself wrong about the whole thing, but deep down he knew that this was what it was all about. If he could prove that the ride could take more than five minutes, he wouldn't have to go back in.

At six thirty, he pushed his plate aside and told his parents that he was going out.

'Can't you eat a little more?' Doreen asked, looking at Dave's almost untouched meal. 'You'll make yourself ill if you don't eat. You've got to stay strong David. For Sally. What good will it do if both of you are in hospital?'

'I'm not hungry,' Dave said. 'I'm sorry, but I can't eat. Look, I've got to go out.'

'Where to Dave?' Reggie asked.

'I've got to report the crosses missing for one thing. Then I'm going to the Dragon to see if anyone has seen Phil or Judy.'

But Dave didn't make it to the Dragon.

As he passed the entrance to the car park at the top of Sarum Hill, an arm snaked out and wrapped itself tightly around his neck. The blood pressure inside Dave's head seemed to increase fourfold as the strong arm squeezed and pulled him backward; his vision darkened and his ears sang; the various bruises around his face started to ache agonisingly. The pressure increased until his vision went completely and he thought his head might explode.

He struggled as the noises of the world faded in his ears, but his breath was trapped in his lungs and getting very old so there was no possibility of screaming for help, no point in trying to fight the pressure which was dragging him backwards into the car park.

The strong arm around his neck tugged him along and his heels bounced on the tarmac as he went. He was only conscious of this now; the feeling of weightlessness in his feet as they hit the ground and floated upwards again.

The grip on his neck loosened slightly and something hard hit him in the back. The corkscrew pain flared in his kidneys for an instant and then the pressure on his neck was gone. He gasped in air and hot blood coursed up into his head with a power that unbalanced him. Still blind and semi-conscious, he slid down the smooth, hard thing that he had been propped against until he was in a crouching position. He wanted to bring his arms up and cover his face against the blows that he knew would shortly be coming, but they were way out there to the sides, somewhere a million miles away where he couldn't get to them. He tried to wave them about, to gain control over them again. Time was running out.

Footsteps. A jingling noise like car keys. A voice swearing. He knew the voice but couldn't place it. More steps. A car door opening. Dave swooned and soared through space. He was falling and about to hit the ground at a great speed when the strong arms grabbed him under the armpits and caught him. He was yanked violently to his feet and his vision started to return. The outline of the car park could be seen now, although it was dark like a black and white negative and reeling back and forth in time with the drumming in his ears. He had somehow got to the back end of the car park and he couldn't remember how.

Gradually the scene brightened and took on colour. It was greyish and washed out at first but it rapidly lightened. His head hurt and the cut on his hand was throbbing like crazy.

'C'mon Foureyes, you're all right!' a smooth voice said from just behind his ear. 'Just get in the fucking car.'

More noises. The world spun and Dave hit something soft and springy. It was cool against his face, and his nose was filled with the smell of leather and engine oil. Then he was jolted about, his face bouncing against the springy surface. A door slammed.

'Okay, cunt, you can wake up now,' the familiar voice said.

Dave was hauled into an upright position. A hard hand slapped his face. Not with enough power to damage him, but with enough to sting. Dave opened his eyes.

And found himself face to face with Roddy Johnson.

'We meet again, Foureyes,' Roddy sneered.

'Oh,' Dave said. He suddenly and clearly knew what was happening. He was sitting in the back of Roddy Johnson's blue Vauxhall Victor with Roddy, who looked big and mean. The Vauxhall was parked well away from the road and there was only one other car in the car park. The doors would be locked. Roddy wouldn't have neglected that, not after all those times Dave had escaped him. He looked around the interior of the car for some kind of help, still surprised at finding himself in here. He'd seen the Vauxhall many times from the outside, but had never expected to be in it. The car was famous around the town, mainly for the crash bar Roddy had made up and welded to the front. Where the front bumper used to be, there was now a structure made of three inch square, steel girders which covered the whole area of the lights and radiator grille. Dave knew that the crash bar was painted with Red Oxide primer and bore battle scars in several places. Rumour had it that when you cut up Roddy Johnson, your car would shortly die. The car tilted slightly towards the front because Roddy had jacked the back suspension up. It ran on huge BF Goodrich tyres, and the back axle casing (which could be seen when you followed the car up the road) was painted with the Stars and Stripes and had extra brake lights fitted. The inside of the car was trimmed in red leather with white piping and the carpets were a matching shade. The steering wheel was tiny and made from maple and chrome. Two fluffy black dice hung from the rear view mirror. According to Phil, the engine had been tuned and the Victor was very fast.

There was no escape. Roddy had him now, good and proper. Soon, it would be beating time. Dave sighed.

'What's up, Foureyes? You're pale. You scared?' Roddy mocked.

'Yeah,' Dave said. He felt weary and old. He wondered if another beating would kill him. He looked away from Roddy, stared over the front seats at the small chromed gearchange with the wooden knob. It had a little Vauxhall motif set in the centre of it.

Roddy's hand caught his bottom jaw, thumb on one side and fingers on the other. He turned Dave's head around to face him.

'What do you think then, Foureyes?' Roddy said.

'About what?' Dave said, looking away from Roddy's deep blue eyes.

'About what, he says,' Roddy said, looking at him in disbelief. 'About me capturing you. What the fuck did you think I meant?'

'It hurt,' Dave said.

Roddy smiled. 'Good,' he said. 'Who did you over? That wasn't me. Your shirt lifted when I dragged you over here and you're covered with bruises. Who did it?'

'Fairground people,' Dave said. He wished Roddy would just get it over with and add his marks.

Roddy leaned back against the door and looked at Dave. He took out a packet of Marlboros from his denim jacket and lit one. Dave looked back at him tensely, wondering when it was going to start. Maybe Roddy had something extra special lined up for him. Perhaps he would drive them somewhere quiet and get his flick knife out.

'It's okay, Foureyes, I ain't going to do you up,' Roddy smiled. 'Relax.' He drew on his Marlboro and blew smoke at Dave. 'Want a fag?' he asked.

'Don't smoke,' Dave said. His heart had recovered enough now to start to hammer. It hurt his ribs. If Roddy wasn't going to *do him up*, what *was* he going to do? Murder?

'Don't smoke,' Roddy mimicked. He held the pack out for Dave. 'If you're in my car you smoke,' he said, his voice getting dangerous.

'I don't want to be in your car,' Dave said, ignoring the proffered pack.

231

'Shirty little fucker, ain't you?' Roddy said. He leaned forward and peered into Dave's face from a distance of about two inches. 'Smoke!' he shouted.

Dave jumped. Roddy laughed. 'Nearly shit yourself then, Foureyes, dint ya? Take a cancer stick or I'll break your arm.'

Dave took a cigarette and Roddy lit it for him.

'Inhale then, you little shit,' Roddy told him.

Dave sucked on the cigarette, inhaled and choked.

'Puke in my car and I'll make you eat it,' Roddy told him.

They sat in silence and smoked for a few minutes. Dave felt sick and light headed. He was terrified that he might throw up and too frightened to butt the cigarette.

'What happened?' Roddy said finally.

'When?' Dave asked. The adrenalin in his body was turning him to jelly.

'AdventureLand. Saturday. I want to know.'

'Nothing,' Dave said.

'Sandy saw you on the Ghost Train. You were going apeshit. What happened?'

Dave shrugged.

Roddy carefully butted his cigarette in the ashtray. Then his hand snaked out and slapped Dave hard across the face. Dave's cheek stung and his ear rang. He wished he was dead.

'Like that?' Roddy asked.

'No,' Dave said thickly. He thought he might cry in a minute.

'Tell me then.'

'What?' Dave said sadly.

The next blow was a back-hander on the other side of his face.

'I can keep this up all night,' Roddy said, smiling. 'Can you take it all night? What happened?'

'You wouldn't believe me,' Dave said, wincing. The next blow didn't come. Instead, Roddy's face darkened. 'You don't know what I might believe,' he said. 'Tell me.'

Dave was wondering whether to tell Roddy or not, when he was hit again. It was a knuckle blow this time, although Roddy didn't clench his fist or hit very hard. His hand stuck Dave's nose which popped and fizzed like a bottle of champagne being opened. He saw stars and for a moment didn't realise what had happened. Then tears sprang into his eyes. His nose felt numb and hot and he didn't know it was bleeding until Roddy told him he'd better not soil the upholstery. There was a crumpled tissue in his jeans pocket. He got it out and dabbed his nose, alarmed at the amount of blood which was running from it. Then his spirit broke. He felt dreadful and utterly beaten and he didn't want to say it, but his body had had enough. 'Don't hurt me any more,' he pleaded, not able to look Roddy in the face any more. 'I'll tell you everything. Just don't hit me again.'

Roddy raised his hand and Dave drew back, cowering against the door and sobbing into the blood-soaked tissue. 'Little fucking coward,' Roddy spat contemptuously. 'Five seconds. If you don't start talking by then I'll take some of your rotten wimp teeth out of your head!' He began to count down from five.

'My f-friends and I w-went on the Ghost Train,' Dave stammered. 'We came out and they didn't. I th-think someone killed them in there.'

'Who got out besides you?'

'My girlfriend. S-Sally.'

'Who didn't come out?'

'Phil and Judy, our f-friends. I saw someone in there. Someone with a knife.'

'He killed them?' Roddy asked, matter of factly.

'Yes, I mean n-no, I mean I d-don't know. I saw them in the strobes. He was dressed as a skeleton and he was standing on the back of their engine. The knife came down and the lights went out. I didn't see it go in, but they didn't come out of the Ghost Train and their engine had blood on it.'

'Their car came out?'

'Yes and they weren't in it.'

'Then what happened?'

'I caused a scene and the police came. We looked inside, b-but it was different in there.'

'They weren't in there?'

'No, but it was different. It looked all wrong. None of the things I saw were there when I went back in with the police.' He shook his head. 'It's all wrong in there,' he said.

When he looked up, Roddy looked serious. His chin was cupped in his hands and he was staring out of the window. 'You may not believe this,' he said quietly. 'But Jon and Sandy are gone too.'

'Where?' Dave asked. His fear was beginning to subside.

'Same place as your buddies went I expect,' Roddy said, still looking out the window. 'I waited outside while they went on. Their car came out but they weren't in it. What do you mean, it's all wrong in there?'

'It's too big inside. The ride went on for too long. I worked it out with the computer. It can't take that long. It's not possible.'

'Where does it go?' Roddy asked. He turned to look at Dave. 'You're the clever fucker. Where does it go?'

'Did you go on?'

Roddy nodded. 'I've seen it, too.'

'The rack and the caterpillar thing and the octopus that comes down?'

'Yeah. Weird, ain't it?'

'It isn't in there. At least it wasn't when I went back.'

'Why did they do you over, Foureyes?'

'I went back to measure the ride. Just to make sure with my computer that it couldn't possibly be so big inside.'

'Get the measurements?'

Dave shook his head.

'You will, Foureyes. We'll go and get 'em tonight.'

'What?'

'What do you mean *what*, you little fucker? Jon and Sandy are in there somewhere. They never came home, did they? Just like your fat buddy and his chick with the tits. They never came out so they're still in there. We'll get your measurements then we'll go in and look for them. Me and you and your chick. We're going in.'

Dave sighed. Now he was going to have to go in. He knew what would happen if he tried to tell Roddy no. If Roddy had

234

decided to go in and take him along, there was no alternative. 'Not Sally,' he said. 'Something's happened to her. She fell asleep and won't wake up.'

Roddy nodded. 'I been watching you, Foureyes. I wondered where she was.'

'Roddy,'

'What?'

'Do you know what it means if we prove it's bigger inside than it is outside?'

'It proves that Fred's Ghost Train is impossible,' Roddy said.

'Does that mean anything to you?'

Roddy shrugged and his face set. 'I got lots of ideas about it. I'm not telling you any of 'em. All I know is, my sister and my best mate are in there somewhere. I'm going to get 'em back. Even if it means killing someone.'

Dave stood outside the park gates at midnight waiting for Roddy. He was wearing the bloodstained overalls and carrying the three cell and the tape measure. He was very scared. Roddy could fight, but there was only one of him and at least four or five hefty roustabouts. George Dale's sons could probably take care of him without having to draft in extra help. And Dave himself would be of no use if it came to a fight. His ribs still hurt, his hand was sore and his ankle had started playing him up where he twisted it last night on the cleat.

Roddy had let Dave go shortly after he'd promised to kill people to get his sister and Jon Kott back, but first he had made Dave swear to turn up at midnight to get the measurements. He had promised to make breaking Dave's bones his life's work if he let him down. Dave didn't want anything to do with Roddy but his intuition told him that Roddy might be of some use in getting the measurements. As for actually going inside the Ghost Train, well, he could think about that later. Best just to take it as it came.

He had gone to the Dragon after meeting Roddy, but no one there had seen or heard from Phil and Judy – not that Dave had

235

expected them to. He was grasping at straws and he knew it. He had drunk two large Scotches then gone to the police station and logged the missing crosses. Nothing had turned up there yet. The duty officer promised to phone him if they were handed in. Dave doubted whether he would ever see them again. And that was another good reason for not going back inside the Ghost Train. He didn't think there was any chance at all of coming out again if he went in without them.

He heard Roddy coming a good long time before Roddy arrived. The night was quiet and the breeze carried the low roar of the Vauxhall all the way from the Black Dam roundabout.

The car arrived a few minutes later and turned into the small parking area next to the Park gates, its engine idling unevenly. Roddy killed the motor and coasted the last few yards into the space. He got out of the car smiling. He was wearing greasy car mechanic overalls and carrying a monkey wrench which he slapped into an open palm as he approached Dave. 'Hiya, Foureyes,' he said. 'Set?'

Dave nodded. Roddy looked businesslike and tough and it gave him a sense of confidence he would never have imagined he could have felt in this kind of a situation.

'Which way shall we go in?' Dave asked. He listed all the possible routes.

Roddy listened impatiently then said. 'Fuck all that creeping about. We'll go straight in through the middle. If they come out and start anything, I'll keep 'em busy. You get the measurements. And if you fuck it up, Foureyes, you'll get this wrapped around your head.' He slapped the monkey wrench into his hand again. It made a dull, meaty thud.

Don't fuck it up, Dave told himself. *He means that.*

Roddy walked past him and strode into the park, not even bothering to look around to see if Dave was following. Dave caught a whiff of gearbox oil mingled with stale sweat as Roddy passed. He stood there for a moment watching Roddy walking jauntily down the tarmac path into the park. His heart was in his mouth and all his bruises and cuts were throbbing. He was suddenly certain that they wouldn't get away with it, and that he didn't want to have anything to do with Roddy Johnson at all – even if his sister and friend had vanished under identical circumstances to Phil and Judy's. Roddy was dangerous. If the fairground people came out tonight, it wasn't going to end up with just cuts and bruised ribs. Quite possibly someone would get seriously hurt. Roddy didn't care what he did. He'd said that he was willing to kill to get Sandy and Jon Kott back, and Dave believed him. He had no wish to be present if the monkey wrench was going to stave in someone's skull. But even worse than that was the possibility that Roddy would injure someone then be overcome by weight of numbers. If one of the roustabouts got badly hurt, his mates would inflict the same kind of damage on Roddy and him if they could.

As Roddy's shape began to merge with the shadows cast by the trees lining the path, Dave seriously considered running away. All the confidence he had felt when Roddy arrived seemed to be vanishing as Roddy disappeared into the darkness. All he had to do now was turn and flee.

And then what, Davey boy? he asked himself. *Spend the rest of your life running away from Roddy? Face up to it, if you're going to go back inside the Ghost Train without Sally and without the crosses, there's no one better to go with than Roddy. He may be a bit psycho, but he's on your side at the moment. Stick with it.*

Then his mind was made up for him. 'C'mon shithead!' Roddy's voice called from the darkness of the park.

He went after Roddy into the dark park and followed his silhouetted shape across the grass towards AdventureLand, finally realising that this was another of those inescapable events, another of those things that seemed to have been plotted out for him when he accepted the cross from Sally. He had the feeling that somewhere, someone knew exactly what was happening to him. He hoped that whoever they were they had worked it all out properly.

They walked through the AdventureLand arch into the dark fairground, Roddy leading and keeping right in the middle of the perimeter pathway as they passed the side stalls and rides. At first, Dave thought it was just bravado on Roddy's part that he was keeping well clear of the stands and walking where he could easily be seen should anyone be keeping a lookout, then it dawned on him that this was the sensible thing to do. By keeping to the middle of the pathway, Roddy was precluding any ambush that the fairground people might have planned. They could jump out from the gaps between the stalls, sure, but they couldn't reach him in one movement, so he would have time to ready himself for them. Dave's confidence level rose again when he realised this and he confessed to himself a sneaking admiration for Roddy's knowledge of tactics.

They stopped in front of the Ghost Train and Roddy scanned the surrounding area, checking both sides of the ride and the nearby stalls. Not a word had been spoken since Dave fell in behind him at the park gates. Roddy broke the silence. 'Do it, Foureyes,' he said quietly and nodded at the Ghost Train.

Dave fumbled around in his overall pocket and got the tape measure out.

From somewhere on the other side of AdventureLand came the noise of a diesel generator starting up. Dave froze, but Roddy was unimpressed. 'Don't worry,' he said. 'Right on the other side. Won't hear us.'

Dave hooked the claw end of the tape measure on the corner of the Ghost Train's platform and walked backwards to the other end, paying out the steel tape as he did so. When he got there, he realised he couldn't see the numbers engraved on the tape. He crouched down and tried to work the three cell torch out of his overalls pocket. As he struggled to extract it with one hand, the hand holding the tape measure waved up and down. The tape bucked and flapped along its length and the metallic springing noise sounded incredibly loud in the silence.

'Shut it up,' Roddy hissed. Then he added, 'What the fuck are you doing, you stupid bastard? Just measure it.'

Behind the Ghost Train, a caravan door opened. Deep laughter issued forth along with the sound of a radio playing the Troggs old sixties hit 'Wild Thing'.

The three cell finally came out of Dave's pocket. It came out suddenly and the excess motion made the tape rattle again. Dave dropped the three cell as he tried to still the tape. It hit the ground and against all the odds, turned itself on. The beam shone straight past the gap at the end of the Ghost Train and he knew that it could be seen from the caravan directly behind, should anyone care to look.

The sound of milk bottles being knocked over came from behind the Ghost Train, and the raucous laughter increased. The laughter was joined by a female voice. Milk bottles clattered and the woman shouted good-naturedly. Dave thought it sounded like Sean and his girlfriend or wife or whatever she was.

Roddy got the torch. He pounced on it while Dave was listening to the clatter of glass bottles and wondering if they were going to spot the beam. Roddy noiselessly fell on the torch, then got up again. When he did, the light was off. 'Cunt,' he breathed from the darkness by the gap between the rides.

He slapped the torch back into Dave's hand. Shielding the beam, Dave turned it on again and read the measurement from the steel tape. The Ghost Train was forty-three feet six inches across the front. Dave's mind reeled for a second with the enormity of the knowledge. He knew then that it had been a waste of time coming back to measure up. His figures had been close enough. The inside of the Ghost Train was now proven to be bigger than the outside. The Ghost Train was an impossibility.

'Let's go,' he said, turning the torch off again.

'Finish it first,' Roddy hissed.

'It doesn't matter now,' Dave said. 'I know enough.'

'Do it,' Roddy commanded. 'Measure the rails.'

'But it doesn't . . .'

'Do it, Foureyes, or I'll let you taste this wrench!' Roddy said, producing it and waving it near Dave's face.

Dave went over to the steps up to the platform, climbed them silently.

He felt very exposed up there on the empty Ghost Train, but he pushed his worries aside and measured the rails. They were

239

three foot six wide, just as he had postulated. He wound the tape back in and returned to the ground.

The caravan door slammed behind the Ghost Train and the music stopped.

Roddy was waiting at the bottom of the steps. 'Do the side,' he threatened.

Dave crept down the side of the ride and hooked the tape measure on one of the boards making up the back side. Sean's caravan was right in front of him as he stood there, the end window looking right down at him. The curtains were drawn, but the lights were on. He could hear the muted music playing inside. He retreated down the gap, paying out the tape again. He was just about to turn on the three cell and take the reading, when he heard Sean's voice.

'Okay, stop just where you are,' Sean said.

Dave looked up from his crouched position on the ground, and his heart sank. Sean was standing in front of him, right where Roddy should have been. Roddy had vanished. Dave considered fleeing the other way down the gap. He glanced back toward the end of Sean's caravan and saw that exit was blocked too. Another roustabout was silhouetted in the light from the caravan's window. This one looked even bigger than Sean.

'Who is it, Sean?' another voice asked. This one bore an Irish accent.

'Is it the guy from last night?' yet another voice asked.

'It most certainly is,' Sean said. 'Sorry old mate, but you are about to get yours,' he told Dave. 'Get up and come out here.'

Dave got to his feet, winding the metal tape measure back in the case. He didn't realise he was doing this. His mind was screaming out at Roddy who hadn't proved to be as tough as everyone thought he was. At the first sight of trouble Roddy had left. What a hard man!

The three roustabouts surrounded him when he came out of the gap, and the fourth was picking his way between the guy ropes in the gap, making his way out too. All three of the men were three sizes bigger than Dave, all of them looked extremely tough. Dave didn't recognise any of them except Sean.

Sean grabbed the front of Dave's overalls and drew him close. 'Didn't get enough last night then, fucker?' he asked. His breath smelled of onions again. Distantly, Dave wondered if he ate the same thing every day of his life.

'Came back for some more,' the Irishman said.

'What were you doing, eh?' a third man asked, looking into Dave's face over Sean's shoulder. This one was big. He looked like he might be related to Fred Purdue, but he was too old to be his son. *Brother perhaps*, Dave thought crazily.

'What do you keep coming around here for, son?' the man asked. 'What is it you're looking for?'

'People all over the fucking place just lately,' Sean said.

'Yeah,' the fourth man agreed. 'Like that fucking loony looking for his son that got kidnapped. We'll do the same to this one as we did to him, shall we?'

'And what happened to him?' the Irishman asked.

'This!' Sean said, and brought his knee up into Dave's groin.

Dave's balls and penis felt like they had exploded and the terrible agony surged up into his intestines. Dave groaned. From somewhere just behind Sean came a hollow sound like the wooden balls had made when they hit the coconuts the other day.

The Irishman yelled and collapsed in an untidy heap.

'Hi, guys,' Roddy said calmly. The monkey wrench was held loosely in his right hand.

Sean let go of Dave and Dave doubled up, clutching his guts. His penis felt hot and wet and he dimly wondered if that was blood running from it or urine. He looked up just in time to see Sean throw a punch at Roddy's face. Roddy's timing was impeccable. He leaned over at exactly the right moment and exactly the right distance for the punch to miss him. But he didn't leave it at that. He caught the arm that sailed by his head and pulled it around the back of his neck, dragging Sean towards him, using the momentum of the punch to keep the man moving. Then his head bobbed down so that the top of it was in the way of Sean's rapidly approaching face. Sean's face

241

bounced off Roddy's head. Blood sprayed from his nose as he fell to the ground.

Someone kicked Dave in his bruised ribs then and this new pain diverted his attention from his crotch.

The man that looked like Fred Purdue's brother charged at Roddy, yelling. Roddy sidestepped and kicked his legs from under him. The man slid across the grass and crashed into one of the darts stalls' kick-boards. Roddy spun to finish the job and the fourth man ran up behind him. This one was armed with a four by two piece of wood. He swung hard and caught Roddy on the turn. The wood hit him in the small of the back and Roddy went down without making a sound.

That's it, Dave's mind screamed. *It's all over! We've had it now!* He struggled to get to his feet, but the hot pain shot through his ribs, making his movements slow and agonising.

The man with the wooden joist stood over Roddy. He raised the wood as Roddy tried to get up. Dave didn't see what happened next, it was just a blur through his tear-filled eyes, but Roddy's hand shot up and the man doubled up and began to scream.

Roddy leapt to his feet and ran across to Dave.

'Get up, fucker!' he shouted. 'We've gotta go!' The monkey wrench wasn't in his hand any more, but his flick knife was. The blade was out and it was wet. A drop of the fluid fell on Dave's face as Roddy hauled him to his feet. Dave wiped it off and looked at it. It was blood.

'Run,' Roddy said, starting into an easy jog.

Dave found he could run very fast, in spite of the pain in his ribs and groin.

Back in the main area of the park, Roddy headed for the trees. He stopped after a while and waited for Dave to join him.

'Get the measurements?' he asked.

'Yeah,' said Dave breathlessly. 'But I didn't need them. My figures were close enough.' He looked over at Roddy who was wiping the blade of his flick knife on his overalls. 'What happened?' he asked, knowing that Roddy had stuck the knife in

the man with the four by two and hoping that it was just a
a haphazard slash that had made the man scream so.

Roddy shrugged and smiled, showing his teeth. His grin
looked evil in the dim light. His eyes had that dangerous look
Dave had seen in Sally when the cross zapped her. Except that
Sally's eyes didn't possess the malevolence that radiated from
Roddy's.

'Had to,' Roddy said. 'He was going to crack my fucking
skull with that wood.'

'You stabbed him?'

'In the bollocks, Foureyes. He won't be fucking any chicks
for a good long time,' Roddy smiled. He clicked the knife shut
and pocketed it. 'Whaddya think?'

'What about?' Dave grimaced. His ribs were hurting like
hell.

'About going inside tomorrow.' Roddy said.

Chapter Ten
The Other Side Of Dead

Anne Cousins woke up fighting. A sheer terror had suddenly descended on what had been the first solid eight hours she'd slept for over a fortnight. Her sleep had been dreamless and velvety black, and what the horror was that woke her, she didn't know. She came awake punching and kicking and when her eyes opened, for a few seconds she didn't recognise her surroundings.

Then she remembered she was in the Ladbroke Lodge motel in Basingstoke and, although her heartbeat took a long time to return to normal, the terror faded almost instantly, leaving a warm, sure feeling that everything was going to be just fine.

Although the room faced away from the morning sunshine, the temperature was almost unbearable and she was drenched with sweat. She threw back the sheets and sat up on the bed, remembering that she'd slept with the windows closed last night and remembering why.

AdventureLand was too near, *that* was why. A five minute walk across the common and past the football pitches would bring her to the funfair where she had spent yesterday evening walking through the stalls and rides, hoping to see her husband. She had spoken to no one, but some of the fair people had looked at her as if they recognised her. She knew it was probably paranoia on her part but she had still been too frightened of what *might* happen to sleep with the windows open.

There had been an atmosphere surrounding Adventure-Land. She had become very sensitive to atmospheres over the past fortnight and the one around the fair was dirty and threatening. The air seemed to be thick with nastiness just waiting to happen.

But that was last night in the sultry summer heat and the flashing-light-filled rowdiness of AdventureLand. Now, sitting on her bed in the bright little motel room, everything felt as if it was going to be okay.

Anne got up and opened the windows, hoping for a cooling breeze. The air was still outside, and the heat haze was already rising from the car park although it was not yet eight thirty. She watched two business types – a man and a woman – loading document cases and overnight bags into the boot of a Granada. The man was thin and in his early fifties, the woman much younger – probably his secretary, Anne thought. As she spied on them, the woman bent over to load a case and the man goosed her. The woman shot up and hit her head on the over-hanging curve of the boot. She turned to the man – whose face had taken on a sheepish look – and began to tell him what was what, her face like thunder and her finger wagging furiously at him. Anne smiled to herself and realised how good it was to feel normal. Now she had finally made the decision to do what was necessary and find Derek, her guilt had vanished.

She padded to the bathroom, deciding to take a shower before breakfast. And that was another thing. Her appetite had made a miraculous recovery since she had walked out and left her mother.

Standing in the cool rain of the shower, she thought about Derek. He wasn't at the fair last night, she was sure of that. She had spent more than two hours wandering through the stalls peering at faces and wondering which one of them knew where Tommy was and which of them Derek had questioned. There was a possibility that Derek had vanished off the face of the earth in the same way that her son had, but she didn't allow herself to think such thoughts. And anyway, just because she hadn't spotted Derek in the crowded funfair, it didn't mean that he *wasn't* there – he may have been doing the same thing as she was on the other side of the fairground, unwittingly matching her pace so they never caught one another up. Nothing would have happened to Derek; he knew how to take care of himself. She would find him tonight and together they would get Tommy back.

It was in the restaurant, halfway through her second fried egg, that she remembered the man from the Ghost Train. She had been mentally listing the faces she had seen last night and deciding who looked like a possible child-snatcher. She had walked past the Ghost Train three times, but it wasn't until now that she remembered the man she'd seen in the pay booth when she first went to AdventureLand. The huge man hadn't been in the box last night. The man taking the money yesterday evening was sandy-haired and in his mid-twenties, she could remember his face clearly. He hadn't looked like a potential kidnapper but the older man, the one she'd seen on the first visit, did.

As she delicately removed the fat from a pink rasher of bacon, she re-formed the fat man's image in her mind. By the time she had assembled him like a photo-fit picture, plucking his features from thin air and slotting them onto that huge balding head, she knew that he had to be the prime suspect. She remembered how he had bellowed at Tommy and how her son had hid behind Derek's legs, looking up at the man with huge, scared eyes. At the time, she had thought Tommy was frightened of what might happen inside the Ghost Train, now she was sure it was the man himself that Tommy had been scared of. She didn't know what she could do about it, even if the fat man was the kidnapper. Would the police take any notice of her? Would they search his caravan if she told them she suspected him? She doubted it. The police would do nothing without some hard evidence to go on, and she had none. It looked like it would come down to sneaking about in the parking area that surrounded the funfair, listening for Tommy's cries or peering through windows on the off-chance of seeing him. That didn't seem very satisfactory, so she resolved to find Derek first and let him handle it. Derek would know what to do.

When she had finished her breakfast, she realised she had a whole day left to fill before AdventureLand opened in the early evening. She could go into the park and look for Derek now, but she doubted that he would be there. He was probably in a hotel like this one having his breakfast and wondering what she was doing. She sent out a mental message to him, apologising and begging his forgiveness. She promised never to do anything like that to him again.

Anne returned to her room. She would go shopping, she decided. She had her real money and the plastic stuff too. Perhaps a few clothes would cheer her up.

But she didn't buy clothes in Basingstoke shopping centre. She bought something else.

Dave sat at Sally's bedside all morning. Sleep had only come to him in fits and starts that night; the image of Roddy's knife hand striking upwards like a cobra into the roustabout's crotch kept coming back to him. Dave knew that Roddy would do that to him, too, if the fancy took him. The crazy look in Roddy's eyes frightened him almost as much as the prospect of going back into the Ghost Train and he thought that someone might die tonight if they went back. He had asked Roddy how they were going to get inside the Ghost Train. Surely all the fairground people would be keeping a lookout for them? They wouldn't just be able to pay their fifty pence admission charge and walk up the steps and climb into an engine. Roddy had just laughed that terrifying low chuckle and said, 'Don't worry about it, Foureyes, we'll get in.'

Once during the night, Dave thought he heard a dog bark. The single bark sounded familiar, and he sleepily told himself that Lucy had heard something unusual. Then he chided himself because there was no dog in the house. Lucy was dead.

He rose early and walked to the hospital. The nurses didn't want to let him in, but he told them that he would be going away for a few days and wouldn't have a chance to see Sally again. He had intended this as a lie, but it was much nearer the truth than he realised. After keeping him waiting for half an hour they had relented, but they said he'd have to be out by lunchtime because Smythe and Parker were coming to run some tests.

When he went in he was shocked to see that Sally was lying on her side. She had moved! A young nurse explained that they had turned Sally. They had to alter her position often to keep her from developing bedsores, she said. They also had to massage her regularly. Dave sat down and watched the nurse rearrange Sally so that she was in what he now thought of as 'the visiting position'.

Sally's tan had almost vanished, and her face looked waxy and pale. In spite of the drip in her arm, she had lost some weight and her cheekbones seemed more prominent, her nose more beaky than before.

Dave began to talk to Sally as soon as the nurse left them alone. He reached out and squeezed her cool hand and told her he'd missed her. Then he leaned over her and tried the old Prince Charming trick again, kissing her soft cool lips. He told her all about his escapade last night and how Roddy was going to make him go along tonight and investigate the inside of the Ghost Train. He told her that he didn't expect to find anything of interest in there – which was a lie – and he told her he wished she could go with him. He explained about the kick he took in the balls and how relieved he was when he found no serious damage. He told her about his sore ribs and the cut on his hand which was now healing nicely, thank you. Sally remained impassive throughout. Once, he thought he saw an eyelid flutter but it didn't happen again and the hope which had flashed through him soon died.

Dave left the hospital at two when the young nurse came back to move Sally. He had already kissed her goodbye and as he walked out into the bright sunlight he suddenly wondered if he would ever see Sally again.

A grim determination settled on him as he walked home from the hospital. The Ghost Train and its owner, fat Fred Purdue, were at the centre of all this and he would make them pay. He would prepare himself.

There was a small yellow nylon rucksack in the attic at home and he climbed up there and got it. Things had to be put in the rucksack. He didn't know why, and the reasons wouldn't come to him when he tried to work them out. All he knew was the rucksack had to be filled. It felt *right*, just like the cross had when it burned on his chest. He had decided to respect these intuitive feelings and act on them from now on. The cross seemed to have left him with some of its strange magic, and he would now do anything that felt right, no matter how outrageous it seemed.

There was money in his hedgehog bank. He had been saving this money for a long time and it was known as his emergency money. His mother had often asked him what emergency he was saving it for and his stock answer was that he would know when the emergency came along. The money had so far survived three Christmases and birthdays and five holidays. Even when Sally's Mini had had all the tyres slashed and her bank account was at an all-time low, she wouldn't let him take a hammer to the hedgehog. Now it felt as if the right emergency *had* come along.

Dave picked up the ceramic hedgehog and took it to the bottom of the garden where he got a hammer from the shed. He stood the hedgehog on the garden path and told it he was sorry. Then he hit it gently with the hammer. Some of its spines broke off, but the hedgehog stayed in one piece. Dave hit it again, harder this time. The money bank shattered. There was more inside than Dave had bargained for. He picked up forty-two pounds seventy-three from the path.

And his silver cross.

He wasn't really surprised to find the cross inside – even though it couldn't have possibly fitted through the coin slot in the hedgehog's back. Even though it couldn't have got back here on its own, and even though he was sure he'd lost it in AdventureLand. Neither was he surprised to find that Sally's cross was missing from its place in the back of his. The message was clear: he was going to have to go without her.

The gleaming red eye of the cross was open again, re-charged and ready for action. He picked it up and put it around his neck, feeling the power and the peace flow through him, just as it had the first time he'd put it on. *Perhaps I ought to take it to the hospital and put it on Sally,* he thought. But he knew he shouldn't. It wouldn't work; it was his cross, not hers. He wasn't supposed to see Sally again, he *knew* that.

He put the hammer back in the shed then returned to pick up the shards of hedgehog. Its pointy little face remained intact and he decided to keep this part. Until now the hedgehog's mouth had been pulled down at the corners so that it looked grumpy, as if it knew you were one day going to smash its head in. Now (and he believed it, simply because it *was*) the hedge-hog was smiling. Its grim mouth looked pleased.

Dave went upstairs and put on the slimfit jeans his parents had got him for his birthday and the Hi-Tec Slammers Sally had given him. That was something else that felt right to do. He transferred the Swiss Army knife and the money from the hedgehog to the trouser pockets of his jeans, and put on a white tee shirt. He put the empty rucksack on his back, went down-stairs and got the three cell from its place under the sink. Then he went back out into the garden to the shed, not knowing why.

There was an old wooden box under the workbench in the shed. It had once been painted olive green, but now almost all the paint had flaked off, revealing the damp wood beneath. Reggie kept all the old tools he didn't use in it and, as far as Dave knew, it hadn't been opened for years. He applied a liberal coating of Three-in-One to the rusty hinges, then levered the lid up with a big screwdriver. Inside the box, amongst the junk, was a selection of rusty saws, a dismantled electric drill, a BSF tap and die set and a lot of broken Dinky toy cars and lorries that had once been Dave's pride and joy. He felt a brief moment of nostalgia when he saw his favourite truck. It was a Bedford car transporter. He touched the cool steel of its cab and smiled. But this wasn't what he was looking for.

The item he had been brought out here to get was in a cardboard box in the corner. As soon as he picked the box up he knew it. Inside was his compass. He remembered Reggie buying it for him when he was eight. They had been on holiday in Falmouth at the time and he had spotted it in a gift shop and spent the remainder of the week worrying at his parents to buy it for him. Reggie had relented on the last day.

He held the compass in his hand and remembered how pleased he had been when his dad had given it to him. The compass was made of brass and was about the size of a pocket watch. It had a flip-up lid covering the glass face and a little ring on the side to tie a string through. Dave had worn the compass around his neck on a length of twine for months. Now, the brass casing had gone green with corrosion. He flipped up the lid and looked at the compass face. Some sort of algae had grown on the inside of the glass, and it was streaked with a greeny- black substance, but the face and the needle were still visible. A few blooms of rust had formed on the end of the needle that wasn't blue and on the face, but that didn't stop it working. The needle tried to swing around to what Dave supposed must be magnetic north, but bottomed out on the rusted white face before it got there. He tilted it, until the needle swung free and then worked out that he was facing north-north-west. If the compass still worked properly, that was. Not wondering why he needed it, he clipped the lid down and put it in his rucksack to keep the torch company. There were a few other things he gathered together from the shed, but he didn't know why he might need these either. When he was done, he walked into town to do some shopping.

Dave passed within fifteen feet of Anne Cousins in Basingstoke shopping centre. He was coming out of Marks & Spencer's food hall when Anne was going in. He had just bought provisions – cans of beans, tins of corned beef and a few packets of crisps. Anne Cousins was going to do likewise. She had just come from Kingdon's hardware shop, where for some reason unknown to her, she had bought herself a new kitchen knife (an eight-inch Kitchen Devil which was identical to the one she had at home) and a wood chisel. From a Cut Price Chemist she had purchased a large bottle of Coppertone suntan lotion, some Airstrip plasters, and a tube of Savlon. She had almost bought a new hairbrush, but had decided against it at the last moment.

When Dave had finished his shopping, he went into the

cafeteria in Owen Owen and ordered plaice and chips and a Coke. He ate the food in a daze, not tasting it at all. Afterwards he still felt hungry, so he bought a portion of apple pie and cream and ate that on remote control, too.

Now he was ready. He walked through the town to the Memorial Park, where he sat on one of the benches that faced the empty bandstand. He felt fit and relaxed. A kind of numb confidence had been building in him all morning and now it peaked. After an hour of mindless sitting he realised he was tired and lay down in the shade behind the park bench.

It was quiet in the park; only the sounds of distant lawn sprinklers and the twittering of birds in the surrounding trees came across the empty expanse of grass. Within five minutes Dave had fallen into a deep dreamless sleep.

Dave was still sound asleep when Anne Cousins walked through the park gates at six thirty. For the second time that day she passed within fifteen feet of him. She saw his sleeping form behind the park bench from a distance and her heart leapt. It wasn't until she was quite close to him that she realised it wasn't her husband Derek at all.

She stood looking at Dave, her plastic Marks & Spencer bag full of shopping in her right hand and her heart in her boots. She shook her head wondering how she could have made such a mistake and got her hopes up so high. *How could you have possibly thought that could be Derek?* she asked herself. *It's only a kid. He doesn't look anything like Derek.*

She turned away and headed across the grass toward AdventureLand, realising that you sometimes saw what you wanted to see rather than what was really there. It took her half an hour to check the perimeter of the funfair and everywhere else she could think of. Derek was nowhere to be found. It didn't look as if he was going to turn up either. Surely he would have been here last night—

Unless—

Unless what, Anne? she asked herself and then she started quickly to recite The Rime of the Ancient Mariner to try and block out the answer. She had learned the poem when she was six and had recited it in the school's Christmas revue. This was the first time she'd tried to recite it since. She was surprised at how it all came back to her. She made it all the way through to the part where the albatross was slain before her mind saw a gap big enough to slip in what it wanted to say to her.

Unless he's over the other side with Tommy, she thought. The Ancient Mariner took a few more faltering steps, cracked into pieces inside her head then dissolved, leaving a picture of a grinning giant for her to consider. The giant wouldn't go away, no matter how hard she tried to bring the poem back.

Derek's over the other side with Tiger, she thought in spite of herself. *On the other side of AdventureLand and you know where that is Annie oh Annie, don't you? The other side of AdventureLand is hell. It's where the bad things live. That's where they are, and that's where you're going to go. You are going to cross the Styx. The river that separates the living and the dead. You've got to go and get them back, Annie; even if it means fighting the giant to get them. That's what it's all about, my girl. Now, you know what you've got to do, so what's keeping you?*

'I'm scared,' she said aloud. 'I'm so scared.' But she turned around and headed back towards the funfair where the generators had started to run and the sound of music drifted over the low throbbing.

There were few people in AdventureLand when Anne walked through the arch and most of the rides weren't yet running. The ones that were doing business were half empty. The Frogger stall's staff hadn't even taken its side shutters down yet. She passed it by, remembering winning a goldfish and losing Tommy. It seemed like years ago.

The Ghost Train drew her like a magnet. She hadn't intended to go there, but she arrived in front of its gaudy facade anyway. She stood there for a minute looking at the horrors inscribed on the walls, knowing that she would have to go in. The sum total of the Ghost Train scared her far more than its various facets should have done. She realised then that this was because it was the *focus*: the centre of the almost palpable evil she had felt before and was feeling now.

But the Ghost Train didn't look all that impressive. Two engines stood on the platform, one red and one white. The roustabouts were perched atop the white one, smoking and waiting for trade. Both of them looked extremely bored. The fat man was in the pay booth, his huge arms folded in front of him and a hand-rolled cigarette dangling from his thick lips. He was the one that really scared her. He had already spotted her and there was a knowing look in those penetrating blue eyes.

He's the one, Annie my girl. He's the prime suspect. The kidnapper. The one who knows where Tiger and Derek are. He's the one that's been doing the bad stuff. That's the person you got the Kitchen Devil for.

She felt a terrible cold hatred toward Fred Purdue and had to fight off an overwhelming urge to take the knife from her carrier bag and sink it into the fat man's neck, right up to the white plastic handle. He deserved that. She felt this intuitively. Even if she didn't know what he'd done or what he was, she knew that he deserved to be stuck through the throat; slaughtered like a rabid animal. She could imagine the look of surprise in his eyes when the knife went in and the blood that would pour from his mouth when he opened it. Perhaps he would talk if she did that. Perhaps Tommy and Derek would come back from wherever he'd made them vanish to.

Purdue caught her eye then and nodded slowly. Anne gasped and put her hand to her mouth, feeling as though her innermost thoughts had been read. She blushed with embarrassment, but her anger towards him increased. It was almost as if *he* was putting those thoughts into her mind.

Her hand went down into the depths of the Marks & Spencer carrier, found the Kitchen Devil. Then she knew that it wouldn't work. Purdue wouldn't let that happen if she was to try it. He was baiting her somehow. Using the power of his mind, perhaps. He *wanted* her to try and kill him. And when she went for him, he would move quickly. The knife would turn through one hundred and eighty degrees as Purdue snapped the bones in her arm. Her head would bob forward and the knife would pierce her left eye, grind against bone, then slip through the socket and into her brain. The pictures formed in her head without her help. They were clean and didn't cause her distress like her feelings of violence had. It was almost as if there was another force putting them there. Not Purdue and not herself, but something else. Something that was on her side. Her hatred vanished and her fear came back.

Purdue winked at her and nodded.

She walked toward the pay booth muttering, 'The Lord is my shepherd, I shall not want, He maketh me to lie down in green pastures . . .'

'You going on lady?' Purdue growled, smiling knowingly.

Anne nodded. *Yea though I walk through the valley of the shadow of death . . .*

'That'll be fifty pence. Normally it's a pound for a single rider, but it's early yet and we ain't very busy, so I'll let you on for fifty.'

. . . I will fear no evil . . . Anne found her purse, opened it and shook. A fifty pence piece appeared above the rest of the coins. She took it out and handed it to Purdue.

Purdue took the coin and looked at Anne carefully. The sausage-like fingers of his other hand tapped three times on the counter.

For thou art with me . . .

'Thanks,' Purdue said, staring into Anne's eyes.

Thy rod and staff, they comfort me . . .

'Take the first car,' Purdue said.

Anne nodded. The words of the psalm died in her mind as though they had been switched off. They left a terrible emptiness which Purdue's corruption threatened to fill at any moment. Anne went quickly up the steps and got in the red engine.

'Enjoy your ride,' the roustabout called after her as the engine gathered speed and careered around the corner towards the first set of doors.

The engine hit the doors and they crashed open, splitting the painted wolfman in two. The strobe lights came on making the skeleton on the inner doors dance. Then she was through and into a long straight corridor. A light pulsed at the far end and Anne could see that the corridor was empty. It was wooden walled and floorboarded. And it was impossibly long.

The red engine trundled toward the distant flashing light and Anne suddenly knew what she had to do.

'Get up, Foureyes!' Roddy toed Dave in the back with his pointed boot.

Dave came awake, his kidneys grumbling in protest at the gentle kick. For a dazed second he wondered what Roddy Johnson was doing in his bedroom, and why his bedroom had got so big.

He sat up, rubbing his eyes and realising that he was in the park and that he could hear the dull noise of AdventureLand working away in the background. That was what he was doing here. They were going in. A small nagging fear started in the pit of his stomach.

Roddy was dressed in his usual attire of jean jacket over white tee shirt, jeans and pointed-toed boots. 'What's with the back pack then, wimp?' he asked.

Dave shrugged. 'Stuff,' he said.

Roddy squatted down beside him. 'What stuff is that?' he said.

'Just things I felt I ought to bring with me.'

'Such as?'

'Food. A compass.'

'A compass?' Roddy scorned. 'What for? Where do you think we're going then?'

'Inside.'

'We ain't gonna get lost in there, squirt. We're coming out again. Tonight. You won't need food and a compass.'

'I'll take it anyway,' Dave said.

Roddy rolled his eyes. '*Jesus*!' he said, exasperated. 'You try and put the shits up me, Foureyes, and I'll slap you.'

'I won't,' Dave promised, realising that Roddy was scared,

too. His confidence level dropped four points on an internal scale. He thought about asking Roddy if he was scared and then thought better of it. Roddy would probably hit him by way of a reply. He wasn't the kind of person who would talk about his innermost fears.

'Come on then, we ain't got all night,' Roddy said, standing up. 'I got some young clit waiting for me in the pub. I'm on a promise and I'm getting a hard-on just thinking about it.'

'How are we going to get in?' Dave asked, getting to his feet. His stomach felt strangely shrunken considering the food he'd packed away earlier.

Roddy sneered at him. 'You do exactly as I tell you,' he said. 'Leave the thinking up to me. I know how we're going to get in. All you do is what I say. If you fuck it up, the fairground people will get you. They won't get me though, and I'll come after you, too. So just do as I say when I say.'

'But . . .'

Roddy glared at him. 'Shut the fuck up,' he warned.

Dave remembered Billy Bowen's head going through the glass pane in the pub. He shook his head and shrugged.

'That's better, asshole. C'mon!'

Roddy strode away towards AdventureLand and Dave followed.

They didn't walk around the perimeter to the Ghost Train. Roddy led Dave into the fairground on the other side to the ride and cut across through the middle. They stopped when they came to the two darts stalls just across from the ride. A number of people were queuing up the Ghost Train's steps.

'They'll never let us on,' Dave said.

'They might,' Roddy replied. 'If we went over and paid, they might let us in. While we were queuing the word might go around. By the time we got inside, half the guys in the ground would be in there waiting for us with knives and coshes. So, whaddya want to do? Pay, or do it my way?'

'Your way,' Dave said.

'Do exactly as I do,' Roddy said. 'Whatever happens, stay on my tail.'

Dave nodded.

Roddy patted his trousers pockets, buttoned down the flaps on his jacket pockets and ran.

He had gone more than five paces before Dave realised what was going on and started after him.

There was no chance of catching him up. Roddy was big and fast. Dave watched from behind as Roddy launched himself at the crowded steps up to the platform. People scattered and fell over. Those that remained in Roddy's way were wrenched bodily from the steps.

The two roustabouts left the car they were pushing and ran toward the steps from the other end of the platform.

Dave arrived at the bottom step just a moment too late. From a distance of three yards he had seen his way up the steps. There was a clear corridor through the people for him to follow. By the time he got there the space had vanished. It was now filled with people trying to keep their places in the queue against the flow of people who were frightened and wanted to get off.

Shit! Dave thought.

'FOUREYES!' Roddy screamed from the platform, searching the crowd for sight of Dave. His fists were balled and held high. He looked extremely pissed off. The two roustabouts were almost on him. One of them – the one called Charlie who had the red devil tattooed on his arm – was carrying what looked like a cricket stump. Dave hadn't noticed him get it.

He tried to push his way through the people on the steps as Roddy had done, but he was too slight and mild-looking and no one took any notice of him in the confusion. He gave that approach up when someone poked him hard in the back and told him to '*get to the back of the fucking queue!*'

The front of the platform was the only way up now. It was just below chest height on Dave and he felt sure he could vault up there. But that would bring him up with the roustabouts between him and the entrance doors, and one of them had spotted him anyway and was coming back.

Tattooed Charlie swung the cricket stump at Roddy. Roddy ducked.

Dave took two paces back and launched himself at the platform.

He was in midair when he saw the stump skim across the top of Roddy's head. He hit the platform and rolled.

If he hadn't been wearing the rucksack, he would have rolled right over and been out of range of the second roustabout's feet. But the back pack bit into the wooden platform and stopped him so that he was lying sideways, his face pressed against the smooth bare wood. As he struggled to get to his feet, the roustabout kicked him hard in the back.

Dave screamed.

Anne Cousins ran toward the light.

Her breath was coming in ragged sobs and her lungs felt fit to burst, but she kept on running, just as she had since she got out of the engine. The engine was gone now, lost from view. Five minutes ago, after what seemed like an age of running, she had turned to see if it was still behind her. All she could see was miles and miles of empty wooden corridor with two metal rails running down the centre.

But there was something in that empty space. Something evil that had formed as soon as she'd left the car. She couldn't see it, but she could sense it wanted her. So she ran.

And as she ran, the corridor expanded before her, keeping her the same distance from the pulsing white light of the strobe. She had increased her speed but the corridor just expanded faster and the invisible thing that followed her moved more quickly, too.

It went on and on and Anne ran on and on, hoping that eventually she would come to the end. The blood sang in her ears and her legs were turning to iron, but still she ran. Her lungs began to scream with each breath she drew, and her throat became raw. Her heart was beating far faster than it had ever gone before. It fluttered in her chest like a caged hummingbird.

She tried to jettison the Marks & Spencer bag which swung crazily from her wrist and banged against her side in time with the swinging motion of her body, but her hand had somehow gone right through the handle loops so that it was firmly attached to her wrist. She let go of the top of the plastic bag and it swung more forcefully still, biting into the skin on her wrist.

She tried to recite the psalm to herself as she ran, but the words were gone and far away, sucked into the backwaters of her brain by Fred Purdue's influence. Then she tried the Lord's Prayer.

'Our father,' she hissed, breathing out.

'. . . which—,'

'Our father—,'

'Our father—,'

No more would come. Purdue had apparently wiped that one, too. She stormed down the corridor, keeping in front of the thing chasing her and not gaining on the light at the end of the tunnel.

And the light went out.

Anne ran in total darkness for a few seconds then crashed headlong into a wall. The impact knocked her to the ground and she slid on the wooden floor, skinning her knees and hands. She would have given up there and then, would have just lay there and cried and screamed for help. Except for the low laugh she heard behind her.

It was a sound that was oddly familiar to her. It was a voice that she hadn't heard before, but she knew it just the same. It was the voice she had given to the Devil when she was a four-year-old child. It was the voice she *knew* the Devil would use. And the Devil breathed her name.

Anne got to her feet quickly and ran into the blackness, wanting to scream, but not daring to in case it slowed down her flight.

Then the floorboard under her pounding feet changed to something more uneven. The surface was rough and loose and warm. She could feel the heat through the soles of her shoes.

Then it was light and she wasn't in the Ghost Train any more.

She was in Hell.

The river ran on her left hand side, dark and wide. She had crossed it somehow. Probably the Ghost Train was a way across. She had run right underneath the black waters of the Styx and come out on the Hell side.

She veered away from the river and ran towards the red horizon, knowing that her worst nightmares were true and that Tiger and Derek were being held by Satan himself. The thing that had been herding her this way was gone now, but Anne didn't stop running, although her nose was filled with the stench of brimstone and burning flesh.

The landscape that lay ahead was flat and empty. All that existed was the dark earth and the boiling black sky which turned red on the horizon. She turned once and could no longer see the river. She was now in the centre of a vast desert and the way back had vanished.

Her pace slowed a little and she began to cough. She stopped running and stood there panting in the foul air.

'Help me,' she shouted, when she could manage to control her breath again. 'For God's sake, help me!'

At the word God, thunder pealed and an eye-searing flash of lightning struck the ground in front of her. The ground opened up revealing red molten rock below. The surface began to crack around her feet and she started to run again.

The ground was getting hotter now, burning her feet. To stop again would mean certain death. And the further she ran, the hotter it got. Puffs of fine black ash started to rise with her footsteps, billowing out before her and choking her as she inhaled. She tried to slow down, but the heat beneath her feet was immense and the ground fractured each time she put a foot to it.

She increased her speed even more when her shoes caught fire. Soon, melted plastic scalded her toes and the soles of her feet. She could smell her flesh burning as she ran and the pain was agonising.

She began to totter, screaming with pain. One of her shoes passed too near the hem of her dress and it burst into flame. The fire ran up towards her waist in a slender line, moving like a live thing. Her lower half seemed to be totally engulfed in dirty yellow flames which gave off an acrid smoke. She could feel her nylon panties melting around her, peeling the flesh off as they shrank.

Anne Cousins stopped running.

Her legs folded up beneath her and her raw knees broke the crust of the ground. She screamed as she sank slowly into the boiling fires of Hell.

And the Devil's laughter rang in her ears.

Dave opened his eyes again, just in time to see Roddy crumple to the ground. The pain flared in his kidneys and he knew that he would be pissing blood again tonight.

Charlie Tattoo raised his cricket stump over Roddy, preparing to strike again.

'NO!' Dave yelled in a thunderous voice he didn't even know he possessed. The wooden planks of the platform vibrated with the power of his vocal chords.

Tattoo paused, stump still in the air, and wheeled around to face Dave, a questioning expression on his face. Dave tried to get up and collected another kick in the back. The pain was excruciating. He fell down again and his head hit the floorboards, bounced and hit them again. *That's it, we've had it. We're finished*! he told himself.

Behind him, inside the ride, a siren screamed. The exit doors crashed open and an engine clattered out.

'NO!' he yelled again, ignoring a fresh burst of pain in his back as the roustabout got another good kick in.

'Leave him alone!' someone shouted from the direction of the steps.

Dave managed to get his face off the floor and look over towards the queue. It was a girl who was shouting. She was about fifteen and she looked terrified.

Charlie Tattoo, who was advancing towards Dave, turned and told her to piss off. The girl shouted back that he was a bastard.

The roustabout turned back to where Roddy was lying, raising the stump over his head like he really meant business this time. Dave saw the man's muscles flex in his arm.

'RODDY!' Dave bellowed. Fresh pain burst in his back and his vision blurred. Distantly he wondered why nobody was coming to save them. The fairground people were clearly intent on beating them to death in front of at least thirty witnesses. That wasn't possible. Surely it wasn't?

Roddy had been playing dead.

He athletically twisted himself out of the way as the cricket stump came down. It glanced off his shoulder, hit the platform and broke in two. Tattoo didn't get a chance to use it again. Roddy leaned back on his shoulders and kicked a pointed boot into the man's crotch. Tattoo dropped to his knees and doubled up.

Dave's assailant gave him one last kick in the back and ran over to help his mate. Roddy was on his feet now. Dave saw that he'd noted the one running towards him then turned back to the business in hand.

Roddy's knee came up. It wasn't fast, but it caught the kneeling roustabout right in the face. His head snapped back and he fell over backwards, curled into a tight ball. Blood was streaming from his nose.

Dave got to his feet just in time to see the second man plough into Roddy. Roddy didn't dodge this time, just stood there and took the full force of the man's momentum. Dave hurried across the platform, expecting Roddy and the roustabout to both fall to the ground. But Roddy absorbed the blow, taking one pace backward as the man hit him. Then they just stayed there locked in one another's arms like long lost brothers, their heads on each other's shoulders.

Fred Purdue was out of the pay booth now and picking his way through the crowd of people on the steps, a grim expression on his heavy jowled face. The sunlight flashed on the red stone of his ring.

Roddy let go of the roustabout when Dave drew level with him. The man slid to the ground, his eyes closed. There was no blood, but he looked terribly pale. Dave wondered if Roddy had asphyxiated him somehow.

'Hey!'

Purdue was at the top of the stairs. There was a steak knife in his left hand.

'Run, Foureyes,' Roddy said smiling. He looked as if he was enjoying himself. That malevolent gleam was back in his eyes again and for a second Dave wondered if Roddy was an incarnation of the evil thing he was up against and not on his side at all.

Roddy turned and ran towards the entrance doors, Dave following hot on his heels. Behind them, Purdue was giving chase. He moved with surprising speed for such a huge man, but they were too far away for him to catch them.

Roddy hit the Ghost Train doors, his arms outstretched before him. The doors flew open and the two of them shot through into the darkness.

They came to a halt in front of the second set of doors.

'Ready, Foureyes?' Roddy said.

'Yes,' Dave replied. He wished Roddy would hurry up and go through. At any second now, Purdue would burst in through the doors waving his steak knife. There were no witnesses in here to see. *None that could stand up in court and testify, anyway,* Dave told himself.

'There's something I've been meaning to ask you, Foureyes,' Roddy said from the darkness in front of Dave.

'What is it? Hurry up, Roddy, Purdue will be in here in a minute.'

Roddy didn't answer straight away, and Dave stood two paces to his left, reasoning that if Purdue came in brandishing the knife, he might just run straight past him. After a few more seconds, he realised that Purdue wasn't coming in after all, and he began to wonder why. *Perhaps it's because Purdue knows what's waiting for us in here is far worse than anything he could do to us,* he thought. The darkness made him feel dizzy, and his cut hand felt hot and wet – probably the fight had made it bleed again. Suddenly he couldn't bear the dark any more and he had to know what his cut was doing. He slid an arm out of one of the rucksack's loops and swung it around in front of him. He managed to get his hand inside without undoing the ties that held the top flap down, but the three cell torch was too big to fit through the gap. Cursing silently, he pulled the knotted strings apart and took out the torch.

Roddy sounded embarrassed when he spoke. 'It'll be alright Foureyes, won't it?' he said.

What are you asking me for? Dave thought. All he could think of was how he didn't want to fall over and how he would if he didn't soon see something. *How the hell should I know if it will be alright?* he thought. 'What do you mean?' he asked.

'The rails. I don't want to get electrocuted or anything. They won't be switched on, will they?'

'There are no electric rails,' Dave replied. 'It's mechanical. At least I *think* it's mechanical.'

'Okay,' Roddy grunted. 'But if I get a shock, it had better do me in because I'll take your balls off otherwise.'

Dave turned the three cell on, casting a pool of yellow light into the darkness. The inner doors were right in front of them. The painting of the skeleton with the Bowie knife looked old and badly drawn. Dave couldn't imagine how the strobe lights could animate it so. He shone the torch at the inside of the outer doors which were just plain wood, and then at the side walls which were made from dirty canvas, strung with rope at the top and pegged into the floor with loops and hooks.

'Inside?' he asked.

'You go first, chicken shit,' Roddy said, stepping aside. 'And don't blind me with that fucking torch.'

Dave walked up to the inner doors and pushed them open. A cool draught wafted out. The air smelt stale and tainted. He stepped through and turned right into the long enclosed corridor.

They walked along keeping between the rails, their footsteps banging noisily on the floorboards. Dave expected the skeleton with the knife to jump out in front of them at any second and he was ready to dodge at a moment's notice.

They reached the far end of the corridor without incident. After the line of dangling wet cloth, they followed a sharp turn to the left at the end of the corridor and passed the model of the man with his intestines hanging out, then they turned right.

'Hey, Foureyes,' Roddy called from behind him, 'spooky ain't it?'

The track straightened out again and began to go downhill. *This is it*, Dave told himself. *This is where it all starts*. The torch beam shone out into the vast emptiness that lay before them.

'It's too far!' Roddy complained. 'This ain't possible. Is it?'

'It's here,' Dave replied.

'Getting chilly, too,' Roddy said. He didn't sound quite so brave now, Dave thought. At last Roddy Johnson was out of his depth. His internal confidence register dropped another two points with that thought.

They followed the track into the darkness, trudging along slowly and quietly. Dave didn't want to have to speak any more if he could avoid it. Roddy's voice sounded like it was coming to him from a long way away, and even his own voice sounded distorted in his ears.

That was when the siren sounded and the strobes came on.

'JESUS!' Roddy shouted. Both of them ducked. The empty corridor reeled in front of them, its shape and dimensions altered by the powerful flashing lights.

Dave staggered sideways and hit something hard. *The wall, it's only the wall*! he told himself.

'WHAT THE FUCK IS HAPPENING, FOUREYES?' Roddy shouted from behind him.

The wall behind Dave slid away and he staggered through the gap, unable to stop himself. 'Here!' he shouted. 'In here!'

The three cell dimmed and went out.

The siren died and the flashing lights stopped. From his position just inside the new corridor, Dave could hear Roddy crashing about outside.

'Where the fuck are you?' he screamed.

'Here!' Dave shouted. '*I'm in here!*'

Then Roddy was on top of him, grabbing his shirt. 'For Christ's sake, what did you do that for?' he yelled shaking Dave until his head rattled. Dave thought Roddy was going to hit him, but he was released and pushed roughly away.

'I couldn't help it,' he said. 'I just sort of fell through and the torch went out.'

'Well, let's get the fuck out of here. Get back out on the main track. Too fucking chilly in here, man.'

'I don't think we can.'

'Whaddya mean?'

'It seems to be some kind of a one-way door. The torch was on when I came in but even then I couldn't see how I'd come through. It just looked like a plain wall. I didn't think you could get in.'

'Switch the torch on,' Roddy commanded. 'We got in, we can fucking well get out again.'

Dave stabbed at the three cell's on button. It was depressed already. He banged the torch against his hand, admonishing himself for not getting new batteries for it today. The bulb lit, but the light was faint and reddish. The torch was suddenly yanked from Dave's hands.

'Give it here, dickhead,' Roddy said. He pointed it in the direction they had just come from and found a plain, seamless wooden wall in front of him. 'That's not possible. There was a hole there a minute ago. It's some kind of a trick!'

'A good trick too,' Dave said sourly.

'Shaddup!' Roddy began feeling the panel, probing the edges and pushing it here and there. 'It's a swinging door,' he announced. 'Like you see in the films. Y'know, it rotates.'

'There's no gap around it,' Dave told him. 'I can see that from here.'

'There *is*!' Roddy shouted, sounding like a spoiled child. Then: 'I just can't open it, that's all.'

Dave looked over at Roddy and saw his breath blooming out in the dim light of the torch. The temperature had dropped severely since they came in here. And the rotting smell had increased.

'What *is* that?' Roddy asked, looking over his shoulder and shining the torch at Dave. 'Did you shit yourself?'

Dave didn't answer. Because his cross was getting hot and something had started to scratch at the other side of the panel blocking their way. The scratching became louder until it was a regular squealing scrape, like fingernails on a blackboard. Dave could hear the wood on the far side begin to splinter.

THE CLAW!

He could visualise the ebony nails cutting the wood away, the tendons standing out on the shiny black skin. Whatever was attached to The Claw was probably out there too. This wouldn't just be the hand part of it, this would be the whole thing. It was out there and it wanted to get in.

'What the fuck is that?' Roddy said nervously.

'We can't go back that way,' Dave said. 'It's The Claw. It wants to get us.'

'The *what?*'

'Forget it. *We just can't go that way*!' Dave yelled. 'C'mon!'

He started down the new corridor, jogging along quickly so that the fear wouldn't freeze him and keep him there watching the wood splinter and the hand come through. Roddy followed.

The track branched three times. Dave chose the left hand fork on each occasion, letting his intuition guide him. There were rails for the Ghost Train engine set into the floor, but Dave hadn't seen this part of it before. This wasn't the way he and Sally had come when the skeleton got Phil and Judy, nor was it the way he'd come with the policemen. He tried to calculate how it could exist as he trotted into the darkness, but was forced to give up. The answer that kept coming to him was simple: it *couldn't* exist. Unless they had crossed over into another dimension or something and he couldn't comprehend what that meant. Nor did he want to.

'Wait!' Roddy called. 'Listen!'

Dave stopped. He could hear the distant rumble of an engine approaching, its click-clacking muted. It rolled around the corner from behind them. Its front light was on and blinded Dave as it approached.

'Get to the side!' Roddy shouted.

Dave pressed against the wall beside Roddy. The gap between them and the engine was just about big enough for it to pass without hitting them.

Dave groaned.

'What?'

'What if the fairground people are on it?' Dave said. *And what if The Claw is sitting in it? What will you do then, Davey boy?*

'Don't worry,' Roddy said. 'I can handle them.'

The engine was empty though. It trundled past them slowly, its left hand edge scraping their knees. Roddy shone the torch into the seat to make sure no one was hiding in there. 'Let's get in!' he said, starting off after the engine.

'We can't!' Dave said breathlessly as he ran along behind.

'Why not, dickhead?'

'It's white!'

'So what?'

'It's the death engine. They've only got one white one and this is it. Phil and Judy were on it when they vanished. So were Jon Kott and your sister, I should think.'

'All the more reason to get on!' Roddy called back as he leapt onto the engine's back bumper. 'We want to find them, don't we?'

Dave jumped on too. The cross told him that Roddy was right by scalding his chest until he was safely on the bumper next to him.

The engine turned right and slowed in front of the worm thing Dave had seen on his first trip. It extended its slimy-ridged body and looked at them with its baleful eye. 'It's a model, too,' Roddy said uncertainly. 'Fuck off!' he shouted at it.

The worm drooled on the front of the engine. 'Uck off!' it grated. It blinked its eye, and the engine passed it by.

It was in the next corridor that the skeleton man appeared.

The stroboscopic lighting began to flash, burning an after-image of the empty corridor onto their retinas, and Dave couldn't be certain where the skeleton man had jumped out from. He did the same thing as last time though, leaping onto the front of the engine and crawling up towards them.

'It's the guy in the skeleton suit!' Dave said. 'We must be near the end!'

The man crawled up the tank of the engine and got into the seat.

Dave heard the familiar metallic *click* and realised that

Roddy's flick knife was out and ready. 'Get off,' he growled.

The skeleton man stood up in front of them, his skull face inches away from theirs. The Bowie knife was in his hand.

'Fuck off!' Roddy shouted.

The skeleton raised the Bowie. Each inch of its movement was burned onto the back of Dave's eyes by the regular blinding flashes of the overhead strobe light.

Roddy struck at the skeleton man first, his right arm snaking out so fast that Dave only had time to collect two flashes of it as it moved. First it was next to Roddy's waist, then it was there in the centre of skeleton suit's stomach. Except that there was no stomach there for the flick knife to sink into. The knife went right through, pulling Roddy off balance with its lack of resistance, and struck the skeleton man's spine. Dave heard the clatter of steel striking bone and saw the knife skid off the skeleton's backbone in jerky movements. Roddy yelled.

It's not a suit! Dave thought, his mind reeling as the skeleton's bony hand clamped down on Roddy's wrist. *It's not a suit, it's for real! The skeleton is REAL!* Through the waves of horror at being face to face with a live skeleton, he found that he wasn't as surprised as he'd expected to be. Too many weird things had happened already for this to be a real surprise.

His cross began to throb steadily, sending waves of heat across his chest, and he could see the dull red gleam of its eye shining through the fabric of his shirt. His kidneys hurt; the flashes of power from the recharged cross seemed to be stronger than before and they reached right down to his crotch and extended almost all the way around his back. His head felt terribly cool and his thoughts were clear and quick.

The skeleton pulled Roddy's knife hand back from its non-existent guts easily, even though his arm was straight and locked at the elbow. Roddy shouted as his arm bent and tried to pry the skeleton fingers away from his wrist with his other hand. Dave saw him slump forward as the skeleton suddenly reversed the direction of its thrust and dragged his hand clear through the gap at the bottom of its ribs and out past where its back should have been. Skeletal fingers buried themselves in

Roddy's hair and dragged his head over the seat, exposing the back of his neck. The Bowie knife flashed high in the strobes.

'No!' Dave yelled. He struck wildly at the skeleton's jawbone with the back of his left hand and shouted with pain as his hand bounced off. Blood flowed from his knuckles and there was a smear left on the skeleton's grinning countenance.

The Bowie started to fall. At each flash of the lights it was a little lower.

'Stop it!' Dave screamed and struck again, at the arm bones this time. The Bowie was deflected by the blow and sliced into the seat back. The skeleton glanced over at Dave, regarded him through deep empty eye sockets, then turned its attention back to Roddy's squirming figure.

Dave launched himself at the skeleton before the Bowie had time to rise again. His fingers looped through its ribcage and he pulled, hoping to take it off its feet. He fought his revulsion at holding onto cold, bare bone and pulled as hard as he could, his biceps bulging, his mouth frozen into a determined grimace. He felt the cut on his hand pop open again as he strained against the resistance. The skeleton was immovable.

The Ghost Train engine rattled around a corner into a huge empty room lit with dim red lights.

The skeleton struck at Dave with the Bowie as the tight turn loosened his grip. Dave saw the blade cannon toward him and knew he was dead. The knife was going to strike him square in the left temple and drive right into his brain. There wasn't time to bring up a hand to block its passage. He tried to duck and his face smashed into the skeleton's collar bone, puncturing the thin skin just under his right eyebrow.

Dave closed his eyes against the flow of blood that instantly sprang from the wound and waited for the knife to end it for him.

Nancy Willis was tired and her feet felt as if they had swollen again inside her tight leather shoes. That happened a lot in this weather. The inside of the hospital was warm at the best of times and ever since the hot spell had started it had been

271

like a furnace in here, even though the windows were open.

On the way back to the nursing station, she poked her head around the door of the Sleeping Beauty girl's room. There was no change. The girl was in exactly the same position that Smythe and Parker had left her. It didn't look as if the two specialists were going to get her to wake up in the near future after all. She had heard great things about Smythe and Parker, but having met them, she had to admit that great men they might be, but she didn't like either of them very much. They were both a bit *too* clever, and both were masters of the art of the cutting remark.

She did feel very sorry for the Harrison girl though. They were almost the same age and she could identify with her. What must it be like to suddenly fall asleep and never wake up? She shuddered and put the matter out of her mind. This was easy to do; nurses weren't supposed to get involved with the problems of the patients, and after the incident at training college with the old man that had died, she had discovered why. It was much too painful to become tied up in other people's lives. She had developed the knack of putting patients right out of her mind as soon as she went off duty. It was the only way you could survive all the horrors you came in contact with. She supposed soldiers and others whose jobs revolved around death did the same thing.

She was hobbling out of the building thirty minutes later when something made her shudder. She spun round and saw an old man with a little white dog. The dog was trotting along on a blue extendible lead about six feet in front of his master.

She watched dumbstruck as the pair of them turned into a side corridor. They looked like they knew where they were going.

Bold as brass! she thought to herself in amazement. *They look as if they have done that a thousand times before! Dogs aren't allowed in the hospital – why didn't someone on the reception stop them coming in? God,* she thought angrily, *this place is getting more and more like a bus station every day!*

She started back in the direction she'd come from, intending to give the man a piece of her mind. The old man was just going around the corner at the bottom of the corridor and the dog had already made the turn. The man looked like someone was tugging him along on a blue string.

'Hey!' Nancy called out, breaking into a trot.

The old man went round the corner without looking back.

Nancy caught a whiff of smoke as she hurried down the corridor. *He's smoking!* she thought, outraged. *Not only has he brought a dog in here but he's smoking a pipe!*

At the end of the corridor past the intersection was the morgue. Nancy had a terrible thought then, that the old man might be taking his dog there to find it something tasty to eat.

The morgue was windowless and dark; the light from the corridor illuminated only the first few feet of the room. She stood in the doorway listening for any noises and smelling the air for a trace of pipe smoke.

A chill ran up her back. She'd seen enough dead bodies in her time but the morgue always made her uncomfortable. Some of the doctors called it the Breaker's Yard and Nancy didn't like that. This was where they cut people up into slices to find out what had gone wrong. Although she knew that these things had to be done, she had a blind spot for autopsies, thinking that the dead ought to be shown more respect and be buried in one piece.

What made it worse was the fact that whenever she came in here she had the irrational fear that she might tread in something squishy. Something that the pathologists might have dropped and forgotten to pick up again. Not only that, but the place was full of corpses. There was no work going on here tonight, but there were probably several bodies in the big drawers.

'Hello?' Nancy said uncertainly. Her voice echoed across the tiled floor.

She reached inside the door, groping for the light switch and feeling very exposed. The old man might be hiding against the wall, waiting to grab her and drag her in there with him. There were tools in there to dismantle people. A picture of the old man towering over her with the skull saw in his hands popped into her mind.

Nancy screamed.

The lights blinked and came on. And the room was empty apart from the tool cabinets and stainless steel tables and lighting rigs.

There's no one here, Nancy. Calm down! she told herself, starting to feel silly. She was glad that no one had witnessed her yelling.

She turned the lights off again and hurried back to the intersection in the corridor. As she trotted along, her anger began to return. Smokey Joe was going to pay for this aggravation when she got him.

She got him sooner than she had expected.

The little white dog came sailing out of the next junction and turned in her direction, its tail wagging furiously. Nancy stopped and waited for the old man to appear, her arms folded and her face set. In a second he toddled round after the dog.

Nancy took a deep breath to let fly at him, but she wasn't quite quick enough. The old man's face creased into a rueful grin. 'Hello, love,' he said, 'I wonder if you can help me. I seem to have got myself lost.'

The little dog stopped at Nancy's feet and looked up at her, its tail brushing the floor. The old man caught up with it, reeling in the lead as he approached. He stopped in front of Nancy looking rather like an ageing naughty schoolboy. His pipe was nowhere to be seen.

'Dogs are not allowed in this hospital,' Nancy pointed out, speaking slowly and keeping a hard edge to her voice.

'I'm sorry, love, I know that. It's just that I got lost,' he said. 'I asked at the reception if I could take him in to visit his friend and they told me no. I was trying to find a short cut back to the car park so I could put him in the car.'

'Smoking is not allowed either!' Nancy said sharply. 'And you should have taken the dog out through the reception.'

'Oh, my pipe,' the man said, patting his jacket pocket. 'Sorry. Force of habit. Forgot where I was.'

'You'll have to leave.'

The man smiled at her. She thought she detected a look of cunning in his eyes. 'I was just going,' he said.

I'll bet you were, Nancy thought. *If you think I'm going to go away and let you leave on your own, you've got another think coming, matey! I'm not letting you wander around here any more.*

'I'll escort you to the door,' she said shortly.

He nodded and his eyes twinkled.

He's eyeing me up, Nancy thought indignantly. *The dirty old sod is mentally undressing me!* She folded her arms higher, covering her breasts and started down the corridor toward reception. 'Come on,' she said, stepping around the dog who looked as smug as his owner.

The man fell in step beside her, playing the lead out so the dog trotted along in front.

'Keep him close!' Nancy commanded officiously. 'We don't want him doing his business in here!'

'Sorry,' the man said, starting to reel in the lead. 'He won't do anything though, he's house-trained. Or hospital-trained if you like.'

'I don't like.

'Who were you going to visit?' Nancy asked.

'A friend,' he said vaguely.

'Who exactly?'

'A girl. A girlfriend.'

'Which ward?'

The old man thought for a moment. 'Funny,' he said. 'I seem to have forgotten. The old memory isn't what it used to be.'

'If you remember and you still want to see her, ask at the reception,' Nancy said, not believing him in the slightest.

'Warm again today,' he said conversationally.

Nancy didn't reply.

'It'll break. End of this week,' he said with conviction.

'What are you, a weather man?' Nancy said.

The man ignored this. 'You have a car, don't you?' he asked in a tone that suggested he knew already.

'I don't see what that's got to do with anything,' Nancy said.

He shook his head. 'No,' he said thoughtfully. 'I don't suppose you would. Well, just supposing you *do* have a car. Like a yellow Datsun Sunny—'

Nancy started. Her Datsun was parked by the nurses' quarters. How did he know that?

'– and just supposing you decide to go to the movies and see the new Robert de Niro film on Friday night with your friend. Just supposing that, don't park your car in the multistorey car park.'

Nancy didn't know what to say. She was horrified. How did this old man know so much about her? She *had* decided to go and see the film on Friday. She had already made the date with June Whitley who was a dyed-in-the-wool de Niro fan. They were going in her car because June's Fiat was sick – the big ends had gone or something. Her mind whirled with half-formed thoughts and questions.

'Why shouldn't I park in the multi?' she asked, wide-eyed and suspicious.

'Because it's going to fall down.'

Nancy shivered. *What if he's right?* her mind asked. *He might be – he knows all about you, so why shouldn't he know about the car park?*

'How do you know?' she said.

The old man shrugged. 'I've got a feeling,' he said happily. Then he added, 'Don't worry though, only part of it will fall down and no one should be hurt. Except you and your friend if you park there.' He didn't look quite so sure about this part of his prediction however.

'I'll park elsewhere. If I go,' Nancy said.

They reached the reception area and the old man turned to her and smiled. 'Goodbye Nancy. Take care on Friday. And watch out for Geoff.' Then he walked towards the swing doors, the little dog straining on its leash.

Nancy stared at his back, a kind of daze settling over her. *Geoff? Who's Geoff?* she thought.

*　　*　　*

In the depths of the Ghost Train Dave waited for the knife to swing lazily across Roddy's bent over body and fill his head with its cold length. Now was the end. Of that he was sure.

His eyes were closed, so he didn't see Roddy's arm fly up and block the skeleton's thrust. He did hear the brittle crack as the skeleton's arm met Roddy's and by the time Roddy shouted with pain, his eyes were open again.

Roddy was struggling to rise but the skeleton's fingers were still buried deep in his hair.

Dave flicked the blood away from the cut over his right eye and felt the cross pulse against his chest. It seemed to be injecting pure anger into him.

The skeleton raised the Bowie again, and Dave knew that if he didn't act, this time the knife would be plunged into Roddy's neck. He reached for the leather strap that held the cross. The Ghost Train engine pulled up sharply and took a right hand turn, throwing Dave off balance. The leather thong slipped from his fingers as he grabbed the engine's seat back to stop himself being thrown right off it.

'YOU BASTARD!' he swore as the knife reached its zenith and started to descend for the last time on Roddy's neck.

The skeleton let go of Roddy's hair and struck at Dave, its bony fist clenched. Dave leaned back as the fist swung towards him and the bare knuckles just grazed against his chin. It felt hot where he was scraped, and he knew he was bleeding, but the cross was pouring outrage into his veins and the pain meant nothing. He remembered what Sally had told him about the thing in the back of her car then. He remembered it clearly and in full detail.

'YOU CAN'T EXIST HERE!' he screamed. 'GO AWAY!'

The skeleton looked at him and cocked its grinning head to one side as if the statement interested it.

It isn't going away! Dave thought bitterly. *Sally was damn well wrong! It didn't fucking work*!

The Bowie sliced through the air, arcing towards Dave's throat and making a low whooshing noise as it came.

Roddy stood up and punched the skeleton. Dave witnessed

the blow as he ducked away from the knife. It was one of Roddy's best; a short snapping punch a middleweight boxer would have been proud to throw. The punch hit the skeleton square in the sternum and Dave heard bone splinter.

Roddy shouted, drawing back his fist quickly. The skeleton didn't even pause in its striking action.

Dave ducked and the Bowie passed over his head. He felt the breeze from it as it sped by. He stood up again, his right hand busy at his throat, his eyes fixed to the knife.

NO! he thought. *IT ISN'T POSSIBLE!*

The skeleton's swing with the knife stopped dead, regardless of momentum, and reversed its direction. It would take Dave's throat out this time and there wasn't time to dodge again.

'Foureyes!' Roddy shouted, ducking.

Then the cross was out of Dave's shirt and in his hand. Its pencil thin red beam sliced through the dimly-lit great hall and Dave caught a glimpse of a wall that might have been as far away as a mile.

'YOU CAN'T EXIST HERE!' Dave screamed.

The knife didn't stop coming.

Of course, of course! his mind yelled. *It doesn't work because it can exist here. We're not home any more. We're in its world!*

He turned the cross, and the beam touched the Bowie's blade. The burst of red light reflecting off it seared his eyes.

And the knife stopped dead in the skeleton's outstretched hand. It just froze in midair as if it had hit a brick wall.

The skeleton's bones creaked and the Bowie slowly turned upwards until it was held vertical in the bony hand.

There was a squealing of tortured metal and the Bowie shattered like glass. Some of the hot shards of metal rained down on Dave's face, blistering his skin.

'We've done it!' he yelled triumphantly.

The skeleton's other hand hit him in the face.

Dave's vision blurred and his balance went. He started to crumple, but Roddy had hold of him.

'Finish it off! For Christ's sake, finish it off!' Roddy shouted.

278

Dave swung the cross round so that the beam played on the skeleton's skull.

The skeleton froze, its bottom jaw dangling as if it were disappointed.

'KILL IT, FOR FUCK'S SAKE!' Roddy screamed.

Dave flashed the beam across the skull.

The bottom jaw flipped up with a distinct *clack*! and the skeleton began to quiver as if a great force was rattling it. Its bottom jaw began to vibrate so that its teeth clattered like castanets.

Die, Dave thought calmly, ignoring the blood that flowed into his right eye and the pain that burned in his knuckles and chin.

The world flashed white.

And the skeleton exploded.

There was no noise, just a violent blast of scalding air that blew both of them off the back of the engine.

The engine reached a bend and clattered back past them, going back the way they'd come.

'What the fuck was all that about?' Roddy said, pulling himself up to a sitting position. He sounded shaken. But not as shaken as Dave felt.

'We're not in Kansas any more, Toto,' Dave said. 'And that's a fact.' He sat up, gingerly inspecting himself for damage. He felt like an empty husk and everything he had hurt like hell. Someone had picked him up and dropped him in the middle of the worst nightmare he'd ever had. Apparently there was no waking up from this one.

'What?' Roddy said.

'Forget it,' Dave told him. 'Just be thankful you're still alive.'

'What now? The engine got away.'

'We find our way out,' Dave said. 'It's as simple as that.'

'No! We stay until we find Jon and my sister!'

'I don't think they're here, Roddy.'

Roddy sounded suspicious, 'Whaddya mean?'

'I think there's more to this. We aren't in good old

Basingstoke in good old Hampshire in good old England anymore, Roddy. This is somewhere else.'

'Where?'

'I don't know yet. It's not another country though. It's another *place*.'

'No. Shut up, Foureyes. If we go outside, Basingstoke is out there.'

Dave shook his head. Blood ran into his eye. Wiping it out, he said, 'I don't think so. I think we've crossed over.'

'What do you mean?' Roddy shouted.

'I think we're on the other side.'

'The other side of what? The fairground?'

Dave shrugged. 'I think it's worse than that. I think we're on the other side of dead.'

Chapter Eleven
Limbo

The Sleeping Beauty woke up at half past eight.

Sally yawned, stretched and opened her eyes. 'Dave?' she said, looking around at the unfamiliar surroundings. The last thing she remembered was falling asleep on his bed while he was programming the computer. For the moment she couldn't remember what he had been doing that kept her from her own cosy bed for so long. It was important – she could recall that. But what it was escaped her. She shivered, wondering why both the windows in front of her were open on such a cold day. She realised that she was only covered by a sheet and thought, *no wonder it's so chilly in here*. Even though the windows were open, there was a burning smell in the room. She knew she ought to be able to identify it but she couldn't.

Her attention was caught by the noise coming from her right. She heard the steady bleeping of the monitoring equipment and hissing of the graph pens swishing away in the corner before she realised what it was.

Sounds like you're in hospital, Sally girl, she told herself. *I wonder what happened?* The fact that she was in an isolation ward in a hospital didn't worry her in the least, although she knew it ought to. She didn't feel at all unwell. Reasoning that *something* must be wrong with her, she lay still for a while, mentally ticking off her various body parts. She started at the bottom by wiggling her toes. They wiggled okay. *Hello toes*, Sally thought to them, and giggled. Her feet moved up and down, too, although the joints were a bit stiff. *Not stiff enough to be in hospital with all this bleeping and buzzing going on though,* she thought.

The first sign of trouble showed when she tried to pull her legs up. They felt as though someone had nailed them to the bed and her thigh muscles hurt as she forced them into action. She could raise her knees no more than a few inches under the covers before she had to give up.

She pulled in her stomach muscles then. These too felt a bit rusty, but there was no stabbing pain or dull ache to suggest this part of her might have suffered some kind of injury or illness. *Must be your back or your arms then,* she told herself, rotating her shoulders. No pain came from her back; not even when she tried to sit up. Sitting up seemed to be out of the question – her stomach muscles didn't seem to be strong enough to supply the required amount of pull to get her up, and her arms wouldn't co-operate and flopped about at her sides as though they'd been struck spastic.

Ah, we're getting there now, Sal. Something has gone wrong with your arms. Maybe you've had an accident. In the car on the way home from Dave's house. Fell asleep at the wheel and hit a lamp post or something. Hurt your neck maybe and damaged the nerves that go down into your arms. She wondered how she was taking this so calmly and eventually decided they must have pumped her full of pain-killing pills.

Try the head, girl. There were electrodes and wires connecting her head to the gadgetry, but she could easily move it and her head turned to face the closed door. She turned her head the other way and looked at the stack of high-tech machinery on the other side of the bed. Whatever was wrong with her must be pretty serious if it required this amount of gadgetry. She looked for red tubes that might be taking her blood away for cleansing, but there were none. She didn't even have a drip in her arm, but there was a bruise which suggested one had been there until recently. There was no oxygen mask on her face, so it couldn't be lung trouble.

What is it then? she wondered.

Her fingers wiggled when she tried them, although her

hands felt fat and stiff, and that just about concluded the testing.

Must be some kind of a mistake, she thought. *There's nothing wrong with me at all. Except that I'm a bit cold – but that's not really surprising since the windows are open. Why did they do that?*

She thought about it for a while and suddenly remembered they were in the midst of a heatwave.

But it's cold in here, her mind protested. Perhaps it was her that was cold, and not the room. Perhaps she was suffering from some tropical disease.

'OUCH!' she shouted suddenly. It felt like someone had dropped a flaring match on her left breast. After a few seconds the burning sensation faded to a dull throb. *That's better,* she thought, feeling the corners of her mouth begin to tilt upwards again. She didn't know what drugs they had been pumping into her since she'd been here (*How long have I been here?*) but she liked them very much. Her head was clear and she felt euphoric. She didn't even feel quite as cold now.

She lay there for ten minutes. Ten minutes was quite enough; the bleeping of the EEG and the scratching of the plotter was like Japanese water torture. No one looked in on her to explain what it was she was suffering from and the pain in her breast kept on coming back.

Sod this, I'm getting up! Sally thought finally.

She rallied her arms (which still felt like blocks of wood) and tried to coax them out from under the cover. This took a considerable time and a large amount of energy. At some point, Sally stopped feeling cold and started to sweat.

She stopped for a breather when her hands were tucked up under her chin in two clumsy splay-fingered bunches.

That was when she realised that something was around her neck. She moved her hand slowly down the thin cord to where her silver cross lay against her left breast.

The cross! she thought. *I've got it back. Dave must have brought it and put it on me!* Then she started to remember what he'd been doing with the computer that night back – back when?

It didn't matter when. What mattered was she remembered that Dave had been calculating the size of the Ghost Train when she fell asleep. But what had happened since? Had the funfair left town? Had Dave gone to investigate the Ghost Train in more detail? Suddenly she had to know.

Help! she thought.

The cross vibrated into life on her chest, just like she knew it would. The warm silver beat like a bee's wings. Its power flooded through her, invigorating her, easing her stiff limbs, clearing her mind. Making her feel alive.

Then it stopped. It gave off a brief flare of heat that was more intense than anything she'd got from it before, and died instantly. *Bugger*! Sally thought. *Just when you need the magic, it vanishes.*

But her arms had loosened up quite a lot and now she was able to sit up. She did so and looking down at her naked body, realised that she'd lost some weight. That meant that she'd probably been in here for a long time. Perhaps too long. There was no time to waste. She had to get out and find out what was going on.

She tore herself free of the electrodes and wires, swung her feet over the side of the bed and put them down on the cool floor. They wouldn't go right down though – the balls of her feet were on the floor, but the tendons at the heels seemed to be too tight to let them sit flat, like feet should. She decided that they would flatten out when she got her weight on them, and pushed herself off the bed. Her legs screamed at her to stop. She tottered across the room on tiptoes, her Achilles tendons tight and feeling as if they might rip at any moment. Then she fell over.

'Bugger it!' she swore, rolling on the bare floor and realising she wasn't hurt badly. Then she started to giggle and couldn't stop. Her eyes streamed. She chortled and snorted and finally had a sneezing fit.

It's the smoke. That damn pipe smoke! The last time she'd smelled it, she remembered, was on the riverbank at Laverstoke when Phil had nearly drowned. It had made her nose run then, too.

She wiped her nose with the back of her hand, got to a crouch, then stood up, ignoring the pain. Grimacing, she raised and lowered herself on tiptoe, stretching her tendons so her feet flattened out.

'Yes,' she said when her heels touched the floor for the first time. 'That's it, girl. Ten out of ten!'

There was a small cupboard beside her bed. She opened the door, hoping that her clothes were inside. There was a tattered pair of shorts in the cupboard and a cut-down tee shirt, freshly ironed and neatly folded. These were not what she had been wearing at Dave's, she was sure of that. She took them out, hoping her underwear and shoes were beneath them. *No such luck*, she thought, disappointed. Her mother must have taken her clothes away to be washed and left these in their place.

All that remained in the cupboard now was a small tin of Leichner eyeshadow, her leather wallet and a few coins. She put the wallet in the back pocket of the shorts and the change in the right hand front one. The make-up she left in the cupboard; she wouldn't be needing that where she was going.

She pulled on the shorts and shirt and padded across the floor. Before she could do anything else she was going to have to find a toilet and pee; her bladder felt like it was currently storing a week's worth. She closed the door of the room behind her wondering if it was.

No one challenged her on her way out of the hospital, although she passed several nurses and orderlies. All of them walked by her as if she didn't exist. The soles of her feet were tough from walking in sandals (and barefoot since the heatwave began) and it felt good to have the solid ground beneath them.

She walked out of the hospital grounds and onto the Tadley road, heading in the direction of town. She hadn't consciously thought about where she was going, but an inner part of her seemed to know, so she just followed her nose, breathing in the warm evening air and enjoying the sights and sounds of the summer's evening. The stiffness in her limbs faded as she walked.

Forty minutes later, she found herself padding through the

town centre and for the first time admitted to herself that she was heading for AdventureLand. This brought a small knot of fear to her stomach, but the adrenalin which poured into her veins as she drew closer to the fair made her feel more alive than ever.

She sauntered under the AdventureLand arch feeling good. There were a lot of people in the fair, and she pushed through the crowds towards the Ghost Train knowing that she might never see crowds of people again. This thought didn't concern her. All she knew was that her destiny lay inside the ride and now was the right time to go and meet it – whatever it was.

About halfway there, her nose caught the odour of frying hamburgers. Her stomach instantly took over her guidance system and soon she was queuing for food.

Later, she would look back at those few minutes and wonder why she hadn't kept to her original plan and forgotten about the pull of her stomach.

There were two elderly women serving in the hamburger trailer. One of the women noticed Sally as soon as she joined the queue. Sally saw her looking down from the stall and smiled, but the old woman didn't meet her gaze and quickly looked away. When Sally was third from the front of the line of hungry punters, the woman left the van. Sally wasn't worried – there was only one person in front of her now, so it wouldn't take very long to get served.

'Yes, love?' the remaining server asked, smiling.

'Could I have two cheeseburgers with everything on and a Coke?' Sally said.

'Of course you can, my dear,' the woman answered. 'Just let me put some more patties on the heat, and I'll be with you. You don't mind waiting for a couple of minutes, do you?'

'No, of course not,' Sally said happily. She was in no hurry.

'It's been very busy, you see dear,' the old woman said, separating the burgers and putting them into the fat. 'I was only just saying to Dotty – that's my partner – how busy it's been tonight. We've been run off our feet.' She picked up a spatula and began to scrape the chopped onions to one side of the hot plate. The burgers sizzled. Sally's stomach rumbled.

'You're a pretty girl, aren't you?' the woman said, looking up from her work. 'I was only just saying to Dotty what a pretty girl you were. Have you got a boyfriend?'

Sally laughed, pleased and embarrassed at the same time by the old woman's compliments. 'Yes, yes I have,' she replied.

'Is he here?' the woman asked.

'Sorry?' Sally said.

'Your boyfriend. Is he here with you?' She looked genuinely concerned.

Perhaps she thinks I'll get raped walking around dressed like this, Sally thought, glancing down to see if her nipples were erect. They weren't, but it was plain she wasn't wearing a bra, and there was a fair expanse of lightly tanned bare flesh showing around her midriff.

She nodded and smiled reassuringly at the woman. 'Yes, he's here somewhere.'

Dotty came back then, and climbed up into the stall. She glanced at Sally – who caught her eye this time – and smiled. 'Who's next?' she asked briskly, turning her attention to the boys behind Sally.

'There you are dear,' the old lady said, handing her the cheeseburgers and the Coke. 'Didn't take long, did it?'

Sally paid the woman and took her meal into the middle of the fairground where she sat on the bottom step of the Noah's Ark and ate ravenously. When she had finished, she dabbed the tomato sauce from her mouth with the paper serviette, drained the dregs of the Coke, belched and stood up.

Right, Sal, here we go then! she told herself. She marched to the edge of the fair and began to make her way toward the Ghost Train, striding out purposefully.

But Sally didn't get to ride the Ghost Train that evening. As she passed the gap at the side of the ride through which Dave had fled the night before last, Fred Purdue's arms shot out and grabbed her by the neck.

Sally squealed as she was dragged forcefully into the gap and was rewarded with a slap around the face that made her head spin. For a few seconds her senses were filled with the smell of sweat and the sound of heavy breathing. When her vision cleared, she was halfway down the gap. There were two men there; Purdue had her under the shoulders and was dragging her along backwards, and another, younger man blocked the way back to the fairground. Sally recognised the younger man by the little red devil tattooed on his right arm. He had an evil grin.

Sally began to struggle. She kicked her feet out and wriggled from side to side, but Purdue was too strong; his sausage-like fingers interlocked across her breasts and his arms crushed her ribs.

'Lemmego!' she squealed.

The tattooed man ran forward when Sally shouted and punched her in the stomach. The blow wasn't very hard, but it winded her severely and she spent the rest of the journey back to the caravan area fighting to draw breath.

They dragged her quite a distance. She didn't notice exactly how far they took her because her eyes were streaming tears and her breath just wouldn't fill her lungs. She hoped dimly that someone would see what was going on and rescue her, but there seemed to be no other people amongst the caravans and trailers.

She moaned. Purdue's knee came up and hit her in the small of the back. The pain was tremendous. Then her hips and legs began to sizzle like the hamburgers had done on the fryer, and she was quite sure that her back had been broken.

Purdue adjusted his grip, taking her body with one arm and supporting her head in the crook of the other's elbow. His forearm came up so that his hand was near her mouth. His fat fingers found her lips, penetrated them, prised open her jaw and filled her mouth. They felt like hot oily carrots and they tasted nasty. Sally wanted to throw up, but she couldn't because the fingers wouldn't let her and her stomach was numb. She let out a muffled gagging noise, and Purdue chuckled, thrusting his fingers in further.

The other man took her legs then, sinking his fingers into the soft flesh of her inner thighs. Sally tried to resist, but her legs were still fizzing and sizzling and the muscles had stopped working. The younger man splayed her legs apart forcefully and Sally dimly realised she was going to be raped.

But, instead of raping her, Purdue's accomplice took one leg on either side of his hips and carried her along wheelbarrow fashion.

Behind her, Purdue started to climb some steps, grunting and muttering as he dragged her up. The two men carried her up the stairs between them and into a dark caravan which smelt of rotting vegetation. They swung her once and let her go.

Sally fell heavily on her back onto a pile of what felt like sacking. Her hips and legs started to fizz and pop again. She saw the pain before her eyes in what seemed to be big ragged blue flashes.

'Gotcha!' Purdue growled. He towered over her in the darkened caravan, his breath whistling in and out through his nostrils.

'Pretty little thing, ain't she?' the roustabout muttered from somewhere outside Sally's blurred field of vision.

Sally threw up her cheeseburgers.

'Shame,' Purdue grunted. 'Last thing you'll be eating for some time, dear.'

'Can I have her?' Tattoo asked.

Purdue shook his head. 'She's mine while she's this side. To have and to hold. To love and to cherish.'

Both men laughed.

'You gonna keep her then, boss?'

'Depends,' Purdue rasped. 'I'll know soon enough. If I get to have her it'll be Knife Time.'

'See you later, lover,' Purdue told Sally. The men left and the door slammed shut. She heard the click of a padlock being fastened.

She rolled over onto her side and threw up again. This time though, there was nothing to come up. When her retching stopped she lay back on the sacking and peered into the gloom of the caravan's interior, wondering what Knife Time might be.

'Okay, clever fucking dicky, which way do we go now?' Roddy spat, pulling his cigarette pack from his denim jacket pocket.

Dave looked at Roddy who now had a Marlboro between his

lips and was groping about in his jeans for his lighter. There was a graze on Roddy's left cheek and a dried trickle of blood traced the side of his face from his hairline to his jaw. This, Dave knew, was from when the roustabout had clipped him around the head with the cricket stump.

The damage that had been inflicted on Roddy didn't seem to bother him one little bit; he just stood there, tall and proud and relaxed. His knuckles were scraped raw from where he'd hit the skeleton, but even these didn't seem to hurt him as he thrust his hands into the tight pockets of his jeans.

Dave hated him for being so tough – personally he wanted to die. The cut above his eye had stopped bleeding, but the dull ache in his kidneys had not lessened, his left cheek felt swollen where the skeleton had hit him and the wound on his hand stung. He had wrapped his hand in a couple of Kleenex from his rucksack, hoping to staunch the flow of blood that had been running down his wrist while he walked. Roddy had watched this patching up operation balefully, contempt shining in his eyes, but he had made no comment.

It could be worse, Dave told himself, *we could both be dead now*.

Roddy's lighter flared and his cigarette end glowed bright in the red gloom. He exhaled the first lungful of smoke into Dave's face and said, 'Let's face it, Foureyes, you're as lost as I am.'

They had been walking, Dave estimated, for twenty minutes. He had checked his wristwatch regularly, but it was still stopped at five fifteen, the time when he'd completed the computer program that verified the ride's physical impossibility.

After the Ghost Train engine had vanished, Dave had led Roddy in the direction in which he'd seen the wall by the beam from the cross. They hadn't yet come to it and Dave wished the cross would work. He needed to check that they were still heading in the right direction, but the cross wouldn't play. It only seemed to be of value and burst into life when things got very shitty.

He'd tried lots of ways of coercing it into life since they'd been walking through the vast wooden-floored room – rubbing it like a magic lamp, shutting his eyes and wishing, silently telling it that he did believe in it and needed its help, praying and, finally, cursing it. Nothing had any effect. Now Roddy was getting stroppy.

'It's this way,' Dave said tiredly, pointing ahead of him.

'How do you know, clever clogs?'

Dave shrugged. 'I just do, that's all.' But he didn't and he was worried because, soon, Roddy's patience would run out. He peered ahead into the reddish gloom, wondering if they were going the right way after all. They had been following the train lines since they had been walking, and that was something else that was weird. After they'd fallen off the engine and it had reached a turn and gone back the other way, there were no lines. They had discovered that interesting fact when they'd got up. All that could be seen were bare floorboards in every direction, the dark wood tinged red by the hidden light source. They had checked each direction for railway lines, one of them staying put and the other walking three hundred paces before turning and coming back again. Dave had found the lines on his third turn; they were three hundred and fourteen paces to the right from where Roddy stood. These rails weren't shiny like the ones they were used to seeing. They were set above the level of the floorboards, held together with sleepers and had a disused look to them. The rails were dull and unpolished and the sleepers black and dirty.

'I think we're going around in circles,' Roddy said. 'That's why we ain't getting anywhere.'

Dave shook his head. 'No, it's this way. It must be.'

'But you don't know, do you? You don't fucking know any more than I do. We're lost. Face it, Foureyes, we're lost and it's your fault. You can't even see the fucking sides from here. For Christ's sake man, admit it, we're lost!'

Roddy dropped his cigarette end to the floor and ground it out with the heel of one pointed boot. 'HEY!' he yelled at the top of his voice. The sound was flat and empty as if they were in a soundproof box. 'HEY, WE'RE OVER HERE!' he shouted.

'Don't,' Dave said quietly.

'Don't you don't me, man!' Roddy warned, pointing a finger. 'I'm getting a little bit sick of you, Foureyes.'

'You'll attract someone,' Dave said. *Or some*-thing, his mind added, reminding him of the hump that had cruised under his bathroom carpet to the sound of rending wood.

'Ain't that what we want?' Roddy said. 'Someone can get us out of here. When they come, I'll knock 'em about a bit. They'll soon see it my way.'

'You didn't do too well with the skeleton,' Dave said.

'It went, didn't it?' Roddy said sullenly.

'The cross did it.'

'Well, why don't you get your battery-operated gizmo out again and make it get us out of here?' Roddy shouted. He'd seen the cross work, but he didn't believe it. He swore it was some kind of a trick, even when Dave had showed it to him to prove there were no batteries or wires.

'Just another twenty minutes,' Dave said. 'Please. Then if we don't get anywhere, we'll do whatever you like.'

Roddy thought about it for a while then nodded.

They set off along the disused line again, Dave leading and Roddy coming up behind, muttering and swearing occasionally.

After about another five minutes of walking (Dave had counted seven hundred and forty-three paces) they found out what the red light source was.

Dave stopped dead. Roddy, who evidently had been watching his feet, thudded into Dave's back and swore. 'What the . . .' he tailed off as he peered over Dave's shoulder.

'What the fuck is *that*?' he finished.

The railway line kept on going, but the floorboards stopped at the point where Dave had halted. There was no ground beneath the lines and nothing holding them up. The floorboards stopped at the edge of a chasm which was hundreds of feet deep and which extended out in front of them farther than they could see. The chasm ran from left to right adjacent to the lines and blurred into the reddened distance either side. At the bottom of the drop, orange molten rock boiled and bubbled.

Dave could feel the heat on his face, even from up here, and the brilliance hurt his eyes. He peered down into the chasm, and the sheer drop made him instantly dizzy. He fought the sensation of vertigo and took a step backwards, bumping into Roddy.

Roddy stepped back, too. 'Oh fuck,' he said.

'Here we are,' Dave said.

'*What is that*?' Roddy demanded.

'That's where the orange light has been coming from. That's what we have to cross. That's the fires of Hell, Roddy.' He had an urge to forget all about this silly quest then, and wondered how it would feel to run three steps forward and jump off the railway line. It would be over quickly; nothing could survive that molten lava, or whatever it was down there. Only the fear of the fall put him off.

'We can't go over there,' Roddy protested. 'The lines will fall in. There ain't nothing holding them up. We gotta go back, man!'

'You go back if you like, I'm going over,' Dave said with more courage than he was feeling. Even when he only considered crossing the chasm, the invisible force snuck out and made him dizzy, made him want to fall over. He wasn't sure he could make it.

'Fuck you, Foureyes! You go!' Roddy said, reaching for his cigarettes again.

Dave glanced up at Roddy's orange lit face, then turned and looked into the pit. This was the way. This was the right thing to do. He *knew* it. He took a deep breath.

And stepped out onto the first sleeper.

'Wait!' Roddy shouted.

Dave paused, feeling the heat warming his feet through the thick soles of his shoes. There would be no stopping once he got out over the chasm, no more pauses to collect his thoughts or take a breather – it would be too hot. He looked down at the dull rails, knowing they would burn him if he touched them.

'What?' he asked. The vertigo was building in him and if he didn't move soon, he wouldn't be able to. All he would be able to do was topple over the side.

'Listen!'

Dave listened. There was the distant sound of the lava glugging and boiling beneath him, but nothing else.

'Can't you hear it?' Roddy shouted. He sounded angry.

Dave tried to speak, but the words died in his throat. He suddenly knew that if he opened his mouth, his balance would vanish. He shook his head instead. His vision reeled with the movement of his head and he staggered a step to the side. His left Hi-Tec touched the inside of the rail and a smell of burning leather and melting rubber assailed his nose. He shifted his foot away and stepped onto the next sleeper, being careful only to look down at the wooden tie and not at the gap in between. He pushed forward and brought his right foot over.

Simple, he thought sarcastically. *All you've got to do now is keep going until the chasm is behind you.*

He had crossed fifteen sleepers when Roddy yelled again, and the heat was making his feet sweat inside the Hi-Tecs.

'Listen!' Roddy yelled. 'Something ... Something creaking.'

Dave took another slow and careful step. He couldn't look round at Roddy for fear of falling, and he couldn't stop because the heat was tremendous.

'NO!' Roddy yelled.

Dave kept right on going. It was too far to go back now, even if something terrible happened to Roddy.

Three steps later he plainly heard the wooden floorboards behind him splitting and squealing as something forced its way up through them. He thought he knew what it was. He glanced up in front of him. The railway seemed to go on forever, straight ahead into the red glow. About five sleepers up, the lines started to gleam a frightening orange colour through the dirt that crusted them.

He took another pace and, as his right foot crossed the gap, the railway line wobbled, rocking him up and down. He planted his foot on the sleeper and froze in position, waiting for the movement to subside. He knew what had happened. Roddy had decided to come after all. 'Slow down!' he shouted, riding out the rocking motion, his arms outstretched and his knees bent like a surfer. 'It won't come on here after you!'

'I got it!' Roddy shouted breathlessly from behind him. 'It came out of the floor and I cut it. I slashed it and slashed it and it just kept on coming out! It's coming after me!'

The rails jolted as Roddy leapt from sleeper to sleeper. Dave's Hi-Tecs started to smell hot again, but he couldn't move on.

'It's okay, Foureyes, it's gone!' Roddy shouted triumphantly. Then: 'Oh God, fuck me,'

'What?' Dave said.

'I'm getting giddy,' Roddy called.

In spite of his predicament, Dave smiled. Not just because Roddy had said giddy instead of dizzy like Dave's grandmother always had done, but because Roddy was genuinely terrified for the first time. Not even the skeleton had scared him, and Dave had been beginning to think he was impervious to fright.

'Don't look down,' Dave advised, sneaking a look into the depths of the chasm where the molten rock boiled far below. His sense of balance deserted him immediately and the falling sensation made him clench his eyes tightly. He seemed to fall for a long time but, when his eyes flicked open again, he was only a few degrees off the vertical and his balance had returned. 'Shit,' he muttered.

'I think it's back again,' Roddy shouted. 'I can hear something behind me.' The rails began to sway again and Dave assumed the surfer position reflexively, ignoring the burning rubber smell from his Hi-Tecs.

'It's on the track!' Roddy shouted.

The unsupported railway line began to buck crazily and the metal started to squeal. The humps that had been formed in it by extreme pressure somewhere behind Roddy, flowed along and passed under Dave like waves, first tilting him forwards, then back. Hot ash flew from the sides of the corroded metal, forming a sparking grey fog as the hump vanished into the distance. Some of the ashes fell on Dave's face and bare arms. He shouted and frantically brushed them away, batting at his hair as some of the cinders singed it.

Dave rode out the third wave that passed beneath him, wondering just what it was that was coming after them. Whatever it was, it was *big* to be sending out these steel shockwaves. He wanted to turn and look, but knew he would fall if he did. Roddy was approaching quickly, sending smaller waves ahead of him. His fear of heights had apparently vanished in the face of whatever was chasing him.

Estimating that the next wave would arrive in three seconds, Dave quickly crossed two more of the hot sleepers.

That was when Roddy, leaping from sleeper to sleeper, hit him full tilt in the back.

Dave's knees buckled and he sprawled full length across the next two sleepers. His head was over the next gap and he stared down at the boiling lava far below. The sleeper under his legs started to make his drain-pipe jeans very hot, and the heat from the one supporting his chest charred the thin material of his tee shirt. The heat was intense. Yelling and cursing, he fought to push himself up.

'Get out of it, you shit!' Roddy screamed and began to walk across him, stepping onto the backs of his legs, then onto his buttocks. The Cuban heels of his pointed leather shoes ground into Dave's kidneys, and Dave collapsed back onto the rails, fighting off the waves of nausea and dizziness.

Roddy leapt from Dave's shoulders to the next sleeper, clipping the back of Dave's head with his foot as he jumped. For a moment Dave sailed through cool velvety darkness, then his head cleared again and he shouted. 'Get me up! I'm burning. Help me!'

Roddy didn't pause.

The next big shockwave dislodged Dave's feet and shifted his position so that the sleeper under his chest was now under his stomach. His legs fell into empty space and Dave hung there, the sleeper now burning his stomach and the backs of his arms. 'Roddy!' he called. 'I'm stuck!'

But Roddy seemed to be prepared to sacrifice Dave to whatever was coming up the line in order to save his own life. He kept moving fast, hopping from sleeper to sleeper without stopping.

The cross flared then, hurting the skin at the base of his neck. 'Come on!' Dave yelled. 'Help me!'

The cross poured its energy into Dave's body, calming him and relieving some of the pain he was in. *Keep it coming, keep it coming!* Dave told it.

The cross died.

'You bastard!' Dave screamed as his last hope of survival failed him. 'You fucking bastard!' If he'd had a hand free he would have torn the cross from his neck and cast it into the lava below. He gripped the front edge of the next sleeper along, and pulled himself forward, his rage at being deserted giving him newfound reserves of strength.

Another steel wave washed past him. Whatever was coming up the lines must be pretty close by now, he realised, renewing his efforts. The waistband of his jeans became caught on the edge of the sleeper as he dragged himself upwards, and pulled them down a little. The hot wood burnt the flesh of his stomach. Dave screamed, but kept pulling, kicking his legs out behind him to untangle his trousers. The waistband came free of the wood and Dave dragged himself up. There were only a few inches to go now until he was in his original position, but his right hand was hurting terribly. He adjusted his grip so that it was more comfortable, but it was nearer the rail now, and seemed to be drawing the heat directly into itself.

PULL! Dave screamed silently to himself. His body moved up another inch. And the tissue around his right hand burst into flame.

He smelled the burning paper and the hairs on his hand singeing long before he felt the pain.

Suddenly he was back to the position from where he'd fallen, and his feet had found the sleeper behind him. He pushed himself back so that he was on all fours, gave one last do-or-die shove and tottered to a standing position. He stood there for a moment, swaying back and forth and whirling his flaming hand through the air. The flames guttered and spat as his hand circled in the air, but the Kleenex stayed alight.

'Go out!' he screamed, nearly losing his balance again

as the next wave washed by. 'For Christ's sake, go out!'

Still burning, the tissue fell from his hand, floated on the currents of hot air for a while, then fell through the gaps in the sleepers and vanished.

Too late, Dave thought hysterically. *It's going to get you now. All that and it's too late to get away!'*

He wheeled around as the next steel wave crested beneath him.

The railway line was empty.

Dave laughed until his eyes filled with tears and his sore chest ached.

Face it down, Davey. Face it down and scare it away, he thought crazily. *Come back, Roddy, you bastard you, your monster has gone away!*

The laughter stopped then and turned instantly to tears.

Dave wiped his eyes with the back of his good hand, turned around and began to leap from sleeper to sleeper again, because that was the only option open to him.

His mind closed down to a mere pinprick of consciousness as he walked and he fell into a rhythm after a while, one that put one Hi-Tec in front of the other in the exact centre of the next sleeper each time. The movement became so certain and inevitable that it didn't even require him to keep his eyes open any more and he coasted along with his eyes closed and the smell of charred flesh and singed hair filling his nose. Pain racked his whole body and distantly he wondered how much more of this he could take.

The walk across the chasm seemed to go on forever and Dave plodded on, unaware of the dull ache in his kidneys and the throbbing heat in his right hand and the thin trickle of blood that still ran from the wound over his right eye. Roddy was nowhere to be seen. He might have fallen to his death for all Dave knew – or the monster might have caught him and torn him limb from limb. Dave didn't care either way. All he knew was that one leg had to go in front of the other, and after that the same again and after that and after . . .

Dave, Sally said. *I'm stuck. I wanted to help you. I wanted to*

come in after you. You said you couldn't do it alone, so when I woke
up I knew I just had to come. What was I doing in there, Dave? In
hospital. I've never been in hospital. I was cold. Something made me
cold. So cold. But I'm stuck now. They got me Dave, did they get you,
too? What happened what is going on what were you doing . . .?

The voice changed to that of Sally's father, Ed.

. . . all night in your bedroom. I won't be mad, I just want to
know.

Then to his mother.

Bad Eddie's got it . . .

His own voice.

Got what, mum? What's Bad Eddie got?

A sharp stinging pain on his left cheek blew away the voices.
Bee, Dave thought. *Stung by a bee. Or a wasp. Swell up like the*
Goodyear Blimp now. Hate bees.

He heard the next crack of pain and it made his eyelids shoot
up like suddenly-released roller blinds. He shook his head and
his sight came back. The vision in front of him made him scream.
It was a wild-eyed thing with a blood-streaked face and very
white teeth.

The thing struck him again and his nose started to run.

'Wake up, you little bastard! What the fuck is the matter with
you?'

Now he knew what was going on: Roddy had hold of him by the
shirt front and was slapping his face.

'Okay, I'm okay,' he said, flinching as Roddy's palm came up
again.

Roddy let go of him. 'Shit,' he said. 'I didn't think you was
ever going to wake up. I dunno how you got across that bridge in
that state.'

'Well it was no thanks to you, shithead!' Dave spat, remembering how Roddy had knocked him down and trampled over
him. Something deep inside him hurt like it was going to stop
working soon.

Roddy slapped his face again. Hard this time. Dave's ear
screamed and his balance vanished. When his senses returned,
he was on his back on the ground.

'Mind your language,' Roddy said sullenly. 'Now get up and get us out of here.'

Dave stayed on the floor where Roddy couldn't hit him again. He wanted to be angry with Roddy, but he was far too tired and his body felt like it had been ground up in a mincer. The hurting thing in his chest didn't hurt any more; it now felt loose and dead. He looked around, wondering what had happened to the chasm. The place he was in now was a blank corridor like the one they had started from. The wooden walls and floor were lit by the orange glow from the volcanic pit, but they were dim, so the chasm was obviously far behind them. There were no markings in the corridor and no Ghost Train tracks.

'Where are we?' Dave asked, peering back down the enclosed corridor. His breathing didn't seem to be working properly and the words had a sibilant hiss to them.

'We're at the end, that's where we are,' Roddy said. 'We're stuck. The track went into this corridor on the other side of that pit. It stopped at some buffers, but the corridor went on. There's no way out. I don't know why I let you talk me into coming in here.'

'We'll have to go back,' Dave whispered, knowing that they couldn't. There was just no way he could make that crossing again.

'I tried kicking the boards down,' Roddy said. 'They're too strong. It must go somewhere behind here. It must. You're the clever little fucker, you get us out. You got us in here, you can get us out. Get up!'

'I can't,' Dave said quietly. It hurt to speak.

'GET UP!' Roddy shouted.

Dave's legs wouldn't work any more and his head suddenly weighed a ton. 'I'm hurt,' he said. 'You'll have to pick me up.'

'Fuck off.'

'I can't help while I'm lying down, can I?' He began to cough. Something liquid and tasting coppery came up from his lungs and he spat. Blood. 'I think I'm hurt pretty badly,' he croaked, coughing again.

'Get up yourself,' Roddy commanded.

Dave spat more blood. His head was feeling very light now. He knew he wouldn't be making the return trip.

'You need me, you pick me up,' he said.

'I don't need you, shithead!' Roddy spat. 'I don't need no one!'

'Then go away and leave me alone. I think I'm dying.'

'You ain't dying, you little fucker. Now get up!'

Dave shook his head.

Roddy kicked him hard in the ribs.

Something inside Dave pulled tight and drew him up into a ball. His mouth filled with blood and he groaned in agony as the liquid ran from the corner of his mouth. 'You've done it now,' he gasped. 'You've killed me, Roddy.'

'Don't you die on me, you cunt!' Roddy screamed. 'DON'T DO IT!'

His leg swung back to take another kick.

And he froze.

Dave lay there on the bare floorboards, shivering with the pain. His internal organs felt like an old, worn out car engine and the blood kept filling his mouth. His lungs wheezed and flared agonisingly when he tried to breathe in. As he watched Roddy's frozen frame, his vision started to grey out.

He coughed. 'Goodbye, Roddy,' he said.

'I can get you out. Get you out. You out,' the voice promised. It went on for a long time saying the same words over and over before Anne Cousins heard it. Eventually, through the darkness that filled her eyes and blocked her ears, she became aware of it. But not before she smelled the smell of charred plastic and singed hair or felt the pain and soreness of her burnt skin. She lay there on the hard, cold floor for a long time, listening to the hollow, somehow lifeless, voice chanting away, and wondered what had happened to her now. Her mind was thick and confused and her thoughts were disjointed and flowed like ants struggling through treacle. The fact that her skin seemed to be tight and burnt puzzled her a lot more than the muffled voice that offered her salvation. Gradually the memory of what had gone before came back to her, and offered a view of her trip across the burning wastes of Hell for her to consider. 'Oh God, help me,' she moaned through a parched throat as she remembered sinking into the molten ground, the extreme heat peeling the flesh from her body like melting polythene.

At the sound of her voice, a single flash of lightning hit the ground at her feet accompanied by a clap of thunder which blew her back against a hard wall. The air smelled strongly of ozone and the odour made her want to vomit. She lay there, ears deafened by the blast, head throbbing where it had hit the wall, and examined the picture of the room she was in that remained etched on her retinas after the flash. The picture was already breaking up, but the three sides of the room she could see were plain brick capped with rough concrete. No doors or windows offered a way out. 'Oh God,' she said again, but this time the words didn't find their way to her mouth so there was no thunder and lightning, just the absolute certainty that she was indeed in hell.

'You didn't ought to say that. Didn't ought to say that. Say that,' the muffled voice intoned. The screeching in Anne's ears didn't subside until a long time after the clap of thunder and she wondered how long the voice had been repeating that.

Your legs, Annie oh Annie, what's happened to your legs? she asked herself as the voice droned away. *Are they still there? Did they really burn off when you fell into the fires?* She wasn't sure, but she was too frightened to put her hand down to feel in case they weren't. She had seen them dissolve earlier, but the pain that was coming from them suggested they were still in place. *Ghost pains, isn't that what they call them? Isn't that exactly what happens when you lose a limb? You can still feel it after it's gone.*

She moved her hands from the cold ground and laid them across her face, realising they were clawed and that the fingers were stuck in that position where the skin had shrunk. They hurt terribly and felt as stiff and sharp as briar against the tender skin of her face. But she could still feel with the fingertips. She drew a deep breath of the ozone-laden air and touched her chest, which appeared to be intact, if a little raw. She screamed when she laid her hands on her breasts, and her scream ripped at her vocal chords and made her choke. Instead of two soft breasts beneath her dress there were two malformed lumps of plastic, bubbled and lumpy with many sharp edges.

'Let me die,' she moaned, 'Please just let me die! I don't want any of this. I can't take it! Just let me be dead.'

Outside, the chant changed back to the original promise of release.

Anne rolled on the ground, coughing and crying. *You can't die, Annie,* her mind told her. *You're already dead. Dead but not buried. You crossed over to Hell of your own accord and it's your own fault that you're here. Now you've got to sit in this cold room forever, feeling your burnt body ache and listening to the chanting of your very own personal devil. And it'll probably get worse too. What happens next? Oh Annie, why did you have to do this to yourself? You were a good girl, weren't you? You could have made it to heaven if you'd just left it all alone like your mother wanted you to. Why did you have to go and ruin it all?*

'I can get you out. Get you out. You out.'

'Shut *up!*' Anne wailed. The mental torture had come as a complete surprise to her. Pain, she had expected, deformity too – she knew all about what Hell had in store for those who went there – but the incessant chanting was something she hadn't bargained on. It made things even worse. Wasn't it enough that her breasts had been melted and her lower half probably burnt away? Why did this scream-making chanting have to go on and on as well. Wasn't the physical agony price enough for whatever sin she had committed?

With the dull voice ringing in her ears, she touched her deformed breasts again. And screamed.

The chant stopped.

The reek of ozone had cleared now, replaced by the charred hair and skin smell and the odour of melting plastic again. Anne sniffed and remembered the bag she had been carrying. *That's where that smell is coming from!* she told herself. *The plastic Marks & Spencer bag. It's in here somewhere.*

She reached out to the sides of her, feeling across the stone

303

floor for the bag. If she could reach it she could get the Kitchen Devil. The eight inch chef's knife she had bought thousands of years ago in a hardware store called Kingdon's not Kingdom's as she had first thought on reading the sign. *Perhaps Kingdom's would have been a better name*, she thought bitterly. *As in Kingdom come.*

She didn't know if it would work or not, but if she could find the big Kitchen Devil she would plunge its length in under her deformed plastic left breast and carve her still-beating heart in two. But would it get her out of here? She didn't know. Could you die if you were already dead?

But you're not already dead, Annie, are you? Your little heart is still tick-tocking away under that mess that used to be one of the thirty-six Bs that used to drive Derek so wild. Oh Derek, where are you? Are you and Tommy here too? Locked away somewhere in a room like this?

There was no plastic Marks & Spencer bag within arm's length, just bare concrete floor.

You'll have to get up, Annie.

But what about my legs? I saw them melt. I saw the skin come off like strips of rubber. I saw the bone show through.

You'll just have to crawl then, she told herself roughly. *You'll just have to drag your raw stumps across the concrete until you find it.*

But what if I can't?

There's plenty of time, Annie, plenty of time.

'Eternity if that's how long it takes!' the voice from outside said, whipping the words from her mind as she thought them.

'It can hear what I'm thinking!' the voice said, mimicking her next thought. Then it added: 'And it knows everything, so there's no use trying to fool it.'

'You're going to be sick now,' the voice from outside told her. 'But don't worry, nothing will come up.'

Anne heaved, bending double with the cramp. When she had finished trying to puke, she strengthened her resolve to find the knife.

She rolled back onto her back and felt down below her

breasts with her clawed hands, assessing the damage before she moved. Her belly felt okay down as far as the waist band of her skirt. After that things began to feel sore and lumpy. Her hips and pubic region seemed to be in a similar condition to her breasts but, to her surprise, her legs were whole and, apart from being extremely sensitive to the touch, seemed to be undamaged. And her shoes were still on, even though the soles had melted and become fused onto the bottoms of her feet. Her feet didn't start hurting until she realised what had happened to them, then it was agony.

She forced herself to a sitting position, then up to a crouch. The pain was terrible, but she fought it and told herself that soon there would be no more pain. Ever.

Something popped above her left breast as she forced herself to an upright position. She gasped and put a fingertip up to feel what had happened, thinking, *it's falling off. One of my boobs is falling off!*

She put her hand inside her dress and gingerly touched her hardened breast. A shell-like structure seemed to have formed over it, and it was this top layer of burnt skin that was the cause of all the lumps and edges. Apparently it was now becoming detached from the raw flesh underneath. She probed along one scalloped edge, working up the courage to push her finger underneath and find out what was there. *Oh God, help me*, she thought, horrified as her finger touched something soft and wet.

'Shouldn't ought to think that, think that!' the outside voice warned.

Anne didn't hear it, she was too absorbed in what might now be residing inside her charred body. Was there something under there, waiting to spring out? Some kind of flesh-eating maggot? She pushed her finger deeper inside and gasped.

Then she pushed another two in to join the first, hooking them beneath the hard deformed part. She knew what it was now. Gently she pulled on the tough material and prised it away from the soft skin beneath. It ripped and crunched as she pulled it, and the pain was immense. But the perseverance paid off. In another thirty seconds she had prised the melted left cup of her 36B Playtex bra away from her breast and was working on detaching the shoulder strap.

Thank you, thank you! she thought as she took off her sweater to work on the melted brassiere. *Oh God, thank you*!

'Shouldn't ought to think that!' her devil told her.

The nylon panties that had fused to her skin were harder to remove. It might have taken two hours to unstick the material from her skin, or it might have taken four. There was no way of telling. All the while she worked, her devil spoke to her, making suggestions, promising it could get her out of here, telling her what she was thinking. She hardly noticed it, her mind was barely ticking over as she worked on the melted nylon.

'You won't kill yourself,' the devil told her as she ripped the last blackened piece of nylon from her hip. Her body had gone completely numb now, but she was still being careful. Some of the material was tugging off strips of skin with it. In the dark she wasn't sure how much.

'I hurt,' she said, dropping the tattered cotton dress back down over her scarred skin.

'Man-made material,' the demon explained at last. 'It melts.'

'I hurt all over,' Anne said.

'I hurt all over,' the demon said simultaneously.

'Not for long though.'

'You won't kill yourself,' her devil's muffled voice said.

'I will,' Anne told it. 'And you can't stop me.'

She staggered across the room and hit the far wall. Then she staggered back again, hit the other wall and fell to her knees. She started to search the floor, crawling on her raw knees and the heels of her clawed hands, occasionally sweeping her right hand out before her, feeling for the M & S bag.

'I can get you out,' her devil told her.

'For Christ's sake, shut up!' Anne yelled.

The immediate flash of lightning showed her where the bag was and the clap of thunder whisked it up and moved it.

'Shouldn't ought to say that!' the devil warned.

Anne crawled after the bag. She banged her head on the wall again before she found it.

The Marks & Spencer bag had melted around its contents, just as her underwear had melted around her body. She could feel the bottle of Coppertone and the box that contained the tube of Savlon, she could feel the handle of the chisel and the blade of the Kitchen Devil but she couldn't pick the melted plastic away with her damaged hands.

'I can get you out,' the dull voice offered.

'Fuck off!' Anne told it, forgetting her lifelong aversion to the F word. It seemed like the most powerful and fitting thing she could say at that moment and, with a distant fascination, she realised there were worse words than that queuing up inside her head.

She tried to pull the melted plastic bag away from the knife with her teeth. It didn't work. The plastic had shrunk around the stuff inside and had become much thicker as it shrunk. She could bite into the plastic but she wasn't strong enough to pull it away. After an age of screaming at it, pleading with it, snapping her teeth on it and ripping her nails on it, it was evident that she wasn't going to kill herself, just like her personal devil had told her. She sat back on her sore bottom and wept.

'Get you out!'

'Then what?' Anne asked. She was defeated and she knew it. Her devil had apparently known it all along.

'Then you'll have to do something for me.'

'What?' she said dully.

'You'll have to swear never to hurt me. Never to let anyone hurt me. You'll have to be my friend and look after me. Help me. Help me find *him*. And you'll have to kiss me.'

'What are you?' Anne said.

'Whatever you think I am.'

'I think you are evil.'

'There's no such thing. Just degrees of knowledge.'

'I'll stay here, thank you,' Anne said. 'I'm dying anyway.'

'No you won't and no you're not,' the devil's muffled voice said.

'I'll stay here.'

'You think I'm a minor devil or demon of some kind don't you? I'm not.'

'What else is there in hell?'

'You're not in hell. Neither am I.'

Anne sighed. 'Where are we then?'

'We're nowhere. And I'm not the devil.'

'What are you then?' Anne said tiredly.

'I'm your friend.'

'Why are you here?'

'Why are you here?' the dull voice asked back.

'I won't say.'

'You're here looking for Derek your husband and Tommy your child.' The devil sounded jubilant. It had been waiting for the conversation to take this turn. It had known all along that this part would arrive and now it was getting close to what it wanted.

'How did you know?' Anne asked, suddenly feeling alert.

'I know everything,' the demon said.

'Do you know where they are?'

'Yes.'

'Get me out!'

'You'll have to kiss me,' the devil said. 'And swear allegiance to me. And there's two more things.'

'What are they?' Anne asked suspiciously.

'If I get you out, you will be sworn to me until you can guess my name. You can't go free until you guess my name. And you must guess what I want from you most before I can get you out and promise to give it to me.'

'Why?' Anne said, thinking, *if he can take me to Tommy and Derek, I'll do whatever he wants*.

'Of course you will,' the voice replied. 'I know everything.'

'Then you know I'll guess what you want most from me, don't you?'

There was a pause. 'Yes,' came the reply.

'Then why don't you tell me and save all the bother. I'm dying in here. I'm not in the mood for guessing games.'

'That's the way it is. That's the way it has to be.'

'You want to fuck me,' Anne said. The devil was obviously going to wait for the best offer it could get from her, so she offered her body at once, hoping to get out quickly.

A longer pause this time.

'That's not it.'

'Give me a clue, for Ch – for my sake,' she said, quickly biting off the 'Christ' before it got out. Her ears were still hissing from the last blast.

'Can't.'

'Something sexual.'

'No.'

'Physical then?'

'Yes.'

'You want to do something with my body, but it's not sexual?'

'Yes.'

'You want to beat me up or something,' she said.

'No.'

She thought for a while. 'No pain or violence involved and it's to do with my body.'

'Is that a question?'

'A statement.'

'Yes, then.'

'Give me a clue!' she wailed. 'I *hurt*!'

'Can't. You have to guess.'

'You want to look at a part of me? That's not physical though, is it? You want to touch a part of me, but it's not a sexual kind of touching.'

'Right.'

'You want to cuddle me.'

'Close,' the devil said.

'You want to . . . put your head on my shoulder while I cuddle you.'

'Closer,' the devil said.

'You want to put your head on my breast and fall asleep.'

'Which one?'

Anne thought about it. 'The left one. Like a baby.'

'So . . .'

309

'So you feel secure. So . . . so you can hear my heartbeat?'

'That's it!'

'No,' Anne said.

'Why not?' the devil whined. Anne began to think that it didn't know the outcome of this conversation after all.

'Because you're warped or something. You're tricking me. You'll get me outside and torture me. Hurt me some more. I hurt enough already, and my breasts are almost skinned.'

'There's nothing wrong with your skin. It's all in your mind.'

'Liar.'

'We can help each other, Anne.'

'I won't do it. Get thee behind me Satan!'

'I'm not tempting you. I'm making a business arrangement,' the voice sniggered.

'I don't want to play, thanks.'

'What option do you have?'

'I can stay here.'

'I can wait. I can get you out. Get you out. You out. I can get you out.'

The flat sing-song voice went on and on and on and Anne's pain got worse. She held out for a long time, and when she could stand the agony no longer, she put her hand to her breast and felt her steady heartbeat. 'Okay,' she said. 'You win. I'll do it.'

'Pick your bag up and walk to the wall in front of you,' the demon – or whatever it was – told her.

'You don't know which way I'm facing,' Anne whined. She didn't understand the rules of this place but she was aware of the fact that there were rules, and frightened that she might inadvertently do something which would endanger her life. All her previous thoughts of suicide were gone now. She realised somewhere in the back of her mind that her devil had got her well and truly hooked. Since it mentioned that it could help her find Tommy and Derek, she had been putty in its hands.

'What if I go to the wrong wall?' she pleaded, wanting to remain alive more than anything she'd ever wanted in the world before. 'What if I do it wrong? I'll be killed.'

'Just walk to the wall in front of you,' the voice said. 'It doesn't matter which one it is, just walk to it. You'll come out in the same place whichever wall you go to.'

'But how?' she said, suspecting treachery after all.

'It's too complicated to explain,' the voice admonished. 'Just do it if you want to get out, and remember what you promised. If you go back on your promise, I'll excoriate you.'

'What?' Anne said, groping on the dark ground for the melted M & S bag.

'I'll peel off the rest of your skin. You won't like that much. It'll be pain beyond belief.'

'I'll just die if you do that,' Anne said defiantly. 'And what use will that be to either of us?'

'You won't die, I can assure you of that,' the demon giggled. 'I know a way to cause you the ultimate pain without killing you. I'll still get my way, and you'll suffer for as long as I want you to. And that will be a great amount of time. So, no tricks.'

'No tricks,' Anne agreed.

'You won't kill me?' the demon asked.

'I can't, can I?' Anne said, walking forwards until she felt the rough brick wall before her. The bricks were warm.

'No,' the demon said, not sounding very sure of itself.

'What do I do now?' Anne asked.

'You have to believe,' the muffled voice said.

'In what?' Anne groaned.

'In getting out.'

'I don't think I can.'

'You can. Then you have to knock three times on the wall and walk through it.'

'Oh,' Anne said, feeling the solidity of the brickwork with her fingertips. This wasn't going to work. Perhaps this *was* hell after all. Perhaps this would go on throughout eternity; her being stuck in here and dying in agony and an annoying voice promising it could get her out and lead her to her family. That sounded like hell if anything did.

'Do you believe?' the voice asked.

Anne nodded. 'Yes. I believe in getting out.'

'Go on then.'

Anne tapped the wall three times with her raw knuckles and walked into it.

Her knees hit solid brickwork an instant before her flayed breasts and hurt a thousand times less. Her head was carried forward by the momentum and her forehead whacked the bricks sharply. Anne rocked back on her heels, feeling the warm blood running into her eyes and the life draining from her body. She sat down hard on her burned buttocks and screamed. 'YOU BASTARD! YOU MOTHERFUCKER! YOU SHITTING LIAR!'

'You didn't believe, did you?' the voice said, its tone mocking.

Anne's next scream died in her throat while it was still only half formed. Suddenly, her small prison was gone, along with its sounds and smell, as she lost consciousness and toppled backwards to the ground.

Something warm and wet. Rough. Rasping. Rasping across skin. It was a good feeling, but a feeling that came from a long long way away. Maybe too far away to ever get back to. There was black, empty space; a universe full of it. A *wrong* universe, but it hardly mattered at all. It existed and it was huge and airless and a long way back to that faint wet rasping.

But the rough damp feeling went on, scratching against a skin that no longer existed. There was no skin here, just emptiness. Skin was long gone. A million years gone, except that years had no meaning in this vacuum either. There was only nothing.

Rasping. Nice. Closer now, much closer, but oh the *pain*!

A noise. Sound. Huffing puffing. What used to do that? Something good. Something loved. Cold! A thrill of wet cold against face. Much nearer than before.

There was no sensation of movement, but he had been pulled back through his empty universe, to a point in space much closer to the source of the pleasurable feeling.

Licking! That's what it was. A dog's tongue was slurping across his face. If the pain had been less, he could have imagined he was at home in bed with Lucy trying to wake him up in the morning. He was almost near enough now to open his eyes.

The dog's cold nose pressed against his hot cheek, and Dave Carter's eyelids parted. With the return of his consciousness came the full weight of the broken ribs and collapsed lung Roddy had inflicted on him. He coughed and his mouth filled with blood. The dog that stood before him, snuffling and licking, was out of focus and he tried to move to get a clearer look at it, but the pain skewered him to the ground. *Glasses*, he thought, *glasses have gone*. He screwed up his eyes to sharpen his vision of the dog. It was white and fairly small. A blue lead extended from its leather collar and disappeared behind it out of sight.

'Lucky,' Dave croaked, feeling blood run from his mouth.

The dog barked, a single low woof! of greeting and wagged its out-of-focus tail.

'You are in a state, aren't you?' Lucky's owner came up behind the dog, reeling in the blue lead. Dave looked up at the old man's smiling features.

'What . . .' Dave said, trying to ask what he was doing here. He choked after the first word and was racked by a coughing fit that seemed to drive broken bone through soft lung tissue. Fresh blood filled his throat.

'I'm dying,' he grated, looking up at the old man.

'No, I don't think so,' the man said and knelt down beside Dave's ruined body just as he had knelt beside Phil's drowned one less than a fortnight ago. Dave looked up at him, pleading for help with his eyes and knowing at the same time that this wasn't going to be just a matter of a little artificial respiration. The damage here was much worse.

The old man leaned over him, his gaunt face swimming in and out of focus. 'My, my,' he said. To Dave's utter amazement, the man produced his missing wire-rimmed spectacles and put them on him.

'They're not broken,' Lucky's dad said. 'That was fortunate.'

'Heppp,' Dave said and coughed blood.

'Lie still, David.' The old man looked down at him and shook his head. 'I thought you were big enough for the job, son. I really did. You couldn't do it, could you? You just couldn't make yourself believe.' He nodded his head towards Roddy, who stood frozen to the spot, and said, 'I could believe it of him. He's a cynic and a doubter. The Wrong Stuff. But you . . .' He put his hand to Dave's neck and pulled the leather thong of the cross until he had it in his hand. He gazed down at it while Dave wheezed and gurgled and then shook his head once more. 'See what happens when you don't believe?' He turned the cross and showed it to Dave. The silver eyelids had closed over the eyeball again. 'You know it's real,' the old man said, 'and you know it works, so why don't you trust it? You can feel its power, son. All you need is a little faith to keep the magic flowing.'

He pressed the cross against his heart then and closed his eyes in concentration. When he took it away again, the eyelids were open and the red iris shone once more. He tucked it back in Dave's shirt, face against his chest.

The warmth flowed instantly, charging though the pain in Dave's chest and kidneys and annulling it. A pink aura formed around Dave's body, pulsing and sparkling in the dank air. The warmth in his body built into heat and the pain went.

The heat gradually increased, tingling into Dave's arms and legs, refreshing and revitalising. His breathing became easier until it felt natural again, and still the heat built, pouring up into his head and healing the cut above his eye, racing around the depths of his brain and chasing away the fear and clarifying his thoughts.

Then it stopped. The pink aura vanished and the healing heat was gone. Dave drew a deep painless breath and exhaled. The air still tasted fresh and clean.

'That's it,' Lucky's dad said. 'You're okay.'

Dave drew himself up to a sitting position and looked over at Roddy, who was frozen in mid kick. His arms were outstretched for balance and his right leg was drawn as far back as it would go, ready to lash out. His face was masked with dried blood.

Lucky barked and jumped onto Dave's lap, panting and

wagging. Dave tickled his ears, still staring at Roddy.

'Don't worry about him,' the old man said, 'I just had to suspend him for a tick. It's allowed here. I'll let him go after we've talked.'

'Who are you?' Dave asked.

'Who or what I am and what I'm doing here don't matter, son. Please don't ask questions, it weakens my grip.'

'Sorry,' Dave said. His right hand had stolen into his tee shirt and was furtively checking for damage. Good reports were coming back and he was wondering how it was done.

'You want to know where you are and what you should do, of course,' the old man said.

Dave nodded.

'Those are complicated questions, David. Let's just say that we're neither here nor there.' He pointed back down towards where the railway lines finished, 'There's the Ghost Train.' Then he pointed at the wall behind Roddy, 'There's where you're going. At the moment we're standing in one of the more tenuous corners of the Bad Side.'

'We can't get through,' Dave said, nodding at the wall. Lucky jumped off him and went to sniff Roddy's left leg. Then he cocked his own leg and pissed on it.

'No respect, that dog,' the old man said, shaking his head again.

'We can't get out,' Dave repeated.

'No such word as *can't*.'

Dave looked hard at the old man, wondering who he reminded him of. It was someone he liked, but he couldn't place the face. 'What's your name?' he asked, blushing at his own impertinence.

The old man frowned. 'It isn't at all important. I answer to anything. You can call me Cyril, if you like. That's as good as anything.'

'Cyril,' Dave said, turning the name over with his tongue. It wasn't the right one, he *knew* this. This man's name would have more power than Cyril did. Still, if Cyril was what he wanted, Cyril was what he would have.

'Cyril Hardesty,' the old man said, sounding as if it amused him.

'What's going on, Cyril?' Dave asked. 'What is all this stuff?'

'You know what it is, David. If you would only let yourself believe it would become apparent. You know where you are and where you're going to. You know what for. All you have to do is trust yourself. Believe in yourself and believe in the magic. Sally does. It's much easier for Sally. She believes.'

'Where is she?' Dave asked, remembering the dangerous glint that came into her eyes when her cross started working; remembering that she was asleep in hospital and wouldn't wake up.

'I can't tell you, David. I can tell you nothing, it's not allowed. Don't ask me questions, because it weakens my grip.'

'Is she alright?' Dave demanded.

Lucky barked and both of them turned to look at him. His small white form had become translucent. Dave could see the outline of one of Roddy's legs through the dog.

'I haven't much time and I can't answer questions, David,' Cyril said sharply. 'You've started Lucky vanishing already. Now just listen!'

Dave nodded apologetically.

'Listen carefully, because I shan't be able to help you again. I have interfered three times, and that is the limit. If I had not interfered this time, you and your friend would have surely died. There was no need for that to happen. It is your own fault and I have been forced to save you from yourselves. I might have been able to help you later, if you had trusted your instincts, but now you will have to do it alone. You were doing so well, David. For a boy, of course. I suppose I should bear that in mind. Boys don't have such a well-developed sense of intuition as girls, do they?'

'No,' Dave agreed, not really sure what the old man was getting at.

'Well, you must make sure you develop yours, David! Your existence depends on it.'

He didn't say my life, Dave told himself, *he said my existence.*

He means my soul and everything. That's the game we're playing here: immortal souls. He sighed. He had started to feel very insecure. What was on the other side of that wall? Was it hell?

'Beware, David. I can tell you nothing of what you must do. All I can do is warn you to be careful. You must not lose.'

'But what *is it*? What's behind the wall?' Dave demanded.

Lucky barked. The sound was hollow. Dave looked over at him, just in time to see him become completely transparent. The dog's wagging tail vanished, followed by his haunches, body and head. For a moment his two brown eyes were suspended in mid-air, then they too vanished.

'What did I do to him?' Dave, pleaded.

'Don't ask!' Cyril Hardesty said sharply. Dave looked at the old man, and realised it was happening to him, too. His face was getting paler each second.

'Say nothing! Just listen!' he said.

Dave bit his lip.

'Limbo,' the old man said. 'Some call it purgatory. Limbo is by definition the term that comes closest to describing it. It is a place that bridges and links other places. It is a no man's land. There are representations there that balance the earth, but life must not exist in that place. That is a simple rule which must be adhered to if the status quo is to be maintained. Understand?'

Dave shook his head. 'Not a word.'

'You will,' the old man replied, smiling. 'You *must*.'

As Dave looked up at him, his face started to fade. He spoke again, quickly this time. 'You are going over. You need to know nothing else now. What you will need to know later will be revealed to you. Just remember to trust your intuition and believe.'

'You said I was no good at it though,' Dave protested. 'You said I almost got myself killed. But it's you isn't it? You're the one responsible for sending me. You're the one that knows what's going on, the one that knows all about the crosses and The Claw and Fred Purdue. If you arranged it so this would happen and I came over here, why didn't you pick someone that *could* do it without screwing it up? That's what I want to know! Why me?'

The old man smiled. And faded a little. 'It had to be you. And Sally. The crosses found you two, I didn't. No one else is capable of doing the job or the crosses would have chosen them. Just accept it. You're the ones because you're special. You have an affinity for the power. Now go and do it. You know what to do.'

On the last five words, the vanishing speeded up. Only the old man's lips and yellowed teeth were still visible by the time he said 'what to do'.

'Wait!' Dave cried, as the lips disappeared. 'I still don't know what it's all about!'

The teeth parted as if they were about to say something important, but they vanished too, still open, the words unspoken. All that was left of Cyril Hardesty was a faint reek of pipe tobacco.

'Shit!' Dave said.

'What? Who's a shit?' Roddy demanded. He was shaking his head and touching the injured spot on his head where the cricket stump had struck him.

'Hiya Roddy,' Dave said miserably.

'Get us out of here, Foureyes. You got us in, now get us out.' He glared at Dave, but he seemed to have forgotten the reason his foot was in the air when he woke up. Dave didn't remind him.

'You're starting to sound like a record, Roddy,' Dave said quietly.

'Get us out!' Roddy shouted, taking his hand away from his head and inspecting it for fresh bleeding.

'I can fix that for you,' Dave told him.

'Got some Elastoplast in our rucksack, have we?' Roddy said sarcastically.

'Yes, but that's not what I meant. I meant I can *heal* it.'

'Fuck off, Foureyes.'

'I can.'

'Go on then. Got healing hands or something?'

Dave took the cross out of his shirt. Its eye twinkled. 'Let me put this on the wound. It'll do the trick.'

'You're mental, Foureyes. I knew I shouldn't have come in here with you. You're a grade A head case.'

'I can do it!' Dave insisted.

'What's going on?' Roddy moaned. 'I can't make it out.' He waved his hand around him indicating the railway line and the boarded wall behind him. 'I don't know what it all is. I can't fucking stand it. Just get us the fuck out of here. I've had enough.'

'Let me heal you. You'll feel better.'

Roddy shook his head. 'Fuck off!' he said very slowly. 'I'm going back.'

'Try it,' Dave said, feeling the power of the cross flowing up his arm and into his chest. 'Try and cross that chasm again.' Unlike the earlier instance in the Dragon, the charge from the cross was smoother now, and it let Dave's thoughts flow freely. He knew exactly how far he could push Roddy without getting hit. It felt good. *You're learning, Davey boy*, he told himself.

'Okay, make my head better,' Roddy said.

'Sit down.'

Roddy sat. But not before he'd taken his flick knife from his pocket and released the blade. 'Don't try anything,' he muttered darkly. 'There's a big artery in your leg, and I know where to find it.'

Dave went over to him and laid the cross on his blood-matted hair.

'Christ man, that feels funny!' Roddy said suspiciously. Then, surprised: 'Hey, it doesn't hurt anymore!'

Dave took the cross away, inspected its still-glowing eye, and tucked it back in his shirt. He took off his back pack and got a tube of Wet Ones out, uncapped it, drew out one of the damp cloths and handed it to Roddy. 'You can get the blood off with this,' he said, getting the next one out to wipe his own face.

'What is that thing?' Roddy asked, wiping his face. 'I mean, how does it work?'

Look out, he's getting interested in the cross, Dave told himself. *He'll want me to give it to him in a minute*. 'I don't know how it works,' he said. 'It just does, that's all.'

319

'Shit,' Roddy said with obvious distaste. 'You give me the creeps, Foureyes.'

Dave carried the back pack over to the wall, crouched down and took the brass toy compass from it. He had packed a tube of Smarties that had been lying around in his bedroom for ages. He had packed them for the same reason he'd packed the compass and worn his new jeans and his Hi-Tecs. It *felt* right. Now he knew what the tube of Smarties was for.

'Give me some, Foureyes,' Roddy said from behind him. Dave looked over his shoulder at him; the flick knife was gone now, back in its trouser pocket and Roddy's face was clean again. He had a Marlboro in his mouth and his lighter in his hand and looked as relaxed as if he were in a pub.

You don't know, Dave thought. *You just have no concept of the amount of trouble we're in. What is going on inside that thick skull of yours, Roddy?*

'They're not for eating,' Dave said.

'Whaddya mean? You may not want to eat them, but I do. Here!' He held out his free hand for the tube.

'No,' Dave said. 'If you want to get out of here, the tube has to stay full.'

'Do you think I'm stupid?' Roddy asked. 'I'm not standing here letting you eat them all on your own. Gimme!'

Here's the guy who thought I was crazy to bring stuff to eat with me, Dave thought. *Good one, Roddy.* His heart speeded up slightly, and he felt his old fear of his adversary start to rise. Then he clamped down hard on it.

'Just a minute ago you were whining because you couldn't get out. I'm getting us out and I need the Smarties to do it. Now shut up and wait.' He turned back to his rucksack and winced, expecting to feel Roddy's toe in his recently-healed kidneys at any moment. The blow didn't come though.

'You're crazy,' Roddy said and lit his cigarette.

Dave stood the tube of Smarties on its cardboard end so that the blue plastic cap was at the top. *How many Smarties does it take to fill Wembley Stadium?* he asked himself, remembering the old advertising campaign. *Only Smarties have the answer*, he sung mentally.

The brass compass was warm where he'd been clutching it tightly. He unclipped the lid and lifted it. 'Oh,' he said, looking at the rusted needle.

'What? What is it?' Roddy demanded, coming up close behind him and peering over his shoulder.

The compass needle had been pointing to the east when Dave lifted the lid, but as soon as he looked at it, it started to spin. Slowly at first, bottoming out on the warped and bubbled backing paper where the compass points were marked. He straightened the compass so that it was level, but the needle didn't stop at magnetic north, it spun right around the dial, a full three hundred and sixty degrees. It wobbled when it was pointing at Dave, but kept going, gaining speed.

'S'fucked,' Roddy said as the needle completed its second rotation.

Dave stared at it in amazement, not knowing if this was a condition of what he wanted to use the compass for, or an aberration caused by God knew what.

The needle continued to move, still getting faster. It started to wobble on its axis as it went, so that it rattled. Soon it was moving so fast that it blurred, the wobbling setting up a humming noise like an angry bee.

The needle was just a blue smear now, and the noise was getting more and more intense. Heat was being generated by the movement and the case began to get hot. *It's going to blow!* Dave thought and snapped the lid shut before the needle burst through the glass and lacerated his face.

The noise stopped instantly.

'Don't tell me that's magic, too,' Roddy said in exasperation.

Dave opened the compass lid again. The needle started to rotate. He stood the compass on top of the tube of Smarties, realising instantly that it wouldn't work. 'Three things,' he said. 'Of course it is. Everything is three things. Fred Purdue tapping on the counter. Separating the crosses. The amount of times the old man could help. All threes.'

'What are you going on about?' Roddy flicked his cigarette butt against the wall sending a shower of orange sparks cascading down the wooden panels.

'It needs to be stood on three things,' Dave said, already sorting through the rucksack. There didn't seem to be anything in there that would make a good tripod with the Smarties tube though. He made do with the Wet Ones canister and a small packet of McVitie's digestive biscuits which he cut in half with the Swiss Army knife to make it more or less the same height as the tube.

He leaned the three packets together and had a flash of inspiration. There was something else that had to be done. He opened the large blade of the Swiss Army knife and laid it on top of the crude tripod with the blade pointing at the wooden wall. Then he unsnapped the compass lid and balanced it on top of the knife and stood back. The needle started to spin, then wobble as well, and the buzzing noise started again.

He shuffled away from it, walking backwards, his eyes never leaving the face of the compass.

'What's gonna happen?' Roddy asked, keeping a pace behind Dave at all times.

'Dunno,' Dave said, feeling a strange kind of delight. This was what it was all about. This was why he'd been chosen. He realised he'd always known things like this were possible. Perhaps he'd known the compass would be useful all those years ago when he spotted it in the shop in Falmouth. You *knew* things like this could happen when you were a kid; it was just that they became more and more impossible as you got bigger. He felt freed from the constraints of logic and the chains of reason, and he knew suddenly why Sally got that glint in her eye when things went mad. Because anything was possible again, just like it was when you were a little kid. And it wasn't illusion like t.v. conjurers, it was fact. The power existed. All you had to do was believe in it and you could use it. And it felt great. Even if by that train of thought it meant monsters and bad things could exist. The risk was worth it.

It's madness, that's what it is, Dave, his grown-up's voice told him. *You're not experiencing anything except the descent into lunacy! You fool, you utter idiot!*

He squashed the thought before it could take hold, and revelled in his new freedom.

Over on the tripod of tubes the compass needle was just a blur again, and the pitch of the buzzing was rising to a shriek. Wisps of smoke had started to rise from the biscuit packet, but the Wet Ones and the Smarties tube were holding out admirably.

'It's moving!' Roddy shouted.

As they watched, the compass and the knife shuffled forward. The biscuits and the Wet Ones canister fell away, but the tube of Smarties didn't. It leaned at an impossible angle for a second as the compass (with the knife still underneath) worked its way on top of it, then it stood up straight. The compass and knife combination adjusted its angle until the blue cap of the Smarties tube was central beneath it. The noise was hurting Dave's ears now. Roddy was tugging at his shoulder and yelling something at him, but he couldn't make out what it was.

I'm going to explode, Dave thought calmly. *This vibration is going to make me go off pop!*

The compass began to scream. Its blurred brass casing seemed to be expanding and filling the air with its colour. Dave could smell it from here, as strongly as if he'd just taken it from its box in the garden shed. A cool musty smell.

Go on, do it! he yelled mentally, not knowing what was going to happen, and not really caring.

The compass and the knife began to levitate. The knife seemed to have become a part of it, and they moved as one, rising slowly into the air above the Smarties tube. Six inches. Nine. A foot.

Go on! Dave yelled.

The compass and knife had risen to head height now, about three feet from the wall. The knife began to swing back and forth in a small arc, as if it was seeking something.

The weak point! That's what it's doing, it's looking for a weak point!

The knife stopped with a jolt. It was pointing slightly to the right of centre and its blade had taken on the colour of the compass case.

Roddy pulled Dave to the ground then, yelling 'Look out!' Dave fell on his front, but his eyes never left the compass.

The screaming vibration became a roar and Dave's vision began to blur.

'FIRE!' he shouted.

What looked like about two gallons of molten brass shot from the pointed tip of the Swiss Army knife blade and smashed against the wall. There was a blinding blue flash and the noise stopped.

Dave's ears recovered before his eyes. Roddy was shouting at the top of his voice that this couldn't fucking well happen. He was still pressed against Dave's back. Dave wriggled out from under him, wondering if he should have closed his eyes to prevent him being struck permanently blind. But his vision returned gradually.

There was blue smoke. A lot of it, mainly in the area where the compass had been. It smelled of brass.

Dave sat up and rubbed his eyes. The smoke was clearing when he looked again, and the compass and knife were perched on top of the Smarties tube again. The packet of McVitie's had spilled broken biscuits across the floor and the top of the Wet Ones dispenser was slightly melted.

And the wall was gone. There was no trace of it at all; no burning edges, no debris, no dust. It had just ceased to exist. Behind the vanished wall was a short corridor with a double door at the end. Dave could see light shining around the edges. 'We're out!' he shouted. 'We've got out!'

He turned back to Roddy, who was on his feet now, but looking quite ill. 'I don't believe it,' he muttered. 'Fuck, my ears hurt. I'm nearly deaf.'

'But you're out,' Dave said. 'Wasn't it worth it?' He walked back to the compass and knife. The compass had almost stopped spinning; the needle was revolving slowly, but there was no vibration now. The knife looked as good as new. Dave reached out and touched the compass face, expecting it to be hot. It was cool. He picked it up, snapped the lid shut and put the compass back in his rucksack. The Swiss Army knife was also undamaged. The point of the blade showed no signs of having recently delivered a slug of molten brass, and was cool and clean. He shut it, put it in his jeans pocket and picked up the Smarties tube.

The tube didn't rattle. Dave shook it. It was empty; all the little chocolate sweets had gone. 'Christ,' Dave said, putting the tube back into the rucksack and going over to gather up the spilled Digestives, 'we just shot down a wall with a blast of molten Smarties.'

Roddy didn't hear. He had lost interest in how the wall had vanished as soon as he saw the light coming in around the exit doors and he was heading down the railway tracks towards them.

Dave quickly picked up the biscuits, shoved them in the rucksack with the Wet Ones dispenser and hurried after Roddy, worrying in case the wall decided to re-form before he got past it.

He caught Roddy up at the doors.

'Someone is going to suffer for all this hassle!' Roddy said. He drew himself to his full height and pushed hard on the exit doors, then strode through, Dave hot on his heels.

He stopped suddenly when he was outside and Dave walked into his back. Roddy didn't seem to notice. He stood stock still for a moment then said in a choked voice, 'What have you done, Foureyes? What the fuck have you done?'

AdventureLand was not as they'd left it. When they crashed their way into the Ghost Train it was early evening and the fair was warming up; there was music, flashing lights, rides working and people beginning to fill the walkways. Now it was empty. Closed. Deserted. None of the neon lights were on, none of the multi-coloured bulbs shone. The covers and boards were all off the rides and stalls as if they were ready for action, but there were no customers and no proprietors.

A thick silence lay over AdventureLand like groundmist.

Dave could hear his heartbeat in his ears and the sounds of Roddy's breathing. Nothing else.

'Where is everyone?' Roddy asked, his disbelief and uncertainty evident in his voice. 'Where have they all gone?'

Dave shrugged. 'It's just like what happened outside Ziegfeld's restaurant,' he said in wonder.

'Why isn't it getting dark?' Roddy demanded. 'It should be getting dark. It was evening when we went in.'

Dave looked up at the sky and shivered. They were somewhere else, that much was evident. This was not the sky they'd had over them on their way in. Their sky hadn't seen a cloud for weeks; this one was filled with a flat grey layer of featureless cloud, so even that it might have been applied with a paint roller. And the light was wrong too. It should have been dim down here with cloud cover like that, but it was bright. Almost as bright as midday. Dave looked around the deserted fair, wondering what time it was. You should have been able to tell roughly how late it was by the direction the shadows fell in. But there were no shadows, in spite of the fact that it was bright enough for them.

Roddy must have been thinking the same thing because he said, 'What time is it?' and turned to look at Dave for the first time since they'd escaped. His face was ashen.

Dave looked at his watch. Five fifteen. When it had stopped. 'My watch says a quarter past five in the morning,' he said, 'but it always says that now.'

'It is,' Roddy said hopefully. 'That's what it is. That explains everything. We've been inside this damn ride all night, that's why there's no one here. You're right, it's quarter past five in the morning.'

'Roddy,' Dave said gently. 'If you're right, then I'm afraid it's going to be a quarter past five in the morning forever. If the world is now taking its time from my watch it will be, anyway. My watch is broken, Roddy.'

'Shaddup, squirt. I'm right about the time. I never said anything about the world running from your watch, did I?'

'No, you didn't,' Dave agreed.

'It's colder,' Roddy said, fishing in his pocket for his Marlboros.

'Yeah,' Dave nodded. The temperature here was at least fifteen degrees cooler than Basingstoke had experienced in the last few weeks. But it still seemed to be Basingstoke out there. Dave could see the trees of the Memorial Park looming over the far side of the fairground and was certain that if he walked around the fair and out through the entrance arch he would find everything in its rightful place. If it wasn't for the dead sky and the absolute silence he could have believed what Roddy said about it being a normal early morning.

Roddy lit up and coughed.

'We're not out, y'know,' Dave said quietly. 'We're not home.'

'What are you talking about? We just came through those doors didn't we?' Roddy said spinning around and pointing at the exit doors. 'Of course we're out!'

'We got out of the Ghost Train, Roddy, but we didn't come out in the same universe as the one we went in from.'

'You've flipped, Foureyes.'

'This isn't home, Roddy. It looks the same – it's identical in fact – but it isn't our Basingstoke. It can't be. There's no sound. There should be some sound, some background noise. There always is, no matter what time of day or night it is. The sky's clouded over. Look up at it. Have you ever seen a sky like that before?'

'So the good spell broke. So what?'

'That's not it, and you know it. That sky is *wrong*. The light is *wrong*. The temperature is *wrong*. Don't you see?'

'All I see is an empty fairground in front of me and a nutter beside me,' Roddy said, blowing smoke down his nostrils.

'So what are we going to do now?' Dave asked, wondering how long it was going to take before Roddy would admit that this Basingstoke wasn't their Basingstoke. This place was what the old man had been going on about. It was another dimension or something. He wasn't sure yet quite what it was, but he was prepared to wait for the knowledge to come to him and certain

327

that it would in time. He was surprised at how easy it was becoming to accept things now. The turning point seemed to have been the moment he managed to blow the wall away with the knife and compass. Now, a new confidence had come to him and although he was anxious about what might lie in store, he was keen to get on with it.

'I dunno about you, Foureyes, but I'm going home for some kip,' Roddy said, starting toward the wooden steps down to the fairground.

Dave looked after him, dumbfounded. 'But what about Jon and your sister?' he called. 'What about getting them back? Aren't you going to bother now?'

Roddy turned around and grinned up at him. 'They ain't in there, are they?' he said, nodding at the silent Ghost Train. 'Neither are your fat friend and his chick with the tits. If they was in there we would have seen them and we didn't. If they was in there for any length of time, they'd most likely be dead or end up mad like you. I know when to give up, Foureyes, I know when I'm beat. They're probably all at home now laughing at us for being so fucking stupid.'

'You're frightened,' Dave said as Roddy started down the steps again. 'You're too scared to go back in there and look for them.'

'Fuck off,' Roddy called, not looking back.

'Chicken shit!' Dave yelled angrily, knowing that going back into the ride was the wrong thing to do, but angry at Roddy for giving up so easily.

Roddy turned and came back up the stairs, his movements quick and smooth. To Dave's eyes, he almost floated across the platform. When he was close, he launched himself at Dave who had noted him in action often enough by now to know what he was going to do and nimbly sidestepped. He hadn't reckoned with Roddy's speed on the ground though and he hadn't moved far enough away. Roddy snaked across the boards, grabbed both Dave's ankles and yanked them out from under him. Dave fell heavily on his back pack and in less than a second, Roddy was on top of him, pinning his arms to the ground with his knees and glowering down at him.

'Don't you ever call me chicken shit again,' he hissed. 'Not unless you want to die afterwards!' He drew back a balled fist. Dave closed his eyes and waited for the punch to hammer home, wondering what it would feel like and where it would strike. He decided the nose was probably the best bet and imagined the fizzing pain so vividly, he didn't notice Roddy's weight vanish from his chest.

'Get up, dickhead,' Roddy said.

Dave opened his eyes and looked up at his companion in confusion. *He never hit me*! he thought. *Why on earth didn't he hit me*!

'I'm gonna leave you in one piece for the moment,' Roddy said. 'Because I ain't sure what's going on at the moment. I dunno if I ought to believe all this shit about being somewhere else or not so I'm going to go home and see what happens.' He shrugged. 'Jesus, this looks like Basingstoke, but it looks wrong too and I can't work it out. I just dunno what's going on. I'm dog tired, Foureyes. I gotta sleep before I can do anything else. You can do whatever you like, but I'm going home.'

'I'll come with you,' Dave said, suddenly terrified at being left alone in this strange place that looked like the AdventureLand funfair in the Memorial Park in Basingstoke, but wasn't.

'No you won't. I want some time to calm down. I ain't sure about you. You keep putting the shits up me for some reason. I don't trust you.' He turned and went down the steps again. Dave watched his wide, denim-clad back as he made his way past the empty darts stalls and cut through to the centre of the dead funfair. He got up when Roddy was out of sight and stood wondering what to do.

After a long time he, too, walked down the steps and made his way back towards the AdventureLand arch, heading for home and wondering if Sally was still asleep in her hospital bed in another land.

Sally lay on the pile of stinking sacking in the dingy caravan listening to the sounds of the fairground outside and wondering how she was going to escape when her legs didn't feel as if they belonged to her at all. She didn't doubt for a moment that she *would* escape – the alternative after all was most likely going to be Knife Time, and she didn't like the game-show sound of that one little bit. It was just that she couldn't for the life of her think up a *way* to escape.

She tried to draw up her knees, but the pain in her back where Purdue had kicked her was too intense and her thighs started to pop and fizzle again.

She lay back, groaning at both the pain and the stench of vomit that assailed her nostrils when she put her head back down on the sacking. *Teach you to eat cheeseburgers when you know you shouldn't!* she told herself harshly, and wriggled across the sacking away from where she'd puked up earlier. She timed herself as she moved, assessing her speed of mobility and trying to keep her mind off the agony. By the time she was three feet nearer the boarded-over window, she had counted to three hundred and forty. *And that's not going to be good enough to do a runner now, is it?*

Lying back again in the foul sacking, she thought about Purdue and what he had said to his kidnapping accomplice. What had he meant about her being his while she was *this side*? She knew what he meant about her being his – that much didn't take a lot of working out, but *this side* puzzled her. Was it really that there were two sides to the Ghost Train then? Were there really alternate fields of existence?

Of course there are she told herself, not doubting her instincts for a moment. *What d'you think this is all about if it isn't a struggle between the big forces: Positive and Negative, Good and Bad, Heaven and Hell? Call 'em what you like, girl, but that's what it boils down to. The only problem is that there doesn't seem to be much evidence of the Good Stuff being about. It's all been Bad with a capital B so far. Surely it just can't be Dave and me against all this evil? Can it?*

She thought about this for a long time and decided that yes, it probably was. If someone or something had pitted ordinary old her and nearly as ordinary old Dave up against some big Bad force or other, they had a far higher opinion of them than she did. Either that or they didn't know their ass from a hole in the ground. In spite of its terrifying implications, this thought amused her and she began to giggle as she imagined a completely stupid God of a lower order than the Ultimate being talked into choosing two Joe averages as his emissaries by a bespectacled accountant type. *These are the right ones, G!* the accountant type would be saying enthusiastically. *They're young, they're fit, they're alert and best of all they are prepared to believe anything and do what we tell 'em! Give it a go, huh? I'm telling you, these two have qualities you haven't dreamed of!* God would frown and say: *Hmm, Dave Carter and Sally Harrison, I don't remember them. Must be losing my grip. Okay, Jackson, if you think they're right, you give them a go. But don't come running to me if there's a Fall.*

Someone banged on the door then, a single hard blow. Sally shrieked and flinched, and her sudden muscular contractions made her legs fizz again. From outside came the sound of Purdue's grating laughter. 'Just checking,' he growled. 'Just making sure you were still there, my little rosebud.'

Sally waited for the sounds of the padlock being unlocked, thinking that Knife Time might have arrived earlier than she expected, but Purdue didn't come in, merely walked the length of the caravan, chuckling and scraping something metal against the caravan's thin skin.

Sally lay still on the sacking, her muscles tensed and her legs popping. There was a final clatter as Purdue reached the end of the caravan, then silence.

She listened for a long time before she was sure that Purdue was gone. *Got to get out of here in a hurry!* she told herself. The cross was good, but she didn't know if it would enable her to face up to Purdue if he was to come back with his knife. After all, it hadn't warned her of Purdue's ambush, nor had it started work on her legs yet, although she waited patiently for it to start buzzing and throbbing on her chest. Perhaps the flashing red stone that Purdue had in his ring had negated the power of her cross's green eye. Maybe that's what it was. Maybe that was why Purdue hadn't taken the cross from her.

Her hand went up to her neck to touch the cross, to feel its

331

cool reassurance. She gasped when her hand touched bare skin. There was no leather thong around her neck, no comforting bulge between her breasts.

'But he didn't take if off me!' Sally wailed. 'He didn't. He *didn't*! It can't have gone!'

It fell off, Sal, that's what happened. It fell off between the side show stalls when they dragged you along. Purdue and his friend didn't notice it. He just thought you weren't wearing it. That's why you didn't feel him take it from your neck.

'But what if he *did* take it off you, Sal?' she asked tearfully. It was quite possible that he had. She had been so terrified and in so much pain when they dragged her in here that she might not have noticed him stealing it.

Steal it or not, it's gone and you'll have to put up with the pain, my dear, she answered herself. *You'll have to face it – you've got no help now. No magical talisman to give you courage or heal your wounds. You'll have to do it alone. Now get those long pretty legs of yours working!*

It hurt. It hurt like merry hell, and it took a slow count of four hundred.

A Diana Ross single was playing somewhere across the fairground and the music drifted into her prison, carried on the low roar of many diesel generators. Diana Ross finished, Stevie Wonder started and finished and Marvin Gaye was halfway through hearing it Through the Grapevine before she got her knees up to her stomach. Getting them down again took one crash of the Ghost Train doors opening and the pain took another Tamla Motown oldie to subside.

The heat inside the sealed caravan was oppressive and all of Sally's pores seemed to have opened up at once, soaking her shorts and shirt and leaking her precious body fluids into the smelly sacking, but she got her knees up again. Then a third time. Then a fourth.

Exhausted, she dozed fitfully for a while, dreaming of terrible dark things that lurked in shadowed corners of her cell. When she awoke, she wasn't sure if the dreams had been real or if she was still asleep. Outside, the music and humming of the diesels had ceased. Only the going-home voices of the last punters who had *died a thousand deaths and lived to tell the tale* disturbed the silence that had fallen on AdventureLand.

He'll come now, Sally thought. *He'll come back now and let himself in and stick his oily-tasting fingers down my throat again. Then he'll rape me. Then his friend will rape me too, you can tell from the silence. There are no other caravans near – I'd be able to hear voices if there were. No one will hear me if I scream. He can rape me or kill me or both and no one will know. So get UP!*

Her legs were stiff and her back still hurt, but the popping and fizzing that she'd thought were signs of a broken spine or at least a severely damaged spinal cord, were gone. It took twenty-five to get up, another ten to walk to the single boarded-up window that showed chinks of light between the planks.

Sally peered through a gap in the boards and waited for her eyes to focus.

From here she could see the back of the Ghost Train over to the left and the ride beside it. Between the two was the alleyway Purdue and his friend had dragged her through. In front of her, standing to the right of the stall next to the Ghost Train she could see the back of another stall – probably the Hall of Mirrors. And that was the limit of her vision. There was no telling what lay to either side of her caravan or behind it.

She wondered if she could make it back into the fairground if she ever got out. There was a space of about ten feet of yellowed grass between the caravan and the stalls – but the alleyway between the Ghost Train and the stall next to it was easily twenty feet away, probably more. Her chances of out-distancing a pursuer with her stiff legs were nil. That meant she couldn't make a break for it when Purdue opened the door to feed and water her or rape and kill her – whichever came first. Unless—

– *Unless you can disable him, Sal*, she thought. *Unless you can catch him a straight right to the balls before you run.* It didn't seem very likely, but what alternative was there?

None Sal, right? she thought, smiling grimly and flexing her legs.

But there was an alternative. It didn't occur to Sally for another hour, by which time she had exercised so much that she was swimming in sweat and too tired to try it. She could attempt to prise the wooden planks off the window and scramble out. There might even be something lying about in here that she could use as a lever.

The search began when she woke up again. It was still dark outside, but her back was feeling a little better. She went to the far right corner of the caravan, got down on her hands and knees and crawled along, feeling the floor ahead of her as she went. At the far end of the caravan in the centre she found a metal chain with a handcuff attached. The chain was bolted to the wall about six feet from the ground. Purdue obviously wasn't a stranger to this kind of kidnapping. *And probably torture, too,* she noted coolly. *Why else would you chain someone up?*

She eventually found herself back at the pile of sacking she'd been lying on and just as she was about to stop and sniff to avoid the puke, she put her hand in it.

She had to fight with herself not to throw up again as she cleaned her hands on the sacking. She dragged the material over the area of puke, mentally noting its position so she could avoid it in future.

As she moved it, something was released from beneath the sacking and rolled across the bare floor stopping with a glassy *chink* when it hit the wall.

Sally scuttled over to it and picked it up. An empty beer bottle.

No good for knocking off boards, but good for knocking off Purdue bollocks, she decided.

She took the bottle over to the boarded window anyway and worked the neck into the gap between the frame and the bottom board. She took the body of the bottle in both hands and levered against the board, using all her strength. The wood creaked. Sally put her knee against the wall to gain more leverage. The board groaned and moved out half an inch.

That's it! You've got it!

Placing the bottle on the floor at her feet, she peered into the gap she had made. Her heart sank. The board hadn't broken at all. It was attached to the aluminium of the caravan body with screws and all her levering had done was pull the side sheet of metal out from its flat position, screws and all. She looked at the puckered places where the screws had pulled at the metal and groaned. All her strength and weight had been used and this was all that had happened.

Keep going, Sal, her inner voice told her. *You've got it worried, so have another go. Just another little tug!*

Twenty-four more little tugs later the board was still in place and Sally was starting to feel that it might soon be Knife Time. She sat down under the window, the beer bottle in her lap, and wondered who Purdue had to contact for his instructions.

Probably whatever it is that lives on the other side of the Ghost Train, she answered herself. *And I've got a feeling that whatever it is doesn't want me over there. If it did, Purdue would have let me go on and vanish just like Phil and Judy.*

She wondered if Phil and Judy were still alive over there on the Bad Side and whether she would ever see them again. At this rate it seemed unlikely.

She intended to start work again as soon as she had caught her breath and stopped sweating but instead she fell asleep, still cradling the bottle between her legs.

'Hello, lover.'

Purdue! Sally woke instantly. He stood in front of her at the open door holding a battered tray on which stood a steaming mug of tea and a cooked breakfast that smelled terrific. Eggs, bacon, fried bread. 'Oh,' Sally said.

Purdue towered over her. She looked up at him, and for the first time saw the handle of the steak knife which was tucked in the wasitband of his trousers.

'I gotta keep you fit 'n fat if you're going to be my little plaything,' he growled.

'What do you mean?' Sally said sharply, glancing from his knife to the shining stone in the ring on his hand, then to the open door.

335

'I mean I brought your breakfast,' he said. 'Take it!'

Run around him, Sal. The door's open, his hands are full, he can't get the knife. You can outdistance him easily! Get up and look as if you're going to take the tray, then leg it!

'Take this fucking tray, or I'll throw it away,' Purdue said.

Sally stood up, glancing past Purdue's huge frame at the open door.

'It's another beautiful day out there,' Purdue said. 'Pity you can't go out and look.'

'I need a toilet,' Sally said. 'I'm bursting.'

'Piss on the floor,' he grated.

'I can't,' she said smelling the food and glancing at the door again. Her stomach began to rumble. She could almost taste that bacon.

'I'll get you a bucket,' Purdue said. 'Take this fucking food.'

Sally's heart began to sing. Her ears hammered with the pounding blood. Her nose was filled with the smell of good food and freedom. She ran.

Purdue's six foot, seventeen stone frame blocked her path. She darted to his right, remembering that she'd seen him use his left hand before to do things with – give change, tap three times on the counter, for instance.

Left-handed, Sal, stay away from that one.

But she had forgotten about her legs. They didn't hurt, but they weren't better, and her run was more of a quick hobble. But even so, she was sure she was out. She stumbled around Purdue and headed for the door, favouring her right leg so that she ran tilted over. Purdue turned slowly around behind her. 'Stop!' he said.

Sally was having none of it. The door was less than five feet away.

You're free! Sally shouted to herself and hopped onto the top step.

That was when Purdue's friend's fist shot out and thudded into her stomach. He had been standing on the ground to one side, waiting for this very thing to happen.

It took Sally a few moments to realise where the cramping

pain had come from and what it was. While this happened, she stared blankly at the man who had hit her, suddenly recognising him as the older roustabout from the Ghost Train. Then she fell back into the caravan, clutching her belly.

'Did you piss yourself?' Purdue asked. 'Because if you did, I'm not going to bother with your bucket.'

'You gotta believe. You can't do it if you don't believe. Believe me, you gotta believe.'

Anne Cousins' eyelids flicked open and showed her darkness. For a second she was surprised she still existed.

Outside, the demon's voice droned on and on like a stuck record. It had almost certainly been chanting about believing since she blacked out. She thought she could remember it chattering against her unconscious ear drums, in a kind of vocal Chinese water torture.

'Shut up!' she screamed, but her throat was raw and dry and all that came out was a croak.

The chanting stopped. There was a pause while her tormentor thought up a plan of action. 'Try again,' it said. 'Try again.'

'I can't,' Anne croaked.

'Try again.'

'I can't do it. I can't believe.'

Another pause while her demon considered the situation. Anne sat up on the raw flesh of her buttocks and sobbed. No tears came though; there didn't seem to be enough fluid left in her body for that.

'What *do* you believe?' the voice asked slowly. It sounded sly and its deliberate tone frightened Anne.

'I . . . I don't know what I believe. I don't believe anything anymore.'

'Think about it. You must believe something or you wouldn't exist. If nobody believed anything there wouldn't be anything.'

'You're trying to trick me,' Anne sobbed.

'Nope,' the voice said. 'Simple law of Physics. At the Quantum level. Things are what you perceive them to be. Nothing more, nothing less. Of course it's not quite as simple as that. Some things are better at believing than others and they force their reality onto lesser things. But everything believes something. Even if it's only what it is. Control is the key you see. As ye sow so shall ye reap. As ye think, so shall ye be.'

'I don't know what you're talking about.'

'What is your name?'

'You already know it.'

'Tell me.'

'Anne Cousins.'

'No, you're not.'

'Yes I am,' Anne croaked.

'See? I told you you believed. Easy isn't it?'

Anne said nothing.

'Do you believe you will remain where you are forever, suffering terrible pain and that there will be no respite?'

'Yes,' Anne said. 'Now shut up.'

'You know what you've got to do then, don't you?'

'Yes,' Anne said. 'But I can't do it.'

The voice didn't reply. Anne thought about what it had said. After a time she crawled back to the wall that there was no door in and found her melted Marks & Spencer carrier bag. She picked it up, then painfully got to her feet.

Empty your mind, Annie, she told herself. *It might be right. Just empty your mind and stop it thinking of pain and imprisonment. Believe there's a door. Just for a second. Try it!*

But her mind refused.

What if, Annie? she asked herself, driving the doubts from her mind with real words. *What if you could make the wall open? What if you could do magic?*

But there was no such thing as magic, was there?

'I believe,' she said, clenching her deformed hand as much as she could. 'I believe there is no pain.' Her mind's grip lessened and her willpower increased. 'I believe I can get through,' she said quietly. Her words rang in her ears and sounded *right*. 'I believe I can get out!' she yelled and knocked three times on the solid wall before her, ignoring the blasts of pain that shot up her arm and made her breasts throb in sympathy. For a second, her disbelief was connected to a steel rope and hauled high above her until it was suspended well out of harm's way.

'I believe in getting out!' she cried and walked forwards.

Her right knee grazed against the cold rough brickwork and, as she started to cry out in pain, it sunk into the wall. The leg went right through, foot and ankle first, thigh following knee. Anne's shout of pain died in her throat as both her arms penetrated the wall. There was resistance, but only a little. It felt like walking into a huge blancmange and she found it strangely pleasant. She took a deep breath and held it as her face sank into the soft cool brickwork, but she didn't close her eyes. One push from her left leg and she was completely immersed in wall. It was grey in there and there was nothing to see except more grey ahead. She glanced down as she moved through, but her body and legs and arms didn't seem to exist at all. She pushed forward another step, moving slowly like a lead-booted diver on the sea bed. On the third step she knew that the wall was much thicker than she had anticipated. Already she had walked a good six feet and the breath in her lungs was stale. If she could just hold it for one more step, she would be through.

The next pace didn't take her out the other side though, but it used up the remaining oxygen in her lungs and they started to burn.

Don't breathe out, she told herself, forcing her legs through the grey. *One more step.*

She kept her breath in her lungs for three more paces, then could hold it no more. No bubbles formed in the soft material as she breathed out, her air just vanished without trace. She kept it under control and made three more paces while she exhaled, but it wasn't enough. She was still deep in the grey when her lungs were empty and needed to breathe in again.

Can't Annie. Can't breathe in again, she told herself. *Not in here. Not in the concrete. Kill you, Annie, so don't!*

Two more paces. Her lungs screamed at her stupidity and her head was filled with the sound of her heart, under pressure and making do on hardly any oxygen at all. As she glided along, the tone of her heart changed from making do to fighting a battle and losing.

Nearly out now. Just another couple of paces. Ignore the screaming lungs and bursting heart because you'll soon be out. Spelt O-U-T. That's where you'll be!

But what if you're not? her sensible voice asked her.

The steel rope suspending her disbelief began to fray. Threads of fine wire began to snap and her imagination dropped a couple of inches.

That was when the concrete began to harden around her.

It's not real concrete, it's not! Anne screamed inwardly to herself, as her movements began to slow even further.

Stuck Annie, stuck forever! Encased in solid stone! How could you do that to yourself? Why did you let it slip?

The next forward movement of her leg was almost impossible. All her muscles ached with lack of oxygen, her lungs were collapsing and her heart was cramping.

It's not solid, she thought crazily. *How can it be? How can you walk through solid rock? You got in here so it can't be solid!*

The grey became softer and her leg sneaked ahead of her. Her mouth opened, the grey flowed in between her lips and tasted gritty and bad. Not breathable. She closed her mouth and pursed her lips, forcing the substance out through them with her tongue.

One more step and I'm out! Just one more step!

Sparks were igniting before her eyes now, and the pained throbbing in her skull was slow and unsteady. Her ears were ringing and her limbs and chest were on fire. The right leg again. That was the one to move. For a moment she forgot how to move her leg. It was so far away from the pinprick of consciousness that it seemed impossible.

But she felt it move. It moved in spite of the fact that it was wooden, in spite of the fact that the nerves had died and the muscles had ripped. It moved for Derek. It moved for Tommy.

Then it was out. Free of the wall. Her other leg followed and the rest of her slipped out at the same moment. The light was too intense after the darkness and her eyelids clamped down over her eyes, shutting out the brightness. Anne took a massive lungful of clean air and fell to the ground.

'See, I told you I could get you out!' her demon's voice said from very nearby. 'You're mine now. Just like you promised. For always and always. Mine. Forever!'

Chapter Twelve
Traps

Sally sat in the corner next to the handcuff and chain nursing the fresh bruises Purdue had given her and cursing her eating habits. He hadn't beaten her up too badly, but her top lip was swollen from a backhanded slap across the face and her stomach ached where Charlie, Purdue's tattooed friend, had thumped her in the guts. She had numerous other aches and pains too, but it was the lip and stomach that bothered her most. Her upper left canine tooth seemed to have a bit of a wobble now as well, but this didn't hurt, and she thought it would probably tighten up again.

All in all, she decided, she hadn't done too badly. They hadn't even put the handcuff on her. And Purdue had left her breakfast. She had told him to stuff his breakfast up his back passage but Purdue had just shaken his head and left. She told herself that under no circumstances would she eat the food, but after a while that delicious aroma of fried bacon had got the better of her.

Now she had indigestion which she tried to ignore while she wondered what was bothering Purdue. The beating he'd given her (*although it hurt – God, did it hurt!*) seemed to have been lackadaisical and offhand. It was as if he had been preoccupied with more important matters and didn't want to hurt her too badly. *Perhaps he's saving you for Knife Time, Sal,* she thought and shuddered.

Outside, someone started fiddling with the padlock. Sally wondered if Purdue had decided to come back and beat her up some more. Or knife her. Or rape her. But in spite of these worries, she wasn't frightened. She was angry at being kept captive, depressed about losing the cross and worried about her safety but she wasn't the quivering wreck she had always imagined she would be if something like this happened. She was ready to fight tooth and nail if the opportunity for escape arose and never mind the pain. Maybe it took extreme circumstances for you to find out just how you would react under pressure.

The caravan door creaked open and Charlie the roustabout came in. He had a plastic bottle of water in one hand and a yellow plastic child's potty in the other. He set them down on the floor at his end of the van, his eyes never leaving Sally's and said. 'You can piss in here if you still want to go. There's water in the bottle if you're thirsty.'

'Thanks,' Sally said. 'What about some toilet paper?'

'You're lucky you got this,' Charlie said, his voice low and growling in what was only a pale imitation of his boss. He backed towards the door slowly, looking ready for a fight.

'It's okay, I won't hurt you,' Sally said. 'No need to be frightened of me.'

Charlie grunted.

'What are you going to do with me?' Sally said conversationally.

'Nothin,' Charlie said. 'But Fred might.'

'Why hasn't he done it already? He says I'm his to love and cherish, so why hasn't he loved and cherished me?' Sally said, fighting off the sickening picture that came into her mind of what Fred Purdue might look like naked.

'He's waiting,' Charlie said, backing away further.

Purdue must have told him I'm dangerous or something, she thought. *Why is he so wary of me?*

He was right at the door now, ready to leave. Sally had to speak to him, had to draw his attention away from the door if she was going to get out. She cursed herself for not having the bottle ready when he came in. Even though he hadn't come near her, she should have picked it up. She could have thrown it at him. And hit him. She was sure of that.

343

'Is he outside like you were?' Sally said, rising to her feet and thrusting her thinly clad breasts forward.

Charlie goggled at her. 'What?'

'Fred. Your boss. Is he waiting out there?'

'What d'you wanna know for?' Charlie asked suspiciously.

'Do you fancy me, Charlie? Do you want me? You can have me if you want.'

The roustabout looked as if he'd been punched in the mouth by a ghost.

The bottle, Sal, where's the damn bottle?

She toyed with the button on her shorts, ran her fingers over her bruised stomach.

'Shut the fuck up! I can't!' Charlie blurted.

'Yes, you can. Come over here and hold me,' she whispered, running her hands down her hips to her legs and wondering if she looked as silly as she felt. Judging by Charlie's face, she didn't.

The bottle was to her right, partially hidden under the sacking. If Charlie came across the room into the dimly lit part of the caravan, his eyes would probably be temporarily blinded. She could be over to the bottle in two paces and wrap it around Charlie's head in one more. Purdue wasn't outside or Charlie wouldn't have shown his interest at all, he would have already gone.

The roustabout took a hesitant step towards her. And stopped.

Come on, Charlie, what are you made of? she thought.

He shook his head. 'I can't,' he said.

'Why not?'

'He's saving you.'

'What for?' But she knew what for. Knife Time.

'Never you mind,' Charlie said, some of his confidence returning.

'He's waiting for instructions isn't he? From his boss.' Suddenly it all fell into place. His boss was on the other side of the Ghost Train. The Bad Side. His boss was the thing that everyone was frightened of. The thing that all this was about. The

344

thing that had appeared in her car and that had left all that slime in Davey's bathroom on his birthday. And Fred Purdue fed it living bodies each time it got hungry. He was waiting to see if it wanted her or not. Apparently it couldn't make up its mind about how she would taste.

'What's Knife Time, Charlie?' she asked, abandoning her role as siren.

'You'll see.'

Why isn't it sure about me? she wondered. *Why is it taking so long to make up its mind?* But she didn't have to articulate the answer, she knew it well enough intuitively: the thing that was running the whole show wasn't sure about her because of the cross. She knew how to use it. She was a natural. She understood it better than Dave and thus represented more of a threat than he did. When it lit up, the cross filled her whole being and she let it because she loved the power. Dave fought it because it was strange. Dave's belief in it was flawed, and the thing could beat him while he was like that. That's why they let him in and not her.

There was something else she knew intuitively, and that was that to beat the Bad Thing, both she and Dave would have to be present, with both of the crosses. They would have to be linked and controlled with perfect faith to win. That was why they'd taken her cross from her and why Knife Time seemed to be the most likely outcome of her stay here.

'He'll kill me with a knife, is that it?'

Charlie shook his head. 'Knife, yes, but he won't kill you. Not enough energy generated. Not enough pain. It doesn't last long enough.' He smiled at her as if he was discussing a forthcoming dinner party.

'What then?' Sally said, her mind throwing up possibilities and jettisoning them. Each one had to do with a knife and her and each was more horrific than the last. Most of them were of a sexual nature.

'You'll get flayed. Flayed, not laid. That'll come later.'

'He's intending to *skin* me?' Sally asked, knowing her eyes were shining with terror and unable to do anything about it.

'Then he'll really love and cherish you, girl. Don't worry, they don't usually last more than a fortnight and he won't take all your skin at once.'

'But why?'

'You really want to know? They don't usually.'

'Yes. Tell me!'

'Energy. He gets it from skin. He eats it. Raw. Keeps him going. He's different you see. Different to you and me. But you have to be alive. Alive and in agony for it to work. He does other things, too, but I can't tell you what those are, he does them alone. They hurt though. I've heard. Now you know. Don't tell him I told you.' He looked at Sally with something approaching contempt for a moment, then smiled again, and backed towards the door. In a few moments he had shut and locked it, leaving Sally alone with her mental picture of Purdue skinning her bit by bit and wondering what the other things he did were.

Some time later Sally began to feel a little better. She used the plastic potty, then drank most of the water from the bottle Charlie had left. She emptied the rest over her face, rubbed it with her hands and let it evaporate. The water didn't take long to dry in the sweltering heat inside the caravan and it left her face feeling stiff and sticky instead of clean and refreshed.

It was when she carried the potty over to the door that she spotted the chinks of light shining in through the centre of it.

A letter box! she thought, trying to remember if caravans usually had letter boxes. She didn't think so, but this one was big enough to be one of those semi-permanent mobile homes, so she supposed it was in order.

She bent down and peered into the letter box, hoping that it wasn't blocked off. She poked her fingers into the hole and swore. Solid wood covered the opening. She prodded and probed, but the wood was well fixed. 'Shit!' she said, trying to see out through the tiny gap at the top of the wood and failing.

She retired to the other end of the caravan and sat on the floor, wondering how she could get to see through the letter box.

If she could make a hole in it that no one noticed, it would give her a distinct advantage because she would be able to see Purdue's caravan and watch his movements. If she knew he was far away, she could lay into the boards across the window with the beer bottle and maybe break them down.

The beer bottle, Sal! You can get the wood off the letter box with that!

Excited, she half stood up, then sat down again slowly. She could probably prise the wood off the letter box with it, but whoever came to the caravan next would almost certainly notice it was missing.

'So what are you going to do then?' she asked aloud. 'Just sit and wait for Purdue to come in and start removing your skin?'

She took the bottle from beneath the sacking and rammed the neck into the letter box, holding the body with both hands.

The noise it made must have been heard at the other end of town, she decided, but no one came to investigate.

Standing solid before the letter box, she rammed the bottle home again. She hit harder this time and the shock of the blow hurt her arms and hands.

With a creak of protest, the wood gave way.

Sally wiped the fresh sweat from her forehead and dropped to her knees to inspect her handiwork. The crack of light at the top of the board had widened slightly where the screws had given. She tested with her fingers, but the wood was still held tightly in place.

She held the bottle firmly and drove it in the letter box again. This time it jarred her hands so much that she dropped it. It rolled away down the caravan, but Sally hardly noticed. She was already crouching before the letter box, eager to know if she could see out.

'Yes!' she breathed. This time, the wood had moved far enough to afford her a view of Purdue's caravan's front door and steps. She couldn't see any of his windows, neither could she see the expanse of grass that lay between here and there, but she could see exactly what she needed to see and the beauty of it was that the wood hadn't come off: it had only moved slightly so the chances were that the two men wouldn't notice.

Opposite her, Purdue's caravan door was closed. Maybe he was inside, washing and shaving or something. He probably had the radio on too and that was why he hadn't heard her bashing the wood.

She retrieved her glass friend from where it had rolled against the wall and knelt in front of the letter box to wait.

The count was slow, but she reached nine thousand and there was no sign of Purdue and no one else passed the caravan. She could hear movements not too far away – voices, doors slamming, cars being started. She thought the time might be about nine o'clock, because she could hear lots of cars swishing by on the Ringway which was less than fifty yards behind the fairground.

The heat grew inside the caravan and Sally sat down on the floor to rest her aching knees. She was beginning to doubt the wisdom of using the last of the water to wash her face. She was thirsty already and it didn't look as if anyone was likely to come over with more water for her during the day. She doubted if the other fairground people even knew she was here. Could you die of dehydration in one day? If it was hot and you had nothing to drink, could you?

There was no answer to that question, but judging by the amount of perspiration running from her already she was going to find out, whether she wanted to or not.

She began to get desperate. *What if I shout for help?* she asked herself. *Someone will hear me, won't they? They can't all be in on it, surely. If I shout, they'll come and rescue me. Won't they?*

Then she asked herself who she was trying to fool. This wasn't the first time Purdue had done this – Charlie had said as much – and none of the others, the people you read about in the papers and saw on the *Nine o'clock News*, had escaped to tell the tale, had they? Using that train of logic meant that everyone in the fairground must also be involved.

Of course they are, Sal. What about that old woman at the hamburger stand? That's how Purdue knew I was coming. That's why he was waiting for me in the alley. She tipped him off.

Sally didn't yell.

The traffic noises had lessened now, so it must be later than nine thirty, the time it usually abated. That meant another eleven hours of searing heat before the sun went down. Sally didn't know if she could make it.

Somewhere out there, someone began to hammer. *Driving in tent pegs in the fairground,* Sally told herself. *Mending the machinery or whatever they do during the daytime.*

She listened to the steady hammering. Metal hitting metal with a bright, sharp tone; the gaps between the noises long, indicating that the hammer was rising slowly between each blow and falling under its own weight. Sally imagined a muscular roustabout sheened in sweat and wielding a heavy sledge-hammer, his biceps bulging as he raised the hammer high. The silence as it fell. Then the *clang!* Then silence.

It took Sally too long to realise. Longer than it should. 'I can use the sound!' she said, finally understanding that the steady sound of the hammer falling would mask the sound of her hitting the boarded-up window with her beer bottle.

She stood before the window, the bottle clutched in her right hand by its neck, biting her bottom lip in concentration as she timed herself to the rhythm of the hammer blows, tensing her shoulder muscles at the sound.

After three dry runs, she swung the bottle at the window boards. The sound seemed incredibly loud and the shock wave made her elbow ache. She had to fight off an urge to run back to the letter box and see if Purdue was coming out of his caravan, a grim expression on his big round face. He *must* have heard that if he was in there.

But she stood her ground, and got the next blow in at exactly the right moment.

There seemed to be more daylight showing through the gaps between the boards now, but they weren't coming off yet.

It's the metal, Sally told herself as she swung at the wooden boards again. *The screws are holding them to the metal of the caravan. They'll go though. Just keep hammering and think of metal fatigue!*

The bottle was getting slippery with sweat now, and

between blows she swapped hands and wiped her right on her shorts, getting the bottle back again in time for the next swing. *Wouldn't do to drop the damn thing*, she thought as she pivoted from the waist, her arm held crooked to absorb the shock.

The gap between the boards got bigger. Sally found her rhythm and swung the bottle again, effortlessly this time. It whacked into the wood and she killed the bounce-back with her wrist muscles as she swung it away again.

Another blow. Sweat ran into her eyes, but Sally was smiling. It felt good to work like this. She was strong and fit and her heart pounded in her chest sending fresh blood to her working muscles. She seemed to have tapped into unknown reserves of energy and knew that she could stand here and hammer the boards for as long as it took and still have enough left in her to climb out and run for her life.

She swung again, feeling the giggles rise to her throat and knowing that she must look like a mad woman. But she didn't care. She didn't care because what she was doing was *right* and *good* and she loved doing it. She was a human piledriver, a battering ram.

The sledgehammer out in the fairground stopped, but Sally didn't know it until after she'd struck the next blow, and then she didn't care because more light was shining through the gaps. Soon the boards would be off.

She struck four more blows, each one harder than the last. 'Go!' she hissed as her pal the beer bottle bounced on the boards again. 'Go!'

Then the bottle broke.

She stood looking at what she had left in her hand. The neck. The rest of the bottle had shattered into thousands of pieces and sprayed itself across the bottom of the caravan. One of the shards had cut her wrist and a line of blood was forming on her skin.

The boards weren't coming off after all.

Sally wiped the blood from her wrist and dropped the bottle neck on the floor. Two big tears formed in her eyes, swelled and overflowed. More moisture loss. She looked down at the shattered bottle in despair.

'Some kind of friend you were,' she told it bitterly.

Anne was lying face down on the floor when she came to. The intense pain was the first thing she became aware of and she tried vainly to get her weight off her raw chest. Her arms and legs were tight where her skin had shrunk on them and wouldn't move far enough to let her get up. The second thing she noticed was that she was out of the Ghost Train and lying on the platform. The third thing was that she was not alone. Two feet stood in front of her, encased in worn-out suede desert boots. The lace was undone on the right foot, but both boots were filthy. Thin ankles showed between the tops of the boots and the bottoms of the ragged brown trousers that were much too short. Anne tried to tip her head back to look up at her demon, but her neck was stiff and she could see no higher than the knees and the hem of an ancient herringbone pattern overcoat. She could hear breathing. Her devil seemed to have some kind of a sinus infection or a heavy cold, judging by the snotty rattle she heard as it drew its breath. There was no way she could get up but she managed to roll over onto her back so she could look up at it.

'Hello Annie, my Annie,' it said, swimming into focus before her blurred eyes.

Anne wanted to scream. It wasn't a devil or demon at all. It was a man. But something terrible had happened to his face. Knowing the promises she had made to him, knowing that she'd sworn to be his until she could guess his name, Anne didn't allow herself to scream; she choked it off in her throat and just whimpered while she told herself that there must be some mistake. People couldn't look like this and it must be her eyes playing tricks on her, *so wait, Annie, just wait and things will sort themselves out*.

But her vision was as good as it was going to get. She stared up into the man's vacant eyes and let the horrific look of his skin sink in. *You can't, Annie*, she told herself. *You can't let him*

351

touch you. There's something wrong with him and you'll get like it too, if he touches you!

The man was about six feet tall and very thin. His ruined overcoat hung open to the waist where it was tied with string and the skin of his chest was as bad as that of his face. His wiry arms were crossed in front of him, cradling a grubby child's dolly to his chest, and he moved from side to side, rocking it, as if he was soothing it to sleep. His hair – what there was of it – had the colour of rotten straw and the texture of candyfloss and his scalp showed through it here and there like a rotten pink balloon. His dull skin was a deathly grey as though it had died in place, and it was peeling off showing dark meat beneath. The infection – or whatever it was – was widespread and the wounds glistened with a yellowish discharge. His eyes which looked as if they had once been blue, were pale, almost colourless. She stared into them, knowing there was something wrong with this man even more dreadful than the state of his skin. The eyes were blank and empty. But they *knew*. They raged with a vacant knowing that chilled Anne to the bone.

'Didn't work,' the man said.

Anne wasn't sure whether those cracked and weeping lips had moved or if this thing had imparted the words telepathically. His voice seemed to come from somewhere other than his mouth.

'I'm out,' she said, trying not to think of how his grey, peeling skin would feel against her raw breast.

'Didn't get it. There's a gap in the Knowledge. You didn't fill it. Not yet. Have to wait. Be patient.'

'What are you talking about?' Anne said. She could smell him now. He smelt more rotten than he looked. It was a kind of sweet odour that spoke of decay and death and again Anne's mind refused to let him touch her.

'You won't kill me, will you?' he asked.

'No,' Anne said, thinking, *I won't have to, you're half dead already.*

'Promise,' the man said, his voice still not being formed in the normal way.

'I promise. What are you going to do with me?'

'If you say my name, I'll die. Can't die until I become *One*.'

'I won't say it!' Anne said, tears coming to her eyes. This man was mad; his mind was as rotten as his body. Yet there was something lying underneath the putrescence of his whole being; behind the knowledge that choked him and the total darkness that shone in him, there was a kind of sadness, a vulnerability. A tiny glimmer of humanity still existed in him, but it encompassed only pain and woe. Perhaps it was what was left of his soul. Perhaps this was the gap in the Knowledge that he was seeking to remove. This would doubtless happen when he became *One*, whatever *One* was.

'Get up.'

'I can't,' Anne sobbed. 'I'm hurt. Most of my skin has come off.'

'The bag,' the madman said. 'It's in the bag. I know.'

He dropped to his knees, and laid the doll gently on the ground next to Anne's head. The doll was naked and its plastic chest was thudding up and down as if it had a real heart. Anne quickly looked away from it, fearing that it might become animated.

The man was kneeling by Anne's side, and she tensed herself, waiting for his scabby hands to lift her shirt so that he could lay his head on her breast and hear her heartbeat. But the man was busy doing something else. Plastic rustled. Anne turned her head, but it wouldn't go far enough for her to see what he was doing. It did go far enough for her to get a full force blast of his sweet rotting vegetation smell though, and she had to swallow hard.

'What are you doing?' she asked.

'Opening.' His voice seemed to be coming from about a foot and a half to the right of his head. He leaned over then, showing her the melted Marks & Spencer bag she had brought through the wall with her. He was trying to pull the hardened plastic apart and his fingers had split open where he had dug them in. The bag was running with blood that looked much too dark to be human.

The chisel came out first. The man looked at it blankly then discarded it and ripped more plastic away. The bottle of Coppertone suntan lotion was the next to be freed and the madman hissed when he saw it and set it down on Anne's stomach, right on the raw flesh where the buttons of her dress had come undone. Anne screamed. The madman paused, the bag in his bleeding hands and his ear cocked as if the sound had come from a distance, then took the bottle off her and laid it beside her.

The handle of the Kitchen Devil seemed to be welded right into the plastic of the bag. The madman ripped it free and this, too, he threw to one side. Next came the tube of Savlon. Apparently this was what he had been after from the start, because he let out a peal of high-pitched laughter.

He leaned over Anne, putting his peeling face close to hers, and peered into her eyes, grinning. 'Here we are, of course,' he said. This time Anne was sure he was talking telepathically because he was breathing in when he said it.

He darted away from her then, leaving her wondering what he was going to do. She screamed when he started to pull her dress up and kept on screaming until the dress covered her face and his bleeding fingers had forced a wad of it into her open mouth.

She started to fight as he straddled her body, batting at him with her sore arms but there was no shifting him. Her clawed hands caught him across the face once, then he squealed and slapped her head so hard her ears rang. She started to pray inwardly and the taunting voice said, 'Shouldn't ought to say that!'

So she relaxed, thinking about other things. Thinking about Tommy and Derek. The weight on her body shifted then and something cold dropped onto her belly. More cold drops followed. On her raw breasts, on her thighs and crotch. The cold drew the fire from her blistered and burnt skin and quickly removed the pain.

'Hands,' the madman said.

Anne gave him her hands. More cool drops. She felt the skin

354

become more elastic and her clawed fingers loosened. The madman took her right hand and gently massaged it, smoothing the coolness across it with his rough fingers, bending her own fingers painlessly back so they were straight again. He repeated the procedure with her other hand, then got off her and pulled her dress down.

Anne looked at him staring blankly at her then at her hands. They were completely restored and moved without hurting.

'Now you can do it,' the madman said, staring past her into the middle distance. He held out his hand, offering her the tube of Savlon.

Anne turned away from him and looked at the front of her body. Where the drops of the cream had fallen, the skin was healed. She rubbed it across the wounds in long sweeps marvelling at how it instantly mended the skin.

'Do me,' the madman said as Anne rubbed the last of the tube into her thighs. 'Heal me.'

'Run out,' Anne replied, looking at the crunched up tube and feeling guilty.

'Coppertone,' he replied.

Anne picked up the Coppertone bottle and turned around. The madman had taken off all his clothes and stood naked before her. He looked as though he'd been shredded by a combine harvester and brownish-yellow pus oozed from his wounds.

'I can't,' she told him, shaking her head.

'You start it. I can finish but you have to start. You have to touch me to heal me.'

She went over to him, holding her breath against the terrible smell. For the first time she realised the two of them were alone in the funfair and she wondered what had happened to everyone.

She unscrewed the bottle cap and held the bottle over the madman's head, squeezing it so that liquid ran out. Then she poured a stream over his shoulders and down his chest. He didn't heal, but flakes of skin fell off him as the lotion spread.

'Touch,' he said. 'You have to touch.'

355

Anne reached out and put her hand on his flaking chest. It felt rough and nasty and awfully cold.

Just pretend you're somewhere else, Annie, she told herself. *Just close your eyes and make out it's a game.*

But she couldn't close her eyes because she wanted to see if she could heal that terrible skin as he had healed hers. She ran her hand down his lumpy and broken flesh towards his stomach. The lesions and scores on the skin healed as she moved her hands, but the skin stayed that sick grey colour. Anne was delighted in a horrified way that she was doing this. She was *powerful*. This madman's very life depended on her healing hands. Her fingers trailed across his navel and ran back up the other side of his cold chest, mending the skin. For a second she felt a dreadful urge to run her hands around his back and embrace him to feel the thrill of his coolness against her. The shock made her step back and take her hands off him and she stood there blushing, the spell broken.

The madman smiled. 'Remember your pledge,' he said, starting to rub the oil into himself.

Anne thought about running while the madman still wasn't healed enough to catch her, but the feel of the place prevented her. This wasn't the same fairground. This was the other side. The side she'd always known existed; the side she thought was hell. Now she wasn't so sure what it was, except that it was somewhere else and that Tommy and Derek were here somewhere.

Would the madman really be able to take her to them?

'Who are you?' she asked, half hoping he would tell her his name by mistake.

The madman smiled. 'Rumpelstiltskin,' he said. 'You can call me R if you want. But you don't want to know my real name. You don't want to kill me, do you. You promised.'

'All I want is to find my husband and my child. Do you know where they are?'

'They are where I need to go. I thought this was it, but we aren't there. Not quite. We're on the edge, you see and they've crossed.'

'Where are we?' Anne asked, not wanting to watch the man rubbing the Coppertone into his genitals but unable to look away.

'We're in Limbo, the vast dead land. The land that separates the Good Land and the Bad Land and balances our Earth. Nothing lives here. Limbo is empty.'

'But we're here and we're alive.'

'Things have changed. Things are changing still. The power balance is altering. The Knowledge has touched Limbo and I can become *One*.'

'I don't know what you mean,' Anne said, shivering and looking up at the grey sky.

'You cannot know yet, my true love. But you, too, will take the Knowledge and then you will know, then you will fill me. We will become *One*.'

'What about finding Derek and Tommy?'

'We will find them. They are *One* already. We will become *One*.'

'I don't think you're going to take me to them at all,' Anne said. 'I think you've tricked me. I don't know where we are or what's going on, but I'm damn well going to find out. I'm going!'

She turned away from the madman and walked towards the steps. She had gone no more than three yards from him when she found she could go no farther. Her feet worked, but she walked on the spot. It was as if an invisible steel rope joined her to him.

'It's your promise,' the madman said. 'You can't break your promises here.'

Anne turned around. The madman was rubbing the Coppertone into his wispy hair and looking pleased with himself. 'Then I'm damn well going to kill you!' she hissed, running for the Kitchen Devil, which lay at the edge of the platform where the madman had thrown it. He made no move to stop her. She grabbed the knife, intending to plunge it into him and sever her bonds to him. She ran right up to him, the knife held out before her and punched it into his guts. It met meaty resistance, but it

357

went in, right up to the hilt. Anne screamed and twisted it. And noticed she was still a good four feet away from him.

'Promised, you did,' the man said.

Anne walked slowly up to him, put out her free hand and felt his cold chest. Then she drove the other hand into his belly. And was four feet away from him again.

'You bastard!' she screamed.

'You made the promise, I didn't,' he said. 'There's only one way you can go free and that is to guess my name.'

'George,' Anne said, hopelessly.

The man shook his head. 'I think it's time to go back to your hotel. I think I want to sleep with my ear against your heart.' He stepped into his ragged trousers and picked up his dolly.

'Simon,' Anne said.

The madman put on his coat, then his desert boots. 'Come along!' He set off down the platform towards the steps.

'I'm not going!' Anne shouted defiantly. She replaced the chisel and the rest of the stuff inside the melted M & S bag. She stood on the platform refusing to go.

But when the madman got to the steps, her promise reeled itself in and she was drawn along behind him.

Just before Anne Cousins walked through the wall of her prison, Roddy Johnson strode through the empty town centre, wondering what it was all about and cursing whoever had taken his car. He'd left it in the Kiosk car park just outside the Memorial Park, but it was gone when he got back there, so he'd walked back through the park to the police station – which was just across the road from the main entrance – to report it. The park gates had been chained shut and were ten feet or more high with spiked tops, but they had presented little problem to Roddy. The real problem was that the police station was closed. That wasn't possible, because the police station didn't close. It stayed open twenty-four hours a day, whatever day it was; Roddy knew from experience.

He had stood in front of the locked doors for a time, trying to puzzle out why it was closed, then walked back down the path and looked up at the windows of the deserted building. None of the lights was burning. He'd looked around the back through the chain wire fence of the car pool to see what was happening out there. Maybe his car had already been recovered and was inside. It was no go there either; the car park was totally empty.

So he'd decided to walk home.

Popley was a good two mile walk, but that wouldn't hurt, he'd done it thousands of times before. It was the emptiness of everything that worried him. That and the feeling of being watched.

He passed by Woolworths and looked into a gutted store. There was no window display, no counters, nothing to buy. He could have believed that Woolworths had decided to close the store if it hadn't been for the fact that all the other shops were empty, too. Dixons, Boots, Owen Owen where Foureyes' tasty girlfriend worked – all were empty.

He passed Sainsburys, heading in the direction of the railway station, thinking there might be someone there who could tell him what was going on in the shopping centre.

It wasn't until he had left the underpass on the station side that he realised it was the damn multistorey car park that had been worrying him. All the time it had been in sight he had felt as if he were being watched. Now it was behind him the odd sensation had gone away.

The railway station was empty, too. There were no red Post Office vans outside, their drivers standing around in groups, smoking and chatting. The paper shop was locked and all the lights in the station building were off. The front doors stood open and Roddy walked into the foyer, expecting to be challenged at any moment. Nothing stirred. He walked past the empty ticket collector's box and up the stone steps to the platforms. It was deserted up there, too. Not only were there no trains and no people, but there was no equipment around there. Usually there was a variety of trolleys and trucks lying about – now there wasn't even a waste paper basket to be seen.

Roddy looked down the empty tracks towards Southampton. There was an overhead set of signals about a mile down the track which usually shone red when no trains were passing. They weren't even turned on.

'Shit!' Roddy said to himself, noticing how odd his voice sounded in the complete silence. He shrugged and went back down the platform to the steps. And stopped.

He stared down at the steps for a long time before he moved again. They had been there forever, those steps. They were made of stone, marble or something, and over the years they had been worn away by the pressure of countless commuter feet. The indentations in them were smooth and concave and that was why Roddy couldn't believe what he saw. In front of him were his own shoe prints as fresh and plain as if he'd stepped into wet concrete. He knew they were his because of the pointed toe and square heel with a rounded back edge. Just to make sure, he slipped off one of his boots and placed it in the indentation on the top step. The fit was perfect. This was impossible. But then again, everything that had happened since Foureyes had got them out of the Ghost Train was impossible. Shops didn't leave town overnight, and police stations didn't close. And there was always someone around in a railway station.

He put his boot back on, wondering if he'd been drugged somewhere along the way. What other explanation was there? Unless Foureyes was right and they had landed in some kind of an alternate universe. Roddy felt incredibly tired as he tried to work out what being in an alternate universe meant. It just wouldn't wash. There was no reasoning it out; each time he tried to think about it, his mind went cloudy, fuzzing his thoughts.

He quickly left the station and walked the rest of the way back to Popley in a daze, not really noticing his surroundings, not looking up at the gunmetal dawn sky that seemed stuck in position so that you could permanently see light to the east and dark to the west. He ignored the odd way things sounded, like the flattened tone as the steel nails in his heels clicked against the pavement and the unreal loudness of his breath roaring in and out of his lungs. He did turn twice to see if he was leaving footprints in the pavement that could be followed by whatever had been watching him from the car park, but it was only the station steps that seemed to have gone soggy on him.

Nothing remarkable happened until he was almost back at his flat. He was crossing the empty square to his front door when the feeling he was being watched returned. He froze, his keys in his right hand, and slowly turned around, the hairs on the back of his neck bristling.

Something moved. Over in the corner of the square, in the alley he'd just come through. There was no noise but, as he turned, he caught a glimpse of red near the ground.

His flick-knife was out in less than two seconds. He ran back towards the alley, feeling the adrenalin rush into his blood. He moved swiftly and silently into the alley, taking the corner wide in case whoever it was was still there, but knowing the watcher had gone.

He ran out of the other end of the alley and into the road. There was no cover here, just a wire fence across the road behind which lay the flat open grass of school playing fields. The watcher couldn't have crossed the road or Roddy would have been able to see him. That meant that he'd concealed himself in one of the back gardens of the houses that faced the road.

Roddy turned and went back up the alley slowly, dragging his heels along the paving stones so that the hidden watcher could hear him coming and know that he wasn't frightened. He opened the first gate he came to and stepped into the tiny garden. It was empty. So was the next. The third one was locked and, knowing no one would hear because there *was* no one to hear, Roddy kicked it hard, breaking the bolt from the wood. The gate flew open and Roddy ran into the garden.

A sheet of corrugated iron leant up against the fence which separated this garden from the next. The watcher was behind it. Something red showed at the bottom right hand corner.

'Okay fucker, come out!' Roddy said contemptuously. The knife felt good in his hand. It seemed almost to have a life of its own, and it made his arm want to slash and stab.

The piece of red material didn't move.

'I know you're in there,' Roddy warned, 'and if you come out now, I won't hurt you.' This wasn't true, but it often worked. Terrified people almost always believed you if you told them you wouldn't hurt them. 'Come on, I can *see* you, for Christ's sake!'

The red thing still didn't move. Whoever it was in there was obviously going to wait for him to get closer then push the sheet of metal down on him, hoping to flee while he struggled out from under it.

Roddy skirted the sheet of iron and wrenched it away from the wall. It fell with a clatter and left Roddy staring down at his prize.

The red thing was a sock. An empty sock. He picked it up and sniffed it. It smelt of foot, so it hadn't been here very long. The watcher had obviously left it here to slow him down while he made his escape. He'd probably gone over this fence into the next door garden and back out into the square.

'Bastard!' Roddy shouted. 'I'll get you, you motherfucker!' He held the sock out and slashed it to ribbons with the knife. On his way out he hung it on the gate latch so the watcher would know what was coming to him.

On the way back to the flat, Roddy thought he heard running footsteps and he froze again and held his breath while he listened. The only thing that broke the silence was the thudding of his heart in his ears.

For some reason he couldn't fathom, he didn't expect to get into the flat. He put the key in the lock and turned it. The hairs on the back of his neck were erect and his senses were screaming *TRAP!*, so he stepped back before he pushed the door open.

The door opened and gave him a view of his hall. Everything looked normal, everything was in its place. Jon Kott's old Doc Martens stood against the wall under the coat rack next to Sandy's spike heel lace-up boots. Winter overcoats hung on the rack, and the old yellow Bex Bissel carpet sweeper stood beside them.

Roddy went down the hall and opened the bathroom door.

Normal. The bath had a grimy ring and an empty toilet roll sat in the holder.

In the room Sandy shared with Jon the bed clothes were heaped around the foot of the bed and a grubby pair of Jon's underpants lay in the middle of the bottom sheet. Sandy's clothes were strewn about the room as usual. The red dial of the clock-radio on Jon's side was pulsing on and off – obviously the power had gone off and come on again.

Somewhere, something was making a crackling, buzzing noise. Roddy hurried down the hall to the kitchen/dining area at the rear of the house. This too seemed normal; the table and sink were loaded with dirty plates, cornflakes were scattered on the floor, the ashtrays were overflowing. There was no sign of whatever had made the noise. Roddy held his breath and listened again, but heard only the buzzing of the electric clock on the cooker. Roddy looked at it and shuddered in spite of himself. It read five fifteen, the same as Foureyes' watch. He waited for the big hand to advance to five sixteen, but although the second hand went around three times as he watched, the big hand didn't move at all. 'Bust,' Roddy told himself, and went over to the cooker and slapped the face plate. It made no difference. The clock still read five fifteen.

The lounge was empty, too. 'No one home then,' Roddy said, heading back out into the hall. The only place left now was his bedroom.

As he left the lounge he heard the crackling noise again, and he shot back inside, hoping to see whatever was doing it. Nothing looked any different.

His bed was unmade, but it looked inviting anyway. Suddenly, Roddy was dog tired. He yawned, took off his denim jacket and shirt and slung them over a chair. He put his flick knife on the little bedside table next to the lamp and the Seiko watch his mother had given him and he never wore. He noted with distaste that the Seiko's hands had stopped at five fifteen.

He cupped his hand under his armpit, put his nose down and sniffed. They were sticky, but they didn't reek too badly. He'd wash when he woke up. Sitting on the unmade bed, he pulled

363

off his boots, then peeled off the damp socks. He took off his jeans and underpants and tossed them on the chair with his shirt and jacket. Then he rolled into bed, pulled the sheets up around him and fell into a deep, dreamless sleep.

Some time later someone sat down on Roddy Johnson's bed. Roddy didn't wake up properly, but he became conscious of the weight next to him.

'I've missed you, darling.'

The voice belonged to Sandy. Roddy tried to wake up but he seemed to be caught on the border of wakefulness and sleep and he couldn't break through.

He felt her cool hand on his face, felt her long nails delicately trace the contours of his lips. He could smell her perfume now; the sharp odour of Poison. Still he couldn't wake up.

'It's okay Roddy, I'm here,' her voice soothed as her nails drifted down to the skin of his neck. 'We're together again and I'm alright.'

Her voice had a distinct crackle as she finished her sentences. It reminded him of the noise from the cooker.

'Sandy,' he said. His voice sounded a long way away.

The cool hand pushed the bedclothes from his chest and sharp nails pinched his left nipple. Roddy started to get an erection. The thrilling nails described a gentle arc across his chest and lingered at his right nipple.

'I still love you, Roddy,' his sister's voice said. 'Just like I always have.'

Roddy's eyes opened. The curtains had been closed and the room was dim, but there was no mistaking Sandy. She was dressed in the same black leather mini skirt and fawn halter top she had been wearing when she went on the Ghost Train with Jon. Her nipples were erect. She smiled down at him.

'You're here,' Roddy said. His penis felt like an iron bar and ached for her touch.

Sandy's hand strayed down to his navel and she dug her nails in. 'We can be together now,' she said.

364

'Where's Jon?' Roddy asked, not really caring in the least where Jon was.

'Somewhere,' Sandy said softly. 'It doesn't matter now. What matters is us.' Her nails nipped the flesh of his abdomen. Roddy gasped.

'I know what you want,' Sandy said. 'It's what you've always wanted, isn't it? This is what you've dreamed of since I grew up.'

Roddy said nothing. He was staring into Sandy's eyes, wondering what colour they used to be. They were electric blue now, but he wasn't sure they were always that colour. It didn't matter anyhow, because they suited her like that, made her look more sexy. As her fingertips reached his pubic hair, he marvelled at how the colour of her eyes seemed to pulse and fluctuate so that sometimes they were flat and greyish, sometimes sparkling and blue. She said something else, but Roddy couldn't make out what it was; the fuzziness drowned the words.

'What did you say, Sandy?' he asked, not wanting to break the atmosphere.

Her voice was clearer this time. 'I said I've always known you wanted me. I knew when you were spying on me in the bath. I knew when you were listening to me and Jon fucking. I used to groan louder when I knew you were there. I wanted you to want me. Now we can have each other.' Her cool fingers slipped around his erection, squeezed and pumped once.

Roddy gasped. The pleasure was more intense than anything he'd felt before. 'But Sandy,' he groaned as the hand pulled back towards the tip.

'It's incest,' she said, 'isn't it? It doesn't matter. Not here.'

She let go of him and took off her halter top. 'We can be together, Roddy, for ever and ever. But there's something you have to do for me first.' She took her breast in one hand and pulled Roddy's head up to it with the other. Roddy tasted his sister's flesh. Her nipple was as cold as ice. She groaned and pulled his head away, looked down at him with those sparkling eyes. 'Will you?' she asked.

'Will I what?' Roddy said. Something was wrong, and it wasn't just that he was about to fuck his sister – although that was enough to fill his mind with all kinds of conflicting emotions, the least of which was the illegality of the act. It was something more serious than that. There was a sort of built-in biological revulsion to the idea of wanting Sandy and, in a vague way, he understood that he was being offered a choice. He could either have the thing he'd most wanted all his adult life (and Sandy had been right on the button with that – he'd wanted her since she was eleven and he was thirteen) or he could turn it down. He understood that if he took what he was being offered nothing would ever be the same again and if he turned it down he would never have that chance again.

'Will you do what I ask? You must promise to if you want to have me,' Sandy said, pulling the sheets off the lower half of Roddy's body and gazing down at his throbbing erection.

It looked as if Sandy already knew what his reply would be. 'Ask me,' he said.

Sandy got off the bed and pulled her leather skirt up over her hips. She wasn't wearing panties. She watched Roddy staring at her for a time then got onto the bed, straddling his ankles. She was wet and cold. 'I love you, Roddy,' she said, and leaned forward so that her painted lips were a fraction of an inch away from the tip of his penis. Her breath was cold, too. It sent shivers of pleasure coursing through Roddy.

'Ask me,' Roddy groaned, frightened to move in case the spell was broken.

Sandy's chilly pink tongue flicked out and lapped at him. She brought her head up, licking her lips. 'Get the cross and bring it to me,' she said.

'What?' Roddy said.

'The cross. The boy's cross. I want it. I need it. *We* need it.' She tickled his balls with her nails. Roddy's muscles contracted and his penis throbbed. 'What for?' he asked.

'To stop him ruining it for us. We have to take it off him.' She licked him again.

'But what is it all about? What's happening, Sandy?' Roddy groaned.

'Trust me,' she said, looking up at him.

'Okay,' he said, ignoring the doubts that were trying to fill his confused mind. 'I'll get it.'

'Something else,' Sandy said, grinning.

'What?'

'There's a young boy outside.'

'I know. I almost caught him,' Roddy said, feeling the heaven as Sandy's fingers ran up and down his erection.

'He got away. He's trying to ruin it, too. Kill him for me.' She squeezed. And pumped. 'Kill him, Roddy!'

'Yesss!' Roddy shouted.

The sex was ecstatic. When Sandy rolled off him, he was shivering and the sheets beneath him were stiff with frost. He could see his breath in the air and although his teeth were chattering and his skin was almost all gooseflesh he couldn't get up. Not yet.

Sandy pulled her skirt down, picked up her top and slipped it on. She walked to the middle of the room and turned around, smiling. 'I love you,' she said, but her voice buzzed and crackled and the words were indistinct. When she finished speaking, the ragged buzzing continued.

Roddy worked himself up to a sitting position, feeling the icy sheet biting into his back, but not caring. He noticed that most of his skin was blue with the cold. 'What are you doing?' he asked, looking at his sister.

'I must go. Remember your promise. Bring me the cross.'

'No, Sandy!' Roddy began to protest. Then he knew what the buzzing was. The electricity. It was the electricity escaping from the socket on the other side of the room. It was alive and blue like Sandy's eyes and it was creeping out of the two bottom pin holes of the socket like stealthy lightning. He watched in horror as the two ribbons of sparking, flexing electricity extended from the socket and crept through the air towards Sandy, filling the room with the smell of ozone and burning wire.

'Look out, San!' he shouted.

367

Sandy chuckled. 'Remember your promises!' she said.

The two bands of electric current split apart as they reached her ankles, each one winding around them like serpents, rising and going up under her skirt. Sandy screamed as the currents joined at the top of her legs – a scream of ecstasy rather than of agony.

'San!' Roddy yelled.

The streams of power shot out of the top of Sandy's skirt and wound around her body, crackling and fizzing. Sandy began to change. Underneath the layer of blue power, her body became elongated and thin and began to turn black. Her head took on the shape of a sideways-up egg. 'You fool!' she said, but it wasn't her voice. This voice was low and powerful. A nightmare voice.

'San!' Roddy shouted. He was off the bed now and on his feet, but he didn't approach the Sandy/Monster thing.

'I have her!' the voice boomed, sending a freezing wind from the vortex that had formed around the shape. Roddy's hair started to freeze. He peered at the swirling electricity, but couldn't make out what it was in there.

'You touched *me*!' the thing thundered. 'You promised *me*! Remember your promise, fool. Do as you pledged and I will give you Sandy for all time. And power beyond your wildest imaginings. Get me the cross! Bring it to me and you shall have your sister.'

'Where? Where to?' Roddy yelled, suddenly finding his voice. 'Bring it where?'

'You will know. Follow the boy!'

The dark shape lost its colour beneath the electrical shield and its form flowed back to that of Sandy. She was naked and she looked terrified.

And there was a gaping rent in her front that ran from the bottom of her neck to the top of her pubic hair.

'Sandy!' Roddy screamed, but the power was flowing back into the plughole, melting his sister and drawing her back with it. He watched her pink flesh ripple and stretch like rubber as it flowed from her into the socket.

Then she was gone. All that was left in the room was a thick coating of frost and a faint smell of Sandy's Poison.

Shivering, Roddy pulled on his stiff trousers, his almost solid tee shirt and denim jacket. He couldn't get his feet into his socks, so he slung them aside and put his bare feet into his boots. He felt sick and the only thought inside his head was to get outside the house. He'd been tricked, well and truly. He'd fucked some monster or something, and not Sandy at all.

'You bastard!' he shouted, as he crossed the room. 'I'll kill you! If you want the cross you can fucking well whistle for it.' He directed this last comment towards the switch socket, since that was where all the action had come from. Now he knew why he'd heard all that buzzing earlier. It had been that *thing* forming Sandy where he couldn't see it being done.

The electricity shot out of the plughole again. Not slowly this time, not in a curving line, but in a straight beam like a blue laser. It seared the front of his freezing trousers as it passed him and disappeared under the bed. The jeans caught alight and Roddy jumped back out of the line of fire and beat them out with his hands.

Above him, the lightbulb exploded, showering him with glass. He knew what was coming next and dodged before the new beam of electricity could shoot down through his head.

He ran out into the hall and sighed. There were three sockets there, and the laser-like beams were coming from all of them. To add to the trouble, a beam shone out of the kitchen at head height (from the cooker switch, he supposed) then ran right up the hall to the front door. He kept close to the wall and edged his way towards the door.

He glanced down at the sputtering beam just in front of his legs, then up at the one at head height. It was closing in on him. He bent himself double and hopped over the cross beam, searing the back of one heel as he came down.

'I'll do it. I'll get the cross!' he yelled, knowing he couldn't make it out of the house.

The high beam touched his hair. It singed and he ducked lower. The cross-beams in front of him had risen somehow so they were like upside-down 'U's. He knew what would happen if he tried to fling himself under them. They would fall like guillotines.

'I'll DO IT!' he screamed as the beam touched his hair again and burnt his scalp.

The electricity died. Roddy decided to keep his comments to himself until he got outside.

The square was still empty when he closed the front door behind him. He walked to the middle of it and sat down on one of the two wooden benches. He had hardly caught his breath when the watcher appeared from the alley.

The boy was about ten years old. He had black hair and was dressed in a red tee shirt and black trousers. He had no shoes on his feet. His face was pale and wary and he looked as though he'd recently escaped from a coal mine.

Roddy stayed where he was, looking at the boy. The boy looked back at him, obviously debating whether or not he should come over. He looked as if he wanted to.

Roddy took out his Marlboros from his jacket pocket and carefully extracted one of the damp cigarettes. He placed it between his lips and tried to make it burn.

When he looked up again, the boy was in front of him. Roddy had followed his progress across the square out of the corner of his eye, being careful not to look up until the boy was near enough to grab.

'Are you Roddy?' the boy asked.

'Yeah,' Roddy grunted. 'How do you know?'

'Your sister . . .'

'What about her?' Roddy said, sitting up straight. The end of his flick knife protruded comfortingly from the top of his right hand trouser pocket.

'They said she's . . .'

'Who said? Who said?' Roddy had a deep-seated suspicion that this kid knew all about what had just happened.

'Some kids. Where the giant is. I got away, see.'

Roddy shot out a hand and grabbed the boy's thin arm. He dragged him close and looked into his eyes. 'You did it, didn't

370

you?' he heard himself say. His mind suddenly flung itself into turmoil. Thoughts didn't work. He was getting a hard-on again because pictures of Sandy sucking his cock were filling his head. 'You fucking did it, kid! You turned on the juice! You know I don't like electricity!'

Then he was shaking the boy and his vision was blank and Sandy was humping his face and something was happening under his skin. Things were crawling about under his skin. Creatures. His flesh was bulging with them and the electricity was chasing him and the *itching*! The knife! Where was the knife? The boy was screaming and the railway lines were bucking under him as the *thing* came across behind him and he didn't like heights or the fires down below but if he didn't do something soon it would have him and Sandy. And Foureyes was blocking the way halfway across and the lines were bucking. Fucking. Bucking. And Sandy. And Sandy!

Roddy roared.

When he looked, the boy was dead.

Dave left the fairground just after Roddy had tried to get into the police station. He didn't know exactly what he was supposed to do or where he was meant to go, and although he didn't like being with Roddy, he hated being alone even more. At least Roddy afforded some degree of physical protection against whatever might be lurking in this place waiting to jump out at him.

Getting out of AdventureLand was easy. Although as he walked around the perimeter past the empty stalls and rides he fancied he could feel eyes watching him, the place was totally deserted and incredibly silent. He decided that the feeling of being watched was due to a combination of the emptiness of the fairground and his overactive imagination. Practically everything that had happened so far could have been the work of an overwrought imagination. If he shut his eyes, he could imagine himself lying in bed at home recovering from one of the most intense nightmares he'd ever had.

He tried this once or twice as he walked through the fair

towards the entrance, but each time he opened his eyes he was still here in this Limbo land where nothing moved and there was no sound. Every time his lids covered his eyes he had the terrible sensation that a huge pit had opened in front of him and he was going to step right off the edge into it.

You already did that Davey, he told himself as he glanced around for signs of whatever might be watching him. *You already jumped over the edge of the big pit. You did it a long time ago at Ziegfeld's restaurant. You wanted to do it, so you've just got to see it through now. Think of Phil and Judy and that guy Cousins who's looking for his son. They're over here too somewhere, you know they are.*

He reached the arch and went through. There was a slight resistance to his passage as he stepped out of AdventureLand; a feeling of cobweb strands breaking as he stretched them past their elastic limit. He was pleasantly surprised. He had expected a force field of some kind to appear and confine him to the fairground.

On a whim, he turned and tried to go back through the arch but he found his way blocked. The air in the archway seemed to have half solidified so that it cushioned him and threw him back when he tried to pass.

Dave went around the side of AdventureLand that was farthest away from the Ringway, opposite the Ghost Train. There were plenty of gaps between the rides this side. He picked his way past the silent lorries, through the tangle of thick cables, to the nearest gap. As he had expected, he couldn't go through. He was locked out.

Dave didn't know whether it would be necessary for him and Roddy to go back through the Ghost Train to get back to their own world but he suspected that AdventureLand would be involved in the return trip. It sounded about right, but they would have to worry about that when it came to it. If it ever did.

Dave turned away from the fair and set off across the grass heading for home.

About halfway across the park, he noticed that the grass felt odd under his scorched Hi-Tecs. Wondering what was different about it, he bent down to feel it. The grass didn't have the right texture. It was brittle and dry and turned to a yellowish dust when he rubbed it between his fingers. And yet it didn't seem to be dead.

It's had its soul removed, that's what's happened to it, Dave thought.

The thing that grass possessed that made it grass, seemed to have been extracted from it, leaving it empty and wrong. It reminded Dave of a crab shell with no crab in it that he'd found on the beach at Falmouth, the same summer that his dad had bought him the compass. For some unknown reason the empty crab shell had filled him with a desolation that made him cry. *And you had to wait another eleven years or so to find out what bothered you about it, didn't you?* he said to himself.

He wondered what was happening at home. Were his parents frantic at his disappearance? Were they at this moment talking tearfully to a *News at Ten* camera like Tiger Cousins' dad had done? And what about Sally? What if she'd woken up to find he'd gone the same way as Phil and Judy? She knew about Purdue and the Ghost Train. She'd known even before he had. Would she come and look for him when she woke up? He hoped so, because he didn't think he could do it alone. He needed her here. Perhaps he and Roddy could give The Claw a good run for its money; perhaps they *could* even kill it. But he didn't think they could rescue Phil and Judy and Sandy Johnson and Jon Kott and Tiger and his dad and get them all out again unless Sally was here.

But thinking ahead was going to do no good at all.

The best thing you can do, Davey boy, is go home and see what develops. Take it as it comes and don't worry about the rest.

The front door of his house wasn't locked – which was a good thing because Dave never carried a key. He pushed the door open and looked into the hallway. *Go on then, Dave, go in like you're supposed to*, he told himself. *Go in and see what's in there.*

He took his Swiss Army knife from his pocket, opened the big blade and went into the house slowly, leading with the knife. The cross got hotter as he passed the threshold, stinging his chest. Its power strengthened his resolve and he swung the lounge door open, ready for a fight. The lounge furniture was in place, the books were still on the shelf, the television stood in the corner and Dave's old sneakers were in the hearth. Everything was just tickety-boo. Except that one of the arms of his father's chair had collapsed and had shed crumbly yellow foam. There was an indentation in the middle of it that roughly mirrored the shape of someone's bottom. His mother's probably; this was where she liked to perch to be close to her husband while they were watching telly.

Dave left the room, closing the door firmly, and checked the dining room and the kitchen. There was no food in the refrigerator and nothing to drink. Other than that nothing was out of place.

Upstairs he told himself, knowing that this was where it was going to happen. His stomach tightened itself into a small fearful knot at the thought of going up there, but it had to be done.

He went back to the hall, Swiss Army knife still held before him. Then, the cross pulsing in time with his quickening heartbeat, he started up the stairs.

There were twenty-one stairs from the bottom to the top but it looked like a lot more. The temperature drop was noticeable two stairs up. His breath started to show on the third stair and by the fifth he was sure that The Claw was waiting up there for him.

There was a coating of frost on the top two stairs. From where he stood, one stair down, he could see that the landing and the lower half of the walls were frosted too.

We can talk, he thought hopefully. *Maybe it'll let my friends go if I ask nicely. Maybe we can make a deal*.

But there would be no deal-making, he knew that. If The Claw was up there, there would be a fight to the death.

He reached the landing and ran to the bathroom, yelling at the top of his voice. He threw the door open and charged in, intending to lunge at The Claw before it could strike at him.

The Claw wasn't there.

But it had been.

Dave stopped in the middle of the bathroom. 'Fuck,' he said.

The bathroom looked exactly as it had done when The Claw had appeared on the night of his nineteenth birthday. The carpet was ripped and broken floorboards showed through. The shower pipe was distorted where the bulge of goo had travelled up it, and several strands of the gelatinous substance still hung from the shower head. There was more of the greenish black slime on the carpet and its stench filled his nostrils. Even the broken toilet brush handle still lay on the floor where he had dropped it.

The mirrored door of the bathroom cabinet caught his eye then and he wanted to go and look inside. There was something in there for him, some nasty surprise, but he wasn't going to look, even though he knew he was supposed to. He wasn't going to look because what was in there would probably kill him and he suddenly wasn't ready to die. He would go and look in his bedroom first. Say hello and goodbye to his Amstrad. Maybe play a last game of Space Pirates for an hour or three. Perhaps the thing in the cabinet would have gone by then. Maybe it would have eaten all the Preparation H and the aspirins and his mother's Ex-Lax and retreated to find a toilet somewhere.

He trotted down the frosty landing and went into his bedroom.

Which was a mistake of the first order.

As the door closed behind him, pushed shut by the weight of what he was now knee deep in, Dave wished he'd opened the bathroom cabinet door after all.

Moths. A solid brown sea of them, two feet deep, filled his bedroom. Nowhere amongst the writhing, flapping insects could the carpet be seen.

The room was filled with the sound of their wings fluttering as the top layer of them took to the air. Swarms of the brown creatures started to climb up Dave's legs.

'OH MY GOD, GET THEM OFF ME!' Dave screamed. He took an involuntary step backward and almost fell.

'Help, HELP!' he screamed, flailing wildly with the knife at the flying moths. Each time he moved his feet he crushed hundreds of them and the floor felt squelchy under his Hi-Tecs.

He turned and tried to pull the door open, but the weight of the insects against it was too great and although it came open a little way, he couldn't get out.

The flying moths were starting to land on his head now and he slapped at his hair with his free hand, brushing them away, but each time he got them off another swarm landed. The sensation of moth bodies crawling though his hair and finding their way down his neck was almost too much to stand and he screamed, stomping up and down across the writhing floor as he fought them off.

The ones that were swarming up his legs had reached the waistband of his trousers now and were tickling their way underneath his tee shirt and crawling on the bare flesh of his belly.

'Cross! C'mon cross!' he squealed, slashing at the fluttering air with the knife and brushing moths from his face with his free hand.

A particularly large moth alighted on the tip of his nose, and he swiped at it and missed somehow. He opened his mouth to scream when it crawled up inside the frame of his glasses and his mouth was instantly filled with more moths.

You've got live moths in your mouth, his mind coolly informed him from some distance away. *Feel them crawling. Feel their fluttering wings!*

He meant to spit, meant to cough and blow the invaders out of his mouth, but a reflex action caused a spasm of his muscles and his jaws clamped down firmly on a mouthful of moths. Their bodies broke between his teeth and Dave tasted a bitter liquid before he was able to spit them out.

The big moth which was wriggling between the inside of his glasses and his eyeball began to do something which made his eye sting terribly. Either it was trying to eat its way through his closed eyelid, or it had released some kind of digestive acid. Screaming though gritted teeth, Dave pushed his glasses up and took the squirming creature between finger and thumb.

That's right, Dave, pull it off, mate, his detached inner voice told him. Hissing and squealing in panic, Dave tugged at the creature. As he pulled it away from his eye, the lid came out too. Before his blurred eye, he saw the moth's mandibles gnashing at the skin of his eyelid.

Can't be happening, his mind told him calmly, *moths don't have jaws, mandibles or anything to bite you with.*

Dave moaned. He increased the pressure of his thumb and finger, but the moth didn't die, just matched the force he was using by quickening its nibbling movements.

Dave screamed long and hard. He pinched the struggling insect with as much force as he could muster, realising dimly that his underpants had been invaded too.

The moth popped. Dark brown liquid squirted into his eye and burnt like acid. There was a sudden flurry of wings and more, smaller moths alighted on his eye. His swiped them away and put his glasses back down again.

He swung crazily around and, with his good eye, noticed the rolled-up copy of the newspaper he kept to kill moths on the bedside table. He grabbed it and set about smashing the flying insects from the air, swiping first with the knife, then in the opposite direction with the paper.

The cross lit up then. Its energy flowed through Dave's tired arms, and its red beam glowed through his shirt.

Should have got it out, no good in there! Dave thought, but there was no time to whip the cross out.

The cold, marble-like feeling left his flesh and Dave fought tirelessly, swiping and slashing and stamping. Insect corpses began to pepper the walls and he'd got most of them off his body now, but the ones inside his underpants were still alive and starting to bite, even though moths weren't supposed to.

He felt a brief stab of heat at his sternum and smelled smoke. The cross had scorched a hole clean through the front of his tee shirt and the red beam shone out, flickering across the room as he moved and incinerating the moths as it struck them. The smell was awful, but Dave ignored it and increased his efforts with the paper and knife. His mind went blank and he fought furiously, no longer feeling anything, no longer even seeing what he was doing. He could smell the smoke of the charred moths, hear the soft *pop* as the red beam struck them and exploded them but everything else was a blur.

It took a long time for Dave to realise that the moths were all dead.

'Oh,' he said when his good eye finally took in the carnage that lay before him. The rolled up paper, now black and sticky with moth entrails, fell from his hand and dropped into the knee-deep pile of dead insects. The cross's beam had gone out somewhere along the line – he hadn't noticed it. He stood there panting and surveying the scene. A pall of evil-smelling blue smoke hung in the room. Moths were splattered all over every surface; dead bodies still smoked on the top of his Amstrad and his clothes were stained with moth juice. Nothing moved. He kicked his leg out and the pile of dead moths surged across the room, rustling like a deep pile of autumn leaves.

That'll teach you, Davey, he admonished himself, thinking of the waiting bathroom cabinet. *That'll teach you to run away from what you're supposed to do. Go back into the bathroom and open the cabinet door. You should have done that in the first place.*

He took off his glasses and felt his left eye which was swollen shut. He couldn't tell how bad the damage was, but it hurt when he touched it. There was Optrex in the bathroom cabinet, and a tube of Golden Eye Ointment and wasn't that funny, because that was exactly what he wasn't going to get when he pulled that mirrored door open. Whatever was waiting in there for him, it wasn't Golden Eye Ointment, that was for sure.

He undid his trousers and pulled them down to his thighs, taking his cotton underpants down with them. His lower abdomen and his crotch were covered in red boil-like swellings, each of which showed a pinprick of blood at the top. It didn't hurt. Yet. Dave wondered if the moths had infected him with anything; malaria or something. He decided that the best policy would be to heal himself, so he took the cross off and – having checked that its deep red eye was still open and ready for

378

action – held it to his penis. He could feel its warmth and vibrancy on the tender flesh, but no burst of power issued forth to heal him.

'I believe I can heal myself,' Dave said, realising he could still taste moth in his mouth and starting to feel ill.

The cross didn't cure him. He wondered if it might not work on his private parts for some obscure reason, so he held it up to his sore eye.

'C'mon cross, I *believe!*' he told it, but the cross didn't flare.

Something was rustling down by his feet. The sound was neither loud nor threatening. It sounded like thousands of dead moth carcasses settling.

Dave shut his good eye and concentrated the way he'd seen Cyril Hardesty do. Nothing happened. Dave didn't give up and he didn't curse the cross. He didn't do that any more. It had saved him just now and he believed in it implicitly. The cross had chosen him to do its work and he had agreed – subconsciously at first, but now consciously too. He was patient now, he had faith.

So why wasn't it working?

Rustling.

Come on cross, do your stuff! he thought.

The cross lit and shot a needle-slender red beam into his eye. He smelt burning flesh and the pain was intense. He screamed and staggered backwards.

His eye was not healed, but the two paces he took saved his life.

Because the moth to end all moths had just crept out from under his bed and its open maw was snapping at the floor where Dave's legs had just been. Dave looked down at it and forgot the pain in his eye. The moth was brown and five feet long. Its body was perhaps eighteen inches in diameter, and its delta shape wings were as wide as the bed. Its legs were long and bristle-haired. But the most horrific thing about the moth was its head, which was as large as Dave's and had huge multi-faceted eyes and sharp cruel-looking jaws. It looked up at Dave, its eyes shining rainbow colours and its mouth opening in a kind of silent I've-got-you-now leer.

For something so large, it moved with astounding speed,

snapping at Dave's legs while he was still in shock.

He moved by will of survival alone, leaping backwards as the moth's jaws shut with a bony *click!*

The moth moved forward and Dave knew that this was it. The cross had failed him this time.

In desperation, Dave kicked at the moth's head, not even thinking about what might happen to his foot if it was caught.

The moth's maw opened, but it wasn't quick enough to catch the Hi-Tec which flashed around the side of its head and hit its left eye.

'Fuck you!' Dave shouted, bringing his foot back again. It was like kicking a rock. The moth's eye had dented, but it didn't seem to be worrying unduly about *that*. It was advancing on him again.

Dave dropped to his knees.

The moth came closer. It beat its wings making a horrid soft flapping that raised the hairs on the back of Dave's neck.

'You can't win, motherfucker!' Dave assured the beast. The Swiss Army knife felt good in his hand. Felt as if it could kill.

The moth snapped, jutting its head forward like a dog. Dave was ready for it. He'd played slaps with Lucy the dog enough times to know where the moth would strike. The moth wasn't quite as fast as Lucy, and his reactions had speeded up, so that when the jaws closed, Dave's hand was well out of the way.

Just as he would have done when play-fighting with Lucy the dog, Dave brought his other hand round and slapped the opposite side of the moth's head to the direction its jaws were pointing in. Except that, instead of tapping lightly, catching the moth upside its head as he would have done with the dog, Dave punched hard with his balled fist. This technique would drive Lucy mad and she would swing her head back in the other direction, miss his hand again and collect another slap around the other ear. It worked just as well with the moth. It turned, spotted the fist that had just punched it still lingering in the air and snapped its head back again after it, not realising that it could have pounced forward and easily taken Dave's neck.

The knife was in his other hand and as the moth's jaw

clamped down on empty air again, Dave punched the blade of the Swiss Army knife into the back of its already dented left eye.

The moth shook its head. Dave held on and tugged, but the knife wouldn't come out again. He grabbed it with both hands and pulled, fighting both to extricate the knife, and stop the moth's head coming back. The blade moved a little, slicing into the rainbow-coloured eye. Black pus oozed out.

'KILL YOU, MOTHERFUCKER!' Dave screamed.

The moth shook its head again and the knife was wrenched from Dave's grasp. Unbalanced, he slid down into the carpet of dead insects. The moth was quicker this time and its jaws closed over his left forearm while he was still falling.

The bones broke. He felt them snap as the moth's jaws exerted incredible pressure. He pulled with the broken arm, dragging himself to a crouched position so that his face was inches from the moth's. His arm was bleeding, and blood was running out of the moth's iron jaws but it didn't hurt at all. It was another arm – it belonged to someone else. But it was attached to his shoulder and it was crunching and it would come right off soon if he didn't do something.

The knife! The knife was still in the moth's eye! He reached for it and the moth saw his other arm coming and ducked, pulling him off his feet again.

He could feel the pain now, an agonising dull ache, deep in his arm which felt as though someone was filling his veins with molten lead.

Each time he reached for the knife, the moth ducked and bit tighter on his arm, repaying him for what he'd done to it earlier. There was blood in his eyes now, up his nose and in his mouth. He could smell blood, taste it, and his vision was red.

He lay on the floor and the moth walked onto him, its weight crushing the breath from his lungs. His right arm punched and gouged at its head, making no impression.

He couldn't breathe any more. Blood was gone. There was just the smell of moth, the weight of moth. Moth filled his whole being.

And his probing fingers touched cool steel.

He grabbed the handle and pulled. The moth shook. The knife was released. He struck with the knife, pulled and struck again, each blow tearing into the moth's eye.

The moth let go of his arm and he suddenly felt the full measure of the damage it had inflicted. His brain reeled, but his right arm knew what it had to do. Strike and pull.

The moth retreated and the next strike glanced off hardened jaw.

Dave dragged himself to his knees, still punching out with the knife, still connecting.

The moth's eye was in shreds and the stinking black pus was oozing freely and running like melted plastic, but it still wasn't dead.

Dave glanced down at his injured arm. The wrist was a mass of tattered flesh and hung at an angle of about forty-five degrees from his forearm. He tried to move his fingers, but they didn't seem to be joined on any more; he could feel tendons working in his arm, but his fingers stayed still.

'Motherfucker!' he screamed again, and this time he plunged the knife into the moth's head between its eyes.

There was a sound like an eggshell breaking and the moth collapsed. Dave withdrew the knife and watched a mixture of yellow fluid and grey brain seep through the tiny slit he had made in the head. The moth's wings fluttered and the rainbow colours left its eyes.

Dave tugged the bedroom door open, ran into the wrecked and frosted bathroom and threw up into the stinking toilet.

When eventually he got to his feet he knew he was done for. He could taste moth and blood and bile in his mouth and tears of pain stung his eyes. His left arm flapped uselessly from halfway down the forearm and it was still bleeding freely. The ache was terrible. At that moment he would gladly have hacked the arm off at the wrist had someone told him it would stop the pain. Whatever was in the cabinet was going to kill him now; he didn't stand a chance.

He went over to the sink holding the gash in his left wrist with his right hand to staunch the flow of blood and looked at his face in the mirror of the bathroom cabinet. His left eye was swollen so badly it was pressing on the lens of his glasses, his face was a mass of moth bites and it was smeared liberally with the blood from his torn arm.

'Shit,' he said in a small voice. He let go of his arm and turned on the hot tap, intending to bathe some of the blood and moth gore away from the wound before looking in the cabinet. If nothing was wrong inside there, he could get bandages and stuff for his eye and bites. *If nothing is wrong, ha ha*, he thought bitterly.

The hot tap glugged and sputtered. And black slime ran out.

'Fuck you!' Dave shouted, and tugged the mirror door of the cabinet open reasoning that he might as well die now. There was nothing else left to do.

The mirrored door fell off when he opened it and broke into thousands of pieces which lay shining amongst the slime in the sink.

And left Dave staring into what was inside.

There was nothing in there.

Nothing, Dave thought stupidly, peering into a black vacuum and listening to the air start to roar through in an attempt to fill the emptiness that stood before him.

The roaring flow of air into the void reached a crescendo and the stuff in the bathroom began to be sucked in. Towels and pieces of carpet whistled by his head and vanished into the blackness. Tubes of toothpaste hit him in the back and bounced off the walls, rising again in the rush of air and cartwheeling into the void. A razor nicked his face as it passed. The shower curtains were ripped from their rails and sucked in, one of them wrapping itself around Dave's head as it passed so that he had to fight it off.

The air pressure in the bathroom dropped to such a degree that the slime on the floor was ripped up and sucked into the void. Dave braced himself against the tiled wall with his good hand and tried to inhale some of the passing air.

Behind him, the heated towel rail was ripped from its mountings and cannoned across the room towards him. Dave ducked as it smashed against the cabinet, folded up and went through.

It was the wickerwork linen basket that knocked Dave's good arm from the wall. It careered across the room, hit the back of his knees and made him stumble. It rose instantly to the cabinet and forced its way through the small hole, blocking it for long enough for Dave to fill his lungs one last time.

It went through into the void with a pop, and then Dave was on his feet again, trying to brace himself so that he didn't get sucked in. His good arm missed the edge and waved hello to the void. He managed to support his weight against the tremendous vacuum with his broken arm for a moment, jamming it straight out against the tiles. The arm began to fold and Dave's head was drawn towards the opening, his hair upright and flapping. He saw the bones start to protrude through the gash in his wrist, then the arm folded double and he was up there, stuck halfway through the cabinet so that his hips and legs were in one world and his body and head in another.

Things hit him in the back and sailed by him, falling not downwards, but outwards into the vacuum. He could see them for only a few feet. After that they vanished into perfect darkness.

His arms were extended in front of him, the blood of the damaged one being pulled from his veins in red ribbons. The hurting in his hips was terrible. His last breath was ripped from his lungs and vanished into the void.

Something was breaking. He didn't know if it was the bathroom cabinet or his body, but he could feel it beginning to give.

Then he was free and sailing into the darkness. Not falling. Sailing.

Sailing.

Chapter Thirteen
Chasing The Dark

'You said it melts, but it doesn't, does it?' Anne Cousins accused her captor as she staggered along behind him, drawn by her invisible bonds. Her demon had decided to leave the empty and crumbling Ladbroke Lodge Motor Inn. He had told her the dark had fallen. It was dawn. Five fifteen by Anne's watch. Five fifteen by all the clocks in the hotel. It was always five fifteen. Time had passed, lots of it, but it still looked the same outside. It was still dawn.

'You lied to me, you bastard,' Anne continued. 'You told me that my underwear melted because it was man-made, but it melted because you arranged it, didn't you?' He said nothing. She trotted along behind him, keeping pace because she was attached to him somehow and it hurt when she tried to stop.

She looked at his balding head bobbing up and down and his dirty raincoat flapping as he hurried across the playing fields towards the park and AdventureLand and she hated him. Hated him more than she'd ever hated anything before in her life. 'Answer me!' she shouted, her tough tone cracking into a sob.

'That's the rules. Nothing to do with me,' he replied without turning, still speaking in his flat, toneless voice that was either ventriloquism or telepathy.

'The fucking bottle of Coppertone didn't melt, and that was man-made!' she stormed. 'Neither did the handle of the kitchen knife!'

'Skin,' he replied. 'Melts if it's touching skin.'

That was possible, she realised, hating him even more for having an answer that fitted. They reached the rusted kissing gate at the edge of the park and, as she waited for him to go through, she fought off an urge to stick the chisel into his ear. Not yet. She still had the knife, too. Her captor (whose name didn't begin with an A because she'd called him all the A's she could think of in last night's fruitless attempt to break the hold he had over her) had let her keep both implements, knowing full well that she wouldn't be able to use them against him. At least, not until she guessed his name.

'Where are we going?' she asked, finally realising that her madman wasn't taking her back into the fairground.

'Sky,' he said. '*One!*'

Anne didn't bother to ask what he meant because most of what he had said last night had been incomprehensible. There was a traffic jam of knowledge inside the madman's head. He knew everything about this place, but he wouldn't or couldn't tell. Couldn't seemed more likely.

She staggered along behind him across the crisp and crumbling grass, wondering if those two sets of shoe tracks they were following belonged to him or to someone else. The footprints were quite clear and where the feet had trodden the grass had turned to grey ash. The grass had obviously turned to ash some time after it had been trodden on, because there were no sole patterns to be seen, just the outline of the shoe. All of them looked like they could have been made by the madman's desert boots although the stride spaces were longer in one and scuffed in the other as if the thing that had made them was too tired to pick its feet up. Neither set of tracks looked like they belonged to Derek or Tommy.

'Are these your footprints?' Anne demanded.

Her captor didn't reply, just kept trudging along.

Anne looked behind her at the tracks they were leaving now and knew that the two pairs of feet that had walked across here before them weren't her madman's. 'They're not yours, are they?' she said.

'Yes, they are,' he replied.

Anne bit her tongue, not wanting him to decide to go back to the hotel. She was feeling dirty enough as it was without a repeat performance.

The madman hadn't raped her, but what he had done felt just as bad. He'd taken her back to her room, made her undress, undressed himself and laid on top of her on the rickety bed, his cold face against her breast and his beating-heart dolly against his own chest. He stank of something rotting and his breath smelled awful. He'd lain like that for hours, wriggling his cold, bony body against her warm skin from time to time as he slept. Eventually Anne had fallen asleep, too. When she woke up she was sickened and horrified with herself because his face was pressed against hers and she had one arm around his neck. But what was worse was that her left hand had a firm grip on his cold, flaccid penis.

She had been dreaming of Derek. That was the only excuse she had to offer. In her dream they had been making love in a carriage which was stuck at the top of the huge Ferris wheel in AdventureLand. Derek had been the biggest and hardest he'd ever been, and the thrill of sex in the open air with the crowds walking about below had given her orgasm after orgasm.

When she woke up with the madman's cold body sleeping on top of her, she was wet and hot and unsure if she'd been doing it with him or not. Totally disgusted with herself, she had wriggled out from under him, knocking his dolly onto the floor as she ran to the bathroom where she'd left the knife and the chisel. The knife hadn't worked before, but the chisel might. She drove it onto his right eye seventeen times before she realised the chisel wouldn't work either. Then she'd tried it on herself, but found that she didn't have the courage to take her own life.

Now, walking across the park, dressed in the only change of clothes she'd brought with her (Levis and a too tight tee shirt) she could feel the madman's disease attacking her left breast. There was a cold patch where his ear had touched her and where she'd poked the chisel, and she was sure his badness had got in through the wound and was changing her so she would soon be like him.

The Coppertone healing had only been temporary. His skin

had started to split and bulge again. She first noticed it while she was trying to pierce his eye, but it wasn't too bad then. Now his face was starting to flake off and his hair was falling out. From her position behind him, she could see dark flesh behind the splits forming in his neck. They gaped when he turned his head, but he hadn't noticed yet. She didn't intend to tell him. Nor did she intend to tell him that there was still some Coppertone left in the bottle.

They reached a point about halfway across the grass and the madman stopped.

His beating heart doll peered at her over his shoulder, its rubber face mocking her.

The two sets of tracks split here, and she thought he was wondering which one to follow, but his head was leaning back as he looked into the air.

'What is it, John?' she asked, following his gaze.

His name wasn't John. She knew that, because he didn't die. Or writhe in pain or anything. She badly wanted to see him writhe in pain.

'Dark,' he said.

Anne looked up at the sky. About a mile or so away to the west, the sky *was* dark. She hadn't noticed it before. Thunder clouds seemed to be forming.

'What is it?' Anne asked, shivering.

'The Knowledge,' the madman replied. His arm went up and he pointed through the gap in the trees. Anne followed the line of his finger and gasped.

Across the other side of the town, the black sky was pulled down in a kind of whirlwind vortex which didn't seem to be moving. The stationary twister reached right up to the dark sky and merged with it. The ground end was slender and bent. Trees and the roof line of the nearby buildings prevented Anne from seeing where it joined the ground but she had a horrible feeling she was going to find out.

'Where are we going, Billy?' Anne asked, starting on the B's and hoping that they weren't going to see what the bottom of that twister looked like.

'The Dark,' he replied, setting off again and dragging her behind him.

The walk took less than twenty minutes. Anne spent the time hypnotised by the sheer scale of the whirlwind. As they drew closer, its height and darkness seemed immense. It looked as if it were five miles high, and the unmoving tubular form cast a shadow of darkness which reached almost all the way to the park. The already chilly temperature dropped again and got even colder as they progressed.

The sharp end of the whirlwind completely covered a big terraced house, almost obliterating it from view.

They stood in front of the twister, looking up into the black sky.

'Knowledge,' the madman said, his flat voice sounding sad somehow. He moved towards the gate, dragging Anne along with him.

'No! I don't want to go!' Anne screamed, but the man's hand was opening the gate.

It's frozen, she thought, in spite of her terror. The gate was white with frost, some of which crumbled away under the madman's hand, revealing the black paint beneath. He walked onto the garden path, still looking up at the huge silent whirlwind.

'Fill me!' he said, walking towards where the darkness touched the ground. 'Fill the spaces in me. I shall become *One!*'

'No!' Anne squealed.

The madman touched the darkness. For a second, half his body was engulfed in the twister's night-time blackness. Anne felt searing cold shoot through her.

Then the frozen twister lifted. It shot back up into the sky as if someone had reversed the film and vanished into the looming black cloud miles above.

The house was still standing. Every pane of glass was thickly coated in sparkling white frost and huge icicles hung from the eaves. The very walls seemed to have been sculpted from clear ice. From somewhere on the other side of the house, Anne heard a loud *crack!* as the ice began to melt.

The covering of ice began to steam, letting off clouds of white fog which drifted around the figure of the madman. He was standing in the same position as he had been when he entered the dark wind – legs apart, the beating heart doll looking back over his shoulder, one skinny arm sticking out of the herringbone overcoat and raised skywards.

The doll's face was white with frost.

He's dead! Anne told herself. *It's killed him, whatever it was. He's dead and he's frozen in place.* She tried to walk away from him, and found that her bonds were just as tight.

You've still got to guess his name to escape him, Annie! He's dead and you're stuck here with him!

The madman moved. He took a stiff step forwards, then turned to face her. Anne's heart sank when she saw that he was still alive.

'Help,' he said to her, but he was smiling.

What had happened to him was terrible. There was a sharp line drawn down the sides of his head, so the back of it – where the darkness hadn't touched him – looked normal. But his face was in ragged ribbons. His coat was open, and the skin of his chest was torn apart, too, although he wasn't bleeding. It was worse than that. His skin had become transparent.

The hand that held the dolly had somehow escaped, but the one waving madly in the air at the clouds had changed. Anne could see through the skin to the translucent muscles and tendons; beneath those shone the grey-white of his bones.

'Help!' he said happily, and Anne watched his jaw muscles flex, saw the bone and teeth moving inside. All his internal organs showed through his chest: the white heart beating inside the cage of grey ribs; the shrunken and empty stomach; the ropes of intestine; the bronchioles of his lungs, filled with pale pink blood which changed colour as he breathed.

'Die!' Anne shouted. 'For Christ's sake, why won't you die!'

'Didn't ought to say that!' he replied, turning away from her and heading into the house.

As she was dragged down the path, the blackness overhead swept away. Anne glanced back towards the town and saw the darkness re-form over the town centre. A spike of whirlwind dropped to the ground, disappearing behind the rooftops. Between here and there, the sky had changed colour slightly as though the darkness had tainted it somehow.

That was when she heard Tommy.

He knew she was there. He must have!

'Mummy!' he cried. 'THE BIG GIANT!' His voice was distant; much too far away for her to go to, even if the madman didn't have her in his power. She might have even heard it inside her head, but that didn't matter: he was *alive!*

'TIGER!' she screamed at the top of her voice. 'I'm coming! Mummy's coming!'

'Help me!' Tommy's small voice pleaded. 'He's killing them!'

She knew it was inside her head then. She also knew where Tommy was – where the darkness had just landed. His voice had come to her over the track the whirlwind had left in the sky.

'Wait!' she called at the madman who was now inside the hall of the frozen house. 'The Knowledge! It's over there!'

'Do you think I don't know that, cow?' the madman asked, using his real voice again. Touching the darkness had changed him, and not only physically; he sounded threatening now and very dangerous. His pale eyes bored into her. She could see his brain behind them through the window in the front of his skull. It was mainly pink and white and it was flexing and moving. In the very centre of it, a dark spot had formed and was beginning to grow.

The madman led her straight up the iced stairs which cracked and complained beneath their feet. He seemed to know exactly where the bathroom was, and once inside headed straight for the medicine cabinet.

'What is it?' she asked, as he thrust his head into the doorless cabinet. 'What's wrong?'

'SHADDUP!' he shouted, and began to fling the contents of the cabinet onto the floor. Tubes and pots hit the layer of ice on the carpet and broke. Toothbrushes followed, bandages, a tube of Golden Eye Ointment. Finally the cupboard was empty.

The madman stood in front of it, thrusting his transparent hand in amongst the shelves as if he expected it to pass through.

'What is it?' Anne asked, frightened by his new violence.

'Gone! It's fucking gone!'

'What is?'

He turned and glowered at her. 'You silly bitch, don't you know? The doorway! The doorway to the Bad Side!'

'I thought we were there already,' Anne said quietly, backing away as far as she could.

'Limbo!' the madman roared. 'Not the Good Side, not Earth Side, not the Bad Side! We're stuck halfway and the doorway is gone!'

He dropped his beating heart dolly, turned back to the cabinet, held it in both hands and wrenched it from the wall. There was a hole behind it the size of his finger. 'All that's left now. All that's left!' he shouted, thrusting his forefinger into the hole and taking it out again. As soon as his finger was removed, the hole closed down and vanished.

'Gone!' the madman cried, pointing at the bare wall. 'Gone, gone gone gone GONE!'

'I'm sorry,' Anne lied.

'Where is it?'

'What?' she looked around the wrecked bathroom, following the madman's crazed eye movements.

'The Darkness. The Knowledge! Where is it?' He ran out of the room and down the stairs, dragging Anne behind him. Outside, on the pavement, both of them looked towards the town centre, searching the bland grey sky.

The whirlwind was gone too.

It was evening. Friday evening. Sally thought the sun would never go down. Since she had broken her friend the brown ale bottle she had been lying on the floor, trying to keep cool and preserve her fluid supply. Neither Purdue nor Charlie had turned up to give her more water or food. Around midday the heat in the boarded-up caravan had become unbearable and Sally had known she was going to die of dehydration before anyone came again.

She had spent the afternoon lying on the stinking pile of damp rags in a mental state that changed from sleep to delirium and back again. She dreamed of Dave and the cross and the thing on the back seat of her Mini that wanted both of them dead. In her dreams, the thing had chased them across a darkened landscape. Neither of them had known what it was and it was impossible to see anything other than a dark icy smear following them as they ran and ran. It caught them and she had watched its claws rip Dave's guts from his belly several times, and each time had been unable to move, unable to avert her eyes as the terrible knowledge that it was her turn next washed over her.

But now it was evening and, although the rank air in the caravan was still as thick as butter, the heat had subsided a little, taking her fever with it. Her mouth was still terribly dry and her whole body ached, but her mind was clearing.

Purdue had come back some time after the roar of the home-going rush hour traffic had died out; she had heard him muttering to someone, then heard the door of his caravan open and slam shut again. While he was out there talking, she had tried to attract his attention by shouting, hoping that if he heard her he would bring her some water. She had no voice though. Her larynx had turned to sandpaper and all she could squeeze from it was a rough cough. Purdue didn't hear.

Sally began to count again, partly to keep herself conscious and partly to take her mind off the awful dryness of her mouth and throat. Seven thousand. More than two hours and Purdue still didn't come out of his caravan. The sounds of AdventureLand warming up for the evening began to filter into the caravan.

Purdue's caravan door opened and banged against the side of the van. She knew it was him because he had a brief coughing fit and muttered darkly when he'd finished.

Sally waited patiently, imagining him standing on the top

step holding a tray on which would be a jug of iced water, droplets of condensation fogging the side. There would be a tall glass tumbler with ice cubes rattling in the bottom and beside the jug and glass a small wicker bowl piled high with fresh fruit: oranges, apples, *grapes*!

And what if it's Knife Time, Sal? a small doubting voice chipped in. *What are you going to do then? Purdue won't come mincing across with drinks and fruit to make you feel better, he'll come over brandishing a steak knife.*

Her mental picture of a benevolent Purdue abruptly changed. She imagined him cutting a square around her navel with a sharp knife, then digging the point in under a corner and lifting the skin so he could peel a section away. Would he eat it raw on the spot where she could see him doing it? Would he stuff her skin into his mouth, all bloody and soft, her navel facing her and flapping against his bottom jaw? Probably.

So get up Sal! Get off your sore back and get ready to fight him. Sure you're weak, sure you're hurting, but Purdue is big and slow. You can dodge him, you can Sal!

She got to her knees, but her head was floating somewhere above her and her balance had gone on strike and she just flopped down again in a crumpled heap.

'Hey Charlie!' Purdue's gruff voice shouted from close by. 'Hurry it up! Work to do!'

They're going to kill me, Sally thought sadly, *and there's nothing I can do about it. I'm finished*!

But the terrible thought of having her skin ripped from her living body gave her strength. She got to her knees.

'Come *on*!' Purdue yelled, just outside the door.

'Okay, okay,' Charlie's voice replied from farther away.

Sally's rubber legs straightened and just about supported her weight. Now she knew just how a newborn foal felt.

Purdue hammered on the side of the caravan and Sally gasped.

'Later, lover!' he shouted and chuckled.

Charlie's running footsteps stopped. 'Sorry Fred,' he said breathlessly. 'Fucking generator playing up again. Injectors want a good dig out.'

'Long as it's running now,' Purdue grumbled.

'Yeah. What about . . .?'

'Her? She's not to go in. She's okay out here, but she's dangerous inside. It can't tell about her. It says she's strong. The boy's strong, too, but he's fucked without her there. We got to keep 'em apart. She's to go in when she's skinned. It wants her alive. So she's mine for now. I'll start tonight.'

'And me?' Charlie asked. 'I've been waiting long enough.'

Purdue chuckled. 'Yeah, and you. It's time. I'll leave you some. When it's finished with the boy, we'll take the other two stones over and it'll have the set.'

'What then?'

'Then it can cross. Then we'll have everything.'

Sally's legs dropped her.

'Take care, darling!' Purdue yelled. 'Be seeing you!'

'Water,' Sally croaked, but the two men had gone. There was going to be no water. Only pain and more pain and then death. Or something worse.

It was an hour before her legs would get her up again. She counted.

Purdue and Charlie didn't come back. They had started the Ghost Train. She wondered how many cars would be coming out empty tonight.

She stood there in the semi-darkness wondering what she was going to do. The boards weren't going to come off the window – she'd proved that with the beer bottle – the door was padlocked and the floor was solid from end to end. And to make matters worse, it sounded as if Purdue had possession of her cross. That meant absolutely no help at all.

'You can't do this to me,' she said, hoping that the cross would magically appear around her neck as it had done in the hospital. Suddenly she remembered what had happened in Dave's bedroom when he was working on his computer programme to calculate the size of the Ghost Train. That arm had come out from under the bed. That long thin black arm with the clawed hand that was a part of the thing which had waited for her in the back seat of her Mini. She had been lying on

Dave's bed, half asleep and it had snaked out and plucked the cross from her neck. Then it had swooped down and touched her nose. It seemed dream-like and unclear, but it *had* happened. She could remember the sensation of extreme cold, but after that her memory was blank.

But what's that got to do with anything? she complained to herself. The fact that her cross had been stolen and then returned while she was sleeping in the hospital seemed to have nothing to do with this, unless the phantom pipe smoker was going to help her out again, and she had a gut feeling that this wasn't about to happen.

Nothing's impossible, her mind informed her. *That's the message. Even if things were once impossible, they're not any more. Which means you can escape, if you believe you can. You're alive, Sal, and that's impossible enough on its own. You could be – should be – dead by now. Purdue didn't kill you. He gave you just enough water to get you through the day. You didn't vanish inside the Ghost Train like Phil and Judy. You didn't get killed by the thing in your car. Nothing is impossible!*

With that cockeyed revelation still burning brightly in her mind, Sally balled the fist of her skinny right arm, drew it back and punched the boards across the window with all her might.

Much later, Sally would remember striking out at the boards with her slender fist and tell herself that she simply didn't remember the pain anymore and that she'd been lucky and caught them just right.

One punch was all it took and there was no pain whatsoever. Her fist smashed into the join in two of the boards and, instead of pure agony, there was joy and triumph. The boards shattered as if they'd been blasted with a 12-gauge shotgun. In slow motion time she saw her undamaged fist, wavering in the empty space where the wood had been and looking like something from one of those old Bruce Lee movies. Her knuckles were white and the veins and tendons in her upturned wrist stood out like cables. Around this magnificent hand, small chips of wood and larger sections of broken board flew outwards like planets created by the Big Bang, each one of them separate and distinct, each one spinning and arcing alone but in unison with every other part. In front of her through the flying debris she could see the back of the Mirror Maze and the alley between this and the Ghost Train's rear end.

A lucky punch.

Sally was not surprised in the least. Ecstatic, yes. Surprised, no.

You're out, Sal, she told herself. *Just like I said you would be. Say thanks, Sal!*

'Thanks,' she murmured to whoever might be watching over her, and scrambled out of the window into the fresh air.

Miraculously, the noise of the wood shattering hadn't drawn anyone's attention. Forgetting her still rubbery legs in her excitement, Sally jumped to the ground and collapsed.

She struggled to her feet and ran over to Purdue's caravan. There was a light burning inside but the van was probably empty. If there *was* someone inside, she decided, she would poke their eyes out with her strong fingers.

Purdue's front door was locked. Sally stood on the top step feeling very exposed and wondering what she should do. She needed to pee. In spite of her dehydration, the need to urinate was almost overpowering.

Open, you fucker! she mentally told the door. *Or I'll huff and I'll puff! I'm warning you!*

The door didn't open.

Still drunk on the power that resided in her right arm, Sally punched the aluminium door. The noise sounded like a bomb going off. The blow didn't hurt her, but the door didn't give way either. She punched it again, then looked at the big dent she'd made in it. *Please let there be a toilet inside, and please don't let anyone look out and see me,* she pleaded, punching the door again.

The door stayed put.

Sally punched the window that was right next to it, shattering the glass. She put her arm through and found the door catch.

The door swung open and Sally entered quickly, closing it

397

behind her. She ran through the filthy lounge, past the bedroom (*what was that hanging on his bedroom wall, Sal? A girl's shrunken head with the blond hair still on? Surely not!*), down the hall and into the tiny toilet. The stainless steel pan was seatless and its inside was smeared with shit, but Sally was too far gone to care. She wrestled her way out of her tight shorts and squatted, sighing with relief.

There were ropes in Purdue's caravan. Handcuffs. Knives. Rusted tools were scattered about in the lounge – a brace and bit; drills, a lorry jack. There was a paint-stained bible lying on a crusty coffee table next to a well-thumbed pornographic magazine featuring young children. That sent a thrill of disgust through Sally in spite of her heightened state.

There were ragged books and dirty plates; cups with mould growing from them; a vacuum cleaner with its dust bag protruding from the open top.

But there was no green-eyed cross.

'Where are you, cross?' Sally shouted, beginning to feel desperate. She had to find it and get out of here before Purdue could stomp back here to lock her up again.

There was a dressing table in Purdue's bedroom. She opened the top drawer and shut it again.

Criminals open from bottom up, your mum told you that! Saves shutting the drawer before you open the next one. Open them from bottom up and you don't have to close them again!

The bottom drawer was heavy. There were more pornographic magazines in there and a collection of what looked like surgical instruments. Most of them had blades of some description and, although Sally didn't recognise them, she could guess what they were for. Perhaps good ole Fred had brought them from a plastic surgeon.

The next drawer held baggy underpants, string vests and socks with holes in the heels. The next was empty. The fourth drawer out of five was the one. The one that held Purdue's American Express and Diner's Club cards and his wallet and spare keys and blood pressure pills and aspirin and Elastoplast and Anusol cream. *Ha ha, Fred, sore arse? I hope it kills you!*

But the cross wasn't there.

The top drawer held jeans and shirts but no cross.

'C'mon cross, come to mama!' Sally called, frantically turning out the contents of the dresser in case she'd missed it somewhere.

Calm down, Sal, she told herself after she'd wrecked the bedroom and found nothing. *The mountain won't come to Mohammed, so what does Mohammed do? He thinks, that's what he does.*

She went into the tiny corridor and fought to empty her mind of everything except the cross. It wasn't easy because Purdue might burst in at any moment but she did it.

She took a deep breath, exhaled slowly, took another and exhaled again, drawing a mental white sheet across her crowded mind so that it covered everything except the cross. Then she called out to it.

Her feet started to move. She let them take her into the kitchen, being careful not to hear the approaching footsteps. She let them stand her in front of the worktop next to the dirty sink full of unwashed plates, not hearing the key being fitted into the door. Then she let her left arm reach up and slide open the glass door of the cupboard above the worktop.

She didn't allow herself to hear Purdue's grating voice say, 'And who's been sleeping in my bed?'

Her hand took down the tea tin and placed it in front of her on the worktop, and her other hand sailed forward and opened it.

She saw the green gleam of the shining eye before the lid was properly open, before Purdue's voice didn't say, 'And who's been eating my porridge?'

Her hand stole in and picked up her cross, drew it out of the brown covering of tea leaves. She felt its power flow through her as she hung it in its rightful place around her neck.

Not hearing Purdue come stomping down the small hall towards the kitchen, she turned on the tap at the sink, ducked her head down and drank.

'What have we got here, then?' Purdue rasped from the kitchen doorway.

Sally slurped at the cool flow of water, sure she could feel it rushing from her swollen stomach straight into her bloodstream and her dehydrated cells. The water was swelling her dried-up body back to its proper size.

'It's poisoned,' Purdue said from behind her. 'I put Warfarin in the tank because I knew you would come in here. It'll hurt in a minute.'

He was lying. Sally could tell. This water was *good*. She finished drinking, stood up straight, turned the tap off and opened one of the drawers in the sink unit, knowing it was the cutlery drawer before she even thought about what she was doing. She was *alive* now, back to normal and then some. Her vision had improved and the things in the caravan were sharp and clear; her nerve endings crackled with energy and her blood sang in her ears. Her muscles were limber and strong, ready for whatever she needed them to do and her thoughts came with crystal clarity.

There was a red plastic cutlery tray in the drawer, but it was empty except for a wooden handled corkscrew. That was okay. That was what she'd expected to find. She grabbed the corkscrew with her right hand and balled her fist so that the tee bar handle was gripped firmly in her hand and the business end protruded between her first and second fingers. She looked down at her small bright weapon, nodded and turned to face Purdue.

He was leaning against the door jamb, shirtsleeves rolled up and top trouser button undone, his bulky six foot frame blocking her only exit. His huge arms were crossed on his chest and the upright blade of his steak knife lay against his left shoulder. His big round face was pale and expressionless, but his tiny blue eyes with their pin-prick pupils glittered as dangerously as the blade of his knife.

'You won't get away, y'know. Put the corkscrew down and go back to the caravan, I won't hurt you.'

'I know exactly what you do to girls,' Sally hissed. 'I've seen your tools. Well, it won't work with this little girl. The best thing you can do is to try and kill me, because I won't let you strip my skin off while I'm still alive.'

Purdue laughed through his clenched teeth. It was a wheezing, choked lungs laugh and it looked as if it hurt him to do it. Purdue wasn't the laughing kind. 'Makes no difference to me, lover,' he said tonelessly, but his facial expression changed, giving the game away. Sally knew that what he wanted more than anything at this moment was to strip off a little bit of her skin, perhaps from the back of the knees or the armpit. Purdue was *hungry*!

'So kill me then, if you think you can,' she challenged. 'Because I'm going across if you don't.'

Purdue stood up and came into the room, glowering. He tapped the red stone in his gold ring with the point of the knife and advanced one pace. Another tap, another pace. A third tap.

His ring lit up and he directed its red beam into Sally's eyes. Her retinas screamed and she thought her eyes would melt. The beam flicked away from her and she couldn't see Purdue through the red blotches before her eyes.

'The third stone,' he growled. 'You know there has to be three, don't you? Even if you get inside you can't do anything without the third stone. And the third stone is mine.'

'I'll kill it,' Sally said uncertainly.

Purdue flashed the thin red beam at her again, damaging her vision some more. 'Not without this you won't.' While Sally was still blinded, he walked to the centre of the kitchen and pushed the lightweight table aside. He was three feet away from her now. He balled his fist and played the red beam across Sally's face. The piercing light flickered back and forth over her skin, burning her.

Then he swung at her with the knife.

Sally didn't see the knife coming, but she felt the disturbance of the air. She dodged back, hitting the sink. The knife missed her bare midriff by a hair's- breadth.

Purdue swung again and Sally's cross lit up before the blade reached her. She smelt burning flesh and heard Purdue scream as he staggered backwards.

Her eyes opened again and she was mildly surprised that she could see. Purdue was by the door, gasping and clutching at a tiny black mark in the hollow of his throat. As he moved, the red beam from his ring shot back and forth across the room like a searchlight raking the sky. The green beam from her own cross flexed and wavered, blocking the red light's passage each time it shone in her direction. She moved to the middle of the room and adopted a fighter's stance, her corkscrew held out like Roddy Johnson's flick knife.

'C'mon Fred, what's the matter, fatso, sore throat? Come'n get me, if you're man enough!'

Purdue charged at her, knife first. Sally sidestepped and raked his muscular right forearm with the corkscrew as she dodged to the other side of the kitchen.

'Missed me!' she said breathlessly as Purdue inspected the long scratch on his arm. He touched his blood with his ring finger and stroked a line of it from his forehead down his nose.

His ring beam found a gap in Sally's cross's defences and scorched her corkscrew hand. Sally yelped.

Purdue charged again.

Sally dodged and lashed out with the corkscrew. She missed this time and it wasn't until she was squaring up to him again that she realised he'd got her with the knife. Warm blood was running down her left leg from the top of her thigh. She glanced down. *Only a scratch, Sal. Nothing to worry about.*

Power surged through Sally and she advanced across the room determined to leave Purdue's dead body lying on the ground.

Purdue came forward, too, and slashed with the knife. Sally didn't dodge this time, but held the corkscrew out in front of the arc his arm was describing, then dropped to her knees. It worked. The point of the corkscrew caught Purdue's muscular wrist and dug in, the power of his swing driving it deep.

The man screamed. Sally yanked the corkscrew back, but it wouldn't come out of his arm. She tugged with all the force she could muster but the weapon was stuck fast.

Then he had her. His other hand came down, the ring's red beam flashing, and grabbed her by the throat. He pulled her to her feet, and kept lifting. Her head was exploding with the pressure of the trapped blood and her throat seemed to have collapsed. Her feet left the ground.

He stabbed the steak knife at her stomach, but she still had hold of the corkscrew in his arm and managed to divert the blow. He tugged the knife back and her fingers were ripped from the wooden handle.

Sally brought both knees up hard into his crotch before he could strike again, but he didn't let her go, just lifted her higher, choking off her senses, stopping the flow of her thoughts. She kneed again, and again. And felt the steak knife graze across her belly.

Her hands grabbed the wrist before the knife could do anything more than split the skin, and she pushed herself away from him and brought her knees up again. Purdue's shouts rang in her ears.

So you are human after all, Sally thought groggily. *You have got balls!*

Her hands crept down the knife wrist of their own accord and found the corkscrew handle. Then they did something that surprised her. Fighting against Purdue's resistance, they unscrewed it.

Her head was screaming for mercy now, and her eyes had clouded over, but her hands were still busy down there somewhere. It wasn't until Purdue dropped her that she realised she'd dragged the corkscrew's point down his chest, opening a rent in the thin skin of his sternum.

She rolled on the floor, gasping as Purdue staggered towards her again. He dived at her and she rolled away, then found her feet and stood up. Across the room, Purdue was up too. His face was a mask of pure rage and his white shirt was drenched with his own blood. The green and red beams clashed and parted, bouncing off walls, dancing on the ceiling, meeting in the reflective metal of the stainless steel sink.

'Not doing too well today, Fred, are we?' she heard herself saying as she regarded him through the living latticework of flaring red and green beams. Her right fist had balled. The strong one. She ran over to him and thumped him hard in the

403

rip in his breast bone, rejoicing in the pain of the shockwave that ran up her arm. Purdue's ring went out. He staggered backwards into the wall and stopped. Sally stepped forward and hit him again in the chest with what seemed like a tremendous force. He slumped to the floor, groaning and coughing. A thin trickle of blood ran from one corner of his mouth.

The ring, Sal, get the ring! she told herself.

She crouched beside the semi-conscious man, peeled his hand from the steak knife and tried to work the ring off his stubby finger. It was useless. The ring had been on there for a good long time and his finger had fattened around it. There were only two options. The first was to cut the ring away, and the second didn't bear thinking about.

Do it, Sal! she told herself. *It's the only way!*

She had the knife in one hand and Purdue's fat ring finger in the other, but it seemed too horrific to contemplate. It felt *wrong.*

But he said you can't kill the thing in the Ghost Train without it! Cut his finger off!

Purdue groaned, took a shuddering, whistling breath.

I can't do it. It isn't right! But three, Sally, it's all in threes. He must be right! She looked at him and shook her head. 'I can't do it,' she said.

She dropped the knife and his hand and stood up. Taking his ring wasn't what she was supposed to do, she was sure of it, in spite of what he had said.

Purdue's eyes popped open. He regarded her with those gimlet pupils and then gave a whistling laugh. 'You can't do it,' he grated. 'You'll die!' His arm came up and tried to grab her bleeding leg.

Sally fled.

Charlie wasn't waiting outside as she had imagined he would be. Sally leapt off the top step and as she landed on the dried grass something sharp dug into her bare foot. She didn't stop to inspect the damage; there wasn't time. Limping slightly, she ran for the gap in the side stalls, wondering how the hell she would get inside the Ghost Train.

It was crowded in the funfair and Sally was forced to slow her pace. She worked her way through the throngs of people, pushing and shoving each hapless punter that got in her way.

'Hey, leave it out!' a teenager in a white summer naval uniform shouted as she elbowed past him. 'What are you, crazy?'

Sally turned and glared as him. He would have been good-looking, she decided distantly, if it wasn't for the terminal acne which reached right down to his shirt collar. 'Go sink a ship!' she called at him, pushing her way through a group of greasers that may or may not have been Dragon users. She crashed out of the other side of the tight circle to a chorus of wolf whistles and lewd remarks, barged past an elderly special policeman, and began to run again.

She had almost reached the centre of AdventureLand when a leg shot out in front of her. She fell, rolled and sprang up again, her cross pouring power into her and searing her chest. Before she realised what she was doing, she had hold of the front of the acned sailor's shirt with her left hand and her strong right fist was cocked ready to mash his nose.

'Okay, lady!' the sailor yelled, his voice terrified and both his hands held up in front of him with the palms out. 'It was just a joke! Lemme go now!'

She released him and he hurried away muttering that she was a fucking psychopath.

Cool down, Sal, she told herself. *It wasn't Purdue, it was a kid. You might have killed him or something. Get a grip on it!*

She took a deep breath and checked the surrounding area for fairground people. George Dale's famous Octopus was to her left and she spotted the wizened figure of Dale himself in the control booth. He was fiddling with something below her line of vision, a dead roll-up dangling from his mouth. He knew. She was sure of it.

She looked at the gaudy facade of the Ghost Train, knowing that she had to get inside quickly. If she waited too long, Purdue might just be waiting for her with his steak knife.

A hand grabbed her right arm from behind. Sally yelped and

405

reflexively struck back with her elbow, but the cross had suddenly gone cold and there was no power in her thrust.

'Steady down, steady down!' a thin voice said. Sally wheeled around and was thankful her extra strength had deserted her. It was the old special that had hold of her.

'What's wrong?' he said, letting go of her arm but looking as if he was ready to grab her again should she try and flee. 'Have you been attacked?'

'No,' Sally said. 'I'm okay. Really.'

'You are, are you?' the special said in obvious disbelief. 'You are filthy. Your leg is bleeding, your hand is burnt and there's a mark that looks like a knife cut on your tummy. Why don't you tell me about it? I can help you, you know.'

'I'm alright,' Sally insisted, knowing she looked scared and wild-eyed and wanting to give it all up. It would be so easy to have him escort her from the fairground. No one would stop a policeman. They could go to the safety of the Police Station and she could tell him all about Fred Purdue and what he did to young girls. Then she wouldn't have to go in the Ghost Train again.

'It's . . .' she stammered. Her throat closed up and her eyes filled with long overdue tears. Suddenly she felt like a lost little girl wanting her father's comforting arms around her. It would be so easy to give up.

And if you give up here you might just as well not have started, a harsh inner voice told her. *What about Phil and Judy and Dave? Will they come back if you give in? Will the police be able to sort it out? You know the answer to that one, girl, don't you?*

'Come on,' the special said gently, 'tell me all about it.'

How will you live, Sal? How will you handle the rest of your life if you give it up? Dave's life depends on you, y'know. You know he's over there and you know he needs you there, too. How will you live with that if you don't go?

'*But I'll die,*' she answered herself aloud. 'I'll die if I go.'

'Now now! No one is going to die,' the policeman said, taking her arm again, gently this time. 'Why don't you tell me what is bothering you?' He began to lead her back the way she had come, back towards the Ghost Train.

*So what if you do die? Everyone dies, Sal. Your mum, your dad,
this special, Dave, all of them are going to die. The only difference
is when. Everyone goes sooner or later and some are going to go
earlier than others. Maybe it's your turn. You can't odds it girl.
You're damned if you stay, damned – quite possibly – if you go.
So what are you gonna do?*

'It's just that . . .' Sally said, still meaning to let it all go.

'Just what?' the cop asked. Up ahead, the pizza-faced sailor
was standing on the bottom step of the Noah's Ark and glaring
at them.

'It's just that I fell over,' Sally heard herself say. 'I'm okay
now, really I am.' She shrugged the special's arm away from
her shoulder and looked deep into his old grey eyes. The cross
warmed her. She wiped the tears away and smiled at him.
'Thank you,' she said, her voice seemingly working on its own.
'But perhaps you'd better forget you ever saw me.'

The special looked confused. Stunned, even. Sally wondered
what she'd done to him.

'Sorry, madam,' he said distantly, stepping aside. 'I didn't
see you there.' He nodded and backed away, then turned and
walked off into the crowd.

He thinks he bumped into you, Sal, she thought. *You hypnotised him.*

The energy was flowing steadily from the cross now, filling
her with power like a battery charger. Her self-confidence
returned. Her mind was made up and it didn't matter whether
she'd done it or the cross had done it for her. She was going
over.

She made her way back to the Ghost Train and stood in the
crowd looking up at the engines filled with white-faced riders
coming crashing out of the doors, and then going back in with a
fresh load. Charlie the roustabout was in the pay booth and the
younger man was helping the people in and out of the engines.
Purdue was nowhere to be seen. The only problem was getting
past Charlie.

In through the out doors, Sal, she thought, looking up at them.

There was a low fence that ran along the front of the ride, but she thought she could scramble up and leap over it before Charlie had time to get to her.

'Hey!'

She was in front of the fence when she heard the shout. She glanced to her right and saw Purdue emerging from the gap between the rides, just feet away from where she stood. There was blood on the front of his shirt and on his face, but he was on his feet and looked dangerous. 'Hey!' he yelled again, and Sally saw the inside of his mouth as he shouted. His teeth and tongue were red with fresh blood. *Internal injuries, Sal. You hurt him good. Ruptured his stomach or something. Punctured a lung, maybe.*

Purdue came towards her waving his knife.

Sally leapt to the edge of the platform and grabbed the top of the fence. Her arms yanked hard and her feet left the ground, scrambling up the side of the ride.

'Stop her someone!' Purdue yelled, slashing wildly.

Sally was over the fence and up on her feet by the time Charlie got out of the paybooth, and halfway across the platform to the exit doors by the time Purdue reached the fence.

Inside the Ghost Train a siren wailed.

One coming out, Sal, look out! she told herself, but Charlie was approaching and it was too late to stop now. She dodged to one side as the doors crashed open then leapt onto the boiler of the engine as it emerged. The two girl riders screamed as the maddened, bleeding apparition landed on their engine. This was one shock they hadn't bargained for.

Sally never came close to losing her balance. She was a mountain goat, a tightrope walker, a nine-lived cat. She leapt from the boiler to the top of the low cab and the girls screamed again. Then she flung herself into the darkness of the Ghost Train's interior, knowing that she would land on her feet.

The doors swung shut behind her as she landed and the light was gone. But Sally didn't need light. She knew where her feet would land, knew where the turnings and the walls were without having to be able to see them. She sprinted through the darkness easily and gracefully, feeling a powerful sense of *right-*

ness. Her injuries had stopped hurting and blood pounded through her body making her nerve endings sparkle and her brain feel huge. The cross was glowing madly, its green beam flickering off the walls and ceilings as it bounced against her skin and she loved it. She was bigger now; she had been magnified by the force from the cross and she was invincible. She would get Dave out. She would free Judy and Phil. She was too alive to fail. Nothing could stop her, not even The Claw!

It grew colder as she ran and the chill breeze that lifted her hair was damp against her skin. She turned right, digging her feet into the cold ground and leaning hard to keep her balance. Somewhere behind her people were shouting and sirens were sounding, but they were a long way away. Too far to catch up.

Her breath came easily and she increased her pace, twisting and turning through the maze of dark corridors. The beam from the cross no longer shone on rails. The rails were way behind her now. She had left them behind forever. Up ahead, the emptiness was filled with a deep red glow and she knew she would have to jump for her life, knew she wouldn't hesitate when the time came.

The gap across the chasm wasn't huge, but it was further than it was possible to leap. But she trusted herself. She ran to the very edge and turned right, closing her eyes against the molten rock below. Her feet knew the way. They didn't falter and she let them take her miles along the chasm, her bare left foot rising and falling half on and half off the twisted edge. The heat was intense, but it didn't burn her.

Sally felt wonderful.

Then she stopped. Before her lay red-tinged darkness. She stood there looking at nothing and wondering what had happened.

Well, feet, where am I? she thought. *This isn't it!*

Her feet turned her around. The chasm was in front of her now, a long way off. Her right leg lifted from the ground and, with a thrill of anticipation, Sally realised she was going to make the jump. She had brought herself here to get a good run up.

Her legs flew beneath her, barely touching the ground as she sped towards the chasm. The wind began to whistle through her hair which rippled out behind her. Her breath began to hurt her lungs as it was sucked in and expelled and her heart didn't seem to be beating properly any more, just vibrating against her ribs.

The red glow of the chasm drew nearer. Sally's arms pumped up and down like pistons as they kept pace with her legs. Sweat began to pop out of her pores. Her muscles were stiffening now, but her legs were still speeding up.

No more! she thought. *I'm not fit and my body can't take this!*

But she wanted her body to move faster, wanted it to scream out in agony. Because this was how it was *supposed* to be.

Muscles screamed and ripped. Tendons popped and tore and her heart was a maddened hummingbird, shrieking to be set free. Her brain had expanded so that it was forcing itself up against the inside of her skull, the pressure surely distorting the bone.

Then the pain went and Sally's body was a balanced, pounding machine with no upper limit of acceleration.

The chasm ripped towards her across the darkened floor at an astounding speed. There was no going back now. No stopping.

The jump seemed to take a long time. Sally sailed through the air head first in a parabolic trajectory, knowing that she was going to make it. Miles down below her, the molten rock swirled and smoked. Her cross flapped against her chin, blinding her with its good green light. Sally screamed with laughter and excitement.

She pushed her arms out before her as she began to come down again. She was going to land on flat grey rock. She hit the other side hands first. Her arms buckled and she rolled head over heels twice, absorbing the impact easily. At the end of the second roll, she straightened up and her legs took over again, using the remaining impetus to start her running again.

The doors came up quicker than she had expected them to, and her hands shot out in front of her at the last moment, knocking them open.

She ran out onto the platform in the grey world where – she knew – Dave and Phil and Judy were imprisoned, and stopped.

'Here we are then,' she said, breathlessly, looking around her at the deserted AdventureLand and feeling very happy indeed. 'What do I do now?'

Then she noticed the black sky which had been sucked down in a funnel over the multistorey car park in the town centre. She stood looking at it for a time, knowing that it pointed the way for her. After a time, the dark whirlwind of sky drew itself quickly aloft and boiled in the still air. Then the blackness vanished.

Sally shivered. A picture of a huge ugly giant had come into her mind. It was over there. Perhaps Dave was over there, too.

She set off across the crumbling park feeling the badness hanging in the still air.

Chapter Fourteen
Dave On The Bad Side

The long fall in the vacuum didn't hurt. Landing did.

Dave hit the uneven ground face down, skidding along through the dust and stones, his chin bouncing off the ground and his half-severed arm trapped under his chest. His body was now filled with a kind of crushing numbness that he thought might be a precursor to death. His mind seemed to have become detached and hung in the air over his body as it skidded towards a big boulder.

He watched dispassionately as his head cracked against the rock and folded under his chest. His body curled and flipped over, coming to a halt lying face up. The rucksack had been torn off his back and lay on the ground nearby surrounded by junk that had been sucked from the bathroom. He could see Doreen's pink Wisdom toothbrush down there and a crimped up tube of Signal toothpaste with the top missing. A cake-icing piping of red and white striped paste decorated the scene.

Take more than Germolene to fix what's happened to me now, he thought bitterly, looking down at the crushed tin of ointment that lay beside his body.

His attention was abruptly drawn by a small pile of items that stood a little way away from the stuff that had arrived with him.

Dave *recognised* these things. There was the gold pocket watch that had belonged to his grandfather and which his father had kept in the china cupboard for years until it got lost. There was Dave's own silver identity bracelet – the one he'd lost on the school football field when running away from Roddy. There were knitting needles, two pairs of glasses and the plastic soldier with the flame-thrower which Dave had poked into the bathroom sink overflow when he was five.

My soldier! he thought.

Then he was back inside his body again and his good arm was groping beside him for his glasses. They wouldn't fit though, because of the swelling where the moth had bitten him. He hooked one arm of the glasses around his ear and left the other side flapping.

He was in something that looked like a tunnel, or a cave. Whatever it was, it was subterranean and had rock walls. It was dimly lit by what seemed to be a spotlight which shone upwards from a raised column of rock about three feet high and four feet across. The dish of light was blue-white and shimmered on the cave roof high above. It diffused off the roof and made the cave look as if it was running with liquid.

Cradling his mangled arm, Dave looked back in the direction he'd come from.

A hundred yards away, the cavern narrowed to a small corridor which twisted out of sight. Set at head height in the wall back there, he could see the small square opening he'd been forced through. He knew it was his bathroom because he could make out the pattern of the wallpaper in there.

He started to walk towards the opening, wondering if he could get back through with his arm in this state. It was steadily pumping out blood and the loss was starting to make him feel lightheaded. There wasn't much time. The pain was dull and distant, he felt terribly cold which meant he'd lost a great deal of blood.

He clamped the edges of the wound in his wrist together with his good hand and walked towards the opening. The flow of blood slowed, but didn't stop and was soon dripping steadily through his fingers. He increased the pressure, knowing he could improvise a tourniquet with the stuff in his rucksack if he only had time. But the hole in the rock seemed to be getting

413

smaller and if he stopped to attend to the bleeding, it would probably disappear altogether.

By the time he was halfway there, the window into Limbo had closed down to half its previous size. Another few paces and all that was left of it was a tiny white dot. There was still a chance that he could get a finger in through that little hole and ease it open again. If he got there in time.

He tried to run, but only managed a shuffling, rocking gait that increased his giddiness and made the dot leap around wildly. When he stopped the dot was gone.

Dave turned around again and started dizzily making his way back towards the light source.

Another corridor ran out of the cavern in the other direction. He had noted it while he was living outside his body, and now he could see it with his one open eye. There was no chance of exploring that though, he was far too weak. As he approached it, wavering in and out of consciousness, the flat dish of light seemed to blink on and off like the strobe lights in the Ghost Train. Except that this time it was *him* blinking on and off while the light shone steadily.

He tripped over his rucksack on the way to the light and fell heavily. It didn't hurt. The hard ground seemed to have gone spongy. But it was too cold to die here. He got up again and staggered across to the light.

When his own inner lights turned themselves on again, he was kneeling before the blue-white pool, his bad arm dangling awkwardly beside him and his good one supporting him on the flat and smooth border of rock at the edge of it.

With the last of his strength, he leaned forward and peered into the brightness.

He gasped as an incredibly ugly face swam before him, then grunted, realising that it was his reflection. His face resembled nothing so much as a huge loganberry. It was completely covered in red lumps and scratches where the moths had bitten him. The ripe swelling that held his eye shut paled into insignificance as he saw what had happened to his lips. They were four times their normal size, bruised black and they hung away from his front teeth like mangled inner tubes.

Got bit, Davey, he thought drawing them up into a malformed smile of defeat.

The old boy said you weren't good enough, and he was right! Come on, cross, do your worst, he asked, dimly realising it wasn't going to work. *I believe, y'know. I do.*

His face began to change. Another face overlaid it. A woman's face. He watched interestedly as his nose grew shorter and his lips thinner and his long blond hair began to take off and wave in the air around his head. He was turning into a middle-aged woman.

Then the face vanished into the depths of the light and he was staring into his own good eye again.

He heard splashing noises and the flat light began to ripple and splash at the sides of the rock.

Water, Davey, it's not a light, it's water!

The water splashed some more and there was a noise like something dropping into it. Or breaking the surface.

'Hello again.'

Dave looked out across the shining pool of water into the face of Jean the Mermaid – the AMAZING FISH WOMAN from the other side of the funfair. She shook her hair away from her face and looked at him, her head bobbing up and down as she flipped her tail in a kind of treading water motion. Dave could see the silver-skinned tail beating beneath the water.

He peered at her through his good eye, no longer questioning how it was done. A mermaid was a mermaid. 'Help,' he coughed.

'Not me,' the Amazing Fish Woman said. Her voice was much softer than it had been in the sideshow.

Dave looked at her and saw that she was worried. 'What then?' he asked.

'I can't help you. I'll suffer if I do,' she said, her face taking on a grim expression. 'It can do that.'

'I'll die,' Dave said.

'Welcome to the club,' Jean said. She hesitated and frowned. 'It's good stuff you know,' she said, 'this water. It's *very* good stuff.'

'Help me,' Dave pleaded. Half the time he was in total darkness now and he didn't like it at all.

'It's very good water,' Jean said. She lay back and flipped her fish tail out of the water, then slapped it down again and vanished beneath it.

Some of the splash hit Dave's face. It was cold and stung his skin. The next time he came back from the darkness, Jean was in front of him. Close up, she looked more than worried: she looked petrified. 'I'll help you if you help me,' she said.

'Okay,' Dave replied.

'You'll have to give me the cross,' she said. 'You'll have to, if I help you. I can tell you what to do, but you'll have to give me the cross afterwards.'

'Trick,' Dave croaked. 'Can't.'

'I won't trick you. I'll bring it back.'

'When?'

'Soon.' Her voice became urgent now. 'Give it to me and I'll help you.'

He shook his head.

'You have to. I've helped you already. Look at your face!' She ducked back into the water. It had cleared when Dave's consciousness came back again. His reflection showed that where the water had touched him, his face was back to normal. He still had the closed eye and the fat lips though, and his life was still trickling steadily out of his arm.

The Fish Woman bobbed up beside him. 'Give me the cross.'

'I know how it's done,' Dave mumbled. 'Do it myself.'

'You'll drown.'

'Won't.' His consciousness was coming and going like a slowly revolving lighthouse beam. He was only alive when the beam was in line with his eyes. The rest of the time he felt dead.

'You have to breathe it in. You'll drown if I don't help you.'

Dave dipped his cupped hand into the water and splashed his face. He could *feel* the swelling going down. He tried to get his bad arm up high enough to dip it in, but it wouldn't work, so he wet his hand again and rubbed the water into the wound.

416

'You'll die,' the mermaid said. 'And so will I if you don't give me the cross. It'll know now. It'll hurt me. There are others down here, too. Lots of them. We'll be extinct.'

'Won't die,' Dave said, getting another cupped handful of water and trickling it down his bad arm.

'It's inside,' she said urgently. 'The damage is inside. It's cosmetic, what you're doing. You have to breathe it in.'

Dave ducked his head forward, but his legs wouldn't lift him high enough to get his face into the pool.

'I can help you do it,' Jean offered. 'You just have to lend me the cross. If you don't lend it to me, you'll die. If I help you and you don't lend it to me, I'll die. And so will all my people. It has us, just like it has you and your friends.'

There was a long darkness then as the lighthouse beam slowed down. On the next pass he could only see dimly and he realised he had no choice.

'Fuck it,' Dave said, and took the cross from his neck. Its red light was winking on and off in time with his slowing heartbeat. He held it out for her.

'Throw it to me,' she said, swimming to the centre of the pool, 'I can't touch it while it's connected to you. It has to fall onto my neck to be any good.' She vanished under the water.

Dave threw it. The leather thong made a loop as it whirled through the air. Dave didn't believe she could catch it, but just when he thought it was too late, Jean's head broke the surface again and the loop fell neatly over it. She gasped when the cross touched her body, then she laughed. Dave could almost see the cross's power filling the mermaid. Her eyes took on the same excited distant look that Sally's had got all that time ago in the Dragon car park when Roddy was after them.

Jean swam back to Dave looking ten years younger. 'You don't know what you've just done,' she said. 'You've freed us! Give me your arm! Quick!'

Us? Who was us? Dave held out his good arm and Jean took it firmly. Her skin was slick and cold, fish-like.

With a powerful flick of her tail, she dragged Dave up and over the low wall and into the water.

417

He choked as water filled his mouth and nose and struggled feebly, but Jean's grip was strong and she swam down into the stinging water towing him behind her.

The blue-white water surrounded him, pressed in on him from all sides. His face hurt, his legs hurt and the small pockets of air trapped in his lungs burned like fire. Still the mermaid dragged him down. His eyes opened and he could see nothing except the mermaid beneath him, the red blood from his half severed arm fanning out in a thin streamer and an endless blue world expanding in every direction.

The mermaid had lost another ten years and now looked no older than Dave. Down here, her skin was smooth and the angular lines of her face had filled out, making her look angelic. She stopped dragging him down and took his bad arm with both of hers. *Let your breath out!* she told him, her voice clear inside his head. *Let it go!*

Can't! Dave replied, his mouth opening by mistake as he thought the words back to her. *Drown!*

Jean held his bad arm tightly at the wrist and drew it away from him. The pain was excruciating, but Dave managed to keep his breath. He looked down at his extended arm and found he could see the broken bones, now that the blood had been washed away. His wrist was at almost a forty-five degree angle facing inwards to the rest of his arm and the distortion made him look as if he was now the proud owner of two elbows.

The mermaid swam downwards, tugging at his arm.

Pulling it off, Dave thought. *It'll come off if she pulls it any more.*

He wanted to fight back, but the pain was tremendous. All he could think about was his wrist and hand which were shortly going to become completely detached from his arm.

Jean swam back up to him, nodding her head at him. She still had hold of his wrist.

I'm drowning, you tricked me! Dave told her.

She swam back from him, nodded again, then with a single strong flip of her tail, drove herself from him, yanking his arm out straight.

Dave screamed, but there was no sound. A few bubbles flew past his eyes heading for the surface. All the air in his lungs was gone. Jean was near him again, pointing to his straightened arm and nodding at him, but he didn't know what she'd done to him and he didn't care because his chest was trying to make him breathe in. He locked his lungs solid, forced his body upright and straight. All his other pain vanished as he fought not to breathe in. There were only a few seconds left now to get back to the surface and stay alive.

But Jean the Fish Woman wouldn't let him go.

Dave's mouth opened. A small bubble came out, and the astringent water replaced it.

Let it go! Jean said. *Relax. You won't die. You'll heal.*

He looked at his cross on her neck. Red in silver dangling between shell clad breasts. Its eye was open and steady circular pulses of light were winking at him. He looked down the centre of them into the eye's black pupil. The darkness seemed to expand so that it covered his whole field of vision and the pulses of light passed him by. The depth of that velvety darkness was both mind-numbing and comforting. For an instant he gazed into infinity, then he was looking at Sally. She was alone, walking down Wote Street towards the town centre. She was grubby and barefoot and her hair was a mess. She was dressed in shorts and a cut-off tee shirt and there was a deep scratch across her belly. At first he thought that one of her legs was clad in a tan and dark red stocking, then he realised her thigh was cut and he was looking at dried blood. Her little silver cross hung outside her tee shirt in the cleavage of her breasts, its green eye pulsing, and that mad, defiant look shone in her eyes. She strode purposefully past the empty shops, a half smile on her face.

Then the vision was gone and Jean's face swam before him again. She came closer to him, took him in her arms and her lips found his.

Kissing me! She's kissing me before she finishes me off! Dave thought.

Jean's lips were soft and cool, her tongue rough and

muscular. She probed his lips apart with it, forced it between his teeth, opening his mouth.

Then she blew, filling his empty lungs with water.

There was no pain, just a cool, clear feeling which soothed away the rupturing sensation in his chest.

Jean drew her face away and smiled at him. *You didn't die!* she told him. *You can breathe underwater and it's healing you.* She let go of him and swam away. *Two more breaths*, she told him, looking back over her shoulder as she plunged into the depths. *That's all you can take. Just two more. Now get out and wait for me. I'll be back!*

Dave's body seemed to have woken up again. It felt strong and flexible. He struck out for the surface, realising that his mangled arm was straight and unscarred again, and knowing that his face was cured too.

He had taken his second and third breaths of the water before he reached the top of the pool, and he realised as his head broke the surface that he still had a lungful of water. He paddled towards the edge, letting it flow from his nose and mouth. He reached the edge and clung on, not daring to breathe in again in case the change from water to air was painful. He'd had enough pain to last him several lifetimes and he wasn't keen on having any more. He dragged himself out of the pool and lay on the flat edge before he breathed in.

The transition was painless.

While he waited for the mermaid to come back, he gathered up the things that had fallen out of his rucksack and packed them neatly in place. He left the pile of lost things where they were, reasoning that they had been sucked over here from his house over the years and he wasn't supposed to have them. The mechanism that had achieved this gathering of missing objects puzzled him though. He formed the idea that the place he was in now was a permanent dimension that stayed beneath his known universe, co-existing with the real world. It was another facet of the Limbo Land.

The plastic soldier with the flame-thrower which he'd lost

down the sink overflow kept attracting his attention and his gaze wandered to it frequently. He peered closely at it, being careful not to touch it.

The little figure was exactly as he remembered it; two or three inches high and made of olive green plastic. It had once been painted but most of the paint had come off in the endless games of war he'd played.

It wanted to be picked up. Without the cross, Dave wasn't sure if picking it up was the right thing to do or not. He wasn't used to his own judgement exclusively any more; there was too much doubt, too much uncertainty. He left the soldier on the ground.

His watch read five fifteen. The mermaid seemed to have been gone for hours, but he had no way of telling if this was so. It seemed like a long time though, even if time didn't exist here in the normal sense.

He'd been tricked. The damn mermaid, or whatever it was, had tricked him. She had been gone too long now. She'd got the cross and she wasn't coming back at all. Why should she? What was there here for her except a dumb nineteen-year-old? He'd been a fool ever to have given it to her.

But what alternative was there? he asked himself, as he picked up a small rock and threw it into the pool.

The alternative was to keep the cross, dummy, he thought back to himself. *You could have done it. You could have healed yourself.*

But that was wrong. The cross wouldn't have healed him this time. It wasn't because he didn't believe, it was because he wasn't in Limbo any more. This was somewhere else again. This was the Bad Place. This was where the owner of The Claw lived. He could *feel* that.

It was still five fifteen.

It was still five fifteen and something horrible was happening. It was happening everywhere, but it was mainly happening down by the far corridor just beyond where he'd come in. He could *feel* a presence. Something had entered down there and it was standing still and watching him. His flesh began to creep and, without the cross, he felt completely naked.

He tried to turn his head and see what it was, but his head didn't want to be turned. His breath hung in the air as he exhaled. It always got cold when The Claw came out to play, didn't it?

What're you going to do now, Davey boy? Run for it? Forget about the cross and leg it? Okay, which way are you going to run? In the other direction, of course, just like it wants you to. It wants you to run away because it wants the cross even more desperately than you do. You know that, don't you? You've known it all along. It can beat you as you are now, and it isn't trying because it needs the cross. Hang loose Davey, it ain't going to get you.

Gooseflesh covered his body as he stared straight ahead of him, too scared to look in case he was turned to stone. 'You can go get fucked, Claw old chap,' he said to the empty air in front of him.

There was a rush of fetid air. The flat water in the pool behind him froze. He heard the ice cracking as it expanded.

'You need them ole crosses babe, don't you?' he told it. 'You're as stuck without 'em as the fish in this pond. Think again. You ain't gonna get 'em, pal!'

The hair on the right side of his head began to freeze. The compass inside the rucksack was beginning to spin again – he could feel it vibrating as the needle spun crazily around. It was working even though he didn't have the cross on!

'My compass doesn't like you, pal,' he told The Claw. 'And neither do I. Sally's coming and she's not exactly fond of you either. She's over here. We're going to give you a right royal working over, Claw. We're gonna put you through the mincer!'

He looked over then, but The Claw had gone. The smell and the freezing atmosphere had dissipated.

It went! he told himself in astonishment. *If that was really it. Surely it would have put up more of a fight if that was really it?*

Unless it was just toying with you of course. Just putting the frighteners on and getting a good look at its next lunch.

Dave picked up the rucksack and looked inside. The compass had stopped now. He closed the rucksack again and heard laughter. Nightmare laughter, deep and slow and dangerous. His skin began to crawl again, and involuntarily he glanced over to where he thought The Claw had been. Nothing was there.

Then the laughter ceased and the distant sound of a child's screams rent the still air.

'Oh Christ,' Dave muttered, 'it's killing a kid.'

The tiny wavering scream ended abruptly. Dave felt sick.

Behind him, the ice began to crackle. He turned around.

Below the ice hundreds of minute blue lights were gathering, each as bright as a welding spark. It hurt his eyes to look at them, but he couldn't look away. Each of the tiny sparks was surrounded by a white aura which merged with the rings surrounding the others, but each was separate and distinct with a hue of its own. As he watched, more arrived. They formed into clusters and began pressing up against the covering of ice which cracked and bulged with the pressure.

Dave stood up and took a pace backwards as the ice shattered.

The blue-white lights took to the air in swarms. They had no wings, but they made a noise like a million dragonflies. The air was alive with them, a seething, swirling, sparkling mass. The mass fractured into thousands of individuals, each as bright as a tiny sun. They flew towards Dave and passed over him, following the line of his face, then sweeping down over his neck and body in a million electric shocks. It was a good feeling. A warm *loving* feeling.

Dave laughed as they swamped him and he dissolved into them, willingly becoming a part of their whole. He felt their happiness and thanks, rejoiced in their new freedom, swam in their power, experienced their *life*.

Then he was alone on the ground and the air above him was alive as they headed for the roof of the cavern. The rock didn't stop them. He knew it wouldn't. They passed straight through like hot knives through butter.

'Goodbye!' he called as the last few points of light slipped through the roof and vanished, and then he felt incredibly lonely.

'Cheer up!'

It was Jean the Amazing Fish Woman. She was in the centre of the pool amongst the ice, her head bobbing up and down as her fish tail flapped. She looked radiant. 'We did it!' she called. 'We set my people free! That was them. Did you feel them?'

'Yeah,' Dave said, knowing he was close to tears. 'I felt them.'

'It captured us,' Jean said. 'A long long time ago.'

'In this pool?'

'It's a sea, Dave. The sea of the damned. This is only one of the openings. You knew that, didn't you?'

Dave shook his head. 'I don't know doodley squat about anything,' he said.

Jean smiled. 'You know whatever you want to know,' she said. 'And you're learning all the time. You know that there are such things as Merfolk now, don't you?'

He nodded.

'And you're our patron saint. You freed us from thousands of years on the Bad Side.'

'The cross did it,' he said bashfully.

'*Your* cross did it,' she said. 'We are forever in your debt.'

'That tank,' he said, feeling embarrassed and trying to change the subject. 'The one in the fairground. Was that really you inside?'

She smiled. 'One of Purdue's tricks. It's a representation. A bad one. Trickery. Bad magic. The image is me, but I don't perform. It stole a part of me and let Purdue have it. He made it do those things, but it isn't the real me. Do I look as bad as that?'

'No,' he said, 'but Judy was scared when we were in there. She didn't like it.'

'She felt the evil,' Jean said. 'It's finished now. The cross released the captured part of me. I'm complete and the tank is empty.'

'Can you help me?' Dave asked, glancing up and down the cavern. 'Can you tell me which way to go?'

'You have no need of my help,' she said. 'You know which way to go.'

'Where are we then? I don't know.'

'Yes, you do. We're on the Bad Side. The negative side. Where *it* lives. The Claw's domain.'

'I'm stuck here,' Dave said, 'and I have to get out.'

She looked at him, her face serious once more. 'You will find your way out of the Bad Side. Let your faith guide you.' She took the cross from her neck and threw it to him. The leather thong slapped his ears as it lassoed him. It felt good to have the cross back.

'But what shall I do?' he asked. His mind was reeling and he was wondering if he might have been struck with some kind of mental affliction and was at this moment locked safely into a padded cell in a mental hospital somewhere. He was standing here talking to a mermaid about the way out of hell and if that wasn't a sure sign he'd gone mad, he didn't know what was.

'I have no time to explain, David. I am sorry, but I must follow my people,' she told him. 'Find the girl. Beware of treachery.'

'But . . .' Dave said. It was too late. Jean the Amazing Fish Woman was in the process of transmutation. The blue-white light had formed around her and her body was diminishing. He watched as she rose from the water, shrinking and getting brighter. Now she floated in the air about four feet above the surface of the water. She was tiny; he could only see a dark outline of her body silhouetted against the eye-searing light. Then she was just a dark speck in the centre of the illumination. Then nothing except light. The light flew towards Dave, touched his nose briefly in a goodbye-and-thank-you kiss and headed up to the ceiling where it passed through the rock.

'What now?' Dave asked himself. 'What do I do now?'

He looked at the pile of the Carter household's missing things, wondering if he needed them.

Only the soldier, Dave, his inner voice told him with certainty. *Get the soldier*.

It wasn't until he began to poke the plastic soldier into the damp right hand pocket of his jeans that he realised his Swiss Army knife had gone. 'Oh no!' he shouted, frantically feeling the outside of the pocket for the knife's comforting bulge. It wasn't there. Neither was it in the other pocket. A kind of numb dread filled him. He searched the cavern floor but it wasn't on the ground either. The knife was a part of the puzzle, he realised that. It was one of the keys; one of the fundamental items along with the cross and the compass. Without it there was no chance of escaping this place intact.

Then he remembered where it was and cursed himself for not pulling it out of the moth's head. It was stuck in his Limbo Side bedroom and there was no way he could get back over there to retrieve it.

Go without it then, he thought sickly. *No option.*

He forced the plastic soldier down into the wet lining of his pocket where the knife usually lived. It felt too light and insubstantial to be of any comfort.

Sighing, he picked up his rucksack and took the compass box from it. He extracted the compass from its box, and holding it level, unclipped the brass lid.

It was as he'd expected. The compass seemed alive. Its rusted blue needle swung unerringly to the exit corridor at the opposite end of the cavern, wavering slightly from side to side as it settled.

'That way then,' he said, replacing the compass in the back pack. He put the rucksack on and walked towards the corridor.

The corridor was long and winding and dark. The only illumination came from the red pulsing of the cross which shone in time with his hearbeat and distorted his perception of distance. The flashing burned an ever-changing picture of the way forward onto his retinas and made him feel dizzy. Dave made his way through the corridor moving slowly, stepping high in case of unseen obstacles and keeping his hand against the left hand wall for support like a drunk.

After what seemed like an hour but probably wasn't, the corridor opened out into a large, well-lit cave. Dave sat down on a jutting rock to rest his weary legs.

'Davey! Davey Crockett!'

He recognised the voice, but couldn't place it. Who used to call him Davey Crockett?

He got up and walked across the flat rock towards the far side of the cave, searching his memory for the voice's owner. The floor rose and fell again. He crossed the hummock realising he hadn't noticed it before. Behind it the floor flattened out again, then stopped. There was a chasm there. Another chasm. It wasn't as wide as the one in the Ghost Train, but it was too wide to jump. The chasm was spanned by a curving bridge of ice. The ice bridge had ornately carved bannisters topped with smooth handrails and this was the source of the light which illuminated the cavern. The bridge shone with an inner fire that danced and swirled with every hue imaginable. It was beautiful.

Dave touched the ice which was smooth and sheened with water. He looked down into the chasm. There was nothing down there except darkness. The light penetrated the gloom and Dave could see down to about fifty feet before the dark outweighed it.

'Davey Crockett!'

He looked up and saw a figure breasting the brow of the bridge. A girl. He saw the top of her head first, followed by her pale face. His heart leapt.

He realised – with a pleasant kind of shock – that it was Karen, the girl he'd gone out with in his second year at school. She walked towards him over the bridge of frozen water, skipping across it as though she was weightless. She was wearing a short white dress that looked familiar and, with a start, Dave realised it was the one she'd worn on their first date.

Can't be, he found himself thinking. *That was seven years ago.*

As she drew closer he saw that the dress was dirty and tattered. It was split across the front just above her navel and it opened and closed again as she walked, giving Dave fleeting glimpses of her bare flesh. Her skin looked tight and shiny and was a shade of white that was almost transparent. Her blond hair was ragged and tumbled about her shoulders – it had grown a lot since he'd last seen her.

'Davey,' she called, and he thought he saw her face light up as she recognised him. Her voice was thin and flat and somehow it made Dave uncomfortable.

She's lost a lot of weight, Dave thought, looking at her skinny arms and legs. Her legs were especially thin. Where once they had been full and muscular, they were bony and wasted. Her wholesome athletic appearance had been replaced by this starved, almost anorexic look.

And yet he was absurdly pleased to see her; even when she came close enough for him to see the skull that lurked beneath the skin of her face, even when his cross blinked on and its heat started to burn his chest.

In spite of the ravaged look she was still pretty, and a thrill ran through Dave which was reminiscent of how he'd felt the first time he'd seen her on the school playground all those years ago.

'Karen!' he said. 'You've lost some weight.'

She stopped a pace in front of him, and he wanted to reach out for her and take her in his arms. It was so good to see another human being after all this time alone, and God knew, he needed the comfort, the warmth.

It was the warmth that stopped him taking hold of her though. A nasty idea was beginning to permeate through from his subconscious that Karen might be *cold* to the touch.

'I missed you, Dave. I'm glad you came,' Karen said in her peculiarly flat tone. She smiled and wrapped her arms around her. 'It's so cold here,' she said.

'You missed my birthday this year,' Dave said. 'For the first time in seven years you didn't send a card.'

'I'm sorry. I knew I'd missed your birthday. I couldn't send a card this year,' Karen said.

'Why not?' Dave asked, realising suddenly how absurd it was to be talking about birthday cards in this Godforsaken place with a girl he hadn't seen for years, and who he didn't even know any more.

'Because I'm dead,' Karen said sombrely. 'I couldn't send you a card because I'm dead. I took an overdose of my mother's Mandrax and no one came home in time to save me. But that doesn't matter now, we're together. Let me give you a birthday kiss.'

She opened her mouth. Her tongue was long and black. Snake-like.

Dave screamed.

And she was gone. Where she had been standing, the bridge showed two red footprints in its swirling colours.

Illusion. Only an illusion, Dave told himself, trying to steady down his hammering heart. *Should have taken notice of the cross, shouldn't you? It's The Claw testing you.*

'Hiya fuckface!'

Dave looked up. Jon Kott's beefy frame stood on the brow of the bridge. He was wearing jeans with big Doc Marten's boots and a short-sleeved Ben Sherman shirt, the sleeves of which dug into his massive biceps. His crew cut head looked like a pink bowling ball with currants for eyes, a strip of liquorice for a mouth and a king prawn for a nose. His blond hair was cut so short that his scalp gleamed through it and his whole head was sheened with sweat or water, Dave didn't know which.

'Come on then,' Kott said in a voice that was both frightening and toneless like Karen's had been. 'There's only one way out of here and that's to go past me. Come and try your luck.' He clenched one fist and hit his other palm with a meaty slap.

Is he alive? Or is he dead and an illusion like Karen? Dave thought as he stood rooted to the spot in terror. He waited for the cross to pulse and let him know, but it had fallen silent. Maybe it didn't know either.

Whatever Kott was, there was no way Dave could get past him. His squat body completely blocked the glistening bridge, and it looked slippery up there anyway. Dave doubted whether his tortured Hi-Tecs would provide the required grip on that ice.

'I'm a troll, fol de roll!' Kott cried excitedly, hopping from one big black Doc Marten to the other. 'You gonna come and trip-trap over my rickety bridge? Come on, sucker, come and give it a go. I'll eat you for my supper!'

'You're dead, Jon,' Dave said, hoping Kott would vanish. Kott just stayed there, his currant eyes narrowing as he looked down at Dave.

'You won't get away this time, you squishy little cunt!' he shouted. 'I'm going to pull your head off your fucking shoulders. I'll count to five and then I'm coming after you! One!'

'Roddy's here. He's looking for you. We came in together to get you and Sandy out.'

'TWO!'

Oh shit, save us! Dave thought. If Kott got hold of him there was a very good chance he would be decapitated. A very good chance indeed. Kott was very big and very strong and was fast too.

'I can help you.'

'THREE! I'M GETTING ANGRY NOW!' Kott reached out and grabbed the ornate ice handrails. And squeezed. Two chunks of the rail exploded in gorgeously coloured showers. In the rucksack, the compass began to squeal.

Come on, cross!

'FOUR! TRIP TRAP OVER MY RICKETY BRIDGE!'

Dave's hand was in his pocket looking for the Swiss Army knife. It came out holding the little plastic soldier with the flame thrower.

No, Dave thought. *It can't work! It's a toy soldier for Christ's sake!*

'FIVE AND HERE I COME, SHITHEAD!'

Dave knelt and placed the soldier on the foot of the bridge, glancing up at Kott's huge advancing frame as he did so. This wasn't going to work. He was certain of that. There had to be something else he must do to make it work.

The cross pulsed power into him, but it was only a trickle. *What do I do next?*

Kott was moving steadily closer. 'Piss off, Jon!' Dave yelled desperately. 'STOP!' But Kott kept on coming.

Dave moved backwards, half hypnotised by Kott's advance, deafened by the compass's screaming. The toy soldier looked tiny standing there guarding this side of the bridge.

Kott paused. His liquorice mouth grimaced and he put his left hand into his trouser pocket and brought out something red. 'COME ON TO MY RICKETY RACKETY BRIDGE AND I'LL LET YOU HAVE THIS BACK! I'VE GOT IT NOW, SHITHEAD!'

He fumbled about in front of him with the red object, then waved it above his head. It was Dave's Swiss Army knife. Kott had opened the big blade and it shone as he waved it, reflecting the dancing colours in the bridge.

'I'LL STICK IT IN YOUR BRAIN THROUGH YOUR EYES. FIRST THE LEFT THEN THE RIGHT. I'LL HAVE YOU, SHITHEAD. I'VE GOT YOUR KNIFE AND I'LL HAVE YOUR CROSS TOO! I'LL STICK YOUR BRAIN AND MINCE IT INSIDE YOUR SKULL AND THEN YOU'LL BE LIKE ME. YOU'LL BE LIKE ALL OF US OVER THIS SIDE THEN!'

Dave took another backward pace and prayed for the soldier to do something. Kott was almost on it now.

'I'M A TROLL FOL DE ROL!' Kott shouted in that flat voice. He stood right in front of the soldier now and nothing had happened. He looked down at it sneering.

It failed! Dave thought. *It didn't work!*

Kott bent down and picked up the soldier.

Dave stood there trapped by Kott's presence like a bunny in car headlights. He was feet away from Kott, unable to move, unable to take his eyes from Kott's vacant face. His muscles had deserted him and it was too late for anything else to happen. Kott only had to take one pace and he could grab him and drive the knife through his eye sockets. All Dave could do was stand there and wait.

Kott studied the soldier with a bemused expression. He held it between finger and thumb and turned it over, looking at the back pack tank, then at the rifle type barrel at the front.

Finally, he looked up at Dave. Something had changed about

his face now, but Dave didn't know what it was until afterwards. In that split second of confusion Kott had regained his humanity. 'What *is* this?' he asked in a puzzled tone.

'It's a flame-thrower,' Dave replied.

As soon as the word *flame-thrower* left his lips, Kott's whole head was engulfed in a raging yellow fireball.

Over the sound of the screaming compass, Dave could plainly hear the high pressure hiss of the flame-thrower as it fed a spray of lighted fluid into Kott's flaming face.

Kott dropped the army knife, staggered backwards and sat down heavily on the ice bridge, still holding the soldier between thumb and forefinger, still directing the spray of fire into his face. Something popped and Dave looked away, not wanting to know if it was Kott's eyes or not.

When he looked again, Kott had dropped his arm into his lap and the soldier's weapon was steadily incinerating his chest. The neatly pressed Ben Sherman had blackened and melted away from his skin and the metal button of his charring Levi's was glowing red hot. Thick clouds of reeking black smoke were coming off Kott and still the flame-thrower worked.

Enough! Dave screamed mentally. *He's dead, he's finished! Turn it off!*

He glanced back at Kott just in time to see his burning body roll off the edge of the chasm.

It was some time before the compass stopped screaming.

Chapter Fifteen
Giant Slayer

At the same time as Dave started across the ice bridge and Sally entered the empty town centre, Anne Cousins and her keeper were walking up the Newbury road about four miles from the town centre.

Anne was dog tired, but her semi-transparent captor strode along purposefully, the invisible bonds of Anne's promise dragging her close behind him. At each painful step, Anne thought of a new name for him and called it out. She had seemingly exhausted her supply of men's names some time ago and was now trying women's in case the man was trying to trick her this way.

Nothing worked.

'Where are we going?' she asked for the hundredth time. Persistence might pay off. It hadn't so far, but there was no alternative for her. All she could do was keep guessing names and keep asking the same question until the words seemed meaningless.

It wouldn't have been so bad if the screaming hadn't tormented her so.

When they left the frozen house on Worting Road and started back towards the town centre where the dark twisting sky had come down, the screaming had started again. She wasn't sure if the voice was carried on the still air or if it was coming to her by another route, but she was sure that it belonged to Tommy. It had become louder as they approached the town centre and it reached its peak of clarity when the crazy man had stopped by the big church.

In front of them was the sloped walkway up to the town centre. Tommy was just up there somewhere and something awful was happening to him; his thin screams were ringing inside her head. But the madman didn't want to go up there 'Other way,' he said and turned left, skirting the high brick wall of the shopping precinct's perimeter, taking her away from her son.

She had tried to leave him then, tried to cross the road to the slope. For a while she thought the calls of distress from her son would overpower the bonds of the promise she had made to the madman. Anne had run, thinking she was finally free, and she made it to the far kerb before her invisible bonds yanked her off her feet. She lay on the ground sobbing for a few seconds then realised she was being dragged back towards the madman. The melted M & S bag slipped from her grasp as she was tugged away and she had to fight hard to retrieve it. The bump as she was pulled back down the kerb skinned the back of her knees and she yelled, realising that she would have to get up to avoid further damage. If the madman dragged her very far like this, it would skin her completely.

She rolled over onto her stomach, glancing at him as she struggled to get back on her feet. Dragging her weight along was causing him no apparent strain and he strode out quickly. She screamed and cursed him as she tried to find her feet, but he didn't even turn around.

Now she was tagging along behind him again, trying not to remember how Tommy's frightened yells had ceased when they started to walk away from the town centre again, trying not to think of the pain that burned in her bleeding knees and hands.

'Where are we going?' she asked again.

'*One*,' he replied. 'Don't you listen, you stupid bitch? We will become *One*!'

'I can't walk any more,' she protested wondering how dangerous the man had become. He had been seething with anger since the hole in the wall in the house on Worting Road had closed down in front of him and she didn't know how far she could push him before he became violent. 'My legs are hurting and I'm going to fall over soon,' she said.

'The Bad Side. We will walk to the Bad Side and become *One*. Soon. I *know*!' The empty blue eyes of his dolly regarded her balefully from over his right shoulder.

'Fuck you, Jack!' she said, goading him. Perhaps he would stop, even if it was only to beat her. A beating was what she deserved. A beating was what she needed for being so stupid and making a promise she couldn't break.

I'm sorry, Tommy, she thought. *I'm sorry, Derek, wherever you are. I've failed you. Please forgive me.*

The madman kept right on walking.

There were trees on both sides of the empty road; sycamores, Anne thought, although she couldn't be sure; the trees stood tall and were in leaf, but something was very wrong with them. They looked like trees that had been fashioned by someone who knew nothing about trees. The angles of the branches seemed slightly wrong and the bark was almost smooth. Although she could detect no real signs of damage on them and their colours were more or less right, they seemed blackened and blighted, as though their tree souls had been corrupted. The corruption was more noticeable the farther they walked.

Behind the trees to the left was a row of recently built but crumbling houses, and on the right, just up ahead, she could see a big, ancient building set back in grounds of yellowing grass.

The madman began to slow down when the quality of the light started to change and Anne closed the gap between them, peering over his shoulder.

There was a T-junction in the road before them. The road they were on went straight ahead and the other road led away to the left, marking the border of the town. On one side of this road there were houses and, on the other, a chain link fence. Anne didn't know what used to be behind the fence, but she supposed it must have been a field. There was no field there now. She stood behind the madman and looked out into that terrible landscape, knowing without having to think about it that this was the Bad Side.

The light stopped just the other side of the chain link fence and became darkness. A sharp division between night and day ran across her field of vision from as far as she could see down the road to her left, across the road they were on and out of sight to her right.

This world – Limbo, he'd called it – ended there and became the Bad Side. The land over there was flat and featureless and black. In spite of the darkness she could see for miles across the blasted landscape and it filled her with dread.

'*One!*' the madman said, and started towards the border across the road.

'NO!' Anne shouted. 'YOU CAN'T GO IN THERE! WE'LL DIE!'

He turned and grinned at her with his transparent face. His coat hung open and she could see his heart racing behind his ribs. 'In there,' he said. 'The Knowledge. Complete. *One!*'

'What is it?' she screamed. 'What's in there?'

'God!' he said, and turned away from her, striding forward.

It's not God, I know it's not! Anne thought as she started to stagger after him. *It's wrong. It's the evil side. It's the devil in there or whatever passes for it. The Bad Thing. The monster. This is where it lives. He wants to merge us with evil!*

The madman walked into the wall of darkness and screamed. When Anne opened her eyes, he was sitting down in front of the border, still wailing.

Oh Christ it got him it put out its hand and touched him and now he's a part of it he's merged with it hasn't he God help me help meeee!

'NO!' The madman cried, leaping to his feet and charging at the dark border.

Anne saw him sink into it. It accepted him and wrapped itself around his body like it was a black rubber sheet. Then it tightened and expelled him again.

Thank you thank you he can't get in! Anne thought.

The madman got to his feet again and ran down the side road a few paces, forcing Anne to follow him. He ran at the chain link fence and vaulted at the last moment.

This time he sank further into the darkness before he was thrown out. He hit the tarmac and lay still, his beating heart doll beside him.

He's dead, Anne thought. *He's really dead this time.* She went over and looked down at him.

The madman was alive. But he was completely transparent now. She could see through his bare chest, through his musculature and internal organs and out through the back of his ribs. There was a rip in the lining of his overcoat just behind his left kidney. His eyes were closed, but she could see his eyeballs through them, and behind them the optic nerves and his brain. His eyes were rolled up and she didn't think he could see her through them. Now was the time to act.

She quickly took the chisel from her carrier bag and tried to plunge it into the madman's heart to finish him off.

It still didn't work.

'Didn't ought to do that,' the madman murmured.

Anne moaned and put the chisel away.

Her transparent captor got to his feet. 'Task,' he said in a voice that sounded like his larynx had been shattered. She could see it in there, vibrating as he spoke and for some reason it disgusted her more than the rest of his transparent organs.

'What?' Anne asked dully, looking into his distant raging eyes and wondering where the man was that used to live in there.

'The symbols. Get the symbols. The keys. It wants the keys. Then we can become *One*. Then we can merge and spend eternity together. You and I. I love you, Annie oh Annie.'

'I'll die first,' Anne said.

'Yes,' the madman replied, scooping up his doll.

He turned and started to walk back in the direction they had come from.

Basingstoke town centre was a huge pedestrian-only concrete shopping mall which spanned the quarter mile valley between two hills. It was built above ground level and suspended on hundreds of thick, steel reinforced, concrete pillars. The multistorey car park ran the length of it on its east side and separated the town cinema and the lower market square from the main body of shops. Access for deliveries and services to the shops was provided by two road tunnels which ran beneath it at ground level. Each of these tunnels branched off into a maze of linked drives and connecting alleyways which served the basements of the shops.

The town centre was less than twenty years old and the last time Sally had seen it, it looked as good as new.

Now it was crumbling. The concrete at the edges of the car park was cracked and powdery and some of the paving slabs were broken. All of them felt strangely soft beneath her feet.

Sally had walked into the town centre from the south side with the car park rising on her right. She'd heard the cries as soon as she set foot on the steps up to the precinct. It was the sound of frightened children and she could pick out at least half a dozen different voices. Unafraid and unquestioning, and with the green cross pulsing power into her, she strode past the empty shops toward the source of the cries.

She knew exactly where she was going and had half an idea of what she would find when she got there. The site of the trouble was underneath the town centre in one of the loading bays. Sally had never been down there before, but she found herself able to picture the location in minute detail: a tarmac square, edged on three sides with four foot high concrete loading bays and large enough for an articulated lorry to manoeuvre in. In the centre of the square she knew she would find a hole twelve foot in diameter.

Thinking of nothing, she made her way to the Sports Centre which stood at the top of the rise up which Anne Cousins had tried to run half an hour earlier. She turned right then and walked down the other slope towards the market square and the cinema. Some of the windows of the empty shops were cracked and Playbox 2000 didn't seem to have any glass at all in its window.

The screaming that seemed to have a direct line into her brain increased its volume as she turned right into the empty

438

market square and headed down to the south tunnel under the shopping precinct.

The old Wimpy stood on the corner of the market square and a small car park and Sally paused in front of it, gazing in at the empty white tables and the unoccupied red plastic seats. The screaming inside her head vanished as soon as she stopped and suddenly it didn't seem important any more.

Burgers, Sal, she thought. There was a distinct odour of cheeseburgers and fries coming from somewhere.

She pressed her nose against the glass, half expecting to see one of the cooks at the griddle turning patties and scraping up crispy burnt onions, which was the way she liked them best. Her stomach began to rumble and her mouth filled with saliva.

There was no one there, but two cheese-topped patties sizzled on the hot plate. Beside them stood two halves of a toasted bun.

I'm hungry, Sally thought, glancing behind her guiltily in case anyone was watching. The square was empty. She walked down to the door and pushed, not really expecting it to open. The door swung back and the smell of burgers, onions and hot buns increased. *It won't take long*, she told herself. *What harm can it do? There might even be a Coke in the fridge to wash it down.*

She went inside and walked down the corridor between the tables, her eyes fixed on the hot plate.

The cross zapped her then, good and hard. The force of the shock made her vision blur and gave her an agonising ache deep in the cut on her leg and the burn on the back of her hand. Her head spun for a moment then filled with images of her last stop for food and its consequences.

But Sally didn't want to know.

The green cross gave her another hot blast.

Take it off, Sally. Take it off and eat. Good food. Lovely greasy food. You can taste it, can't you?

And she *could* taste the cheeseburger. The meaty taste mingled with melted cheese and the tang of the piquant sauce filled her mouth and nose. She wanted very much to go and eat the burger, but she paused because those last thoughts didn't seem to belong to her at all.

You never say 'Lovely greasy food', Sal, do you?

Take it off. The cross only hurts you. Look how it's burnt your tits!

Sally glanced down at the cross which had singed its outline in the material of her tee shirt. She pulled the top of her shirt out and looked down at her breasts which were indeed burnt. The edges of the cross's tee bar had blistered a small square on the inside of each breast.

'Tits'? Do I say 'tits'? Don't I usually say 'boobs'? She couldn't remember.

The odour of burger increased and Sally's mouth filled with saliva. She swallowed and took a step towards the counter.

Take it off, Sal, and it won't hurt you any more. Take it off and your boobs will heal instantly. Take it off and you'll never be hungry again. Keep it on and you'll starve. There's no food over here you know. No food at all.

She took the cross in her hand and pulled it up, intending to never be hungry again because it sounded like a much better deal than starving to death. And she was right, too, there was no food over here. She just hadn't noticed until now because she hadn't felt hungry.

She brought the cross up to eye level and stopped. Its green light wasn't shining and the silver lid was half closed.

Not your thoughts, Sal, she told herself. *Something else thought them into your head. Oh shit, shit and double shit!*

She put the cross back on again and noticed that the fine cooking smell had suddenly gone. In the time she took to realise she was being tricked, it had been replaced by a rancid smell like rotting vegetation. She recognised the smell from Dave's bathroom. It was the smell of the stuff that oozed from The Claw.

Take it off. Take off all your clothes. You don't need clothes when you're making love to me!

Now the voice in her head was speaking without disguise. It was low and chilling. She glanced over at the griddle and saw that the burgers weren't burgers any more, but the long slender black fingers of The Claw. Only the top half of the hand existed;

440

it ended just after the knuckles and there was no thumb, but those long nails were there alright. They were scraping against the hot griddle and sending up trails of acrid smoke as it pulled itself towards the edge nearest her.

She spun around just in time to see the door close and the lock snick across. Something that looked like a wave of heat was forming just in front of the door. It was well over six feet tall. The windows misted and the tables nearest the door grew a coating of frost as the shape started to solidify. The figure inside the shimmering haze was thin and very tall and was growing a large ant-like head.

Trapped! Which way, Sal?

Sally turned and ran towards the griddle – there had to be another exit back there somewhere.

As she neared the hot plate, The Half Claw's four fingers suddenly tensed as it drew itself up on the sharp tips of the hooked ebony nails. Then the seamless fingers bent, bringing it into a crouched position like a cat ready to spring.

Mind the fucker, Sal, it's gonna jump! she warned herself as she approached it, still running full tilt. She had to go by it – there was no other way to the back. She veered to her left and ran past the griddle, her shoulder rubbing the cracked porcelain tiles and peeling the glaze from them in a cloud of yellow dust.

The Half Claw leapt as she drew level with it and someone seemed to have slowed time down because her right leg was out in front of her in the air in a running position, and the muscles in her thigh stood out in hard bulges, but it was only moving very slowly. Her arms, which should have been rapidly pistoning back and forth, were moving as slowly as her legs. The Claw's hand was travelling silently through the air towards her, its dangerous talons extended before it. She had time to take in the diving-suit blackness of those long smooth fingers and she could imagine what they would do to her bare midriff when they struck it like four poison-tipped arrows. Very likely they would disembowel her.

She willed herself forward, conscious of the sticky blue floor

441

tiles under her left foot, conscious of the rapidly falling temperature behind her.

She knew instinctively that the airborne Claw was a part of the thing that stood behind her, and that that thing had been the unwelcome passenger in the back seat of her Mini. It had tried to take the cross off her then, too, but at home it had been weaker than it was now. At home it had just frightened her and tried to snatch the cross from her neck; over here it was much more powerful – it had tried to plant those thoughts in her mind, hadn't it?

Yes, Sal, and it very nearly succeeded.

It knew what she was thinking in that slowed down split second, because it started to laugh then.

Sally's right leg came down hard on the blue tiles, and she dug her heel in and pulled her body back. She skidded a foot, but it was enough; The Claw's hand missed her. It hit the wall, cracking the porcelain tiles and slid to the ground.

'I'll kill you!' Sally roared, leaping over the hand. It had worked in the car and it might just work here too. 'You don't belong here!' she yelled as she passed the griddle. 'You can't exist here!' She skidded to a halt, and glanced over her shoulder. The hand had gone. Over by the door, the tall shape still shimmered inside the haze. The far end of the Wimpy looked as if it had just been taken from a deep freeze. Thick ice covered everything.

'But I *can* exist here, Sally,' the low thundering voice told her. 'This *is* my place.'

The hairs on the back of Sally's neck bristled. She was unable to take her eyes from the tall dark shape inside the swirling haze. 'You won't win!' she shouted. 'I'll kill you!'

'Not alone, Sally. You need three stones. One won't do it!'

'Liar,' she hissed. She bumped into a wall behind her and realised she'd been backing away.

'I can give you peace. Eternal peace. Take off the cross and throw it to me.'

'Never! Go eat shit!' Sally shouted angrily. 'This isn't your place, now fuck off! The cross is *mine* and I won't give it up, not to you or anyone!' The cross blinked on then and its thin green beam hit the shrouded figure dead centre. The Claw seemed to solidify for a moment and Sally could see its long muscular legs. Veins stood out through the black skin like ropes.

The Claw roared. Behind it, the plate glass window exploded sending thousands of sharp shards out into the market square.

The spell that had transfixed Sally broke. She turned quickly and ran out through the rest room, frightened to look behind her in case The Claw was there in the flesh and following her.

She ran through a room filled with empty packing cases and out through a fire door into the small car park.

Thanks, cross, she told it. *I'll never give in to my tummy again. Promise.*

The cross's beam went out then, but the eye was still open – to give her confidence, she knew.

She skirted the wall of the building and peered around it to see if the thing was now outside the Wimpy. There was nothing there except the shattered glass strewn on the ground.

'Claw?' she called, feeling extremely confident and exuberant. 'Are you there?' She was in control now. Whatever The Claw was, it wasn't omnipotent. Not here in Limbo, anyway. She'd driven it out of her car, and it looked as if she'd driven it out of the Limbo Land Wimpy, too.

Picking her way carefully through the glass, she looked into the Wimpy. The tables and chairs were still coated with ice and she could feel the cold radiating out, but The Claw was gone. Where the shimmering shape had stood, a pool of thick black gelatinous substance was now spreading across the floor.

That was when the screaming started again. Only a single voice this time.

Sally ran to the gap in the fence that separated the car park from the tunnel which ran under the town centre, and listened to the distant screaming, allowing the picture of the loading bay to come back into her mind. Then she strode into the tunnel, her eyes distant and her face set in determination.

She turned into SERVICE AREA 2 and passed the bays,

following the maze of empty corridors until she came to the northern loading area. She stood on the edge of the dock and looked down at the tarmac marshalling area, nodding to herself. This was it. Down there, out in the centre of the yard, was the huge hole in the ground. It was surrounded by a three foot high pile of rubble and broken tarmac. Just behind the hole and about twenty feet above it, she could see sky. There was an oval opening up there bordered with a wall. That was the level of the shopping precinct, she realised; the oblong opening was situated between Woolworths and the row of shops on the other side of the walkway – she had walked past that wall many times since the town centre had been built and she couldn't remember ever looking over it to see what was below.

What now, Sal? she asked herself, looking at the pit. *That's where the screaming is coming from. Do you climb down it or what?*

'Mummy, the Big Giant!' The thin voice echoed from the mouth of the hole. It hurt her to listen to the plaintive screaming but she wasn't sure if it was a trick or not, so she stood her ground, waiting.

The wait didn't last long.

'FE FI FO FUM, I SMELL THE *BLOOD* OF AN ENGLISHWOMAN!'

The voice was harsh and louder still than that of The Claw. Dust fell from the concrete ceiling with the sheer volume. Sally coughed, taking her cross in her right hand and rubbing it gently like a magic lamp. Suddenly she didn't feel so sure of herself any more. She may have got rid of The Claw, but what was lurking in that hole wasn't going to vanish so easily.

The giant started to emerge from the hole in the ground. Sally saw the crown of its dark-haired head first. The head was almost eight feet across and, as Sally watched, it came up and came up until she was sure it was going to be all hair and nothing else.

'I SMELL THE *BLOOD* OF A LITTLE SALLY HARRISON!' the giant roared. Sally clapped her hands over her ears, but the sound still hurt. As the words cannoned out, her vision blurred with the tremendous vibration. More dust fell from the crumbling concrete and, from behind her, she thought she heard the squealing of tortured metal.

Then the giant's face came out of the hole. It had a prominent forehead with thick, black eyebrows which knitted on the bridge of its nose. Its skin was pale and cheesy and rough. Two small coal-black eyes glowed under that Neanderthal brow. Underneath a squashed nose that was the size of Sally's car hung a slack cavernous mouth. The giant was bearded with black, cable-thick hair. It opened its mouth showing massive yellow teeth and roared: 'WHAT DO YOU MEAN BY DISTURBING MY MEAL, LITTLE SALLY HARRISON?'

Sally groaned as the rush of fetid air blew her hair back and flapped her tee shirt against her body. The giant still had some of its meal in its mouth. Its tongue was red with blood and there was a crushed shape in there that looked like a half-chewed, fully-dressed male teenager. One of the legs was gone and the head was missing, but most of it remained.

It snaps your head off first, Sally, she thought, horrified. *That's what it does, snaps your head off.*

The giant's huge mouth closed and it began to chew, still fixing Sally with its glittering eyes. She looked away, but that didn't prevent her from hearing the crunching of bone, nor the wet swallow as the body was consigned to the giant's stomach.

'WHAT HAVE YOU COME HERE FOR?' the giant demanded.

'I've come to get Dave Carter and the others you've got down there,' she said shakily. 'I've come to rescue them.'

The giant put up a hand as big as a bungalow on a massive muscular arm and scratched his head. 'DON'T THINK I'VE EATEN A DAVE CARTER. WHAT WOULD HE HAVE TASTED LIKE?' he asked, almost blowing Sally over.

'He's down there with the others. I *know* it. I've come to take them away from you!' Sally yelled, wishing the cross would zap him.

'YOU THINK YOU CAN ROB MY LARDER?' the giant laughed. His face became serious as he scratched his head and considered the matter; then it became enraged. 'I'LL GRIND YOUR BONES TO MAKE MY BREAD! I'LL PINCH YOUR BODY TILL YOU'RE DEAD! I'LL SNAP MY TEETH DOWN ON YOUR HEAD!' it shouted.

Sally tried to dodge, but the wind from the giant's lungs had put her off her balance and there was no escaping the huge hand as it swept out and plucked her from the floor. He held her struggling body up in front of his glittering black eyes and peered at her. 'A TASTY MORSEL YOU'LL MAKE. YOU'LL GO IN THE LARDER WITH THE OTHERS. OR SHALL I EAT YOU NOW?'

The cross didn't come on, but it warmed Sally's skin and put words in her mouth.

'You'll choke on me!' she shouted. 'I'm sharp. As sharp as they come!'

'THEN I'LL COOK YOUR FLESH UNTIL YOU'RE DONE!' the giant replied.

'I can give you something better than that,' she said, suddenly remembering her Brer Rabbit. 'Put me down on the edge of your hole and I'll tell you how to get a much tastier morsel than me.'

'I'LL BITE YOUR HEAD OFF FIRST! DO YOU EXPECT ME TO PUT YOU DOWN SO YOU CAN FLEE? YOU CANNOT FLEE FROM ME!'

The cross pulsed. Sally tried to ignore the pain where the giant's fingers were crushing her body and fixed her gaze on his beady eyes. 'I'm sharp and I'm hot,' she said. 'Very hot indeed.'

The giant thrust her away from him quickly, letting her go. She fell the last six feet and landed on the pile of rubble beside the hole.

'Mummy! Heeelp meeeee!' The tinny voice rang in her head as her world swam in front of her eyes.

The giant roared and swiped at her with its huge hand. Sally ducked under it and rolled, fully expecting the killer blow to land.

'GET BACK INSIDE!' the giant roared.

Sally glanced up and saw that a young girl was scrambling

over the pile of rubble. She was dressed in a blue gingham frock and had blond hair. She was about eleven, Sally thought.

'Run!' she yelled, getting to her feet and grabbing a rock from the ground.

'RUN!'

She threw the rock at the giant's head. It struck the bridge of his nose and opened up a large wound from which bright blood gushed.

The young girl almost made it. She was on Sally's side of the pile of rubble and running when the giant's fingers plucked her in the air.

'LET HER GO!' Sally shouted, throwing another rock. It hit the giant under his left eye, opening another wound, but he didn't even blink. His eyes were fixed on the little girl and he was smiling. His mouth opened. The girl squealed.

'NO!' Sally shouted, but the girl was on his tongue and his mouth was closing again. There was a sickening crunch and the girl's screaming stopped.

Dark blood ran from one corner of the giant's smiling mouth.

Sally picked up a bigger rock and weighed it in her hand. 'Right, you fucker, this is the one!' she yelled, and heaved it at him.

The rock hit the giant's left eye and sank in. There was a moment's pause while the giant looked down at Sally and she looked up at him, cursing him. Then the eye burst and gouted black jelly. The rock didn't come out though and Sally wondered if it had gone right back to his optic nerve or further.

'DIE, YOU BASTARD!' she yelled, expecting the giant to collapse.

The giant roared bringing rubble cascading from the concrete roof, and he started to come up out of the hole.

No room, Sal, she thought, running back. *He's too tall to stand in here. He'll bring the roof down!*

The giant was out of the hole now. His body was much too big to fit under the service area roof and he was bent double, his head banging against the ceiling as he staggered around.

447

Sally snatched another chunk of rock from the ground and threw it at the giant's other eye. It missed, hitting him on the cheekbone. A gash that was far too big considering the size of the rock opened up and the giant groaned and clapped his hand over the cut.

It's soft, his skin's soft! Sally told herself, unable to believe her eyes. She scooped up another rock and aimed it, knowing that the top of the giant's head was much harder than his face and that it would soon bring this part of the town centre crashing down on them if it kept on thumping against the ceiling.

The rock hit the giant's neck and it must have struck an artery because a fountain of blood jetted out like red water from a fireman's hose. The giant fell to his knees, screaming so loud that everything became blurred in front of Sally's eyes.

But she saw his huge hand sweeping across towards her and dodged behind one of the concrete support pillars. The giant's hand smashed into the pillar and passed through it. The air was filled with flying debris and dust as the pillar disintegrated and Sally ran along the loading dock away from it. She turned the corner at the end and stood in front of the row of smaller shop loading-doors, facing the giant which was still groping in the dust for her.

'I'LL GRIND YOUR BONES TO MAKE MY BREAD!' it screamed.

Sally's cross shot a bolt of pain down her chest. 'Tell me another!' she hissed, marvelling at how the words came out with no effort or thought on her part. 'I've heard it all before.'

The giant turned to face her. Its good eye gleamed down at her and it opened its mouth, giving her a clear view of its front-door sized yellow teeth.

'Don't touch me because I'm hot!' Sally yelled. 'Don't touch me because you'll burn yourself. YOU'LL DIE IF YOU TOUCH ME!'

The giant's hand swept out towards her again and Sally dropped to the ground and rolled aside. The huge fingers smashed into the first door in the line and ripped through the walls behind her, passing over her. The noise from the exploding walls was deafening and the dust was so thick that she could hardly see now. Just when she thought she'd got away with it, a large chunk of masonry toppled forward from what was left of the wall behind her and trapped her legs.

It won't get you, Sal, it's going to die first, she assured herself as a spray of blood splashed across her face. *It can't live much longer like that!*

Huge fingers came down through the blanket of dust, and pinching shut under her arms dragged her out from under the section of wall.

She was *burning* it. It had *worked*! Grey blooms of acrid smoke were rising from the giant's finger and thumb as it pulled her up and it was shouting with pain and anger.

There was a sharp piece of concrete in her right hand. She didn't remember picking it up, and she was surprised to see it. She looked at it stupidly for a second thinking: *And what if it does 'die? What are you going to do then? You're crippled, Sal. Your legs might not hurt now, but they will in a minute. It's just dragged you out from under a heavy wall. Your hips are bound to be broken and your legs have probably been pulled right off and that's why you can't feel them right now.*

She brought the sharp piece of rock down into the muscle between the giant's smouldering thumb and forefinger. There was little resistance, and it passed right through with no more effort than it would have taken to poke a dessert spoon through a raspberry jelly.

Fighting to draw a breath against the pressure around her ribs, she pulled the shard of concrete back towards her, splitting the muscle in two. It didn't bleed much, but that was probably because the giant didn't have too much blood left in him now. Most of it was coming out of the hole in his neck and cascading around her like smelly red rain.

The giant's grip on her loosened, and she wriggled free, falling a few feet and landing back on the smashed loading bay.

Legs are alright! You're standing, Sal!

Out of the thick dust, the giant's head loomed up before her, its mouth opening and snapping shut again as it tried to bite her. It was lying down – either because it was dying, or because it thought it would be able to move more freely. Its left eye was dribbling down onto its cheek and the deep cut on its nose was bleeding freely. Sally backed away from it, noticing how pale it was now, how ponderous its movements had become.

'I think you made a mistake lying down,' Sally said, dodging back from its snapping teeth. 'Because you're not going to get up again. Ever.' She looked into its one gleaming eye, took aim and threw the rock.

The giant screamed as its eye burst. Huge chunks of concrete began to fall from the roof and Sally ran back into the open shop store room behind her, leaping onto the stairs as the giant's hand smashed into the room after her.

It was five past ten on Friday evening.

State Registered nurse Nancy Willis sat in the third row from the back in the darkened interior of Basingstoke's Cannon cinema with a (very good looking) stranger on her left and her friend, radiologist June Whitley on her right.

The Robert de Niro film was nearing its completion now and it looked as if it was going to be a tragic ending, which was a shame, because de Niro wasn't going to get the girl and he ought to have. In fact it didn't look as if he was even going to be alive when the credits rolled.

Nancy glanced at the rapt face of the man to her left, marking him a very good eight and wishing that circumstances would somehow provide her with an introduction to him. He noticed her watching him and glanced in her direction, his eyebrows lifted questioningly. Nancy quickly looked away, feeling herself flushing and thanking God it was dark in here. He was probably married anyway, she decided, settling down in her seat again.

'You have a car, don't you?' de Niro (who was holed up in the back streets of Chicago and expecting them to come for him at any moment) asked the blonde girl who'd grassed on him two reels earlier.

Nancy shivered as an unpleasant chill of fear ran up her back. Now the evening was ruined because that was what the old man in the hospital had asked her just before the Sleeping Beauty girl vanished earlier in the week. Just when she was beginning to forget, de Niro had to go and remind her again. The words hung shimmering in her head: *You have a car, don't you?* but the voice wasn't de Niro's, it was the dry, crusty, *knowing* voice of the old man.

That old man had got her into a lot of trouble and it was uncomfortable to think about him now. He had obviously had something to do with the Sleeping Beauty girl's disappearance and she deeply regretted ever having seen him at all.

Why hadn't she reported him to the administration who could have, in turn, reported him to the police, they'd asked her. Why hadn't she done *this*, why hadn't she done *that*?

Because I didn't think he was dangerous, she'd told the administrators and the two detectives who were investigating several disappearances of a similar kind. *I did nothing because he was a harmless old man on the edge of senile dementia who thought he knew when the weather would change and who told me not to put my car in the car park on Friday evening because it was going to fall down. We get all sorts of people wandering about in here and usually they don't do any harm. We just lead them out and let them go. There's a mental hospital in these grounds in case you haven't noticed. Having their patients wandering around our wards is a commonplace event.*

The detectives had been abrupt and generally unpleasant to her as if all the disappearances were entirely her fault. One moment the girl who was called Sally Harrison had been sleeping peacefully in her bed, the next she had vanished from the face of the earth. Apparently she had last been sighted just outside the hospital wearing a pair of shorts and a tee shirt last seen in an oak chest under her bed at home. Where did she get the clothes? And where had she gone?

Nancy was unable to answer those questions, any more than the detectives but when she had said so, she'd got a right old dressing down. Didn't she realise it was serious? they asked. Of course she did, but what could *she* do about it?

Then where was the girl's boyfriend, David Carter? He'd vanished a day earlier. And where were their friends, another boy and girl? They'd gone missing last weekend. What did *she* know about it?

Nancy knew nothing about it and she told them so. She'd never heard any of the names they'd mentioned except Sally Harrison the Sleeping Beauty, and someone called Roddy Johnson who was also missing. She'd heard of Roddy Johnson because of his reputation as a hard man. According to June, (who had worked in Basingstoke for much longer than her) he'd once put a kid in intensive care for two weeks by slashing his throat from ear to ear with a piece of glass.

She'd given the detectives a good description of the old man and his little white dog on the long blue lead and the disgusting pipe he'd smoked while wandering about in the hospital. They'd come back yesterday and informed her that the man didn't exist.

Not in Basingstoke perhaps, she told them, *but he does exist because I've seen him*.

You're making it up, what do you know about all this? they'd asked. You're involved aren't you? You can tell us. No harm will come to you.

Perhaps he came from the AdventureLand fairground, she'd said. *Why didn't they look for him there?*

But apparently that was what everyone said.

There *was* no old man of that description working on the fair, nor living with any of the people there.

Eventually the detectives had left her. She was glad she hadn't told them that the old man knew she drove a yellow Datsun Sunny and that her name was Nancy in spite of the fact that she hadn't been wearing her name badge. If she'd opened her mouth about *that* she'd probably still be there answering their questions now.

She didn't believe that the old man had anything to do with Sally Harrison's disappearance, just as she didn't believe what he'd said about the car park falling down tonight – he was an old nutcase, that was all.

452

What worried her was the fact that June's car hadn't been fixed in time for them to use it tonight. It should have been fixed today, and it *would* have been fixed today if it hadn't been for the fact that the mechanic had forgotten to oil the big end bearings before he reassembled the engine this afternoon. Apparently this was a big mistake because if you didn't oil them first, they got ruined when you started the car up. That meant that the old man had *known* what was going to go wrong. He'd been certain that they would use her Sunny tonight.

On the journey here, she had decided to be cussed and park in the multistorey car park just to spite the old man, just to prove that she wasn't superstitious and didn't fall for all that cosmic hooey. Car parks this size didn't fall down. Not in disaster free Basingstoke they didn't, anyway. There were no earthquakes here, not in this part of the country.

But in spite of all the reasoning, she hadn't been able to make herself turn into the up ramp of the multistorey car park when it came to it. She'd indicated and started to make the turn, then changed her mind and cruised by. A feeling of relief had settled on her as she passed the car park entrance.

'Where are you going?' June had demanded. June was a creature of habit and always parked in the same space on the ground floor level of the park opposite the cinema. You could get out of the car, leap the three foot high wall and be in the street opposite the cinema's foyer.

'I'm parking in the market trader's car park behind the Wimpy,' she'd told June.

'What on earth for?' June had wanted to know, obviously imagining the horrors of a two hundred yard walk to the cinema.

'Because the car park is going to fall down,' Nancy replied, feeling stupid.

Up on the silver screen, de Niro was shooting a silver Magnum at the police from a speeding black Packard with blown out windows.

June nudged her and offered her the bag of Butterkist popcorn she'd been rustling for the last half hour. June ate on autopilot when she was watching Bob and didn't notice the noise the bag made as she did it. Nancy had watched her earlier on – her hand was like one of those mechanical grabs as it rose and fell from her mouth. The woman behind them had muttered darkly about the row during a love scene earlier on, but June hadn't paid any attention to her.

De Niro was out of the car now, backed up against a wall in a dead end alley. His Magnum was out of ammo and tears were coursing down his face because he now realised how his lover had betrayed him. There were cops approaching him, bristling with fire power. His girl was with them. 'Put the gun down, Angelo,' she called to him. 'It's over!'

Nancy took some popcorn and the bag was noisily withdrawn.

'Shh!' the woman behind them hissed.

'Why?' de Niro asked, shaking his head sadly.

There was a moment of silence as the two lovers looked at one another.

The roar of the Wimpy's plate glass window exploding two hundred yards away was muffled but distinct. The sound of shattered glass raining down sounded like distant bells.

A ripple of confusion ran through the audience. People started muttering.

'I'm sorry,' de Niro's lover said.

'Put down the gun!' the policeman in charge commanded.

De Niro brought the gun up to his head. The movie cut to a close up of his finger on the trigger.

'What was that?' June whispered.

Nancy was rigid in her seat. 'I didn't hear anything,' she lied.

De Niro pulled the trigger.

The hammer struck an empty chamber.

'Okay, son, it's all over,' the leading cop said, advancing with his own gun held steady in one hand and a pair of cuffs dangling from the other. The picture dissolved and re-formed six months later in a tenement building.

That wasn't the car park falling down, Nancy thought, relaxing slightly. *He was wrong. Something happened out there, but it wasn't the car park falling down.*

The buzz of conversation had died out as the audience became engrossed in the movie again, but Nancy couldn't concentrate on the story any more. Half of her was happy about the car park not falling down, and the other half was telling her that there was still plenty of time for it to happen.

The movie ended unhappily five minutes later – de Niro was jailed for life and his lover had found herself unable to live with what she'd done and committed suicide.

The credits started to roll and people got up to leave. June turned to Nancy and nudged her. There were tears in her eyes. 'C'mon, Nance, let's go,' she said, fishing a tissue from her handbag and blowing her nose.

They were at the end of the row when the power failed and lights went out.

The credits ground to a halt and the downbeat soundtrack slowed and finally stopped. The emergency lights were on, but they only glowed over the exit signs. On the other side of the cinema someone screamed.

'Powercut,' said the tasty guy on Nancy's left, turning in the almost total darkness and grabbing her as she stumbled over a seat arm.

Somewhere down the front panic had taken hold. It had spread quickly, crystallising into terror and the aisles were now packed with frightened people surging towards the foyer where they fought each other to be first out through the doors.

'Keep calm!' someone shouted in a cracked voice. 'We're not on fire. I repeat, we're not on fire! Please keep calm and leave in an orderly fashion!'

The crowd didn't much care whether the cinema was alight or not. The only certain thing was that they didn't intend to stick around to find out.

June and Nancy and the good-looking guy held one another's arms and joined the rush for the doors. Most of the audience was outside by the time they got to the exit, but there were still a few stragglers and Nancy got an elbow in the guts and a sharp kick on her right shin before they got out.

Outside the cinema, the streetlights were off but the air of panic had vanished. It was a clear, mooonlit night and easy to see. Throngs of people stood around on the pavement looking sheepish and embarrassed. More were heading off into the town centre and a few were entering the Nightjar pub intending to calm themselves with a quick drink before last orders were called. The taxi rank was empty.

'False alarm!' the good-looking guy said.

Nancy realised she was still hanging on to his arm, but she didn't let go.

'Nothing to worry about,' he said, smiling down at her. He glanced at her arm linked in his and said, 'We haven't been introduced, have we? My name's Geoff. Who are you?'

'Nancy,' she said looking up at him and just about managing to smile back. 'Nancy Willis.'

'And I'm June Whitley,' June said from behind them.

'Can I give you a lift home, girls? You both look shaken,' he said. 'My car's just down there on Jackson's garage forecourt.'

'Our car is behind the Wimpy,' June said.

'Oh, I'm sorry. Let me walk you to your car then.'

'Thank you,' Nancy said, glancing at June who was pulling a face and rolling her eyes. 'Don't worry about my friend, Geoff. She's in love with Robert de Niro and she's extremely upset,' she told him.

'Ha ha,' June said falling in step with them as they walked toward the market square. Nancy wished she would go away. 'When do you . . .? Oh . . . Look!' she said, pointing across the square.

The area around the Wimpy was cordoned off with day-glo red tape. A big red fire engine stood in the middle of the square and police cars were blocking the entrance to the car park. Police and firemen with torches were swarming around outside the cordoned-off area. Inside the square of red tape, glass and brickwork were strewn everywhere. At first Nancy thought it was her car that had done the damage. It had blown up, that's what it had done. One of the male nurses had told her weeks ago that the carburettor was leaking and might catch fire.

456

The old man knew something bad was going to happen to me, but he didn't quite get it right, she told herself.

'You're hurting my arm. What's wrong?' Geoff asked.

Nancy released her grip on him. 'Nothing,' she said.

As they walked over to the cordoned-off area, a policeman approached them. 'Where are you off to?' he called.

'Going back to my car. It's behind the Wimpy,' Nancy said guiltily. Now they knew who was to blame.

The policeman didn't run forward and arrest her, though. He smiled sympathetically and said, 'I'm afraid it'll have to stay where it is for now, love. We've had an explosion or something. The front of the Wimpy has been blown out. We don't know if it was a bomb or a gas explosion, but no one is allowed near it until the bomb disposal guys have had a look. You'll have to leave the car here until the area is pronounced safe. I suggest you come back in the morning. Sorry.'

'Is the car alright?' Nancy asked.

'Yellow Datsun Sunny? W registration?'

She nodded.

'Yeah. There's no damage back there, love. It'll be alright if the Wimpy doesn't blow up again.'

'Oh, thanks,' Nancy said.

'Now I'll get to give you that lift home, won't I?' Geoff said squeezing her arm reassuringly.

'Look, uh, I think I'll go up to Southern Road and see if Janie and Bill are still up,' June said. 'Perhaps they'll feed me, they usually do. Don't worry about me, I'll get Bill to drive me home later. Okay?'

'Okay, June, thanks,' Nancy said.

'Alone at last,' Geoff said as they watched June go up the ramp to the town centre.

'What kind of a car do you have, Geoff?'

'BMW Series 7. Fuel injected. Mean anything?'

She shook her head. 'Expensive, but that's all.'

'I didn't pay for it,' Geoff said, 'it's a company car. I sell computers. IBMs mainly. It's a tough job but someone's got to do it.'

'Geoff?'

He looked down at her and shook his head. 'I recognise that tone. No Nancy, I'm not married. Not any more anyway. Clean break, no kids.'

There was no one left in front of the cinema and the doors were shut. Nancy stopped outside the taxi cab office. There were no taxis in the rank, but the controller was still in there in the darkness in front of his microphone – she could see the red end of his cigarette glowing.

'Did you feel anything?' she asked.

'Bit early to be talking about love, isn't it?' Geoff quipped.

'No. Seriously.'

'What?' He listened. 'Something squeaked.'

'I felt the ground shudder,' Nancy said. 'It trembled. We can't get earthquakes here, can we? Not in Basingstoke, surely?'

Geoff's face was intent as he peered into the empty depths of the car park across the road. 'Something in there squealed,' he said, frowning.

'I don't like it, let's get out of here,' Nancy said feeling the ground vibrate through the soles of her shoes.

'I think I heard someone scream,' Geoff said distantly. 'Someone's in trouble in there.' He started towards the road and Nancy tugged at his sleeve, trying to stop him.

'NO!' she said. 'Don't go over there! C'mon, let's go!'

'What's going on?' a voice asked from behind them.

It was the taxi controller. He was a grey-haired man in his fifties. His cigarette dangled from the corner of his mouth. 'First there's the bloody power cut, and just now I felt an earth tremor.' He nodded back to the office. 'Stuff is falling over in there. What's going on? That's what I want to know!'

'There it is again!' Geoff said, striding out into the empty road.

'What?' the controller asked.

'Screaming. I heard screaming.' He was on the other side of the road now, peering into the level that Nancy usually parked on. 'Too dark,' he called back. 'Can't see anything.'

'I never heard any screaming,' the controller said, puffing on his cigarette and shrugging. 'Did you?'

Nancy ignored him. 'No Geoff! Come back! Please!'

But Geoff had leapt over the low retaining wall and was going into the darkness. Soon he was out of sight.

'Oh God,' Nancy said.

'Another earth tremor,' the taxi man said. 'S'the heat see? Get Mediterranean weather and what follows? I'll tell you what follows, Mediterranean earthquakes, that's what.' He nodded to himself, took the dog end from his mouth and crushed it out on the bottom of his shoe. 'Think I'll go home,' he said, flicking the butt into a nearby drain cover. 'Tranny's broke and no one can hear me, so I think I'll go home.'

'But where are you?' Geoff's distant voice called.

That was when the section of the multistorey car park in front of Nancy collapsed.

The ground floor level went first, sinking into the ground as though it was falling into a hole. The noise was tremendous. Concrete and dust flew as Nancy watched it sink.

Geoff's dead, she thought.

Then she was running. Running for her life down towards Jackson's garage where Geoff's Series 7 fuel injected BMW was parked. Down towards Churchill Way and safety. On her left, the six levels of the car park were falling like dominoes, folding up their huge support pillars as they went. Dust and debris bloomed out of the gaps between the falling levels, fogging her way forward, but Nancy kept on running, unable to hear anything except the long low rumble that went on and on and on.

On the Limbo Side, Sally was fleeing through the clothes shop she'd entered down in the service area. The giant's hand had missed her as she flew up the stairs and had swept away the bottom of the building from beneath her. The town centre level of the shop had survived the attack temporarily, and she had leapt the gap that had formed between the stairs and the shop floor and kept going.

She knew the door would be locked as she fought her way through the fallen clothes racks, so she ran straight at the plate glass window, hoping that it would break. She pelted across the last few yards to the window and launched herself at it, folding her arms in front of her face and bringing her knees up as she took to the air.

Behind her, half the shop floor had fallen into the yawning chasm. There would be no second chance.

The glass felt warm and soft when she hit it and shattered instantly. She hit the concrete paving slabs of the precinct, rolled and got to her feet still running. When she looked behind her, she could see all the way down to the cinema. Nothing of the town centre or the car park was left between here and there except a pile of grey ash.

'Christ,' she said breathlessly. 'It went all the way through!'

She stood still and listened. The giant might still be alive down there under her. He might be getting his second wind so that he could bring the rest of the precinct down, too.

When she had counted to five hundred and heard nothing except total silence, she was sure the giant was dead. She peered down into the service area above the giant's pit. There were steps leading down to the ground from here, but the bottom half dozen were gone. Most of the service area was gone, too. All she recognised down there was a section of loading dock she had stood on. The rest was a haphazard pile of smashed concrete chunks and grey dust.

Realising what she was going to have to do, she shook her head. 'I don't want to go down there,' she said aloud, looking up at the dull grey sky. 'At least let me rest first. I'm knackered. I can't do anything else today. I've already broken out of a caravan with my bare hands, fought Fred Purdue, run through the Ghost Train and killed a giant. Now you want me to go down that goddamned pit. I'm only a girl, for God's sake!'

But there are people down there in that pit, Sal, and you've got to go down after them, she told herself. *Something terrible is happening to the fabric of this place, Sal; it's all wrong. It's going rotten or something, that's why you broke that plate glass window so easily, that's why the town centre collapsed. There's not much time, you know that, don't you? The Claw is strong and getting stronger and if you don't go now it'll win or this place will fall*

460

apart or both. So off you go. Get your skinny ass in gear and move!

'Bugger it!' she swore, starting toward the gate at the top of the steps.

The gate wouldn't open so she climbed it, muttering that all she ever wanted to be was a make-up girl on films. It wasn't until she was halfway down the steps that she realised the cut on her thigh and the slash across her belly had healed. She still had the burn on her hand where the beam from Fred's ring had hit her though, and she had a feeling that it would stay there for ever.

Chapter Sixteen
Getting The Knowledge

Dave picked up his army knife and looked at the ice bridge. It was beginning to melt. He didn't know whether this was due to his presence or because of the heat from the flame-thrower soldier that had burnt Jon Kott's face off. He started across, pulling himself up the slippery slope by holding onto the freezing handrails to aid the skidding grip of his Hi-Tecs. By the time he reached the brow of the bridge, the ice was cracking and water was running down in hundreds of tiny rivulets. At the top he paused for a moment to rest his arms but he didn't look down into the chasm. He could still hear the sibilant hiss of the tiny soldier's weapon coming from down there somewhere and the thought that Kott might be climbing back up the side, his head nothing but a charred football, was too much for him to take.

He blew on his numb fingers, promised them he wouldn't subject them to so much pain ever again if they would only look after him until he got down the other side, and took hold of the ice bannisters, intending to go slowly down the curved slope, testing the ice under his feet as he went. The bridge was melting quickly now and he wasn't sure the footway would support his weight.

He had taken four steps when the handrails collapsed and toppled over the sides into the chasm, leaving him with a chunk of ice in each hand.

Shit! he thought, realising that his feet were already sliding. He dropped the portions of handrail and crouched, keeping his arms outstretched for balance.

Behind him, the far side of the bridge broke away and fell, spraying his back with needle sharp slivers of frozen water. The shockwave wobbled his side of the bridge and altered his direction so that he was heading for the edge. He turned his foot and dug the outside of one Hi-Tec into the slick surface, hoping it would catch and skate him back to the middle.

For a moment he thought he was going to fall, then the boot caught a crack in the ice and straightened his path. When his Hi-Tecs caught the next fault in the ice, he was moving fast and the edge of the chasm was still fifteen feet away. The toes of his boots dug in and his feet stopped. He fell forwards for what seemed like an incredibly long time before his chest and chin hit the wet walkway. His hands slapped down hard in front of him, raising a shower of ice which blinded him. The remainder of the bridge exploded noisily as his cold hands touched the rock of the far edge.

His body fell into the chasm but his numb fingers had hold of a jutting piece of rock and held on. His body swung down and hit the side hard, knocking the breath from his lungs.

Gonna fall off now, Dave, he told himself with absolute certainty.

His stretched arms ached and his hands must have been cursing him for breaking his promise to them because they'd had enough and were letting go.

C'mon! he thought, trying to force the half-frozen digits to hold on as his legs flapped below him.

Then his right foot found a ridge and he put his weight on it and pushed, pulling his aching arms down and forcing himself up towards the edge.

Come on hands, I'm sorry. Please! Just this once! he pleaded as his unfeeling fingers slipped from the rock a little more.

His left foot scrambled up the rock face and found a crease. He had to turn it sideways to get it in and his ankle complained bitterly as it took his weight, but the alternative was worse. Much worse.

His hands felt like two pieces of wood, but he clapped them around the rock again as he pushed himself up on his left leg.

'COME ON!' he shouted desperately, pulling for all he was worth. He was half on the ledge now, but his foot wouldn't come out of the crack and his arms weren't strong enough to tug him up.

A kind of dull fascination built in him as he watched his fingers peel away from the jutting rock as though they had a life of their own. He slipped backwards slightly and his left ankle felt as though it would break.

Cross! Help!

He didn't know whether the cross buzzed at his chest or if it was just a muscle cramp, but the pain jolted his body and freed his trapped foot. His legs started to scramble crazily up the side of the chasm, regaining the six inches he'd lost. He slapped his hands around the rock once more, and this time it was enough. Seconds later he was lying on the rocky ground choking and sobbing as he fought for breath.

He lay like that for a long time, wondering if the hissing of the flamethrower was getting nearer or if it was just a trick of his imagination.

As his breathing grew more regular, the sound of the weapon vanished and was replaced with what sounded like a child's cries of distress.

Feeling very old and very tired, he got to his feet and went across the small ledge to the tunnel in the rock face from which presumably Jon Kott had emerged.

It wasn't so much a tunnel as a doorway. It was only about four feet deep and the wall behind it was solid rock.

'So what do I do now?' he said aloud. 'I've run out of Smarties, so I can't blow the fucker down.'

Knock, Dave, knock three times.

His fingers were still stiff and aching, but he made a fist and tapped on the rock wall three times, wincing with pain at each blow.

'Open Sesame,' he said wearily.

Well that didn't work, did it? he told his intuitive side. *What now? Dance a jig?*

His cross zapped his chest then, but it didn't fill him with power or heal his wounds – apparently it had got fed up with doing that – this was a jolt of redress.

Now it's telling me off for being sarcastic, he thought indignantly.

The ground started to tremble.

Oh, don't tell me something is going to collapse on me, please! he thought.

The trembling increased and changed into a dull rumble. The rock face rolled aside as if it were on castors. Through the doorway was a huge room, containing four pools like the one that Jean the Mermaid had been trapped in. There was one in each corner.

Dave walked through the doorway, marvelling at the size of the room which was big enough to have accommodated a couple of 747s. The floor was tiled with huge grey flagstones and was empty except for a row of what looked like human-sized bird-cages along the left-hand wall and stacks of bleached bones along the right. The barred cages had small doors which were all open except the one at the other end. Inside this one a small blond-haired boy sat sobbing into his hands. Even from this distance, Dave knew who it was immediately; he'd seen the boy's picture on the *News at Ten* and in the Sunday papers. It was little Tommy Cousins, known as Tiger by his father. Dave remembered meeting the child's dad in the Memorial Park and wondered what had happened to him. Had he found his way over here, too?

He's probably dead by now if he did come over, Dave thought. *You can't survive here for long unless you have help.*

And he'd been almost deranged, back then, hadn't he?

But he was right about the giant, by the look of things, he told himself. *If this place doesn't belong to a giant, I don't know what does. Derek, that was his name. Didn't he say his wife kept on dreaming of giants?*

'It's okay, Tommy, I'm coming!' he called as he hurried toward the other end of the hangar-sized room. The boy didn't look up.

Dave tried not to notice the mess as he went to the boy, but his eyes recorded it anyway. On the opposite side of the room to the cages, there were heaps of bones with pieces of rotting meat clinging to them. The bones looked like parts from human skeletons, but most of them were smashed and he couldn't be sure. There were no skulls there at all.

When he got halfway across and saw the piles of torn and bloodied clothes he *was* sure and he started to feel sick, imagining what that poor kid might have had to watch. The bones here were fresher, and the walls were stained with blood. The further he went, the more he noticed the smell which was sweet and sickly.

'I'm coming, Tiger!' he called, glancing at what might just have been a girl's stockinged leg protruding from under one of the heaps of clothing.

'Mummy help me! He's coming!' the boy screamed. 'He's going to eat me all up!'

Dave ran to the cage. 'It's okay! I'm going to help you! I've come to rescue you and take you back to your mummy!'

He stood in front of the barred enclosure and looked at the shuddering child. 'It's alright,' he said softly. 'I won't hurt you.'

The boy looked up. Frightened blue eyes regarded him from underneath a shock of yellow hair. '*The Big Giant!*' he said. 'He'll come back. He said he'll come back and eat me. He'll eat you first if he sees you, then he'll eat me.' The boy's eyes filled with tears.

'We'll get away!' Dave promised, praying that there was no Big Giant. 'I'm going to rescue you.'

Tommy Cousins wiped his face with the back of his hand and sniffed. 'Jackie got away and the Big Giant caught her and ate her. I heard it,' he said in a tremulous voice. 'Where's my mummy? I want my mummy.'

'I'm going to take you to your mummy,' Dave said.

'I heard her,' Tommy said hopefully. 'She said she was coming to save me.'

'Yes, I expect she is,' Dave replied, looking at the huge lock on the cage and wondering how he was going to get it undone.

There was no chance of bending the bars – they were much too thick.

'We'll just get you out of here first,' he said.

'Jimmy got away, too. He slipped through the bars of his cage. I didn't hear him get ate so I think he's gone to get help. He said he would. He was going to the railway station to get a policeman.'

We'll need more than a policeman to get us out of this lot, Dave thought, taking his rucksack from his back and looking inside. Nothing in there took his fancy, though. It *felt* as if it would be about right to pick the lock with his army knife, so he got it from his pocket and opened the big blade, wishing Roddy was here. He'd know how to pick a lock.

'What are you doing?' Tommy asked, coming to the door side of his cage.

'Picking the lock. Stand back – something weird might happen in a moment.'

He waited until Tommy had gone to the back of the cage, told him to close his eyes and think of Kansas, then inserted the knife blade. He could feel the tumblers inside, but they were big and stiff and the blade would probably break before it flipped them.

'Know any magic words, Tommy?' he asked as the knife blade clicked off the metal tumblers for the fifth time.

'Izzy wizzy let's get busy,' Tommy replied.

'Sooty,' Dave said. 'I used to watch that too when I was a kid. Know any better ones?'

'No.'

'Oh well, worth a try.'

The tip of the knife had caught under the mechanism and it had moved slightly. *Knife don't fail me now!* Dave thought, feeling sweat break out on his forehead. *I can do this, I really can. I know I can do this. It's easy!*

The knife blade flexed and Dave knew just how far he could push it, just how much the blade would take. A part of him seemed to have merged with the knife so that it became an extension of him and he could feel its movements and its point of contact with his own nerves.

The tumbler grated with protest but the knife was just a little stronger. Dave pushed gently and twisted. The tumbler clicked upwards with a loud *tick*!

He took the knife from the lock, shut the blade and pocketed it. 'You're out,' he said, pulling on the heavy door and congratulating himself. The magic *did* work if you believed in it. It was keeping the belief going that was the problem.

You just need more practice, Dave, that's all. You can do it alright, you're just not very consistent at the moment.

Tommy came out of the cage and clutched Dave's legs, sobbing quietly.

'It's okay,' Dave said, peeling the child away, then crouching and cuddling him. 'We're on our way.'

Suddenly the boy stiffened.

'What?' Dave said, his senses straining to hear what the boy had heard.

'It's coming back,' Tommy said. 'It'll get us.'

'Where does it come in?'

Tommy pointed to the wall.

'Through there?'

'It opens up. You have to knock three times and a big doorway comes.'

'Hide in the corner by the pool on the door side,' Dave told him. 'I'll stay here and get him when he comes in. If he gets me, you run. Don't try and help me, just run. Okay?'

Tommy nodded and said nothing. He didn't have to; his expression told Dave everything he wanted to know about what chance he had.

Dave got the Swiss Army knife out again and crouched by where he hoped the edge of the door would be when it opened. There were no seams around the wall, so he wasn't sure if he was in the right place or not. It didn't matter; wherever the door was, he would have the advantage of surprise. When the thing came through it he would leap forward and stab it.

He wasn't really expecting a giant. He suspected that you saw the most frightening thing your mind could imagine and that Tommy had seen a giant because that was his pet fear. What was

468

going to come through that door was going to be worse than a legion of giants. The Claw was coming in.

You've fought it before, you can fight it again, he told himself, remembering slashing at it in his bathroom and banishing it from the mermaid pool by yelling at it. *And maybe this time you can kill it.*

The familiar rumbling noise began and Dave tensed as the wall began to slide. The position he'd taken had been the right one – he was to one side of the door and would be shielded from view by the wall.

Not a giant! he thought as the human-sized shape came through the doorway. The shape was backlit by a strong light and looked slender and black. Something at its neck flashed emerald green in the darkness.

I was right, it's The Claw!

He leapt forward at the dark shape, his Swiss Army knife thrust ahead of him. 'YOU BASTARD!' he screamed, and slashed the knife from right to left at its midriff.

The Claw was faster. It caught his wrist in its left hand and stopped it dead. Dave punched with his free hand, and the blow was intercepted before it had travelled six inches.

'NO!' Tommy yelled. 'STOP!'

But Dave and The Claw were rolling on the floor now, each of them struggling for possession of the knife.

'Dave, stop it! DAVE!'

The voice! Sally's voice! It was using Sally's voice to try and trick him. He snatched the knife back and pressed the tip against The Claw's throat. Except it didn't look like The Claw at all now, it looked just like Sally. Sally had hold of his wrist with both hands and was supporting all his weight as he pressed the knife towards her neck.

'YOU CHEATING BASTARD!' he screamed and pushed down, tensing his whole body for leverage. The Claw's skinny Sally arms began to buckle.

Then the world exploded.

*　　*　　*

'S'okay, you're alright,' Sally's voice was saying in his ears. 'Please Dave, please wake up, you're alright really.'

Dave's head hurt. It felt as though his skull had been split, but he had to know, in spite of the pain, he had to look. He opened his eyes and looked up into Sally's face. His vision was misty and for a moment he wasn't sure if it was Sally or The Claw and he started to struggle.

'It's me, it's really me!' Sally said, pressing him back to the ground.

'Oh Sal, sorry,' he groaned. 'I thought . . .'

'I was The Claw, right?' she said.

'Yeah,' he said. 'Did I hurt you?'

She shook her head. 'Not as much as Tommy hurt you. I can see why they call him Tiger.'

'What happened?' Dave asked.

'He saw you attacking me and hit you with one of those big bones over there,' she said. 'I think they're human,' she added quietly.

'Thanks, Tiger,' Dave said, lifting his head and looking at the boy who was trying to hide behind Sally. 'It's okay, really.'

Tommy looked sheepish. 'She killed the Big Giant,' he said, nodding at Sally.

'Then I came down here to get Tommy. I could hear him calling.'

'There was a giant?'

Sally nodded.

'Christ, Sal, where are we?'

'I think we're on the Border. Between Limbo and the Bad Place. This is one of the entrances.'

Dave nodded. 'I've been over there. Kott's over there. He's dead.'

'What happened to him?' she asked.

Dave shook his head. It felt as if his brain had come loose in there and was thudding from side to side. Tommy Cousins was a demon with a thigh bone, in spite of his size. 'I dunno,' he said. 'He went missing on the Ghost Train like Phil and Judy did. He was with Roddy's sister when he vanished. I suppose

470

The Claw got him. There was a bridge over there, made of ice. He was guarding it like a troll. Weird as it sounds, I set him on fire with a toy soldier.'

'You don't have to tell me about weird,' Sally said smiling grimly, 'I've just fought a giant.'

'What happened?'

She shrugged. 'It's dead. I'll tell you about it later. What about Judy and Phil, were they there?'

'No sign of anything. What are we going to do, Sal?'

'Get out of here before anything else happens. Take Tiger out, then . . .'

'Then what?'

'Then we wait.'

'What for?' Dave said drawing himself up to a sitting position.

'Because something will happen. You know.' She shrugged.

'I don't know,' Dave said. 'That's just it. I haven't a clue about what's going on.'

'Well, we'll find out. Soon. Can you get up?'

'I think so,' Dave said, wincing as he moved his head.

She leaned over, took his head in her hands and kissed him on the lips. 'I love you,' she said.

'I love you too, Sal, but you're hurting my head,' he said grimacing as he returned her kisses. In spite of the pain he was relieved to see Sally awake and in one piece and it felt incredibly good to have her warmth and softness near him.

She let go of his tender head and smiled. 'I tried to heal you. It doesn't work in here. I think I can do it when we're back in the Limbo Basingstoke.'

'Please,' Dave said. 'Which way is out?'

'Follow me.'

Dave got to his feet and wearily put his rucksack back on. Tommy was holding the Swiss Army knife in his cupped hands as if it were a holy relic. He held it out for Dave to take. 'Thanks, Tommy,' Dave said, folding the big blade back and putting it in his pocket.

'It *glowed*,' Tommy said. 'When you were fighting her, it *glowed*.'

Dave nodded. 'It's got a life of its own. I'm thinking of taking it back to the shop and demanding a refund,' he said.

'Come on, dickhead,' Sally said, walking through the doorway into the next room. 'Let's get out of here.'

'I know what it is,' Dave said as they picked their way through the treasure trove of junk that filled the huge hall. It was stacked to bursting with items which were piled against the walls in small mountains. The floor was covered in ballpoint pens of every hue, cheap jewellery (and some not so cheap), knives, forks, pincushions, watches, ashtrays, toys, staplers and scissors. Here was a pair of spectacles with the arms half chewed away and one lens missing; there a pink orthodontic brace, perished brown elastic bands dangling from its metal levers. Dave wondered whose mouth impression was forever indented into its translucent plastic. The only thing all these things had in common was their size. They were all small enough to mislay or lose. There was a worn leather wallet, poking out of the top of an old dog-chewed slipper. Dave bent and picked it up. Inside, there were three five pound notes, a driving licence in the name of Simon Charlesworth, a Barclaycard in the same name and a photo of a pretty woman and two equally pretty children. Between Dave and Sally Tommy was pulling a battered Action Man from under a tangled heap of necklaces.

'Okay, clever clogs, what *is* it?' Sally called back.

'It's where the things you lose come to,' he replied. He held the wallet up for her to see. 'Somewhere there's a guy called Simon Charlesworth who lost his wallet and never found it again. Haven't you ever wondered what happened to all the ballpoints you've ever lost? All the things you used to have that got mislaid? All the things that vanished from the face of the Earth? They all turn up here. Christ, Sal, they make millions of ballpoint pens every year. The world should be snowed under with them by now, but it isn't. It's because they escape. They come over here.'

Sally kicked a heap of red pens. Several glass dolly's eyes rolled across the floor as the biros scattered. 'But this isn't all the pens that have ever got lost, it can't be!' she said.

'We're attached to Basingstoke somehow. The Limbo Basingstoke is outside, isn't it? These are all pens that have vanished in Basingstoke. And all this other stuff, that's local, too. It must be. Look, the guy who lost this wallet comes from Popley.'

Sally frowned. 'But surely this can't be *all* the stuff that got lost?'

'I dunno Sal, perhaps it only lasts for a certain amount of time and then it goes somewhere else. Or maybe the giant stockpiled this and got rid of the rest – all this junk looks fairly new. Maybe it goes over the Bad Side when he's done with it. I found my toy soldier over there and I lost that more than twelve years ago.'

'Does every town have a depository of this stuff underneath it then?' Sally said.

Dave shrugged. 'If that place out there – Limbo the old guy said it was called – is a replica of the real Basingstoke, *our* Basingstoke, then it probably doesn't stop in town. There's probably a whole Limbo world out there, each town with its own store of Limbo items.'

'What old guy?' Sally asked.

'The guy with the pipe and the dog called Lucky. The one that helped us fish Phil out of the river that time. He appeared inside the Ghost Train and gave me a lecture.'

'He woke me up in the hospital,' Sally said. 'I didn't see him, but I could smell his pipe when I came round.'

Dave nodded. 'That's it then. He wouldn't tell me what had happened to you, but he said he'd interfered three times and that was the limit. He helped me in the Ghost Train and he helped us get Phil out of the river, so the third time must have been when he woke you up. Or rather, when he got us our crosses back. It was probably the cross that woke you; the old man just brought it to you.'

'But who is he?'

Dave shook his head. 'I dunno. He was on our side though, Sal. It doesn't matter who he was because he won't be coming to rescue us this time. We're on our own now.'

'Except for Tommy.'

'Oh yeah, and Roddy Johnson. I came over with him,' Dave said apologetically.

'Roddy?' Sally was amazed. 'You came with Roddy?'

'Yeah, he's looking for Kott and his sister. I dunno where he is now. He said he was going home for a sleep. I haven't seen him since. I'll explain all about it later.'

'How does it get here?' Tommy's small quavering voice asked.

Dave glanced at him. 'What?' he said.

'These toys and things. How did they come?'

'I dunno, Tiger. I s'pose this world occupies the same space as ours and there are holes in both of them. Maybe the holes are tiny and little things can slip through.'

'What's the Bad Side?' the child asked. His eyes were saucer wide, his face pale. 'Is that where the devil lives?'

'Don't worry about it, Tiger,' Sally called. 'Let's just get out of here!'

'We won't slip through, will we?' Tommy asked anxiously.

'To where?' Dave said, dropping the wallet and moving over to him.

'To the Bad Side. I'm a little thing, my mum said so. I might slip through the holes.'

'We won't let you, Tiger!' Sally said. 'Now come *on!*'

Tommy was apparently satisfied with this reply. Some of the fear left his face and he said, 'Can I bring my Action Man?'

'No, Tiger, it might be dangerous,' Dave said, realising how easy it was to win a kid's confidence and trust. No wonder they were so easy to kidnap. 'We don't know how things work over here. It would be best if you left it where it is.'

Tommy dropped the Action Man, trotted forward and took Sally's hand.

Ten minutes later the three emerged from the stairway and stepped out into the pedestrian precinct.

'Shit!' Dave said looking out over the carnage which used to be three shops and a large portion of the car park, 'What happened?'

474

'It fell down when the giant came after me. He tunnelled underneath it and it fell on him,' Sally said matter-of-factly.

'He was *big*,' Tommy said nodding gravely.

Dave nodded. 'And you killed it?' he said to Sally, thinking, *this is the girl who hid behind you three weeks ago when you were watching the original version of* Dracula *because she was too scared to look.*

'I helped,' she said.

'Good girl,' he said, loving her for her courage and remembering the wild look that came into her eyes when the cross zapped her. *Yes*, he thought, *you could do that, Sal, you could fight a giant.*

'Do you think the real car park fell down, too? The one in our world, I mean,' she asked worriedly. 'I think it probably did. If they're connected like I think they are, then it did.'

'Not your fault, Sal,' he said.

'Someone might have been killed. It was my fault that the window blew out of the old Wimpy too. What if it happened in the real world and people were outside?'

'Things collapse every day, Sal. You couldn't help it. Forget it.'

She shook her head and chewed her thumbnail as she looked out over the smashed concrete and heaps of grey dust.

'Where to?' she asked finally.

'I don't know,' Dave said, 'but I can find out.' The backpack was already off and open. He took the compass out and unclipped the lid. 'I have a magic tool,' he explained.

Sally grinned, the consequences of her fight with the giant temporarily forgotten. 'You don't have to tell me that,' she said lightly.

'There are children present, Sal,' he said. 'I mean that my old compass does odd things over here. I've already blown a wall down with it. It'll point where we have to go.'

Sally and Tommy came over and peered at the compass. The rusted blue needle spun and settled pointing south.

'We go where it points,' Dave said. 'Trust it.'

'I do,' Sally said. Her hand stole round his waist, then

dropped and goosed him. 'And I trust you,' she added, looking at the needle which remained steady when Dave jumped. 'It's back to the jolly old park then, judging by the way it's pointing,' she said, nodding. 'That's where I would have gone, too.'

'What we need is an oracle,' Dave said, waking up suddenly. He glanced around him and was surprised to find himself sitting on the grassy bank by the crumbling summerhouse in the Memorial Park.

The green and white painted pagoda-style bandstand stood a hundred yards in front of him, and beyond that lay the path to the kiosk gate. He couldn't see the gate because the way was shielded by rows of yellowish bushes which lined the path right up to where it circled the bandstand. This was where he'd crept into the trees on his first night-time visit to AdventureLand. They had chosen this spot because from here they could see the whole grass area of the park – and because the compass had indicated that this was the place to stop simply by starting to spin gently as soon as they stood on the bank.

Since there were trees behind them they were open to attack at their rear. Tommy had pointed out this hole in their defences and had been uncomfortable until Sally assured him that the compass would not let them down. That placated him. If the Giant Killer said it was alright, then that was good enough for Tommy Cousins. He'd settled straight down and fallen asleep.

After they'd swapped notes about their experiences Sally had fallen asleep, too, with the little boy cradled in her arms. Dave didn't know how long they'd lain like that, because his watch still said five fifteen. The clock on the bandstand roof had also stopped at five fifteen but that could have been coincidence – he'd never known a time when the clock had worked properly.

Dave was convinced that the end was getting near. Returning here they had left footprints in the concrete of the precinct and the tarmac of the roads. Brick dust had fallen from creaking buildings as they had passed and when they got to the Kiosk outside the park Sally had made them pause because the vibration of their feet had been making the building tremble alarmingly. The park was as deserted and sick looking as it had been when they arrived, but something else had changed now. The situation had worsened.

'Sal,' he said, prodding her gently. 'Wake up.'

Sally moaned and moved away from him.

It's colder, that's what it is. The temperature has dropped, Dave thought, looking at the privet hedge that surrounded the band-stand. The normally precision-clipped green hedge was now yellow and looked as if it had been fashioned out of coloured paper by a child of five. The large expanse of grass in the centre of the park looked terrible, too. It still had its pale Limbo Side colour, but now each brittle blade looked blackened around the edges.

Dave prodded Sally again, realising how refreshed he felt. Sally had laid her hands on his head when they settled down here and, although her green cross had shone, nothing had happened. Or at least they *thought* nothing had happened; now it was evident that something *had* happened because all his pains were gone.

He examined his arm where the huge moth had bitten it. The scars were still there, but there was no stiffness any more. He shivered and rubbed his hands together. The air was cooler and smelled as if rain might be on the way.

It's coming, Dave, he told himself and refused to think of what that might mean.

'What is it?' Sally said, looking at him blearily. Tommy Cousins was still asleep in her lap.

'It's falling apart,' Dave said. 'This place is starting to crack. We need an oracle, and we need it very soon. Something terrible is happening.'

Sally shook her head. 'What's happening? Oh God, look at the sky!'

The featureless grey sky had darkened slightly. There were tendrils of black, marbling the cloud cover like mould growth on an old slice of bread.

'Shit,' she said, staring up. 'What are we going to do?'

477

'Get advice. That's what we need an oracle for,' Dave said. 'We need something to tell us what to do.'

'That's the trouble with oracles, there's never one around when you need one,' Sally said, picking up her cross and looking into its deep green eye. 'It's gone off,' she said, surprised. 'It was flashing in time with my heartbeat, but it's stopped. It's resting I suppose.'

'So's mine,' Dave said. 'Mine packed up before you came into the giant's store room and it hasn't worked since. I've had a lot of trouble with that damn cross, I think it's faulty or something. It never seems to light up when you want it.'

Sally looked at him and smiled. 'It's you, you dummy. You just don't know how to work it properly. You have to believe.'

'I do believe, Sal,' Dave whined.

'Yeah, but not properly. You're always looking for a logical reason for things to happen. Remember when I gave it to you how you couldn't understand why you couldn't get them to separate unless you tapped them three times?'

'What's that got to do with anything?' he said, looking hurt.

'That's got everything to do with it. You can't believe that some things just happen. There's always got to be a reason, it's always got to be explainable. That's the trouble with you Joe 90 computer types, you can't accept that illogical things sometimes work. What you have to do is trust your intuition and forget logic. Trust yourself. If you can do that, the magic works.'

Dave shrugged. 'I'm trying,' he said, 'but I like to know how I stand. I like to know what things mean.'

Sally took his arm and squeezed it. 'I still love you,' she said, 'even if you are a dimwit.'

'What's happening though, Sal? What's it all about?' he said. 'I can't get a grip on it at all. What are we supposed to be doing?'

She shook her head, her smile suddenly gone. 'Don't ask me, pal, I know as much as you do. Less possibly. I've just been following my nose like you have. I don't know what it's all about either. Not really. I don't know what this place is except that it sure ain't the real world. I don't know where the giant came from or what that place under the ground was or what we're supposed

478

to do now. I know we came looking for Judy and Phil, but it's bigger than that, isn't it? Phil and Judy were only the bait that drew us in here, but there's more . . .'

'What d'you think it is then?' He thought he knew what she was going to say, but he was hoping he was wrong. Perhaps if Sally didn't say it, everything would be okay. Maybe it was just an extended nightmare or something.

Sally sighed. 'There's something wrong with this, place, Dave, and it's getting worse. It's to do with the Ghost Train and Fred Purdue and The Claw. I don't know exactly where we are or what is happening, but I think we've been sorted out to come over here and fix it. Maybe we should have gone the other way out of the giant's room. I've been worrying about that ever since you told me about the other passage where The Claw came from. Perhaps we were supposed to go down it.'

Dave shook his head. 'The compass said no, Sal. It hasn't let us down yet. We couldn't go back down there because it wasn't the right thing to do.'

'If that's it . . . If we've been put here to beat The Claw, then we're in trouble.'

'What do you mean?' Dave said, his heart sinking.

'There's something I didn't tell you. Something Fred Purdue said when I went into his caravan to get my cross back.'

'Oh God, what did he say?' Dave said heavily. Wasn't there any good news to come? It didn't look like it.

'He said we can't kill The Claw unless we have all three of the eye stones. I could have got the third one, Dave, I had a chance to cut off his finger and take his ring when he was stunned. I wanted to but I couldn't make myself do it. I'm sorry.'

'He was lying,' Dave said, watching tears well up in Sally's eyes and trying not to think of how everything always went in threes. 'He was trying to trick you.'

Sally shook her head and wiped her face with the back of her hand. 'I think he was telling the truth,' she said. 'I couldn't make myself do it. I couldn't cut it off!'

He took her hand and pulled her to him thinking, *it's because her cross went off. She's tired and she's frightened because the damn*

479

thing went out. That's all, so don't let her spook you. She's wrong about needing the other stone. She has to be!

He undid the top flap of the rucksack and pulled out the melted cannister of Wet Ones. He drew out a damp tissue and gently wiped Sally's grubby tear-stained face.

'Don't worry, Sal,' he said. 'It'll be alright, you'll see. We'll win through and forget what Purdue said, it doesn't matter.'

'Look!' Sally said, suddenly drawing away from him and pointing towards the park entrance. 'What on earth is that?'

A pair of trousers and an open overcoat appeared to be shambling across the grass towards them. A prostrate figure was somehow being towed along behind the clothes although they didn't seem to be connected. The grass was turning to dust as the fallen body ploughed through it and thick clouds filled the air like grey smoke.

'What *is* it?' Sally said. She sounded frightened.

'There's someone in those clothes,' Dave said, getting to his feet. 'There's someone in there Sal, and he's *transparent*! Look! You can see his head when it moves.'

'What's it dragging behind it? It looks like another man. A dead one. What are we going to do?'

'Dunno, Sal, you tell me,' Dave said taking the Swiss Army knife from his pocket and opening the Claw-slashing blade. He felt calm and knew he could deal with whatever it was.

'It's coming this way,' Sally said. 'Ouch! My cross just came back on.'

Where else would something like that be going? Dave asked himself. *To the funfair to play on the empty rides?* He winced as his cross's eye lit up too and the familiar electric tingle ran down his chest.

Tommy woke up. 'Mummy,' he said in a terrified voice. 'I can hear my mummy.'

'It's okay, Tiger, don't worry,' Sally told him, her eyes never leaving the approaching thing.

Tommy started to cry.

Behind the transparent man, the other figure rolled over and fought to get to its feet.

'It's a woman!' Sally cried as Anne Cousins lost her footing and collapsed onto her back.

'Mummy!' Tommy wailed, pawing at Sally's leg. Sally scooped him up in her arms. 'Is that her?' she asked, pointing at the figure in the centre of the blooming plumes of dust.

She's dragging a plastic bag along with her, Sally thought. *I don't believe this*!

'He's got my mummy!' Tommy shouted burying his head in Sally's chest. 'He's killed h-her!'

'She's going to be okay, Tiger,' Dave said. 'I'll make sure of that. STOP!' he shouted.

The man kept coming. Now he was closer Dave could see his thin transparent body and the pink dolly clutched to his chest with see-through hands.

'What do you want?' Dave called to him. *I can see his innards and all his muscles working*, he thought. *He should be dead, surely*. Or perhaps he *was* dead. Perhaps he was something that had followed Dave over the ice bridge or crawled out of the chasm when Kott fell in. Perhaps it was The Claw dressed up in see-through skin.

'I can smell him,' Sally said. 'It's disgusting. He smells like a rubbish heap on a hot day.'

The transparent man stopped. Tommy's mother ceased moving. 'Symbols!' the man said.

'He's come to hear a brass band, apparently,' Dave muttered murderously.

Sally shook her head. 'No. He's come for the crosses. I can tell.'

'He'll have to fight us for them,' Dave said, and knew instantly that the see-through man would be willing to fight to the death for them. He could feel the *need* for the crosses coming off the man. 'He can't win . . . can he?' he said uncertainly.

Sally shrugged. 'I think I know who it is,' she said.

'Who?'

'Shit! It's gone. It was on the tip of my tongue and it vanished. It was important. We need to know. He knew, Dave. He *knew* what I was thinking and he made it go.'

'He's a b-bad m-man,' Tommy moaned. 'He's got my m-mummy.'

The man's name almost came back to Sally then. And was whisked away again.

The transparent man started towards them.

'What're we gonna do?' Sally said.

Dave felt good about the horrendous man now. An idea was forming in his mind. It was crazy but it felt *right*. 'We can't stop him coming, Sal. And I don't think we should. I think we've got our oracle. Wait and see what happens.'

The man approached the bank and came up, moving effortlessly. The weight of the woman he was dragging along seemed to cause him no difficulty at all. He stopped a pace in front of Dave and regarded him with flat, empty eyes.

Dave could see thin translucent blood pouring through transparent veins deep inside the man's chest. He could see the large heart pumping and the involuntary twitching of the slender muscle under the man's left eye.

He wants them badly, Dave thought. *He wants the crosses.*

'You can't hurt me,' he told the man confidently.

The man grimaced with his see-through lips. Dave watched the different sets of muscles straining against one another in his face. His glass teeth were clenched tightly shut and his tongue worked against the roof of his mouth. Inside his head his brain pulsed.

Strip off your skin, the man said inside Dave's head. *Flay you alive.*

For a second Dave knew exactly how it would feel to have his skin torn from his body. Like being stung by a million bees. Like being immersed in boiling fat. He saw the skin of his arms melting and peeling away in strips, leaving raw red flesh exposed to the air.

'NO!' he shouted and the vision broke.

Symbol, the man thought to him. An empty hand was placed in front of him, palm up. Dave could see the blighted grass through it.

No one said it was going to be easy, Davey boy, he told himself. *No such thing as a free lunch.*

There was a buzzing in his ears that sounded like a voice coming through a corrupted telephone line – all white noise and no substance.

'You can't have it!' he said keeping his voice level and reasonable.

Tommy's mother. I can kill her now. Give me the symbol.

Dave glanced down at the unconscious woman. Her face was dirty and scratched where it had been dragged along the ground and her clothes were tattered. Both her knees had black scabs and one of them was weeping blood. Her face was pale and empty and Dave wasn't sure she wasn't dead already.

'What do you want the cross for?' he asked.

The urgent hissing voice filled his ears again.

What did you say? he thought back mentally.

Kill the woman, kill her dead! the man warned. His eyebrows knitted and his eyelids slid down over his eyes in concentration. Dave could still see his eyes, but they weren't looking at him any more.

Down on the ground, Tommy's mother's body bucked as if she'd been kicked in the stomach. The see-through man grinned and Dave felt the ground vanish from under his feet. Suddenly he was suspended in blank empty space that went on forever in each direction. His mind started to reel. *Lost*, he thought dimly.

'Dave!' Sally shouted. 'Don't look in his eyes! Don't let him inside your head!'

Her voice rang inside his head and the world came back.

One, the man said. *Merge. Give me the symbols. I will be One.*

'Sorry,' Dave said and struck out with his right fist.

The man ducked under the blow easily and blocked as Dave threw his left.

'He can read your mind!' Sally yelled.

Dave dodged back as the transparent man's hand snatched at his cross and kicked at his skinny leg. This, too, was withdrawn long before the blow could land.

Empty it, Davey. Clean out your brain! he told himself, letting his hands fly whichever way they fancied.

483

The man danced and dodged as Dave threw punches at him and with each blow Dave flung, Anne Cousins' body jumped as if he was hitting her.

Trust yourself, Davey. Just empty your mind and let it happen.

'Okay, you win,' Dave said, as he stopped trying to hit the man. 'Take the fucking thing!' He grabbed the leather thong, took the cross from around his neck and held it out for the man.

Merge! the transparent man thought, and took the cross.

Dave's right hand flew up, surprising both him and the see-through man. The punch was quick and sharp and jabbed the man on the point of his chin.

His head snapped back, then came up again and Dave saw shock register in his pale eyes. Then the transparent lids snapped down like roller blinds and the man collapsed.

He's got a glass jaw, Dave told himself and smiled at the pun.

'I thought that was it, then,' Sally said, breathing a sigh of relief and stroking Tommy's hair. 'I thought you were a goner.'

'I did it, Sal. I believed and I let my subconscious do the talking. I *can* do it.'

She nodded. 'Something happened just now. I could hear his thoughts, and I could hear yours, too. I was trying to talk to you mentally, but I couldn't get through to you. I think he was cutting me off.'

'I heard you, but it was all blurred,' Dave said. 'He made the world disappear and I thought that was it. When I heard you shout, it all came back.'

'I know who it is,' she said. 'I thought I knew earlier, but his name went out of my mind. It was like he knew what I was thinking and took the thought away so I couldn't see it. I think we could have stopped him if we'd said his name. He *knew* that Dave and he took it away.'

'Who is it then?'

'It's Bad Eddie. Remember that night your mum was talking in her sleep and she said Bad Eddie had got The Knowledge? It's him, Dave. This is Bad Eddie. He's over here. Oh God, he's disgusting.'

Dave nodded. 'I can see why they call him Bad Eddie,' he

said, looking down at the transparent man. 'What d'you think happened to him?'

'I don't know, Dave, but I don't think you should touch him. He's dangerous. Not just because of his physical condition, but because he's . . .

'Got The Knowledge,' Dave finished for her, nodding.

'What are you going to do?' Sally asked worriedly as Dave knelt down beside the man. Dave was scaring her. He'd got a glowing – almost rapturous – expression on his face and his eyes shone.

'He's got The Knowledge, and I'm going to get it out of him,' Dave replied, smiling. 'I can do it, Sal, I know I can. I can feel the power brewing inside me. I feel good. It's *right* to do it, Sal. Listen.'

He took the compass from his pocket. Inside the dull brass case, the needle was spinning. The sound reminded Sally of the noise her bike spokes had made when, as a kid, she'd attached playing cards to the forks. Dave opened the compass lid and showed her the grimy face. The needle was revolving quickly inside and hammering on the glass as it fluttered up and down.

'It's *right*!' Dave said, putting the compass on the ground beside Bad Eddie's knee.

'What about my mummy?' Tommy wailed, looking up for the first time. He glanced at his mother and looked away quickly. 'She's d-dead,' he moaned.

'No, Tiger, she's just asleep. We'll help her,' Sally said. 'We'll make sure she's alright.' She looked at Dave who was retrieving his cross. The thin red beam was now glowing.

'What about Tommy's mum?' she asked. 'She's bonded to him somehow. I think there's some kind of mental link between them. It'll have to be severed.'

'He'll die if we do that first. I know he will. I'll find some things out before we set her free. I'm going to hook myself up to Bad Eddie.' He pulled the unconscious man up into a slumped sitting position, folding his legs in front of him to keep him upright and placing the limp, see-through hands in his lap. He sat down in front of Bad Eddie and folded his own legs.

485

Sally frowned. 'Dave wait, it might be . . .'

But it was too late. Sally watched as Dave opened his mouth and popped the flaring cross in.

Oh no, it'll burn him, it'll scorch his mouth! she thought, remembering how the beam from Fred Purdue's ring had burned into her flesh. *It gets too hot to do that with!*

Tommy whined in terror and grabbed Sally's hand as Dave closed his mouth on the red beam. For a moment Sally could see the outline of Dave's jawbone and teeth shining through the blood red of his cheeks like an instant x-ray. *Please don't let it hurt him!* she thought helplessly.

Dave reached out like a blind man, his trembling hands searching for the face of the transparent man who sat before him. On the ground beside him, his toy compass began to wail.

He's blind, he's gone blind! Sally thought looking at Dave's eyes. A glossy white film had covered both his irises and Dave's eyes seemed to be boiling and changing. Particles swarmed as cells divided, broke again then re-formed, pairing up in a different order and the colour of Dave's eyes lightened until they were almost as transparent as the man who sat before him.

The compass roared, its siren-like sound splitting the still air and drilling into Sally's eardrums.

Please let him be alright, please! she thought.

Then the movement beneath the white film slowed down. The colour in Dave's eyes deepened and the cataracts began to dissolve. He closed his eyes and gasped and a stray red beam shot out like a laser from between the lids.

'Oh God,' Sally said, as Dave's flailing hands finally clapped home on the transparent man's face and his eyes opened. They were as red as the eye on the cross.

'Tell,' Dave said in a voice loud enough to temporarily drown the scream of the compass. It didn't sound at all like Dave's voice, and Sally knew she was picking up his thoughts telepathically because he hadn't moved his lips.

'Mummy!' Tommy screamed and Sally looked down at the woman's unconscious body which lay to the left of the transparent man. The woman hadn't woken, but her eyes had opened

486

and she was jolting back and forth across the grass as though she was being electrocuted.

'Help her! Mummeee!' Tommy screamed. He started towards her, but Sally grabbed him, yanked him back and held him tightly.

'Don't touch her, Tiger, she'll be alright!' she yelled. 'I promise!'

She wasn't sure whether the woman would be alright or not, but there was nothing she could do now. Dave had thought he'd known what was the right thing to do and he'd done it. She didn't know what was happening, but her instincts told her that to interfere now might well ruin everything – if there was any physical contact all three of them might die. She *knew* that.

Have faith, she told herself. *Just have faith*!

Dave blinked and suddenly two piercing red rays were flowing steadily from his eyes and boring into the empty ones of the transparent man.

'You want to know about faith? I'll tell you about faith!' It was the transparent man speaking, but his voice was coming from the lips of Tommy's mother. Her heels banged the ground in a crazy tap dance as she spoke in the man's toneless voice and her hands flapped like fish on a river bank.

'Faith is a system of belief used by fatalists and the unimaginative to explain the inexplicable and bolster up their flimsy reality,' Tommy's mother said as she writhed on the ground.

'Mummy!' Tommy wailed.

'An act of God, you'll say,' she continued. 'God moves in mysterious ways, his wonders to perform, you'll say. Taken by God to sit at his right hand, you'll say when people die. When you can't assimilate something, when something unimaginable happens what do you do if you have faith? You put your head back in the sand and say it's God moving mysteriously. Faith is what you get when you're stupid enough to believe that there is a God and he's running things. Faith is you saying it'll be alright in the end. There is no God here. Faith is a lie.'

The words stopped coming and Tommy's mother's mouth snapped shut.

Christ, Sally thought, looking from the writhing woman to where Dave sat like a statue, the red beams flowing from his eyes.

'There is no Christ. There never was a Christ,' Anne Cousins spat.

'I've got it,' she whispered. 'I've got the oracle. I can ask the questions. Dave's just making it happen!'

'Two plus two,' Sally said, just to be sure.

Anne Cousins writhed across the grass leaving a patch of flat brown earth behind her. Her mouth worked but only a choking sound came out.

'Come on, what's two plus two?' Sally said, hoping she wasn't killing Tommy's mother.

'Four!' she gasped. Her eyelids fluttered and her jaw snapped shut.

'That's not my mummy talking,' Tommy sobbed. 'What's happened to my mummy?'

'She's okay, Tiger, she's in there somewhere. We'll get her back for you soon,' she promised, pulling Tommy close to her. He buried his hot face in her thighs and clung to her legs.

Right, Sal, now down to the nitty gritty, she thought. 'Where are we?'

Anne's body bucked. 'Shan't say!' she hissed.

'You have to, Eddie, Dave's controlling you and he'll hurt you if you won't play fair.'

'Not Eddie!'

'Okay, Anne then, if you prefer,' Sally said, wondering if Anne was conscious inside her possessed body. What did it feel like, trapped in there with that awful thing and unable to do anything about it? She decided she would probably die if it happened to her.

'What is this place?' she asked.

'Limbo Side,' the strangled voice replied.

'Meaning what?'

'Limbo is the supposed abode of souls not admitted to heaven but not condemned to punishment,' Anne replied.

'I didn't want a dictionary definition. Tell me what Limbo *really* is!'

'The Limbo Side is a separate realm coexisting and underlying the Earth Side. It is an empty land whose sole purpose is to maintain balance.'

'Between what?' Sally said.

'The balance between the Three. Earth Side, the Good Side and the Bad Side.'

Sally shivered. She didn't really want to know this stuff, it was too scary. 'Where are the other two sides?' she asked, half hoping this information would be denied her.

'In and Out,' Anne's mouth said.

'In and Out? What d'you mean?'

'Gap in The Knowledge. Fill gap. Become *One*.'

'What's happening here? Why is the Limbo Side falling apart?' Sally asked.

'Bad Side close. Getting nearer. The balance destroyed. Limbo Side and Bad Side will merge. Become *One*. There can be only One.'

'Why?'

'The answer is unavailable.'

'Liar. It's The Claw, isn't it? The Claw is from the Bad Side and it wants to come through, doesn't it?' she demanded. 'It wants to take over or something. What's it doing?'

'Supreme being.'

'What are you talking about?'

'Take the symbols to the Supreme Being. I will become *One* with the Supreme Being. Symbols are keys.'

Sally bit her bottom lip, wondering how to phrase her questions to get the proper answers. 'Tell me what its plan is,' she said.

'The balance has been altered. Each plane is interconnected. The Three are mixed. The essence can move between the sides at will. There must be uniformity. The One and only The One must exist simultaneously in all sides.'

Well, Sal, that about sums it up. It's quite simple really. It doesn't make any sense at all, but it's quite simple.

'Damn you!' she spat. 'Tell me something I can understand!'

Anne Cousins simply belched, long and hard.

'What should we do?' Sally asked, giving it one last try. She didn't want to have to go in there, too, but she was getting nowhere like this.

'Die,' Anne Cousins said. 'Become *One*!'

'Anne,' Sally said. 'His name is Bad Eddie. Say it.'

'Buud Heggie,' Anne murmured. Her body began to buck and thrash madly.

'Sit down, Tiger,' Sally said, looking at Dave and Bad Eddie who sat facing one another like stone Buddhas. 'And shut your eyes and cover your ears. It might get nasty from now on.'

'What are you going to do?' Tommy said, sitting down. His eyes were closed already.

'I'm going to get inside Bad Eddie's mind. I can't get the information I need like this, so I'm going in to get it. I'll free your mum, too.'

'Heggieeeee!' Anne Cousins screamed as she rolled about on the grass.

Sally put her cross in her mouth like Dave had done and went over to where he and Bad Eddie were sitting, still locked together by the slender red beams from Dave's eyes. She took Dave shoulders and pulled him sideways. His body was rigid and very heavy. She tugged him across the grass until there was a space on the other side, then she went and sat in it, completing the triangle.

She felt her eyes begin to change as soon as she looked at Bad Eddie and she thought, *I hope I'm doing the right thing.*

Then the cross's raw power surged through her insides and she was plunged deep into The Knowledge.

Bad Eddie's personality was in there somewhere and so was Dave's, but The Knowledge was so dense and tightly packed, she couldn't see where.

The Knowledge filled her brain to bursting point and she found she knew how Einstein had arrived at his famous

490

conclusions. She knew his methodology, could follow the train of his thoughts while she watched cells divide and replace themselves while she experienced every play ever acted, every movie ever screened, every sound ever made. She could see the raw material of the universe and the things it *was*. She bathed in the heat from every fire that had ever been lit; was blasted by exploding suns. She experienced each single pain that every individual human being and animal and plant had ever been crushed by. She flowed in a tidal wave of joy. But she was surrounded, cocooned by the crushing thud of Bad Eddie's beating heart doll. And there was something else, too. Something worse. A terrible malignancy. Strands of it ran through The Knowledge, permeating it, and containing it, surrounding it like the hammering of Eddie's doll surrounded Sally. It was vast – far too huge to contemplate – and it was colder than absolute zero and darker than deep space. It was alive, but not in any sense of the word that Sally knew. It just *was*.

I don't think I can get out of here!

She heard Dave's voice through a mish-mash of soundwaves and an ever-deepening block of boiling knowledge. She *knew* now. She *knew*!

Sal! Help!

Races of people lived and died before her eyes. Waves roared. Tornadoes tore the trees from strange lands. She tried to think back to Dave, but there was no room inside her mind to formulate the thought.

Think Out! The words lit up before her, pushing aside seas of molten rock, carving their way through mountain ranges, dulling the brilliance of nuclear explosions and collapsing galaxies.

OUT! Dave replied.

Yes! Sally thought. *OUT!*

She was ripping backwards through millions of years, drawing herself in, solidifying.

There was a mind-shattering thump which seemed to knock her senses from her and she was back on the park grass sitting in a triangle with Dave and Bad Eddie. The beating heart doll lay beside her and, by Eddie's right knee, the compass was slowing down. Eddie's transparent eyelids were still closed and beneath them his eyes were looking up, the pupils pointing at the inside of his forehead. Dave was massaging his temples. His face was pale.

'Christ,' Sally said. Her head ached terribly and she thought she might soon throw up.

'You could say that,' Dave said dully. 'Where's Tiger?'

Tommy Cousins sat on the top of the bank, his eyes tightly closed and his hand pressed against his ears.

'Anne,' Sally said. 'Say Bad Eddie!'

'Heggie baaa,' Anne said. She woke up then, looking confused.

'Say it, quick!' Sally said. 'Say his name.'

Bad Eddie's eyes flicked open. 'NOOOO!' he screamed. 'YOU WON'T KILL ME!'

'I've forgotten it,' Anne said miserably.

'Bad Eddie,' Dave said. 'Say it and the bonds will break.'

'DON'T!' Eddie screamed.

'Bad Eddie,' Anne said, getting to her feet.

Bad Eddie exploded.

Moments before it happened Dave saw something that looked like a shockwave run up through Bad Eddie's internal organs. Then there was a blinding flash and he was blown off his feet. He felt soft pieces of Bad Eddie hit him as he flew through the air, but his eyes had closed and he had no desire to know exactly which parts they were.

When he opened his eyes again, he saw that he was lying close to Sally who was throwing up noisily. Anne Cousins was face down next to her son on the bank. Tiger still sat there, his eyes closed and his hands over his ears, and Dave was thankful for that. The odd thing was that there was a door standing in the position that Bad Eddie had previously occupied.

The door was wooden and was supported in a frame. It was painted white and looked just like any ordinary door. Its handle was made of aluminium and there was no lock.

Dave got up on his elbows, his head still throbbing with the residue of The Knowledge. 'It's okay, Tiger!' he called. 'You can look now!'

Chapter Seventeen
The Doorway

'I know,' Sally said as they walked back towards Anne and Tommy. 'It hurts my head, and it's fading fast, but I know what it all means.'

Anne was sitting up and crushing a tearful Tommy to her bosom by the time Dave and Sally sat down next to her. Her head was buried in Tommy's neck and she was weeping. Both of them were covered in spatters of a clear substance that looked like Clearasil gel. Apparently, that and the doorway was all that was left of Bad Eddie and his beating heart dolly.

Anne looked up when Sally touched her arm. Her face was puffy and red and she looked tired. 'Was it you?' she asked suspiciously.

Dave nodded. 'We got you away from Bad Eddie, if that's what you mean,' he said. 'And there's no need to worry, we're on your side,' he added.

'I'm Sally Harrison and this is Dave Carter,' said Sally. 'Your name is Anne Cousins. We know that.'

Anne didn't seem to be listening. 'He tricked me,' she said thickly. 'He made me promise to be his if he found Tommy and my husband.'

'We know,' Sally said. 'We just got inside his head and looked at The Knowledge. It's okay, you're alright now and so is Tommy.'

'Where are we?' Anne asked, sniffing. Her right hand nervously picked at Tommy's shock of blond hair. 'It's all different.'

Dave gave her one of the moist tissues from the plastic dispenser. 'The Limbo Side,' he said. 'There are no people here. Or at least, there are not meant to be.'

'I came through the Ghost Train. I was looking for Tommy and Derek. I thought I was in hell,' Anne said.

'Fairly close,' Sally said. 'But not quite.'

'Your husband is over here, too?' asked Dave, remembering their meeting with him in the park. Derek was astute; for all his jittery craziness, he'd known what was going on long before Dave and Sally had.

Sorry, Derek, things just didn't work out, Dave thought.

'He vanished,' Anne said, 'Just like Tommy did. He said he was going to look for him, so I suppose he's over here somewhere, unless . . .'

Sally shook her head. 'I knew about him, but it's gone now,' she said. 'It's all fading.'

'We haven't seen him,' Dave said. 'Not since we were on the other side.'

'He must be here somewhere,' Anne said. 'What are we going to do?'

'We'll find him,' Dave said, looking at Sally and then glancing at the darkening sky.

'I want my d-daddy,' Tommy sobbed without looking up. 'He *is* alive. He *is*!'

'Sure he is, Tiger,' Sally said, 'and we'll find him soon. But we're going to have to do something else first; time is running out.'

Anne frowned. 'What do you mean?' she asked, sniffing, then dabbing her nose with the tissue.

'We're in trouble, Anne, and we're going to have to do something soon or . . .'

'Or indeed,' Dave said nodding sombrely.

'Or what?' Anne said, looking from Dave to Sally and quickly back again. Dave noticed that she shared her jerky, nervous movements with her husband. He'd been like that when he'd approached them outside the funfair that day.

'Or the Ultimate negative force of the universe is going to

494

come crashing through from where it resides and change things forever,' Dave said. 'Or maybe a bit longer; the details are a little hazy.'

Anne shook her head, not understanding.

'Don't you know?' Sally asked her. 'Didn't you get The Knowledge?'

Anne sighed. 'I didn't get *anything*. Just pain and fear. I couldn't see inside his mind. He dragged me back and forth across the town. We only stopped once and I thought I was going to die of exhaustion.' She looked up at Dave, her eyes huge and brimming with tears.

Hold on to her or something, Sal, Dave thought. *Comfort her for God's sake. I can't do it.*

He didn't know if Sally had heard him or not, but she went over to Anne and Tommy and encircled them with her arms. 'S'okay,' she said. 'We'll be all right.'

Dave sat and looked up at the sky for what seemed like a long time.

Tommy had fallen asleep by the time Anne had calmed down and she rocked him gently back and forth in her arms. 'What's going to happen?' she asked. 'What's going on?'

Sally took her hand and squeezed it. 'I don't know if I can explain very well, but I'll do my best,' she said. 'I don't know about the rest of the universe, it's too confusing and it doesn't matter anyway, so I'll just tell you what I'm sure of. Okay?'

Anne nodded.

'Our world co-exists with two others, just like the Bible says. Only the rest of it isn't very biblical at all. This Limbo land – where we are now – doesn't figure in the Bible. As far as I can tell, Limbo is a feat of metaphysical engineering that holds the three together.

'There is supposed to be a balance between the three sides – Earth Side, the Good Side and the Bad Side but something has gone wrong. The balance has been lost and the Bad Side is coming out on top. There's something from there that desperately wants to get in here and make this place its own. It wants to do that because it can get to Earth Side – our world – from

495

here. There have always been gaps through which it can exert its influence on our world and it likes to do this. I don't know why. It's too big and too different for us to know why, but it does it and we can see the results.'

'And until now it could only do it in a small way,' Dave added. 'The bad things that happen are because of its weak influence. Tidal waves, hurricanes, people who go mad and run through towns blasting people with Kalashnikov rifles. All the big disasters are caused by the negative influence that filters through from the Bad Side.' He frowned. 'I don't think the little things are though. Are they, Sal?'

'It doesn't matter,' Sally replied. 'The point is this: Fred Purdue and his pals have opened up a passage between Limbo and our side, and the thing we're up against wants to get through in a big way. Fred has stirred it up. Against all the cosmic rules and forces that are there to prevent interference, Fred has opened the way. He's provided the bad thing with the negative energy it needs to get through.'

'But what does it want?' Anne said. 'Souls? Does it want human souls?'

Sally shook her head. 'I think it wants to own everything, it wants everything to be *it*. Bad Eddie said there are gaps in The Knowledge, and he was right, there *are* gaps. We've seen them. Maybe it wants human souls, maybe it just wants to fill those gaps. Whatever it wants, the results will be the same. No more us. No more birds singing in summer trees. No more anything except absolute cold and absolute darkness.'

'And it's going to achieve what it wants unless we stop it,' Dave said. 'There's this thing called The Claw. It's some kind of an incarnation of the negative force. It's the owner of the Bad Side. It's after us because it wants these crosses. It seems to need them to get it through to the real world. Sally and I were unlucky enough to buy them cheaply,' he added sardonically.

'But how can you stop it?' Anne said. 'If it's an embodiment of everything evil, how will you stop it?'

'There are gaps in The Knowledge, that's how,' Sally said. 'The Claw is not omniscient, much as it would like us to believe it is. It doesn't know everything. There are big confusing blanks in The Knowledge where we and the crosses are concerned. I think the crosses are from the Good Side. They are powerful and it wants them. Badly. Like Dave said, the crosses are the key to its escape. And we're going to take them to it and see what happens.'

'We're going through the door,' Dave said. 'The one that used to be Bad Eddie. That's what it's there for, to go through.'

'But why are you going to take the crosses to it?' Anne said.

Dave shrugged and gave her a wan smile. 'It just feels right.'

'Don't you *know* what you're doing?' Anne asked, horrified.

'Not until we do it,' Sally said. 'We don't exist in The Knowledge so we couldn't find out. We have to just follow our noses and hope. All we do know is that we have to go over to the Bad Side and try and stop it before it comes over here. If it breaks through to this side, we're sunk.'

Tommy woke up and looked blearily at his mother. 'Daddy's coming,' he said.

Dave looked out over the blighted grass towards AdventureLand. A tall, upright figure dressed in blue denim was striding purposefully towards them.

'Roddy,' Dave said. 'Here's Roddy.'

Roddy Johnson was carrying the body of a man across his shoulders, but he was moving easily as if the man weighed no more than a sailor's kit bag.

'Daddy!' Tommy cried excitedly, leaping from his mother's lap and running down the bank towards Roddy.

'Tiger, wait!' Anne shouted, but the boy didn't stop. 'What if he's dead?' she moaned piteously.

'He's alive,' Sally said.

'Oh shit!' Dave swore as Tommy Cousins skidded to a halt in front of Roddy. Even from this distance he saw the boy go rigid.

'Something's wrong with Derek!' Anne wailed, getting to her feet. 'I knew it. He's dead!' She swayed back and forth on the spot, her shoulders shuddering. The Marks & Spencer bag was once again clutched firmly in her right hand. Not for the first time, Dave wondered what was inside.

'No!' Tommy screamed, his cracked voice riding clearly through the still air. 'No no no no NOOOO!' He turned away from Roddy and pressed his hands over his ears. Dave guessed his eyes were clamped shut, too.

Roddy strode past Tommy, and Derek Cousins's limp arms and legs waggled at the child as Roddy swaggered by.

'Look at him. Look at him!' Anne screamed. 'He's transparent! It's happened to him too! Oh God, *please*!'

'He's alright,' Sally insisted. 'He'll be okay, Anne. Calm down!' She took the weeping woman in her arms once more while Dave caught Tommy and swept him from the ground. Tommy's face was flushed and tearstained. 'Okay Tiger,' he said, as Roddy drew close.

'Hiya, Foureyes,' Roddy said, striding up the bank. 'Long time no see.' He stopped in front of Dave and dumped Derek Cousins unceremoniously on the grass.

Dave had spotted the stain on the front of Roddy's clothes as he had approached, but he'd thought it was grease or dirt. The oval mark ran up from the tops of the legs of Roddy's jeans and stopped just below his ribs. It was thickest and darkest around the front of his trousers and it could have been any kind of liquid. But where it was crusted on his white tee shirt it was the dirty reddish-brown colour of dried blood.

'What happened?' Dave said.

Roddy cocked his head to one side and screwed his face up into a parody of concentration. 'When exactly?' he said.

Dave pointed to the stain. 'Looks like blood,' he said.

'Oh *that*,' Roddy said. 'Cut myself didn't I?' He pulled up his shirt and showed Dave a thin scabbed line just below his navel that had obviously been made with his flick-knife. He tapped his pocket and grinned. 'I was cleaning it and it went off,' he said.

There's no way it could have bled enough to make that huge mark, Dave thought. But he didn't question Roddy about it any further. Somehow, it didn't seem wise.

'I brought you a present,' Roddy said, digging Derek in the back with the toe of his boot. 'But I see you've got some

498

presents of your own. I thought you said your tart was in hospital,' he added suspiciously.

'She got better, Roddy,' Dave said, looking closely at Roddy's face. He was sweating, but there was something else different about him and Dave couldn't quite put his finger on what it was.

'Who's the other bit of clit?' Roddy asked. He sounded slightly out of breath. 'I could go for her but don't worry, Foureyes, I'd still rather fuck your Sally. Christ, she's got a body on her.'

Dave didn't take offence. Roddy's heart didn't seem to be in it. He sounded as if he was just going through the motions. There was none of his old leering threat present in his voice.

Sally took offence though; she glared at Roddy over Anne's shoulder but said nothing.

'Where did you get to?' Dave asked.

Roddy took off his jean jacket, folded it neatly and laid it on the ground beside Derek. 'Look after that for me, shithead,' he said. Then: 'I went walkabout, Foureyes. I wanted to see just what this place is you've got me into. I found the window man out by Black Dam roundabout. You can't go any further than that. The whole town is surrounded by a weird kind of sheet that you can't get through. You can see through it, but there's nothing out there to see. Just black empty ground. This guy had got caught up in it somehow. His legs were this side of it, but his head was out the other side. I huffed and puffed and pulled the fucker back again. He didn't like it much. He squealed like a stuck pig and then he blanked out. He ain't dead, Foureyes, you can see him breathing and if you open his shirt you can see his insides working. It's fucking horrible. I brought him back. I knew you was going to be here and I thought you might want to see him.'

'It's her husband; the boy's father,' Dave said, hefting Tommy up. He was getting very heavy all of a sudden. Roddy wasn't interested, he was gazing at the doorway.

'Where did that fucking thing come from?' he demanded.

'It just appeared,' Dave said, looking at Roddy's bulging biceps. One of them had a tiny patch of something that looked like mould growth on it.

It's a mole, that's all it is, Dave told himself. *You just didn't notice it before. It's only a mole.*

'What's it doing here?' Roddy asked, wiping the sweat from his face with the back of his hand.

'Dunno,' Dave said, thinking, *did you ever see him sweat before, Davey?* The answer was categorically no.

He had to put Tommy down; his arms were aching.

'Well it must be here for something, f'Chrissakes!' Roddy said, glowering at Dave. 'Now what is it?'

Sally glared at him. 'We don't know yet. We are going to find out but first we have to fix Tiger's dad,' she said. 'Now shut up – you're scaring Tommy!'

Roddy looked over at Sally, his bottom jaw dangling open. He looked as if he'd been slapped hard. Dave expected him to start a fight, but instead Roddy glanced at the doorway, then at Tommy and said, 'Yeah. Okay,' and sat down on the bank next to Derek.

He's got a mole on his right ear, too, Dave told himself. *That definitely wasn't there before. You know that, don't you?*

'Are you feeling okay, Roddy?' Dave asked, setting Tommy down and wishing he would go back to his mother where he would be out of harm's way if Roddy did anything weird. The boy just buried his head in Dave's legs.

'Whaddya mean?' Roddy demanded.

'Nothing,' Dave said, shaking his head. 'Forget it.' He pulled Tommy away from his legs. 'Your dad's going to be alright,' he said. 'We can fix him.' But he didn't know how. He looked down at Derek, who lay in a crumpled heap, still dressed in what looked like his working suit. He was as see-through as Bad Eddie had been. Dave just hoped he wouldn't end up the same way.

Anne Cousins looked at Sally. 'I think I know what to do,' she said.

'About Derek?' Sally asked, wiping her own eyes and

wishing that seeing people crying didn't always make her cry too.

Anne nodded and held out the M & S bag. 'I've been saving this because I thought . . . I thought . . . I don't know what I thought. It won't work, I know it won't.'

She fumbled about in the bag and brought out the bottle of Coppertone suntan lotion. There was still some left in the bottom of the bottle. It was her emergency supply that she'd kept secret from Bad Eddie. 'You rub it on,' she said, instantly wishing she'd kept her mouth shut. What was she thinking of? Suntan lotion didn't bring the dead back to life, did it? Except that Derek wasn't dead – or so Dave and his nasty friend had said. She hadn't had the courage to look for herself until now.

'Suntan lotion,' Sally said, wondering what Anne meant.

'He told me. When I came through, my nylon underwear melted and stuck to my skin. I had to rip it off and a lot of my skin came off too. Bad Eddie told me what to do. I rubbed it on and my skin healed.'

'But will it wake him up?' Sally asked, wondering if he was too far gone to fix. He looked like he might be.

'Yes it will!' Tommy said, leaving Dave and running back to Anne. He hung on to his mother's skirt and glowered at Sally as if she was the worst kind of a traitor to have said such a thing. 'My mummy *can* make my daddy better,' he said defiantly. 'She *can*!'

'Okay, Tiger,' Dave said, trying to keep the doubt from his voice. 'Why don't we give it a go?'

'He'll want more than a rubbing with suntan cream to sort him out,' Roddy said.

'Shut up, Roddy. Please,' Dave said.

Roddy's hand went to the pocket he kept his flick knife in, but he didn't take it out. He paused for a second, his ear slightly cocked as if he was listening. Then he relaxed, dropped his hand and smiled.

'What?' Dave said.

Roddy looked at him innocently, his eyebrows raised. 'What what?' he said, grinning.

'What did you hear?'

501

'I dunno what you're talking about, Foureyes,' Roddy said. He looked confused for a moment and several expressions swept across his face, some of which Dave recognised, but none of which he had ever seen on Roddy before. Fear, for example. Fear looked as out of place on Roddy's face as sweat did on his forehead.

There's something wrong with you, Roddy, and I know it, Dave thought. *I don't know what you've been doing to get all that blood all over you, but you sure as shit didn't bleed like that because you cut yourself. I think you cut yourself afterwards because you knew you were going to get asked about that stain and you wanted to have a reason for it. One that would satisfy us.*

'I gotta headache,' Roddy announced abruptly and walked around to the other side of the nearby summerhouse where he sat against its wall, his arms folded over the bloodstain.

Dave looked at Sally and shrugged. 'What do we have to do with the Coppertone?' he said to Anne.

'Just rub it on him, that's all,' she said quietly.

They undressed Derek Cousins while Roddy looked on, smiling to himself.

'I don't like him,' Sally whispered as she pulled off one of Derek's stiff socks. 'Don't tell him anything.'

'I wasn't planning to,' Dave told her, looking at the tendons inside Derek's right foot. They had little nodules growing from them and you could see them moving smoothly up and down when his toes moved.

Tommy stood watching at a safe distance. His face was blank and pale and his eyes had a faraway look that spoke of shock. His mouth dangled open and his fingers picked at one another agitatedly. Sally realised that he shouldn't really be watching this macabre task at all, but Anne seemed to have forgotten about him temporarily and Sally didn't like to tell him to go somewhere else – especially if it meant him sitting with Roddy. *He'll be alright, Sal,* she told herself as she undid Derek's shirt. *He's seen worse than this.*

Dave and Sally supported Derek's cold body between them while Anne removed his trousers and boxer shorts.

'He looks a little pale, don't he?' Roddy said.

Anne looked at Sally as she uncapped the Coppertone bottle. 'Here goes nothing,' she said, squirting the white fluid into the palm of her hand.

She started on his face, drawing her palm down the centre.

'It works!' Dave said, watching Derek's skin change back to its proper colour where Anne stroked it.

Anne smiled, smoothing the cream into her husband's cheeks.

Please let him wake up, Sally thought.

Sally was counting again. It took six hundred and all the Coppertone for Anne to change Derek's skin back to its original colour. She counted another four hundred while they knelt around his still body and waited for him to wake up.

Roddy got bored, announced that he was going to take a piss and wandered into the creaking trees.

What should we be doing? Sally asked herself. *How can we wake him up?* But no inspiration came. The cross didn't pulse or burst into life and she wondered what had gone wrong.

'Wake up, Daddy,' Tommy pleaded in a shaky voice, but Derek's eyes didn't so much as flicker.

'Sleeping Beauty Syndrome, Sal,' Dave said. 'That's what it is. He's got what you had. The Claw did it, I bet. Just like it did to you.'

Anne looked up. 'How did you wake her?' she asked.

Dave sighed. 'I didn't. There was this old man with a dog called Lucky. He did it.' He shrugged and returned to watching Derek's face.

Sally counted another five hundred, timing herself by watching the unconscious man's shallow breathing. A whole breath took four; two in, two out.

Roddy came back and sat down by the summerhouse. He looked sick and his face was sheened with sweat.

Sally watched Derek's heart beating. He was thin and she could see the skin between his ribs rise and fall with his pulse. She reckoned it was doing thirty a minute, give or take a few.

C'mon, someone give me a hint! she thought, but her mind was a blank.

'Tide's coming in,' Roddy said. No one paid him any attention.

'I might be able to heal him,' Sally said. 'I don't know if it'll work or not, but I can have a go. I healed Dave.'

She went around to Derek's head and took it between her hands. When she had done it to Dave she could feel the power flowing into her from the cross, running through her body and down into her hands from where it entered his head. This time there was nothing. Not even a tingle. *C'mon Sal, you're the one who's supposed to be able to do this. You're the one with the faith in yourself. Think positively.*

'I think he's meant to stay like this,' Dave said, shaking his head.

'Getting dark now,' Roddy called.

Dave looked up and swore softly. The veins of darkness in the cracked grey sky had grown and now filled it with ragged zebra stripes. He could see the darkness expanding slowly as he watched. The light was fading, too. The Claw was nearly here.

'I think we'll have to work on Derek later, Sal,' Dave said. 'That's if there is a later. We'd better move.'

'Tide's coming in, in case you haven't noticed,' Roddy said, nodding toward the park entrance. There was a sick smile on his face. 'It's making my head ache,' he said.

When Dave looked again, the walls of the Bad Side had crept soundlessly up to the perimeter of the park. Dave looked up into the vast empty darkness and followed it around the park. It had completely surrounded them. The dark wall was growing lazily upwards, curving in from all sides. Soon it would meet in the middle and they would be in total darkness.

'It's that clingfilm stuff with nothing behind it,' Roddy said, getting up. 'The stuff I found old Derek half through.'

From somewhere in the woods behind him there came a painful wooden creaking, followed by the crashing sound of a tree falling. Tommy moaned and pressed himself against his mother.

504

'It's getting colder,' Sally said. 'You can see your breath in the air.'

'It's through the door time,' Dave said. 'It's just you and me, Sal, we've got to go through.'

'What about us?' Anne half screamed. 'You can't leave us!'

'We have to, Anne,' Dave said. 'You'll have to stay here with Derek and Tommy. You can't come. You're not *meant* to come. That's probably why Derek won't wake – to keep you here. It's the Bad Side in there and it's showdown time. Claw Time. If we get out again, we'll help Derek. If we don't and The Claw gets these crosses, to put it bluntly it won't matter either way. That's about the size of it, I'm afraid.'

'Oh my God,' Anne said. 'I thought it was going to be alright.'

'Don't worry, it might be!' Sally said.

Dave glanced at her and saw that the eye of her cross had come back on. The green iris was pulsing erratically as though it was trying to find the groove and settle into a rhythm, but Sally's face had already got that glassy, *wild* look which had frightened Dave before. Now it thrilled him and filled him with confidence. A shiver ran up his back as he thought, *that's her Giant Slayer look, Davey*. She suddenly looked big and vibrant and strong against the crumbling and dim backdrop of the Limbo park. And she was smiling.

'Come on!' she said, starting down the bank toward the doorway.

Dave looked down at the deep red iris of his cross's eye and wondered when *that* would happen to him. *It'll come when it's time*, he thought and followed Sally to the doorway.

'Wait!' Roddy was jogging down the bank after them.

'You can't come!' Dave said.

'I'm coming, Foureyes,' Roddy hissed, catching them up. 'And you can't stop me.'

Sally stood in front of the doorway, staring at the handle and shaking her head.

'Sorry, Roddy. You aren't equipped. You can't come with us,' Dave said taking a pace back. He didn't want to have to fight Roddy at this particular moment – or at any particular moment, come to think of it. There was only likely to be one outcome and that was a bad one.

'I want my sister back!' Roddy shouted. 'And I'm fucking well going to get her! I'M COMING!'

The patch of mould growth on Roddy's ear that Dave had thought was only a mole, now ran all the way around the rim. And the mole on his bicep had expanded too. It was a nasty deep green colour and a fine fuzz grew from it.

'You'll be killed,' Dave said. 'Jon Kott went over there and he's dead. I saw him.'

'You liar, you fucking cunting little *liar*!' Roddy said, wiping the sweat from his face with a clenched fist. He looked dizzy for a moment.

Dave shook his head and stepped away again, not liking the fact that Roddy was close enough to hit him.

Roddy's face ran through that odd array of expressions again, then it cracked. Roddy looked like he was ten years old again. Tears welled up in his eyes. 'Please, man,' he said, sniffing. 'I've gotta get Sandy back. You've got to help me. I . . . I love her.'

'He can come,' Sally said, without looking round.

'SEE?' Roddy said, vindicated. His tough guy face was back instantly. His eyes were dry and had his old evil glint. A vein throbbed in his temple. Dave wondered whether he'd imagined the tears.

'Okay, if Sal says so, you can come,' Dave said.

'It's all wrong,' Sally said from in front of the door. 'I don't know how to go through.'

'Pull the handle down and push the door,' Roddy said.

'You can only go one way,' Sally said, 'and I don't know which it is.'

'What's around the other side?' Dave said, skirting Sally and going around to the rear of the door. The door looked exactly the same from both sides. He knocked on it. Just in case it had magical properties, he knocked on it three times.

Nothing happened. The door was just an ordinary white

domestic door made of thin wooden panels and probably with a lining of corrugated cardboard.

He went back to Sally's side. She had her hand on the aluminium handle now, but she was still shaking her head.

'Hurry it up!' Roddy said. Then he strode forward, pushed Sally aside wrenched the door open and went through.

And stepped onto the same faded patch of grass that Dave had just stood on.

'It didn't fucking work!' he shouted. He slammed the door and came back around the outside of the frame.

'Maybe we have to open it from the other side,' Dave said.

'I'm not sure,' Sally said. Her cross was pulsing steadily now and her eyes had changed. The irises were shot with sparkling strands of the same green colour as the cross which glinted almost incandescently in the half light. Dave had never seen her look so gorgeous.

He and Roddy followed her to the other side of the doorway. She put out a hesitant hand and touched the aluminium handle. 'No,' she said, shaking her head, 'it's still wrong. I-I don't know.'

'Concentrate, Sal,' Dave said. 'Relax and concentrate.'

'I *am* concentrating, but I can't get it. There's something stopping me getting it.' She glanced back at him and shrugged.

'Maybe I ought to open it,' Dave suggested, realising he really didn't want to be first through that door at all. 'Perhaps it's one of the conditions.'

Behind Anne and Tommy and the sleeping Derek, another tree began to complain. Dave saw the trembling upper branches silhouetted against the sick sky. This one was near the edge of the woods, two or three trees in. It had gone completely black and the branches were leafless. *Christ, it's gonna fall on them*! Dave thought as the tree squealed and started to move. 'Anne! Look out!' he yelled, waving his arms frantically.

Anne and Tommy looked up from Derek's still form. From here it was hard to read their expressions, but both their faces looked pale, shocked, and both of them looked bemused.

They didn't hear it! Dave thought, nervously pushing his

507

glasses back up to the top of his nose. *It's going to fall on them and they don't even know!*

'Look out! The TREE!' he screamed.

But it was going to be too late. It was falling towards them, smashing its way down through the surrounding trees. Leaves and wood flew, turning to grey ash in the air, but the trunk was stronger than that; it wasn't going to come apart so easily.

They're not moving! Dave thought, unable to believe what he was seeing. *They still haven't heard it!*

'THE TREE!' he screamed above the roar of the falling trunk, jabbing his finger at the air behind them.

Tommy looked at Anne, then waved, moving his hand back and forth from the wrist like royalty.

Dave looked at Tommy's tiny hand then at the massive tree which would shortly pulp all of them. Behind him Roddy muttered, 'They're dead,' in a flat tone.

The tree missed them by a fraction of an inch but Dave didn't see what had become of them afterwards because the tree burst like a bag of flour when it hit the ground and a huge cloud of thick grey-white ash bloomed into the air.

'Come on, man,' Roddy urged. 'Open the fucking door. There ain't much time!'

'But Anne . . . Tommy . . .'

'Too late,' Roddy said. 'Just open the fucking door before this whole place collapses or something.'

The cloud of tree ash rolled down the bank towards them. Dave didn't want to think about what it might do to his lungs but he couldn't tear his eyes away from it.

'COME ON!' Roddy shouted, and thumped him hard between the shoulder blades.

Dave's feet got the message and he staggered over to Sally who still stood in front of the door. She looked as if she had become transfixed. Her eyes were closed and her hand hovered over the handle, not quite touching it.

Dave gently pulled her aside.

'Not this way,' she said as he took her outstretched arm and led her back. 'I can't get what it is, but it's not this way.'

'Which way is it then?' Dave asked.

'Wait,' Sally said without opening her eyes. 'I've nearly got it.'

'There's not *time*!' Roddy screamed. 'Open the fucking door, Foureyes!'

Dave took the door handle in his hand and looked back at Sally and Roddy.

Sally stood off to one side. Her eyes were closed and she was biting her bottom lip in concentration. Her right arm was still outstretched, ready to take the handle that was no longer there. Roddy was close behind Dave, an expression of terror etched on his profusely sweating face. His right ear was completely covered with the green-black mould growth now and the whites of his eyes were darkening. He was extremely agitated and the muscles in both his legs were tensing and relaxing quickly as if he were about to run.

'What's happened to you, Roddy?' Dave asked staring into Roddy's eyes and feeling very exposed and frightened. Roddy's pupils were contracted to black pin pricks that reminded Dave of Fred Purdue.

'Open that motherfucking door!' Roddy screeched, slapping his fist into the open palm of his other hand and making those twitchy movements with his legs.

The door handle was cold under Dave's hand. Too cold.

He glanced up at the oncoming dust cloud and pulled the handle down and pushed open the door thinking, *it opens inwards both ways. I knew it would.*

Then he screamed.

Because the huge pink cyclopean worm from the Ghost Train was waiting behind the door for him. It looked at him out of that travesty of a human face and blinked its single bloodshot blue eye. Its head swivelled on its slender neck as though it was looking out past Dave and he had time to take in the ugliness of its slick pink body with the worm-like sections and the black bristles which grew from the joints. Under its snub nose it had a wide, lipless mouth which now opened, the top half of its head tipping back. This wasn't the same worm-thing from the

Ghost Train though, because that one had black rotted stumps for teeth – this one had a mouthful of glistening, pearl white triangular razor blades. There was no tongue in there, no roof to the mouth, just rows and rows of savage looking, shark-like teeth.

The worm opened its mouth even further until the top of the creature's head was tipped back at an angle of forty degrees or more, and its single eye had extended from the socket on folds of wet flesh, shaped like camera bellows so that it could still see.

Something went *snick*! behind him and he didn't know what it was, but he knew the dust had reached this far because Sally was coughing.

Perhaps that's why she isn't helping you, Dave thought. *It's because she can't see what's going on here.* She coughed again as Dave stared into the worm's maw and this time it sounded as if she was miles away.

The worm tensed, then flexed and struck forward like a cobra. Dave stared in horrified astonishment as the teeth came down at him. There wasn't even time for him to consider what it was going to feel like, let alone get his Swiss Army knife out. Then the ground was gone from beneath his feet and he knew what the familiar noise had been, knew what had saved him.

Roddy had got his flick knife out and decided to go to work.

By the time Dave hit the ground, Roddy was standing in his place, the knife raised high in his right hand. The worm had snapped its head back inside the doorway, but it wasn't going to go away. It was going to fight. Its baleful eye fixed Roddy, while it dodged and ducked like a streetfighter, keeping moving while it searched for a gap in Roddy's defences.

'Fuck off!' Roddy screamed at it.

'Heek eff!' the worm replied through its open mouth, and Dave saw the back of its throat contract as it made the words.

'Get it, Roddy!' Dave yelled, suddenly knowing how Roddy's meathead friends must feel when their role model went into action.

The worm struck fast, coming straight down from above, but Roddy had seen it tense and leapt nimbly to one side, smoothly slashing out backhand with the flick-knife's thin blade. The blade rattled across the layers of teeth and shards of enamel chipped and flew. The worm snapped its mouth shut while Roddy's knife hand was still passing through it, but apparently he'd expected this to happen, and quickly withdrew it. The worm's jaws clamped shut, just missing the knife. Roddy's arm was fully extended and he was moving away from the worm, but he wasn't finished yet. He flicked his wrist back, bringing the blade up under the worm's chin. The tip slipped into the worm's flesh and opened it up in a pencil-thin line. Purple fluid sprayed out and the worm flicked back inside the doorway, bleating terribly.

'Motherfucker!' Roddy yelled, jumping athletically back into position.

'Hudderhucker!' the worm mimicked and struck again, faster this time and without warning.

Roddy yelled and leapt back, but the worm's teeth clamped down on his arm. It pulled Roddy towards the doorway and Dave saw blood ooze from the edges of its mouth.

Roddy leapt into the air, dragging himself up by his trapped arm and kicked the worm, snapping both his feet into its soft pink belly.

The worm made a wet coughing noise and dropped him instantly. He lay on his back half through the doorway, the flick-knife still held firmly although his arm was lacerated badly. The worm looked down at him, blinking its single eye. Dave thought he recognised triumph on the creature's face.

'Roddy! LOOK OUT!' Dave yelled as the worm struck for the final time.

Clouds of tree dust wafted in front of Dave's face and the air felt dry and powdery when he tried to breathe in. The dust prevented him from seeing how Roddy avoided the worm's last strike, but he saw the flick-knife flash and slice clear through the corrugated structure that held the worm's eye and he saw the worm gnashing crazily at empty air, its eye dangling from a bleeding thread.

Now Roddy was back on his feet. Dave could see him

momentarily through the clouds of choking dust; dancing this way and that as he avoided the blind worm's clashing teeth and laughing like the devil as he slashed deep ugly welts into its pink flesh.

The worm didn't fall for a long time.

Not until Roddy had minced its face to bloody ribbons and opened its flaccid body until its insides hung in long purple streamers. When it finally collapsed, it was drawn back inside the doorway as if someone inside was reeling it in on an invisible rope. The door slammed shut when it was gone. There were spatters of purple blood running down the wood.

'I'm okay man, I'm okay!' Roddy said, emerging through the dust. He sounded surprised and his sweaty face was pale and coated with grey ash. The flick-knife was still in his right hand and he was holding his right arm at the elbow with his left. Blood was dripping steadily from the deep abrasions the worm had made in it. There was a central cut on the inside of his arm which ran almost all the way from his wrist to his elbow. Here, the worm's teeth had sheared right down into the thick muscle. Dave thought he could see the tendons deep down inside.

'Thanks, Roddy,' Dave said, trying not to notice how his blackened ear had shrivelled. *Just concentrate on his arm, Dave. Take care of that first.* 'I owe you one.'

Sally came out of the cloud, the emerald beam of her cross dancing and reflecting the way before her. Her eyes were streaming and she was coughing. 'Give me your arm,' she told Roddy. 'I can fix it.'

Roddy obediently held out his damaged arm and Sally grabbed it with both hands.

'Fuck it, girl, you're hurting me,' Roddy complained as she squeezed the edges of the wound together. Sally wasn't listening. Her eyes were closed in concentration again and she was breathing hard, her lungs wheezing as she sucked in the dusty air.

Dave dropped the rucksack from his back and got out the Wet Ones cannister. He extracted one of the moist tissues and put it to his mouth, not expecting to be able to draw a breath through it. In spite of the fine weave of the material, he found he could breathe through it easily and the air tasted fresh and good. He took out three more tissues, handed one to Roddy, held the other over Sally's mouth and nose and used the third to clean the grime from his glasses.

Behind them more trees began to fall and the dust got thicker.

'Oww *shit*!' Roddy shouted as Sally threw his arm forcefully away from her.

Her eyes opened. 'Did I do it?' she coughed through the tissue.

'Yeah, near enough,' Roddy muttered. There were a lot of minor abrasions still bleeding on the inside of his forearm, but the main wound had partially healed. It still looked red and angry and wept clear lymphatic fluid, but the edges had almost grown back together.

'Better go back to Anne and Tommy, see if they're alright,' Dave said.

'No fucking way,' Roddy said, dropping his tissue. His arm was healed enough for him to wave the flick-knife menacingly in front of Dave's nose. 'Just get us in there!' he said, nodding at the almost obscured doorway.

'He's right Dave, there's no time,' Sally said. 'We have to go in and we have to go now. If we delay any longer it'll be too late.'

'Okay,' Dave said heavily. 'Which way in?'

'You have to decide,' Sally said. 'I can't get it. Something doesn't want me to know. There's something blocking me.'

'And my cross isn't working,' Dave said. 'Great.'

'You can do it, Dave. You have to!' she said. Her eyes shone.

'Why me? I already got it wrong once.'

'Because you are the one. Not me, not Roddy. You are the one. Don't you see that? We're only along for the ride. To help. It's your trouble, Dave. You were the one who got picked. And you were picked because you're the right man for the job. It doesn't matter that you aren't as good with the cross as I am, and it doesn't matter that you can't fight like Roddy. You got picked because of something else.'

'Oh yeah, like what?' Dave said.

513

'Because you don't give up. No matter what happens you don't give up. Even when you're beaten and tired and totally depressed, you won't give up. I know you Dave, and that's how you are. You got picked because you have faith.'

'I'm not religious, Sal. You know that. Even now all this good and bad stuff has happened, I'm still not religious. Not in the biblical sense, anyway.'

'But faith isn't about believing in God and stuff. It doesn't have to be religious faith at all. Faith is when, however bad things get, you still believe you'll win. I've got it, and Roddy might have some as well, for all I know, but you've got the largest dose, Dave, you're the one that believes in the magic, you're the one that the compass and the knife work for. Faith in yourself is enough and you've got it, even if you don't think you have. That's one of the reasons I love you. Because you came over here even though you thought you couldn't win. It's courage, but it's more than that. It's *faith*.'

Dave shrugged. 'Stupidity by any other name . . .' he said, nodding and feeling embarrassed. 'Okay, you win.'

Then his cross lit and the power surged through him, burning his chest and flowing through the skin into muscle, then deeper. He smiled as the power filled him and shook hands with his insides like an old friend.

'In through this side,' he said. 'At a guess.'

Sally kissed him.

Trees were falling regularly now, and the thickening dust was beginning to blind as well as choke them as they made their way back to the doorway. Dave's glasses were opaque again, and he found his way across the short expanse of blighted grass by following the beam of his cross.

'Right,' he said, glancing around at them and wondering why Roddy was grinning so enthusiastically, 'here goes.'

He took the cold door handle, swung the door open and stepped through into the Bad Side, wondering where all his legendary faith in himself had gone to.

Chapter Eighteen
Earth Side

Back in the real Basingstoke where the time was eighteen minutes to twelve on Friday night – almost two weeks since Dave's nineteenth birthday – State Registered Nurse Nancy Willis was asleep in her flat at the hospital. She was still fully dressed and coated in concrete dust from the collapsing multistorey car park, because when she arrived home after running the three miles from the town centre she had taken three Librium then thrown herself on her bed. She had lain there for a time, refusing to admit what she had witnessed but unable to force away the terrible reality of the scene.

After a time the shaking had stopped and she had fallen into an uneasy sleep. Now she was locked in the throes of a terrible nightmare in which Robert de Niro caused the multistorey car park to collapse again and again by firing at it with an empty gun.

Each time the huge slabs of concrete fell, Geoff's distant voice would say: 'I think I heard someone scream. There's someone in trouble in there!' and the taxi controller's voice would inform her that what followed after you got Mediterranean weather was Mediterranean earthquakes, that's what. And underneath all that, an old man's voice whispered that the weather would break at the weekend. The old man had a dog, she was sure of that. Neither of them actually appeared in her nightmare, but from time to time she could plainly hear the dog's rasping breathing as it pulled at its extendible lead, and the click-clack of its toenails on the polished hospital floor.

* * *

While Nancy thrashed and moaned in her sleep, at the other end of the town in Cliddesden Road, Ed Harrison was sitting in an old-fashioned wood and canvas deckchair on his back garden patio nursing a chilled can of Fosters and staring out across the dark lawn at the fishpond. Several crushed empties and a pile of violently stubbed out cigarette ends lay at his feet. He had been sitting there all evening. Thinking.

Ed Harrison had done a lot of thinking since his daughter had vanished without trace from the hospital, but it had done him no good whatsoever.

Earlier this evening, while it was still light, he had seen the orange shape of one of the legendary goldfish break the surface of the bottomless garden pond and he hoped it was a good omen. According to Sally, the legendary goldfish had been left in the pond when the previous owners moved out. For months Sally had sworn she regularly saw them just below the surface, but neither he nor Marie had believed her. Seeing the fish now was a sign; it *had* to be. All you had to do was be very patient, that was the message. All things come to he who waits. Even if it was bad news it would be infinitely better than Not Knowing.

Not Knowing was a heartbreaking business that had brought both him and Marie to the very edge of their sanity. Whenever the phone rang, Hope would surge high, closely followed by Dread, and the moment you knew it wasn't news, your insides would collapse again. Not Knowing made you lose your appetite and turned your stomach into a twisted knot. Food wasn't the end of it either: Not Knowing made you lose your appetite for life, too. It turned you into an adrenalin-ravaged shell that hurt and hurt and hurt some more and then, just when you thought the hurting had reached its zenith, it shot higher still, pushing back the barriers and increasing the pain tenfold.

Earlier in the week, Ed and Marie had visited Dave's parents who were coping just as badly. The afternoon had been a disaster. Instead of offering hope and mutual reassurance to one another, the four of them had sat in the Carters's lounge in silence while they all tried hard not to cry.

Ed sipped his Fosters and wondered what had happened downtown. He'd heard the terrible roaring crash earlier on and had thought at first it was a clap of thunder. But it went on too long to be thunder. It sounded as if someone had dropped a bomb on the town centre. Ed didn't care if the town centre was razed to the ground, not even when the pall of white smoke and dust had risen in the sky to the north and the sound of emergency vehicle sirens had split the still air.

One thing was for sure and that was that Sally hadn't been hurt in the explosion.

The burgeoning mushroom of dust or smoke or whatever it was, had drifted east, thinned and finally vanished. Ed had drunk three cans of beer while he watched it and he forgot all about it as soon as it had gone.

Leaning forward in his deckchair, Ed got his cigarettes from the warm stone of the patio, lit one, inhaled and then finished his beer before exhaling again. He was starting to do things like that now. If you did things in a specific order it might just crack some weird magical code and form a spell that would bring his daughter safely back to him.

There were lots of things that could be done to produce magic and he'd tried all of the ones he could think of. Like passing Sally's bedroom door and asking 'Are you back yet?' in a low voice. Perhaps he would do that one day and Sally would emerge, tanned and smiling.

Marie was using a different kind of magic. This was the magic of the unspoken. They hadn't discussed it because you *couldn't* discuss it when you were grasping at magical straws, but Ed knew exactly what his wife was doing.

He crushed his beercan and dropped it by the (left hand, always the left hand) side of his seat. Sighing, he reached to his right and took another can out of the latest six-pack. He held his breath while he pulled the ring and opened the can. Sipping the beer, he wondered if Marie was asleep yet. He'd heard her go to bed about half an hour before the crash, and she hadn't called out when it happened, so sleep must have finally got her.

Staying awake was a part of the magic of the unspoken. Ed

517

had watched his wife closely and he had been able to crack the code of her magic. If she stayed awake, Sally would come home. And she didn't care how long it took. Marie had been tremendously determined – she'd managed five sleepless nights, in spite of taking the downers the doctor had given her and she hadn't complained about how bad she felt. Not even when her tired and bloodshot eyes had started to bulge from her head like eggs and her chewed up lips had developed rows of weeping sores.

Now Marie was asleep and the staying awake part of her personal magic had finished, let her down.

Ed shrugged. 'Fuck it,' he said, examining his cigarette in the summer twilight to see if he'd smoked it down to the lettering just in front of the filter. That was how far the cigarette had to be smoked; no more, no less. He took another drag, examined it, then crushed it out hard between his feet on the patio flagstones.

It had got darker when Ed looked up at the sky again. A lot darker. He didn't see where the clouds had come from, but there were definitely clouds there, in spite of the forecast having said that the hot spell would remain for the foreseeable future. The clouds had no business to be up there, blocking half the starlight and covering the face of the full moon, but there they were, big fluffy thunderheads that hung high in the sky to his left over towards the park. They had apparently formed in position because there wasn't a breath of wind that might have blown them there and there was no other cloudbank in the whole sky. The moonlight shone around the edges of the thunderhead, sharpening them and making unwelcoming yellow-tinged spikes that for some reason caused Ed to shiver.

'Weather's gonna break,' he muttered, staring at the cloud and wondering if it was a trick of the light. 'Fucking depression right in the middle of Basingstoke,' he said bitterly.

Down at the bottomless pool, the stagnant water went *plop*! Ed saw an orange fish tail flip into the air, then slide slowly beneath the surface.

'Getting colder, too,' he said, rolling down his shirtsleeves and glancing up at the cloud.

Over in the park a tree fell down. The park was less than four hundred yards away as the crow flew and the sound of the tree crashing to the ground carried clearly on the still night air.

'Fucking fairground people cutting 'em down for firewood I 'spect,' he said, realising from the slurred tone of his voice that he was more than a little drunk.

Ed knew the faces of all the fairground people off by heart. He'd been there doing the round. Looking at them and wondering – of course he had. It was the television reports that had made him suspicious. All those missing people. First there were two kids in Nottingham, then one in London, then Tommy whatsisname from Bracknell, then Sally and Dave and Phil and his girl from here. All the disappearances had one thing in common. There was a travelling funfair in town at the time. So he'd done exactly what he supposed all the other parents had done before him. Walked round and around the fair, searching the ride owner's faces, hoping to see one with KIDNAPPER written on it. Or any of the alternatives of course, like: MURDERER or: SEX BEAST. But they just looked like fairground people. All of them except the Ghost Train owner, Fred Purdue. That one had fixed him with knowing eyes. It had been enough for Ed who was almost demented by his emptiness. He strode over to the Ghost Train paybooth and told Fred Purdue to give her back or he would kill him. Purdue had smiled and told him he didn't know what he was talking about, pal. That was when Ed had come to his senses. He'd apologised and left feeling very ashamed at having accused an innocent person.

The lightning strike brought down the next tree. Ed could still see the jagged, twisting shape the lightning had made, long after the tree had crashed to the ground. He blinked his eyes, watching the yellow after-image turn blue and counting the seconds to the clap of thunder.

The clap of thunder didn't come. This was impossible. Ed kept counting until he got to thirty-five then gave up, wondering if he'd hallucinated the lightning after all.

The air had cooled noticeably now and, above the park, the

dark cloud had expanded. Its edges were right above his back garden now, and for some reason a thin blade of fear ran up Ed's spine.

'Better go indoors,' he muttered, lighting another cigarette. 'Gonna have a storm.'

Lightning flashed and another tree fell down in the park. No thunder followed.

'Cold,' Ed said, feeling slightly surprised as goosebumps puckered up on his arms. Something was happening here and it wasn't the result of the *specific order* magic he'd been trying to invoke, nor was it the result of Marie's *magic of the unspoken*. This was something much more powerful. This was nature magic: the kind that blew the roof off your house and sucked you out of bed, only to dash you to the ground; the kind that fried you with a lightning strike; the kind that threw billions of gallons of water at you from a tidal wave.

Not only was the weather going to break, it was going to do it in a Big Way.

Ed folded up the deckchair and stored it in the garden shed which was beside the fishpond. One of the big goldfish leapt from the water, then flopped back in as Ed left the shed.

Bubbles formed and popped on the green surface of the fishpond and Ed leaned over, wondering if he would be able to see the fish again.

What happened next took less than five seconds and, afterwards, Ed wasn't sure if it was a trick of his emotionally-drained mind or not. He never mentioned it to anyone.

A face appeared in the pool. He could see it clearly, even through the murky water. It was a girl. She was beautiful and had pale, clear skin, elfin features and long flaxen hair which swirled this way and that in the water as she moved her head. The girl was smiling.

Sally is alive, the girl said. Beneath the water, her mouth moved and bubbles came out, but Ed heard her musical voice right inside his brain.

'Wha . . .?' he gasped.

Sally is alive. Fear not, the girl said.

Then Ed was staring into the empty algae-ridden water wondering if his magic had worked or his mind had gone.

He walked back to the house, shivering with the sudden cold but smiling. For a few seconds, his fear for his daughter *was* gone and he *knew* she was coming back.

Chapter Nineteen
The Skull-Man

In the intense cold of the Limbo Side Memorial Park, Anne Cousins sat closely huddled to Tommy and Derek, hoping the immediate danger was over. Instead of running for the safety of open ground after the first tree had narrowly missed them, she had simply drawn her family close to her and covered their faces as best she could with her thin cotton shirt. The shirt had kept most of the dust out of their lungs, but Tommy was sweating heavily and racked with such coughing that Anne thought it might permanently damage his lungs if it didn't cease soon.

Although she was endangering herself and her son by staying here, running would have meant abandoning Derek, because he was much too heavy to carry. There was simply no choice to make. If Derek was going to die, then they would all die together.

But none of the trees had hit them and now they seemed to have stopped falling so perhaps it was going to be alright for the moment.

Tommy's head was tucked into her armpit and Derek's was in her lap, the boy's burning and her husband's still ice cold. She rocked back and forth, hugging Tommy to her and stroking Derek's smooth, cool forehead with her other hand.

The creaking noises of tortured wood still issued forth from the trees behind her but apart from that and the sound of dust falling lightly like dry misty rain, there was silence. Even Tommy's coughing had subsided.

She waited for a time, killing each new troublesome thought as it grew in her mind and when she was sure nothing further would happen, she pulled her shirt away from her face and opened her eyes.

It was not quite dark. The light had a quality like that which you sometimes saw when the sky was filled with thunderheads on one side and sunshine on the other.

The huge black walls which surrounded the park had curved in and met overhead. What she thought of as the surface of the bubble, which now enclosed the park, appeared to be a very thin membrane. It was moving; bending and flexing slightly like an oversized soap bubble. Where the walls trembled, the surface glistened with a dark sheen. She could see through the thin barrier, and at first she thought she was looking at a clear night sky and wondered why she could see no stars twinkling. When the realisation came that she was staring out into a vast nothingness that might have gone on for eternity, her mind did a stomach-churning cartwheel and she quickly looked away.

Towards the funfair the light was stronger and Anne realised that AdventureLand was its source. She knew that if she walked out across the grass so that she could see the funfair entrance, it would be enclosed in a bubble of its own light – proper daylight. This was because AdventureLand didn't really belong in this godforsaken place. It existed simultaneously here and back on the real Earth and it was an unnatural structure. It had been forced into existence here by the combined efforts of Fred Purdue and what Sally called The Claw. She knew that AdventureLand – and the Ghost Train in particular – was the *real* doorway, the one that mattered. This was the one that had generated its own particular version of Hell inside it; the one The Claw would use to invade her world in person.

Anne wiped the dust from her face and looked at the closed doorway, wondering whether Dave and Sally would ever come out again. There were two possibilities as far as she would allow herself to imagine. The first was that Dave and Sally and Roddy would come back out of that door, having returned things to normal; the second was that they would perish inside and, when the door opened again, The Claw would waltz out and the emptiness that surrounded the park would engulf her and her family as the beast strode towards AdventureLand where Fred would be waiting to welcome it on the real side.

There were other things that could happen, of course, but they were only minor. Derek might wake up, for instance. *And what if he does, Anne?* she asked herself. *Would you really be able to go back inside the Ghost Train and find your way back to the real world? And what if you did and Dave and Sally lost the battle? What then? Would it have been worth it? How long would you survive?*

The thing that happened next, happened very quickly and surprised Anne so much that she didn't have time to prepare herself.

Overhead, the sky stretched as though a huge finger was pressing down on it from the other side. A dark cone swept down like a sudden whirlwind, its point touching the ground in front of the bank they were sitting on.

Anne and Tommy jumped to their feet, but the whirlwind was already shooting back up to the sky and the present it had left them was staggering up the bank towards them.

'What *is* it, Mummy?' Tommy yelled, darting behind her for protection.

'Oh God,' Anne said, looking at the man who was approaching her and feeling the strength flowing steadily away from her arms and legs.

The man's body was beefy and squat with the build of a weightlifter. Anne didn't know what his face looked like because he had a ball of fire where it should have been. His bull-like neck ended three inches below his head and strips of skin dangled from it in crisp tatters that looked and smelled like burnt bacon. He was holding a toy soldier in his right hand and it was shooting a roaring yellow flame into what had once been his face.

'I'm a troll fol de rol!' Jon Kott's blackened, empty skull shouted over the high pressure hiss of the toy flame-thrower.

Each time he opened his mouth to speak, the fire shot through his charred jawbone, distorting his words as it travelled up through his roofless mouth and flared out of his nose and eye sockets. Bone glowed red with the extreme heat.

'Get away!' Anne shouted, wanting to run but not able to desert Derek.

'AND I'LL EAT YOU FOR MY SUPPER!' Kott screamed, stamping his heavy boots up and down in the dust. Some of his red hot front teeth fell out and started tiny fires on the ground.

The knife, Anne, where's the knife? She glanced around and saw the M & S bag was out of easy reach behind Derek. *First time you let go of it, Annie oh Annie. Why didn't you keep it close to you?*

She momentarily considered dashing over there and getting it, but Tommy was clinging to her legs and Derek was in the way and there wasn't going to be enough time because the burning man was coming closer.

'Make him go away, Mummy. I don't like him!' Tommy screamed.

'TRIP TRAP TRIP TRAP!' Kott said leaping up and down excitedly. The soldier moved in his hand as he jumped and the high pressure flame bit into his throat.

Anne saw the pink flesh char and peel away. Blood oozed from the fresh wound and dried in treacley brown strands like burnt sugar as the fire cauterized the veins. The man took two faltering steps towards her and she could feel the heat on her own face now. One more step and her skin would start to singe, too. She tried to move away, but her legs were no longer paying any attention to what she told them.

'Make him go away!' Tommy screamed.

'Go away!' Anne shouted, leaning away from the heat as Kott came forward.

He spoke again, but his vocal chords had been incinerated and this time his voice was almost lost in the sibilant hiss of the flame-thrower. 'Hee whoo hor hi huhher!' he said in a cracked sing-song voice.

'Leave us alone!' Anne screamed. Strength flowed back into her arms and she balled her right fist and smashed it into Kott's stomach as hard as she could. It was like hitting iron and it hurt terribly. When she drew her fist back there were four bloody knuckle marks on the front of his Ben Sherman shirt. The sheer force of the blow knocked Kott backwards.

'Hooo!' his skull said as he tottered back down to the foot of the bank.

'GO AWAY!' Anne yelled, starting to believe she might be able to drive this awful thing away after all.

'Hickety hidge!' Kott breathed, coming up the bank again. 'Hickety hidge. Hickety hidge. Hip hap hip hap!'

'FUCK OFF!' Anne screamed, realising distantly that she was setting a bad example for her son, then – just as distantly – finding the thought hilarious.

Kott was close again and the heat was so bad she nearly fell over backwards, but she waited as he came forward. When he was no more than eighteen inches from her she brought her knee up hard into his groin, missed her target and struck his solid thigh.

'Ha ha,' Kott said, not even feeling the blow this time.

Tommy! Where's Tommy gone! Anne thought, realising he wasn't behind her any more. She hoped he was running away as fast as he could.

She hit Kott in the stomach again, feeling her knuckles split even more as they drove into his hard flesh.

Kott stood his ground but another one of his front teeth jolted out of his mouth. This one landed on Anne's bare foot and she screamed, trying to kick it off as it sizzled and sank into her flesh.

The tooth didn't come off; it was stuck fast. That didn't matter now because her foot had gone numb and Kott was struggling to pull the hand containing the flame-thrower soldier away from his face. Anne knew exactly what he intended to do and, for the second time, she hoped Tommy was a long way away.

She stood transfixed as Kott fought to turn his hand. It was held high in front of him and turned inwards, the little olive soldier grasped between his first three fingers and his thumb. Veins rose and muscles popped up in Kott's powerful hand as he tried to turn the soldier's flame towards Anne. Then the soldier moved and for a moment Anne thought he'd broken the spell that held it in place. She gasped, but the soldier flicked back into position and the roaring yellow flame seemed to increase in intensity.

Kott now used his other hand; first to try and prise his fingers away from the soldier then, when that failed, to pull his whole arm around. His biceps bulged and the tendons in his arms stood out like cables. Anne heard a ripping noise and was certain the man had torn his own arm from its socket. When she realised it was only the sheer bulk of his shoulder muscles bursting through his shirt she became desperate and hit him once more, lower this time, hoping to strike his penis or testes or preferably both. He was as solid here as he was everywhere else and Anne felt a sharp stinging pain as the shock broke something inside her hand.

'Hough!' Kott said, and before Anne knew what was happening his beefy left fist was sailing through the air towards her face.

The blow caught her right temple and its sheer force knocked her clean off her feet. Blue and white stars burst in front of her eyes and she was only dimly conscious of falling and hitting the ground.

Then she was being hauled up again by her shirt. She was right up close to him now, her face against the rough material of his jeans. She knew what he was going to do, even though she was only half conscious. He was going to lift her up between the flame and his face. She wanted to struggle but her body was having nothing to do with her any more and the flames were getting closer and closer. She could already feel the heat on the top of her head, and distantly she wondered if that was her hair she could smell singeing.

Tommy watched what happened from behind the crumbling trunk of one of the dry, papery trees. He was terrified, more terrified than he'd ever been in his life because he knew when the muscle-man with the fiery skull punched his mother that he was going to have to help her. At first he'd been sure that she could vanquish the skull-man and save him and he'd screamed triumphantly when she hit him and made him go back down the bank. But now the skull-man had knocked his mummy out and was dragging her into the path of the flames that turned his skull red hot. He wished that Sally and Dave would come back through the magic door because the skull-man was going to burn his mummy and he wasn't big enough to help her all on his own. Perhaps if he had one of those shining crosses or the Swiss Army knife with the blade that glowed he would get strong enough.

He grasped the bark of the tree and whimpered, knowing that no one was going to come and save him and if he didn't *do* something, the skull-man would burn his mummy and kill her and then he would burn his daddy, too, and then he would come lumbering after him, little Tommy Cousins who'd never hurt anybody. And he would have to run and he *could* run but his legs were too short and too tired for him to stay ahead of the skull-man for very long. And he knew what the skull-man would do to him when he caught him. He would drag him through those flames like he was going to do to his mummy, only he wouldn't do it long enough to kill him, but just enough to fry his skin so it was all black and crispy. Then he would eat him for his supper with those red hot teeth. The skull-man had promised as much, hadn't he?

So he had to do something and do it fast because mummy's hair was getting very close to that roaring yellow fire and soon her face would look like the skull-man's, too. So he had to do something. There was to be no cowering in your cage with your eyes covered when the Big Giant came near now.

Stepping out from behind the tree took a lot of courage and effort and his legs felt rubbery and weak and they wanted to bear him away through the woods so that he was too far for the skull-man to ever catch up, but he forced himself towards his mother's Marks & Spencer carrier bag. She had kept it close to her since she arrived so there must be something important inside; something magical, perhaps, that would make the skull-man go away. Once he'd started to move, some of the fear left him and his legs began to work properly again.

'LET HER GO!' he shouted as he dropped to his knees and skidded to a halt right in front of the carrier bag.

His mother's hair was singeing now. He could smell the acrid stink as she was drawn inexorably nearer to the hissing flames. He thrust his hand inside the bag, not knowing what he would find. His fingers closed around the handle of the Kitchen Devil chef's knife as if they had known it was there all along.

The knife's grip fitted his small hand as if it had been made for him and he withdrew it, glancing at the long triangular blade and the finely honed cutting edge.

Never play with knives! his mother's warning voice rang in his ears. *It'll end in tears if you do. Knives are dangerous. Never touch them, never hold them. You'll cut yourself and have to have stitches and you might even cut your hand right off, so never play with knives. Never never ever!*

And as he ran towards the skull-man, the dusty earth flying beneath his feet he knew why his mother had warned him. She was right: knives *were* dangerous. They were dangerous because when you took a big knife like this one in your hand, it told you to run over and stick it in someone. It sent messages up your arm and into your head and they said: *get angry, get real mad and cut that sucker down because he's hurting your mummy. Slash him and hack at him and pierce that bad man until he's dead!* And the messages took over. They were irresistible and they made you strong and . . .

STICK IT IN YOUR MUMMY!

. . . they made you go crazy because when you had a knife you didn't know what was right and what was wrong and you got thoughts . . .

CUT OUT HER GUTS!

. . . that you couldn't control . . .

SPILL 'EM TO THE FLOOR AND SEE WHAT THEY LOOK LIKE!

. . . and you just wanted to kill your mummy.

Tommy ran towards his mother's back, the big Kitchen Devil held out before him like a lance.

Just before the knife stabbed into her back, Anne moaned.

And Tommy knew he was being manipulated by the Bad Man. The Bogeyman who stalked him through the velvety darkness of his worst dreams.

He didn't think he was going to be able to stop in time. His legs wanted him to run, and the knife wanted him to plunge it into something and he managed to stop his legs, but the ground was wet or frozen or something and he kept on going forward towards his mother. Deep booming laughter rang in his ears but it sounded like it was coming from inside his head.

It was the Bad Man. He was laughing because he knew he'd tricked little Tommy Cousins into stabbing his own mother who loved him at least as much as he loved her and probably more. He was laughing because he knew that Tommy would have to bend his knees and drop to the ground to avoid stabbing her, and the Bad Man had frozen his joints and stuck his fingers to the knife handle.

But in spite of all that, Tommy made his knees bend. They popped and hurt a lot, but they went.

He fell to the ground, rolled and got up again, all in one seamless movement.

He was behind the skull-man now and his mummy had woken up because she was screaming fit to wake the dead. The knife was making his hand tingle now and his arm felt very heavy and incredibly strong. The knife badly wanted him to take it just one step closer to the skull-man so that it could make him put it in the skull-man's back.

Tommy didn't want to hurt anyone. He wasn't allowed to; that had been drummed into him since he was tiny. You could never hurt anyone, no matter how mad you got at them, no matter what they did to you, you weren't supposed to hurt them. Hurting people was spiteful and vicious.

Not even to stop them killing your mummy?

Tommy wasn't sure if it was the knife talking to him, or

someone else. It had a knife-like voice, but it sounded like a grown-up too. A good grown-up.

Tommy still hesitated. Stabbing the skull-man would kill him and didn't you go to hell if you killed someone?

Not this time, the knife whispered. *Have a free go. Put me in him. It's allowed this time.*

Tommy leapt forwards and punched the Kitchen Devil into the skull-man's back. The knife went in easily for a few inches, then it struck bone, glanced off and was nearly ripped from Tommy's hand.

The skull-man screamed and let go of his mother. The hand that didn't have the soldier in it shot around behind him, seeking the blade.

His fingers had closed around it when Tommy yanked it free again and, as it came out, it severed the top joints of two of them.

Tommy expected to see blood, but there was none, just a sticky black substance that coated the knife blade and smelt horrible and a thick purple fluid that dripped from the skull-man's cut fingers.

Then Tommy knew the knife was magic like Dave's Swiss Army knife because it looked alive and had an orange glow on the surface of the metal where there was no black stuff.

The man turned quickly and Tommy darted back, slashing the knife at his grasping hand and missing.

'Hee hoo . . . *for my supper!*' the skull-man said and his voice changed on the last three words. It had the same tone and timbre as the bad thoughts Tommy had thought earlier and it left him in no doubt about what he was up against. It was the voice of his mind, the voice of the giant and the skull-man's voice, all rolled into one. It was the sound of the Bad Man.

'Leave me alone!' Tommy shouted, feinting with the glowing knife.

'GIVE IT UP, YOU LITTLE FUCKER, YOU CAN'T WIN!' the skull-man roared. 'GIVE ME THE KNIFE AND I'LL LET YOU GO! TRY AND FIGHT ME AND I'LL RIP YOUR FACE OFF AND RUB SALT IN YOUR EYES!'

'Go away!' Tommy said uncertainly. He wanted to hand over the knife at once, but it wouldn't let him. Nor would it let him run away.

'I'M A TROLL FOL DE ROL!' the skull-man warned.

Tommy darted forwards and slashed crossways with the knife. The sharp tip bit into the skull-man's shirt and sliced through it as easily as the electric scissors in his mother's work-box would have done. He was shocked to see that he'd also carved a great gash in the man's skin and muscle. The rent was a foot long and it was opening like the petals of a strange purple flower and giving him a glimpse of what lay below. He was so mortified by the man's innards that he didn't realise the gash was opening because the skull-man was moving. He didn't see the swinging fist with the two missing fingertips until it was almost on him.

He dropped to his knees again, but he wasn't quite fast enough and the fist glanced off his nose. His eyes watered and his nose stung as he felt hot blood begin to course down it, but he didn't give up. He was mad now, really mad. He hadn't had a nose bleed since he'd fallen off his trike back in May and that had been an accident. This was on purpose and grown-ups weren't supposed to hit kids hard enough to give them bloody noses – even if they were skull-men. That was *bad*!

He got to his feet, wiping the blood away with the back of his free hand, and squared up to the skull-man.

'I'LL SHOVE THAT KNIFE UP YOUR ARSE IF YOU DON'T HAND IT TO ME NOW!' it yelled.

Suddenly the flame-thrower went out. The skull-man looked at it, his bony bottom jaw dangling in surprise. Grey smoke wafted out of his eye sockets and the collar of his shirt smouldered red. A trickle of purple blood ran from the mangled mass of flesh at his neck.

Now that the constant hissing and roaring had stopped, the silence rang loud in Tommy's ears. Somewhere over on the bank, his mother was sobbing quietly.

'Flame-thrower,' the skull-man's voice said questioningly.

Tommy saw his chance. He darted forward and plunged the

532

knife into the skull-man's chest, right where his heart should be. The knife grated against bone and split it as Tommy forced his weight onto it. Then the glowing blade was sinking right through the skull-man, cleaving his heart in two.

He didn't fall down or turn to dust or anything, but Tommy stepped back, knowing that he'd done what was required of him, knowing that he should leave the knife in place.

The skull-man didn't make a sound. He looked down at the knife and the thick trickle of dark fluid that was running from the wound then he glanced up at Tommy, his blackened empty eye sockets looking confused somehow. Then he turned away from Tommy as if he'd lost interest in the fight and stumbled over towards the doorway.

Sally and Dave will kill you good and proper if you go in there, Tommy thought as the skull-man fumbled with the door handle.

The door opened and the skull-man went through, half turning to close it behind him. For a moment Tommy was looking directly into those evil empty eye sockets and felt frightened again.

'They'll get you!' he called. 'Dave and Sally will get you!'

But after the door had closed he wasn't so sure.

Chapter Twenty
Crossing The Bad Side

'How far d'you think it is?' Sally asked, glancing back over her shoulder at the doorway. They'd been walking for a long time; she'd counted four thousand four hundred and seventy-seven steps and she hadn't started until they'd been going for a while. The doorway was still visible on the horizon behind them, but it was tiny now and dwarfed even further by the immense size of the flat empty plain they were walking across.

'Miles,' Dave said, turning back to look at her. He and Roddy were a few paces ahead of her and walking side by side. Roddy hadn't spoken since they came through into the Bad Side and Sally thought he might be in pain. Her healing hadn't worked properly and his arm had started bleeding again. The blood was seeping from the wound, running down his arm and dripping from his fingertips where it was quickly soaked up by the surface of the ground which seemed to be composed of black cinders. Sally hoped the blood wasn't going to awaken anything that might be slumbering below the surface.

'Don't worry, Sal, we can do it,' Dave said, turning around and walking backwards in an effort to keep pace with Roddy. The ribbon of red light that shone from the eye of his cross danced over her skin, warming her. Dave smiled at her as though he hadn't a care in the world. His eyes shone and she fancied she could see flecks of the beam's clear red in his irises.

'I hope you're right,' she said, looking into the distance and feeling very vulnerable in spite of the cross's power which surged through her with each heartbeat. The three of them seemed so small and insignificant against the vast twilight emptiness that she was beginning to wonder if they could pull it off after all. Fred Purdue's voice rang in her ears, assuring her that she needed the third stone to be able to beat The Claw and she tried – and failed – to push his grating, mocking voice away. It was like a leech on her self-confidence and the more she listened to it the worse she felt. She wondered if The Claw was somehow putting Fred's voice into her mind to sap her strength and she wished Dave would say something to reassure her and drive her doubts away.

'I'm right, Sal, believe me,' Dave said. 'We're going to waltz right up that hill and zap the fucker. We can do it and we *will* do it!'

The hill was more of a small mountain. From this distance it looked like an almost vertically sided column of black rock. Dave had estimated it to be a hundred feet high, but Sally thought it was going to look a good deal taller than that when they got closer.

On top of the mountain there was a tall, slender structure like a lighthouse or a castle tower which shone a brilliant white that hurt your eyes. This was evidently Hell Central – The Claw's home. It was the only feature on the flat burnt-black landscape and they headed towards it. The compass confirmed what Sally was already sure of: this was where they had to go.

'Are you tired?' Dave asked, polishing the lenses of his glasses on the front of his grimy tee shirt. He had dropped back to walk beside her and she felt much better just through having him nearby.

'No, just scared,' she told him. 'Are you?'

Dave grinned. 'I'm terrified,' he said, 'and I keep hearing little voices telling me I can't do it. They whisper in my ears or inside my head or something. That's good.'

She took his arm and squeezed it. 'I keep hearing Fred Purdue saying I can't do it and I think I'm starting to believe him. I hate it. It scares me so. Why is it good?'

'Because it means we've got the fucker worried. It wants to suck the fight out of us before we even get near it. It wants us scared, Sal. It wants us shaking in our shoes. Look, if it was that good, it would have killed us already. We're on its home territory now and we're still alive. I'm not saying we're invulnerable or anything, but it can't kill us easily or it would already have done it. These crosses might only be small, but they're powerful, Sal, believe me. It's frightened, Sal, and that's why it's whispering to us. It wants us to be frightened, too.'

Sally shook her head. 'It might just be toying with us like a cat does with a mouse. What if it's just letting us know that it's aware we're coming and it's ready for us?'

'Then we lose, Sal,' Dave said, pulling her around and kissing her hard. He drew back and looked at her crestfallen face, still grinning, 'What's up, Sal? We've all got to die sooner or later. If we die doing this it's going to be worthwhile. *If* we *do* die. I don't think we will. And whatever happens, we're not going to give up without a fight, are we? I'm gonna rip the balls off that fucker before I go, even if it's the last thing I do.'

'And it very likely will be,' Sally said, but Fred's voice was fading and her confidence was returning. Perhaps she would rip one of The Claw's balls off herself. If it had balls, that was.

'I feel sick,' Roddy said, stopping. 'And my arm hurts like fuckery. Fix it for me.' He turned around and held out his arm in front of him.

'I don't think it'll work here,' Sally said. 'It didn't work on Dave under the town centre and that was a part of the Bad Side.'

Roddy came towards them, glowering. 'Fix it, slut!' he shouted, his face contorted with rage. His other ear was growing mould now and his eyes looked deep and vacant.

'Shut up, Roddy,' Dave said, placing himself between Roddy and Sally.

'FIX IT!' Roddy screamed, his eyes rolling up so that Dave could see their whites. Roddy took two paces forward then bent his head down so that they were almost nose to nose. He smelt of sour sweat and his breath was ripe. His eyes were glassy and black, the pupils – which had been pinpricks when Dave last looked at them – were now so big that only a slender band of colour showed around them.

'Get out of my way,' he growled and Dave got a good look at his even white teeth and the coating on his tongue which may or may not have been more of the green-black mould growth.

'Leave off, Roddy,' Dave said almost casually.

'Make her fix me or I'll bust her arm, then I'll bust you,' Roddy said, and before Dave could react, he had reached around his body and grabbed Sally's wrist.

Sally squealed.

Dave balled his fist and punched. Roddy fell down onto the cinders clutching his stomach.

That's it, I did it! Dave's mind yelled. *I punched Roddy Johnson and he fell down! Give that man a prize! Send a postcard home*!

He stepped back, pushing Sally away from Roddy's writhing body. Roddy was dangerous even when he was on the floor.

But Roddy didn't strike out with that smooth snake-like snap that Dave expected. He got up to a crouching position and wrapped his arms around his knees. His face had lost all its remaining colour and there were tears in his eyes. The blood that oozed from his arm began to stain his jeans. 'Sorry, man, I'm sorry. Help me,' he moaned. 'Just help me.'

'It's okay,' Sally said, and crouched beside him, taking his damaged arm between her hands and closing her eyes.

Roddy sat still, his shoulders rising and falling jerkily as he sobbed.

Five minutes later Sally stood up. Roddy's face was buried in his knees and he didn't seem to notice she'd left him. Sally glanced at Dave and shook her head. 'It doesn't work here,' she said.

'Foureyes, help me, man,' Roddy said looking up at Dave with pleading eyes.

This isn't the Roddy Johnson we know and love, Dave thought. *This is more than just the pain in his arm, that's for sure. This is to do with the old bloodstains on his jeans and the mould stuff growing on him*.

'Is it just your arm? Or is it something else?' Dave asked suspiciously.

Roddy, still sitting on the black ground, wiped the tears from the corners of his eyes. 'Something happened, Foureyes. Help me,' he said.

'What happened?' Dave said looking at the dried blood on the front of Roddy's shirt. 'You didn't cut yourself with your knife, did you? You cut someone else with it. Who was it? Come on, tell me!'

Roddy shook his head. 'I don't remember what happened. A k-k-kid. I cut a kid. Oh, Sandy! Where's Sandy! I love her, man. Get her back for me.'

'What kid? Did you kill him?' Dave demanded.

'Something happened. I don't know what it was. Then there was this kid. I got mad because . . . because . . . Then the kid was dead. Oh Sandy, I can't hear her any more.'

Sally took Dave's hand. 'There was a kid under the car park that got away. Tommy said he'd gone to the railway station to get a policeman. Looks like he met Roddy first.'

'You killed a kid?' Dave said, horrified. 'Jesus, Roddy, you make me sick.' But his mind wasn't on Roddy the murderer, however terrible the crime might have been. His mind was on Roddy the psychic who could hear voices. Roddy the hard-case who cocked his ear when his vanished sister spoke to him.

'I . . . I . . . I dunno what happened. Sandy. I gotta get Sandy. She promised.'

'What do you mean, she promised?' Dave said. 'Has Sandy been talking to you?'

Roddy cringed as if he was going to be whipped. 'I dunno – I . . . Yes, man, yes. She talked to me. She told me to get her back. She said I got to take her the crosses and we can be together. I dunno what's happening man. I'm going nutty. But I love Sandy. She's all I got. Help me, man. She was in my head and now she's gone and all I can hear is screaming. Screaming, screaming and it's driving me mad. You gotta give me them crosses and I can rescue her.'

Dave sighed and shook his head. 'It wasn't Sandy talking, Roddy, it was The Claw. Did it make you kill the kid?'

'No . . . yes . . . I dunno. I want her, Foureyes. I got to get her home. I love her, man.'

'It got to him,' Dave told Sally. 'It got to him and we didn't know. It made him a murderer, made him belong to it. And we brought him right along with us.'

'You were going to kill us before we get there, weren't you?' he shouted at Roddy. 'You were going to take the crosses off us and take them to Sandy, weren't you? Didn't she tell you to let us carry them for you until we were close? Didn't she tell you that you could kill us then if you wanted to, or do what you liked to us?' He glared at Sally. 'Jesus, he probably would have knifed me like he did that kid, and raped you, Sal. Then he would have killed you, too, and taken the crosses to The Claw.'

'What are we going to do?' Sally said.

'What went wrong?' Dave asked Roddy. 'Why did you give up?'

'Because she's gone and there's screaming, Foureyes,' Roddy moaned. 'And I wouldn't kill you. I didn't want to.'

'Oh yeah, and why was that?' Dave said, wondering why he didn't feel extreme hatred for the man, wondering why his righteous rage was leaving him.

Roddy got slowly to his feet and examined the rent in his arm so that he didn't have to look Dave in the eye. 'Because I like you, Foureyes,' he said, glancing up at Dave and shaking his head.

'Tell me another,' Dave said, but for some reason he believed Roddy and felt absurdly flattered.

'What are you gonna do?' Roddy said.

Dave looked at Sally, then at Roddy. 'Take you with us,' he said, knowing it was right to say it and that Sally agreed, but not knowing why. 'Try and get your sister back, if she's up there. What else *can* we do?'

'You could kill me,' Roddy said.

Dave shook his head. 'We only came to kill The Claw,' he said.

Roddy groped in his trouser pocket and took out his flick-knife. He looked at it for a moment and then offered it to Dave.

Dave glanced at Sally who shook her head. Roddy had to stay alive and go with them and he had to keep the knife, too. Dave just hoped that his intuition was coming via the Good Side and not The Claw. 'Keep it,' he said. 'Just don't use it on us.'

'I think I'm gonna die, Foureyes,' Roddy said, smiling sickly. 'There's something gone wrong inside of me.'

'You'll be okay,' Dave said, wondering how he could feel this strange kind of companionship with a guy who killed kids. 'When we get out of here you'll be okay.'

'Give me the knife,' Sally said to Roddy. 'I'll cut your shirt and bandage your arm.'

'Cut my balls off probably,' Roddy said ruefully, but he handed her the flick-knife anyway.

Sally weighed it in the palm of her hand, tossing it up slightly and catching it again like an expert. The combination of the knife and the crazy look that had been in her eyes since her cross lit up worried Dave a little and he thought for a second that she might just do what Roddy had predicted. She threw the knife up, caught it, pressed the button and slipped her hand towards Roddy's throat as the blade sprung out.

'Sal,' Dave said, but the blade had stopped moving a fraction of an inch in front of Roddy's skin and Sally was chuckling. Roddy looked even sicker.

'Just wondered what it would feel like,' Sally said innocently. She turned Roddy around, took hold of his shirt and ran the knife down it in a dead straight line.

Dave watched Sally as she attended to Roddy and finally tied an improvised bandage around his cut arm. He noticed that she had been very careful not to touch Roddy's skin during the operation and he was glad because Roddy's mould growth seemed to be spreading; when he turned and started walking again, his shirt opened at the back where Sally had cut it. The dark green substance now covered most of his spine and was sending out tendrils along the lines of his muscles and ribs.

After another eight thousand steps through the dull, empty cinder plains it began to get cold. The column of rock was much

540

taller than Dave had originally thought, but the sides didn't look quite so steep now. There would be no walking straight up the mountainside, though, that was for sure. What looked like a slender path spiralled up around it. This, apparently, was going to be the only way up. Dave knew they would be very exposed during the climb; the path was narrow and the drop too sheer to survive if something happened to make them fall off. And something probably would happen. He began to doubt the wisdom of letting Roddy come with them. The Bad Side seemed as uninhabited as the Limbo Side, but who was to say that Roddy wouldn't suddenly react to something his sister's voice told him to do when they were halfway up?

Sally coughed, breaking into his private worries.

'Is it the dust?' Dave asked her.

She shook her head. 'It's the smell. Haven't you noticed it?'

Dave sniffed and nodded his head. 'Yeah, but it's faint. I thought it was Roddy. He stinks now,' he whispered, looking at Roddy's infected back. Roddy seemed to have got a second wind and was striding along about twenty yards in front of them, his boots crunching on the cinder ground. He hadn't spoken since Sally bandaged his arm, and the mould was still growing on his ears and his back, but Dave thought he'd recovered somewhat because the last time he had looked around he had seemed like the old Roddy again.

'It's not him,' Sally said. 'I can smell him. It's another smell. It's vague, but it hangs in the air all the time. It's like a combination of burnt coal and something rotting. I catch a blast of it every so often and it makes me want to throw up.'

'Corruption,' Dave said. 'It's the smell of the Bad Side.'

Sally coughed again, long and hard. 'I hope I haven't caught anything,' she said when it had subsided.

'Nah,' Dave said, shaking his head, but he knew what she was thinking. She'd touched Roddy and Roddy had mould growing all over him and she might have breathed in some of the spores or germs or whatever caused the stuff to grow.

'If this is hell – or whatever you want to call it – where are all the tormented souls?' Sally said, changing the subject.

'Dunno,' Dave said. 'I imagine that what we've got here – this big empty plain and the column of rock and the thing on top – is just a physical representation of the *real* hell. I think the real hell is The Knowledge. Bad Eddie's Knowledge. It wasn't nice in there. There were good things in it, but everything was rotten and nasty and it was sort of . . .'

'Desolate,' Sally said. 'Loveless and cruel. Tinged with evil and hatred.'

'Sounds like hell to me,' Dave said, nodding.

'Mile,' Roddy shouted back to them. 'Nearly there.' His breath bloomed in the cold air when he spoke.

'It's moving away from us, isn't it?' Dave said to Sally. They seemed to have been walking forever and one of the soles on his Hi-Tecs had come loose at the heel. Small pieces of cinder were finding their way in through the gap and he kept having to stop to shake them out again. His feet felt raw and blistered, so God only knew how Sally's bare ones were managing to stand the pace. He stole a look at them. They were blackened with the cinders, but otherwise looked okay. Some of her toenails still had bits of red varnish on them. He hoped that the badness of this place wouldn't creep into her through her unprotected soles.

She shook her head. 'We're getting close. I can tell because I'm getting more frightened and it's getting colder.'

Dave looked up at the rock and found he could see the structure on top more clearly now (although the outline was still blurred by its brightness). It was a smooth-sided obelisk that looked rather like an upended cigar tube. There didn't seem to be any doors or windows in it, but perhaps there were and he just couldn't see them because of the light. The ground surrounding the base of the mountain shone, somehow reflecting its light.

It was getting very cold now, and the next time he looked at Sally, she was walking with her arms folded across her chest. This, he knew, was what women did when they became aware that their nipples were erect. Even here where there was no one to look at her except him and Roddy this unconscious ritual was being observed.

542

He felt a sudden flush of love for Sally and realised then that he was never likely to want anyone more than he wanted her now. He stopped walking, caught her arm and pulled her to him, kissing her hard.

'What was that for?' she asked when he broke away.

He glanced over at the towering mountain. Roddy was more than two hundred yards in front of them now, still striding steadily along. Apparently he hadn't noticed they were no longer following.

'Because I love you,' Dave said. 'I just wanted you to know that whatever happens up there, I still love you.'

'It's the cross,' Sally said, smiling. 'It makes you randy. Mr Hard-On.' She pushed her hips against him. 'If we ever get out of here I'll show you a real good time.'

'Why don't you show me one now, just in case?'

'Here?' Sally said sounding shocked, but looking as if she was giving the matter some serious consideration.

'Here,' Dave said. 'It'd be better than the mile high club. Not many people can say they've had it off on the Bad Side. You'll be able to tell your grandchildren.'

Sally laughed and pushed him away. 'When we get out,' she said. 'So make sure you get us out. Come on, Roddy's getting away.'

They tramped through the black cinders after Roddy, neither of them feeling quite as frightened as before.

The ice spread out from the base of the steep mountain for more than a mile, or so Dave estimated. The ice floe was what he'd seen reflecting the tower's light. It was two feet thick and they had to step up onto it where it met the black cinders. Roddy was already on the ice and a good two hundred yards ahead of them.

'Can you?' Dave said, looking at Sally's bare feet.

'You bet your sweet ass,' Sally said, leaping nimbly up onto the floe. The ice crackled.

'It's a mile, Sal, probably more. Then we have to climb the mountain. What about frostbite and stuff?'

'My feet aren't cold,' Sally said. 'Don't worry.' She held

up one of her feet for him to look at. It had already gone blue.

'I dunno, maybe you ought to wait here for us,' Dave said. 'I don't want you losing your feet or anything.'

'I was meant to come dressed like this, and I've got this far so it must have been right, mustn't it? The soles of my feet are hard as nails and they don't feel cold, so quit griping and come on!'

'Okay, boss,' Dave said, climbing up. What was left of the soles of his Hi-Tecs was no match for the ice. The cold hit his feet instantly, numbing them and turning his toes into ten marbles.

'I don't know about your feet, Sal, it's freezing my toes off already,' he said, hopping from foot to foot. 'I don't think I can stand this for very long.'

'Think hot,' Sally said. 'Then follow me!'

Sally began to run, moving quickly and easily across the ice. Dave swore, then fell in behind her, noticing how the backs of her legs and the small of her tanned back had broken out in goosebumps.

The freezing air was starting to hurt his lungs long before they caught up with Roddy. When they soared past him, running close together in Indian file, his legs were starting to ache and he was wondering how Sally was managing it. Then he closed his eyes, consigned the pain and the cold to the back of his mind, and let his legs fall into the rhythm that Sally seemed so certain of. He blanked his mind out and tried to *become* Sally. After a while the agony began to fade and the cool air started to feel good in his lungs. He became aware of his heart thumping steadily in his chest and the blood powering around his arteries to his muscles, but he was no longer sure if it was him or Sally or both of them he was feeling. Whatever it was, it was *good* and he was safe and secure, strong and vibrant and he wanted it to go on for ever. The ice was cold under his bare feet, but it didn't hurt. The air chilled his naked midriff but not too deeply. There was no weight on his back any more – the jiggling rucksack had vanished. And he could feel the power of the cross surging through him just as it was supposed to. Except that it wasn't *his* red power shaking his body as its heat blasted through him. It was a cooler, more controlled flow; one that filled you without hurting you, tingling down nerve paths rather than searing through muscle. It was different to the power from his cross and it wasn't as raw and savage, but it was just as good and it made you strong in other ways.

'How was that?'

Dave realised that the running had finished. He felt dizzy for a moment, then he was being torn away from his safety with a noise that felt, rather than sounded, like a velcro fastener ripping undone. There was an instant when he just didn't seem to exist any more, then he was thudded back into his body and he felt as though someone had clipped him around the head with a baseball bat. He was surprised to find that he was panting hard and that his mouth was dry and coppery tasting. His ears sang and his back was sore where the bottom rucksack stay had jarred it. His head felt as if it would split apart each time he drew a breath.

Sally was standing in front of him, grinning from ear to ear. She didn't look at all out of breath.

'Christ, Sal, what happened?' he panted.

'I had a passenger for a while,' she said. 'I liked it. It was nice.' She pulled him to her and kissed his neck. He cuddled her, panting hard and looking over her shoulder at the towering column of rock. Now they were here it looked more like six hundred feet high than his original estimate of a hundred.

They were at the base of the column, standing on a flat platform which had been hewn from the mountain itself. It looked rather like a jetty. The way upward started at the back of the platform. The path was narrow and steep, but it wasn't sheeted with ice as Dave had feared.

The Claw wasn't going to make it too difficult for them, was it? It wanted them up there with the crosses. He knew then that he needn't have worried that Roddy might push them over the edge of the path. He wouldn't do it unless he went independently mad; The Claw wasn't going to make him do it. Why should it when they were taking the crosses up themselves?

He let go of Sally and turned to face the direction they'd come from. The ice field was six feet below where they were standing and ran out into the distance in a vast frozen sea. The light from the tower reflected off it making it burn like the Arctic when the sun shone. The black speck slowly approaching them across the shining ice was Roddy. He looked very small out there on his own and Dave felt a moment of compassion for him.

'How did we get up here, Sal?' he asked looking down at the ice. There were no steps down.

'We jumped.'

'In one go? Both of us?'

'I did the jumping. You just tagged along,' she said happily.

'What about Roddy?'

'We went past him. I don't think he noticed,' she said, taking his hand.

'No, I meant, should we wait for him or go on ahead?'

'We'll wait. I think he has to come, too.'

Dave frowned. 'Why?'

'I don't know. He just does. Don't worry about it, Davey. Thinking won't get you anywhere. Just do what feels right.'

Dave nodded and looked out past Roddy, past the distant edge of the empty ice to where the cinders started. There didn't seem to be any curvature to this place; no apparent horizon, but he could no longer see the doorway they had come through. It had vanished in the immensity of the black plain which seemed to go on forever.

'What was that?' he said suddenly.

'What?' Sally asked. 'I didn't see anything.'

Dave shook his head. 'Just my eyes playing tricks, I s'pose. Thought I saw something glint in the distance.'

'I didn't see it,' Sally said. 'And my eyesight is better than yours, Foureyes.'

'Don't you start, too,' he said.

They held each other close for warmth while they waited for Roddy. Although there was no ice on the mountain, the air was extremely cold and Dave didn't expect it to get any warmer. The Claw *was* cold. He watched Roddy and thought about his birthday (which seemed like an age ago) and the frosted belt

546

loop on his slimfit jeans after The Claw came out of the toilet pan and grabbed him.

And he hoped the crosses were big enough for the job.

Roddy looked terrible. He leapt at the side of the jetty and hauled himself up by the power of his bulging arms. Dave saw how the patch of mould on his bicep had spread, but it wasn't until Sally gasped that he realised just how awful Roddy looked.

The dark green mould must have been sensitive to nerves – entropic, Dave thought the technical term was – because it had fanned out in needle sharp lines across Roddy's neck and face, following the paths of his nerves so that he looked like a ghoulish road map. His eyes had no iris at all now – just huge, black pupils and in spite of the cold he was sweating profusely.

'Hiya, cocksuckers,' he said, getting to his feet. Somewhere out there he'd pissed himself. The urine had frozen down the left leg of his jeans and then cracked with his movements. Tiny pieces of it clung around the damp patch. The bandage that Sally had applied to his arm had come undone and dangled almost to his feet. The gaping wound in his forearm was plugged with the mould which had now taken on a brown tinge. Dave wondered if it was living on his blood.

'I'm going up first,' Roddy said, smiling. His teeth were stained green and mould tracers filled the cracks in his lips.

'Okay, Roddy,' Dave said, stepping aside because he really didn't want Roddy to come anywhere near either him or Sally. He thought he might scream if Roddy touched him.

'You follow *me*!' Roddy shouted, his huge black eyes glittering dangerously.

'Sure, sure Roddy. You lead,' Dave said, unable to take his eyes from the split that formed in Roddy's hollow left cheek when he shouted. The mould was right inside Roddy and it was fast. Dave watched it boiling deep in the split. It quickly bubbled to the surface and started to solidify. It formed a light green, wet-looking membrane over the gash, then hardened and changed colour. Roddy didn't seem to notice.

547

Sally moaned softly.

'No tricks, cocksuckers,' Roddy said, grinning at Dave then leering at Sally. His voice seemed to have deepened to a booming bass and his other cheek cracked open when he spoke.

'No tricks,' Dave replied as Roddy strode past him, his torn shirt flapping open at the back. The smell was terrible.

They followed Roddy up the steep path, Dave first and Sally behind. Dave kept his eyes on the path because it was better than looking at Roddy's exposed back. Roddy didn't have any skin on his back any more; it was now composed entirely of shiny green-black mould that glistened as he moved.

Dave didn't know how frightened of heights he was until they were halfway up the black mountain. Here, the sides narrowed until they were almost vertical. The rough pathway was about two feet wide and you had to concentrate on where you were putting your feet because the outer edge was crumbling and there was nothing between it and a three hundred foot drop to the mountain's base. Dave had glanced over once or twice, but he was determined he wouldn't do it again because looking over made your balance vanish and somehow drew your feet towards the edge.

So he ignored the panoramic views of the desolate Bad Side and trudged onwards, looking down at the rough black path because if he looked ahead of him he could see Roddy's mouldy skin stretching across his back as he walked steadily up the steep incline.

The path spiralled up the column of rock but from this point the sides were too sheer to look down on the section below. The view across the Bad Side was identical wherever you looked from and after a few more circuits Dave lost his sense of direction. He worried about this for a while and wished they'd left a marker on the jetty above the ice. There might be more jetties each with its own spiral path upwards, and if they came down the wrong one, they might easily set off in the wrong direction.

Behind him he could hear Sally's measured breathing and her bare feet padding on the cold rock. Her breathing was regular and not as fast as his own, but it had a harsher edge. From time to time she coughed, but Dave preferred not to think about what might be going on inside her lungs. She had been through a lot – much more than he had – and the sheer physical exertion was going to take its toll sooner or later. And she had used the power of her cross far more often than he had. Dave didn't know if that was a good thing or not. There might be side effects caused by its use for all they knew. He just hoped she could hold herself together until this was all over. It wouldn't be long now.

'Nearly up, aren't we?' Sally panted.

'My legs sincerely hope you're right,' Dave replied. 'And my thigh muscles would like you to explain exactly why it is you're trying to make me wear them out before they're twenty years old. They're rapidly approaching middle age now. How's your cough?'

There was a pause while Sally charged her lungs up enough to speak. 'Getting better,' she said. 'Higher we go better they feel.'

'You sure? This cold air is making my lungs hurt,' he gasped.

'Don't . . . don't worry about me Davey . . . I'll live . . . till I'm ninety.'

Dave hoped she was right. Whatever the Big Good force was doing for them, it certainly didn't have their physical condition as its first priority. It hadn't exactly gone out of its way to stop them being damaged, had it?

No, Dave, but it's getting you up this mountain. You couldn't have done it without some help, could you? You're not as fit and strong as Roddy. And it lets you heal yourself, and I seem to remember the old boy and his dog getting you out of a fix a while ago. I think it's helped all it can, and the rules are different over here, aren't they? That's why it couldn't do the job on its own. That's why it needed you and Sal, isn't it?

'Yeah, okay,' he muttered. He was in no condition to argue with himself right now.

'What?' Sally asked.

'Just thinking aloud,' he said.

'I think we're nearly up,' Sally said. 'The path isn't as steep now.'

Roddy must have heard her because he speeded up then. Dave tried to increase his pace to keep Roddy in sight, but his legs were working as fast as they intended to go. In less than thirty seconds, Roddy had rounded the bend and disappeared from view.

'Can't catch him up,' Dave panted. 'Too fast.'

He wanted to stop and discuss the matter with Sally, but besides the pain in his legs and back and the raw agony in his lungs, the fear was growing in the pit of his stomach and he knew if he stopped he was going to have a lot of trouble getting started again.

'Don't . . . try,' Sally said.

Ambush, Dave wanted to say. *He's going to get to the top and ambush us; rip our crosses off and push us over the edge.* But he couldn't manage even a short speech and Sally had probably had those thoughts, too. If she wanted to keep going, then it must be right to do it.

There were two more – quite flat – circuits before the path ended. Steps ran up the final six feet or so of the mountain. Dave stopped at the bottom although his thigh muscles kept on trying to jerk his feet from the ground. He sat down heavily on the bottom step and watched Sally as she came up the final few yards, the green light from her cross's eye dancing on the ground before her.

'I'm knackered,' Sally said, sitting down beside him and immediately starting a coughing fit.

Dave put his arm around her cool shoulders and pulled her to him. 'You're going to be okay,' he said.

She smiled at him then and he knew he was right. Sally *was* going to be okay. He could tell by her sparkling emerald-shot eyes. The cough wasn't going to finish her off at all.

'It's going away,' she said, tapping her chest. 'It tried to stop me getting up here, but it's going away now.'

'What was it, Sal?'

'The Claw, I s'pose. I think it put some kind of a hex on my lungs. It wants to split us up. Or at second best it wants us to wait until it's too late. I thought I was going to die, Dave. It hurt terribly. I thought my lungs were going to come bubbling out of my mouth, but then I realised there wasn't anything wrong with me at all. It was being done to me. I fought it. I fought it all the way across the ice, and all the way up here. I didn't say anything to you about it because you would have wanted me to stop. Anyway, I've beaten it now and I feel good again. It's worried Dave. It's frightened of us. I can *feel* it.'

'But it's stronger up here, isn't it? Our crosses are on but I don't feel like I've got any advantage over it any more. It's like it's sucking the extra energy away somehow. I don't feel as strong as I did.'

She shook her head. 'Neither do I. I don't know whether it's illusion or if it's real but even so, I still think we can do it. I really do.'

He looked behind him then, up the steps to where the tall shining tower stood. The brilliance was blinding. He glanced out over the blasted landscape of the Bad Side once more, then he stood up and took the Swiss Army knife from his jeans pocket and opened the big blade. The blade glowed a dull orange colour and looked hot. A slight electrical tingle ran through Dave's hand and into his arm.

Sally got up. Her eyes sparkled and there was a grin on her face that had a kind of jolly malevolence. She looked as if she was capable of dismantling the Empire State building with her bare hands then trashing King Kong if he happened to be on top.

'I'm ready to go. Are you?' she said.

'As ready as I'll ever be,' Dave replied.

They walked up the steps side by side.

Chapter Twenty One
Facing The Claw

The ice started three steps from the top. They could already see the flat, circular plateau of the mountain top as they walked up the final three steps, the thick, slippery ice freezing their feet.

In Dave's pocket, the compass needle started to spin and batter at the glass. He could feel the vibrations against his hip but, for some reason, this time there was no noise.

The mountain top was circular and about fifty feet in diameter. The tower's base took up about half the area and the rest was flat and empty and sheeted with translucent ice that flared with its own inner light. By the time they'd reached the plateau, Dave had already observed that, if you screwed your eyes up against the powerful white light, you could see right down through the ice to the surface of the rock. Writing and symbols were engraved in it, but somehow the words were alive. The markings were in perpetual motion, swirling and swarming, forming words and sentences, then rearranging themselves into further geometric patterns which spun and fragmented again.

The tower itself was tubular and seamless, and coated in thick ice. But *this* ice – or perhaps the very material of the structure itself – shone with a brilliance that made your retinas scream for mercy. You could still feel the light blasting your eyes even if you closed them and the outline of the tower could be seen through the flesh of your eyelids. There were no windows and no doors in the tower.

'Roddy's not here,' Sally said. By the time her voice reached Dave's ears it had been stretched, sliced and pasted together again by the energy of the light which hung heavily in the air like a living thing. She sounded like a baritone Minnie Mouse.

Dave took her arm. 'Where's he gone?' he said and the sound-waves from his own voice battered his eardrums and the meaning of the words was lost.

Don't talk, think, Sally's voice rang in his head. *I've got a feeling that it can target you from your voice. Just think things to me. I can hear them.*

That's fucking weird, Sal, he thought. *What are we going to do?*

We go in. It's in there, isn't it? This is what it's all been about.

The freezing air felt savage on Dave's exposed face and arms. Sally's hair and eyebrows had already taken on a coating of frost which glittered in the intense light like a mantle of tiny stars.

But where's Roddy? Dave thought.

Inside. Gone. It doesn't really matter, does it? Sally replied.

Yes, it does matter. It matters a lot because . . .

Because what? Hurry up, Dave, the feeling is going from my fingers and toes.

Dave shook his head. He almost had it then, but it had vanished. Whatever significance Roddy's disappearance had, there was nothing they could do about it now. They had to move – and do it quickly because they wouldn't be able to survive here for long.

We're a stone short, Sally thought. *Fred Purdue said we couldn't kill it with a stone missing and so did The Claw, in the Wimpy. It taunted me, said we couldn't win.* Then she looked guiltily at Dave. She had forgotten about the telepathy; this thought was meant to be private.

What'd you say? Dave asked, pretending he hadn't heard. But he had caught the thought with crystal clarity, and he had experienced Sally's deepest, darkest worries and fears. He hoped they were misplaced. Earlier he'd had the same thoughts but he'd driven them away. It was true that the magical number over here seemed to be three, but since there was no place in the pair of crosses for the third stone to have fitted he'd convinced himself that this was going to be an exception.

I said we can do it, Sally replied bravely.

How do we get in? Dave thought to her. *There's no door. What about round the back?*

He took her cold hand and they skirted the base of the tower, the words and pictures beneath the ice whirling and changing under their feet. The sides and back of the tower and plateau were identical. There was no trace of Roddy ever having been there.

She shook her head and wiped the frost from her eyelashes. *No doors anywhere here. Waste of time looking. Maybe we ought to knock three times like on the doorway in the park.*

Or in the giant's larder, Dave added. *Come on then.*

They walked right up to the tower, shielding their eyes from the intense light with their hands. This close, there was a sharp smell of ozone in the air and they could feel the ice forming rapidly on their skin.

Who is going to do the honours? Dave asked, knowing he was going to have to touch the tower sooner or later, but really not wanting to.

You are, Sally told him.

It won't burn my hand off or anything, will it? he thought, but he was talking to himself this time.

He clenched his left hand, glanced at Sally and then struck at the tower. There was little resistance. His fist vanished into its surface and a sensation of incredible cold shot up the inside of his arm. He could feel the blood inside beginning to solidify and the muscles and tendons becoming brittle. He withdrew his arm quickly, fully expecting it to be frozen solid.

The pain stopped as soon as his hand was clear of the tower and, apart from a thin coating of ice his arm looked and felt normal. He flexed his muscles just to be sure he wasn't paralysed. The ice cracked and fell away. His cold skin had a bluish tinge to it now and the scar where the moth had bitten him shone an ugly purple.

We'll have to walk through, he thought to Sally. *I don't think it will stop us. Roddy might be frozen in the wall somewhere but we can get through. It hurts and it's very cold, but we can go inside.*

Hold my hand, Sally said.

He took her hand and together they walked through the substance of the tower wall. The one step it took them to pass through the wall seemed to last for ever and the penetrating cold passed through their bodies like a guillotine blade. Chill fingers seemed to search along nerve paths, probe arteries, crush muscle. Dave's heart spasmed momentarily as the probing cold touched it.

Then they were inside, gasping for breath with aching lungs. Shards of ice scattered across the smooth floor ahead of them.

'Oh my God,' Sally gasped.

The room was circular and huge, the floorspace perhaps twice the area it should have been judging from the size of the exterior. The ice floor was mirror flat and crystal clear. The same letters and patterns moved beneath it, but in here the jumbled words seemed to have a power and logic.

Magic words, Dave thought fleetingly as he looked around the room.

The curved wall behind him was composed of the same shining substance as the outside, but the far side of the room – over there behind the stone slabs with the bodies on – was made from The Knowledge. This was the base of The Knowledge, where it was rooted; he knew that without having to think about it. The wall was totally black. No light was reflected from it at all, but Dave could see tendrils of rainbow light drifting towards it from the inert bodies on the slabs, curling laterally like cigarette smoke. But what had shocked Sally stood perhaps twenty feet away from them, in the centre of the room.

There was Roddy, frozen in his fighter's stance, legs apart, one hand held high with the flick-knife extended, the other palm open and raised ready to block. Both his arms were glossy black with the mould and it had formed on his face in the rough outline of a hand as though someone's inky fingers had slapped his cheek.

And in front of him stood The Claw, mimicking his pose.

Not just the arm and hand with the cruel ebony nails this time, but the whole beast.

It was much worse than Dave had imagined – and lately his mind had conjured up some fearsome images of how The Claw might look.

It towered over Roddy, standing perhaps eight feet tall. It was thin and had tight, shiny black skin stretched like latex across its sinewy parody of a human frame. Its arms and legs were long and spindly, but Dave could see the muscle and tendons taut beneath the skin and knew it would be strong enough to crush his skull one-handed. The long, sharp ebony nails curved from its fingers and its toes like twenty cut-throat razors.

But its *head*!

It looked too large to be supported by the long slender neck, even if there were tendons like ropes bulging beneath the skin to support it. The head was almost egg-shaped at the back and sides, but it narrowed down to a long sharp snout that might have been dog-like if it had been capped with a nose. Its eyes were huge flat almonds which hung beneath a prominent bony brow and had red irises, dull whites and yellow pinpricks for pupils. Its lower jaw hung open and the big white teeth – hooked and pointing inwards like those of a shark – glistened wetly.

It looked infinitely evil and infinitely powerful, but it was as unmoving as Roddy.

It's frozen, too, Sally's astonished voice said in Dave's mind as she peered at it from between her fingers.

Must have been Roddy, Dave thought back. *He must have done something*. His heart leapt. Perhaps they were going to manage this after all.

Quick! Over here! Sally said, taking his arm again, and dragging him across the ice floor towards the semi-circle of stone slabs.

There were twenty-seven of them, all but three with an ice-covered frozen body lying on top.

Ours, Dave thought, as Sally dragged him past the three empty slabs. *These were ours. We would have completed the quota if Roddy hadn't somehow stopped The Claw.*

It's getting power or energy or something from them, Sally said, glancing at the woven strands of light which flowed from the bodies to the blackness. *It's drawing the life out of them and using it for itself. It's making itself stronger.*

They're dead, Sal, Dave said as they stopped in front of the first slab. It contained a girl about Sally's age. She was encased in at least six inches of clear ice. Bands of blue and red light shone from her head and belly, out of the ice, and into the black wall behind her. *They're buried in ice from head to toe. They can't possibly still be alive in there: they can't breathe, for Christ's sake!*

Sally turned and glared at him. Her eyes shone. *They aren't dead. We can take them out of here. We can wake them up again! We can! Judy and Phil are in here somewhere, don't you want to try and get them out?*

How? Dave said, shaking his head. His mind was whirling.

Like this! Sally's voice shouted inside his brain. Before he could move, she had punched the ice with her right hand. It shattered and chunks fell away from the girl on the slab. Dave brushed the ice away, but the girl was cold, her skin had a blue tinge and she had no heartbeat or respiration. The bands of light had winked out when the ice broke.

She's dead, Sal, he thought, leaning over and looking into the girl's empty face. There was no reply except a grunt of exertion as Sally punched the next block of ice.

Sally seemed to be in a fury. Her eyes blazed as she moved from one body to the next, and she didn't answer his mental calls for her to stop. Right or wrong, there was no preventing her so Dave followed her along the row, clearing the ice from the bodies and wondering what had possessed her.

By the fifteenth slab, the ice was stained with blood from Sally's cut knuckles. By the twentieth, he had caught her up. Her eyes were wild and her hand was dripping blood onto the smooth floor. Beneath the ice, intricate circular patterns spread like ripples at the fall of each drop of blood.

There were tears in Sally's eyes now, but a look of grim determination was on her face.

We've got to do it, she thought to him. *Even if we can't make them alive again, we have to do it. We're cutting off its energy by doing it.*

Let me finish it then, Dave told her. *You're hurt.*

She nodded, wiped her knuckles on her shirt and inspected the broken skin.

Dave balled his fist and hit the next block of ice. He expected to feel pain, but his hand was suddenly stronger than it had ever been and the ice broke easily. Inside his head he heard a soft sigh as the bands of light ceased to shine and he knew now what was troubling Sally. These people really *were* alive inside that ice and when you broke it, you killed them just as surely as The Claw would have done.

No, Sally's voice insisted. *You don't kill them, they're still alive. I know they are.*

The twenty-third and twenty-fourth slabs contained the bodies of Phil and Judy. Phil was first and although light was coming out of him, it was hard to believe he was still alive because his throat was cut from ear to ear.

Sorry buddy, Dave said, drawing his powerful hand back and driving it into the ice just above Phil's fat belly.

He didn't think he could do Judy, too, but he needn't have worried because Sally was there already.

By the time he realised he should have cracked the ice with the glowing blade of his Swiss Army knife Judy was finished as well.

It tricked us, Sal, he thought. *It made us kill them all. We could have woken them up if we'd used the knife, but we've killed them all now.*

No, it hasn't! she insisted. *They're all alive; we can get them out! I know what to do.*

Do it then, Sal, he thought glancing worriedly over to where Roddy and The Claw still stood facing one another. *Whatever it is, do it before that thing comes alive again.*

Sally nodded, closed her eyes and drew a deep breath. Her clothes and hair were coated with sparkling frost and her skin was steaming like a racehorse after a hard battle. Her arms hung limp at her sides and blood dripped steadily from her grazed

knuckles. Under the clear ice at her feet, a circle of letters –
mostly capital Ws – revolved lazily. When a letter reached the
side where the blood was hitting the ice, it broke from the
formation and skidded away towards the black wall in an
elaborate, ever-changing shockwave.

Dave guessed that The Knowledge was tasting her and he
wished she would hurry up. He wanted to send that thought to
her, but she was obviously trying to attain some kind of a trance
state so he tried to keep his mind empty.

Dave heard a movement. He spun around, dragging the
knife from his pocket by its hot orange blade. Roddy and The
Claw were still stuck in position. He looked at them carefully
for a few seconds, but neither moved.

When he looked back at Sally, words were coming through
the surface of the ice, cruising across her bare feet and entering
the ice again on the other side.

The letters that slipped out of the ice were about three inches
high and printed in Gothic Script. They were coloured scarlet
and edged with gold.

A sentence ran over her left foot as he watched:

SALLY HARRISON IS DEAD

Dave shook his head. He could still see her heart pounding
through her icy top.

Come on, Sal, he thought. *DO IT!*

A thick red, gold-edged streamer emerged from the ice and
curled its way up her left leg like a stripe up a barber's pole.
Dave watched its slow, steady progress until it slid up under the
tight leg of her shorts.

'No!' he shouted, but the word was destroyed as it left his
lips. The sluggish soundwaves came back and beat heavily on
his eardrums. The end of the streamer came out of the ice and
began winding up Sally's leg just before the first end came out
of the other leg of her shorts. It wound back down into the ice,
breaking into letters and forming a message for him as it slid
over her toes:

SALLY TASTED GOOD WHEN I ATE HER INSIDES

It's a trick, it's only a trick, Dave told himself.

Sally's eyes blinked open, but they weren't her eyes any more. Her pupils were tiny and her irises were identical to the shining eye of her cross. They were the purest green and Dave felt drawn toward them as if they had become the sole source of gravity in the room.

You could fall into those eyes and never be seen again, he told himself.

Sal, he called to her, using the verbal part of his mind. *Sally!*

There was no response; either she wasn't in there any more, or she'd changed herself somehow. It looked as if she'd *become* the green-eyed cross.

'Rise!' Sally commanded, spreading her arms. Her voice was sharp and clear and crackled in the air. Her breath bloomed white.

Behind her, twenty-four corpses sat up in perfect unison. Each of them swung their legs over the left side of their slab and pushed themselves to a standing position at precisely the same moment.

She's waking the dead, Dave thought. *She made them get up!* Distantly he wondered if Jesus had ever been in possession of these crosses.

'Line!' Sally said.

The dead people shuffled to the edges of the slabs, turned left with the precision of an army platoon and waited.

Sally turned and walked to the head of the queue.

She was right, she can *take them out of here!* Dave thought, suddenly believing that she would be perfectly capable of waking them up again whenever the fancy took her.

'Walk!' Sally ordered and started across the room towards the shining wall. Dave was stupefied. He watched the conga line of dead people walk past him in amazement until Phil went by. With each step, his head teetered backwards and the gash on his neck opened far enough to give Dave a view of the inside of his windpipe.

He hurried towards the head of the line which Sally was leading dangerously close to Roddy and The Claw.

Sal, he thought, *keep away from them. Keep away!*

But Sally paused before Roddy and it was plain that she was going to try and make him fall in line too. She wasn't going to desert even Roddy who was covered in mould and who had intended to betray them just to get his sister back, who . . .

Isn't even here! his mind told him. *Where is she, then?* it demanded.

His own cross pulsed, searing his chest, and he got a mental picture of Sandy sitting in the Dragon, her long shapely leg pressed close to his and her hot lips brushing his ear while she said, '*Roddy wants to fuck your little girlfriend, how about it?*' The smell of her perfume filled his nose again. *Poison*, that was what it was called, wasn't it? He could smell it now. For real. He was certain. His own voice rang in his ears: 'Go and fuck your sister, she's willing!' he had shouted into Roddy's threatening face that night in the pub.

Poison. Sandy. Roddy.

And then he knew. Knew everything.

And it was too late because good old Sally who always did her best for everyone no matter whether she liked them or not, was looking at Roddy and saying 'Line!'

Sally! Dave shouted mentally. He ran up to her, grabbed her shoulders and heaved her aside.

Sally staggered stiffly sideways and her troop of dead people followed her lead. She stood still, staring blankly back at Dave with her green eyes. The eye in the cross on her chest was almost out and glimmered like a torch with a flat battery.

Dave glanced over his shoulder at The Claw, then plunged the glowing knife blade into Roddy's stomach.

But it was too late. Sally had fallen for the trick and done the damage.

Roddy was waking up.

Except that Roddy wasn't Roddy any more.

Dave yanked the knife from his guts and stood back, not knowing what to do now that it was too late for the hot blade to work. Roddy was writhing on the spot and mewling pathetically as the mould rapidly spread across what little ordinary skin he had left, and kept growing so that it started to dangle from his face and arms in flaps. The odour of *Poison* had increased considerably now and something pink was growing from halfway up Roddy's arms.

Oh shit, save us! Dave thought, frantically wondering what to do.

The mould had now completely engulfed Roddy and it was drying, setting over him in hanging folds like sheets of black rubber.

He swiped at Dave and his fingers clawed away a chunk of hair as Dave ducked.

Sally, get them out of here! Dave screamed mentally.

She stood stock still, staring at what was happening before her with uncomprehending green eyes. Opposite Roddy, The Claw had started to writhe, too, but it was shrinking and its black skin was lightening.

Sally didn't move.

In front of him, Roddy began to grow, shooting upwards with a wet creaking and popping. His arms and legs lengthened and ripped through his clothing; his head began to swell and take up the loose black skin. Clawed hands with hooked ebony nails burst into the empty black finger skin and stretched it taut. A long jaw with sharp white teeth formed. Almond eyes grew.

The Claw had taken over Roddy and hidden inside him, leaving Roddy's empty body dressed up as itself. Dave didn't know what it had expected to achieve by hiding this way, or how it had done it, except that Roddy's sister was involved somehow.

It took another five seconds for the transformation to be completed and then Dave was alone against The Claw, just as he'd always known he would be.

The Claw was stronger now, stronger than it had ever been. It was because of Roddy and Sandy. Roddy was gone now, reduced to a limp heap of flesh and muscle on the floor behind him, but Sandy had survived and The Claw was using her, feeding off her living agony.

Sandy was naked and The Claw was wearing her. It had split her apart somehow and climbed inside her body, yet she still lived. It was grotesque and disgusting and impossible, but Sandy was still alive. The Claw had evidently torn her body open and forced its long, slender arms and legs inside hers and now it wore her like a horrific jumpsuit. Its thin arms protruded from the insides of her forearms and its legs came out through her legs just above the knee so that her bloodstained pink calves dangled behind its own, her twitching toes flapping at the backs of its bony knee joints. Her fingernails were still perfectly manicured and painted red and they scratched and scraped at The Claw's elbows, moving independently of it.

The Claw's chest was narrow and Sandy's splayed open ribcage almost surrounded it. Almost but not quite. There was a gap of almost a foot between her pink-tipped breasts and jagged white ribs which showed where the flesh was ripped away. The points of them dented The Claw's taut skin as it moved. Her lower abdomen had gone because Dave could see the edges of her hip bones. They were wrapped snugly around The Claw's waist and moved up and down slightly, smearing its dark skin with her blood as its legs moved her legs for her.

Sandy's head lolled over The Claw's left shoulder. Her face was unblemished but was distorted with an expression of awful agony. The worst thing was her eyes. Dave thought he could have handled it if Sandy's eyes hadn't been open. They looked at him with recognition and a terrible pleading.

Help me, her voice said inside his head.

GIVE THE SYMBOL TO ME! The Claw demanded, stepping towards Dave and holding out its hand. Sandy's voice screamed in Dave's head as The Claw's flexing tendons split her legs apart. He heard the flesh tear in her wrist. Her head juddered and her lips worked feverishly but no sound came from them. Fresh blood ran from her body, coursing down The Claw's slender legs to fall on the ice.

Sally! Get out of here! Dave shouted. The cross had turned red hot on his neck and it hurt like hell. Its tubular beam played up and down The Claw, but didn't seem to be doing it any harm.

'Help me! It's *hurting* me!' Sandy used her voice this time and it came clearly to Dave's ears. A thin trickle of blood ran from the corner of her mouth.

Dave bit his lip against the searing pain of the cross and struck at The Claw's outstretched hand with the knife.

The beast was quick. It withdrew its hand long before the knife reached it, then flipped its wrist around. The glowing blade flashed as it hit Sandy's left forefinger and lopped it off. Sandy screamed.

'Fucker!' Dave shouted and slashed with the knife again. He was getting good with it now, almost as good as Roddy had been. The knife felt like an extension of his arm rather than a weapon. The tip of it glanced off The Claw's bottom jaw, opening up a thin cut. Teeth snapped and missed. Dark green slime oozed from the cut but, by the time Dave had stepped back out of range, the cut had healed itself.

I CAN DO THIS TO YOUR WOMAN! The Claw said, hunching its shoulders so that Sandy rose on its back. Bone crunched. Sandy squealed, a long plaintive note that Dave thought would go on forever.

You're not getting the crosses, Dave said, concentrating on The Claw's limbs and jaws and being very careful not to look at Sandy's agonised face. He doubted if there was anything that could be done for her now, even if The Claw let her go. Sandy was ruined, good and proper.

I'm here to kill you! Dave added.

GIVE ME THE SYMBOLS OR I WILL PLUCK OUT YOUR WOMAN'S EYES LIKE THIS, it said, and casually gouged one of Sandy's eyes from its socket with an ebony nail.

Run, Sal! RUN! Dave thought over the screams as The Claw crushed the eye between its long thumb and forefinger. Sally didn't move. He glanced at her as she stood there at the head of her legion of zombies. Her eyes shone green and her breath hung in clouds in the cold air.

Go on Sal, run! he thought, but it was no use. She couldn't hear him; she was the cross and his thoughts weren't getting through.

GIVE ME THE SYMBOLS! The Claw shouted holding out the hand with the crushed eye in it.

The cross whacked Dave in the ribs and he leapt forward, slashing with the knife. It went through the long, sinewy finger easily, ground against harder bone but kept going. The Claw's little finger fell to the ice and the monster screamed with rage, raking at Dave's head with its other hand. Dave dodged, sucking in his stomach as the ebony nails whizzed by.

A clawed foot came up quickly and raked his leg, shredding his drainpipe Levis and biting into his flesh. The Claw stamped downwards and Dave almost passed out as the sharp nails grated against his shin bone.

The cross was going mad now and his chest felt as if it was on fire. His tee shirt was smouldering and he was dimly aware of grey smoke rising. The power of the cross flowed through him in great waves, strengthening him, but hurting him with its agonising heat. He knew he was changing, knew that his eyes were shining now, like Sally's, only his would be red instead of green.

He leapt away from the monster, not knowing if his leg had healed instantly but suspecting it had from the lack of pain. All he could feel down there was the same molten heat that filled the rest of him. His brain was starting to boil, but he hadn't gone into a trance like Sally; he could still see, think and act. He had speeded up, too, and his reactions were now as fast as The Claw's. The only thing it had on him was its superior strength and experience.

He jumped forward, parrying with one arm and cutting with the glowing knife, then stood and fought, taking blows to his body that shuddered through him but seemed insignificant against the great hacking, stabbing motions he was making.

He slashed and saw The Claw's belly open and black-green slime start to ooze out; slashed again and lopped off another clawed finger; slashed again and saw black tendons deep beneath the flesh of its thigh.

He was a killing machine. Muscle pulled against muscle as he worked; sinews bulged, tendons sprang up like ropes. He dodged and parried, thrust and hacked, dimly aware of the odour of stinking pus and sickly *Poison* perfume; dimly aware of Sandy's screaming and Sally's mute presence. And he couldn't be beaten because the cross was strong and its power lived in his nerve endings, flowed through his brain like red electricity. He knew where the jaws would strike, knew where the next blow would fall. Something wet hit him in the face and he screamed a triumphant battle cry, knowing that The Claw was breathing its last.

That was when the big black hand caught the right side of his head. Orange sparks wheeled before his eyes and his brain whirled through empty space.

Then he was in its grasp and the battle rage was gone. The Claw had hold of the back of his head in one hand, its slick fingers locked around the back of his skull with bone-crushing pressure. He opened his eyes and realised he'd blown it. The Claw had him now. There was no way he was going to escape that terrible crushing sensation in his head. It hurt just to breathe – fighting back was out of the question.

The Claw regarded him for a moment with its red and yellow eyes. Sandy's single eye accused him from behind its head. Her empty socket was filled with black pus and her mouth was drawn back in a silent scream. Somewhere in there her right cheek had been gouged away and flaps of ragged skin bled onto her pearl white teeth. Dave distantly hoped he hadn't been responsible.

The Claw's pointed jaws clacked open and shut once, the teeth meshing together perfectly.

One bite, Dave thought groggily. He had time to glance down at its body before it lifted him and he saw the damage he'd done to it. It didn't amount to much. There were scars all down its trunk and legs, and the stinking black pus was still dripping, but its wounds were already healing and in places there weren't even any marks at all.

Dave thought he would die when The Claw lifted him. *This*

is what it's like having your head run over by a truck, something informed him unnecessarily as those long fingers bit deeper and pulled him up to the tips of his toes. For some reason he couldn't understand it was being careful. It could have crushed him with one flex of its fingers, but it hadn't. In spite of its care, one of the ebony-tipped nails slashed through his scalp. He felt the skin pop and then part as the nail bit through to the bone. The pain was like a hot needle being inserted into his skull.

The Claw drew him close and looked at him with hypnotic eyes. It stank terribly. Dave could feel the cold being transmitted through the creature's eyes somehow, and the cold was fighting inside him with the power of the cross. The Claw was winning. The red power was gradually being driven back. Dave's biceps already felt like frozen water.

Sandy's ruined face peered over its shoulder. Her lips worked as if they were trying to form words. At first she only managed mewling noises, then she spoke. 'Give . . . it . . . the . . . crosses,' she moaned. Then her head toppled sideways and rested on The Claw's shoulder. Her eyes closed and Dave hoped she was finally dead.

The Claw flicked its shoulder and Sandy's head rose again. 'It's . . . ripping me apart,' she cried. 'It's gone right through . . . my body and . . . into my-my soul. Give it the crosses and it'll let me go. Let me die, *please*.'

'Can't,' Dave hissed through clenched teeth.

'Take it off your bitch,' Sandy said. 'It can't touch her while she's linked. It'll kill them all if it does. They'll escape.'

TAKE IT OFF HER OR I'LL CRUSH YOUR SKULL! The Claw's voice boomed in his ears.

'Make me,' Dave groaned.

The Claw fixed him with its terrible eyes, and squeezed tighter on his skull. He felt the bones begin to give. The fontanelles were cracking apart. The pain was tremendous, and deep inside his head, something felt as if it had come loose.

The cold poured into him, driving the power away and filling him with the most excruciating fear he'd ever felt. Dave was no longer certain it was cold any more because the fillings in his mouth were beginning to boil and the spittle and blood on them were vapourising.

TAKE IT OFF HER, The Claw commanded.

Never, Dave thought back, wondering how long he could stand that boiling feeling inside his head. He was trying to breathe just through his nose but the smoke from his cracking teeth was already finding its way into his lungs. If he started to cough he would totally lose control, so he fought against the need just as he fought against the pain in his head and the agony that was coursing down the nerves under his teeth.

Then The Claw's mind was probing him, looking for a weak spot, searching for a way in. Although he was still more than a foot away from The Claw's terrible face, he could feel the twin pinpricks of those yellow pupils pressing physically against the flesh of his face like two cold needles.

Help Sal, I can't stop it. Help! he thought, but his mind didn't seem attached to him any more; it was floating in space about a mile deep.

The Claw was invading him now. It had found an entry through his eyes and its mind surged in through them in a freezing gale, seeking him out and driving his personality further and further into the back of his boiling brain. Its red and yellow eyes shone before him – shone inside him – alien and knowing.

He kicked out, not sure if his legs were moving or not; there was no feeling in them now, and he couldn't see them because his vision had been corrupted by great circles of penetrating yellow.

A hooked ebony nail touched his neck – even over the pain of his bubbling fillings and the agony of the vice-like grip around his skull he could feel it as it ran down from just above his Adam's apple, tearing the skin and grating against cartilage.

The cross, it's going for the cross and then it will be all over, his distant, freewheeling mind coolly informed him. *You've blown it, Davey boy. You've lost*.

The nail carved a line down his chest, hooked under the leather necklace and pulled the cross away from his skin. He felt its power leave him then and knew the full intensity of the pain and terror. He would die now, but he wouldn't be dead; The Claw would climb into his body like it had done to Sandy and the pain wouldn't go away. Ever. And The Claw's soul – The Bad Knowledge – would possess his own soul and torment it throughout eternity. That was the price to be paid.

The Claw began to pull hard on the leather strap, and it bit into the back of Dave's neck, cutting the skin. Dave tried to pull away from this fresh pain, but he no longer knew what it was or even which way he was facing. He seemed to be submerged in The Claw's yellow eyes.

TAKE IT OFF HER! the voice rang inside his head, and suddenly it seemed the most logical thing he'd ever been asked to do.

Okay, a distant part of him thought back. *That's good, I'll do that*.

The knife spoke then. The Swiss Army knife that Sally had given him for his birthday all that time ago. He still clutched it tightly in his right hand. He knew this only because it spoke – he couldn't feel it at all. Its voice had a chatty, friendly tone, and afterwards Dave couldn't have sworn to anyone that it had spoken at all. It might have only been a part of his mind; a dull, sleeping part that had suddenly woken up to see what all the fuss was about, given advice and then returned to its slumber.

Bad idea, the knife said. *Why don't you stick me in The Claw instead?*

Suddenly he could feel his arm again. It seemed to be the only part of him left alive. And it wasn't just alive; it was *strong*. As strong as it had been when he'd smashed the ice shrouds.

He punched it away from him, not knowing if it was going in the right direction, and not caring at all. The knife seemed to know what it was doing and he trusted it.

It hit something hard, sank in and exploded. There was a momentary flash of searing heat and then the knife was gone. And The Claw was leaving him, roaring terribly as it swirled out of his brain like water down a plug hole. It had let go of his head and he was falling towards the ice, half burned, half frozen, but still alive.

When he opened his eyes an instant later, The Claw was astride him, leaning over towards him so that Sandy's one-eyed head hung right over its shoulder.

Half its midsection was gone – blown out when the knife exploded, Dave realised – and dark entrails hung from the wound, writhing like gooey black, slime-covered snakes. Its slick, sinewy arms were stretched out like a diver's and its ebony nails were descending slowly, irrevocably, down towards Dave's eyes.

Blew a hole in the fucker, Dave thought wearily. *Blew it up, but it won't go down. Cross. CROSS!*

The cross was still on his chest. It flicked back on, glowed brightly like a bulb about to blow, then went off.

Dave grabbed The Claw's slender wrists and tried to force them back, knowing he couldn't beat it. Its shiny black skin was colder than ice and twice as slippery and its arms were much more powerful than his own. Nothing was going to stop them coming down.

Sally! CROSS! HELP ME!

Sally didn't come out of her trance and the cross didn't blink back on. It looked as if he'd had all the help he was going to get. For a moment he experienced a complete blind panic and was sure that he couldn't hold onto those achingly cold limbs any more, then he thought of Roddy. Roddy on the Ghost Train platform, fighting the roustabouts; Roddy beating off the skeleton with the Bowie; Roddy in the pub, moving with a fluid precision as his head snapped down towards Dave's own. Then he was calm and knew exactly what he had to do.

He pushed his arms up as if to drive The Claw's ebony nails higher on his face. He didn't expect to be able to divert them, and he was right. What did happen was what he expected. He slid down the ice a few inches. It wasn't far, but it was enough. In one quick movement, he let go of the powerful wrists, linked his fingers making a vee shape and drove them up between The Claw's arms. The arms parted and the sharp nails smashed deep into the ice floor on either side of his temples.

Dave grabbed hold of those two bulging ankles then and pulled hard, sliding himself through the long spindly legs. He rolled across the ice and quickly got to his feet.

The Claw was slow in turning and Dave got a good look at Sandy's bare back. It was split apart, from her pelvis to her shoulder blades, and deep in the rent her spine glistened.

Dave's head was cool and clear. The pain had subsided now, and his teeth seemed to have cooled. Although the cross was out, he was going to fight. He *could* fight.

He darted in and smacked a fist into The Claw's hip joint as it turned, dodged easily as it struck back. Then he was squaring up to it like a boxer, looking only at its hooked claws and its injured body so its eyes couldn't distract him.

But The Claw didn't want to fight. It raised its right hand, palm up and waited.

Dave glanced at the tight black skin, the taut tendons; at Sandy's manicured nails constantly drumming on the slender arm. He wanted to rush in and tear some of those glistening entrails out of the hole the exploding knife had made, but The Claw's reach was too long. It would swipe at him and take his head off before he was halfway there.

IT'S MINE, the voice told him.

The cross rose from Dave's neck, pulling the leather thong tight. The eye was finished now. The silver lids had closed tightly over it. The cross rose so that it was level with Dave's chin, and started to pull him towards The Claw's open hand. He leaned back, trying to dig the tattered soles of his Hi-Tecs into the ice, but there was no grip to be had and once more he started the slow slide towards The Claw.

You won't get Sally's! he assured the monster.

LOOK! SALLY'S HAS GONE OUT TOO! The Claw's voice said inside his head. *I THINK I WILL.*

Sal! Sally! Wake up. Run, Sal. RUN!

The Claw extended its other hand like a bayonet and lined it up in front of Dave's stomach. He knew he would be cut in half long before The Claw got the cross, knew he could simply duck down and let the leather strap off his neck, but he couldn't admit to himself that he'd lost, couldn't let it go.

The sharp talons were six inches away now and no matter how much he called Sally wouldn't wake up and help him.

Four inches. They were long and curved and black and sharp. *Sally!*

Still he slid towards damnation. The nails dug into his shirt, pressed against his flesh. He pulled his stomach in, back-pedalled with his feet.

The longest claw broke the flesh and the cold started pouring in.

Sorry, Dave thought to anyone who might be listening. He closed his eyes and relaxed then, prepared himself to die.

Chapter Twenty Two
The Zombie Run

What? Sally thought. *What?*

It was too confusing. Distorted echoing sounds came to her from a long way away. Troubled sounds. She didn't want to open all the eyes again, but she was going to have to; there was no way of telling precisely what was going on without looking out.

It had taken all her concentration to flood those empty bodies with her mind, to make them get up and move. But she had done it. She had spread herself away from her body, jumped the gaps like a green electrical spark and found herself inhabiting the bodies.

For a moment she had looked out of twenty-five pairs of eyes, heard through fifty ears. Nothing was clear. Not a damn thing. Her vision was faceted like a fly's and her hearing boomed and echoed so that nothing was clear. So she'd closed her eyes and tried to make her hearing go away. It was warm and green and comforting like that but the strain on her mind was immense. She was thin – a twenty-fifth of her normal volume, and she wasn't sure she was strong enough to do what had to be done, even with the cross guiding her.

She had closed her eyes after she'd filled the bodies and walked them into a line and she'd kept them closed since. She knew the way. Or rather her feet did. It had been fine, tripping across the ice towards the exit, but things had gone wrong since.

First of all there was the last body (the last in here anyway – there was another to climb inside later) and that had thrown her. She had filled it and it was *wrong*. The shape was gone. There were no bones or muscles, nothing to get a grasp on. But this was the last one, and she'd tried and tried because it was supposed to be. She had wormed her way into it, not caring that there was no personality, because they were all like that; suspended. But this one was *wrong*, even if it was supposed to be right. This one was smelly and infected and showed her terrible dark things that she didn't want to see. This one seemed to be The Claw. Even though it was basically a human body, it felt, smelled, and tasted like The Claw in her own mouth. So she'd deserted it.

And after that there was something else she was supposed to do, but with their eyes closed and their hearing turned off she couldn't remember. She'd tried to make them walk again, but it wasn't working properly because of the other thing.

What? she thought. Something was coming through, a kind of distress call, mixed with anger. It was garbled because it was coming through twenty-four drained brains and one terribly tired one.

Concentrate, girl, it's important!

She was going to have to open their eyes again, even if it did make her feel dizzy, even if it did drain her resources. She thought about it for a long time and then let them listen. There were noises; grunts, thumping noises, echoing yells, but she couldn't tell.

So she opened their eyes and got twenty-five split views of what was wrong.

She saw the rear of The Claw, Sandy Johnson's torn and bleeding body riding high on its back. She saw why she couldn't pick up the last corpse. Roddy lay just to one side of The Claw in a crumpled heap of diseased flesh looking for all the world like a deflated balloon. There only appeared to be skin and clothes and hair left of him; he looked as if his skeleton had shucked him off like a suit of dirty clothing.

And with her own eyes she saw Dave being drawn onto The Claw's ebony nails.

His cross was suspended in front of him and almost in The Claw's open hand. His garbled pleading for help had ceased now and silence rang in that part of her brain which could hear his thoughts.

Now she remembered what she had been supposed to do. Help him kill the beast.

Sorry, Dave, she thought and her words reverberated, through twenty-four empty heads.

She was going to have to break the chain if she wanted to help him and she wasn't sure she could. Neither was she sure that she could get them back again, once she got out of them. It might have been a once-only, never to be repeated, occurrence.

From the view of the fourteenth in line, she saw the ebony nails pierce Dave's flesh, saw the blood run down into his torn jeans.

OUT! she thought and her faceted vision wavered like a telly on the blink. She got marginally stronger, but the bodies didn't seem to want to let her go. They clung tight.

OUT! she commanded again. Behind her, one of the bodies shuffled forward. It was a boy of about eighteen – she could feel herself deep inside him.

OUT OUT OUT LET ME GO! she screamed.

She pulled out of Judy with an unpleasant tearing sensation and felt Judy's body fall into the back of number twenty-five – Phil with the cold neck.

With one desperate effort, she ripped herself free along the line, popping out of the bodies like peas bursting from a pod. They fell forward onto one another like dominoes as she left them.

She crashed back into her body with a sickening jolt.

'DAVE!' she shouted, and to her surprise, her voice wasn't distorted, its energy didn't flow towards the black wall.

Her cross wasn't working any more, but she knew why; knew what she had to do.

'DAVE! QUICK!'

He looked around at her, his eyes sad and beaten and full of pain.

Killing me, Sal, he thought to her. *Killing me. Cold. Hurts.*

There was no time. No time at all. Without thinking, Sally

pulled the dead cross from around her neck, aimed and threw it.

'CATCH!' she shouted as the cross whirled through the air towards Dave and The Claw.

It seemed to hang in the air for a long time, the leather thong making a perfect circle. It spun slowly as it arced across the great room and the little silver cross revolved once, twice, three times.

Dave was leaning back at a sharp angle, his heels dug into the ice, straining against the thong of his own cross as it dragged him onto the Claw's fingers. His right hand, blue with the cold, reached out towards the loop.

The Claw's hand came up, too. Its shiny black fingers reached out much further than Dave's. His red blood dripped from its ebony nails.

It's gonna get it first! Sally thought. *Don't let it catch it, don't!*

Dave's hand seemed to be moving in slow motion. He reached out towards the slender black wrist and pushed it away. Sally saw the wrist flex, saw the muscles bulge. Then Dave's hand was flying back, away from the path of the looping cross.

Sally felt the power build quickly inside her. It felt as if her insides had turned into a nuclear reactor melting down. It wasn't the cross's green power this time though, it was her own. She could *do* it! It boiled white hot and rose under phenomenal pressure, finally bursting from her lips in one ear-shattering word.

'TURN!' she screamed.

And the cross obeyed. It was impossible, but the flying circle juddered in mid air and changed direction so that it spun towards Dave's splayed fingers.

Fit it in! Sally thought. *Join them up!*

Then it was in his hand and he was fighting to put it in its place in the back of his own cross.

Powerless to help further, Sally watched Dave fumble in front of him with the small cross. He seemed to be having trouble moving his fingers, and something was making the leather strap whip at his face.

You can't stop me now! she heard Dave yell. His thumbs were pressing the cross home, but it hadn't gone in properly. You had to be very precise because the two crosses were a perfect, seamless fit and if one was a millimetre out of alignment they wouldn't go. And he hadn't got it. It wasn't going in!

The Claw looked at her with its horrendous red and yellow eyes and curled its top lip displaying its row of triangular, hooked teeth. Stark terror flooded through her, borne on a wave of numbing cold. One of the creature's arms reached behind it and took hold of Sandy's head, puncturing it. Its thumb pierced Sandy's other eye. Then it was pulling her forwards, over its shoulder. Its strength was immense. It ripped Sandy's flesh from its body and held her corpse limply in its hand. Both her feet and lower legs were gone and one of her hands was held to the wrist by a strand of flesh. The other was still drumming its red painted nails on The Claw's arm. Her ribs were broken wide open and there were no organs in the cavity. Still gazing into Sally's eyes, The Claw tossed the body aside.

Dave's thumbs were pushing the little cross home, when The Claw's empty hand started to move again, and he still didn't have them lined up correctly.

Look out! Watch out! DAVE! Sally screamed, but her voice didn't seem to reach him this time, he just kept working at the crosses, jiggling his thumbs against the smaller one as he tried to force it home.

The Claw's hand was sailing through the air then; curved ebony nails stretched apart as it arced towards Dave's throat.

Dave! she yelled, stamping her bare feet on the cold ice. Things seemed to have slowed almost to a standstill now and she had time to notice the circle of words revolving lazily around The Claw's feet under the ice; saw the thin black spiral spinning under Dave's Hi-Tecs. She saw his breath hanging in the air, the bright red blood seeping through his slashed tee shirt and colouring the waistband of his Levis.

And the two crosses were apart again. Dave had one in each hand and was gazing at them as a baby might look at a square block it had been trying to insert into a round hole.

His hands were moving very slowly and the two crosses were

577

close again now, but The Claw's talons were closer – almost at Dave's neck.

He isn't going to do it, she thought.

Dave didn't even look round as the five clawed fingers smashed sideways into his face.

Sally saw his cheek burst open and blood fly. There was an instant in which she saw his clenched teeth through the wound and the inside of his throat as those fingers ripped it apart.

Then there was a low *whoomp* like a bomb going off and a brilliant flash of the purest blue light. Sally felt her hair sizzle as the blue energy scorched past her. She saw right through Dave and The Claw in that instant, saw their dull bones moving under their flesh. After that her eyes clamped shut, but flashes of blue played on her eyelids, and The Claw's awesome voice raged in an alien tongue.

When she forced her eyes open again, she almost wet herself with relief. Dave wasn't dead – he wasn't even cut. His glasses lay crushed on the floor beside the now shredded rucksack, but he had somehow pieced the two crosses together and he was holding them high in his right hand. They were alive again and shining like she'd never seen them before. The slender rays of light beamed from the eyes of the joined crosses, one red, one green, and they wove together in a double helix about six inches in front of it. Six inches in front of that, the helix merged into one tubular blue beam about four inches in diameter. This beam was iridescent, sparkling with gold and silver.

Dave was using the beam like a sword and fencing The Claw. The creature was dancing back and forth, defending itself with its arms. As it knocked the solid beam away, Dave's arm jolted outward with the force.

The Claw was coming towards him now, moving quickly, its arm high and forcing the beam to the right. But Dave had anticipated this tactic, and did a single turn, spinning on one foot like an ice skater. The blue ray sizzled around the walls, passed over Sally's head and slashed into The Claw's body from the left. It stopped dead. Acrid smoke and a noise like burgers sizzling filled the air. Black flesh parted and the monster began to topple like a falling tree. As the beam bit into it the creature roared and the sound was like a long rolling explosion of thunder. The noise made the room tremble and the ice started to crack.

Dave brought the beam up and one of The Claw's eyes vapourised; slashed it down and The Claw fell, its chest gaping and spraying green-black slime. It roared and writhed across the ice, trying to wriggle out of the merciless blue beam.

Sally watched Dave slice its limbs off then quarter its body. He played the sparkling ray on its head until there was nothing left but a mound of smoking slime.

When the beam went out The Claw was all but dead. Its limbs twitched reflexively on the floor and its great dark green bladder of a heart trembled slightly. The air was filled with the smell of rotting vegetation.

'Dave,' Sally said.

He stood there gazing open-mouthed at The Claw's remains. His shoulders were slumped and the double cross hung life-lessly from his right hand. There was a spatter of slime on his left cheek.

'Dave! Are you okay?' she said.

He turned slowly and looked at her, slack-faced. 'I killed it,' he said. 'Didn't I?'

'It's gone,' she said, nodding. 'You drove it away.'

Three stones, Sally, it said you needed three stones.

He held up the crosses and looked at them. 'They're finished,' he said. He held them out towards her. The eyes weren't just closed. They were gone. And the crosses looked as though lightning had struck them. They were blackened and twisted out of shape. 'No help now,' he said, shaking his head.

'They've done what we needed them for,' she said, glancing behind her at the fallen bodies and wondering what she was going to do about them without the cross to help her.

He grunted and shook his head, smiling ruefully.

'What?' she asked, going to him and taking him in her arms.

'My glasses. They're bust.' He shook his head.

'S'okay, I'll get you back.'

'I can see, Sal. I can see without my glasses on. My eyes are better. And my fillings . . . Look!' He opened his mouth and showed her thirty-two perfect teeth.

The ice cracked like a rifle shot. Sally glanced back at the slabs and the black wall. The slabs were still in place but the black wall had receded and taken the ice with it. It looked like it was a mile away now. There was no visible top to it. It rose for-ever, a distant perpetual wall.

'You didn't kill the Bad Side, you killed the devil,' she said. 'That was what was supposed to happen. That's why I couldn't take Fred Purdue's ring. They said it took three stones to kill it and I thought they meant The Claw. The Claw was only an incarnation of the Bad Side and that's what we were meant to kill. All we had to do was restore the balance and we've done that. With three stones we probably would have destroyed everything.' She pointed at the black wall. 'Look! That's the source of the evil. That's where all the badness comes from. It's getting further away. We've driven the evil back to where it belongs. We won.'

The ice cracked again and a yawning chasm opened beside them.

'It's coming apart, we ought to leave,' Dave said. 'What about them?' he added, nodding at the bodies.

'I think I can do it again, Dave,' she said. 'I think I can get inside them and move them.'

He shook his head. 'They're dead, Sal. Aren't they?'

She sighed. 'I don't know. I don't think so, but I won't be sure until we get them back on our side. I've got to try to do it. I really have. We can't leave them here.'

'But the crosses . . .' he held the mangled ruins out for her to see.

She shook her head. 'I can do it without them,' she said.

Dave knew she could, she had that *dangerous* look in her eyes again.

'Okay,' he said.

That was when Roddy's body started to inflate. It rose from the ground like it was being pumped up. His head grew from the pile of loose flesh. Except that it wasn't Roddy's head at all, it was The Claw's. A long slender neck and narrow black shoulders emerged as it rose.

Sally screamed.

'Die, you fucker!' Dave shouted, running over to it and stamping on it. It deflated with a wet hiss.

'Go, Sal! Quick!' Dave said.

He watched her fall into that trance state again. It took her longer without the cross. A lot longer. The black wall was miles away now and the words under the ice had vanished. He glanced from Roddy's flesh to Sandy's torn body and back again, wishing Sally would hurry up. The temperature was rising and the ice was cracking like a spring melt. God only knew what the rules of this place were, and God only knew what would happen to them if they didn't get out quickly.

'RISE!' Sally said.

The corpses got to their feet again. She'd done it. She was inside them.

Sally started running towards the shining wall in a slow jog. The corpses followed her, matching her movements like shadows. Dave waited until all the blank-faced, blue-tinged bodies had all trotted past him and joined the end of the queue, fumbling in his pocket for his last magic tool.

He had the compass out when he charged through the cold wall. He ignored the sharp, freezing shock as he passed through, then wiped the coating of frost from the face of the compass. The needle spun and Dave nodded grimly – they were going the right way.

At the top of the steps he gazed in horror at the black cinder land of the Bad Side.

As far as the eye could see, the ground was burning red molten rock. There were darker shapes floating there like black ice floes, but the distances between them were surely too great to leap. Especially if you were carrying a cargo of twenty-four stiffs.

He wanted to give up then, wanted to sit down on the sloping path and cry until death came for him. They had done the job, but there was no escape. Even if they survived the first few jumps, they sure as shit weren't going to go all the way. It was too far. Much too far.

But something was happening to him as he jogged along. It felt like a weight pressing on him. It wasn't unpleasant, so he didn't fight it. After a while he began to feel stronger, happier. His pace loosened and he fell in step with Judy's dead body as it trotted in front of him. His legs started to rise and fall of their own accord – as though he wasn't working them. His arms pumped and his lungs sucked in and blew out, all with no effort. Then his personality began to shrink and his vision to fade. He finally realised that Sally was working her way into him, taking over his body. He felt privileged to have her there.

Hello, Sal, he said as her presence invaded him and took control of his limbs. Then he was somewhere dark and warm in his mind. He could still feel the jolting of his body as Sally carried it along, but now he was safe and secure.

Even when it started to get hot and he felt his body leaping across the floes, he remained relaxed, trusting her and knowing that she would manage. This was her job. Eventually he slept.

The stinging pain in his face brought him back. He was rolling crazily, jerking this way and that with every fresh pain. He spread out again, falling back into himself as Sally departed.

Then the ground tilted. His balance was gone and he was falling to the left. His eyes popped open as he went down. He was toppling in a row with other people. All their movements were identical and they were falling like a team of formation dancers.

He must have gone down quicker as he came to his senses because somehow Judy was on top of him. She was ice cold and a dead weight. He scrambled out from under her just in time to see the remains of Jon Kott booting Sally in the stomach as she lay on the black cinders.

Some of her was still connected to him, because he was as winded by the blow as she was. He managed to stay upright though and, bent double, he hurried past the toppled bodies to Kott who was preparing to kick Sally again.

They were on an island of solid ground surrounded by boiling sea. The doorway, now shrunk to two-thirds of its size, was twenty yards ahead and Kott was barring their way. Obviously he wasn't going to let them pass.

We did it, he thought, ignoring the hot spreading pain in his gut. *We got across. Good old Sal!* He glanced behind him at the molten lava sea as he ran up the line of corpses and marvelled that they'd ever managed it.

Kott kicked again, and Dave gasped. He slowed to a trot.

'Jon!' he called, when he got some of his breath back. He waved his arms over his head.

Kott stopped kicking Sally and Dave was grateful for that. He turned his blackened skull towards Dave, cocked his head to one side and put one hand on his hip like an angry parent waiting for a lost child. His right hand was still holding the little plastic soldier with the flame-thrower, but it was no longer working. He was covered in sticky black blood from his neck to the knees of his trousers. His Ben Sherman shirt was in ribbons and his gashed midriff displayed purple muscle and intestines. A big kitchen knife protruded from his heart.

'Flame-thrower!' Dave shouted, thinking, *this can't be right! The Claw's gone and the balance has been restored. Kott should be dead and merged with the Bad Side like Roddy and his sister.*

But Kott wasn't. Dead and faceless and slashed to bits he might be, but he was standing there with the little plastic soldier waiting to dismantle Dave as soon as possible.

'Flame-thrower!' Dave called again. Why wouldn't the damn thing light?

'Hol!' Kott's open throat hissed. His blackened and toothless lower jaw opened and closed. 'Hol woll he hol!'

'Finished, Jon,' Dave said. His stomach still hurt where Kott had kicked Sally. 'It's all over, Jon. You aren't a troll fol de rol any more. You're dead. Now lie down.'

'Hol,' Kott hissed. He staggered towards Dave, faltered and stopped. He turned his skull to look down at one of the fallen corpses. It was a thin, almost anorexic, girl of about seventeen. She had cropped black hair and wore a singed white dress. Her feet were bare and the soles were terribly blistered.

'Huffer!' Kott said.

Before Dave realised that Kott intended to eat the girl for his supper, he had bent and yanked her to her feet by her hair. She hung limply in Kott's strong hand.

'Put her down,' Dave said, taking a cautious step closer. He suddenly knew that a part of Kott still existed inside that charred skull. And he thought he could restore himself by eating the girl. 'You can't come back to life like that. You're finished, Jon. You're dead. Put her down.'

Kott's head dipped and his jaws clamped around the girl's neck. Dave felt the searing pain as clearly as if Kott had bitten him. He screamed in agony as he ran at Kott.

It was like charging into a brick wall. Kott didn't even shudder as Dave slammed into him. He'd torn half the girl's neck away by the time Dave grabbed the knife handle which protruded from his chest and while Dave yanked it up and down, driving it further in, he worked ravenously at the girl's neck.

Her body fell to the ground as Dave gave a final push. Kott turned his head and looked at Dave with empty eyes. Chunks of red meat hung from his jaws.

'Troll,' he said and toppled over backwards. He hit the ground and burst into a cloud of grey dust.

When Dave looked up again, Sally was watching him from the head of the line of corpses. She was crying and holding her neck. She now knew better than anyone how it felt to have your head chewed off. 'Killed h-her,' she said. 'He j-just ate her neck away and k-k-killed her.'

'The door, Sal!' Dave said, stabbing his finger towards it. There was no time to comfort her. The door was diminishing in size. It remained in proportion as it shrank and it was now only about three feet high and eighteen inches wide. Already they would have to crawl through it and if it got much smaller, they would be stuck here forever. Floating through the Bad Side's molten sea on a floe of black cinders.

'Get them up and get them through the door!' he shouted.

Sally looked at him helplessly. 'I don't think I can do it again,' she whimpered.

'Do it Sal!' he raged. 'Don't even think about it! *Just do it!*'

Sally closed her eyes and put her hands over them. Dave watched her trying to release the tension from her neck and shoulders. Whatever remained of the cross's power was fading fast. He wasn't sure she had enough left.

'Rise,' she said softly.

The corpses got up.

'Good girl!' Dave yelled. 'Good girl!'

They had to crawl through the door.

Dave went to the back of the queue again and watched the door between the Bad Side and the Limbo Side shrinking as the corpses went through on hands and knees. By the time Judy's rear end got there, the door frame was so small that he had to lie on his back and force her through with his feet.

He shot through the gap head first as it slipped down to nothing. The wooden frame jarred his shoulders and scraped his hips. He wasn't quite fast enough and the toe of his right Hi-Tec was caught in the tiny frame. The pressure was tremendous. He crunched his toes up as far as he could and pulled his foot high in the wrecked boot, not knowing if it was enough.

The doorway vanished with a tiny popping noise, guillotining through the toe of the Hi-Tec as it went.

Dave's heart was hammering in his ears and his vision seemed to be pulsating. Someone was screaming a blood-curdling yell. Thunder roared and lightning flashed. Dave thought he might faint. 'Jesus,' he gasped.

That was when the first frog hit him.

The dome of darkness that hung over the Limbo Side hadn't gone away. The Bad Side was still raging over its defeat. Forked lightning crashed down to the dusty ground of the park in a never-ending series of jagged strikes. The sky was low and boiling. In fifteen or twenty places it reached the ground in inverted cones, depositing a plague of large green frogs.

It was Anne Cousins who was screaming. She was fighting

the frogs bare-handed, pulling them off her husband and throwing them aside. Tommy stood in front of her at the top of the mound, frantically kicking the creatures away as they swarmed up the bank.

Dave snatched the frog from his hair and tossed it aside. That was when he realised it wasn't a real frog at all. It was one of the big slimy rubber ones from the Frogger game in AdventureLand.

But they're alive, for God's sake! They're alive!

He got to his feet as Sally's procession of bodies started to run, zigzagging through the lightning strikes across the barren grass field, heading towards the fairground.

'Anne! Tommy!' he screamed over the rolling crashes of thunder, kicking frogs away as they bounded up at his legs. 'RUN! *Follow them!*'

Derek was up now, and Dave realised Sally was inside him, too. He looked unstable, but he was tottering down the bank, heading for the end of the line of zombies.

'Run!' Dave called, pulling a frog from his shoulder. Its painted black eyes revolved in their sockets, looking out lifelessly.

Anne was following Derek across the park, Tommy was in her arms. She had abandoned her Marks & Spencer bag but she held something metal in her hands – Dave could see it glinting as the lightning flashed.

They were halfway back to the fairground now, with Sally's line of zombies leading the way.

As Derek caught up with the line Anne and Tommy went down and were instantly buried under a blanket of leaping and crawling frogs. Derek remained upright and trotted along behind Judy.

Get up, for Christ's sake get up! Dave implored them as he ran towards them. One of Anne's arms broke through the surface of the mass of frogs. The thin shiny thing was clutched in it and she slashed it back and forth, carving the frogs away.

It's a chisel! Where did she get that from? Dave thought as he started to wrestle the frogs away from them. Anne had punctured some of them and these seemed to be dead. He threw them aside, caught hold of her arm, and pulled her up out of the seething mass. Tommy was still clinging to her chest.

Her eyes were wide and hysterical. 'Get us out of here!' she screamed, stabbing frogs as they rose around her knees. One became impaled on the chisel. She looked at its unmoving body and shrieked.

Dave slapped her face and ducked as lightning struck the ground beside him. Hundreds of frog bodies melted instantly and stuck together in a quivering mass. Anne looked at the impaled frog in frozen horror. Dave hit her again, harder this time. Tommy whined.

'Oh God, get us out of here!' Anne moaned.

'Run!' Dave roared at her. 'Follow the line!' He turned her towards her husband and pushed her. Her legs started to move and she staggered clumsily through the carpet of frogs. After a few seconds she started to run.

They were getting close to the AdventureLand entrance when a fork of lightning struck two of the corpses in the middle of the line. One moment they were there, trotting along in file, the next they were nothing more than two piles of drifting dust.

How many more? Dave thought. *We did the job, now give us a break! This isn't fair!*

As if in reply, the next stroke of lightning took off the toe of his left Hi-Tec.

AdventureLand had almost disappeared. The entrance arch looked solid enough but the circle of lorries and generators and rides seemed to have faded and become insubstantial. Dave could see right through the candy floss stall inside the entrance to the stall behind it.

Can't get in through the arch, Sal, he thought to her. *I tried it.*

There was no reply, but a reply wasn't necessary. Sally already knew because she had bounced off the invisible membrane that sealed the funfair and had veered off to the right. Now she was leading her troop of zombies round the outside perimeter of the fairground, heading for the caravans and lorries. And the back of the Ghost Train.

Anne was slowing down now, and Dave had to hold her waist and drive her along to keep her going. Lightning struck at their heels. They had outpaced the main body of the frogs and now there was only the occasional one to kick away. Here the rides and caravans looked more solid. Dave didn't know why. AdventureLand was going to vanish from Limbo, he was sure of that, but he didn't know why it should do it in stages.

'Stop!' Sally shouted. The line of zombies stopped immediately. Anne ran into her husband's back and collapsed. Tommy began to cry.

'I'll take him now,' Dave said. 'I'll carry him through. C'mon Tiger!' he said, lifting the boy up.

Sally was waiting for them at the head of the line. She was standing by the canvas back of a stall two rides away from the Ghost Train. White-faced and bleeding, her eyes were still distant, and Dave knew that she hadn't broken away from the corpses this time. In the back of his mind he wondered whether she ever would.

'In through here,' Sally said in a monotone. She stared at the faded green canvas.

Dave shook his head. 'This isn't the back of the Ghost Train, Sal,' he said doubtfully.

'In through here,' she repeated.

'It's wrong Sal, the Ghost Train is two rides up. We have to go back the way we came in.'

'What's the matter? What's wrong?' Anne said, her voice veering towards hysteria once more.

'In through here,' Sally said.

Anne grabbed hold of Dave's arm. Her fingernails bit into his flesh. 'If she says this is the way to go, then let's go!' she hissed over the constant roar of the thunder.

'But it's wrong,' Dave complained. 'We didn't *come* this way.' He glanced behind him at the tide of approaching frogs. They were less than twenty yards from the queue of bodies. If they didn't move soon they would be swamped.

'Try it! We've got to try it!' Anne screamed. She stuck the chisel in the canvas and hacked open an entrance.

'Oh no, not that,' Dave said, knowing now that Sally had been right all along.

Before him stood another side stall with Fred Purdue's name written on the front hoarding. They were looking into the rear corridor of the Glass Maze.

She got us through it last time, Dave thought, looking into Sally's blank eyes. *But she had the cross then. I wonder if she can do it without.*

Lightning struck the ground nearby. The accompanying clap of thunder came instantly and the pressure wave almost took Dave off his feet. One of the zombies fell over and clumsily regained his feet.

'Okay, Sal,' Dave said. 'Go.'

Sally stayed where she was, facing the rent in the canvas. Dave could feel the tension in her. All her muscles were locked into position as she strained to keep the dead people standing. Her stomach muscles were bunched and ridged and the tendons stood out in her wrists and inner elbows. The skin of her neck was taut and corded and a vein throbbed in her forehead.

'What's she waiting for?' Anne screamed, shaking his arm again. 'Why doesn't she move?'

Realisation dawned on Dave slowly. He placed Tommy on the ground. 'Can you walk?' he asked.

The boy wiped his tear-stained face. He nodded.

'Why? What is it?' Anne yelled, her eyes rolling crazily.

'I have to lead,' Dave said. 'Sally can't get us out while she's hooked up with those people. I have to do it.' He took the compass from his pocket and snapped the brass lid open. The rusted needle revolved once as if getting its bearings, then settled, pointing at the rip in the canvas.

'Can you do it? Can you get us back?' Anne asked.

Dave shrugged – then ducked as lightning crashed beside him. 'I hope so,' he yelled over the roar of thunder.

★   ★   ★

He stepped through the split in the canvas into the back corridor of the Glass Maze. It smelt damp and musty, but there were traces of worn down grass on the floor. The light was bad in here but out through the layers of dusty glass panes he thought he could see the green grass of the Memorial Park. *His* Memorial Park; the *real* one.

'Go on!' Anne urged, shoving him in the back. He glanced down at the compass and turned left even though it felt like the wrong way to go. Anne was close behind him, dragging Tommy along with her free hand. The chisel was still clutched tightly in her right. Behind them was Sally, tense and blank-eyed as she led her line of corpses along after her.

Dave crashed into a pane of glass. He staggered backwards, nose stinging and starting to bleed. Swearing, he glanced down at the compass which was pointing left. He couldn't see whether there was glass to the left or not, and he reached out and felt the space before he moved.

After that he didn't look where he was going at all, he just followed the compass.

Eventually he fell into a jogging rhythm, aware only of the movement of his feet and the swinging of the compass needle. Side corridors swept by to the left and right, trampled grass flew beneath his feet. He was distantly aware that he was chanting 'I can do it,' like Sally had when she'd got them out of here the first time, but his mouth was moving of its own accord.

The compass needle swung right, and Dave turned, matching its movements precisely. Feet were tramping along behind him like an army in slippers marching double time. Somewhere back there he was able to hear Tommy's laboured breathing as he struggled to keep pace. *Not long now,* a part of his mind whispered to him. *Not long now, Davey boy. Soon be out.*

They were deep in the maze now, twisting, turning but always going the right way. He could tell how deep in they were because the sounds had altered, becoming more and more muffled as the glass panes separated the line of running zombies. Soon they would be in the centre.

Lightning was still striking regularly. From the periphery of his vision he could see the flashes both on the Limbo Side and Earth Side. There was a drumming that sounded like rainfall, but he wasn't entirely sure it wasn't the blood singing in his ears.

Then he knew it was raining, because a fat drop of water landed on the glass face of the compass. It touched his fingers and felt cool and refreshing.

He could smell life. Damp and warm after the barren wastes of the other sides; sparkling and fresh and seething like hedgerows after a storm. It was going to be alright. It really was.

Except that the lightning was flashing red on the left.

The lightning flashing red!

He turned through one hundred and eighty degrees at the end of the corridor and came back on the other side. Out of the corner of his eye he saw Sally's bare feet pass in the opposite direction. A girl's feet clad in open-toed sandals followed them. After that, a pair of court shoes, then some low brown brogues with the colour scuffed from the toes.

He'd just noticed some Hi-Tecs identical to his own when the compass needle swung right. He dodged through the gap ahead of him and stopped when Anne screamed.

'Wha . . .?' he said, breaking out of the light trance instantly. But he didn't have to complete the question because he knew what Anne was screaming and screaming about now; knew where the red lightning had come from.

They were in the centre of the maze, an area of about ten feet by ten with gaps into corridors at each corner. They had entered from the bottom left of the square. There was a high tubular steel-framed stool in the centre of the glass room and on it Fred Purdue sat waiting for them.

His huge, ham-hock arms were folded across his broad chest. In one hand – and cradled in his left elbow like James Bond's Walther pistol – was the biggest steak knife Dave had ever seen. His left hand was gripping his right bicep. On his wedding finger was the ring containing the third stone and it was shining.

Shining with a vengeance.

Red lightning, Dave thought, looking at the searing ray that beamed from the ring and passed around the room like a search-light.

Anne's screaming suddenly stopped and the instant silence made Dave feel dizzy for a second.

'Motherfucking little cunt bastard,' Purdue grated. He seemed to be having trouble breathing and blood ran from the corner of his mouth when he spoke. He looked at Dave with those piggy pale blue eyes. The pupils were like pinpricks, even in this light. Dave felt them boring into him, searching him.

'What did you do? You little cunt, what did you do?' Purdue moved his hand and the ruby beam drew a line of fire in the dead grass at Dave's feet.

'I beat it,' Dave said, looking away from Purdue's invading eyes.

What're you gonna do now, Davey, ask him to dance? he thought crazily.

Purdue shook his huge balding head. 'You beat nothing,' he said, his breath whistling. 'I can get it back again. Done it before, do it again.'

The beam flicked over Dave's toes which protruded from his ruined boots. Flesh sizzled. Dave screamed and leapt backwards, crashing into Tommy.

Should have been Anne, where's she gone? She's left him here and run, Dave thought in amazement. *She's deserted him!*

'You're done, Freddy. Finished. Let us go,' Dave heard himself saying in a flat, calm voice.

Purdue looked at him, his lungs bubbling as he breathed.

'Killing starts here,' he said, nodding towards the ground in front of his stool. 'Gets it back. First you, then the kid, then your squeaky little girly. I got scores to settle with that one. I'm gonna take off her skin. I might let you stay to watch that. But I can get it back. I know how.' He played the red beam up Dave's leg.

The pain was terrible. Dave fell to the ground and rolled, but Purdue kept the beam on him, kept it searing his skin. He crawled frantically, his torn trouser legs smouldering

592

around his ankles and the beam stinging his bare back.

'I got scores to settle, too, you fat bastard!'

For a moment Dave didn't know who had shouted. All he knew was that the beam was gone from his legs and was flickering around the roof. Rain was pouring in through the holes it made.

He rolled again. *Anne! It's Anne!* his mind shouted. Now he knew where she'd gone. While Purdue had been trying to put the 'fluence on him she had been creeping around the side of the room. Either Purdue hadn't noticed her, or he'd been confident that he could handle her.

She'd crept in from the side and thrown herself at Purdue, knocking him off his stool in spite of his bulk.

Now they were rolling on the floor, locked in mortal combat. Purdue was underneath Anne, struggling to get up as she knelt on his arms and stabbed at his throat with the chisel. Blood was flying and he was making horrible choking noises, but still he struggled.

Then his right hand was coming up, forcing Anne's body away from him. The steak knife flashed and Anne leapt away, clutching her arm with her free hand. Blood oozed from between her fingers.

But she wasn't finished yet.

'You bastard!' she screamed leaping forwards and striking at Purdue's bald pate as he struggled to get to his feet. His scalp peeled back in a half inch strip and Dave could see his skull beneath.

'Teach you to kidnap children!' Anne screamed, lunging again.

Purdue ducked this time, ran forward on his hands and knees and slashed with the steak knife.

There was silence then, broken only by Purdue's heaving breathing. Anne stared at the gash on her shin while blood coursed from it. Purdue looked at her, grinning. The red beam flickered around the glass walls. The chisel hung limply in Anne's right hand.

'Oh,' she said and her voice bore a distinct note of surprise.

Purdue's grinning countenance turned to glare at Dave, and it was then that Anne struck again. She made the strike without warning and Dave was as surprised as Purdue. In one swift, smooth movement, the chisel slashed down the side of his fat neck, curved back and stopped where it had started from. Her expression hadn't changed and her stance was exactly the same too. She looked as if she hadn't even moved.

Missed, Dave thought. *She missed him!*

And a huge gout of blood shot from the far side of Purdue's neck. It splattered against the glass like water from a high pressure hose. Then stopped, then squirted again. Purdue's ring went out. His arms collapsed and he crumpled to the ground. His blood jetted out in pulses almost a second long. His feet drummed on the ground as if he were having a fit.

Dave glanced from the dying man to the compass – it was indicating that they should exit through the top right hand door. 'Anne!' he shouted. 'COME ON!' He grabbed Anne and dragged her along with him. Tommy ran up to his mother and took her hand. Sally and the zombies started to move after them.

The next corridor took them back past the centre. Dave screamed when he saw Purdue was upright again and hacking at the toughened glass with the knife while his neck jetted blood. Tommy began to cry.

Then they were in the last corridor and the good smells of wet grass and rain swept towards them on a wave of clean, fresh air.

'We did it!' he yelled as they ran out into the pouring rain in what had once been the centre of AdventureLand. 'We did it!' He shut the compass, kissed the case and stuffed it back in his pocket.

The fair was gone except for the Glass Maze and The Ghost Train. Yellow circles and squares of dead grass marked the positions of the departed rides. Behind the two remaining attractions, Dave could see Purdue's Range Rover and his two caravans. Off to one side stood a big Scammell lorry and trailer. The Scammell had a radiator grille which looked to Dave like a friendly face.

Sally was out now, but she kept running, dragging the zombies out behind her. She curved around and came back, collapsing lifelessly into Dave's arms as Derek cleared the exit. She was cold and heavy. The circle of zombies tottered uncertainly, staying on their feet for a few moments more. Then they, too, fell.

Anne limped over to Derek, dragging Tommy with her.

'We did it, Sal!' Dave yelled, glancing back at the maze to make sure Purdue wasn't following them, brandishing his steak knife and ring. Sally didn't move.

'Sal! Wake up! We're out. Sal?'

Her eyes were closed and she didn't seem to be breathing any more. He laid her on the wet grass and tried to find a pulse; first in her wrist, then in her neck. Finally he put his head to her heart. Which was still.

'NOOO! NO! HE CAN'T BE!' Anne screamed. She began to beat on her husband's chest, hands clenched together. Then she massaged. Then listened. Then screamed again.

Dave looked at Sally's chest. It didn't move. He opened one of her eyelids, then shut it again. His right hand bunched into a tight fist.

Just a little! Please let me have just a little bit left!

He walked slowly over to Anne who was weeping on her husband's body. Tommy looked up at him with huge blue eyes. 'Is my daddy dead?' he asked.

'No, Tiger, just asleep,' he said, bending over Anne and taking her right hand.

Anne didn't even notice the chisel being gently taken from her fingers, didn't look up when Dave stood before the Glass Maze and drew back his right fist.

She didn't seem to hear when the first pane of glass shattered into tiny pieces. She was on top of Derek trying to blow life into his body when the second pane went. Massaging his heart again when the third fell.

And she had given up hope when Dave came back out of the maze, the bloody chisel tucked in the pocket of his trousers and the ring with the shining red stone on his wedding finger.

He walked past her, stood in the centre of the zombie circle and spread his arms in front of him like a preacher.

'DO IT!' he yelled.

Lightning struck him and the explosion shook the ground. Anne's world turned ruby red as a shockwave of extreme heat washed over her. For a moment she thought she was dead.

When she looked again, she was sitting in the middle of an empty fairground in the rain, surrounded by dazed and wet people who looked as if they had just woken from a deep and comfortable sleep.

Dave sat down beside Sally and took her in his arms. 'We're back,' he said. 'We did it!' Around him, the zombies were getting to their feet and looking surprised. There was a lot of animated discussion going on. Somebody wanted to know what the fuck he was doing in a field in the rain. Phil and Judy were nearby. Judy was crying and Phil had his arm around her shoulders. He was rubbing at the big white scar on his neck. Derek was sitting up and shaking his head in disbelief as Anne and Tiger smothered him with kisses.

'I was stuck,' Sally said. 'I couldn't break away.'

'I know,' Dave said. 'It doesn't matter, we did it.'

She kissed him. 'I love you, Davey.'

'Yeah, I love you, too,' Dave said, pulling back and smiling. 'We did it, and it can't happen again. I got Purdue's stone.' He showed her the ring. The stone's colour was a dull maroon. 'They can't start without it.'

'What if they try to get it back?' she asked.

He shook his head and smiled. 'They won't. And if they do we'll give 'em a hard time. We know how, don't we?'

She nodded and smiled ruefully. 'Yeah, I s'pose we do.'

Dave glanced at his watch.

Just to be sure.

The second hand was moving again and the digital numbers were advancing steadily.

It was twenty past five.

Extract from the Basingstoke Examiner, Monday 31st July:

FAIRGROUND CAPTIVES FREED IN STORM

Memories Wiped: Some Claim Brainwashing
Early on Saturday morning at the centre of the worst
storm recorded this century, twenty-six people were discovered in Basingstoke's War Memorial Park by local
police. The people, spotted by patrol car driver P.C.
Maurice Greaves, were on the site of the AdventureLand
funfair which had departed during the night.

On investigation, the group, thirteen men, twelve
women and one child, only five of whom live locally,
were discovered to have been reported missing this year
over a period of six months.

Most of them were found to be highly confused and,
when questioned, were unable to remember what had
happened to them. Speaking from hospital where they
are undergoing a period of observation, David Carter, 19,
and his girlfriend, Sally Harrison, claimed they had been
kidnapped and held in one of the fairground caravans
belonging to Mr Frederick Purdue, the proprietor of the
Ghost Train.

Mr Carter said that Purdue seemed to have been crazy
and had tortured several of the captives with knives and
burning cigarette ends for reasons known only to himself.

He also said that Purdue starved the captives and refused them water.

Most of the injured have no recollection of their ordeals, but Mr Carter claims that the memories of most of the captives were wiped. He saw Purdue 'doing something that looked like hypnotism' to them with a brightly-coloured stone. Mr Carter lost consciousness on the third day of his captivity and remembers nothing from then on.

Detectives investigating the disappearances have been alerted and Inspector Grogan of the Bracknell CID who initiated the nationwide search for Tommy 'Tiger' Cousins, 6, a fortnight ago is reported as saying he is now able to resolve 'the greater quantity' of the missing persons cases in which he was involved. He refused to comment when asked if the three local people still missing – Rodney Johnson, 23, his sister Sandra, 21, and their flatmate, bodybuilder Jon Kott, 23 – were believed to be dead.

When asked about the allegations of torture made by some of the captives he said that investigations were under way but so far police had been unable to trace Mr Purdue.

The AdventureLand funfair has moved to a site in Winchester but so far Mr Purdue has not joined it. Funfair colleagues say that they had no idea that Purdue was the subject of a criminal investigation and that they were surprised when he didn't follow them to their next site. Some said that it is not unusual for a ride to break with a funfair in mid-season and thought that Purdue might have taken his Ghost Train, Glass Maze, and optical illusion sideshow to join another fair in Scarborough.

Charles Fisher, an ex-employee on the Ghost Train – famed for its ghastliness – dismissed allegations of abduction and torture as 'plain nonsense' and said that colleagues 'probably would have noticed a caravan full of screaming people if there had been one'. Fisher, sporting a red devil tattoo that he claims Purdue gave him, said that AdventureLand mainstay Purdue was a respectable church-going businessman who kept himself to himself and had never been in trouble of any kind.

Detective Inspector Grogan says that he expects to locate Fred Purdue 'in the near future'.

Meanwhile, the captives are recovering from their ordeal and starting to piece together the threads of their disturbed lives.

A selection of bestsellers from Headline

FICTION

BLOOD STOCK	John Francome & James MacGregor	£3.99 □
THE OLD SILENT	Martha Grimes	£4.50 □
ALL THAT GLITTERS	Katherine Stone	£4.50 □
A FAMILY MATTER	Nigel Rees	£4.50 □
EGYPT GREEN	Christopher Hyde	£4.50 □

NON-FICTION

MY MOUNTBATTEN YEARS	William Evans	£4.50 □
WICKED LADY Salvador Dali's Muse	Tim McGirk	£4.99 □
THE FOOD OF SPAIN AND PORTUGAL	Elisabeth Lambert Ortiz	£5.99 □

SCIENCE FICTION AND FANTASY

REVENGE OF THE FLUFFY BUNNIES Cineverse Cycle Book 3	Craig Shaw Gardner	£3.50 □
BROTHERS IN ARMS	Lois McMaster Bujold	£4.50 □
THE SEA SWORD	Adrienne Martine-Barnes	£3.50 □
NO HAVEN FOR THE GUILTY	Simon Green	£3.50 □
GREENBRIAR QUEEN	Sheila Gilluly	£4.50 □

All Headline books are available at your local bookshop or newsagent, or can be ordered direct from the publisher. Just tick the titles you want and fill in the form below. Prices and availability subject to change without notice.

Headline Book Publishing PLC, Cash Sales Department, PO Box 11, Falmouth, Cornwall, TR10 9EN, England.

Please enclose a cheque or postal order to the value of the cover price and allow the following for postage and packing:
UK: 80p for the first book and 20p for each additional book ordered up to a maximum charge of £2.00
BFPO: 80p for the first book and 20p for each additional book
OVERSEAS & EIRE: £1.50 for the first book, £1.00 for the second book and 30p for each subsequent book.

Name ....

Address ....

....

....